SONIC™ THE HEDGEHOG

THE IDW COLLECTION

01

SEGA®

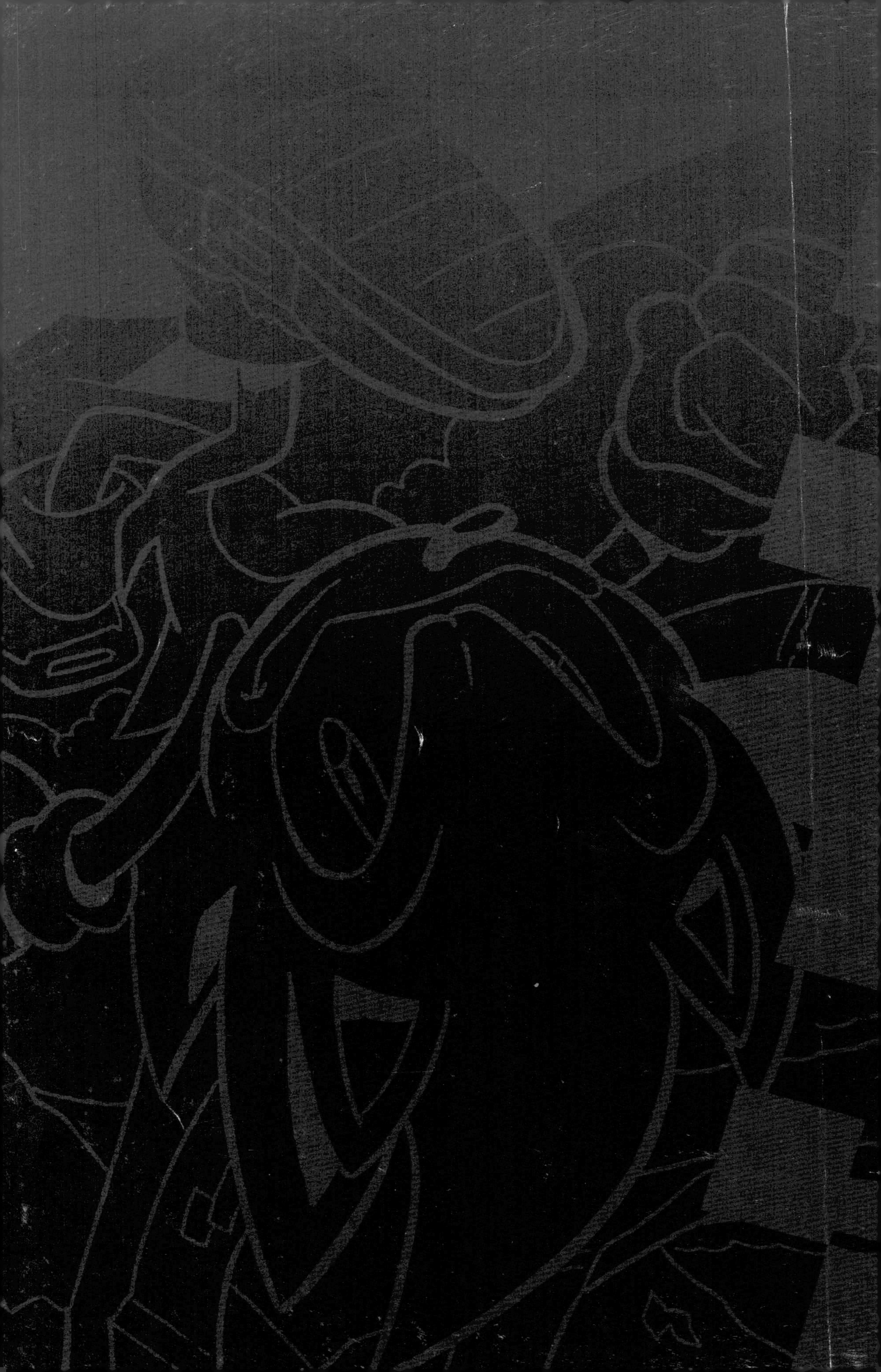

COVER ARTIST **EVAN STANLEY**
SERIES ASSISTANT EDITOR **MEGAN BROWN**
SERIES EDITORS **DAVID MARIOTTE** AND **JOE HUGHES**
COLLECTION EDITORS **ALONZO SIMON** AND **ZAC BOONE**
COLLECTION DESIGNER **SHAWN LEE**

Nachie Marsham, Publisher • Rebekah Cahalin, EVP of Operations • Blake Kobashigawa, VP of Sales
John Barber, Editor-in-Chief • Mark Doyle, Editorial Director, Originals • Justin Eisinger, Editorial Director, Graphic Novels & Collections
Scott Dunbier, Director, Special Projects • Anna Morrow, Sr. Marketing Director
Tara McCrillis, Director of Design & Production • Shauna Monteforte, Sr. Director of Manufacturing Operations

Ted Adams and Robbie Robbins, IDW Founders

IDW
www.idwpublishing.com

Special thanks to Mai Kiyotaki, Michael Cisneros, Sandra Jo, Sonic Team, and everyone at Sega for their invaluable assistance.

Originally published as SONIC THE HEDGEHOG issues #1–12.

Facebook: facebook.com/idwpublishing • Twitter: @idwpublishing • YouTube: youtube.com/idwpublishing • Instagram: @idwpublishing

YouTube

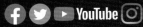

ISBN: 978-1-68405-827-3   24 23 22 21 1 2 3 4

TABLE OF

CONTENTS

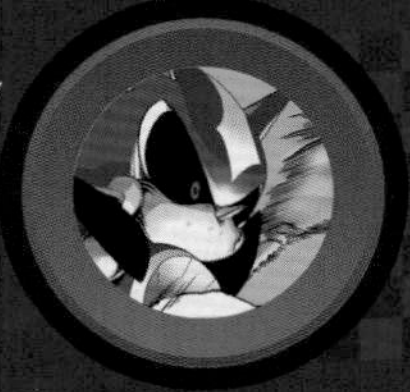

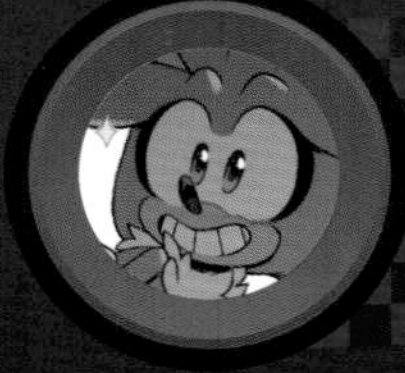

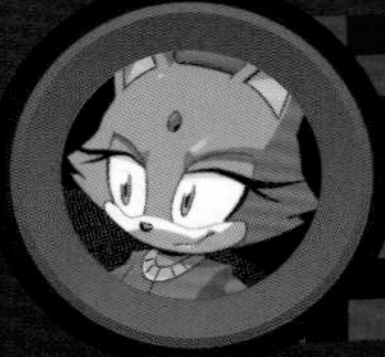

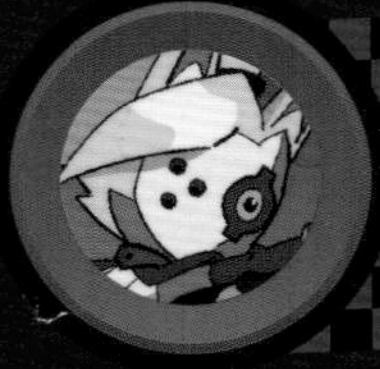

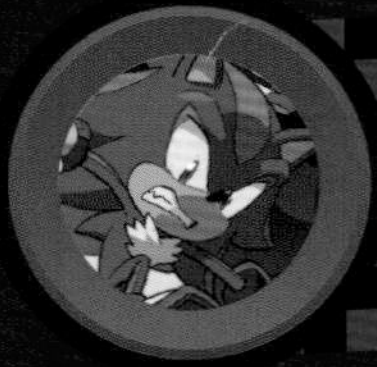

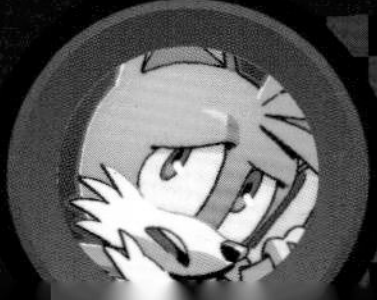

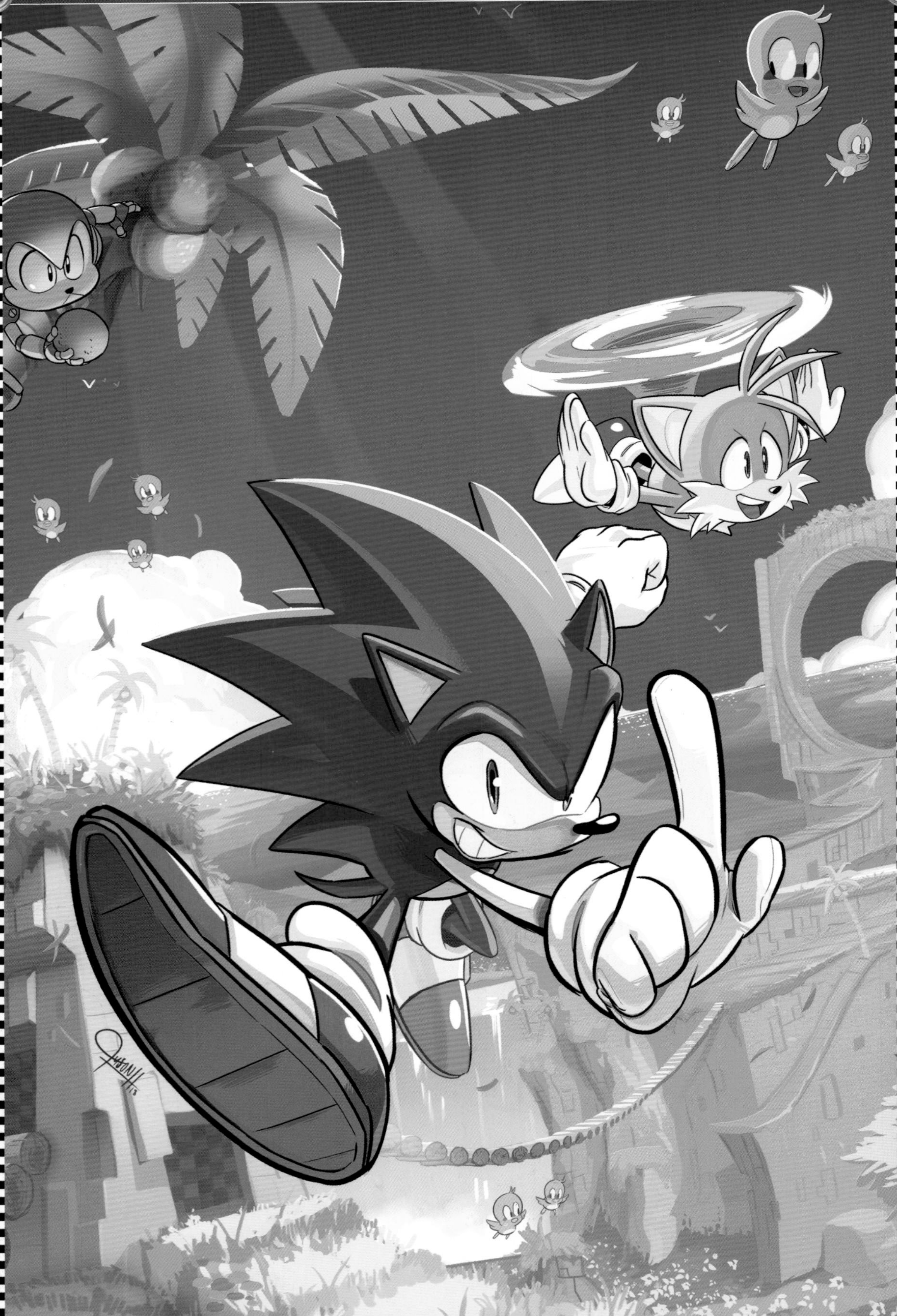

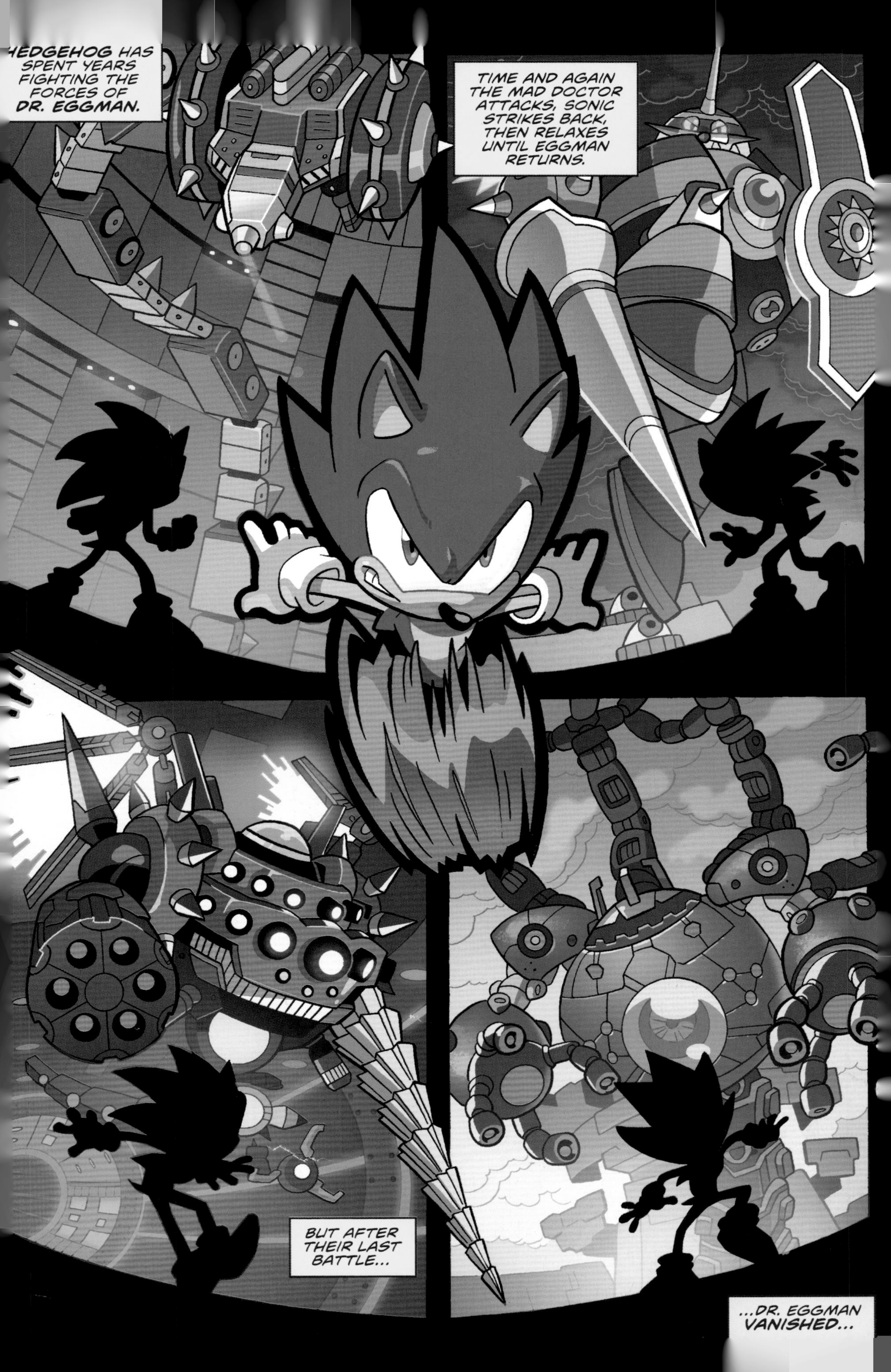
HEDGEHOG HAS SPENT YEARS FIGHTING THE FORCES OF DR. EGGMAN.
TIME AND AGAIN THE MAD DOCTOR ATTACKS, SONIC STRIKES BACK, THEN RELAXES UNTIL EGGMAN RETURNS.
BUT AFTER THEIR LAST BATTLE...
...DR. EGGMAN VANISHED...

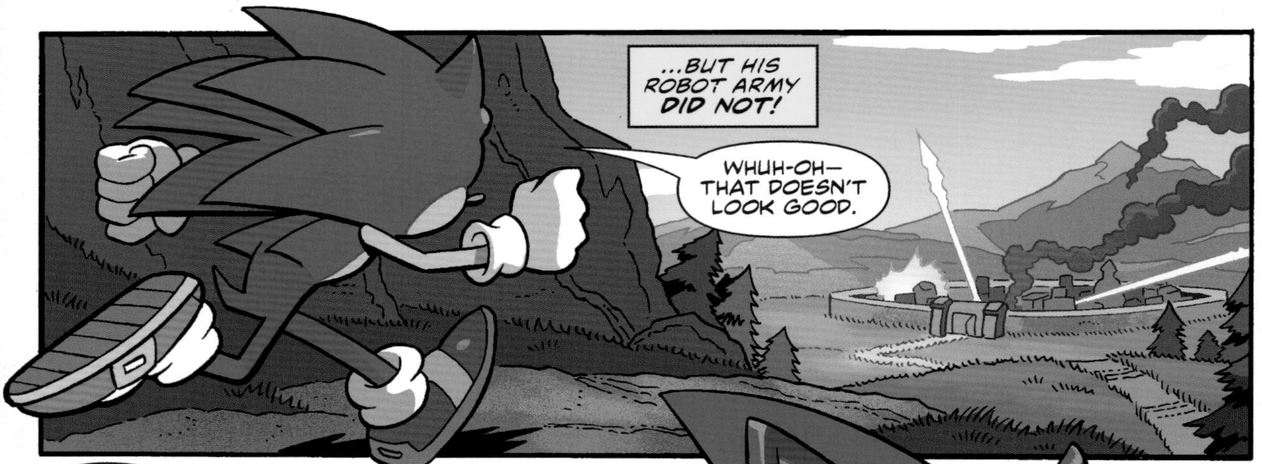
...BUT HIS ROBOT ARMY DID NOT!
WHUH-OH— THAT DOESN'T LOOK GOOD.

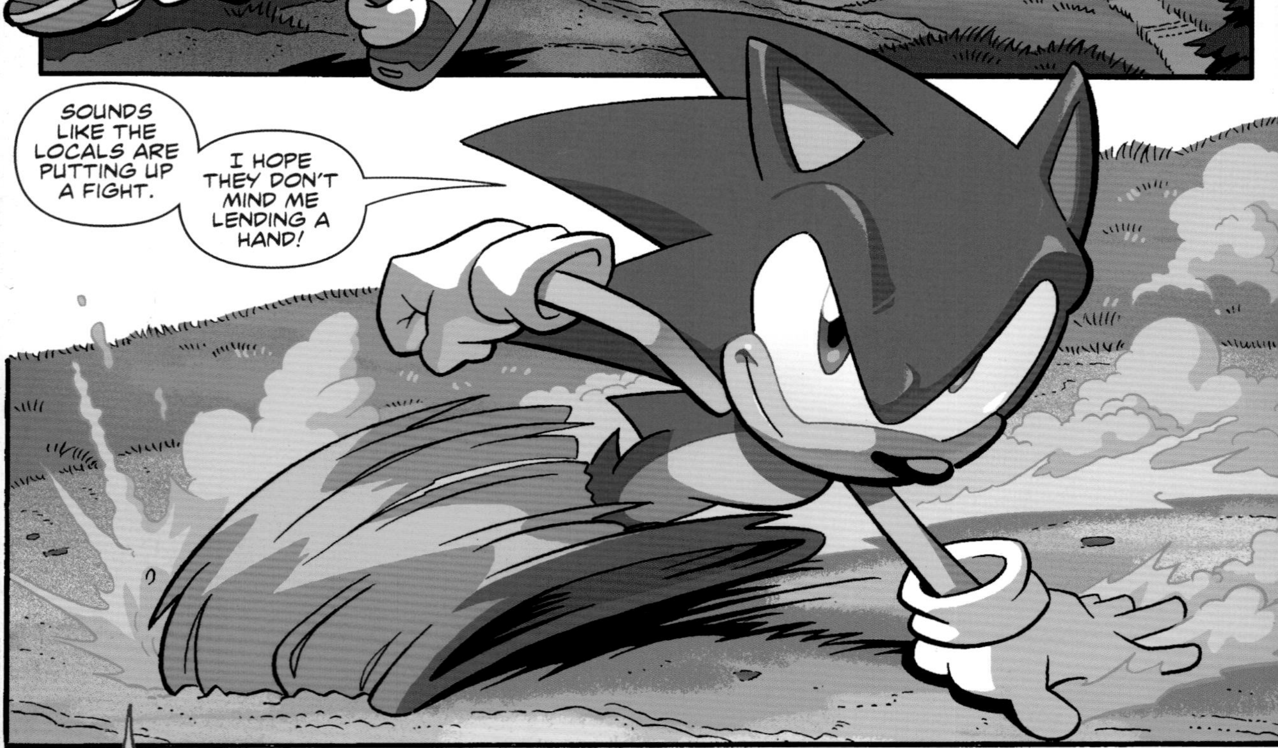
SOUNDS LIKE THE LOCALS ARE PUTTING UP A FIGHT.
I HOPE THEY DON'T MIND ME LENDING A HAND!

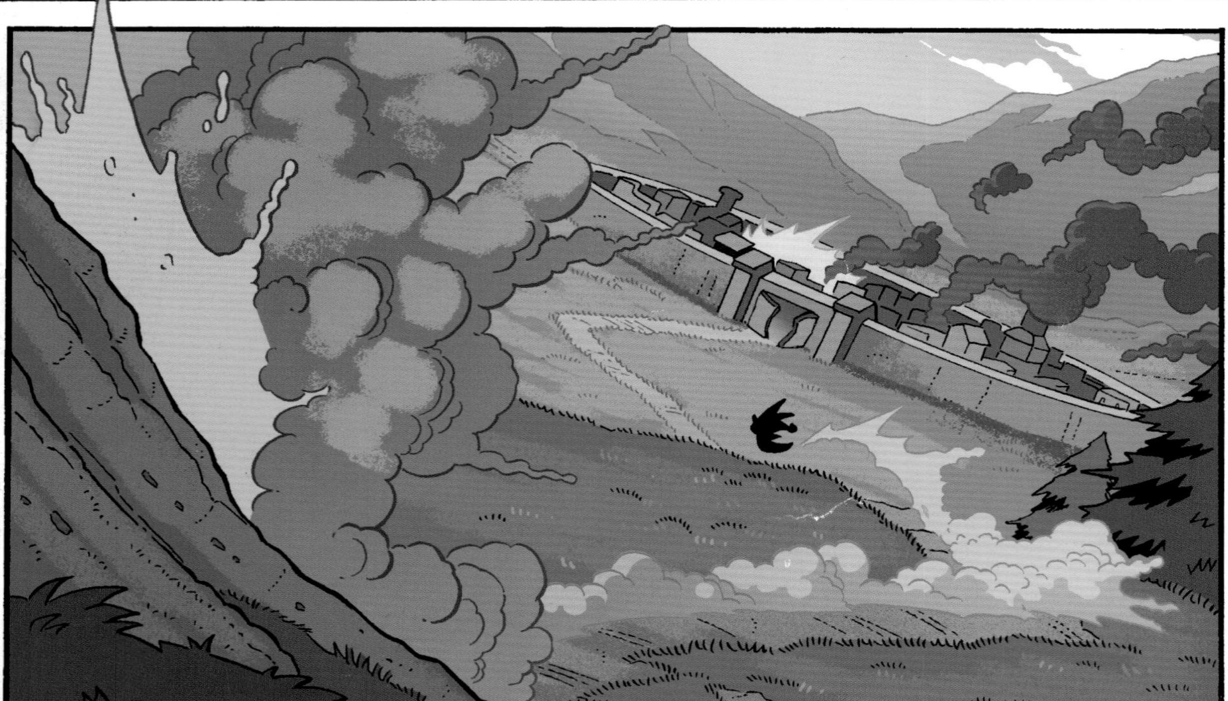

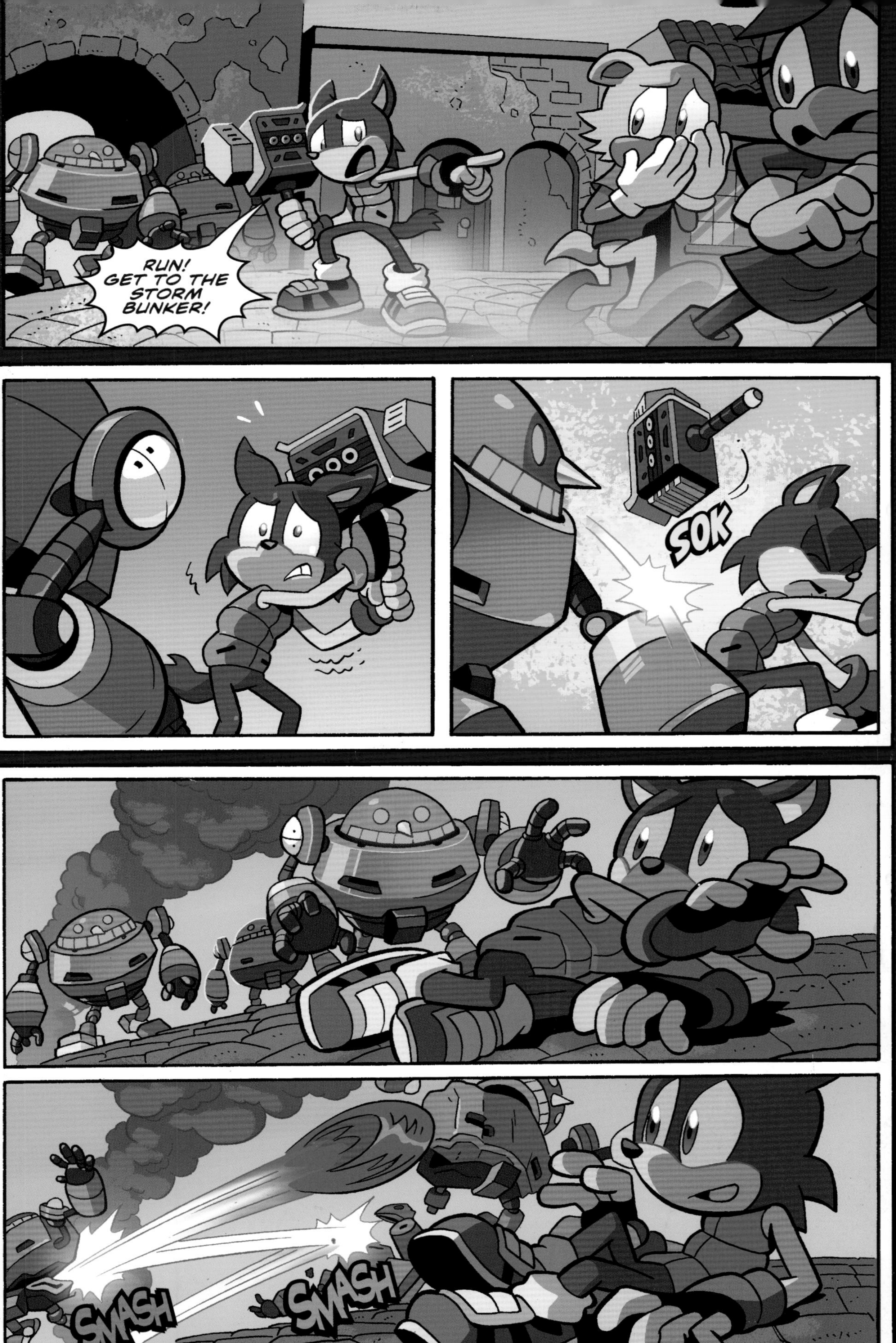
RUN! GET TO THE STORM BUNKER!
SOK
SMASH
SMASH

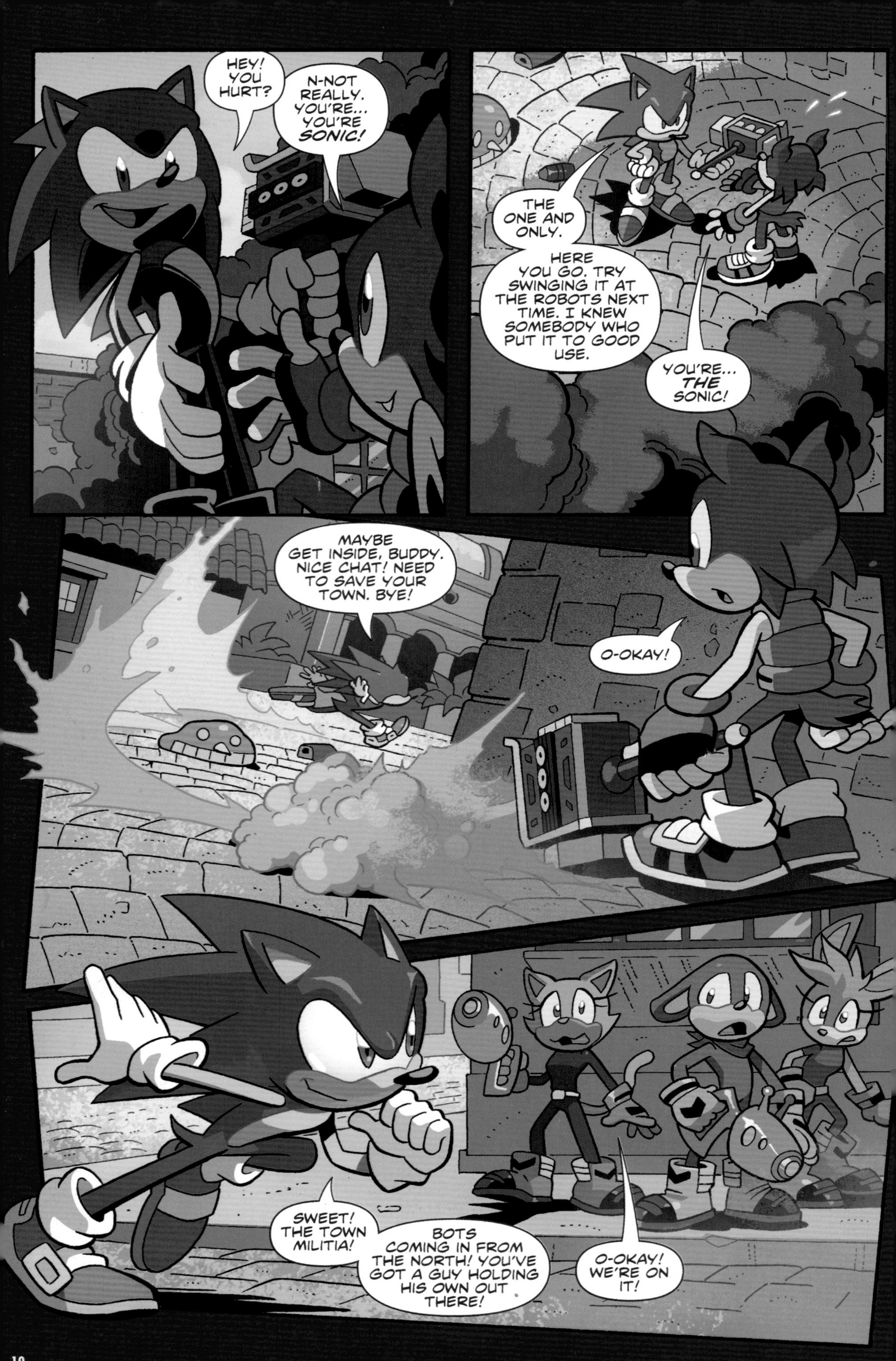
HEY! YOU HURT?
N-NOT REALLY. YOU'RE... YOU'RE SONIC!
THE ONE AND ONLY.
HERE YOU GO. TRY SWINGING IT AT THE ROBOTS NEXT TIME. I KNEW SOMEBODY WHO PUT IT TO GOOD USE.
YOU'RE... THE SONIC!
MAYBE GET INSIDE, BUDDY. NICE CHAT! NEED TO SAVE YOUR TOWN. BYE!
O-OKAY!
SWEET! THE TOWN MILITIA!
BOTS COMING IN FROM THE NORTH! YOU'VE GOT A GUY HOLDING HIS OWN OUT THERE!
O-OKAY! WE'RE ON IT!

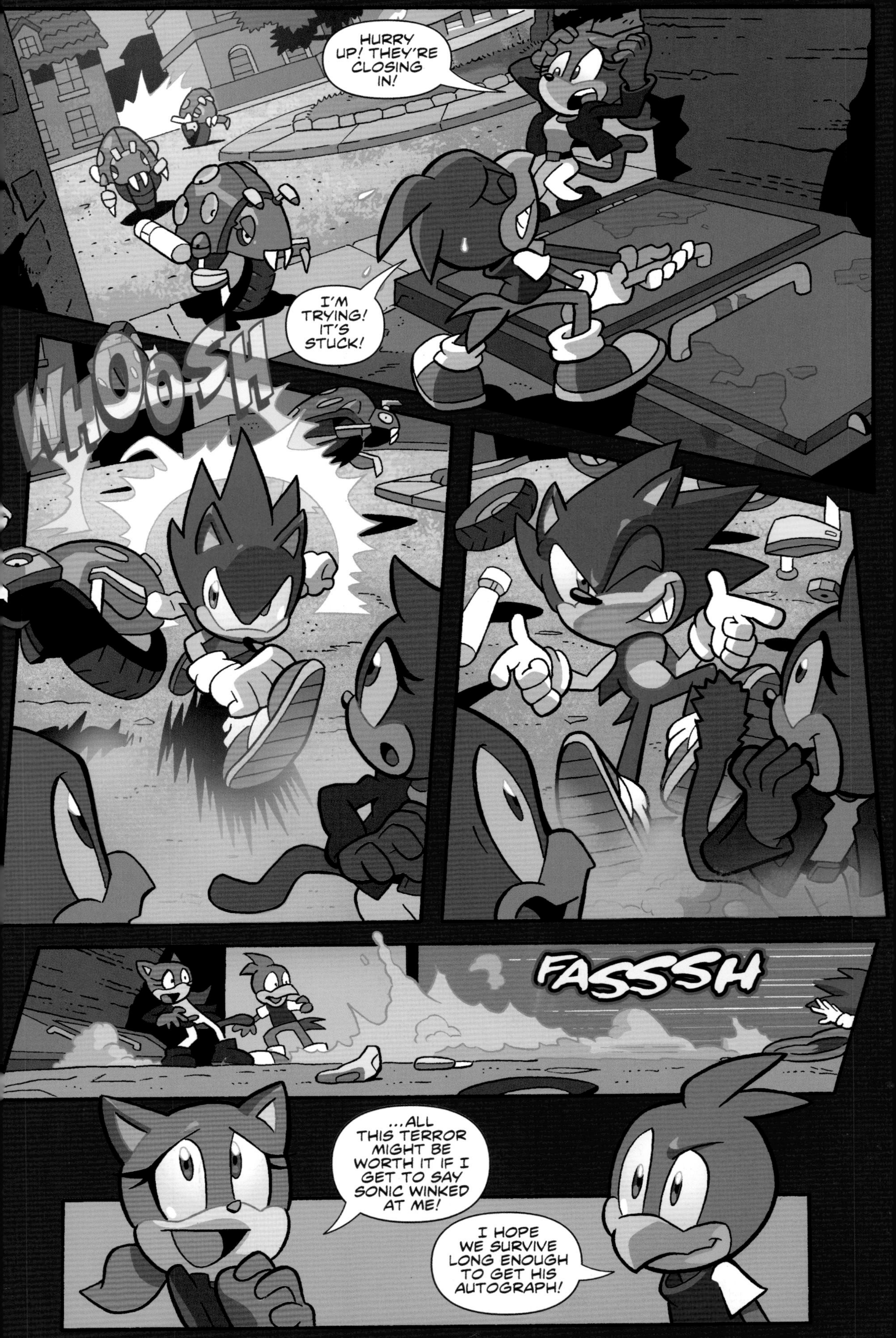
HURRY UP! THEY'RE CLOSING IN!
I'M TRYING! IT'S STUCK!
WHOOSH
FASSSH
...ALL THIS TERROR MIGHT BE WORTH IT IF I GET TO SAY SONIC WINKED AT ME!
I HOPE WE SURVIVE LONG ENOUGH TO GET HIS AUTOGRAPH!

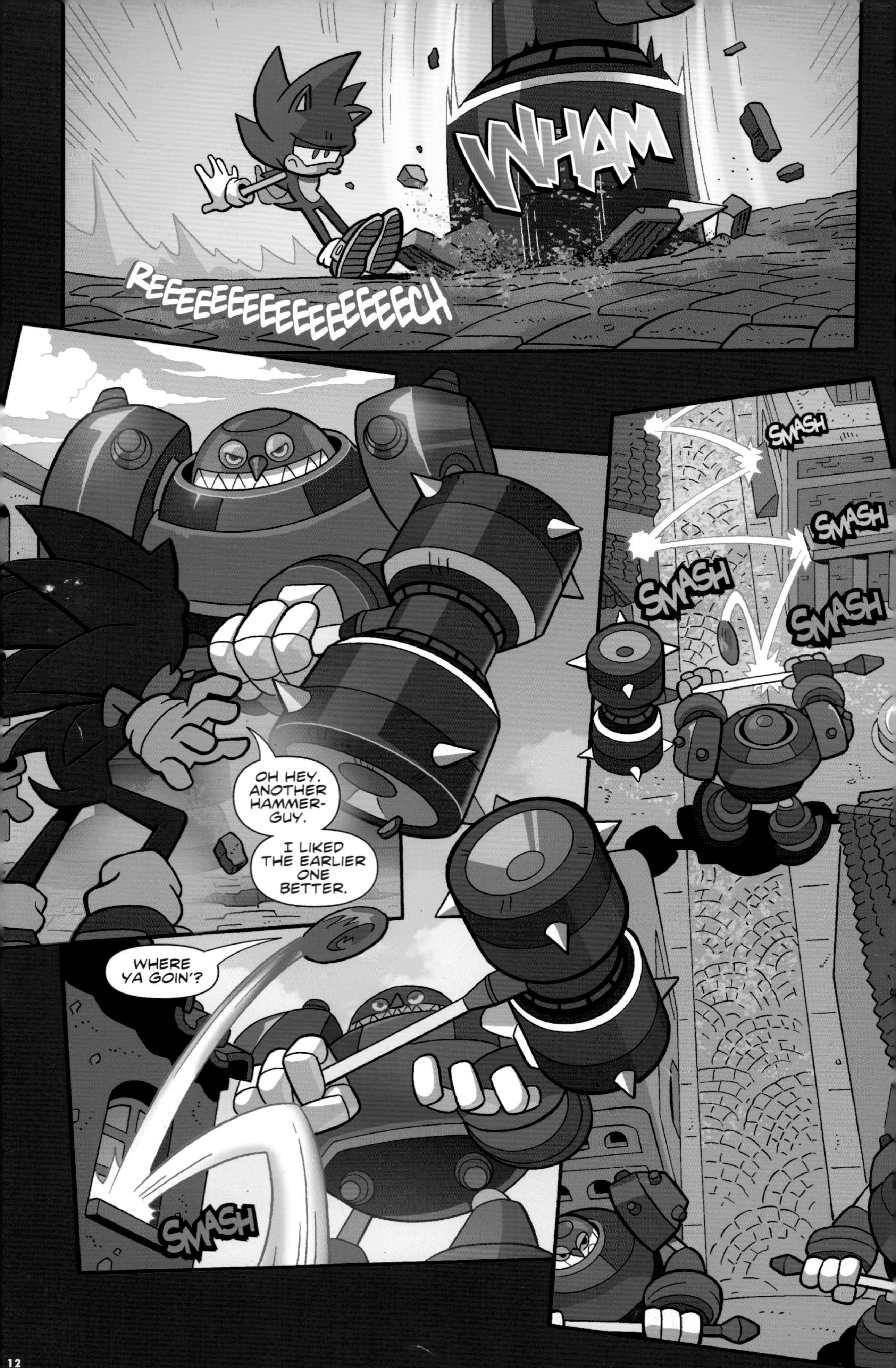
WHAM
REEEEEEEEEEEEEEEEEEEECH
OH HEY. ANOTHER HAMMER-GUY.
I LIKED THE EARLIER ONE BETTER.
SMASH
SMASH
SMASH
SMASH
WHERE YA GOIN'?
SMASH

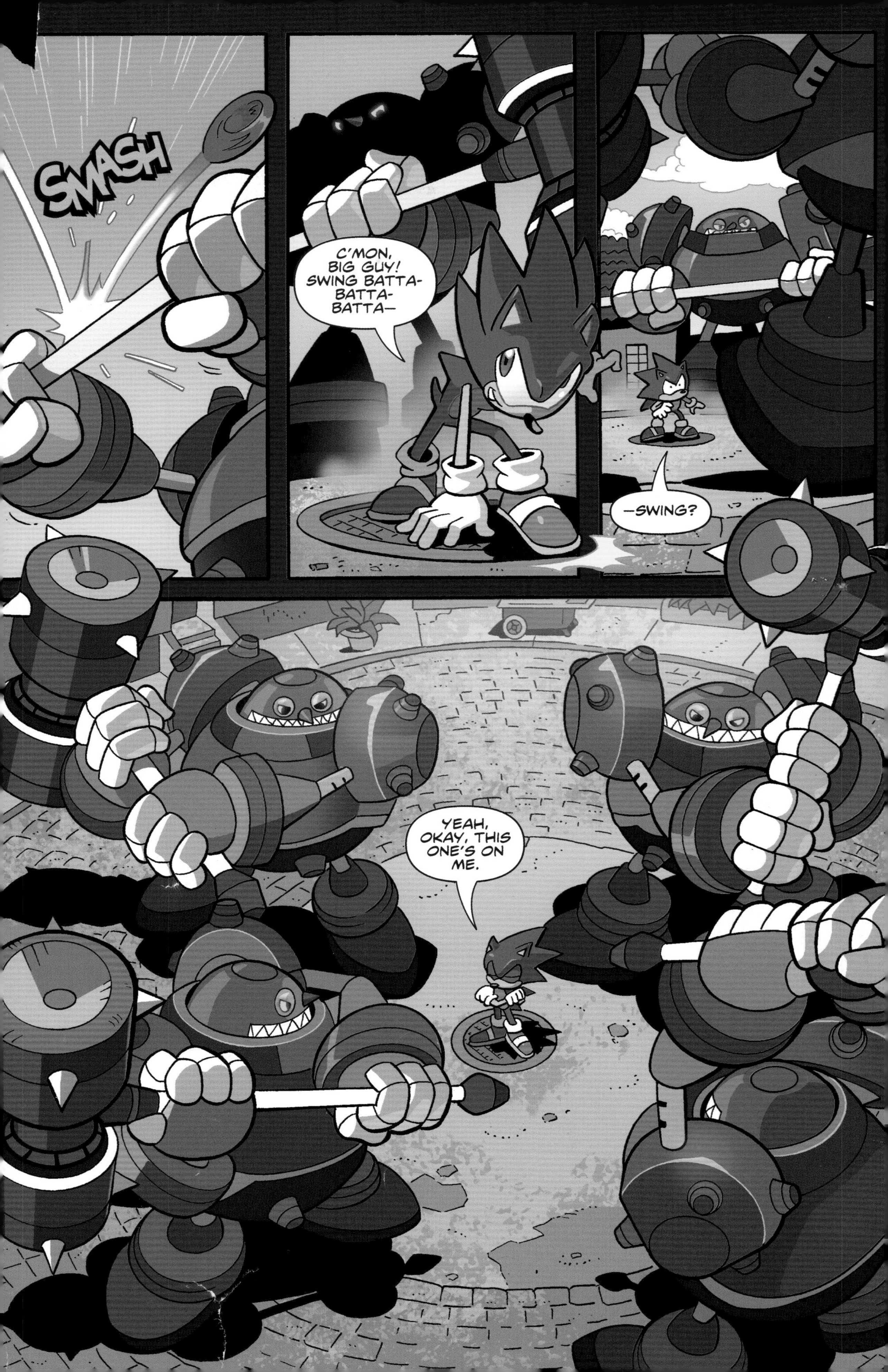
SMASH
C'MON, BIG GUY! SWING BATTA-BATTA-BATTA—
—SWING?
YEAH, OKAY, THIS ONE'S ON ME.

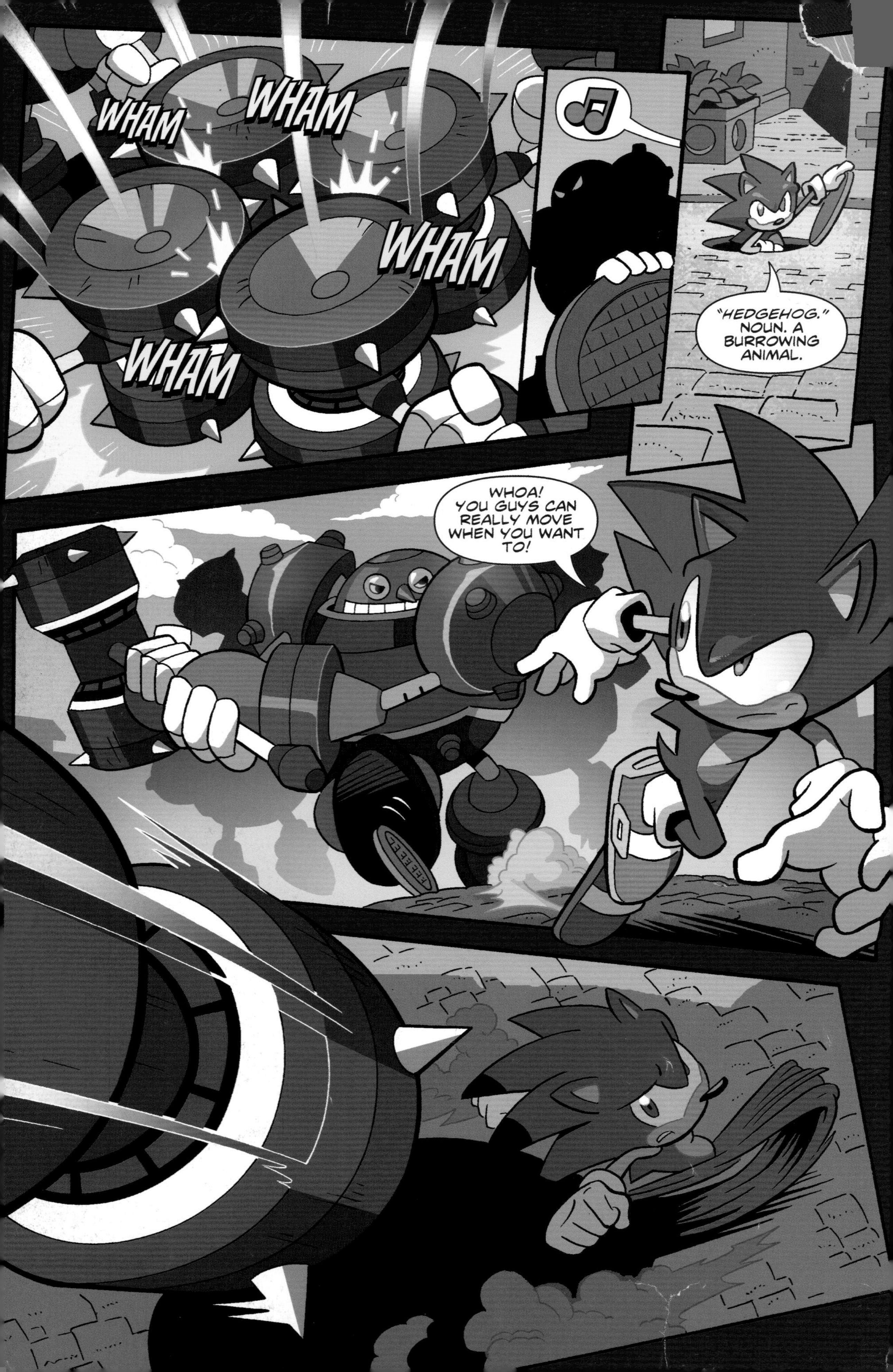
WHAM
WHAM
WHAM
WHAM
"HEDGEHOG." NOUN. A BURROWING ANIMAL.
WHOA! YOU GUYS CAN REALLY MOVE WHEN YOU WANT TO!

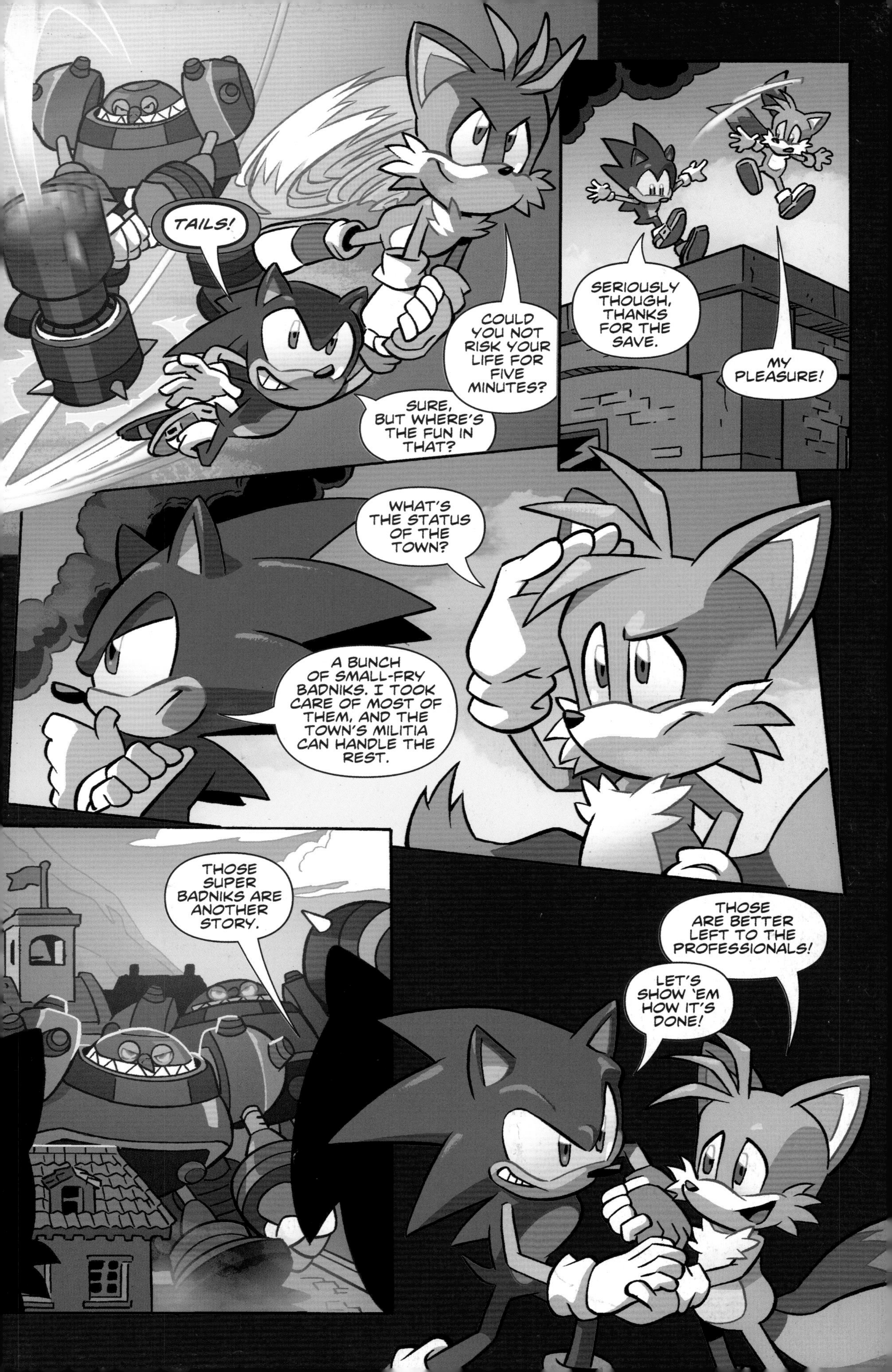
TAILS!
COULD YOU NOT RISK YOUR LIFE FOR FIVE MINUTES?
SURE, BUT WHERE'S THE FUN IN THAT?
SERIOUSLY THOUGH, THANKS FOR THE SAVE.
MY PLEASURE!
WHAT'S THE STATUS OF THE TOWN?
A BUNCH OF SMALL-FRY BADNIKS. I TOOK CARE OF MOST OF THEM, AND THE TOWN'S MILITIA CAN HANDLE THE REST.
THOSE SUPER BADNIKS ARE ANOTHER STORY.
THOSE ARE BETTER LEFT TO THE PROFESSIONALS!
LET'S SHOW 'EM HOW IT'S DONE!

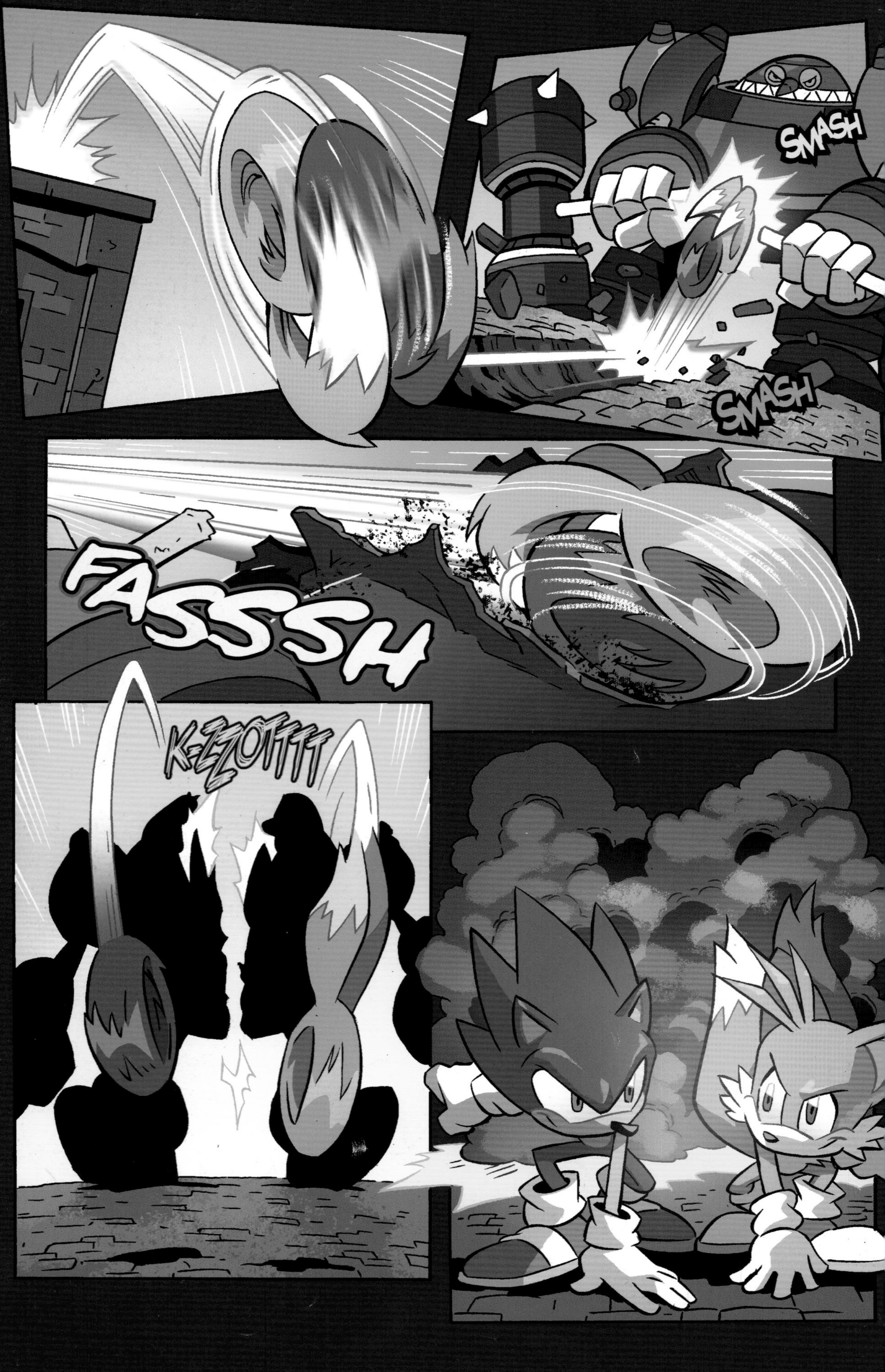
SMASH
SMASH
FASSSH
K-ZZOTTTT

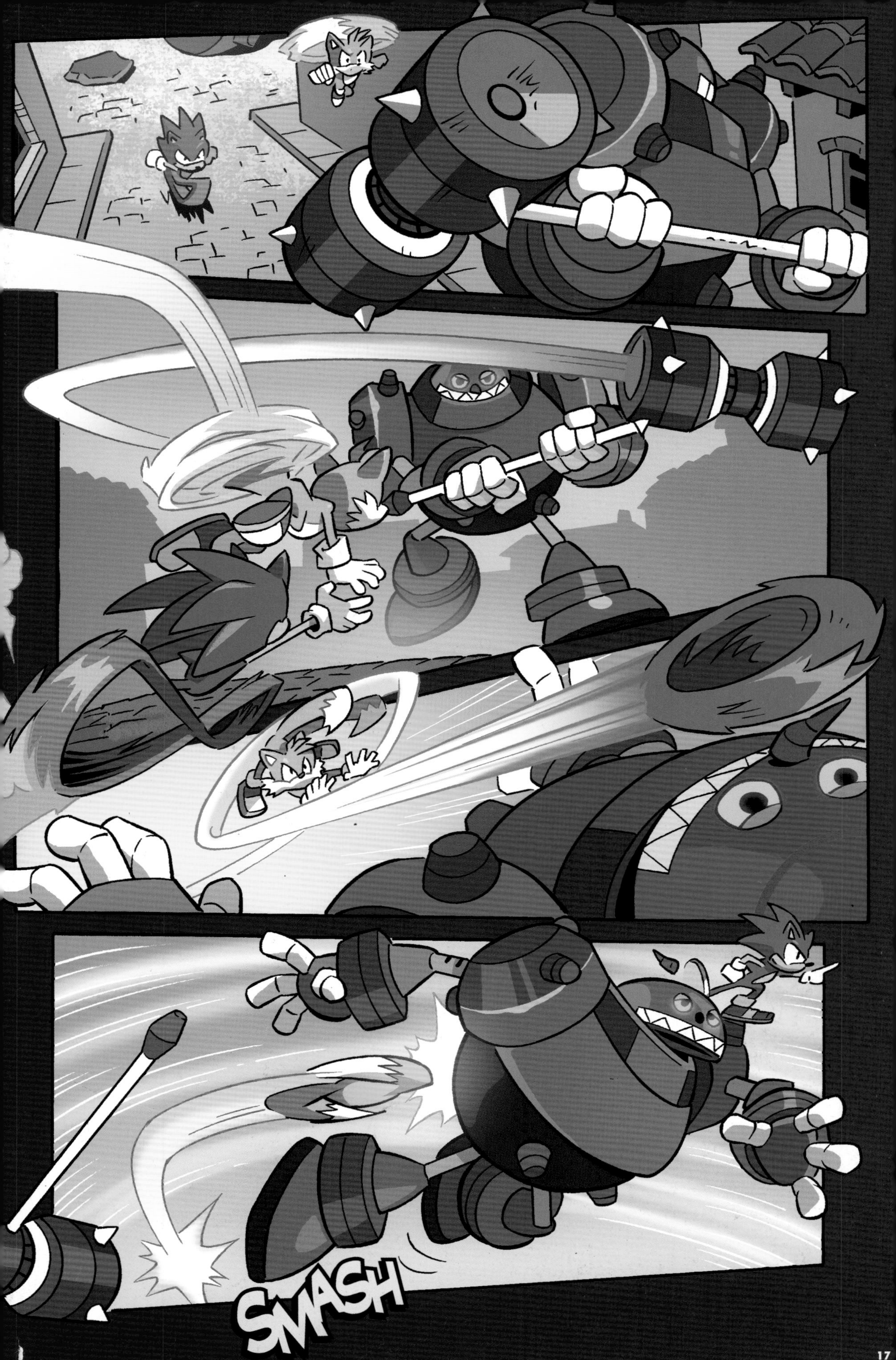
SMASH

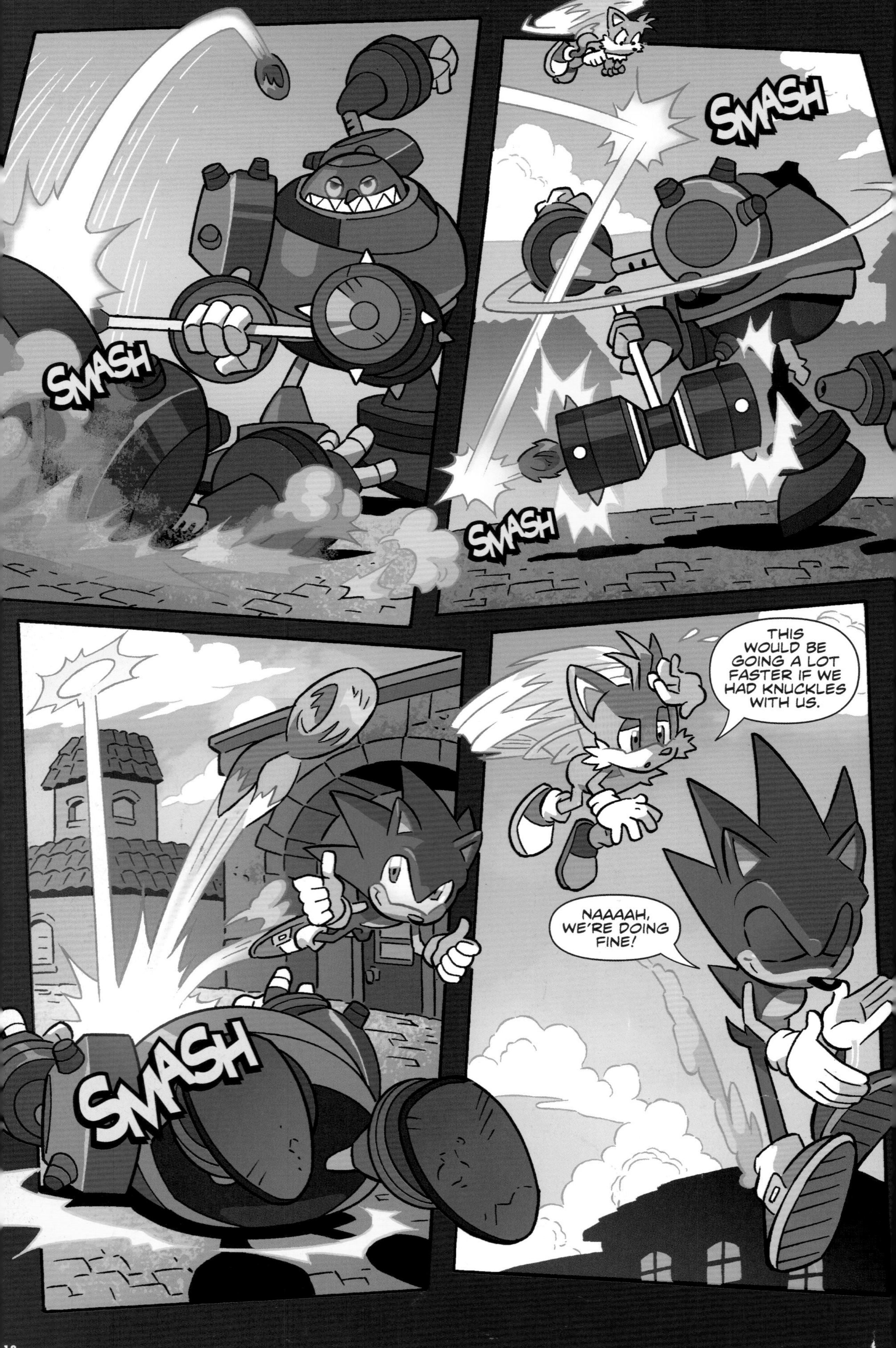
SMASH
SMASH
SMASH
SMASH
THIS WOULD BE GOING A LOT FASTER IF WE HAD KNUCKLES WITH US.
NAAAAH, WE'RE DOING FINE!

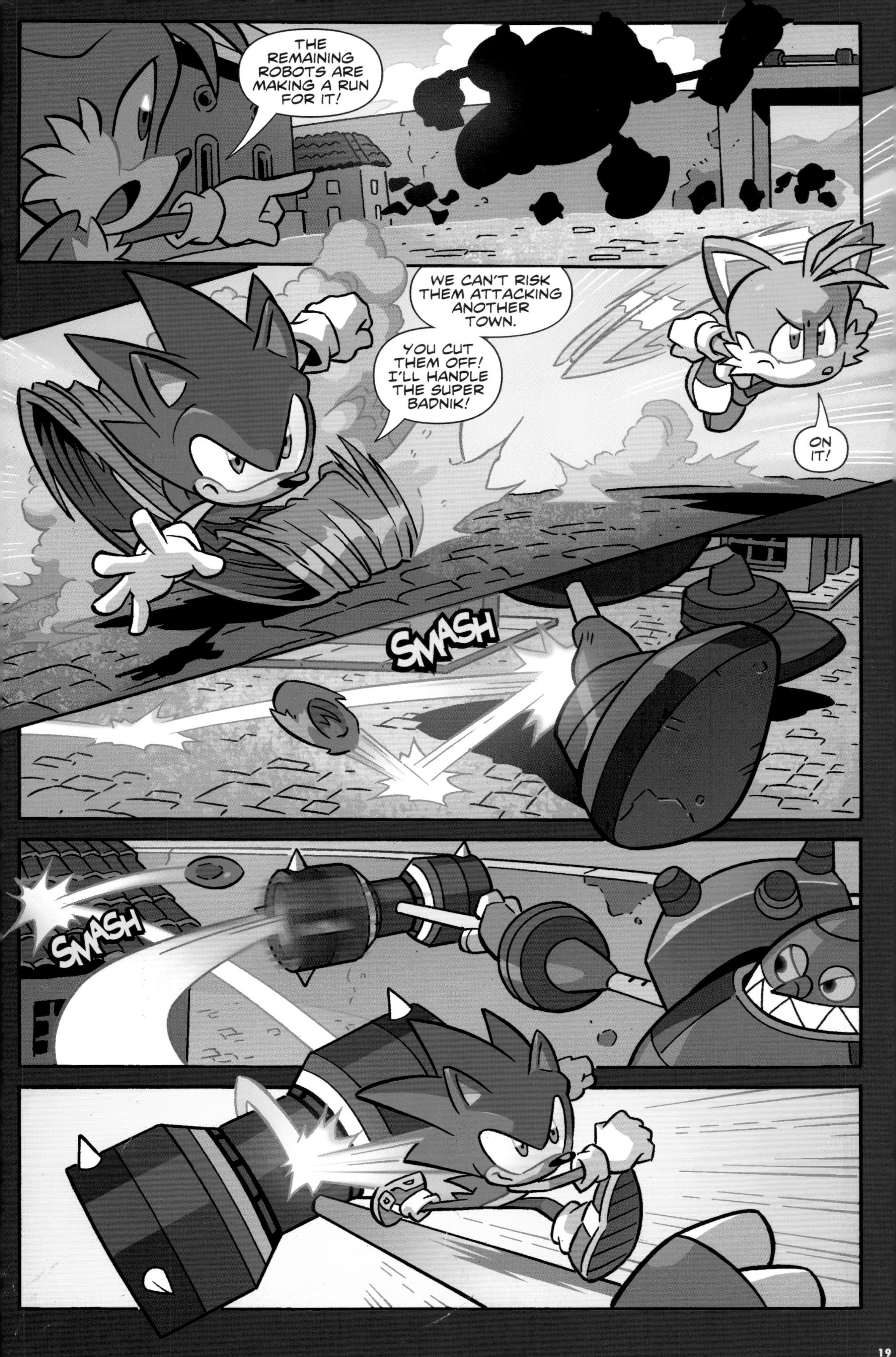
THE REMAINING ROBOTS ARE MAKING A RUN FOR IT!
WE CAN'T RISK THEM ATTACKING ANOTHER TOWN.
YOU CUT THEM OFF! I'LL HANDLE THE SUPER BADNIK!
ON IT!
SMASH
SMASH

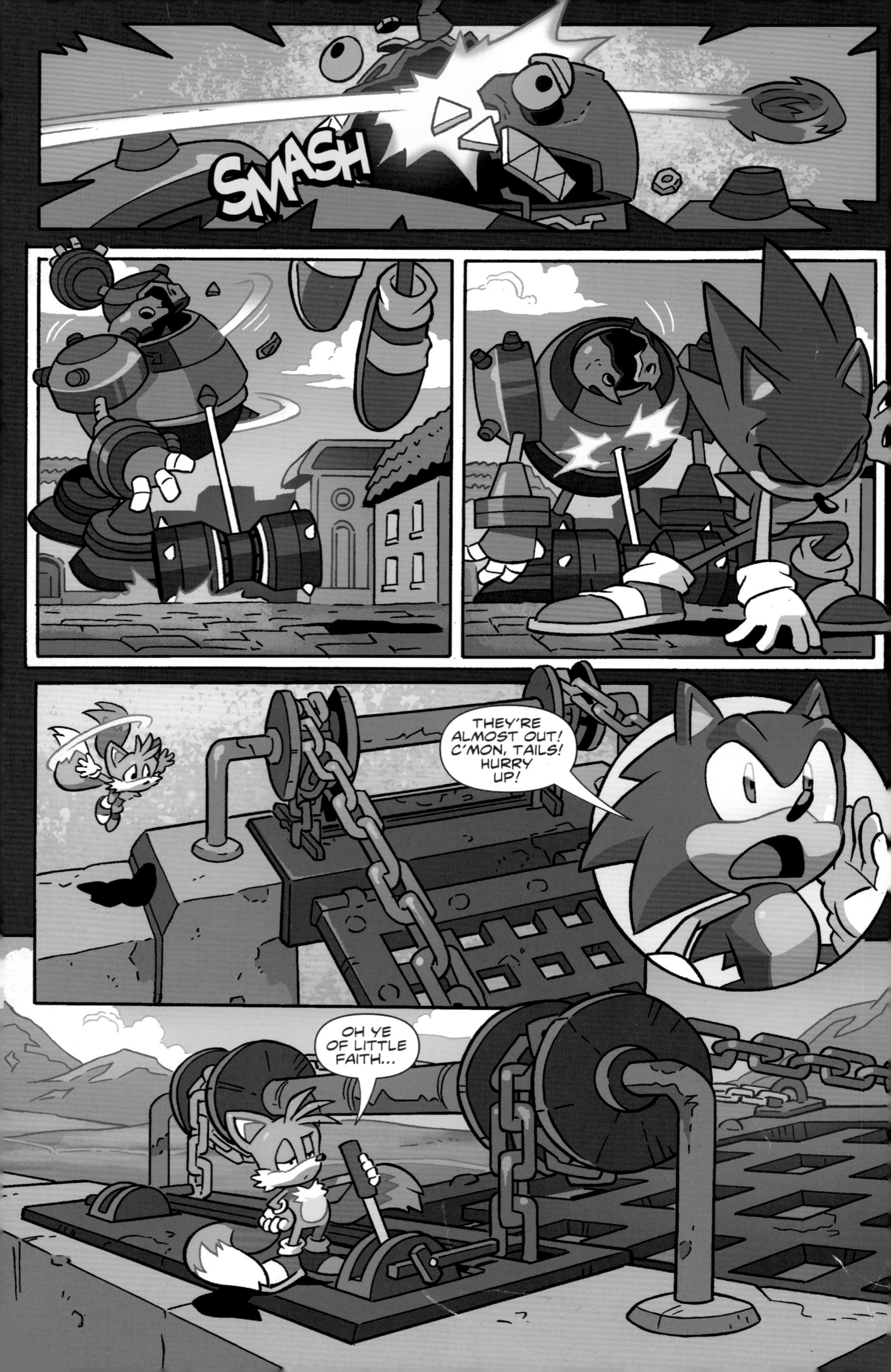
SMASH
THEY'RE ALMOST OUT! C'MON, TAILS! HURRY UP!
OH YE OF LITTLE FAITH...

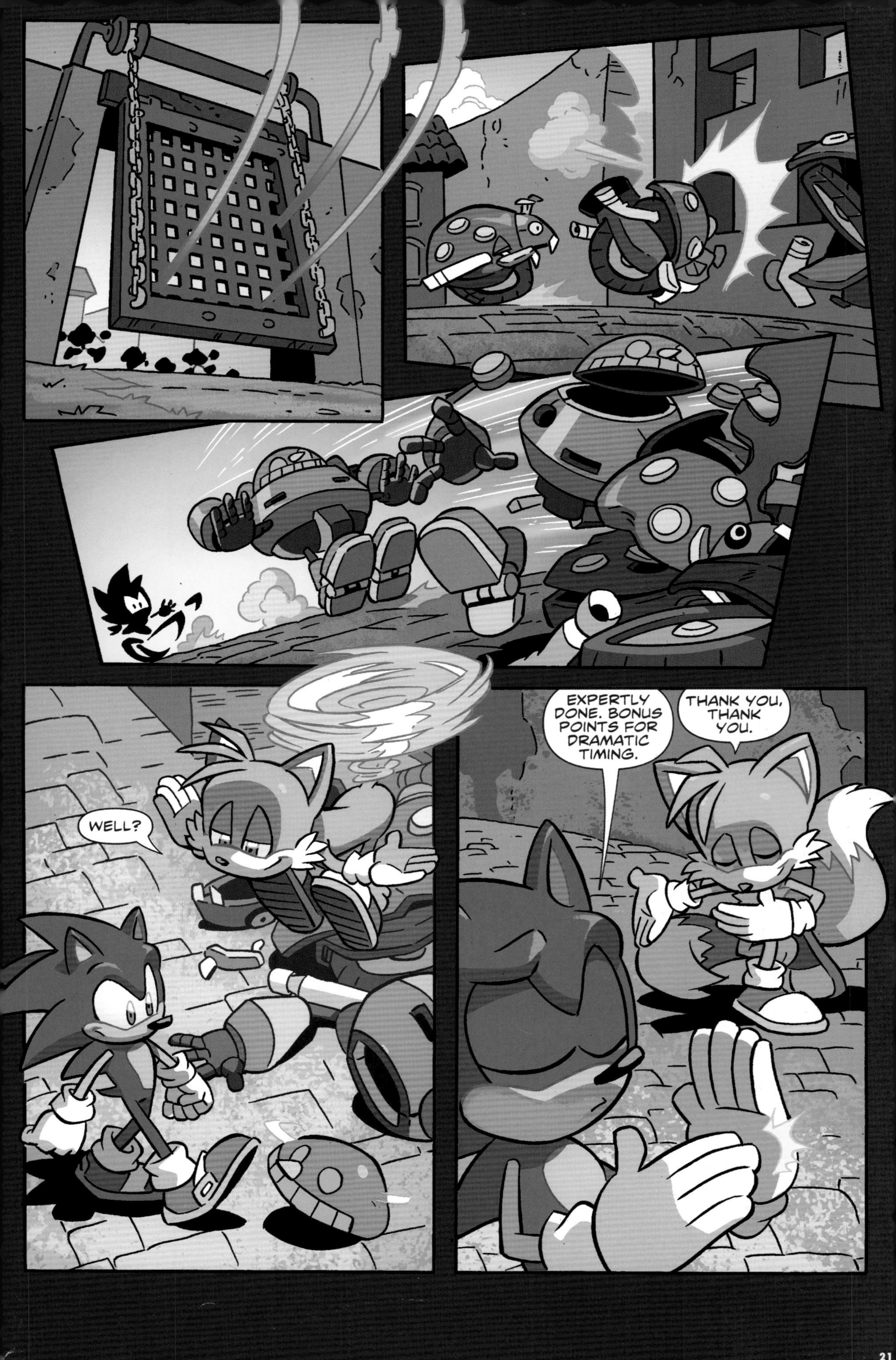
WELL?
EXPERTLY DONE. BONUS POINTS FOR DRAMATIC TIMING.
THANK YOU, THANK YOU.

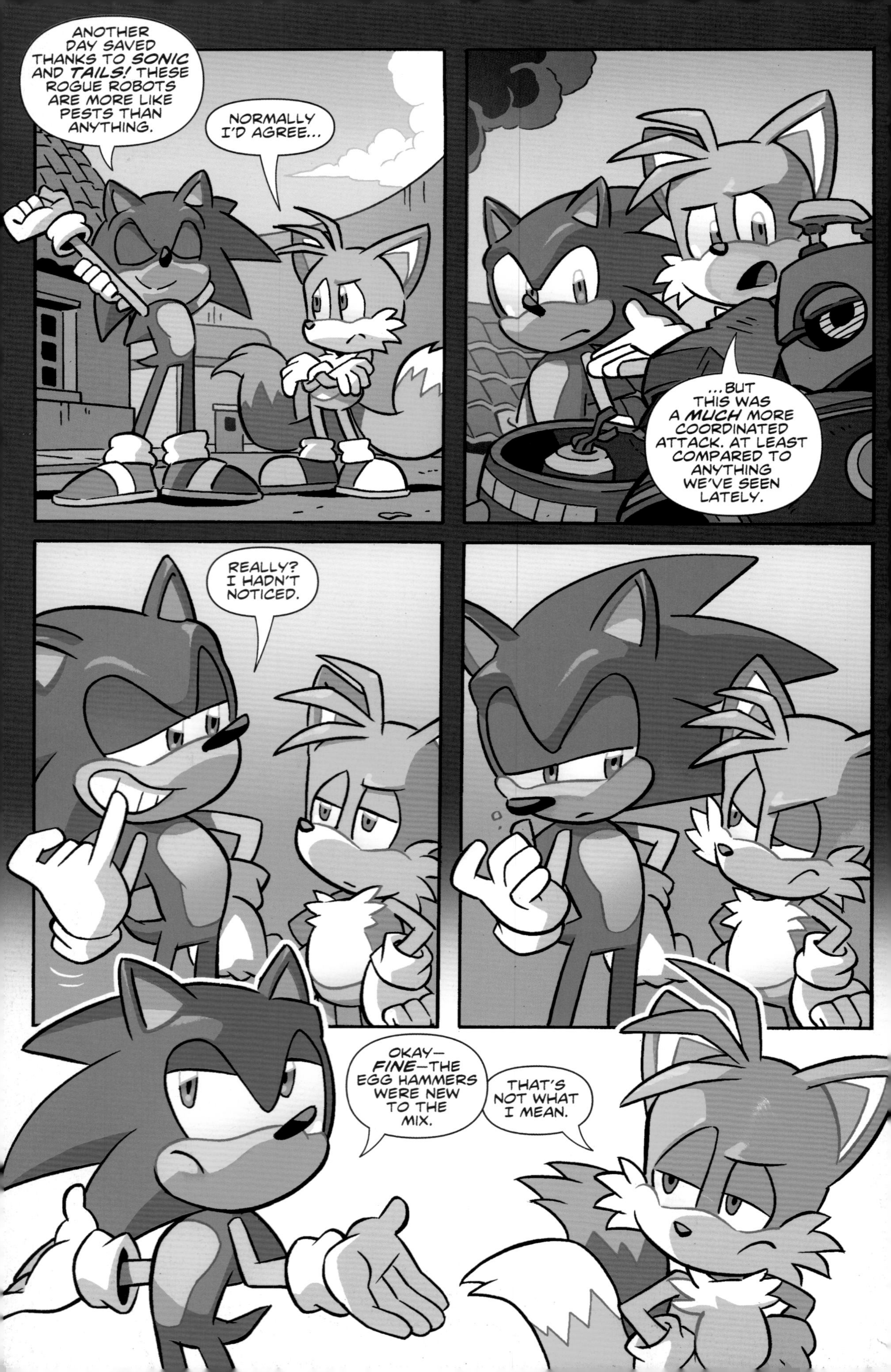
ANOTHER DAY SAVED THANKS TO SONIC AND TAILS! THESE ROGUE ROBOTS ARE MORE LIKE PESTS THAN ANYTHING.
NORMALLY I'D AGREE...
...BUT THIS WAS A MUCH MORE COORDINATED ATTACK. AT LEAST COMPARED TO ANYTHING WE'VE SEEN LATELY.
REALLY? I HADN'T NOTICED.
OKAY— FINE—THE EGG HAMMERS WERE NEW TO THE MIX.
THAT'S NOT WHAT I MEAN.

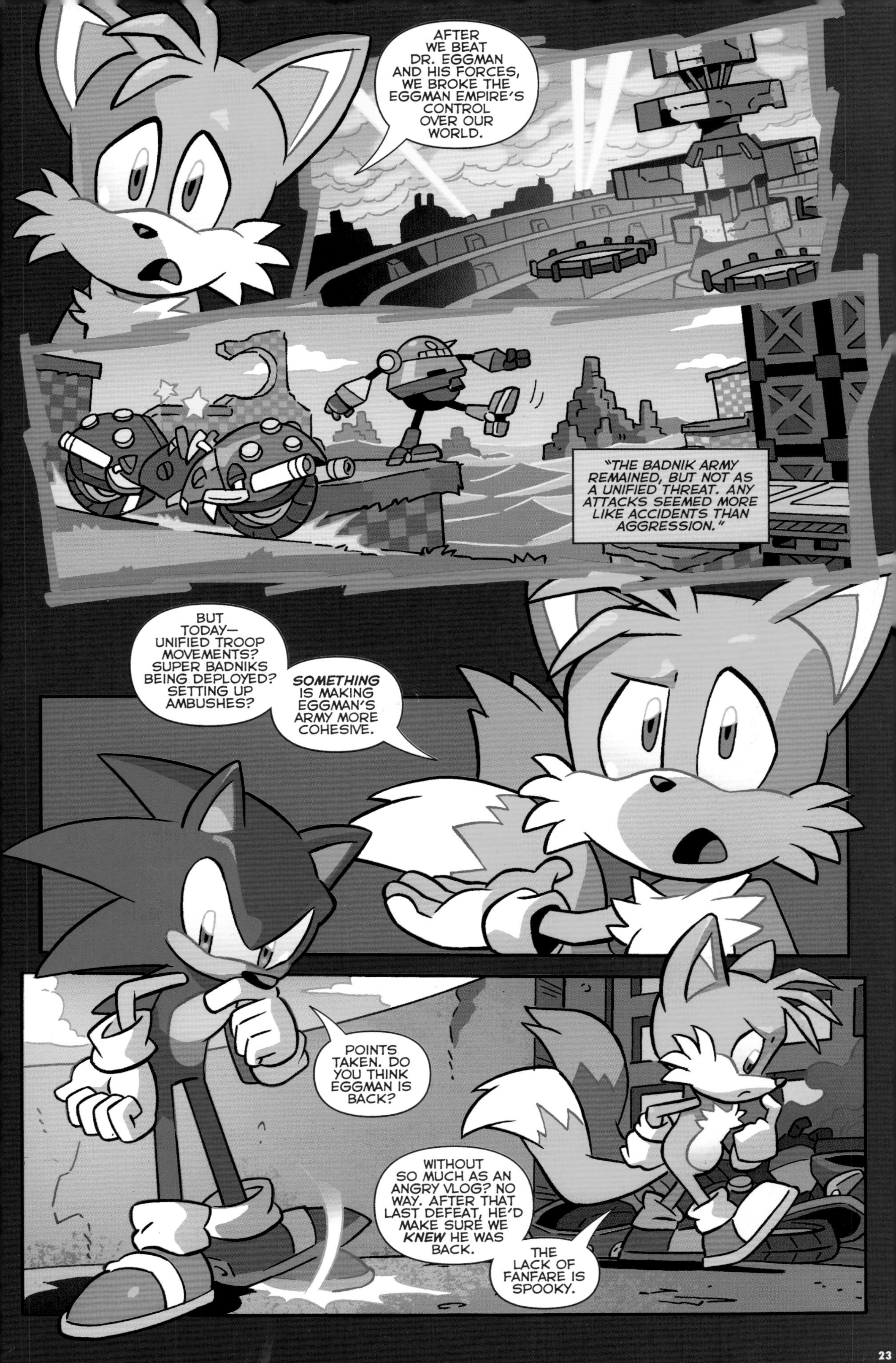
AFTER WE BEAT DR. EGGMAN AND HIS FORCES, WE BROKE THE EGGMAN EMPIRE'S CONTROL OVER OUR WORLD.
"THE BADNIK ARMY REMAINED, BUT NOT AS A UNIFIED THREAT. ANY ATTACKS SEEMED MORE LIKE ACCIDENTS THAN AGGRESSION."
BUT TODAY— UNIFIED TROOP MOVEMENTS? SUPER BADNIKS BEING DEPLOYED? SETTING UP AMBUSHES?
SOMETHING IS MAKING EGGMAN'S ARMY MORE COHESIVE.
POINTS TAKEN. DO YOU THINK EGGMAN IS BACK?
WITHOUT SO MUCH AS AN ANGRY VLOG? NO WAY. AFTER THAT LAST DEFEAT, HE'D MAKE SURE WE *KNEW* HE WAS BACK.
THE LACK OF FANFARE IS SPOOKY.

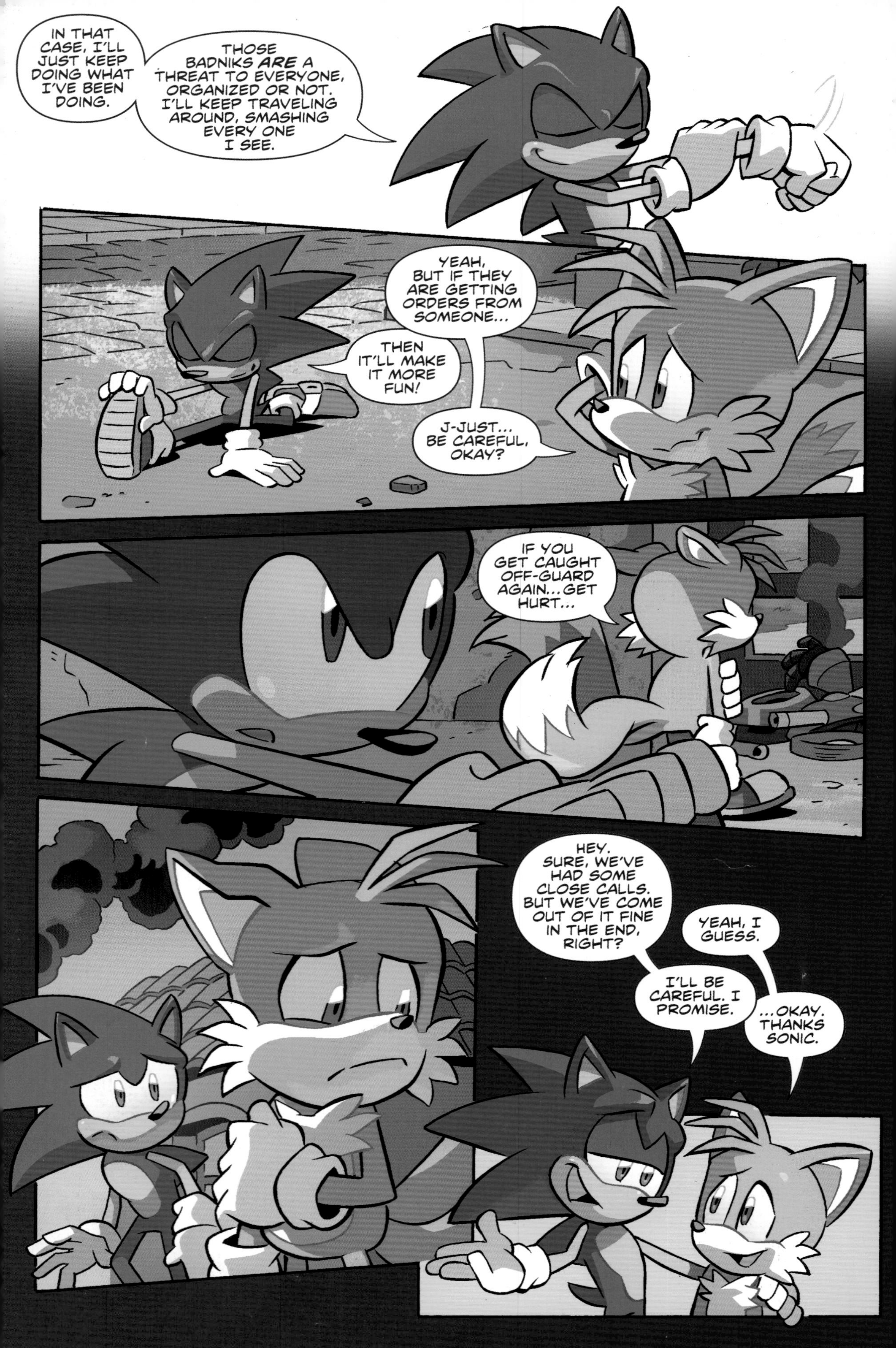
IN THAT CASE, I'LL JUST KEEP DOING WHAT I'VE BEEN DOING.
THOSE BADNIKS ARE A THREAT TO EVERYONE, ORGANIZED OR NOT. I'LL KEEP TRAVELING AROUND, SMASHING EVERY ONE I SEE.
YEAH, BUT IF THEY ARE GETTING ORDERS FROM SOMEONE...
THEN IT'LL MAKE IT MORE FUN!
J-JUST... BE CAREFUL, OKAY?
IF YOU GET CAUGHT OFF-GUARD AGAIN... GET HURT...
HEY. SURE, WE'VE HAD SOME CLOSE CALLS. BUT WE'VE COME OUT OF IT FINE IN THE END, RIGHT?
YEAH, I GUESS.
I'LL BE CAREFUL. I PROMISE.
...OKAY. THANKS SONIC.

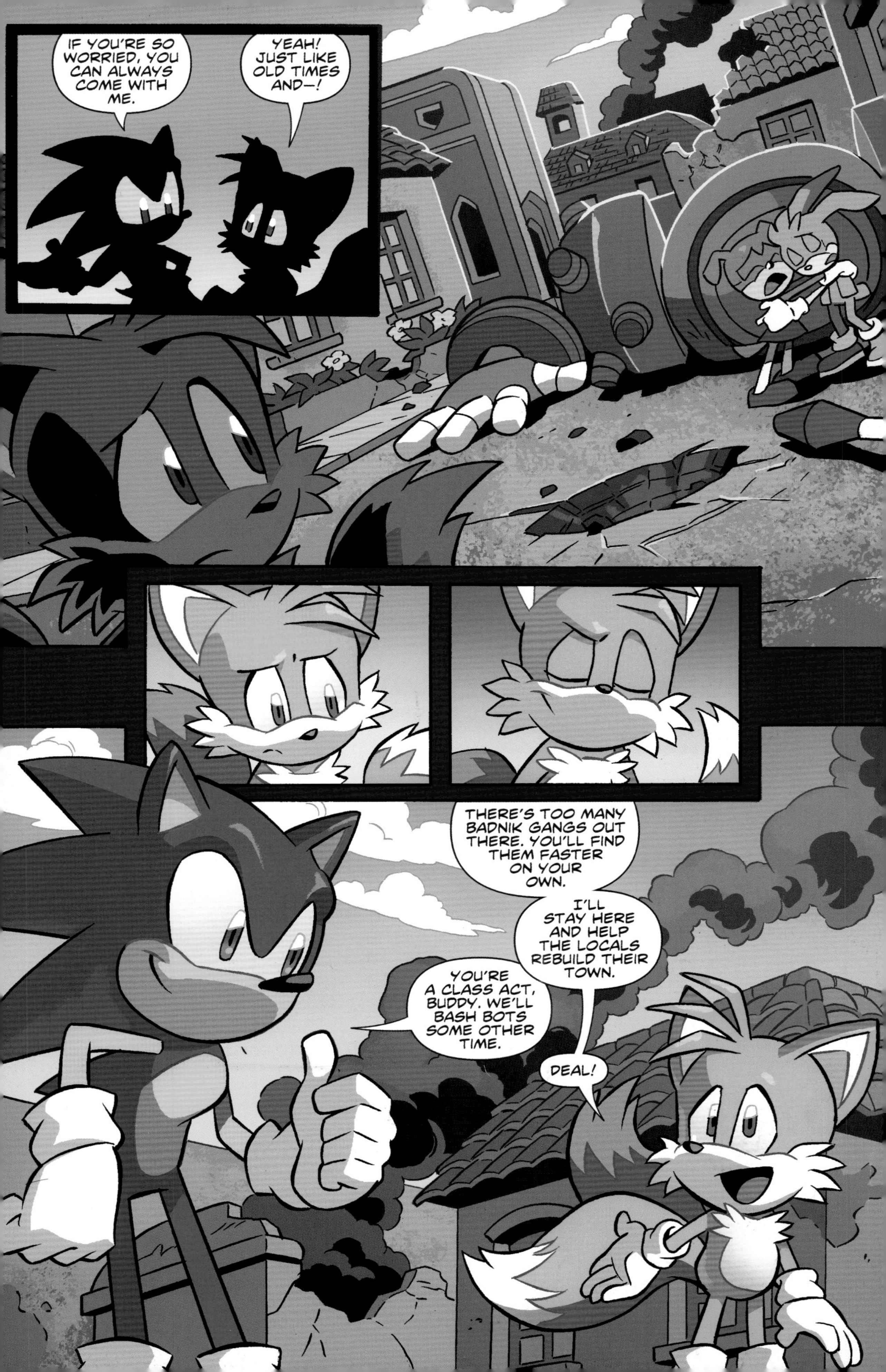
IF YOU'RE SO WORRIED, YOU CAN ALWAYS COME WITH ME.
YEAH! JUST LIKE OLD TIMES AND—!
THERE'S TOO MANY BADNIK GANGS OUT THERE. YOU'LL FIND THEM FASTER ON YOUR OWN.
I'LL STAY HERE AND HELP THE LOCALS REBUILD THEIR TOWN.
YOU'RE A CLASS ACT, BUDDY. WE'LL BASH BOTS SOME OTHER TIME.
DEAL!

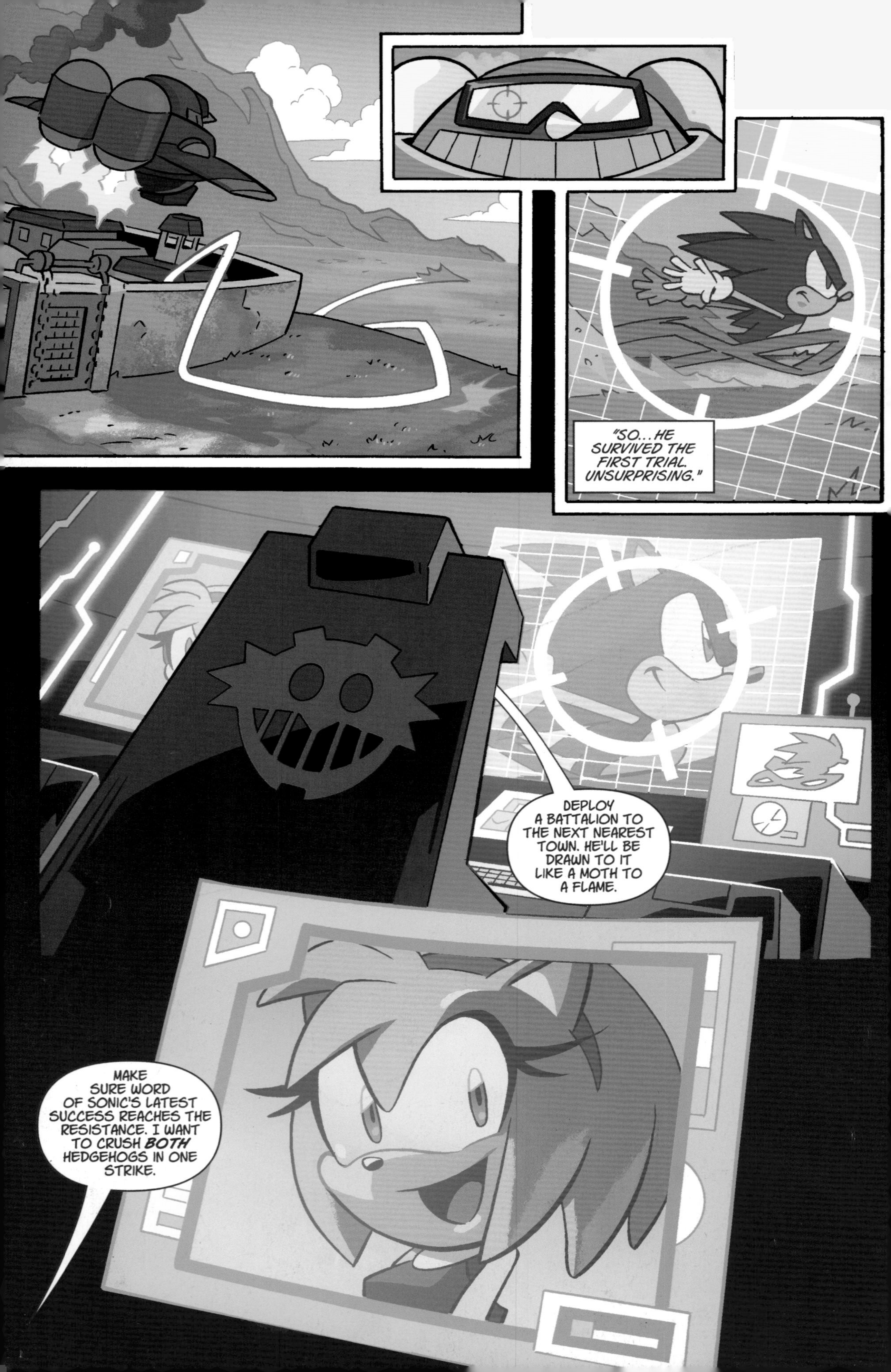
"SO... HE SURVIVED THE FIRST TRIAL. UNSURPRISING."
DEPLOY A BATTALION TO THE NEXT NEAREST TOWN. HE'LL BE DRAWN TO IT LIKE A MOTH TO A FLAME.
MAKE SURE WORD OF SONIC'S LATEST SUCCESS REACHES THE RESISTANCE. I WANT TO CRUSH *BOTH* HEDGEHOGS IN ONE STRIKE.

ART BY NATHALIE FOURDRAINE

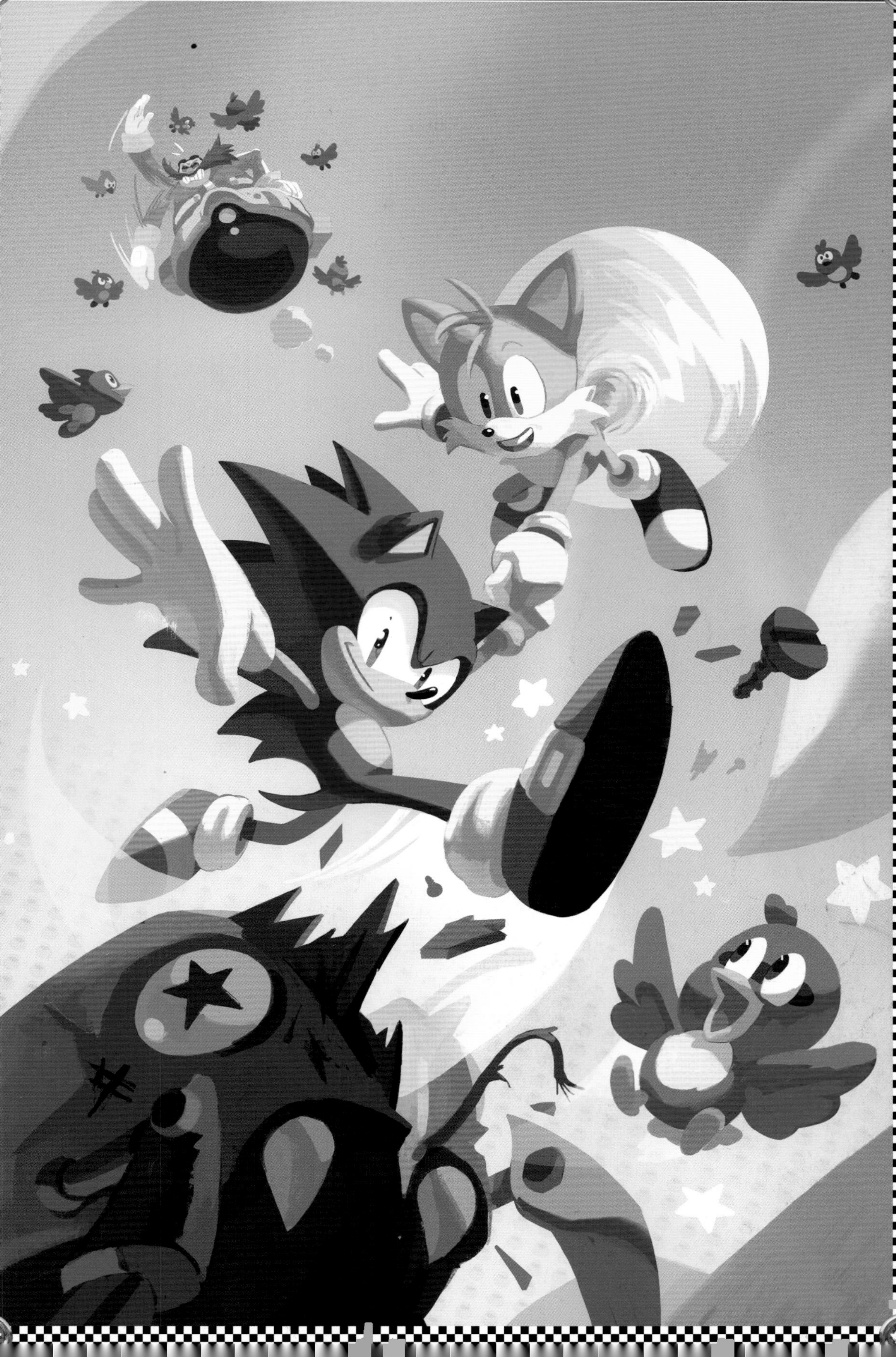

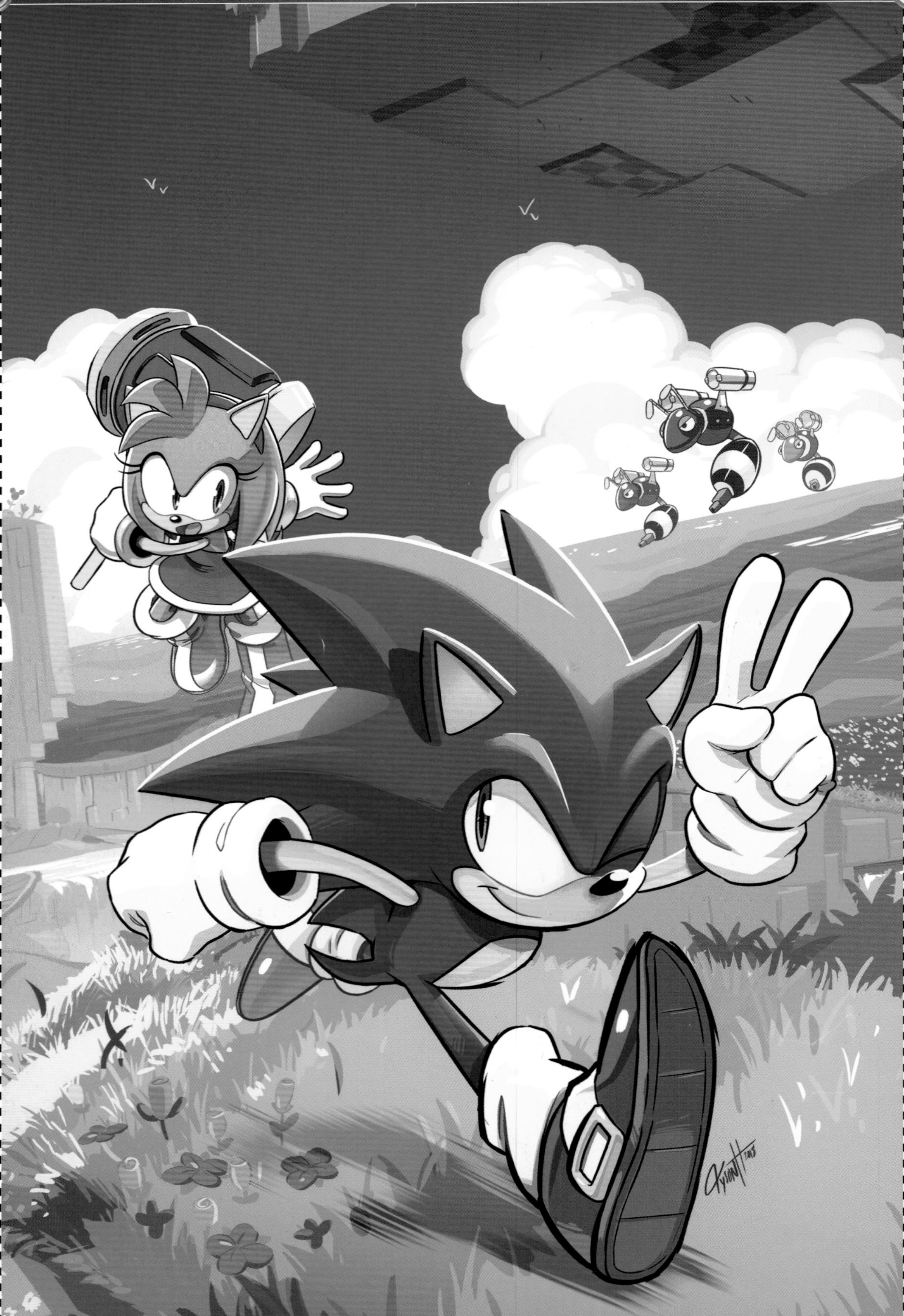

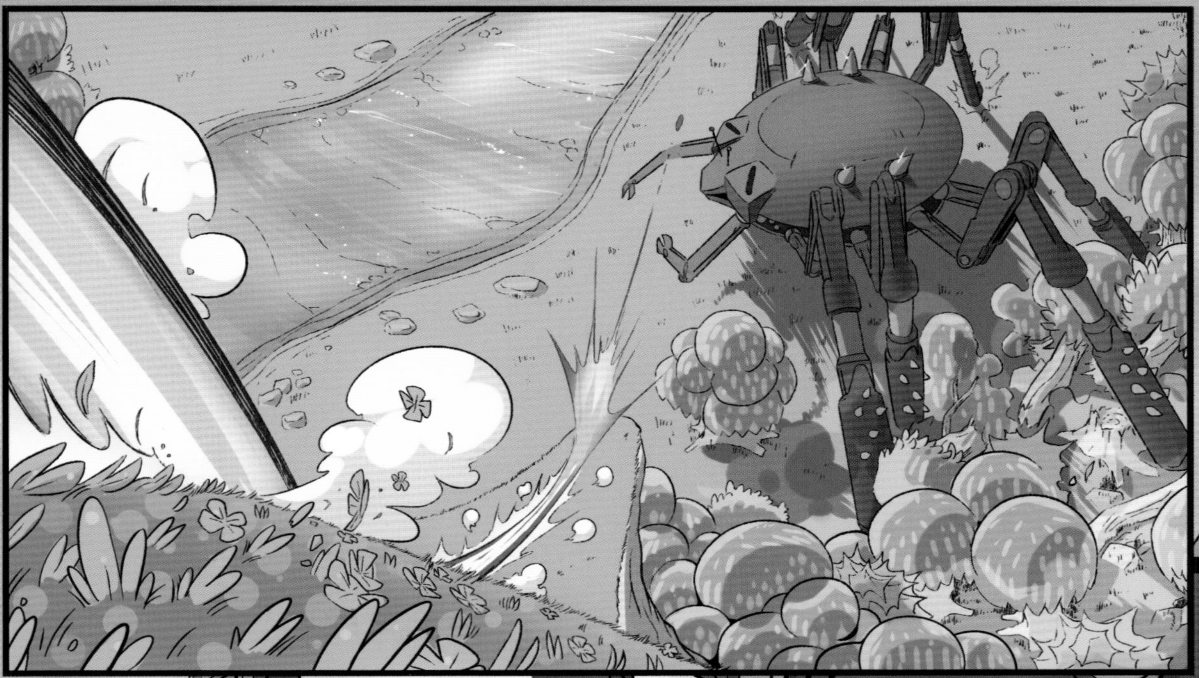

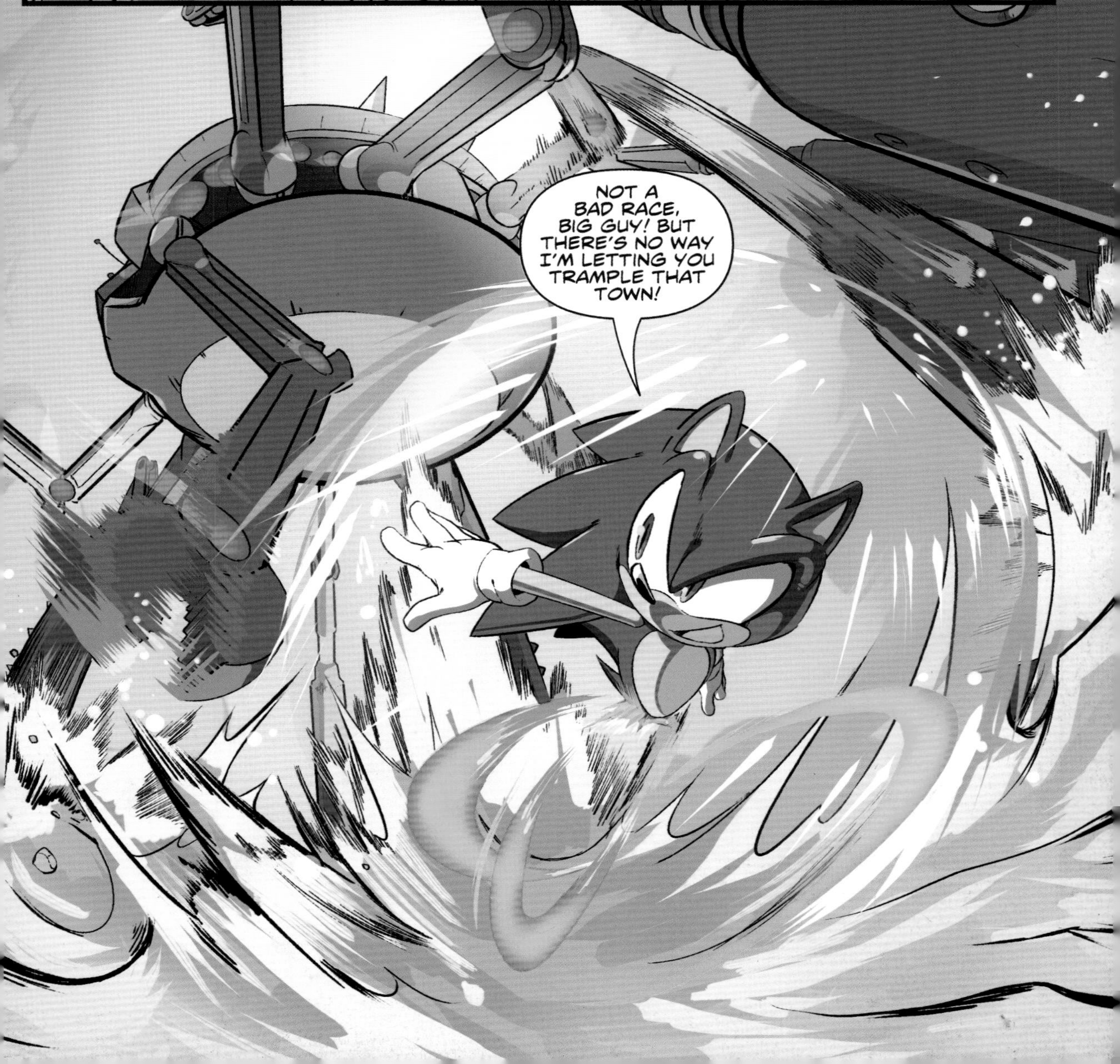
NOT A BAD RACE, BIG GUY! BUT THERE'S NO WAY I'M LETTING YOU TRAMPLE THAT TOWN!

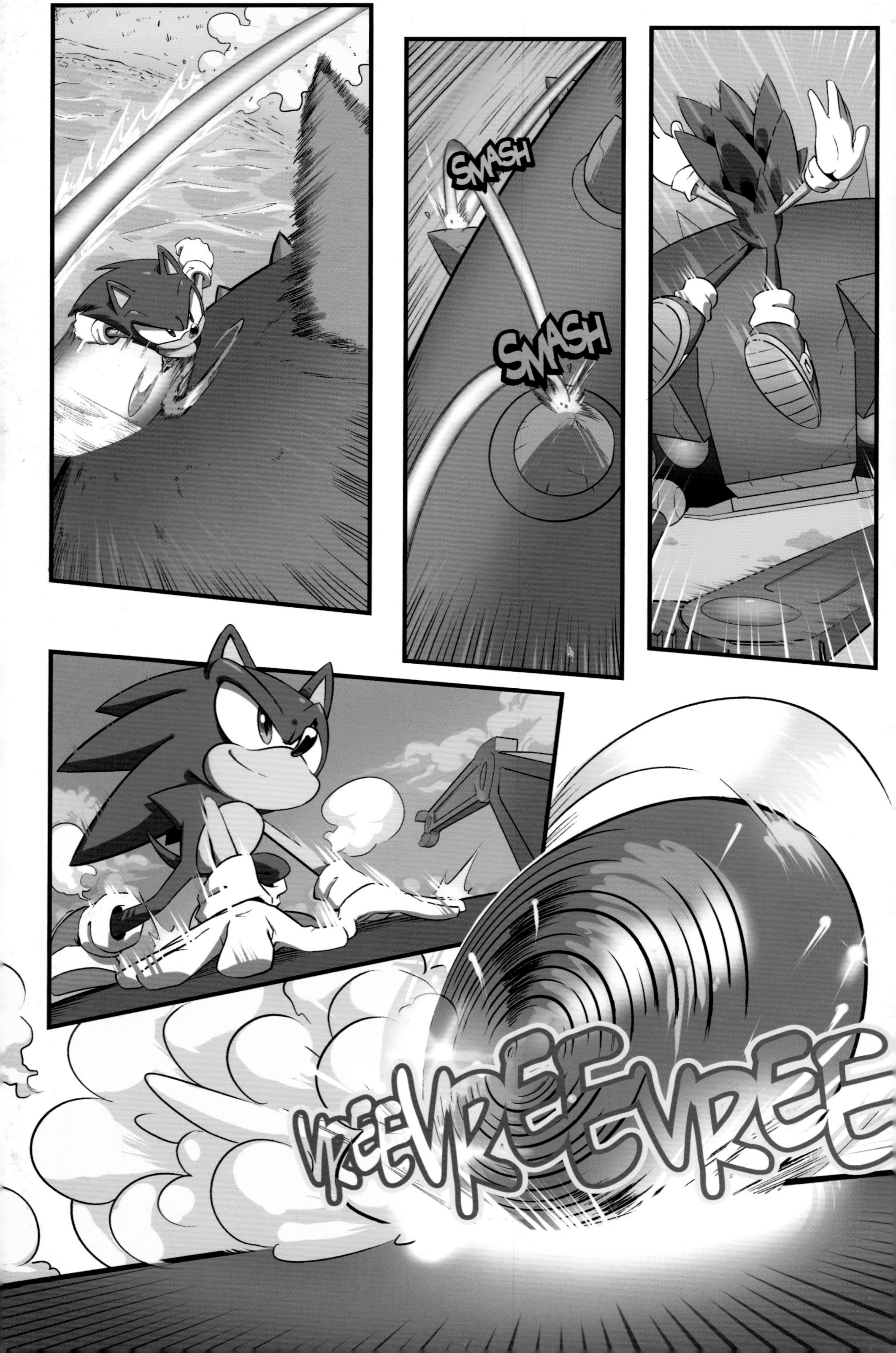
SMASH
SMASH
VREEVREEVREE

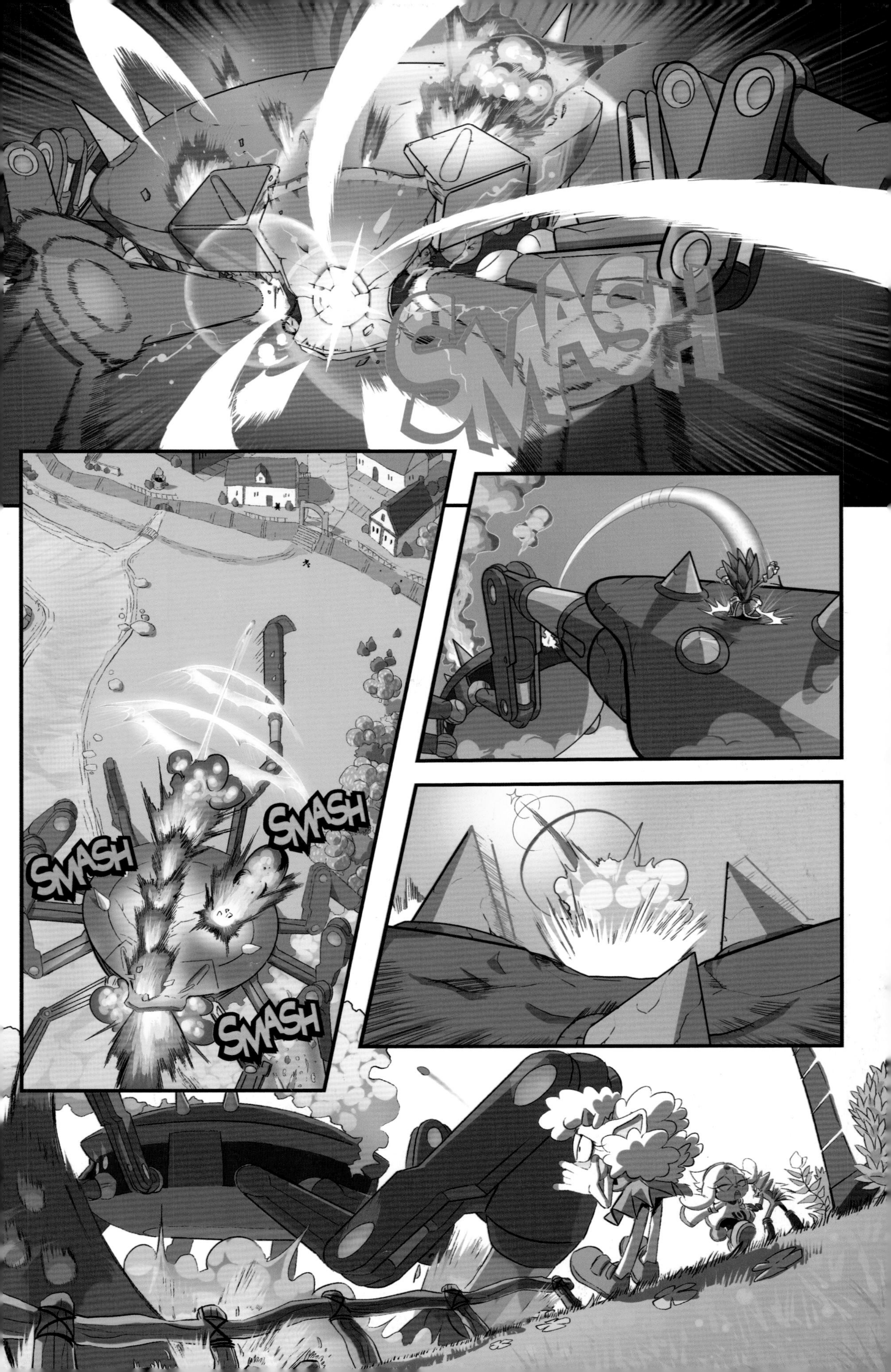
SMASH
SMASH
SMASH
SMASH
SMASH

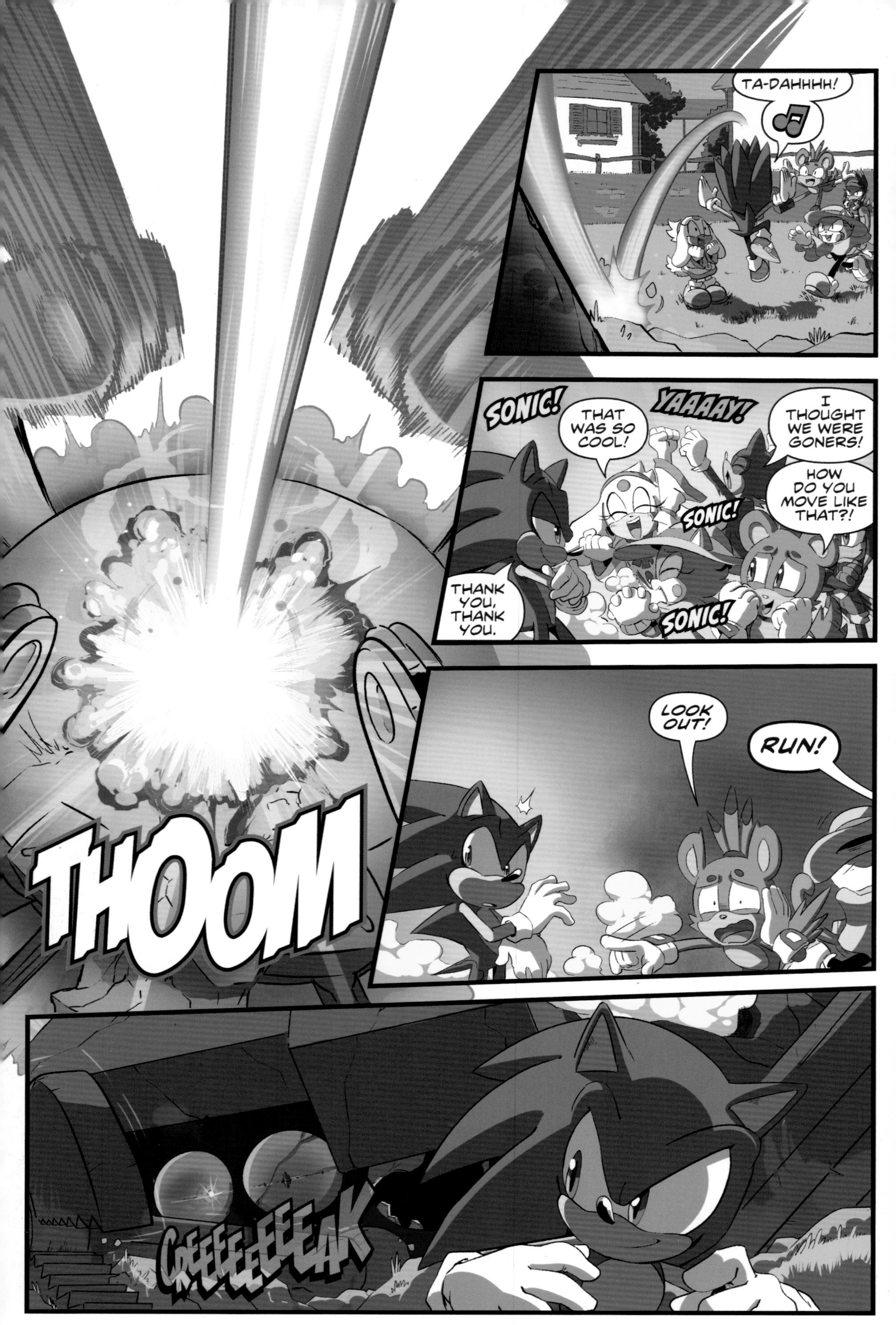
TA-DAHHHH!
SONIC!
THAT WAS SO COOL!
YAAAAY!
I THOUGHT WE WERE GONERS!
HOW DO YOU MOVE LIKE THAT?!
SONIC!
THANK YOU, THANK YOU.
SONIC!
THOOM
LOOK OUT!
RUN!
CREEEEEEEEAK

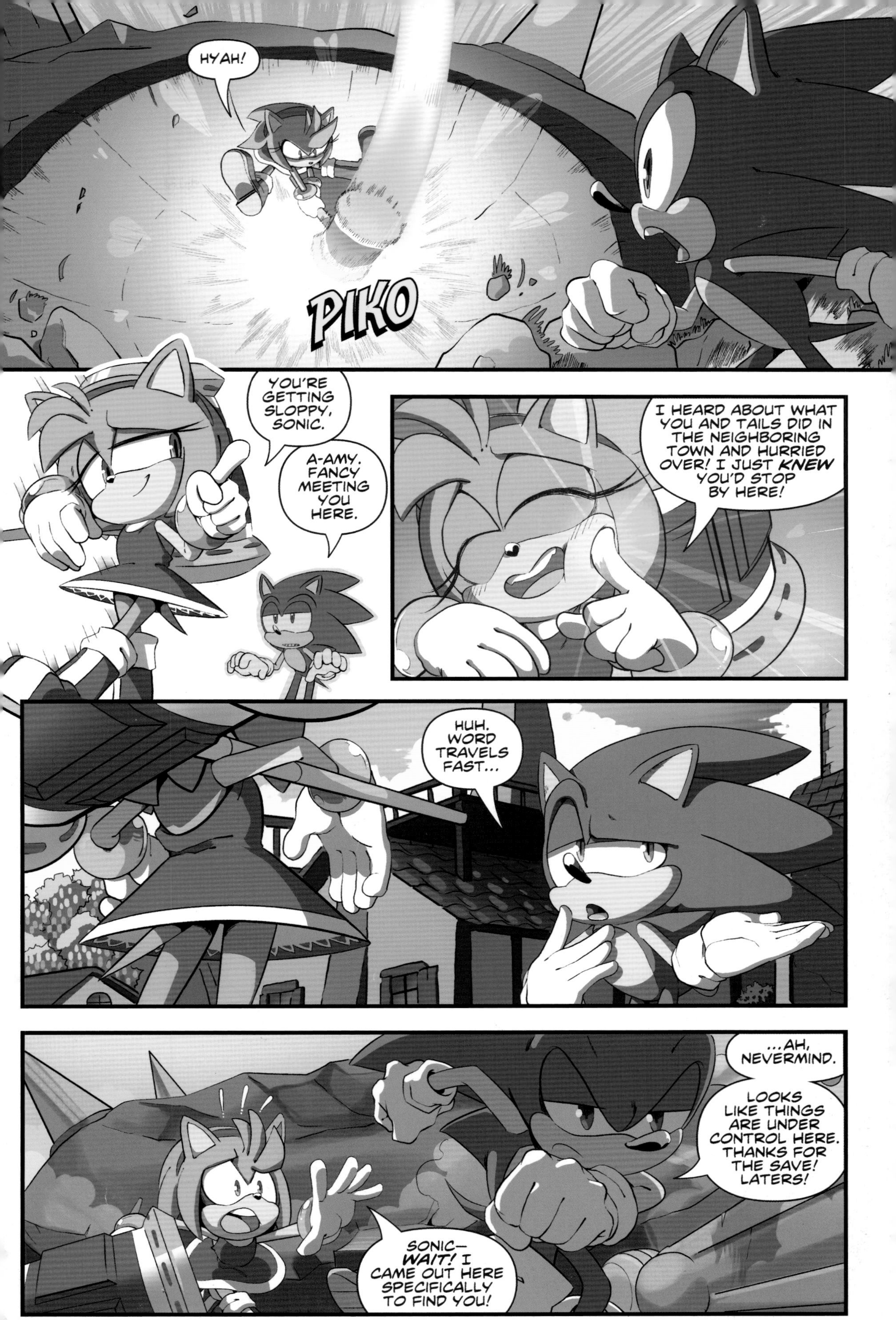
HYAH!
PIKO
YOU'RE GETTING SLOPPY, SONIC.
A-AMY. FANCY MEETING YOU HERE.
I HEARD ABOUT WHAT YOU AND TAILS DID IN THE NEIGHBORING TOWN AND HURRIED OVER! I JUST **KNEW** YOU'D STOP BY HERE!
HUH. WORD TRAVELS FAST...
...AH, NEVERMIND.
LOOKS LIKE THINGS ARE UNDER CONTROL HERE. THANKS FOR THE SAVE! LATERS!
SONIC— **WAIT!** I CAME OUT HERE SPECIFICALLY TO FIND YOU!

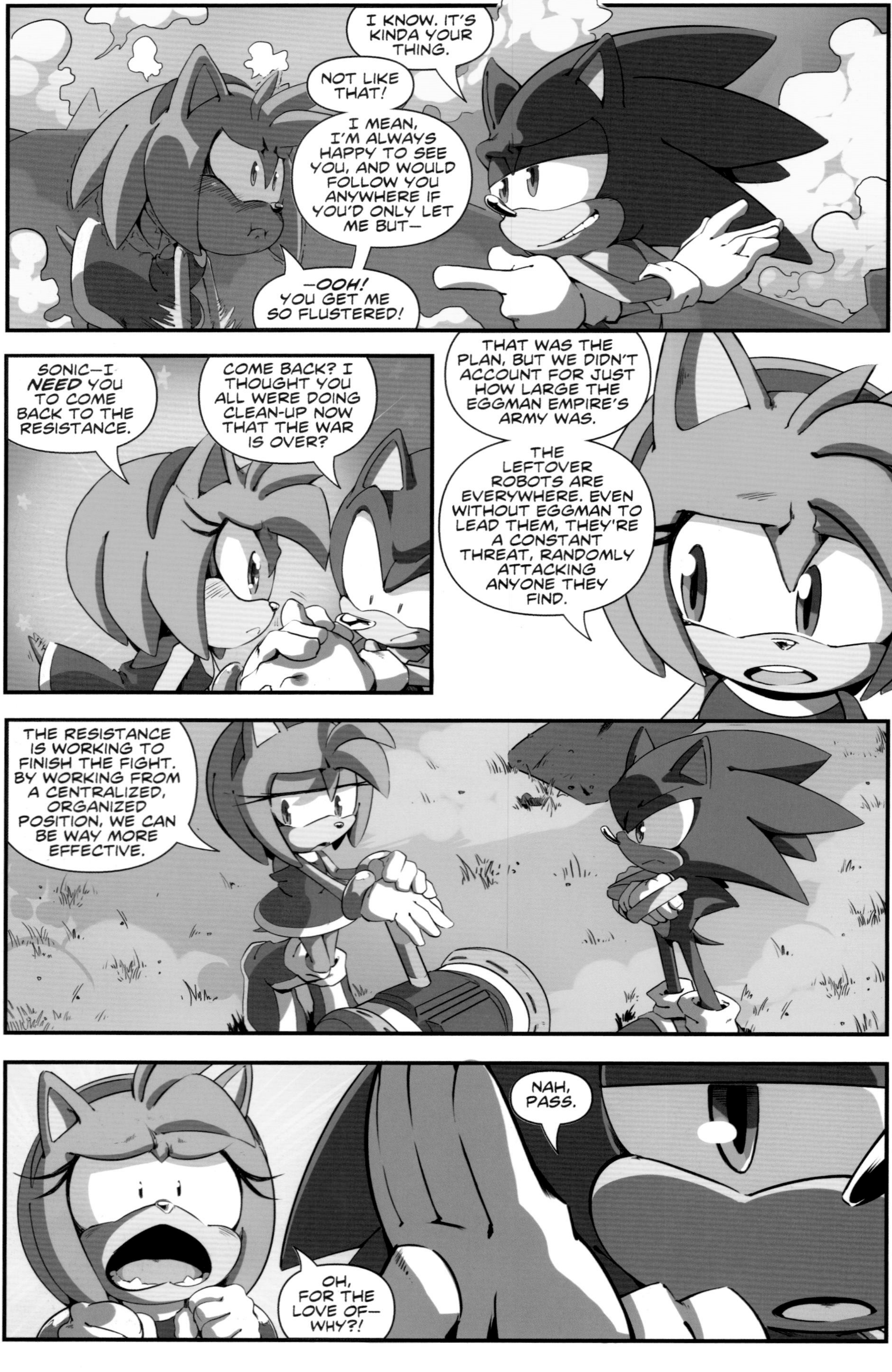

I KNOW. IT'S KINDA YOUR THING.
NOT LIKE THAT!
I MEAN, I'M ALWAYS HAPPY TO SEE YOU, AND WOULD FOLLOW YOU ANYWHERE IF YOU'D ONLY LET ME BUT—
—OOH! YOU GET ME SO FLUSTERED!
SONIC—I NEED YOU TO COME BACK TO THE RESISTANCE.
COME BACK? I THOUGHT YOU ALL WERE DOING CLEAN-UP NOW THAT THE WAR IS OVER?
THAT WAS THE PLAN, BUT WE DIDN'T ACCOUNT FOR JUST HOW LARGE THE EGGMAN EMPIRE'S ARMY WAS.
THE LEFTOVER ROBOTS ARE EVERYWHERE. EVEN WITHOUT EGGMAN TO LEAD THEM, THEY'RE A CONSTANT THREAT, RANDOMLY ATTACKING ANYONE THEY FIND.
THE RESISTANCE IS WORKING TO FINISH THE FIGHT. BY WORKING FROM A CENTRALIZED, ORGANIZED POSITION, WE CAN BE WAY MORE EFFECTIVE.
NAH, PASS.
OH, FOR THE LOVE OF— WHY?!

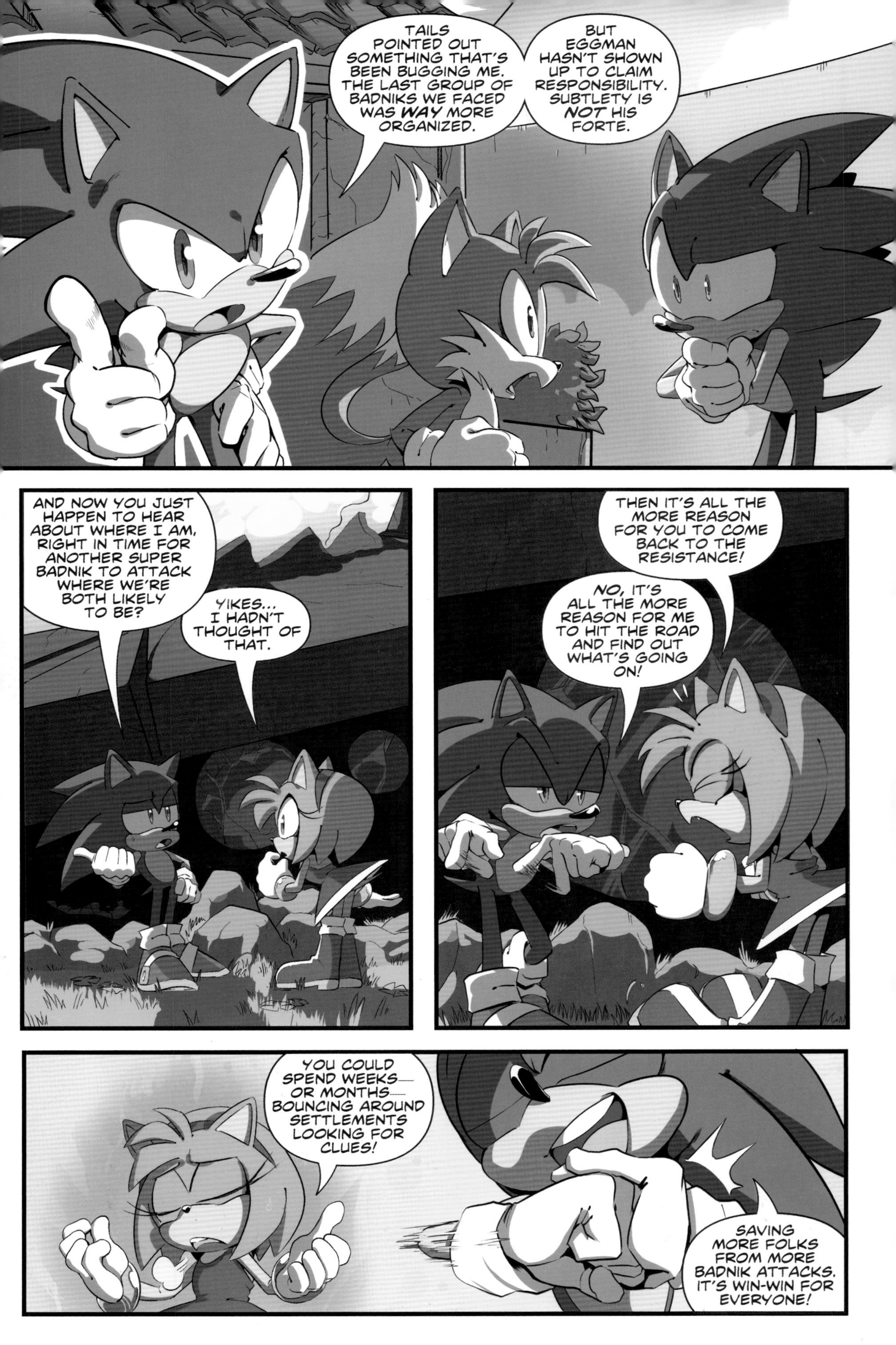

TAILS POINTED OUT SOMETHING THAT'S BEEN BUGGING ME. THE LAST GROUP OF BADNIKS WE FACED WAS **WAY** MORE ORGANIZED.
BUT EGGMAN HASN'T SHOWN UP TO CLAIM RESPONSIBILITY. SUBTLETY IS **NOT** HIS FORTE.
AND NOW YOU JUST HAPPEN TO HEAR ABOUT WHERE I AM, RIGHT IN TIME FOR ANOTHER SUPER BADNIK TO ATTACK WHERE WE'RE BOTH LIKELY TO BE?
YIKES... I HADN'T THOUGHT OF THAT.
THEN IT'S ALL THE MORE REASON FOR YOU TO COME BACK TO THE RESISTANCE!
NO, IT'S ALL THE MORE REASON FOR ME TO HIT THE ROAD AND FIND OUT WHAT'S GOING ON!
YOU COULD SPEND WEEKS— OR MONTHS— BOUNCING AROUND SETTLEMENTS LOOKING FOR CLUES!
SAVING MORE FOLKS FROM MORE BADNIK ATTACKS. IT'S WIN-WIN FOR EVERYONE!

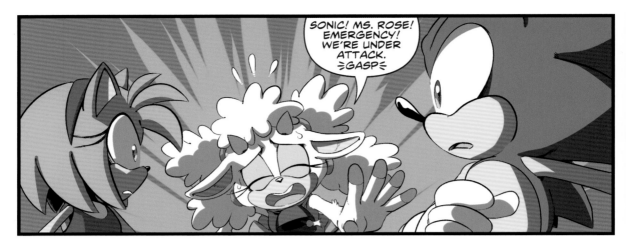

SONIC! MS. ROSE! EMERGENCY! WE'RE UNDER ATTACK. ≋GASP≋

IT'S COOL. WE TOOK OUT THE SUPER BADNIK.

≋PANT≋ NO! I MEAN AN ARMY! INVADING FROM THE WEST!

THE CRAB-BOT WAS A DECOY...

WE'VE GOT TO STOP THE INVASION BEFORE THE CITY IS OVER-RUN!

I'LL RUN AHEAD AND THIN THEM OUT!

DO YOU HAVE ANY KIND OF DEFENSES?

WE TURNED TOWN HALL INTO A BUNKER OF SORTS DURING THE WAR...

TAKE ME THERE!

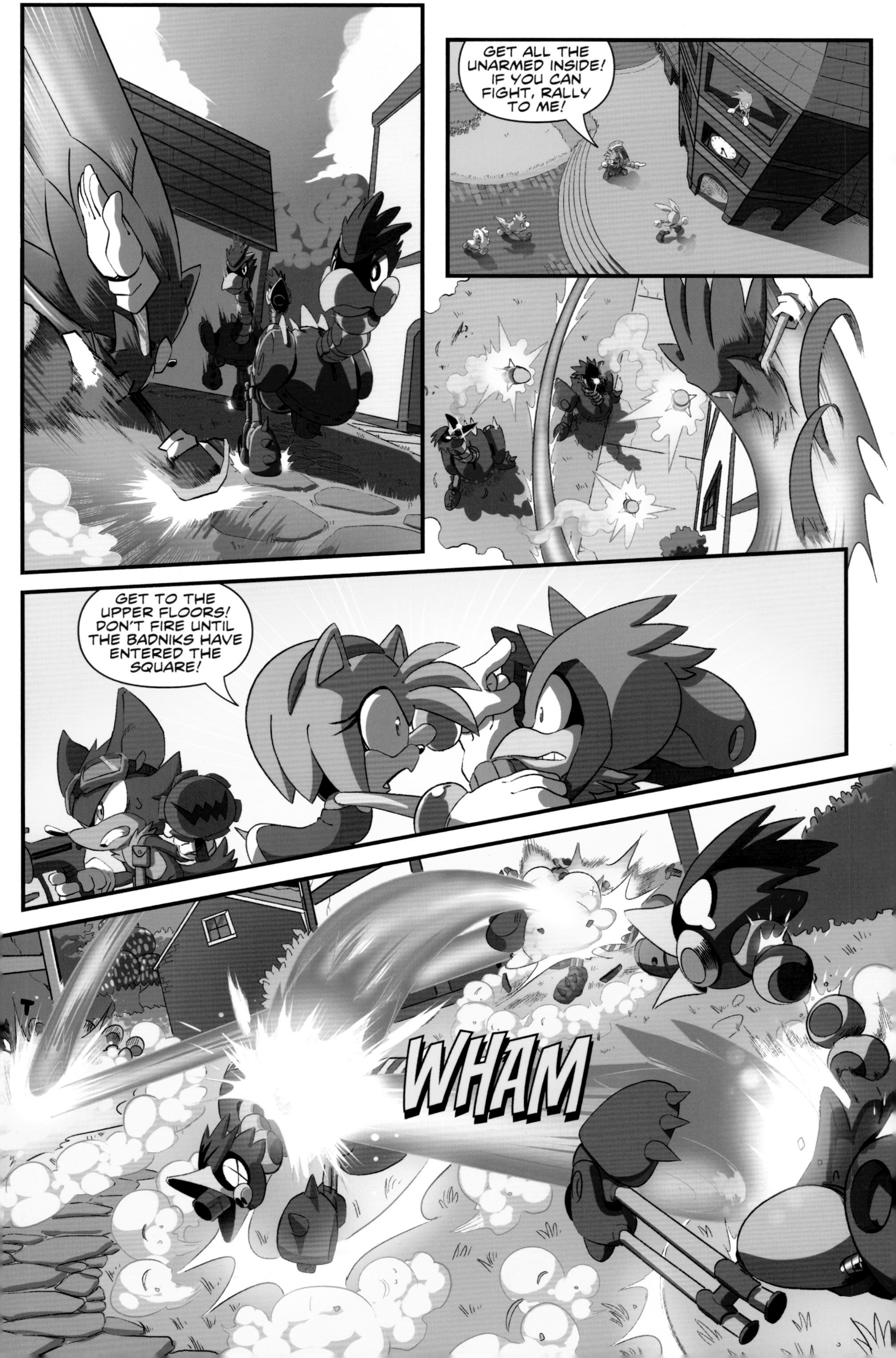
GET ALL THE UNARMED INSIDE! IF YOU CAN FIGHT, RALLY TO ME!
GET TO THE UPPER FLOORS! DON'T FIRE UNTIL THE BADNIKS HAVE ENTERED THE SQUARE!
WHAM

WHOOPS...

NOT EVERYONE IS ACCOUNTED FOR!

PAIR UP! GO DOOR-TO-DOOR AND BRING BACK NO MORE THAN 10 AT A TIME! KEEP LOW AND CHECK YOUR CORNERS!

BLAM

BLAM

BLAM

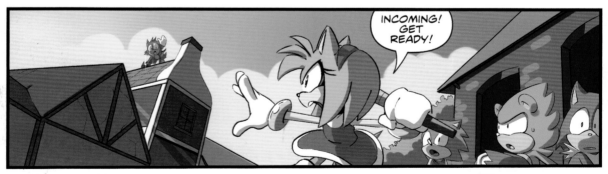

INCOMING! GET READY!

DANG IT! I LET TOO MANY GET PAST ME!

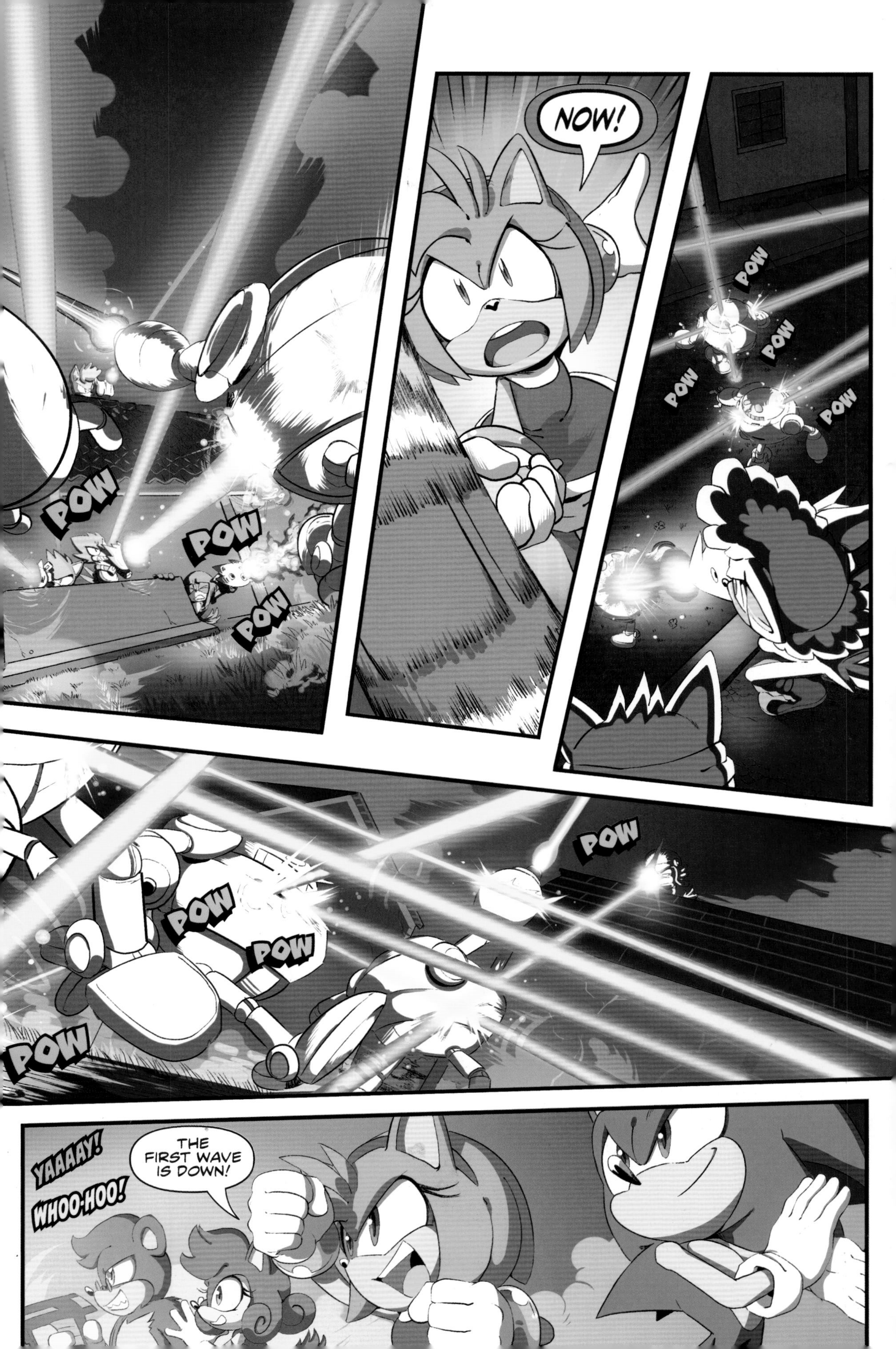

POW
POW
POW
NOW!
POW
POW
POW
POW
POW
POW
POW
POW
YAAAAY!
WHOO-HOO!
THE FIRST WAVE IS DOWN!

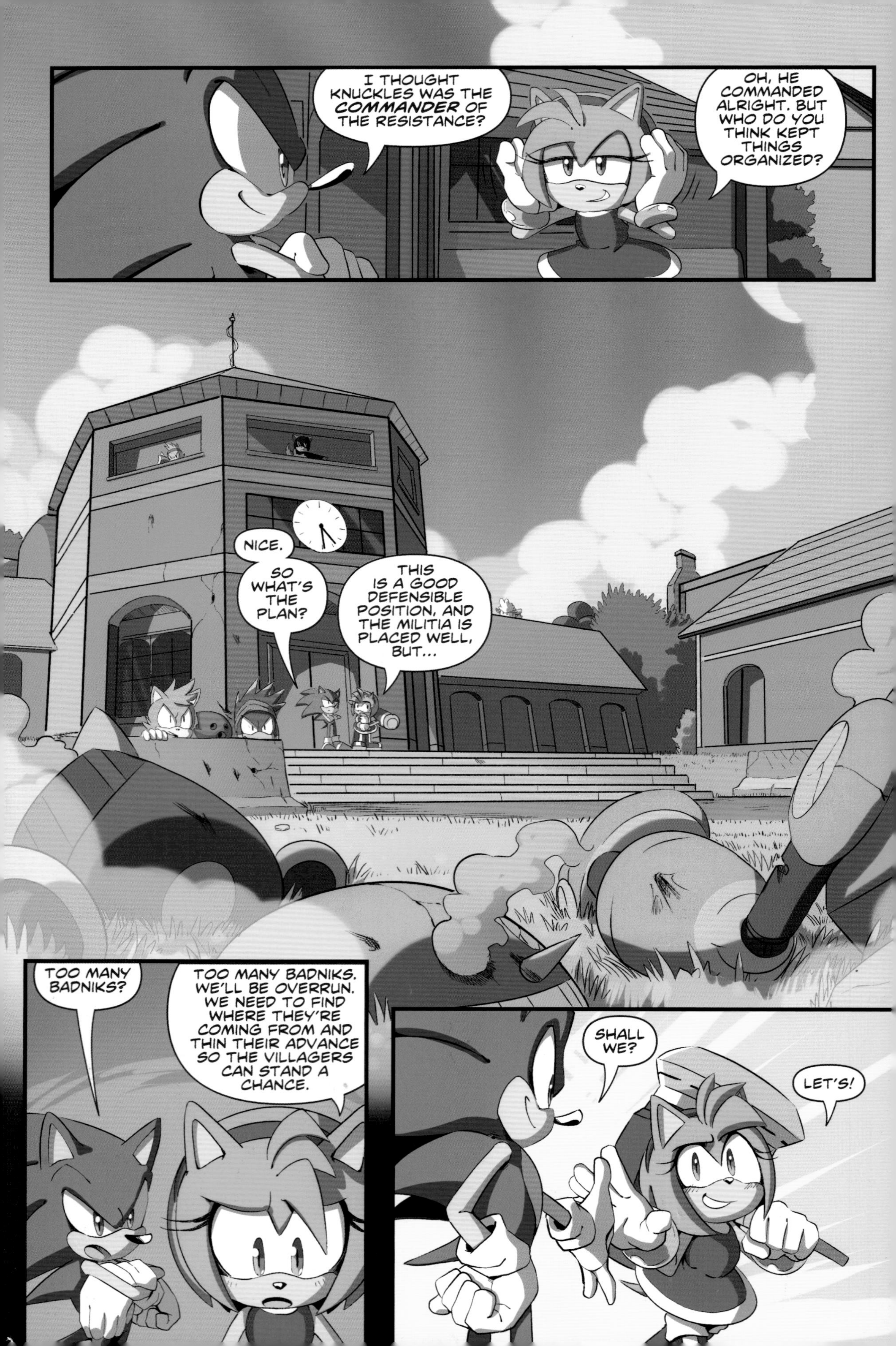
I THOUGHT KNUCKLES WAS THE COMMANDER OF THE RESISTANCE?
OH, HE COMMANDED ALRIGHT. BUT WHO DO YOU THINK KEPT THINGS ORGANIZED?
NICE.
SO WHAT'S THE PLAN?
THIS IS A GOOD DEFENSIBLE POSITION, AND THE MILITIA IS PLACED WELL, BUT...
TOO MANY BADNIKS?
TOO MANY BADNIKS. WE'LL BE OVERRUN. WE NEED TO FIND WHERE THEY'RE COMING FROM AND THIN THEIR ADVANCE SO THE VILLAGERS CAN STAND A CHANCE.
SHALL WE?
LET'S!

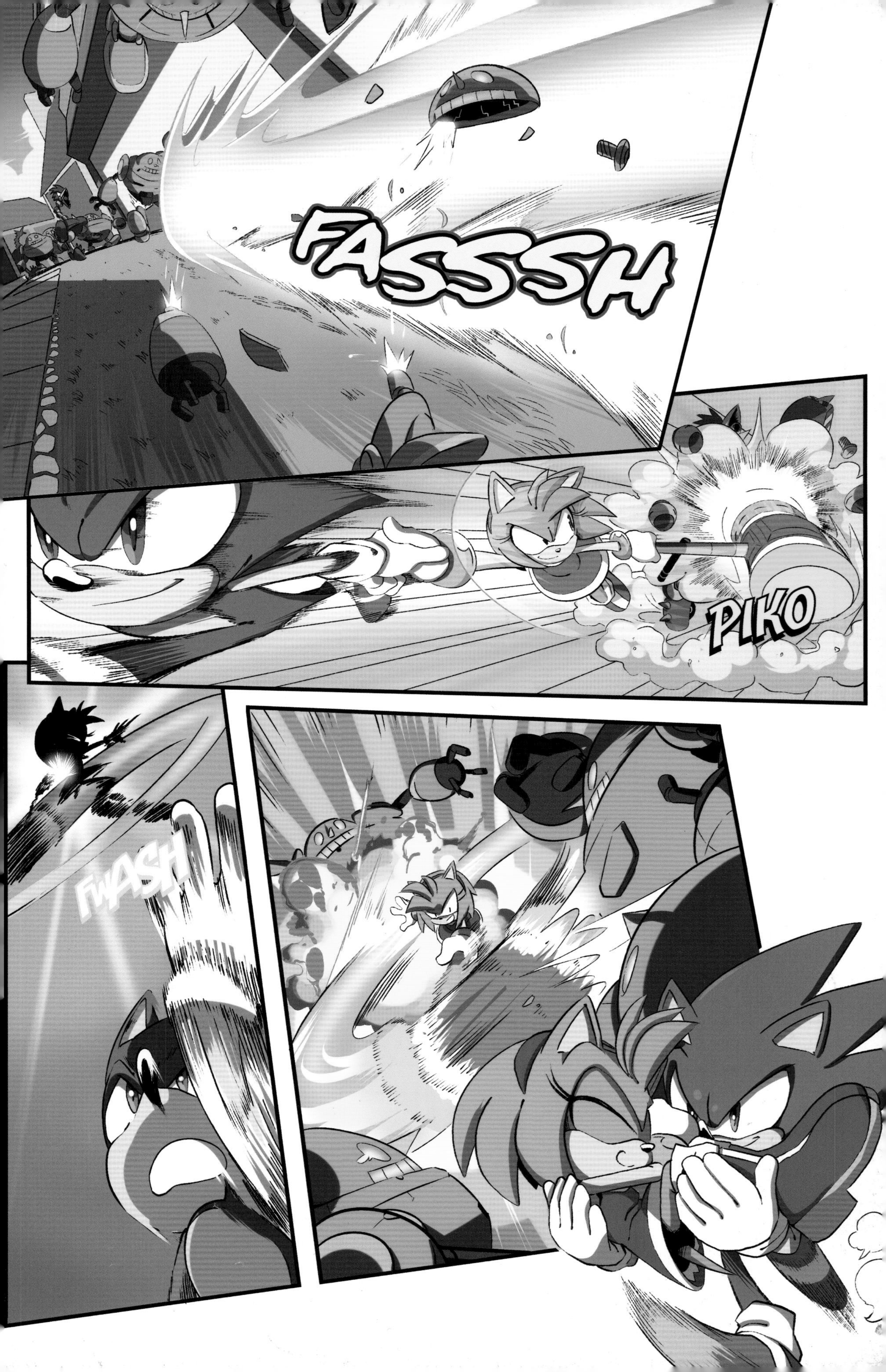
FASSSH
PIKO
FWASH

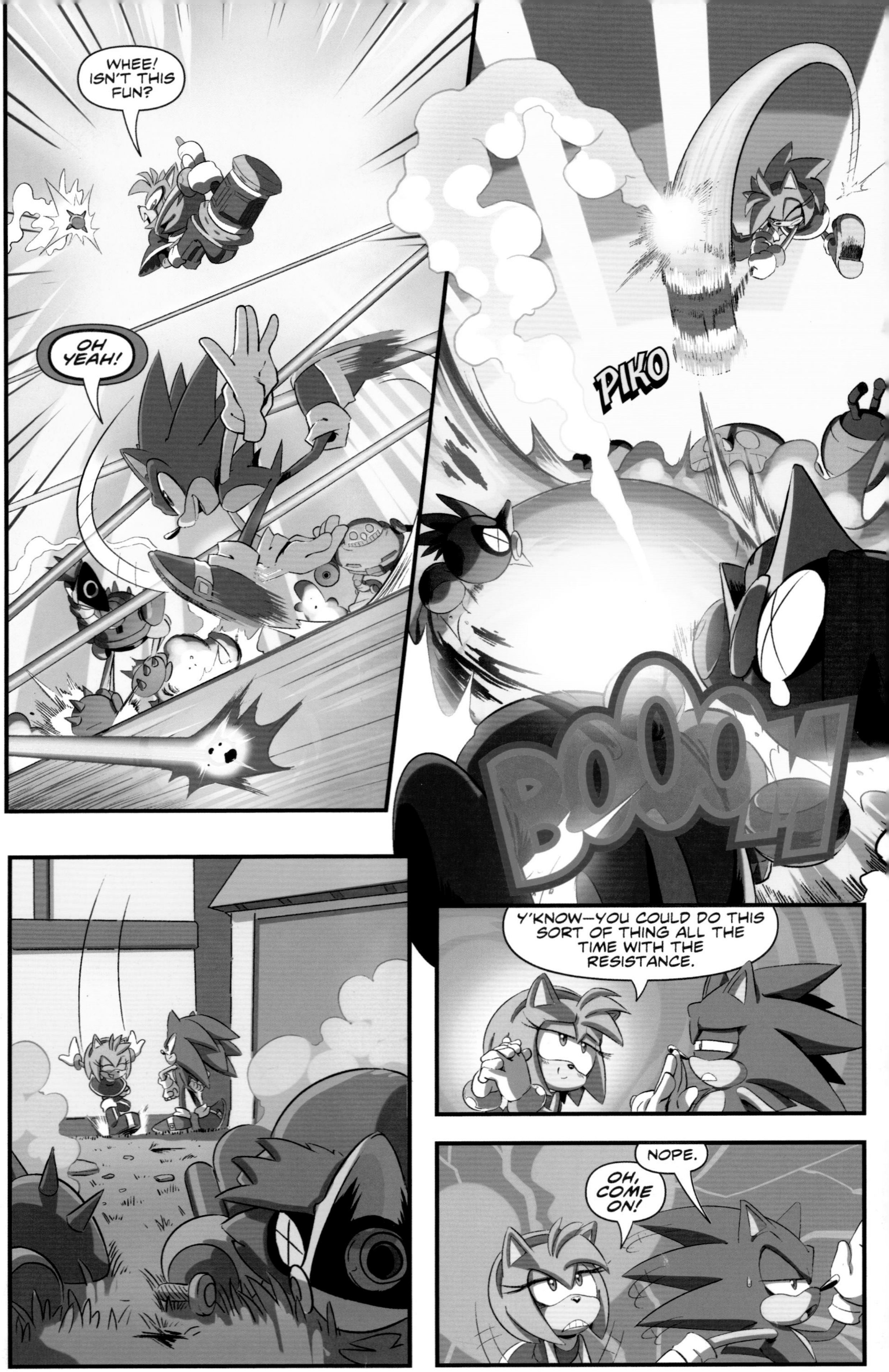
WHEE! ISN'T THIS FUN?
OH YEAH!
PIKO
BOOOM
Y'KNOW—YOU COULD DO THIS SORT OF THING ALL THE TIME WITH THE RESISTANCE.
NOPE.
OH, COME ON!

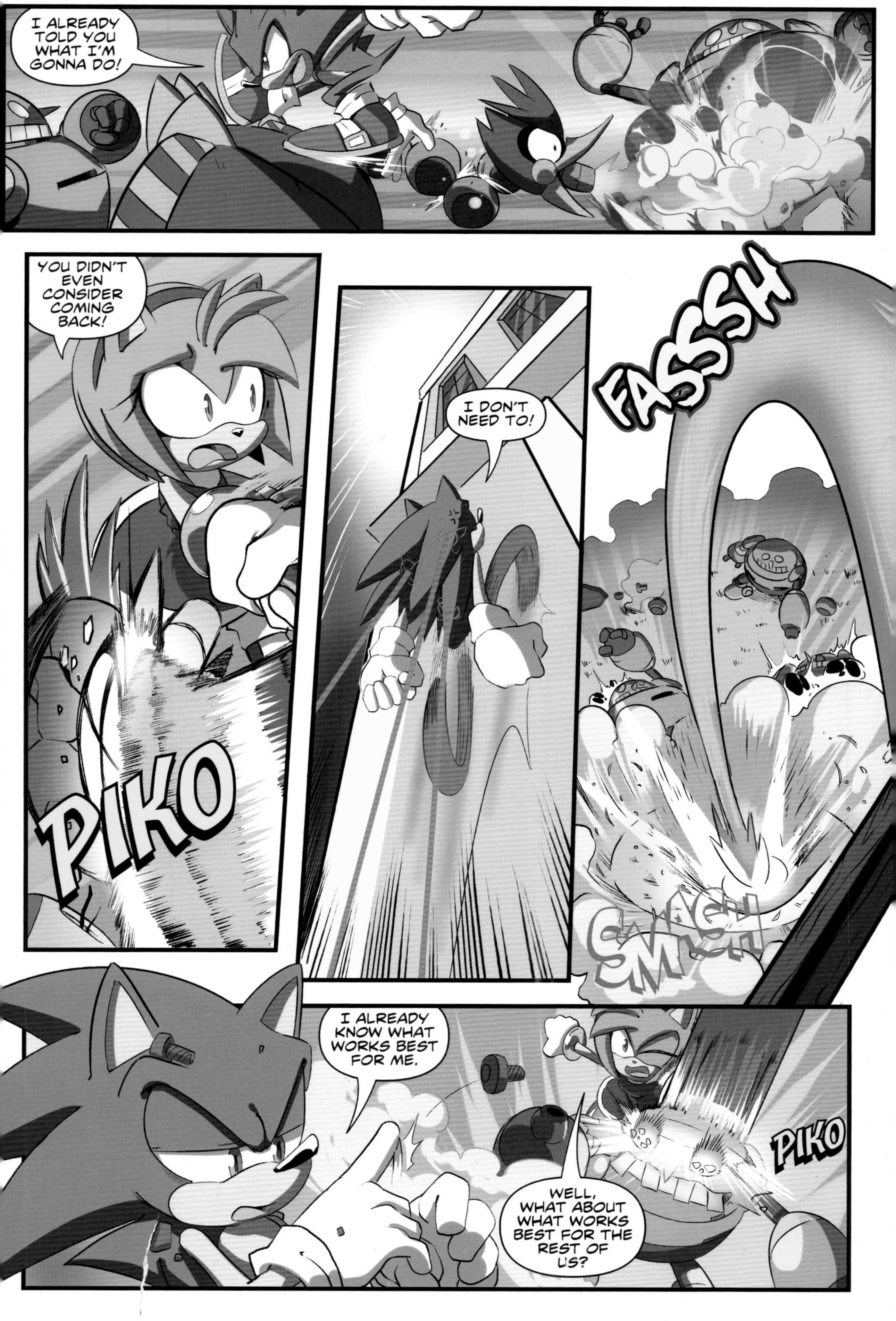
I ALREADY TOLD YOU WHAT I'M GONNA DO!
YOU DIDN'T EVEN CONSIDER COMING BACK!
PIKO
I DON'T NEED TO!
FASSSH
SMASH
I ALREADY KNOW WHAT WORKS BEST FOR ME.
PIKO
WELL, WHAT ABOUT WHAT WORKS BEST FOR THE REST OF US?

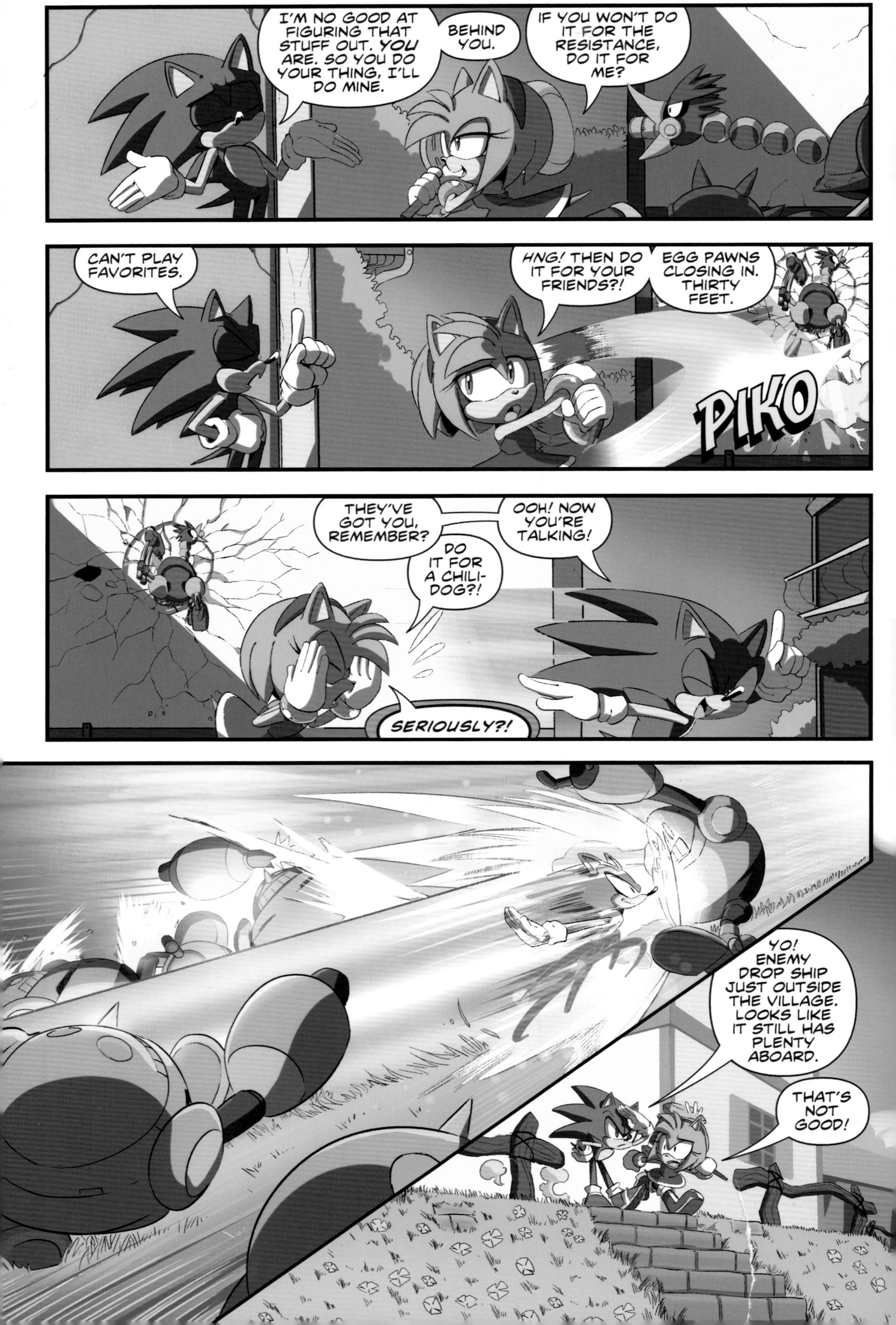
I'M NO GOOD AT FIGURING THAT STUFF OUT. YOU ARE. SO YOU DO YOUR THING, I'LL DO MINE.
BEHIND YOU.
IF YOU WON'T DO IT FOR THE RESISTANCE, DO IT FOR ME?
CAN'T PLAY FAVORITES.
HNG! THEN DO IT FOR YOUR FRIENDS?!
EGG PAWNS CLOSING IN. THIRTY FEET.
PIKO
THEY'VE GOT YOU, REMEMBER?
DO IT FOR A CHILI-DOG?!
OOH! NOW YOU'RE TALKING!
SERIOUSLY?!
YO! ENEMY DROP SHIP JUST OUTSIDE THE VILLAGE. LOOKS LIKE IT STILL HAS PLENTY ABOARD.
THAT'S NOT GOOD!

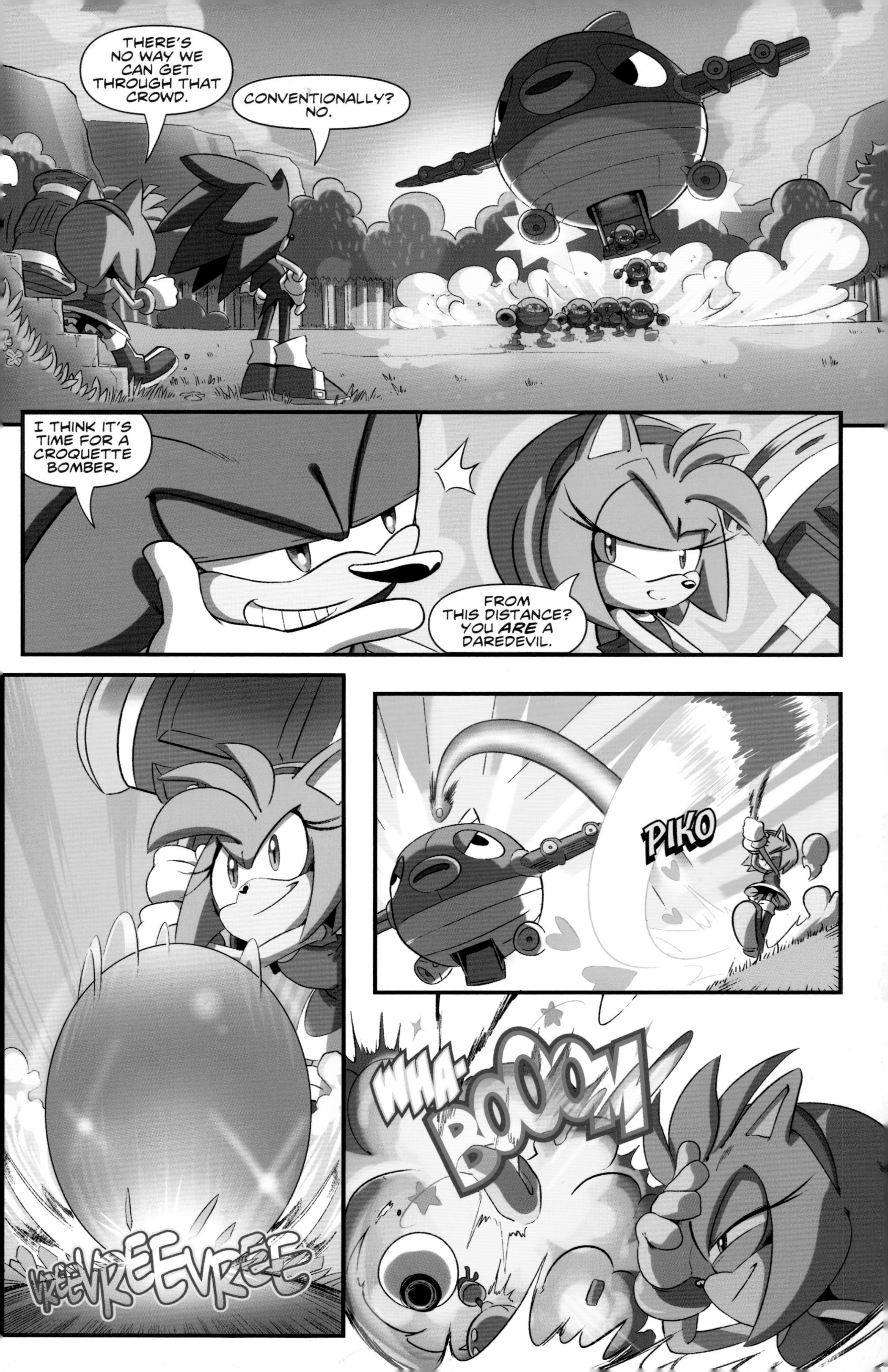
THERE'S NO WAY WE CAN GET THROUGH THAT CROWD.
CONVENTIONALLY? NO.
I THINK IT'S TIME FOR A CROQUETTE BOMBER.
FROM THIS DISTANCE? YOU ARE A DAREDEVIL.
VREEVREEVREE
PIKO
WHA-BOOOOM

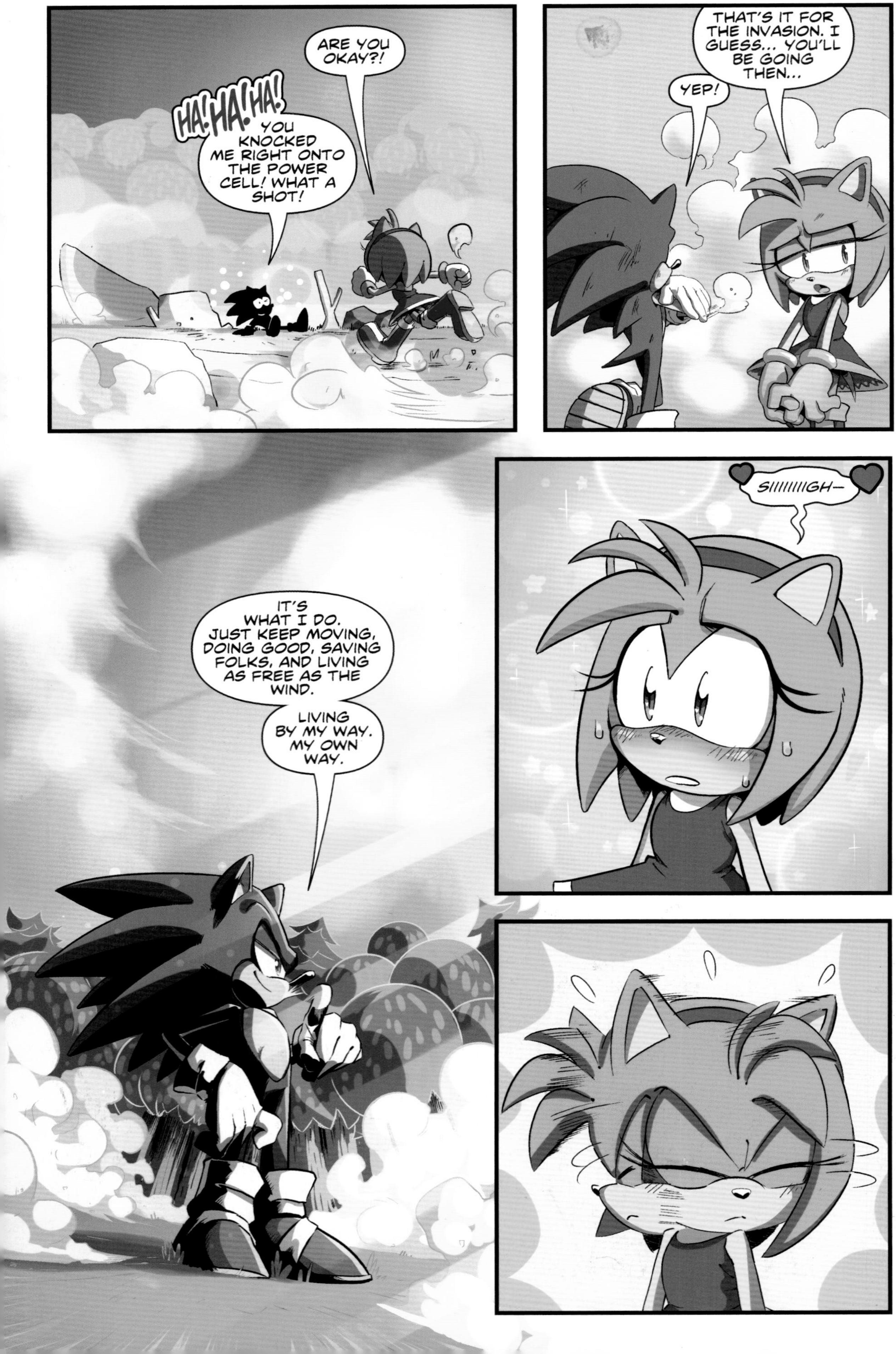
HA! HA! HA!
YOU KNOCKED ME RIGHT ONTO THE POWER CELL! WHAT A SHOT!
ARE YOU OKAY?!
THAT'S IT FOR THE INVASION. I GUESS... YOU'LL BE GOING THEN...
YEP!
IT'S WHAT I DO. JUST KEEP MOVING, DOING GOOD, SAVING FOLKS, AND LIVING AS FREE AS THE WIND.
LIVING BY MY WAY. MY OWN WAY.
SIIIIIIIIGH–

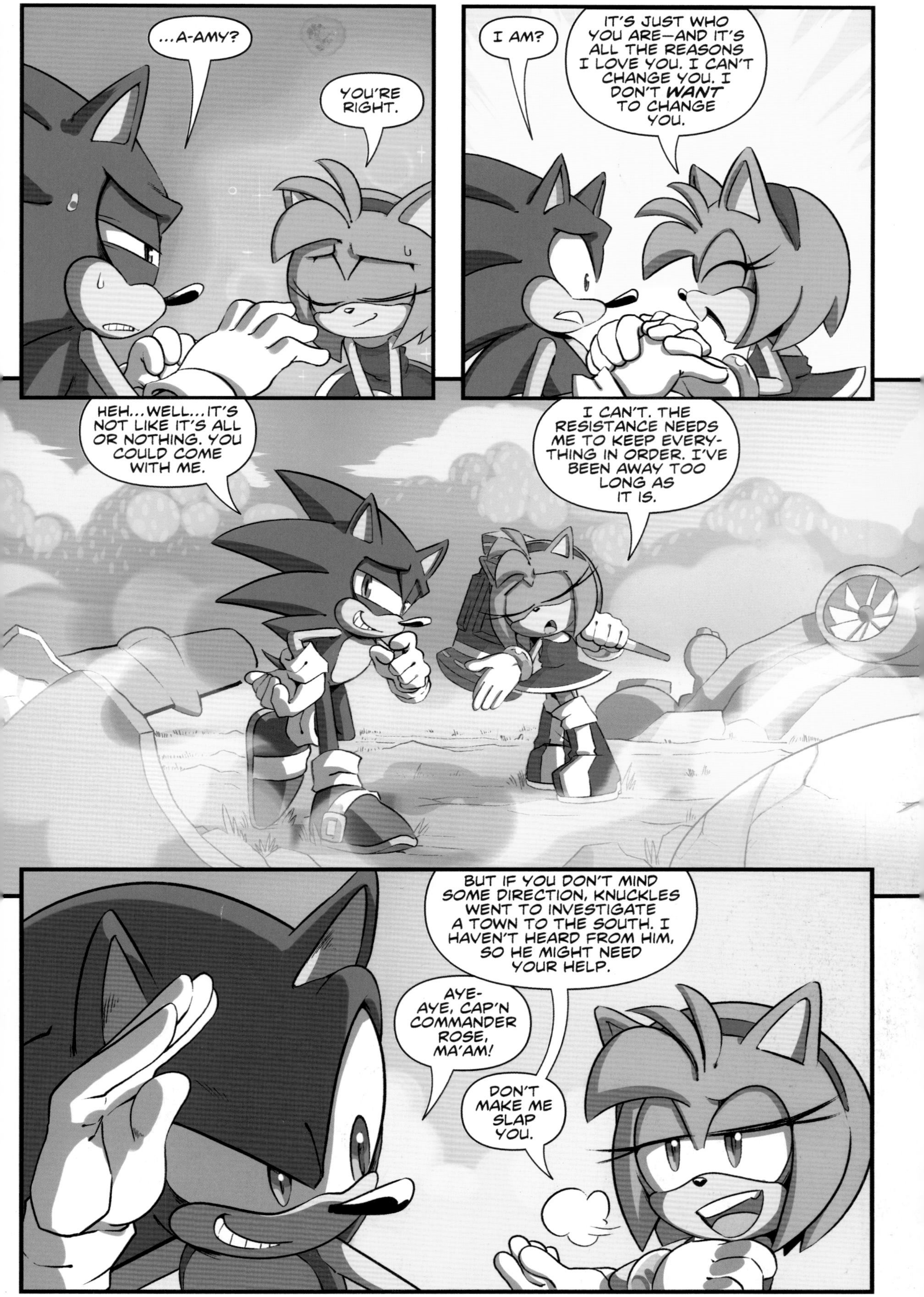

...A-AMY?
YOU'RE RIGHT.
I AM?
IT'S JUST WHO YOU ARE—AND IT'S ALL THE REASONS I LOVE YOU. I CAN'T CHANGE YOU. I DON'T ***WANT*** TO CHANGE YOU.
HEH...WELL...IT'S NOT LIKE IT'S ALL OR NOTHING. YOU COULD COME WITH ME.
I CAN'T. THE RESISTANCE NEEDS ME TO KEEP EVERY-THING IN ORDER. I'VE BEEN AWAY TOO LONG AS IT IS.
BUT IF YOU DON'T MIND SOME DIRECTION, KNUCKLES WENT TO INVESTIGATE A TOWN TO THE SOUTH. I HAVEN'T HEARD FROM HIM, SO HE MIGHT NEED YOUR HELP.
AYE-AYE, CAP'N COMMANDER ROSE, MA'AM!
DON'T MAKE ME SLAP YOU.

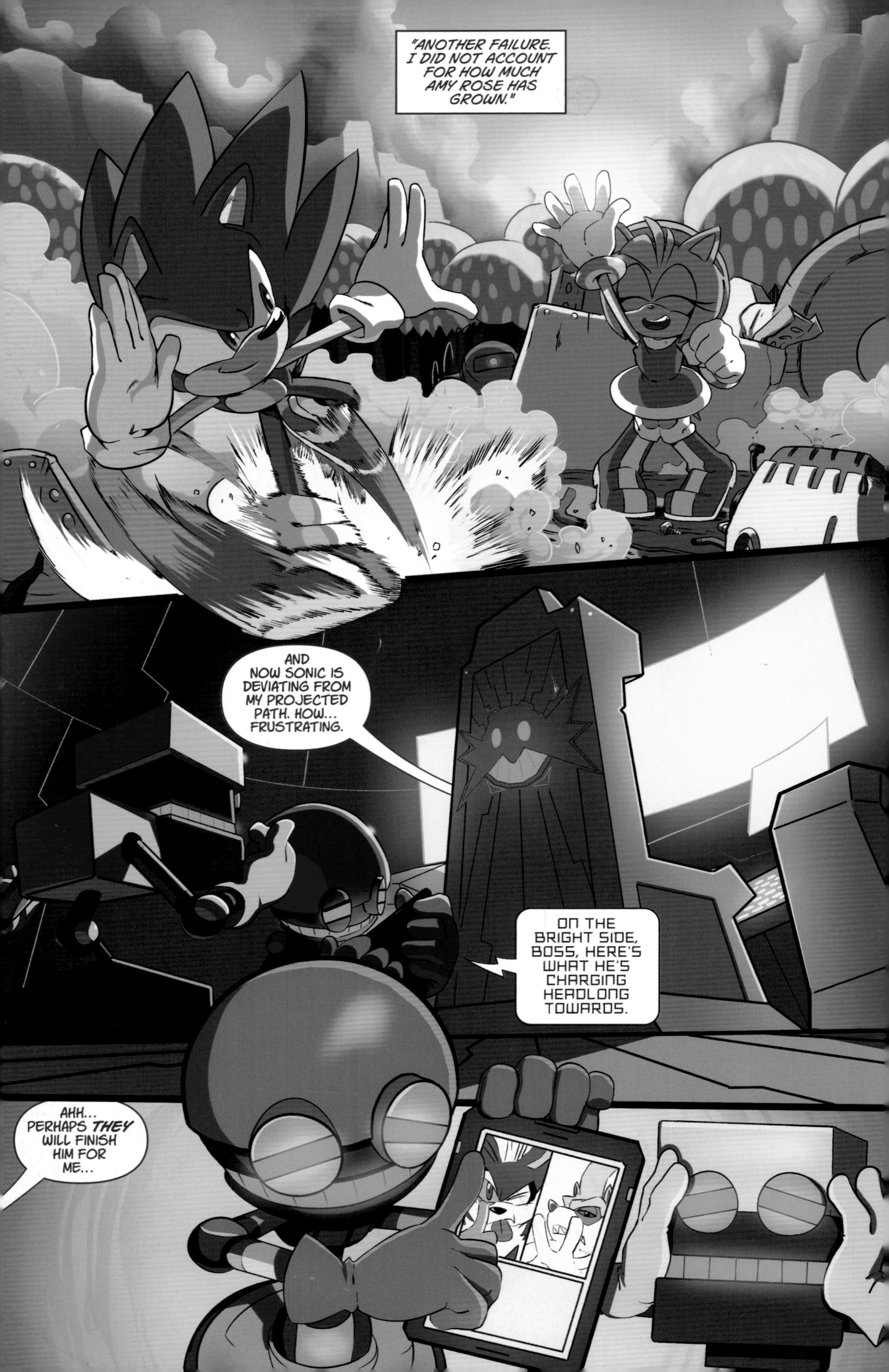
"ANOTHER FAILURE. I DID NOT ACCOUNT FOR HOW MUCH AMY ROSE HAS GROWN."
AND NOW SONIC IS DEVIATING FROM MY PROJECTED PATH. HOW... FRUSTRATING.
ON THE BRIGHT SIDE, BOSS, HERE'S WHAT HE'S CHARGING HEADLONG TOWARDS.
AHH... PERHAPS *THEY* WILL FINISH HIM FOR ME...

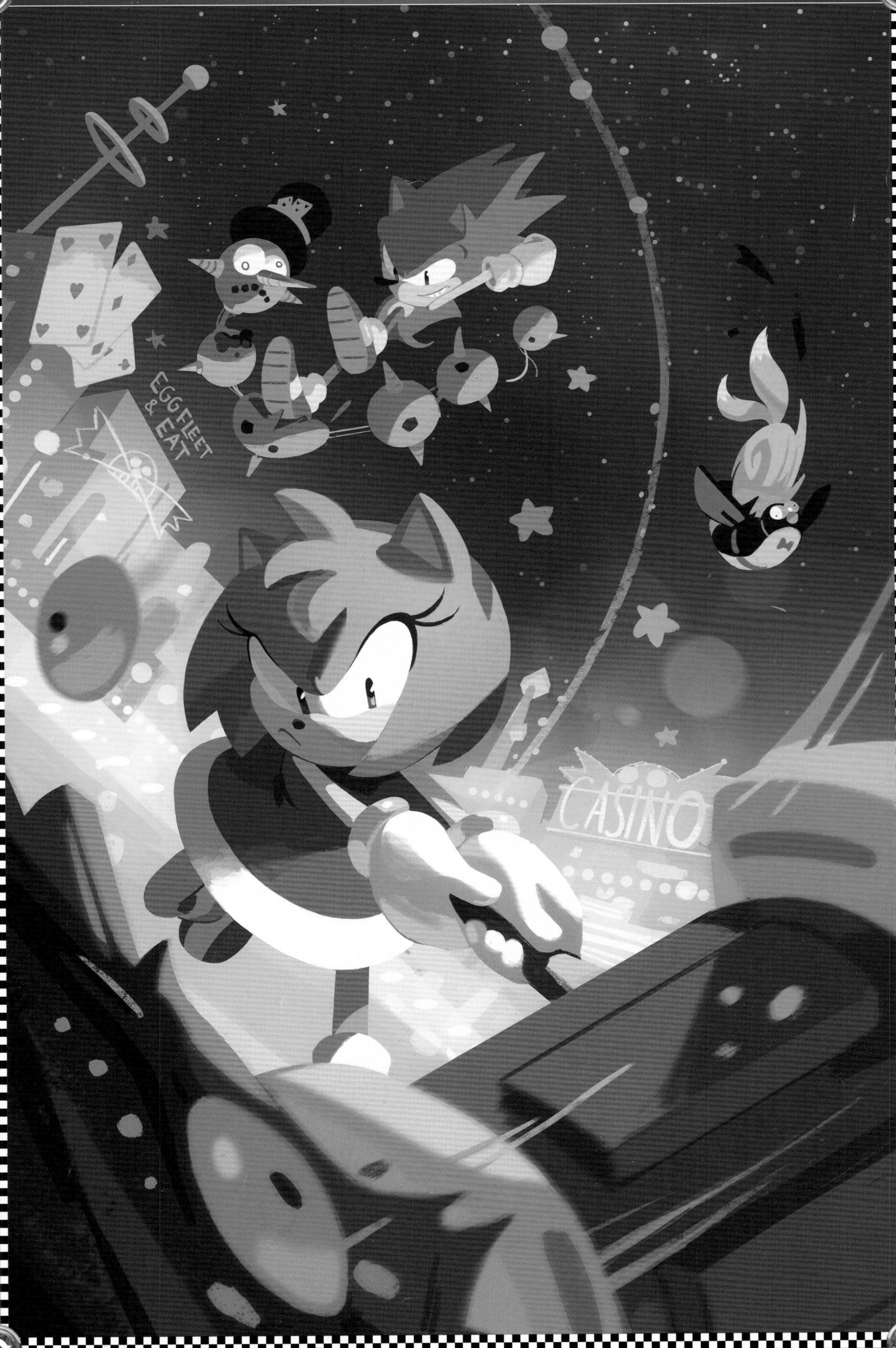
EGG FLEET & EAT
CASINO

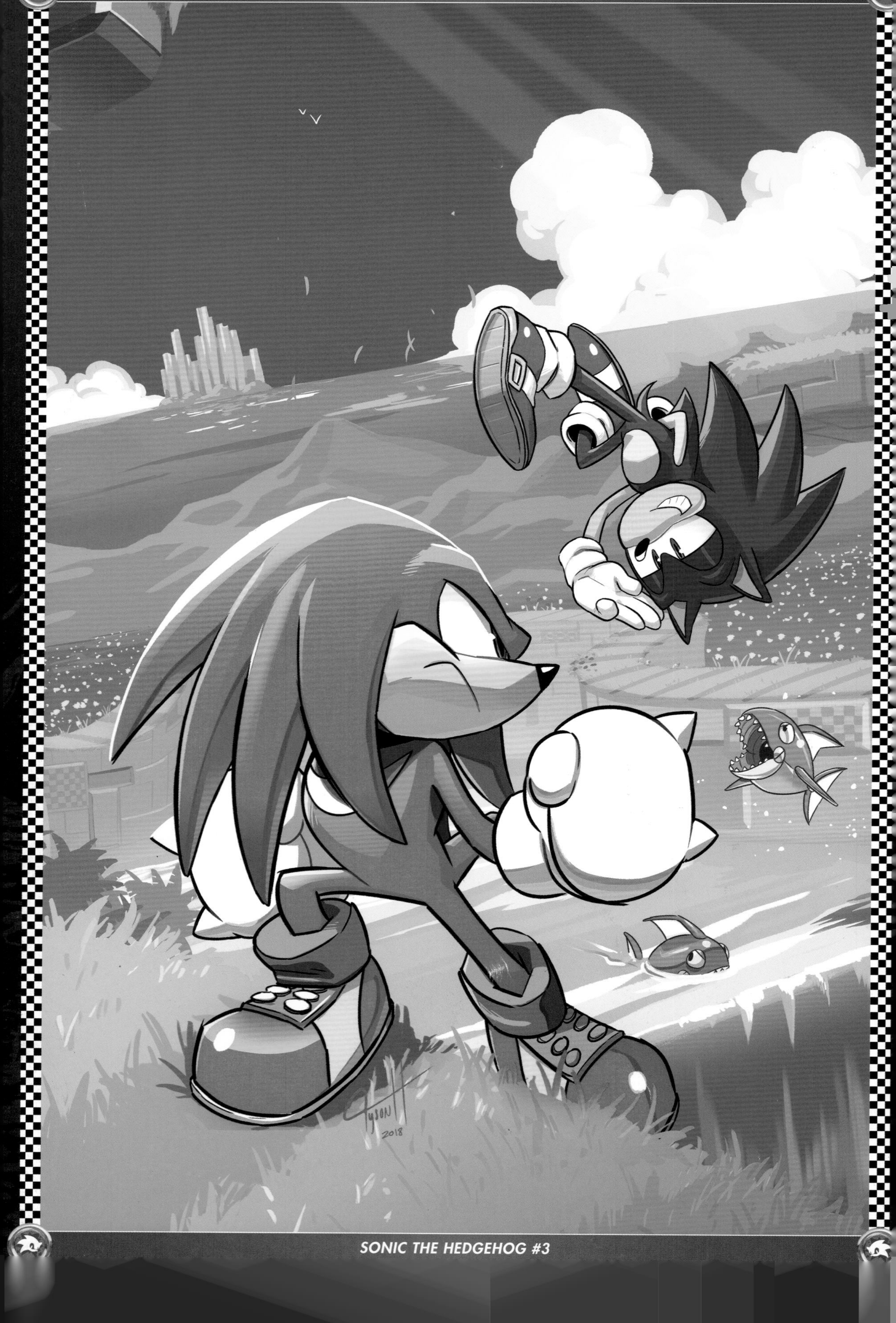
TYSON
2018

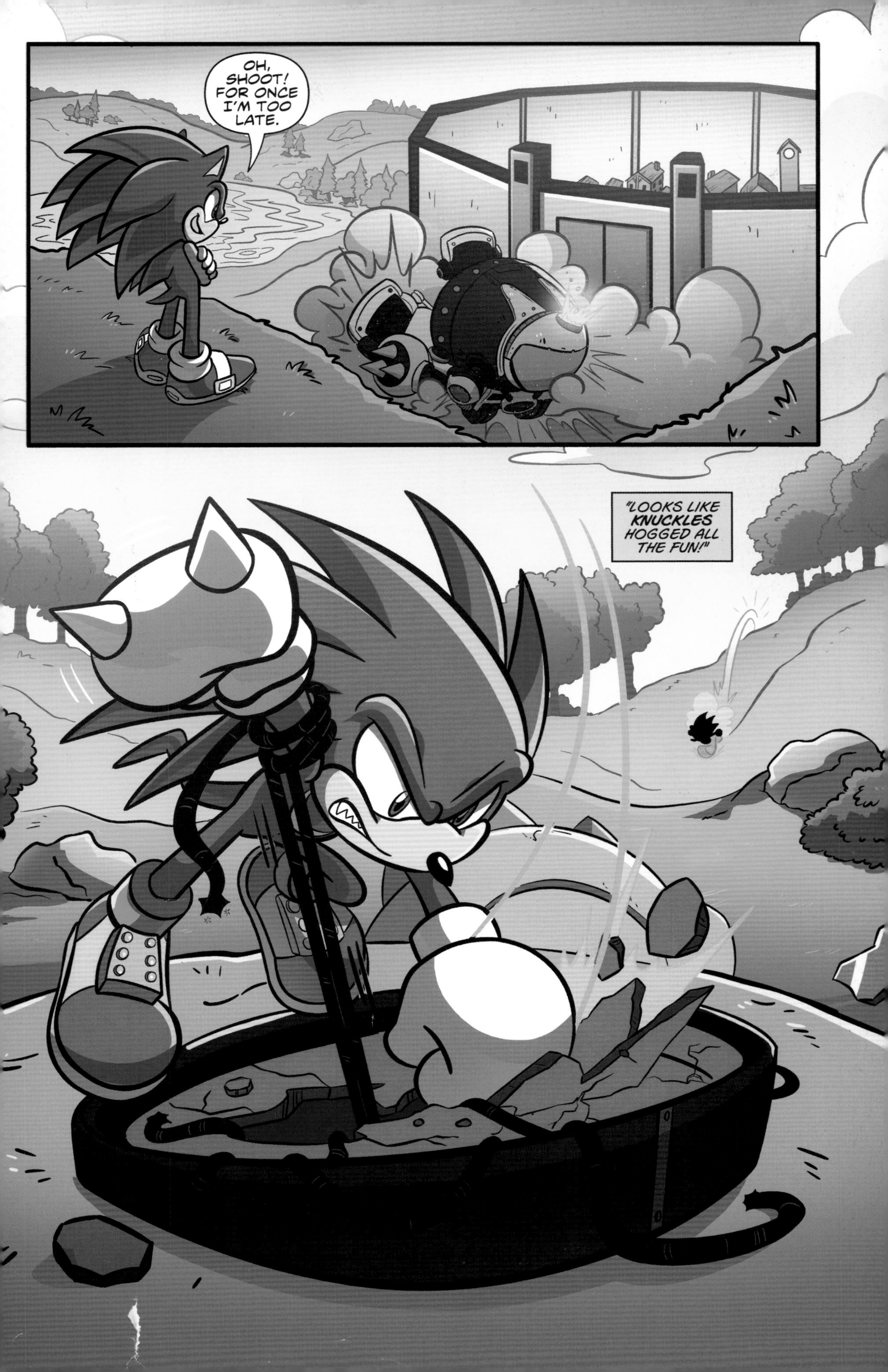
OH, SHOOT! FOR ONCE I'M TOO LATE.
"LOOKS LIKE KNUCKLES HOGGED ALL THE FUN!"

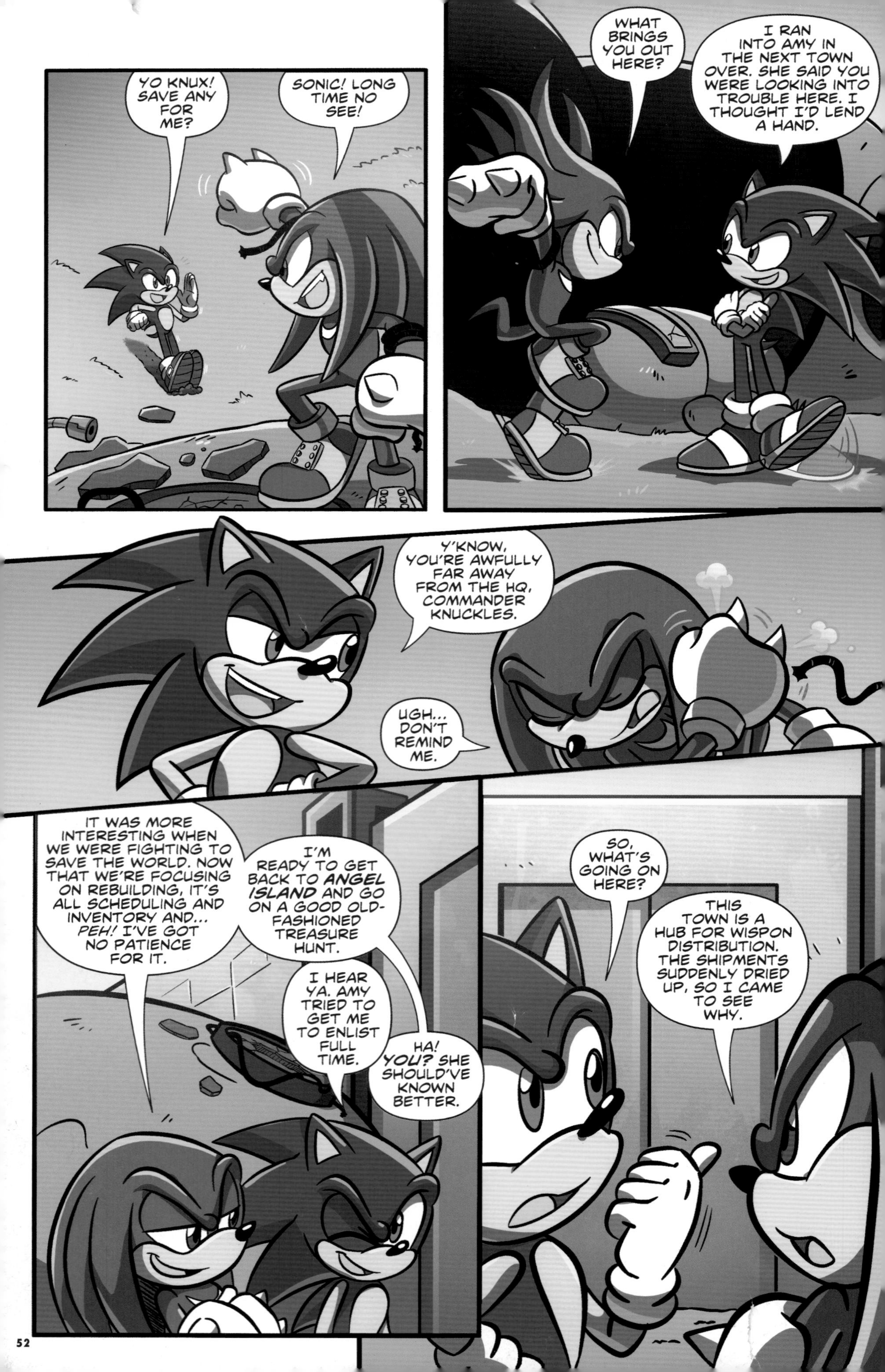
YO KNUX! SAVE ANY FOR ME?
SONIC! LONG TIME NO SEE!
WHAT BRINGS YOU OUT HERE?
I RAN INTO AMY IN THE NEXT TOWN OVER. SHE SAID YOU WERE LOOKING INTO TROUBLE HERE. I THOUGHT I'D LEND A HAND.
Y'KNOW, YOU'RE AWFULLY FAR AWAY FROM THE HQ, COMMANDER KNUCKLES.
UGH... DON'T REMIND ME.
IT WAS MORE INTERESTING WHEN WE WERE FIGHTING TO SAVE THE WORLD. NOW THAT WE'RE FOCUSING ON REBUILDING, IT'S ALL SCHEDULING AND INVENTORY AND... *PEH!* I'VE GOT NO PATIENCE FOR IT.
I'M READY TO GET BACK TO ***ANGEL ISLAND*** AND GO ON A GOOD OLD-FASHIONED TREASURE HUNT.
I HEAR YA. AMY TRIED TO GET ME TO ENLIST FULL TIME.
HA! ***YOU?*** SHE SHOULD'VE KNOWN BETTER.
SO, WHAT'S GOING ON HERE?
THIS TOWN IS A HUB FOR WISPON DISTRIBUTION. THE SHIPMENTS SUDDENLY DRIED UP, SO I CAME TO SEE WHY.

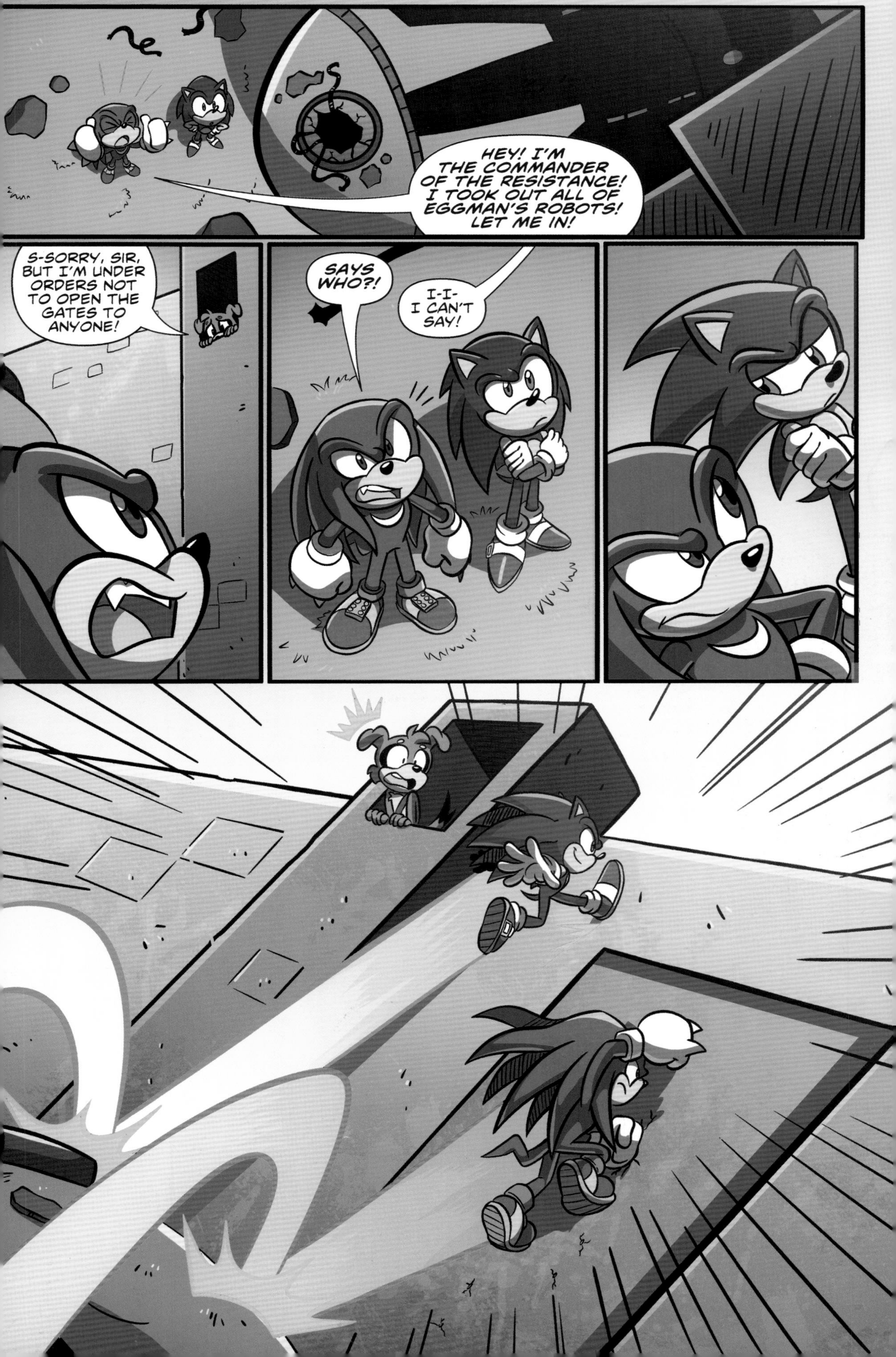
HEY! I'M THE COMMANDER OF THE RESISTANCE! I TOOK OUT ALL OF EGGMAN'S ROBOTS! LET ME IN!
S-SORRY, SIR, BUT I'M UNDER ORDERS NOT TO OPEN THE GATES TO ANYONE!
SAYS WHO?!
I-I- I CAN'T SAY!

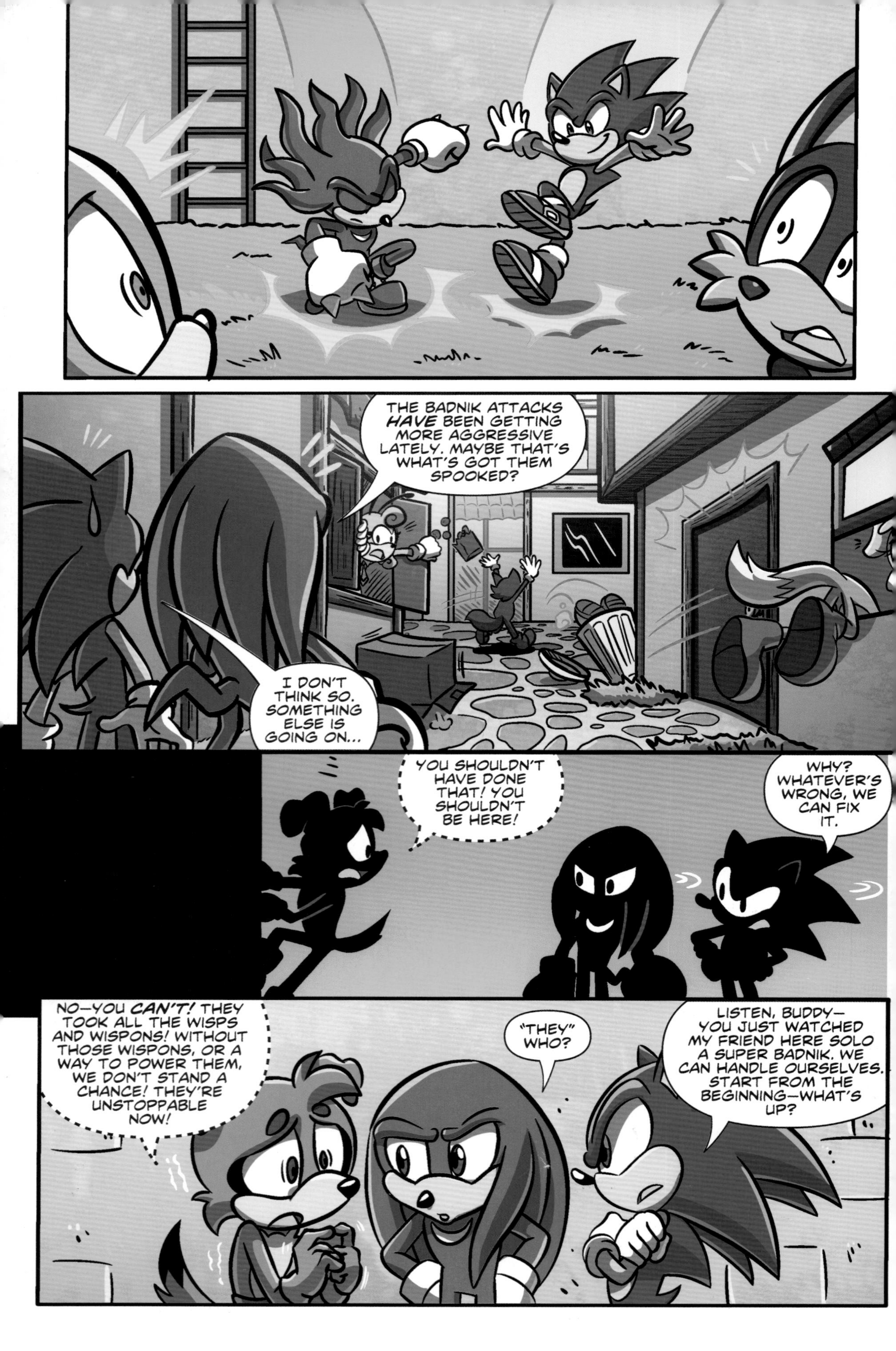
THE BADNIK ATTACKS *HAVE* BEEN GETTING MORE AGGRESSIVE LATELY. MAYBE THAT'S WHAT'S GOT THEM SPOOKED?
I DON'T THINK SO. SOMETHING ELSE IS GOING ON...
YOU SHOULDN'T HAVE DONE THAT! YOU SHOULDN'T BE HERE!
WHY? WHATEVER'S WRONG, WE CAN FIX IT.
NO—YOU *CAN'T!* THEY TOOK ALL THE WISPS AND WISPONS! WITHOUT THOSE WISPONS, OR A WAY TO POWER THEM, WE DON'T STAND A CHANCE! THEY'RE UNSTOPPABLE NOW!
"THEY" WHO?
LISTEN, BUDDY—YOU JUST WATCHED MY FRIEND HERE SOLO A SUPER BADNIK. WE CAN HANDLE OURSELVES. START FROM THE BEGINNING—WHAT'S UP?

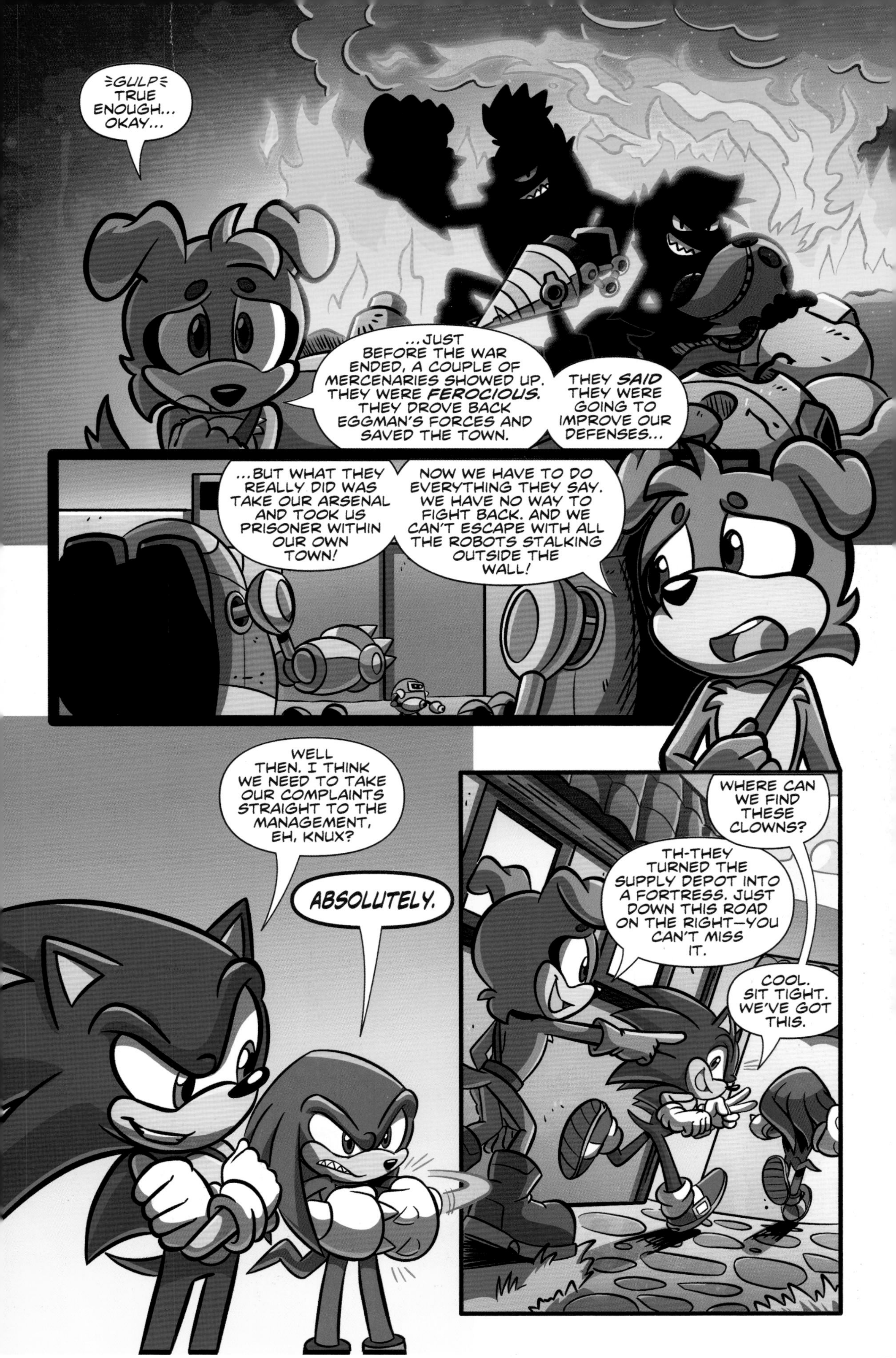
GULP TRUE ENOUGH... OKAY...
...JUST BEFORE THE WAR ENDED, A COUPLE OF MERCENARIES SHOWED UP. THEY WERE FEROCIOUS. THEY DROVE BACK EGGMAN'S FORCES AND SAVED THE TOWN.
THEY SAID THEY WERE GOING TO IMPROVE OUR DEFENSES...
...BUT WHAT THEY REALLY DID WAS TAKE OUR ARSENAL AND TOOK US PRISONER WITHIN OUR OWN TOWN!
NOW WE HAVE TO DO EVERYTHING THEY SAY. WE HAVE NO WAY TO FIGHT BACK. AND WE CAN'T ESCAPE WITH ALL THE ROBOTS STALKING OUTSIDE THE WALL!
WELL THEN. I THINK WE NEED TO TAKE OUR COMPLAINTS STRAIGHT TO THE MANAGEMENT, EH, KNUX?
ABSOLUTELY.
WHERE CAN WE FIND THESE CLOWNS?
TH-THEY TURNED THE SUPPLY DEPOT INTO A FORTRESS. JUST DOWN THIS ROAD ON THE RIGHT—YOU CAN'T MISS IT.
COOL. SIT TIGHT. WE'VE GOT THIS.

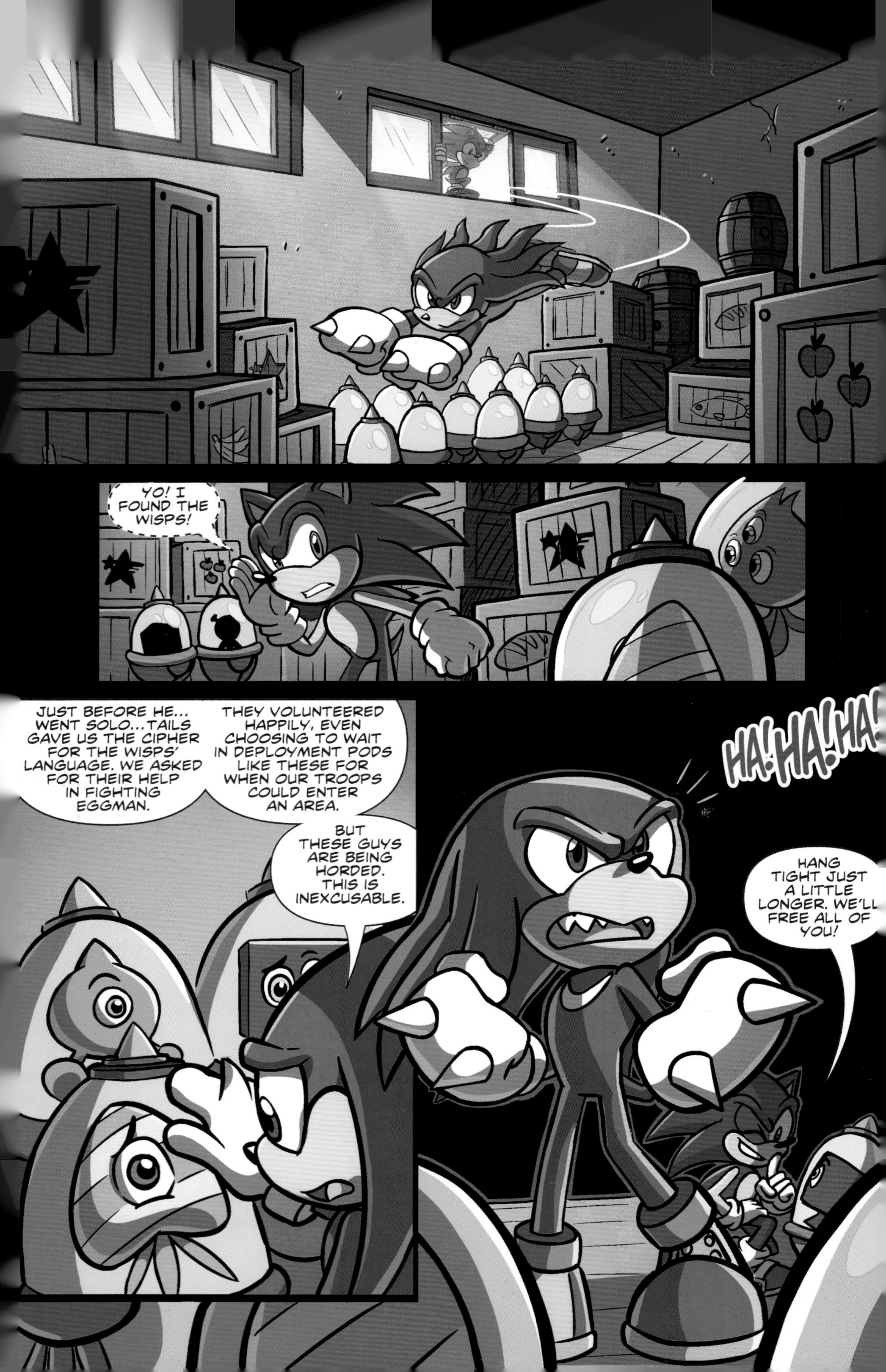
YO! I FOUND THE WISPS!
JUST BEFORE HE... WENT SOLO...TAILS GAVE US THE CIPHER FOR THE WISPS' LANGUAGE. WE ASKED FOR THEIR HELP IN FIGHTING EGGMAN.
THEY VOLUNTEERED HAPPILY, EVEN CHOOSING TO WAIT IN DEPLOYMENT PODS LIKE THESE FOR WHEN OUR TROOPS COULD ENTER AN AREA.
BUT THESE GUYS ARE BEING HORDED. THIS IS INEXCUSABLE.
HA! HA! HA!
HANG TIGHT JUST A LITTLE LONGER. WE'LL FREE ALL OF YOU!

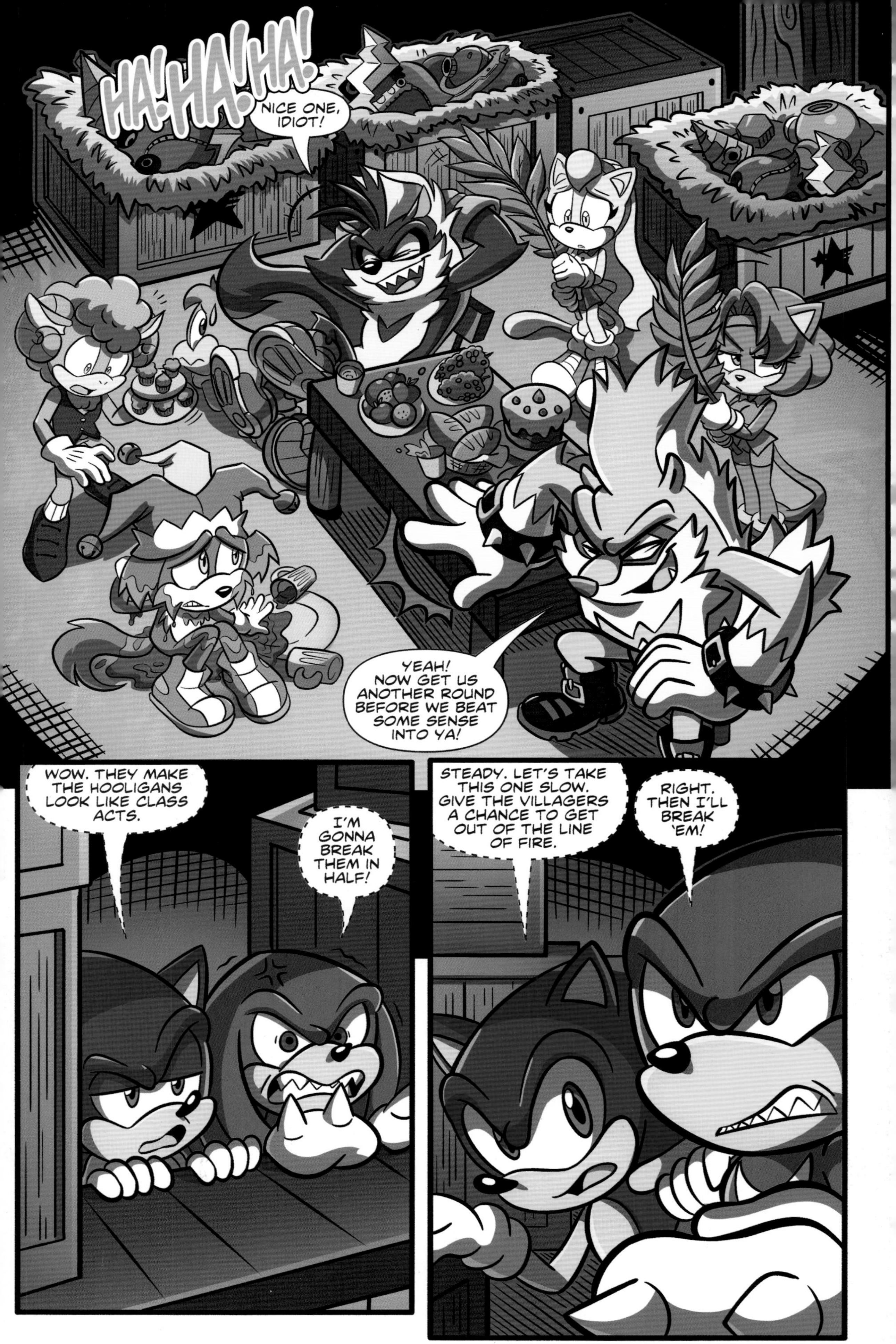

HA! HA! HA!
NICE ONE, IDIOT!
YEAH! NOW GET US ANOTHER ROUND BEFORE WE BEAT SOME SENSE INTO YA!
WOW. THEY MAKE THE HOOLIGANS LOOK LIKE CLASS ACTS.
I'M GONNA BREAK THEM IN HALF!
STEADY. LET'S TAKE THIS ONE SLOW. GIVE THE VILLAGERS A CHANCE TO GET OUT OF THE LINE OF FIRE.
RIGHT. THEN I'LL BREAK 'EM!

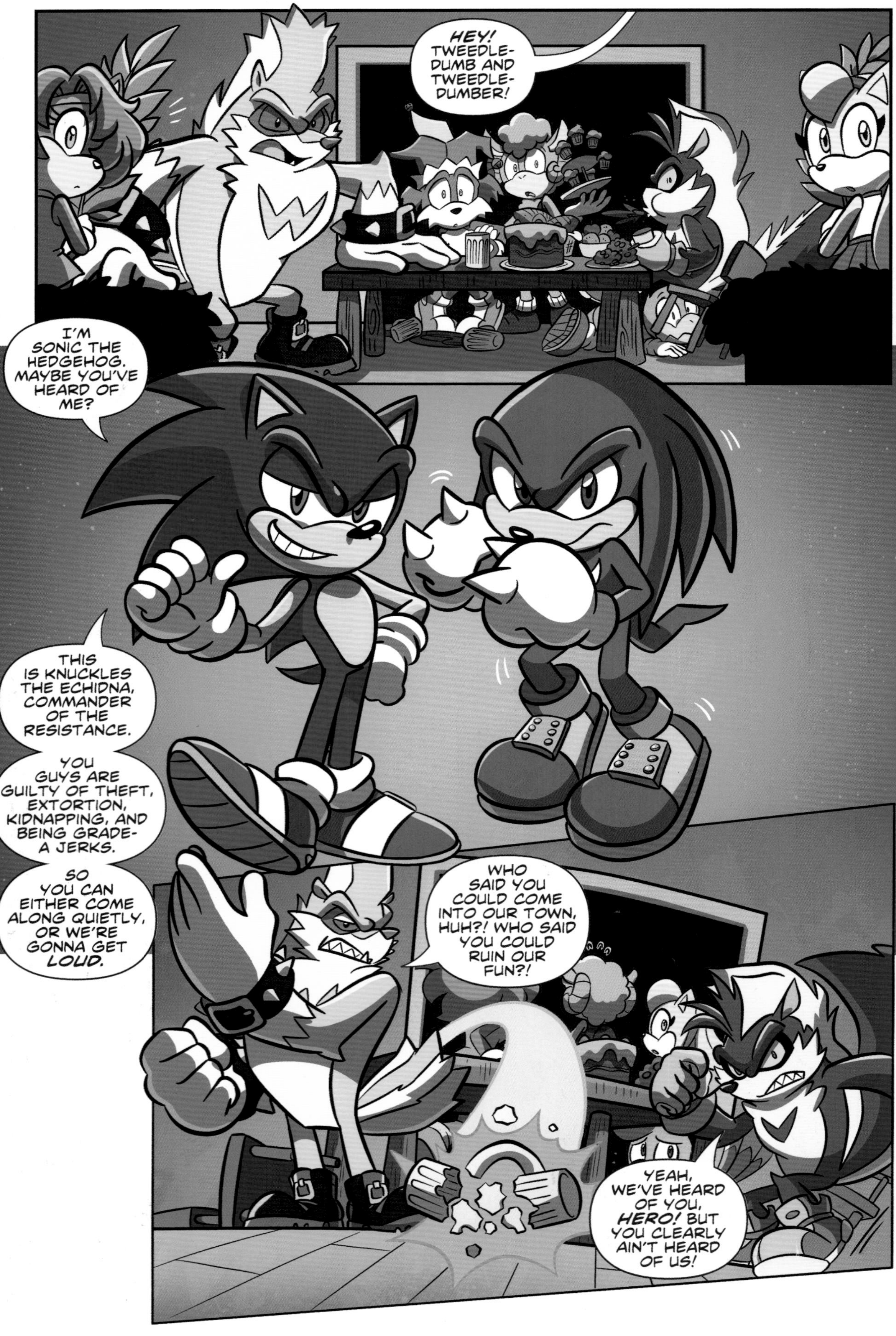
HEY! TWEEDLE-DUMB AND TWEEDLE-DUMBER!
I'M SONIC THE HEDGEHOG. MAYBE YOU'VE HEARD OF ME?
THIS IS KNUCKLES THE ECHIDNA, COMMANDER OF THE RESISTANCE.
YOU GUYS ARE GUILTY OF THEFT, EXTORTION, KIDNAPPING, AND BEING GRADE-A JERKS.
SO YOU CAN EITHER COME ALONG QUIETLY, OR WE'RE GONNA GET LOUD.
WHO SAID YOU COULD COME INTO OUR TOWN, HUH?! WHO SAID YOU COULD RUIN OUR FUN?!
YEAH, WE'VE HEARD OF YOU, HERO! BUT YOU CLEARLY AIN'T HEARD OF US!

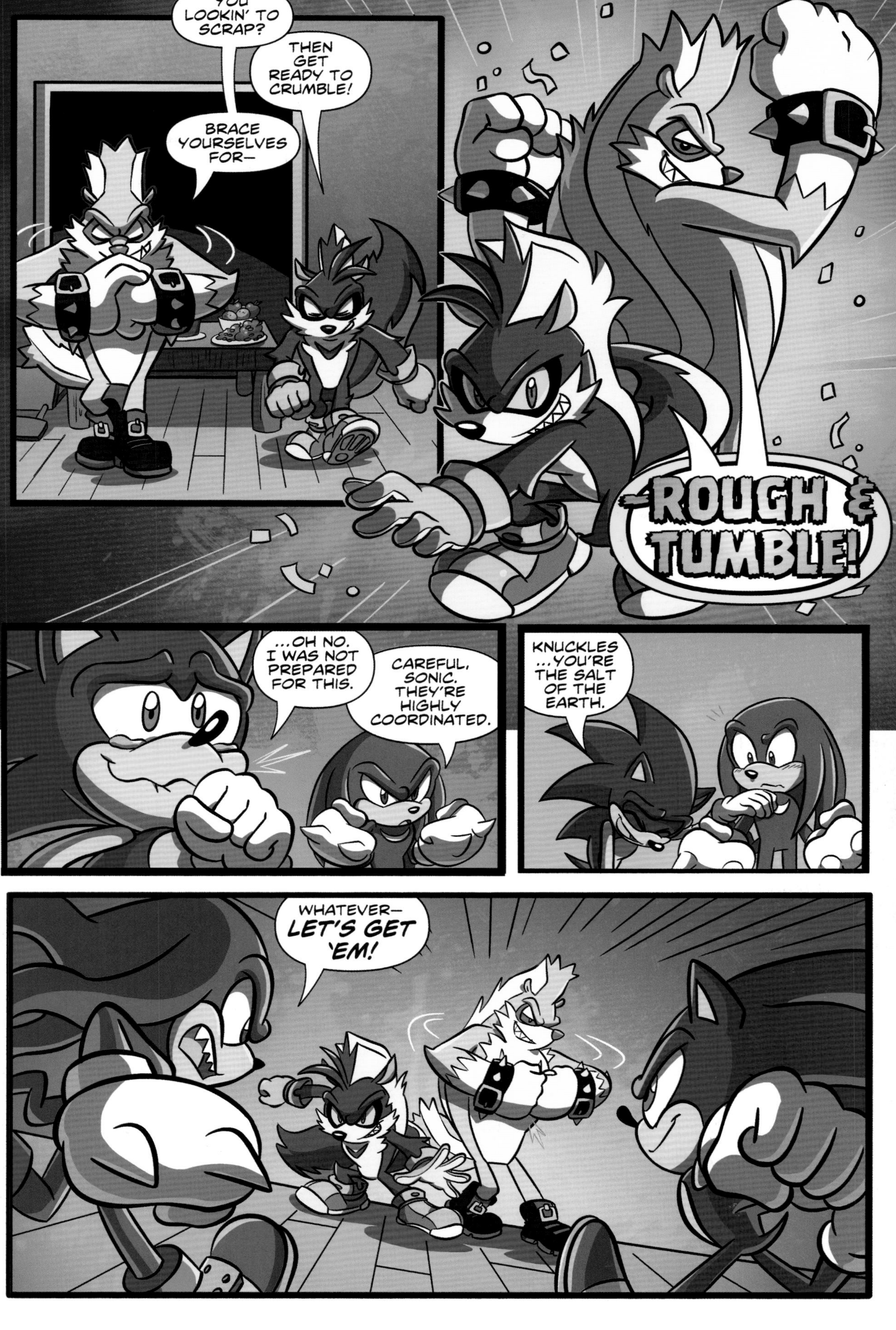
YOU LOOKIN' TO SCRAP?
THEN GET READY TO CRUMBLE!
BRACE YOURSELVES FOR—
—ROUGH & TUMBLE!
...OH NO. I WAS NOT PREPARED FOR THIS.
CAREFUL, SONIC. THEY'RE HIGHLY COORDINATED.
KNUCKLES ...YOU'RE THE SALT OF THE EARTH.
WHATEVER— *LET'S GET 'EM!*

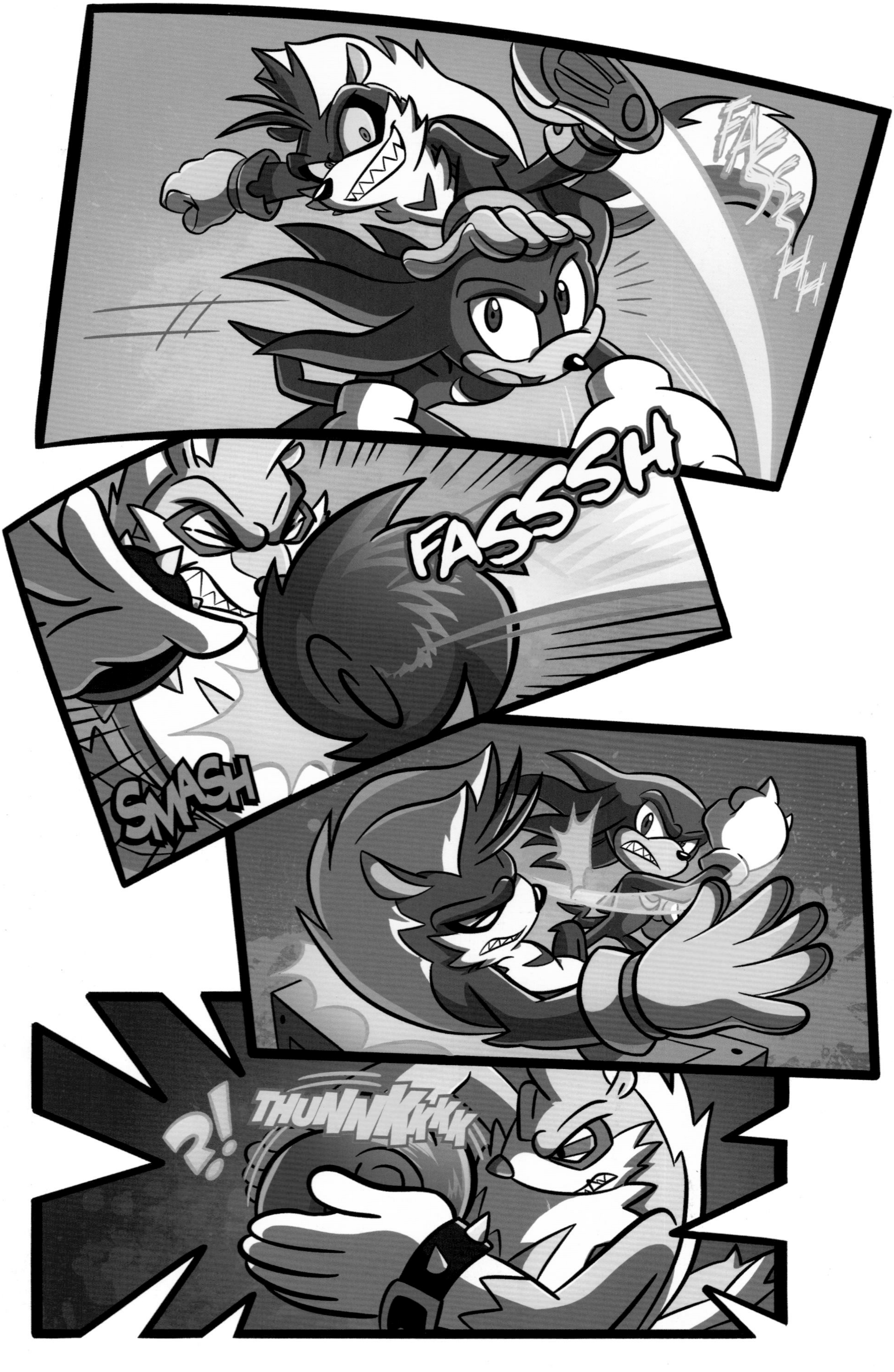
FASSKHH
FASSSH
SMASH
?!
THUNNKKKK

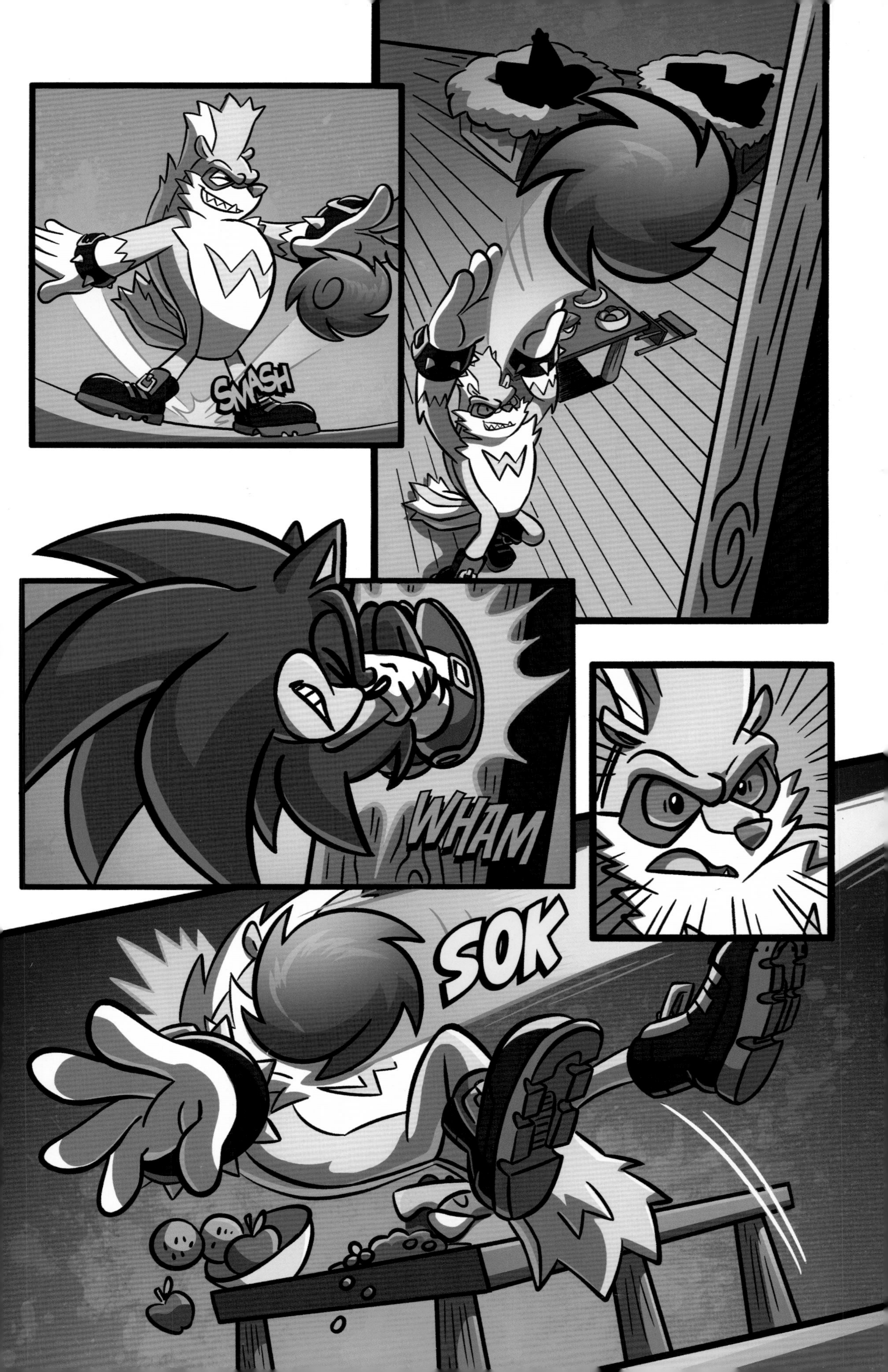
SMASH
WHAM
SOK

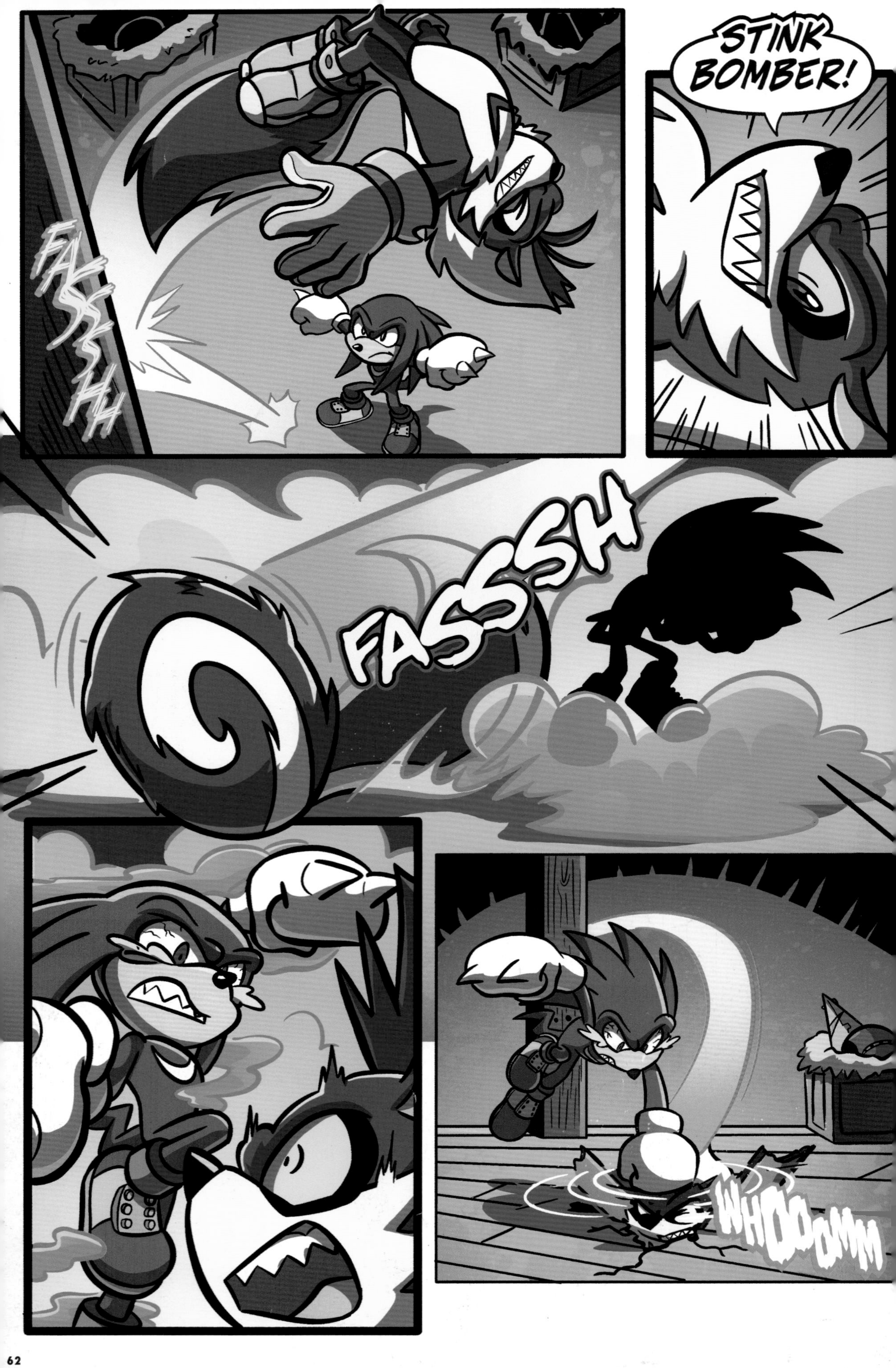
FASSSHHH
STINK BOMBER!
FASSSH
WHOOOMM

C'MON BRO, WE AIN'T DONE YET...

WHUGH... YOU OKAY, DUDE?

I'MB FUHNE.

NO MORE MESSIN' AROUND!

SAY YOUR PRAYERS, CHUMPS!

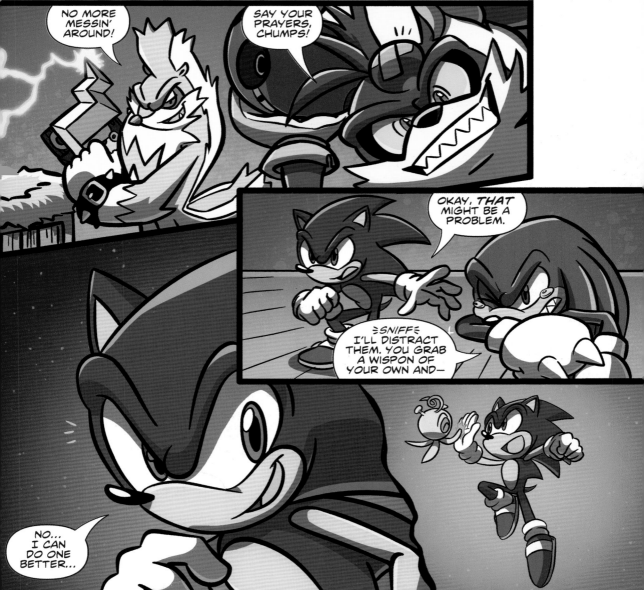

OKAY, THAT MIGHT BE A PROBLEM.

≷SNIFF≷ I'LL DISTRACT THEM. YOU GRAB A WISPON OF YOUR OWN AND—

NO... I CAN DO ONE BETTER...

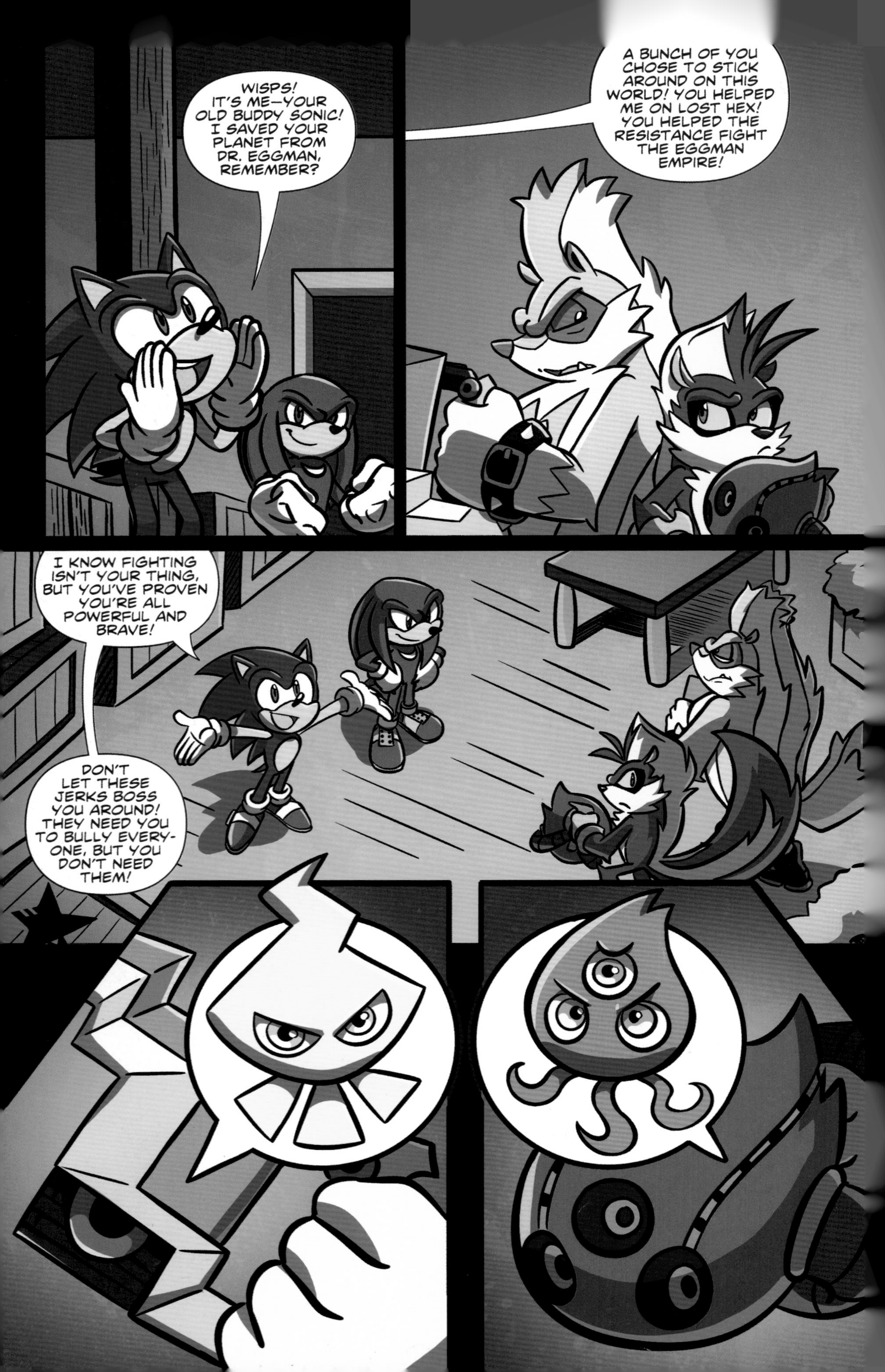
WISPS! IT'S ME—YOUR OLD BUDDY SONIC! I SAVED YOUR PLANET FROM DR. EGGMAN, REMEMBER?
A BUNCH OF YOU CHOSE TO STICK AROUND ON THIS WORLD! YOU HELPED ME ON LOST HEX! YOU HELPED THE RESISTANCE FIGHT THE EGGMAN EMPIRE!
I KNOW FIGHTING ISN'T YOUR THING, BUT YOU'VE PROVEN YOU'RE ALL POWERFUL AND BRAVE!
DON'T LET THESE JERKS BOSS YOU AROUND! THEY NEED YOU TO BULLY EVERY-ONE, BUT YOU DON'T NEED THEM!

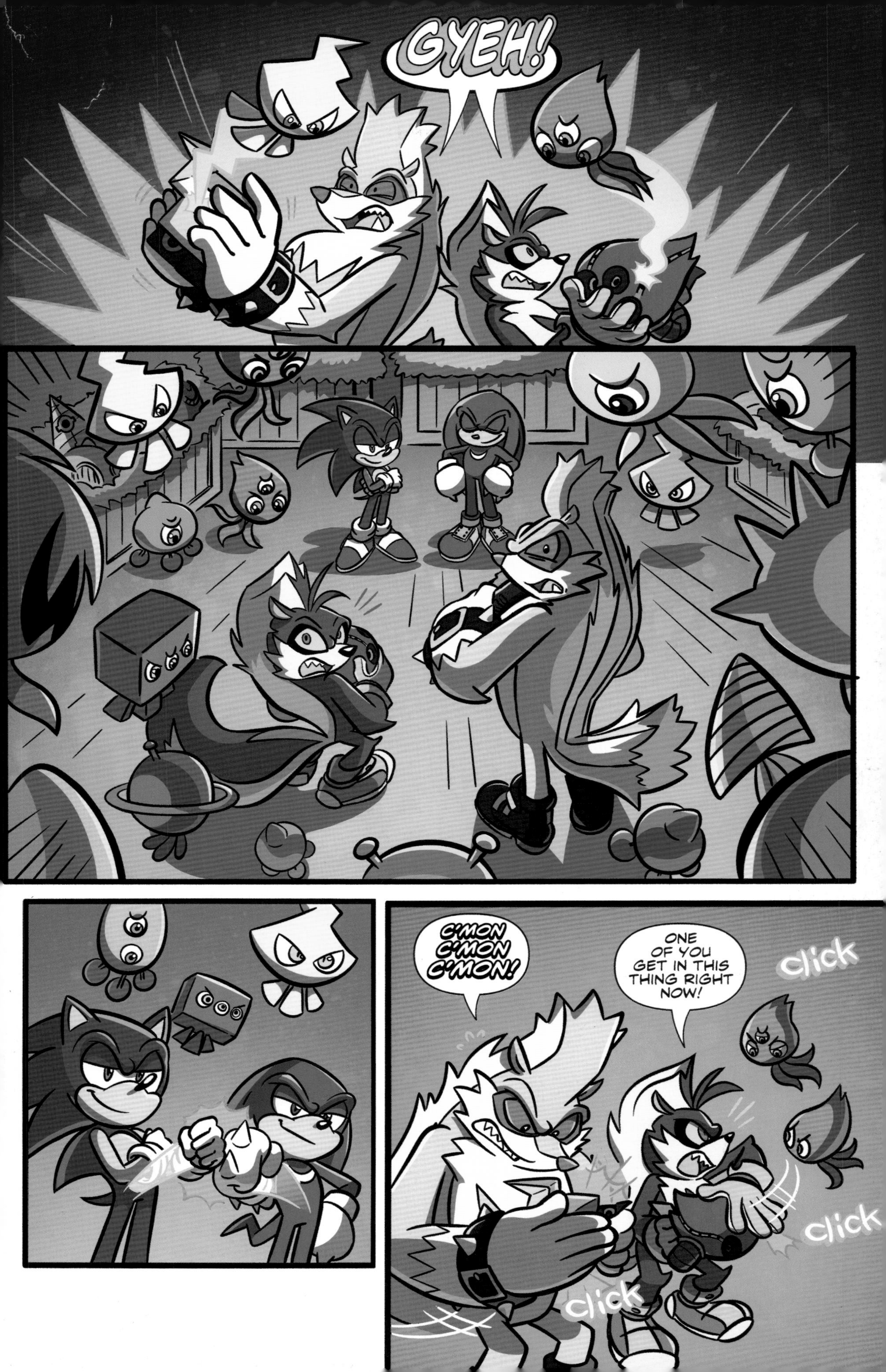
GYEH!
C'MON C'MON C'MON!
ONE OF YOU GET IN THIS THING RIGHT NOW!
click
click
click

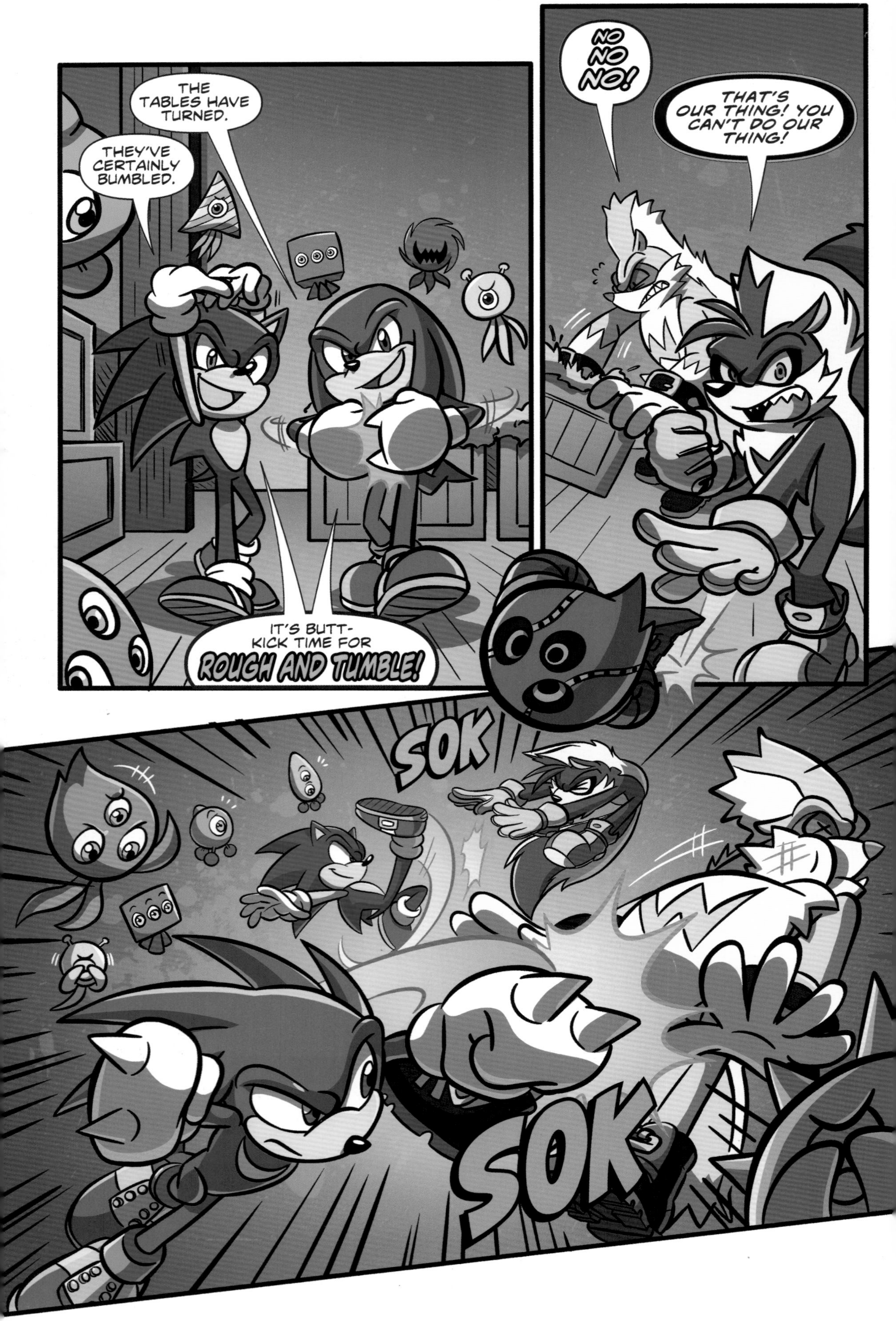

THE TABLES HAVE TURNED.
THEY'VE CERTAINLY BUMBLED.
IT'S BUTT-KICK TIME FOR ROUGH AND TUMBLE!
NO NO NO!
THAT'S OUR THING! YOU CAN'T DO OUR THING!
SOK
SOK

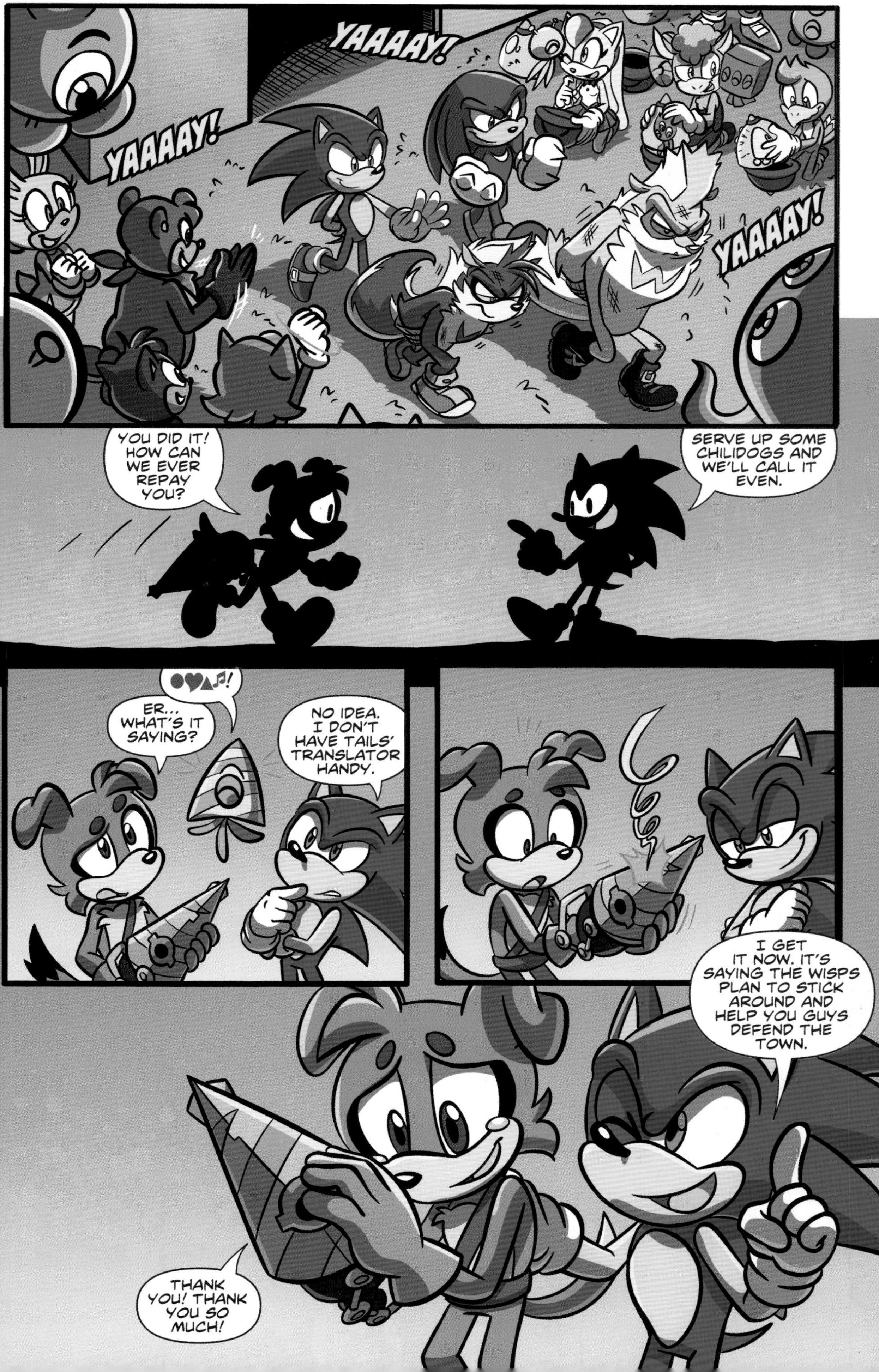
YAAAAY!
YAAAAY!
YAAAAY!
YOU DID IT! HOW CAN WE EVER REPAY YOU?
SERVE UP SOME CHILIDOGS AND WE'LL CALL IT EVEN.
ER... WHAT'S IT SAYING?
NO IDEA. I DON'T HAVE TAILS' TRANSLATOR HANDY.
I GET IT NOW. IT'S SAYING THE WISPS PLAN TO STICK AROUND AND HELP YOU GUYS DEFEND THE TOWN.
THANK YOU! THANK YOU SO MUCH!

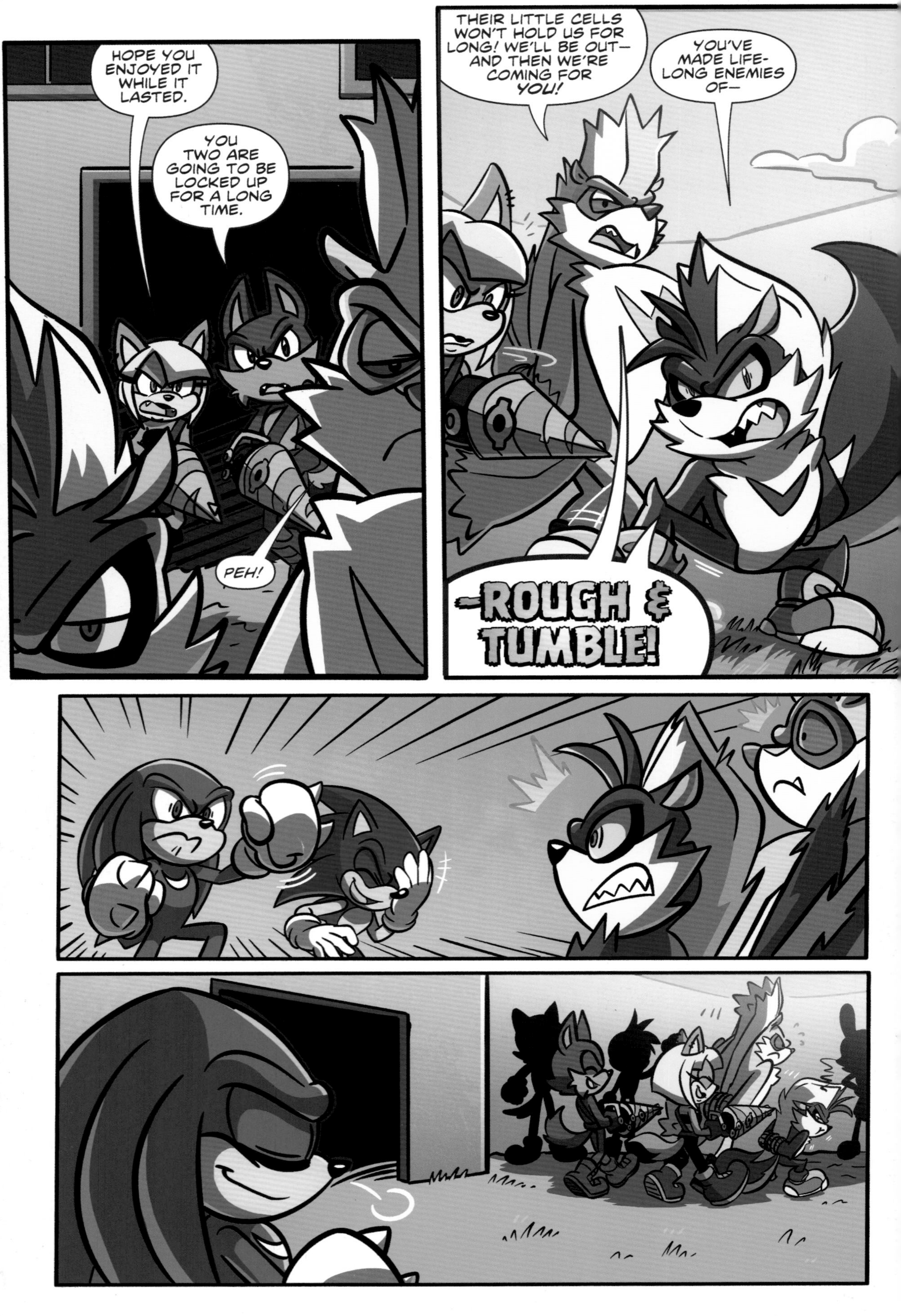
HOPE YOU ENJOYED IT WHILE IT LASTED.
YOU TWO ARE GOING TO BE LOCKED UP FOR A LONG TIME.
PEH!
THEIR LITTLE CELLS WON'T HOLD US FOR LONG! WE'LL BE OUT— AND THEN WE'RE COMING FOR YOU!
YOU'VE MADE LIFE-LONG ENEMIES OF—
—ROUGH & TUMBLE!

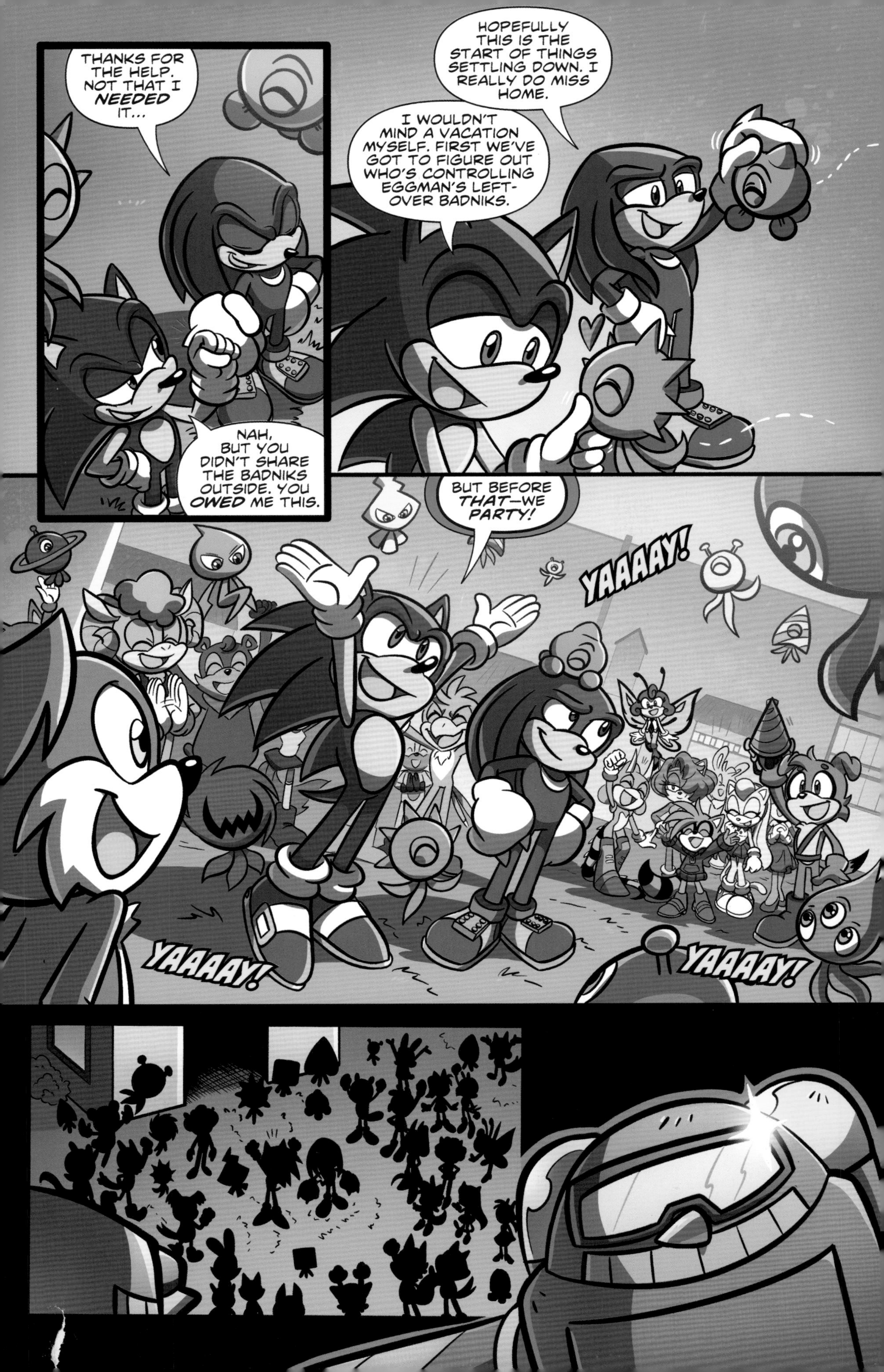
THANKS FOR THE HELP. NOT THAT I NEEDED IT...
NAH, BUT YOU DIDN'T SHARE THE BADNIKS OUTSIDE. YOU OWED ME THIS.
HOPEFULLY THIS IS THE START OF THINGS SETTLING DOWN. I REALLY DO MISS HOME.
I WOULDN'T MIND A VACATION MYSELF. FIRST WE'VE GOT TO FIGURE OUT WHO'S CONTROLLING EGGMAN'S LEFT-OVER BADNIKS.
BUT BEFORE THAT—WE PARTY!
YAAAAY!
YAAAAY!
YAAAAY!

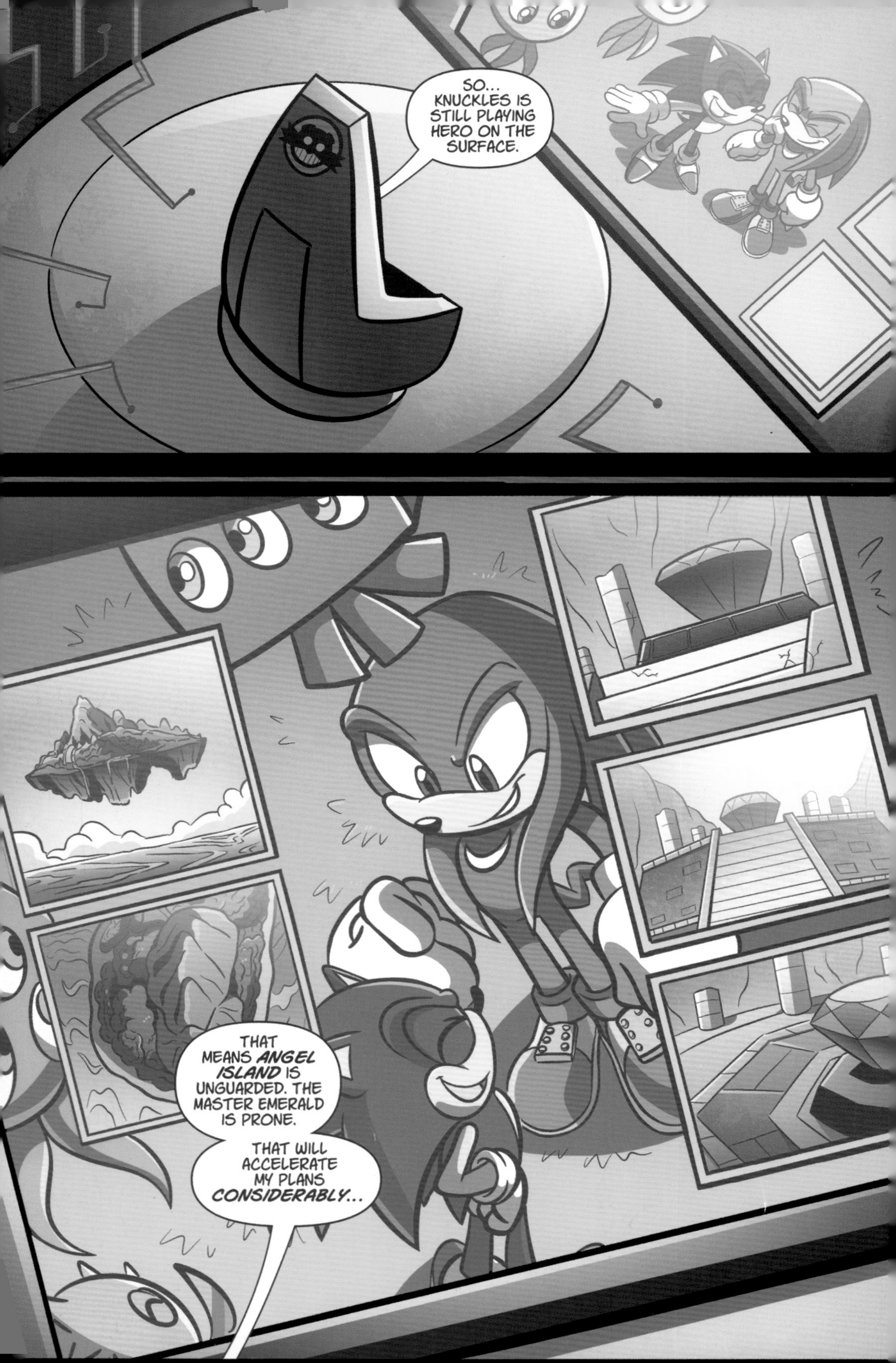
SO... KNUCKLES IS STILL PLAYING HERO ON THE SURFACE.
THAT MEANS ANGEL ISLAND IS UNGUARDED. THE MASTER EMERALD IS PRONE.
THAT WILL ACCELERATE MY PLANS CONSIDERABLY...

ART BY NATHALIE FOURDRAINE

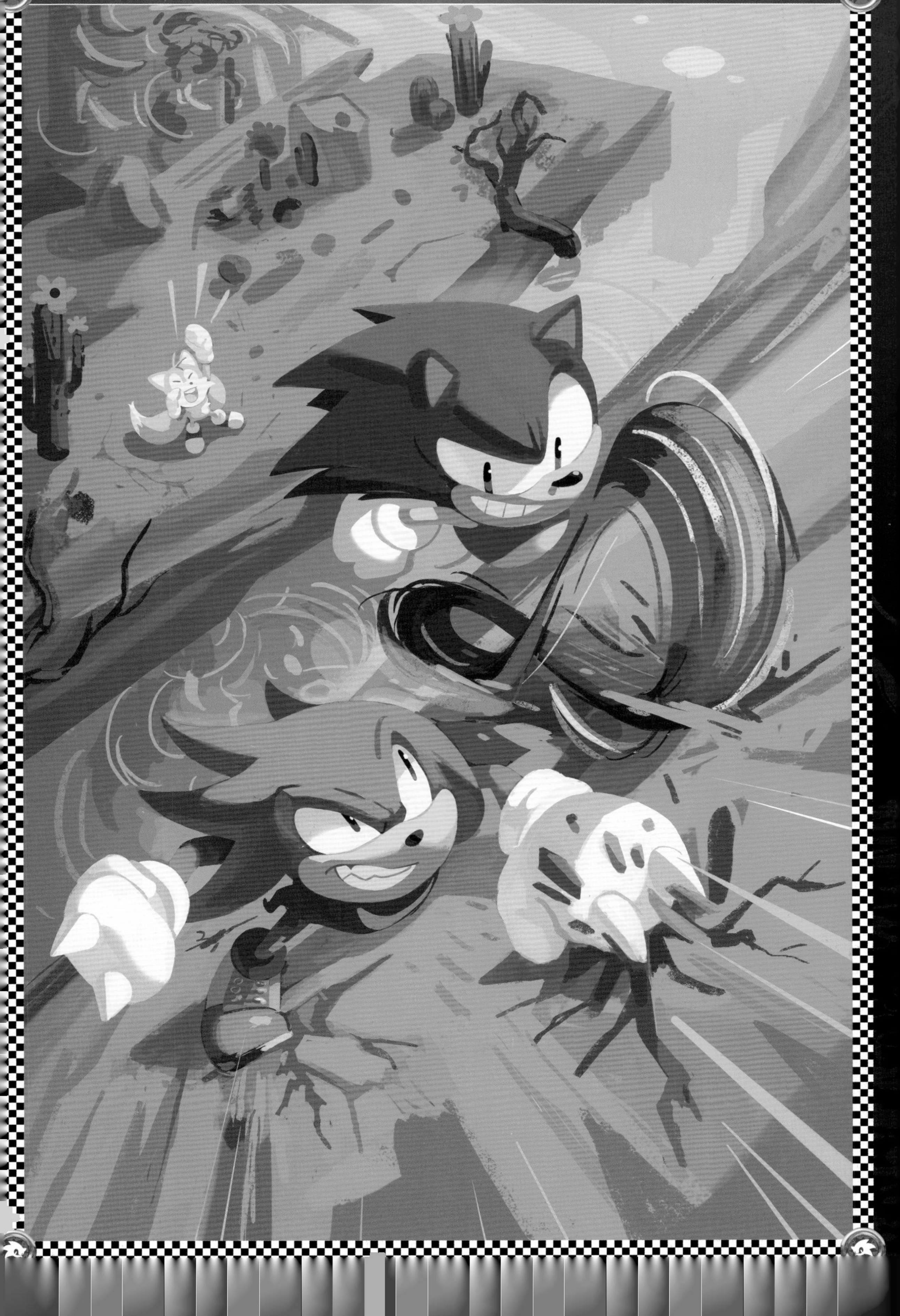

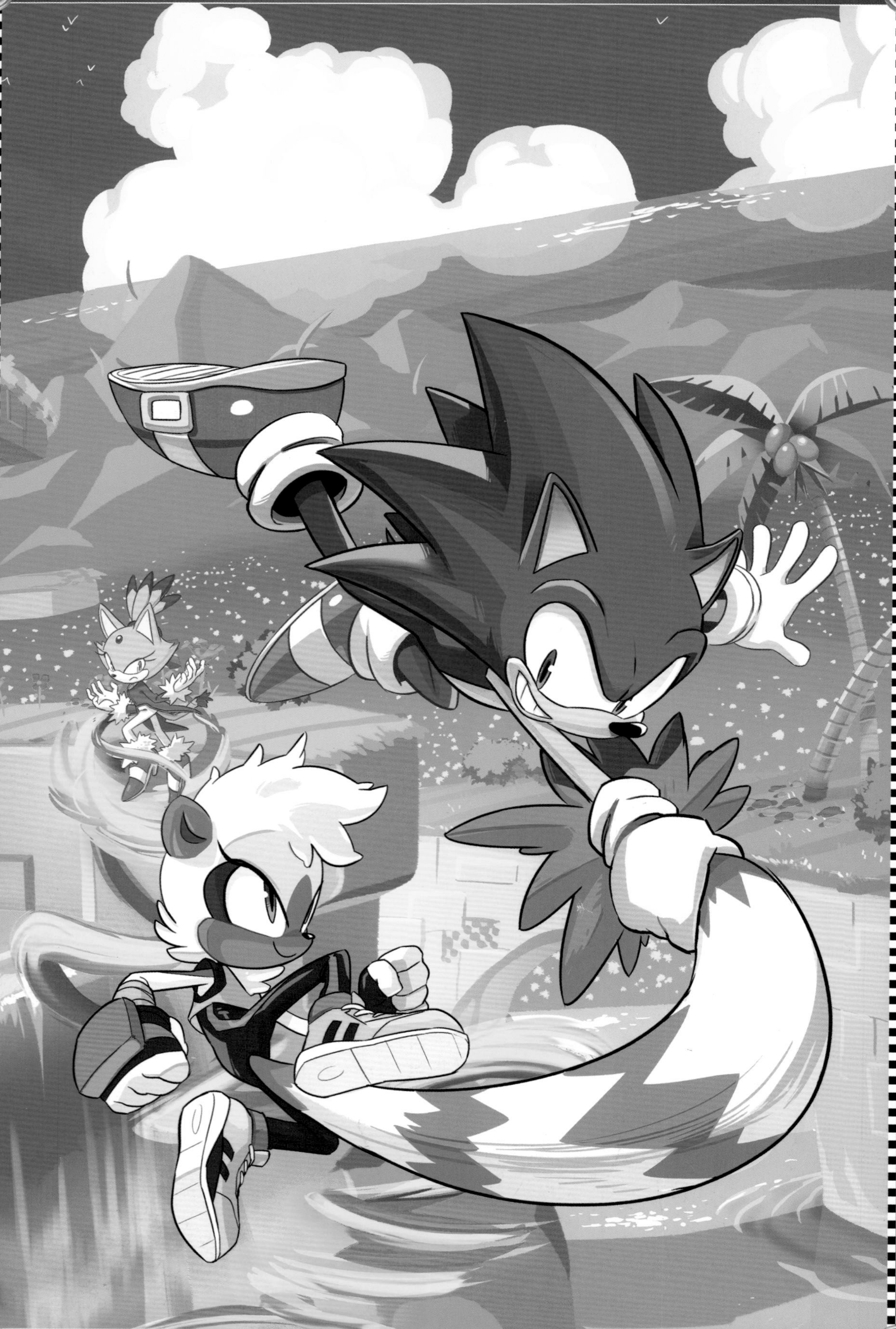

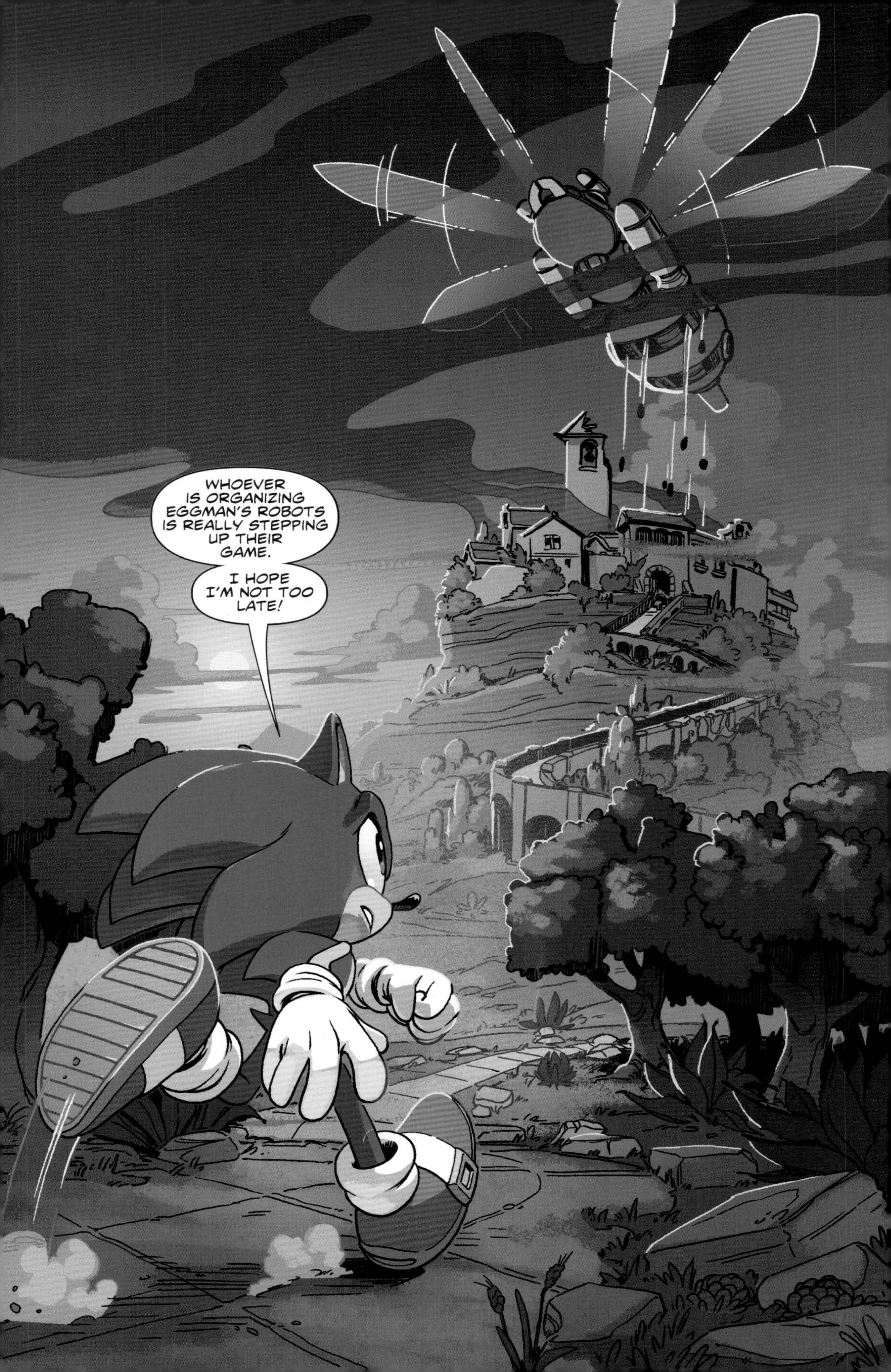
WHOEVER IS ORGANIZING EGGMAN'S ROBOTS IS REALLY STEPPING UP THEIR GAME.
I HOPE I'M NOT TOO LATE!

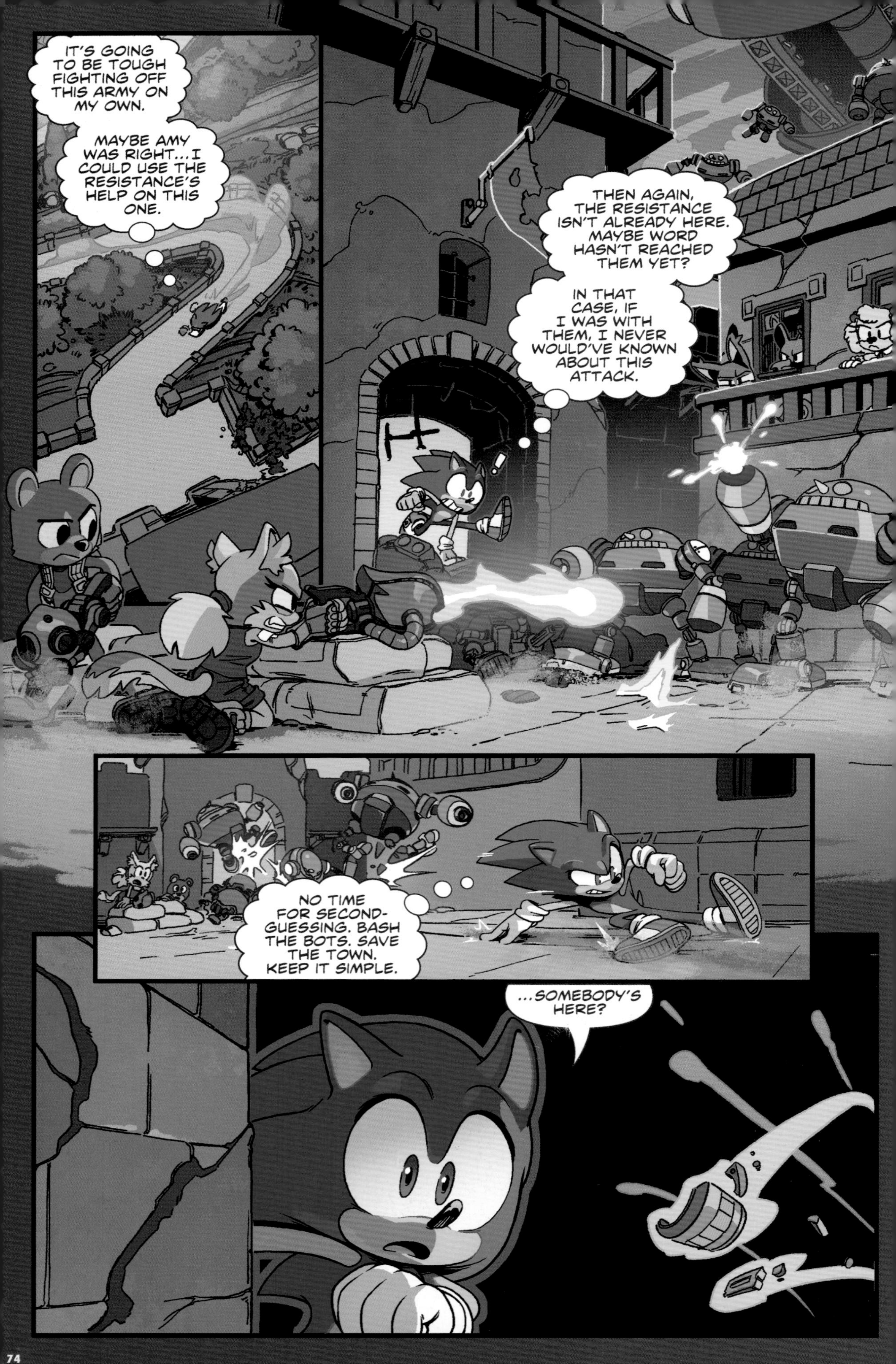
IT'S GOING TO BE TOUGH FIGHTING OFF THIS ARMY ON MY OWN.
MAYBE AMY WAS RIGHT...I COULD USE THE RESISTANCE'S HELP ON THIS ONE.
THEN AGAIN, THE RESISTANCE ISN'T ALREADY HERE. MAYBE WORD HASN'T REACHED THEM YET?
IN THAT CASE, IF I WAS WITH THEM, I NEVER WOULD'VE KNOWN ABOUT THIS ATTACK.
NO TIME FOR SECOND-GUESSING. BASH THE BOTS. SAVE THE TOWN. KEEP IT SIMPLE.
...SOMEBODY'S HERE?

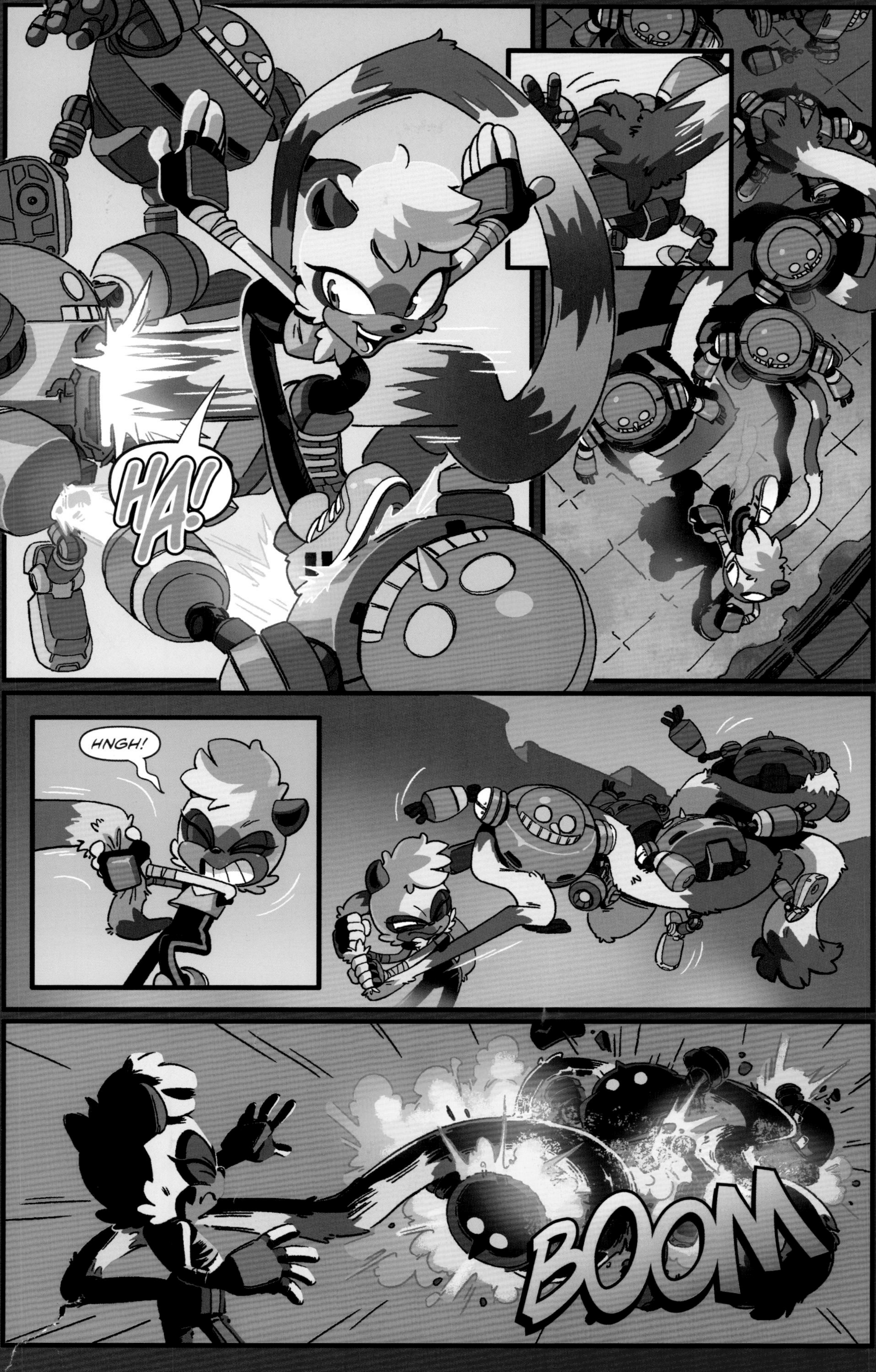
HA!
HNGH!
BOOM

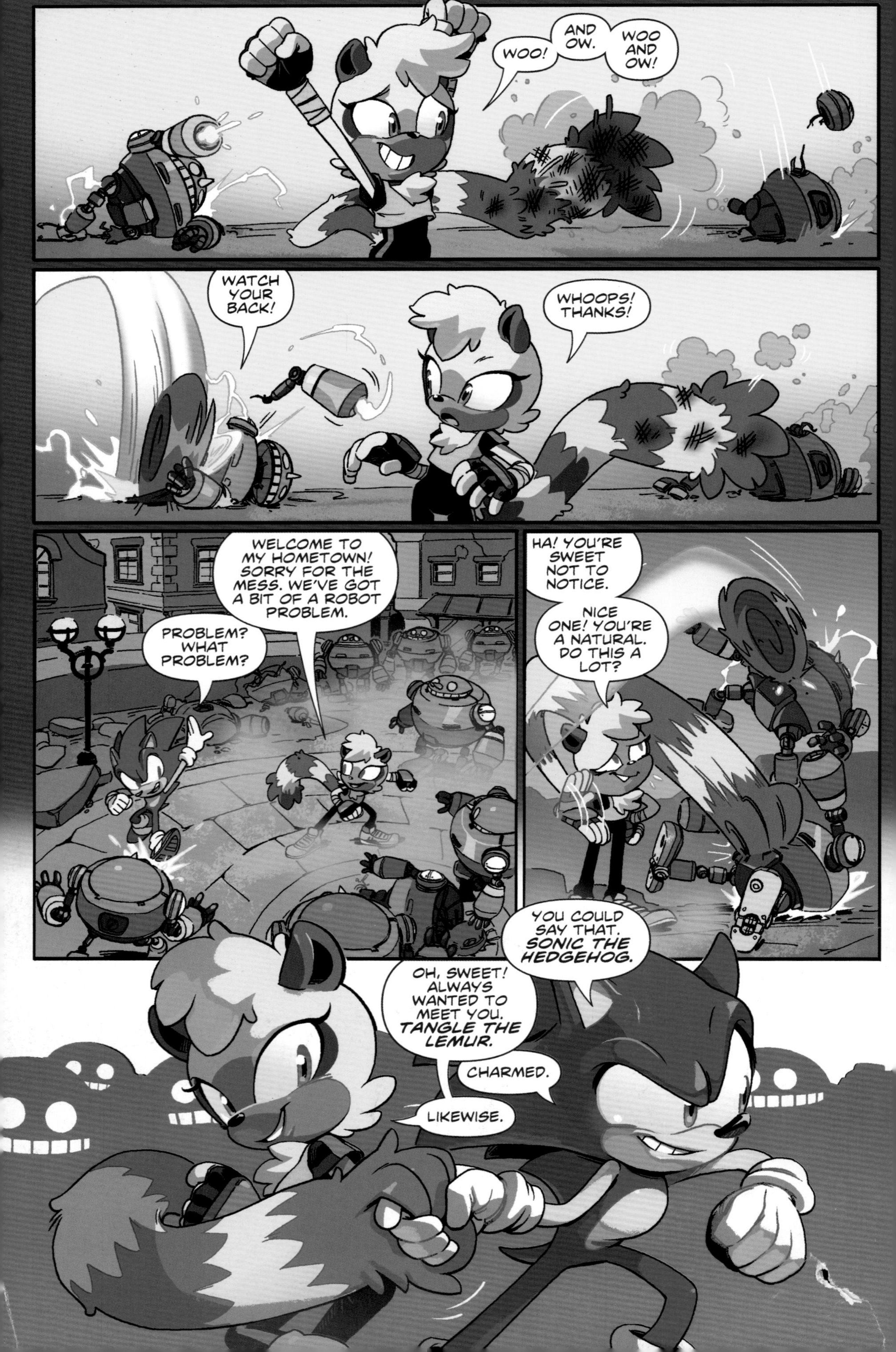

WOO!
AND OW.
WOO AND OW!
WATCH YOUR BACK!
WHOOPS! THANKS!
WELCOME TO MY HOMETOWN! SORRY FOR THE MESS. WE'VE GOT A BIT OF A ROBOT PROBLEM.
PROBLEM? WHAT PROBLEM?
HA! YOU'RE SWEET NOT TO NOTICE.
NICE ONE! YOU'RE A NATURAL. DO THIS A LOT?
YOU COULD SAY THAT. SONIC THE HEDGEHOG.
OH, SWEET! ALWAYS WANTED TO MEET YOU. TANGLE THE LEMUR.
CHARMED.
LIKEWISE.

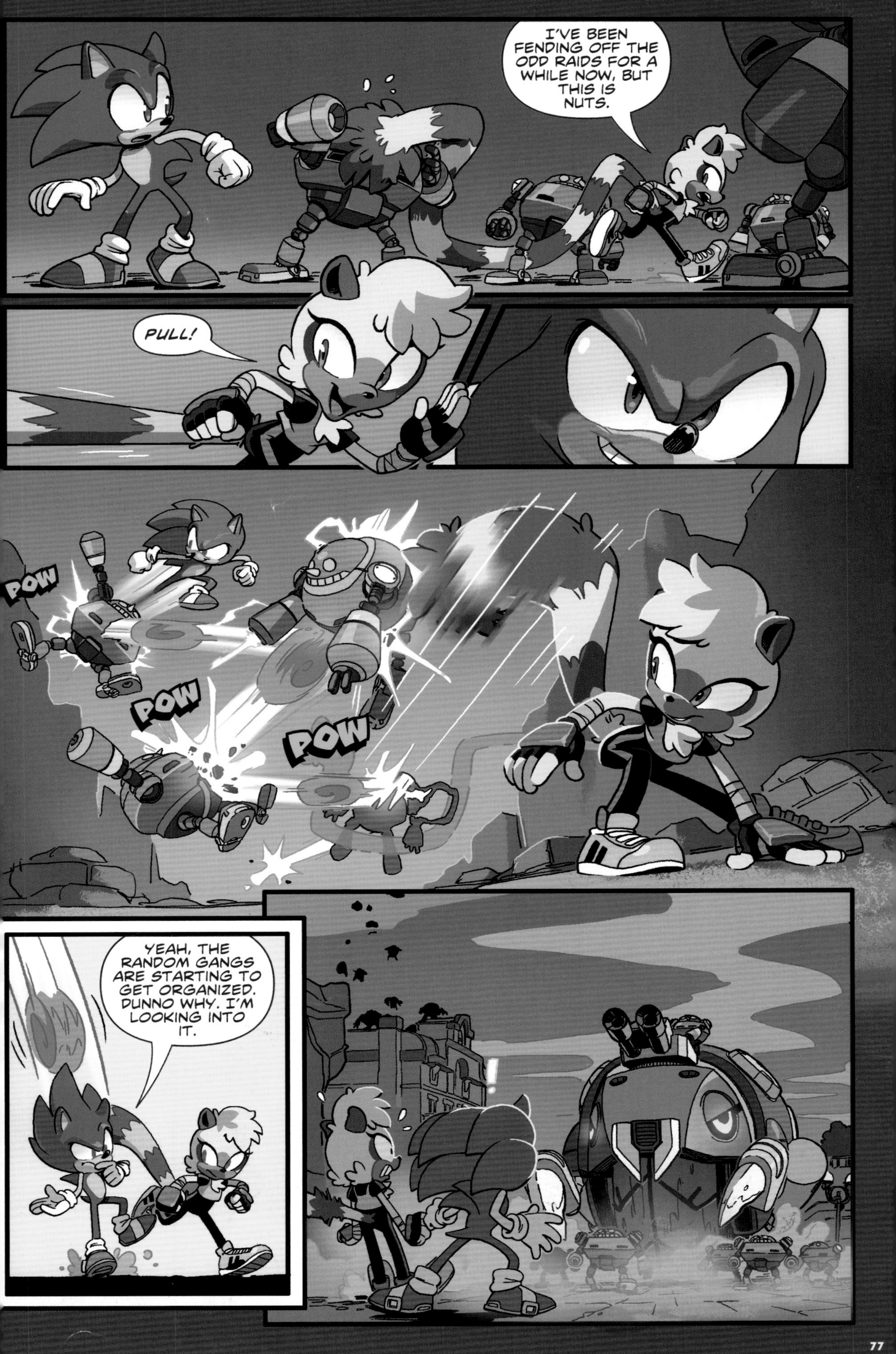
I'VE BEEN FENDING OFF THE ODD RAIDS FOR A WHILE NOW, BUT THIS IS NUTS.
PULL!
POW
POW
POW
YEAH, THE RANDOM GANGS ARE STARTING TO GET ORGANIZED. DUNNO WHY. I'M LOOKING INTO IT.
!

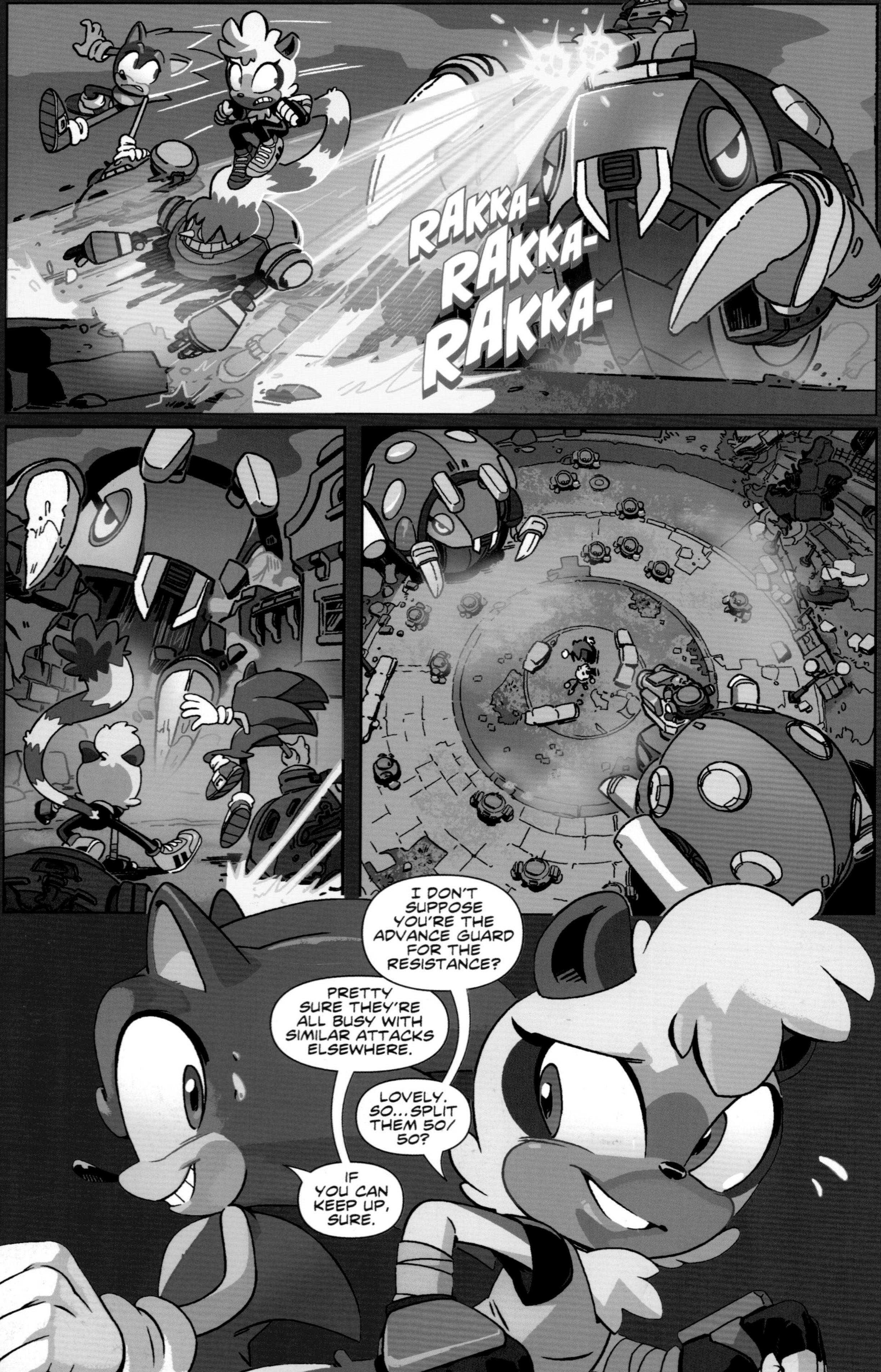

RAKKA-
RAKKA-
RAKKA-
I DON'T SUPPOSE YOU'RE THE ADVANCE GUARD FOR THE RESISTANCE?
PRETTY SURE THEY'RE ALL BUSY WITH SIMILAR ATTACKS ELSEWHERE.
LOVELY. SO...SPLIT THEM 50/50?
IF YOU CAN KEEP UP, SURE.

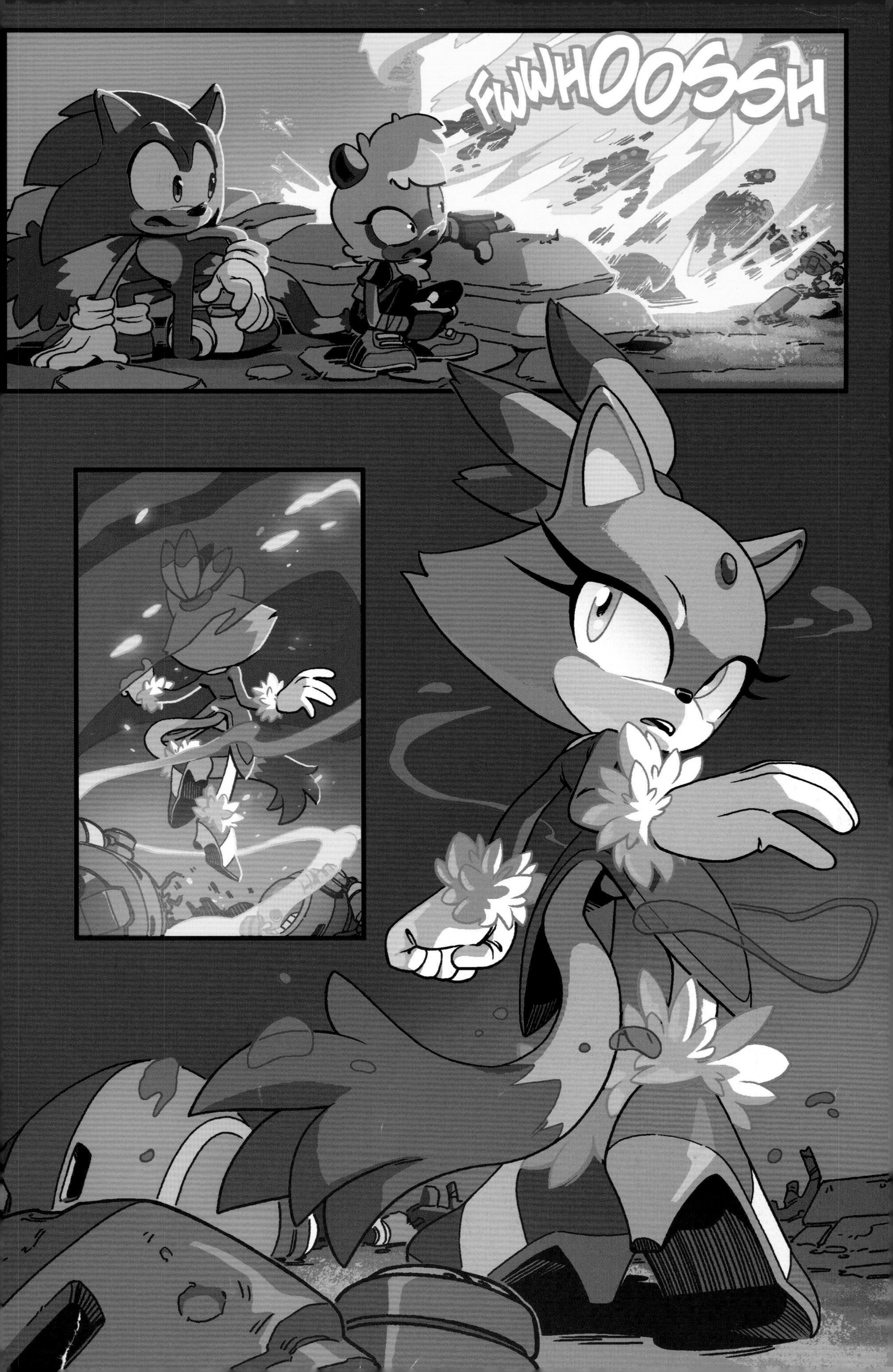
FWWHOOSSH

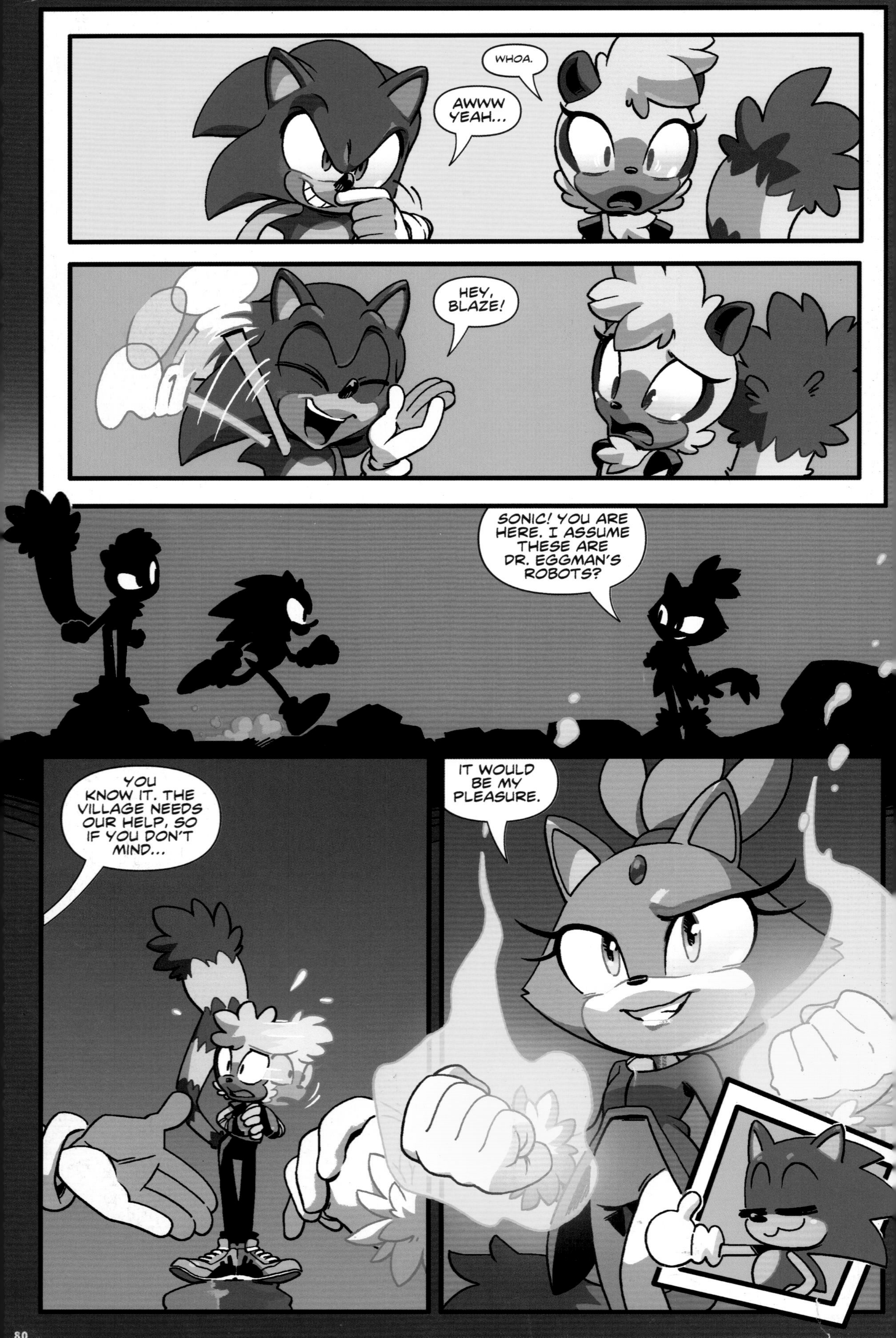
WHOA.
AWWW YEAH...
HEY, BLAZE!
SONIC! YOU ARE HERE. I ASSUME THESE ARE DR. EGGMAN'S ROBOTS?
YOU KNOW IT. THE VILLAGE NEEDS OUR HELP, SO IF YOU DON'T MIND...
IT WOULD BE MY PLEASURE.

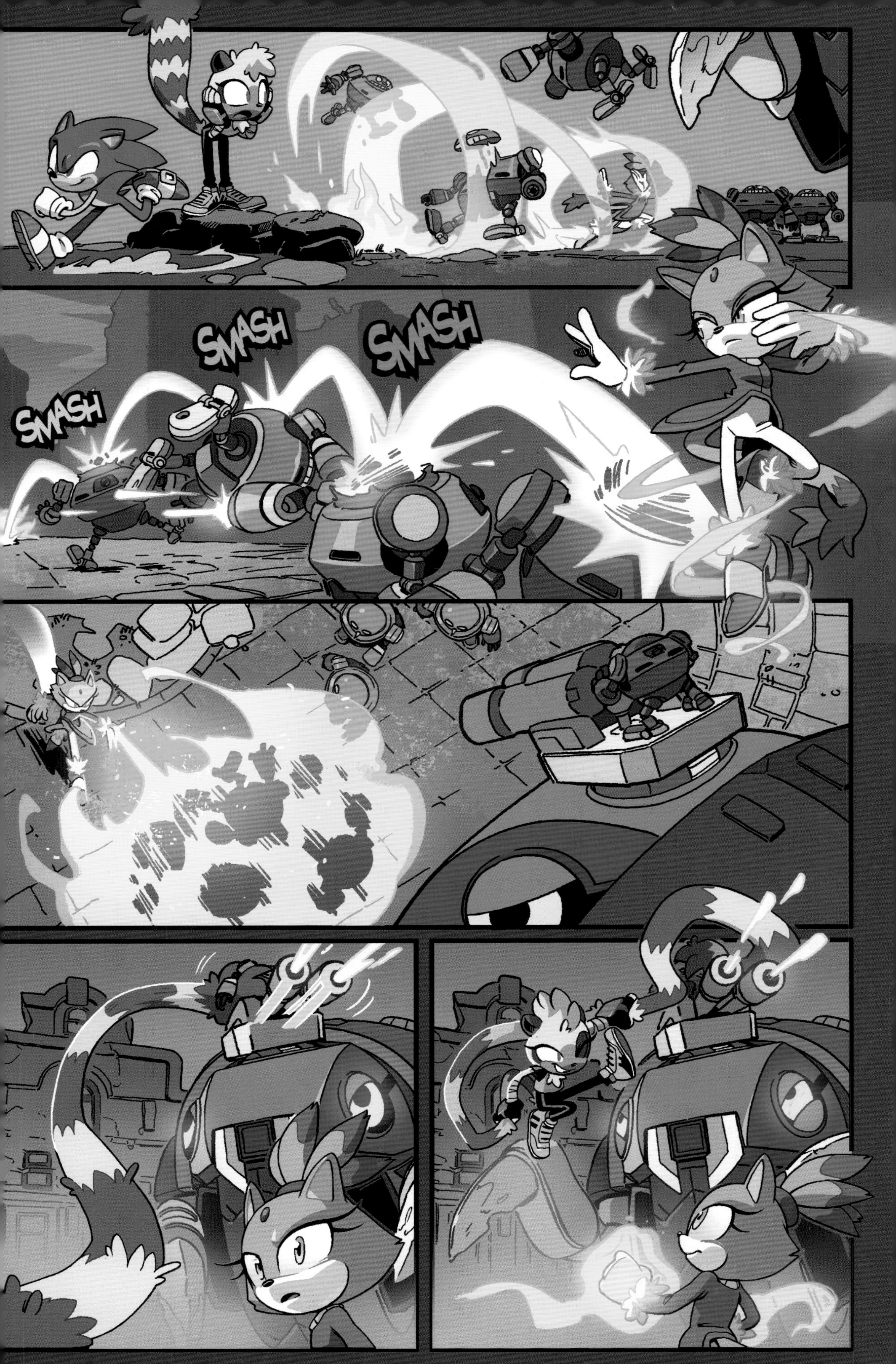
SMASH
SMASH
SMASH

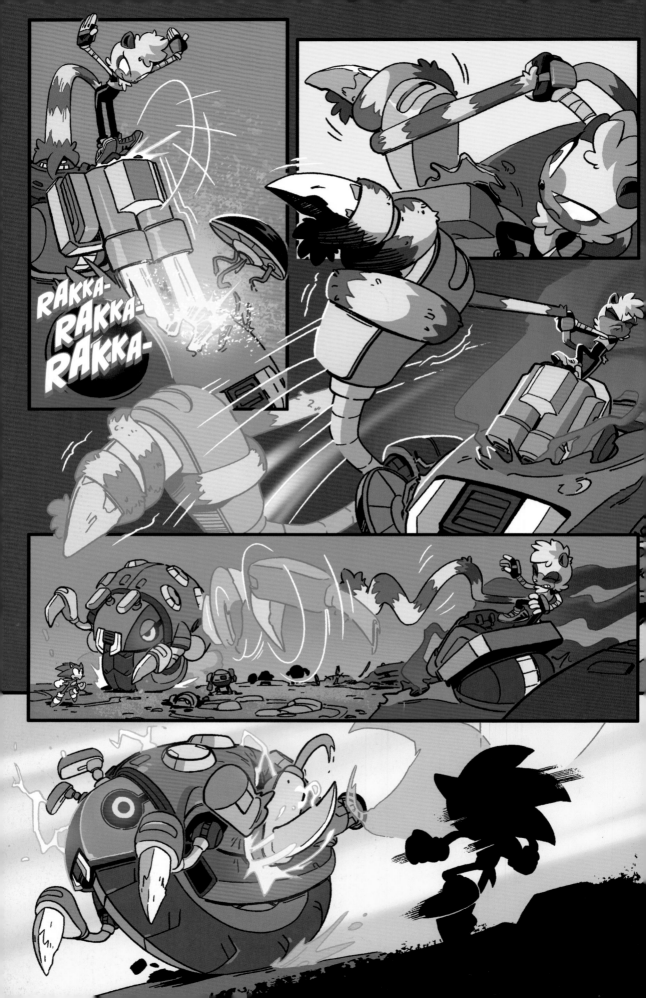

RAKKA-
RAKKA-
RAKKA-

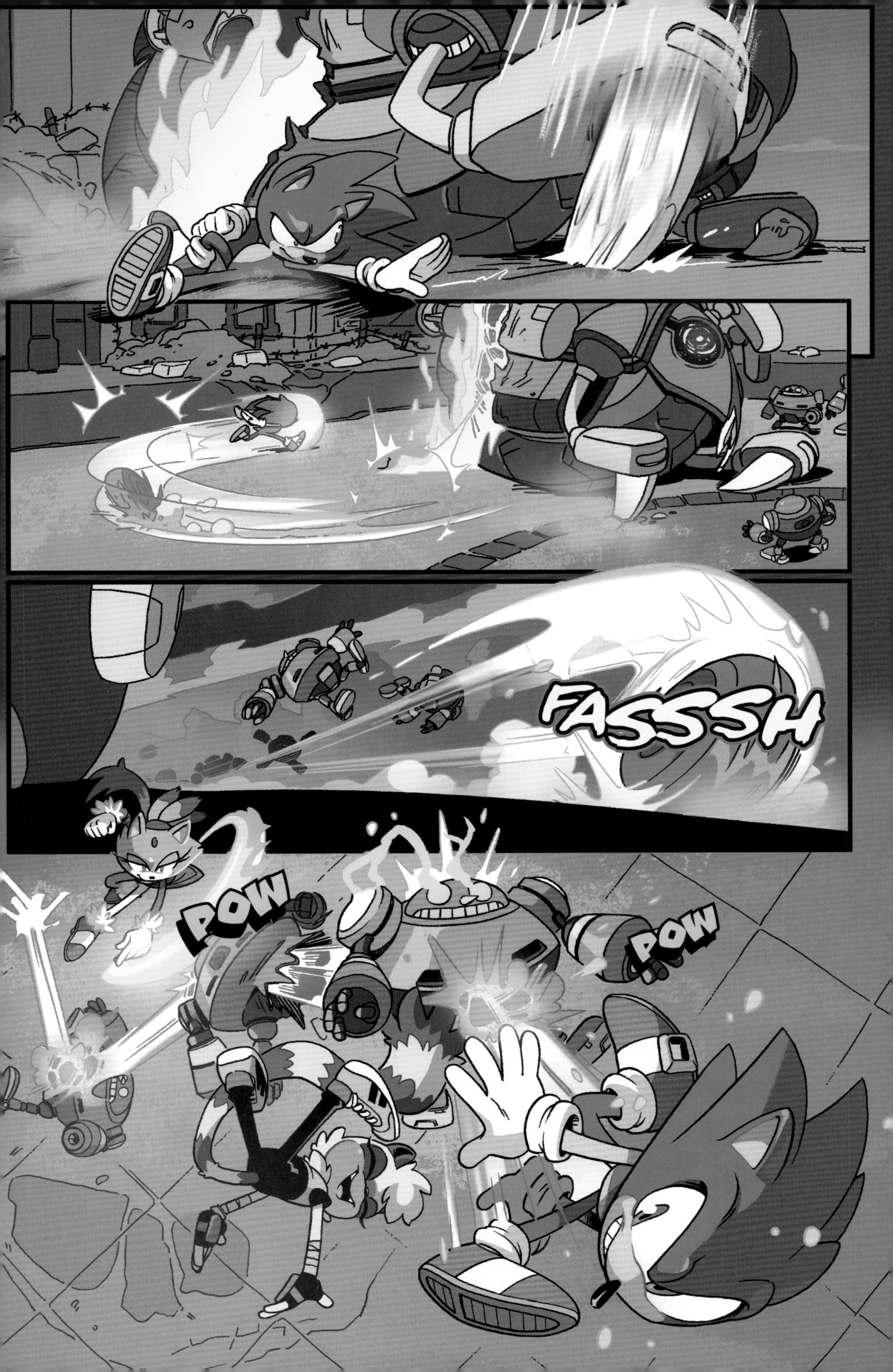
FASSSH
POW
POW

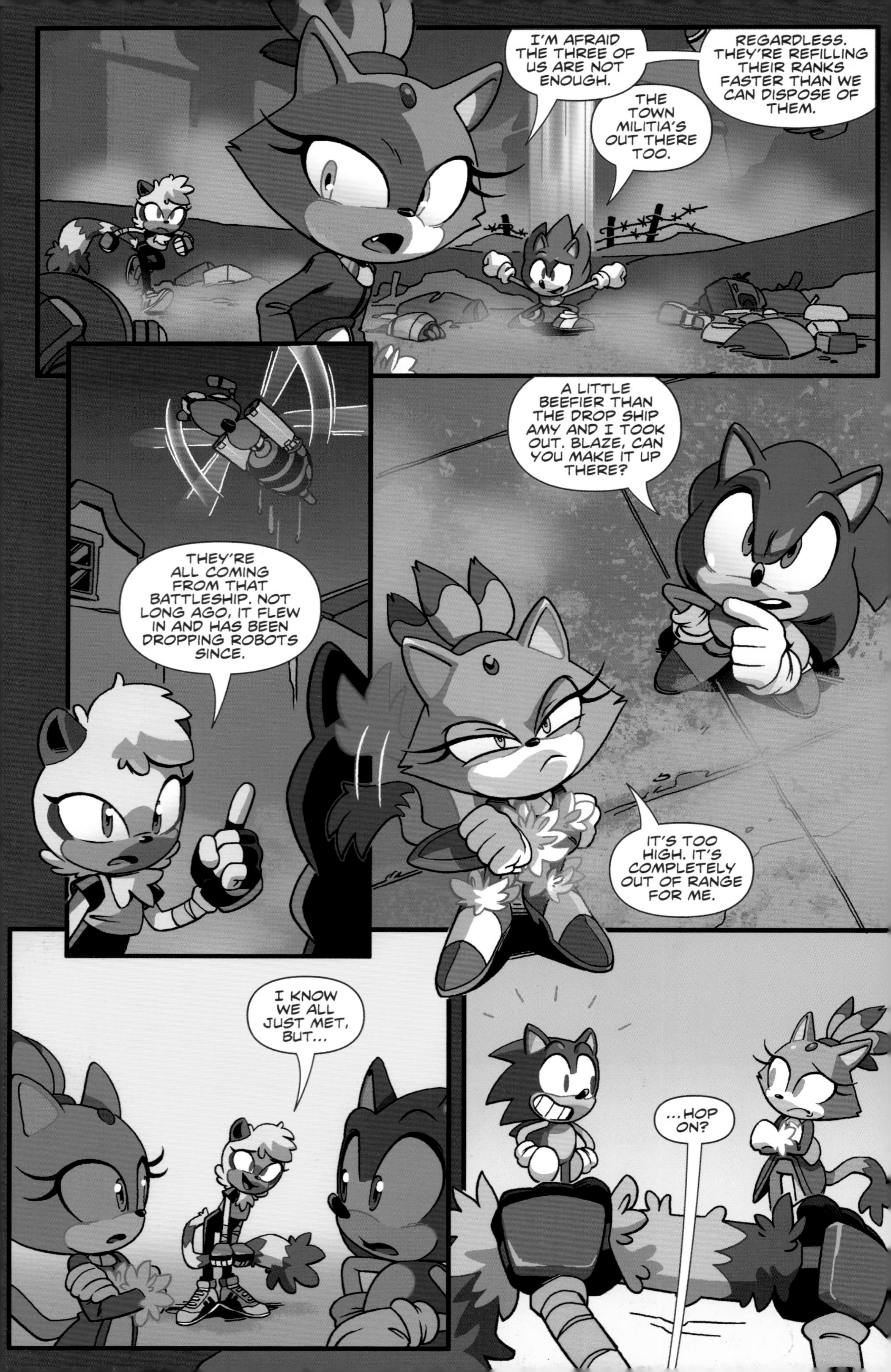
I'M AFRAID THE THREE OF US ARE NOT ENOUGH.
REGARDLESS. THEY'RE REFILLING THEIR RANKS FASTER THAN WE CAN DISPOSE OF THEM.
THE TOWN MILITIA'S OUT THERE TOO.
THEY'RE ALL COMING FROM THAT BATTLESHIP. NOT LONG AGO, IT FLEW IN AND HAS BEEN DROPPING ROBOTS SINCE.
A LITTLE BEEFIER THAN THE DROP SHIP AMY AND I TOOK OUT. BLAZE, CAN YOU MAKE IT UP THERE?
IT'S TOO HIGH. IT'S COMPLETELY OUT OF RANGE FOR ME.
I KNOW WE ALL JUST MET, BUT...
...HOP ON?

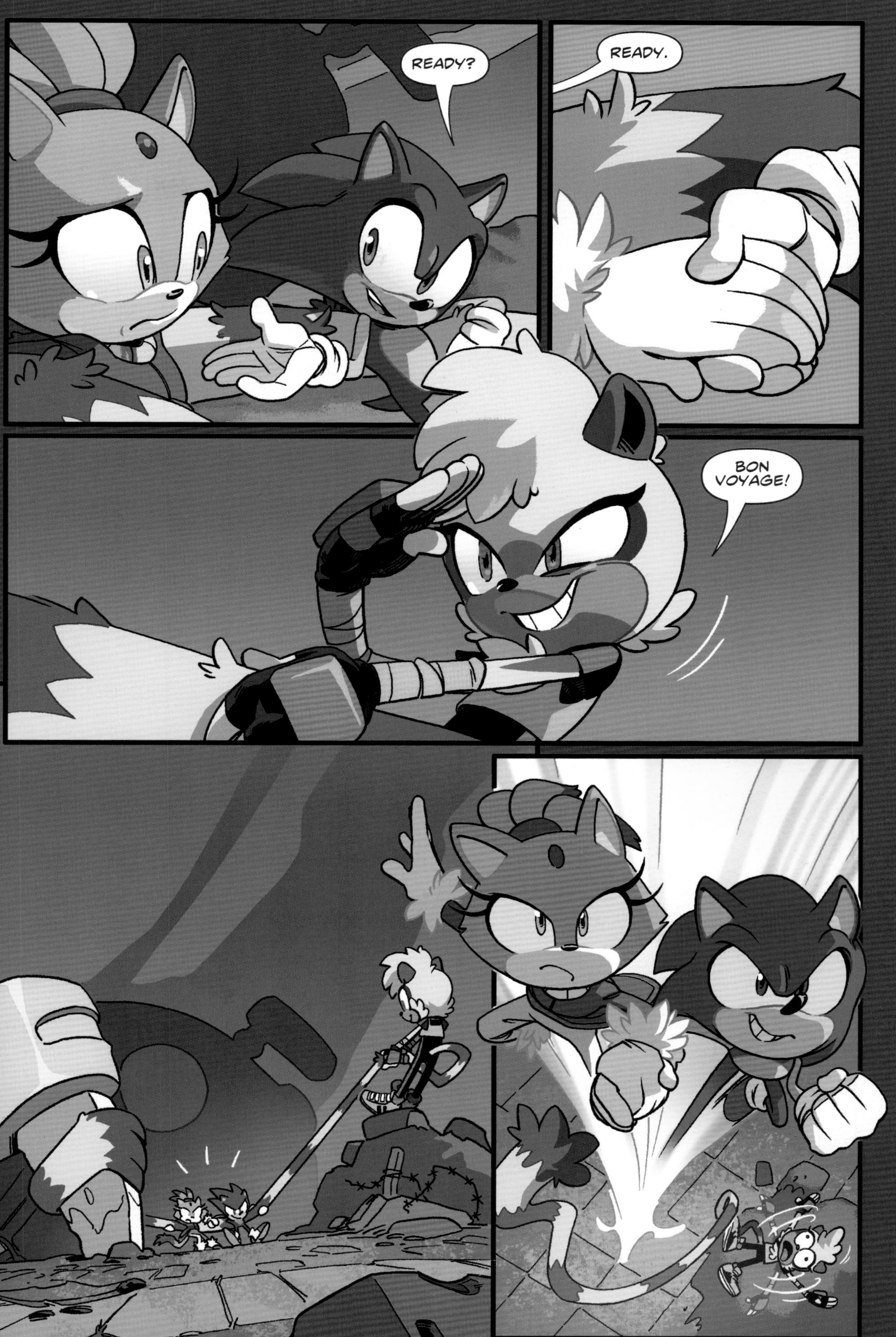
READY?
READY.
BON VOYAGE!

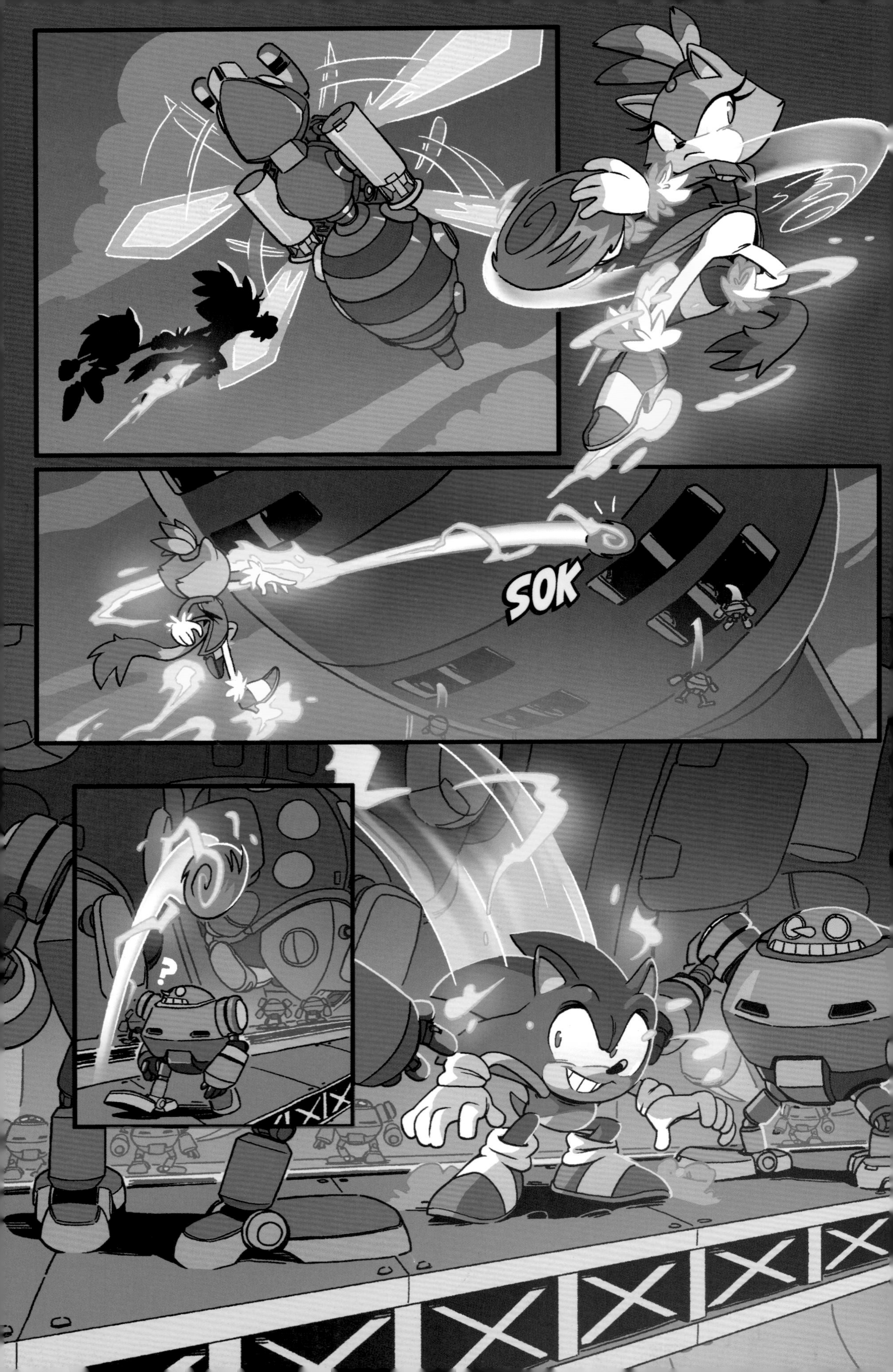
SOK
?

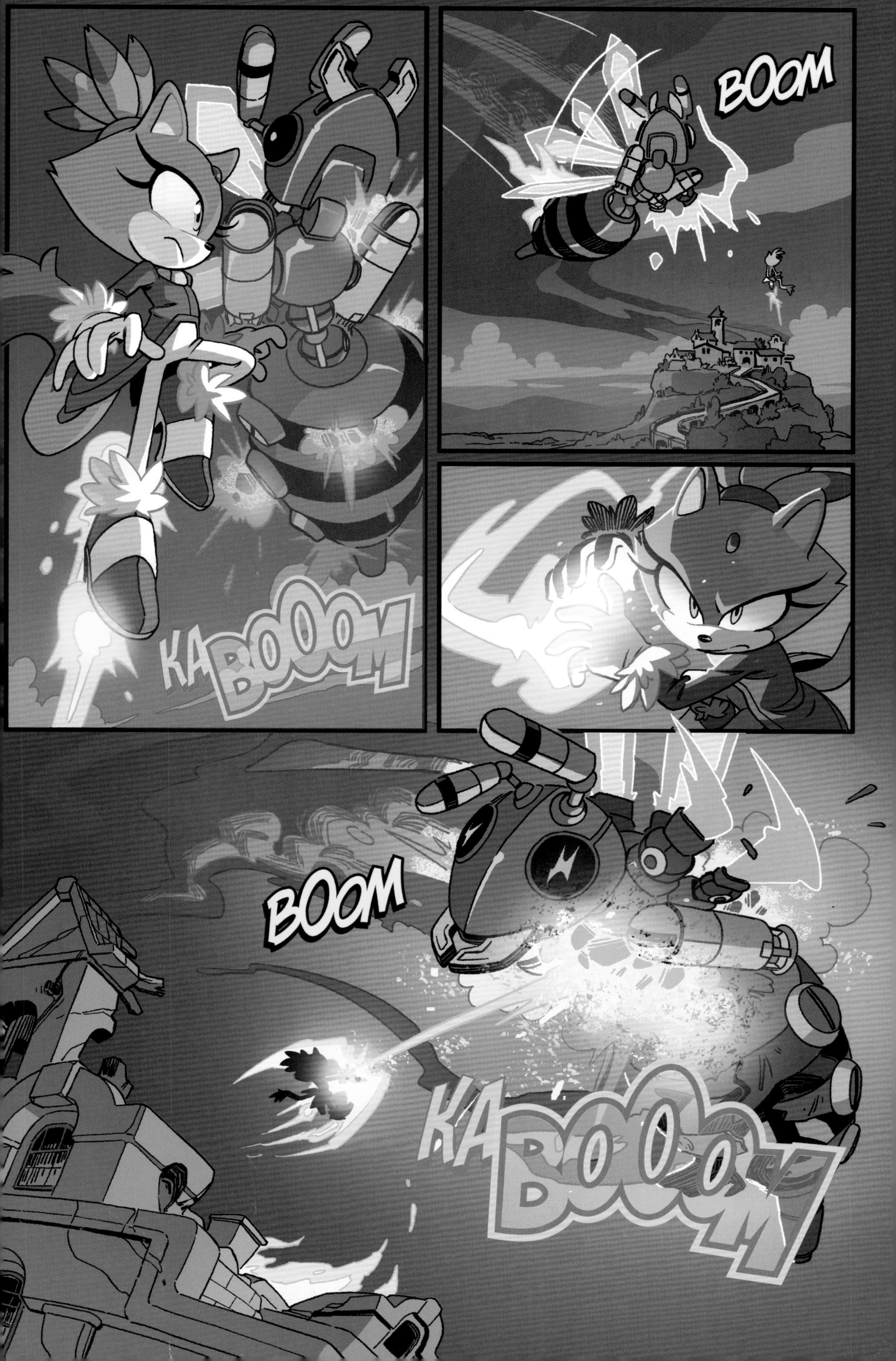
KABOOOM
BOOM
BOOM
KABOOOOM

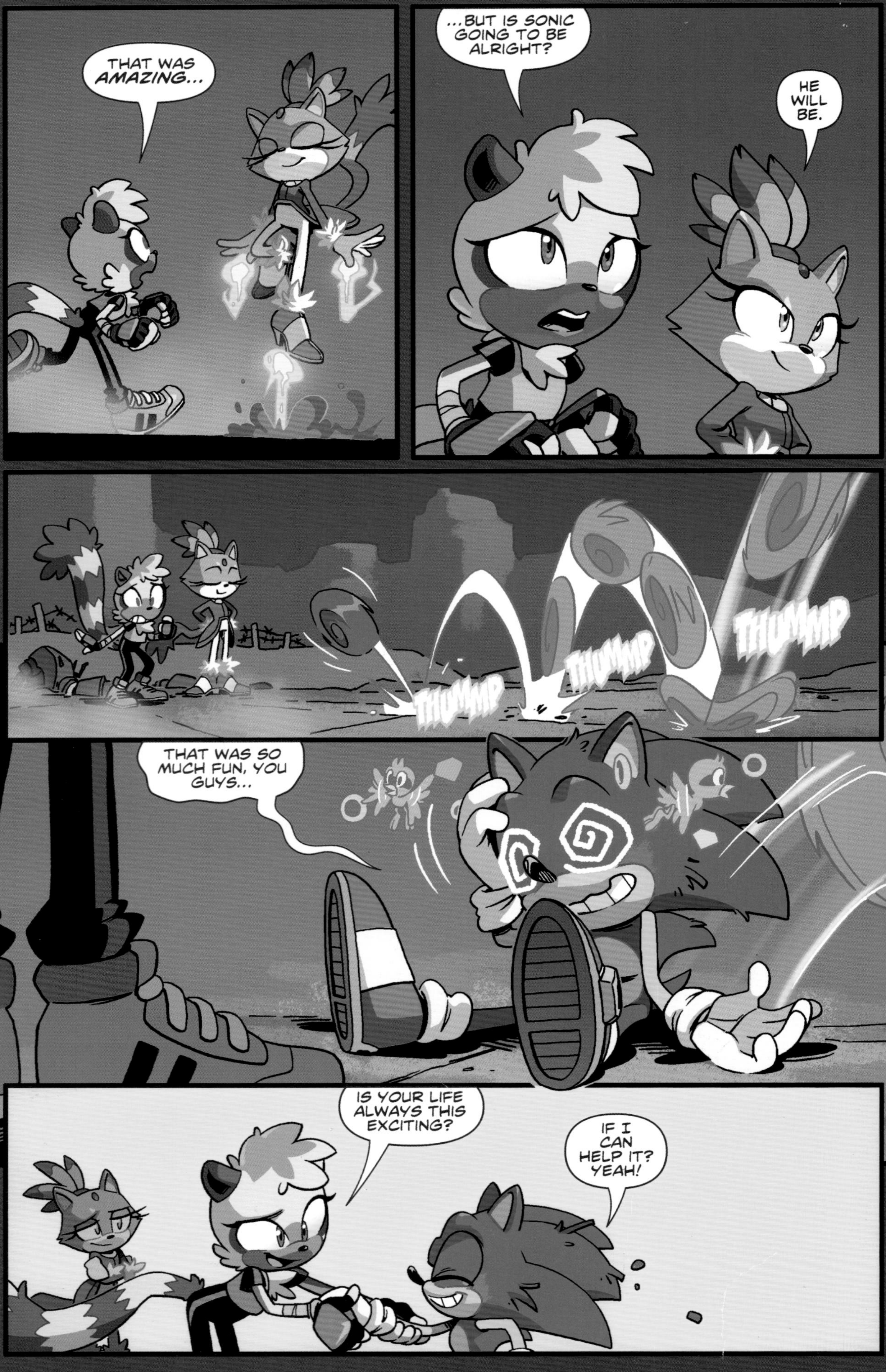
THAT WAS AMAZING...
...BUT IS SONIC GOING TO BE ALRIGHT?
HE WILL BE.
THUMMP
THUMMP
THUMMP
THAT WAS SO MUCH FUN, YOU GUYS...
IS YOUR LIFE ALWAYS THIS EXCITING?
IF I CAN HELP IT? YEAH!

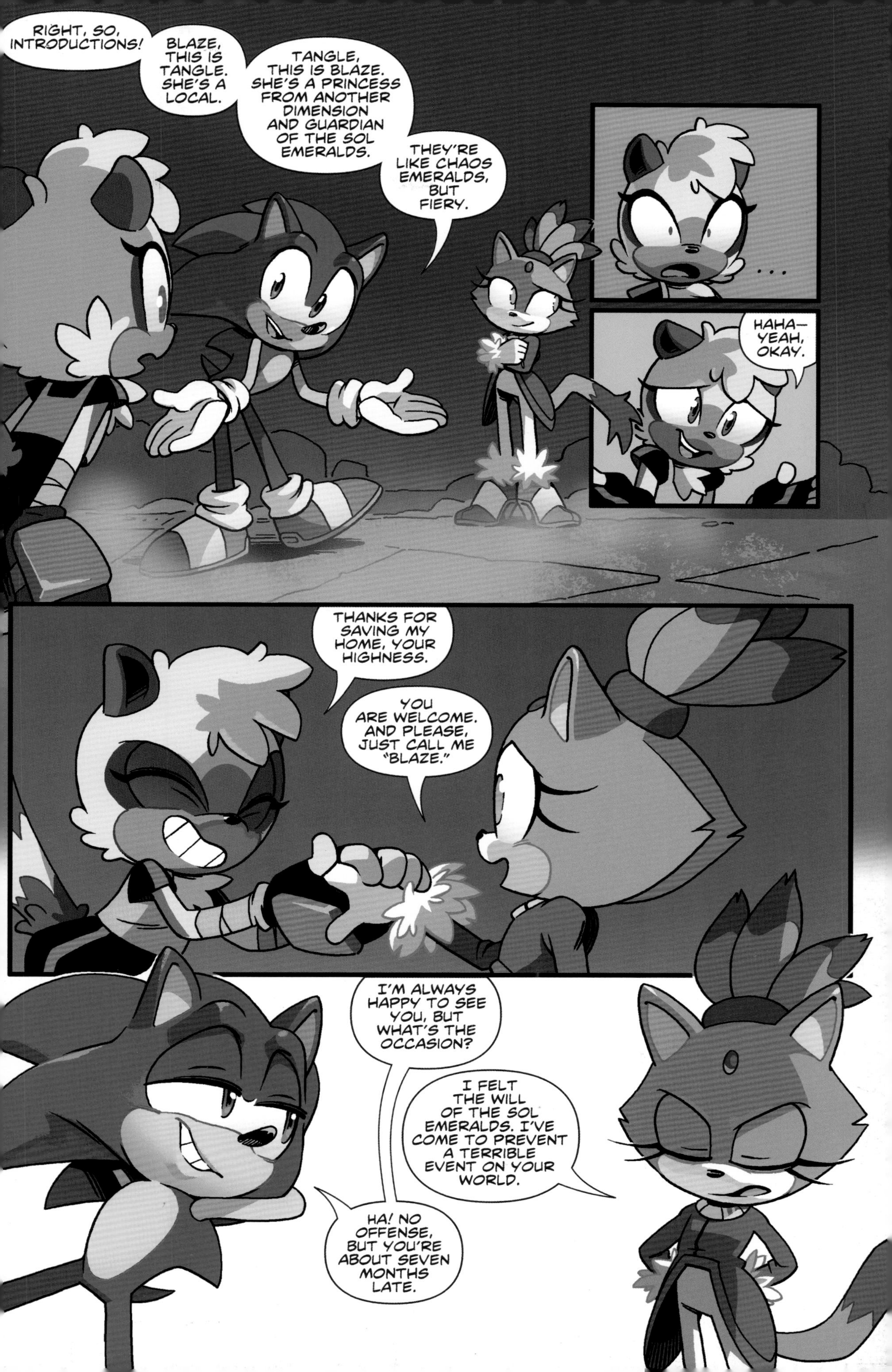
RIGHT, SO, INTRODUCTIONS!
BLAZE, THIS IS TANGLE. SHE'S A LOCAL.
TANGLE, THIS IS BLAZE. SHE'S A PRINCESS FROM ANOTHER DIMENSION AND GUARDIAN OF THE SOL EMERALDS.
THEY'RE LIKE CHAOS EMERALDS, BUT FIERY.
...
HAHA—YEAH, OKAY.
THANKS FOR SAVING MY HOME, YOUR HIGHNESS.
YOU ARE WELCOME. AND PLEASE, JUST CALL ME "BLAZE."
I'M ALWAYS HAPPY TO SEE YOU, BUT WHAT'S THE OCCASION?
I FELT THE WILL OF THE SOL EMERALDS. I'VE COME TO PREVENT A TERRIBLE EVENT ON YOUR WORLD.
HA! NO OFFENSE, BUT YOU'RE ABOUT SEVEN MONTHS LATE.

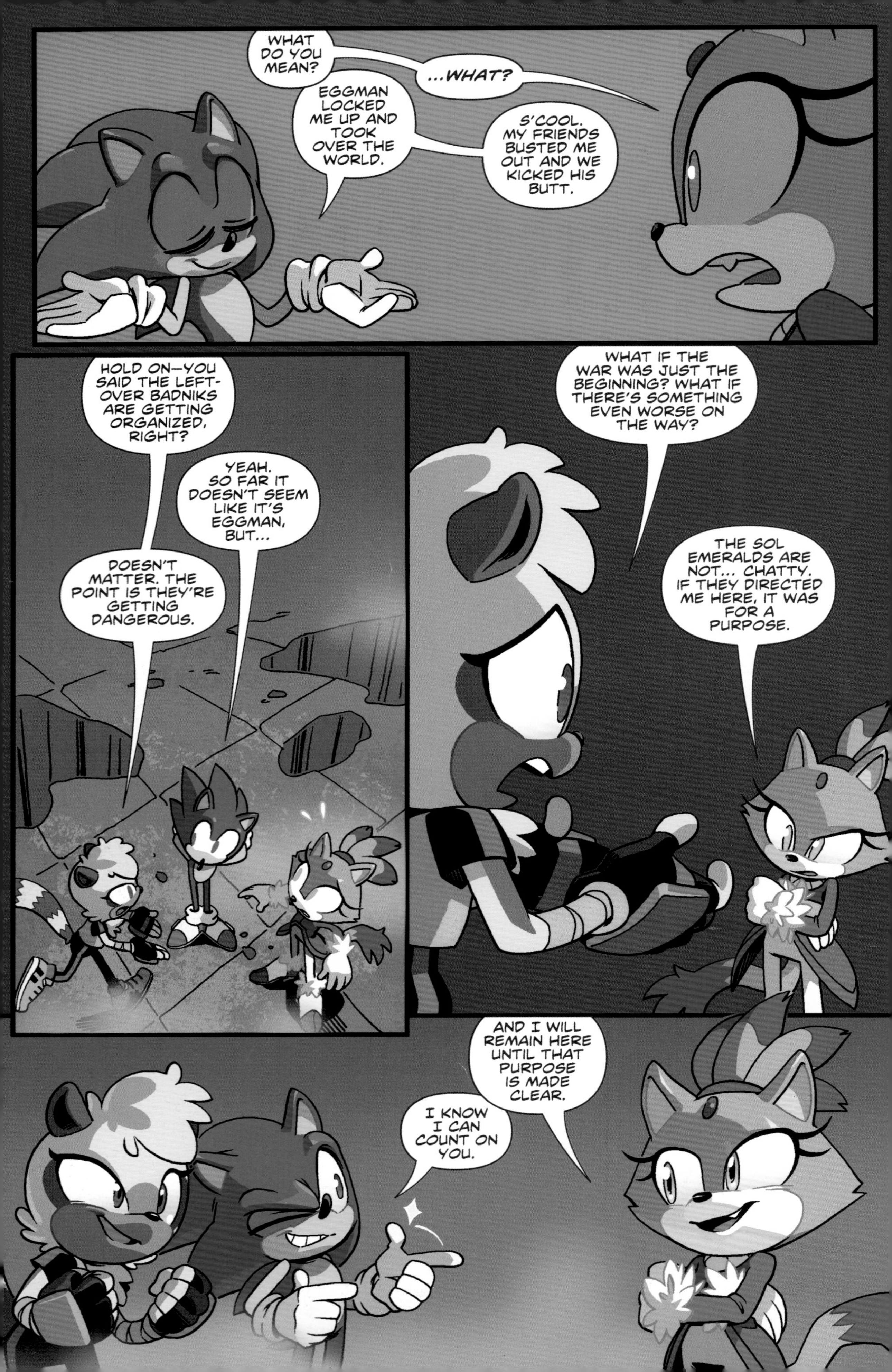
WHAT DO YOU MEAN?
...WHAT?
EGGMAN LOCKED ME UP AND TOOK OVER THE WORLD.
S'COOL. MY FRIENDS BUSTED ME OUT AND WE KICKED HIS BUTT.
HOLD ON—YOU SAID THE LEFT-OVER BADNIKS ARE GETTING ORGANIZED, RIGHT?
YEAH. SO FAR IT DOESN'T SEEM LIKE IT'S EGGMAN, BUT...
DOESN'T MATTER. THE POINT IS THEY'RE GETTING DANGEROUS.
WHAT IF THE WAR WAS JUST THE BEGINNING? WHAT IF THERE'S SOMETHING EVEN WORSE ON THE WAY?
THE SOL EMERALDS ARE NOT... CHATTY. IF THEY DIRECTED ME HERE, IT WAS FOR A PURPOSE.
AND I WILL REMAIN HERE UNTIL THAT PURPOSE IS MADE CLEAR.
I KNOW I CAN COUNT ON YOU.

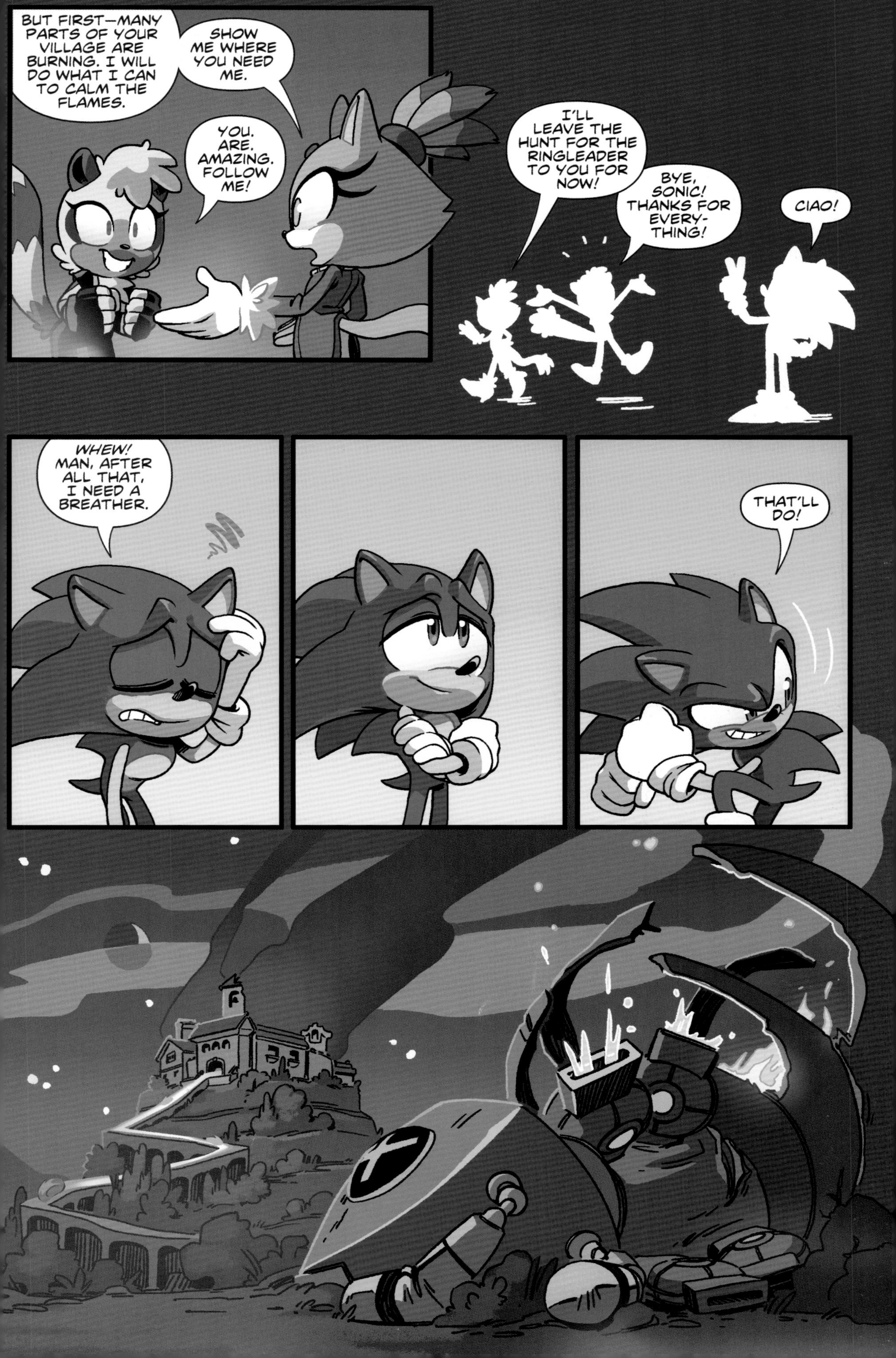
BUT FIRST—MANY PARTS OF YOUR VILLAGE ARE BURNING. I WILL DO WHAT I CAN TO CALM THE FLAMES.
SHOW ME WHERE YOU NEED ME.
YOU. ARE. AMAZING. FOLLOW ME!
I'LL LEAVE THE HUNT FOR THE RINGLEADER TO YOU FOR NOW!
BYE, SONIC! THANKS FOR EVERY-THING!
CIAO!
WHEW! MAN, AFTER ALL THAT, I NEED A BREATHER.
THAT'LL DO!

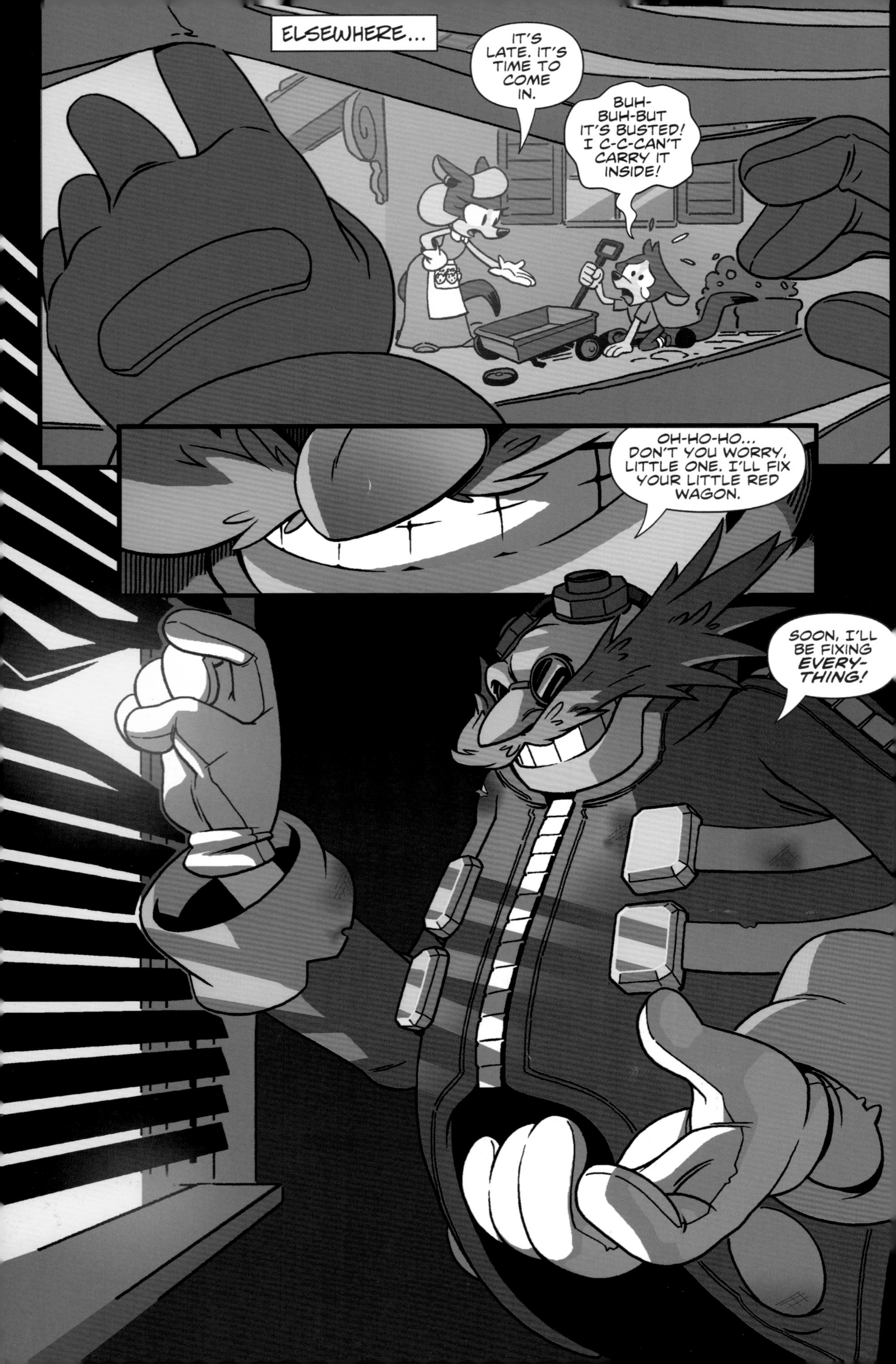
ELSEWHERE...
IT'S LATE. IT'S TIME TO COME IN.
BUH-BUH-BUT IT'S BUSTED! I C-C-CAN'T CARRY IT INSIDE!
OH-HO-HO... DON'T YOU WORRY, LITTLE ONE. I'LL FIX YOUR LITTLE RED WAGON.
SOON, I'LL BE FIXING EVERY-THING!

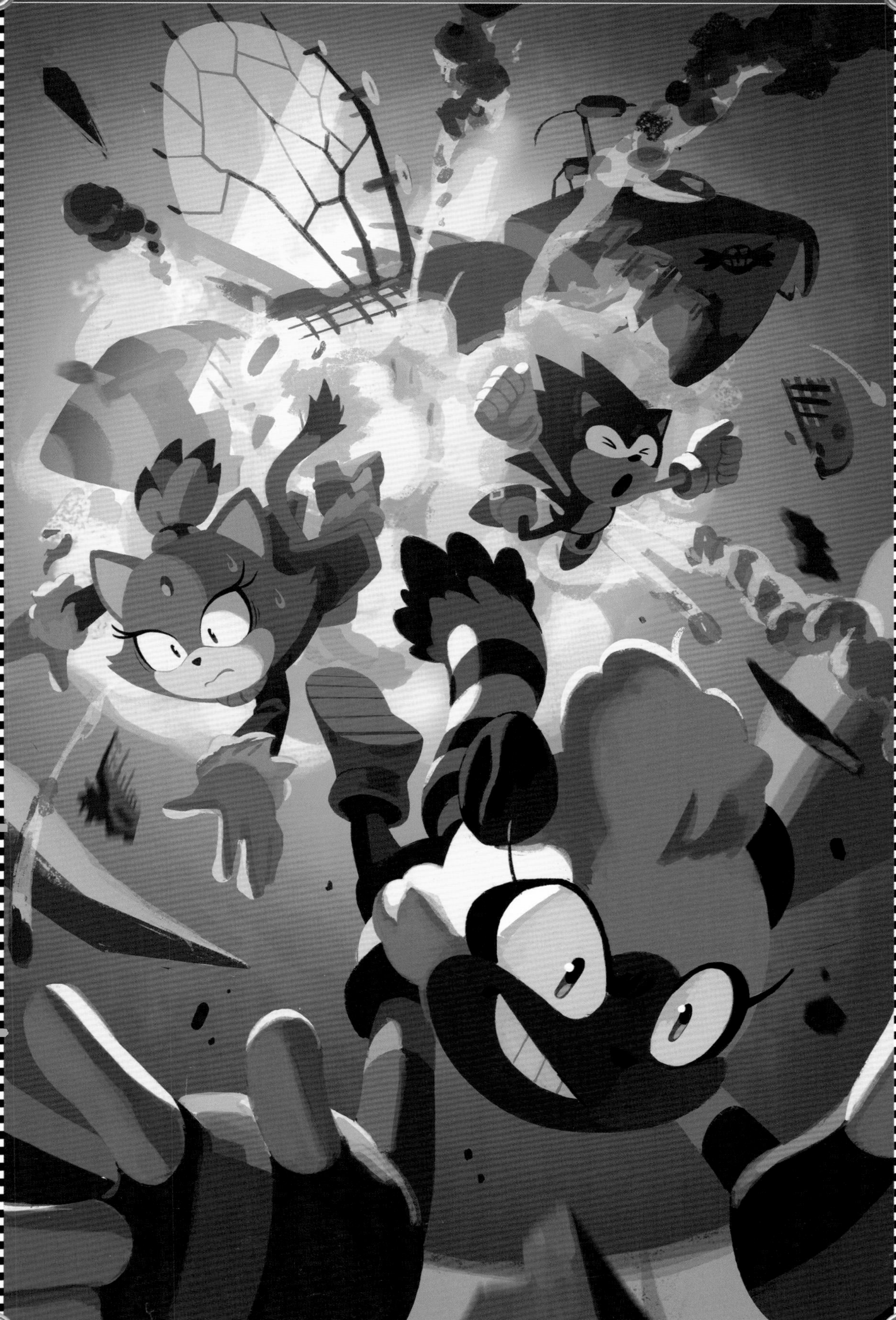

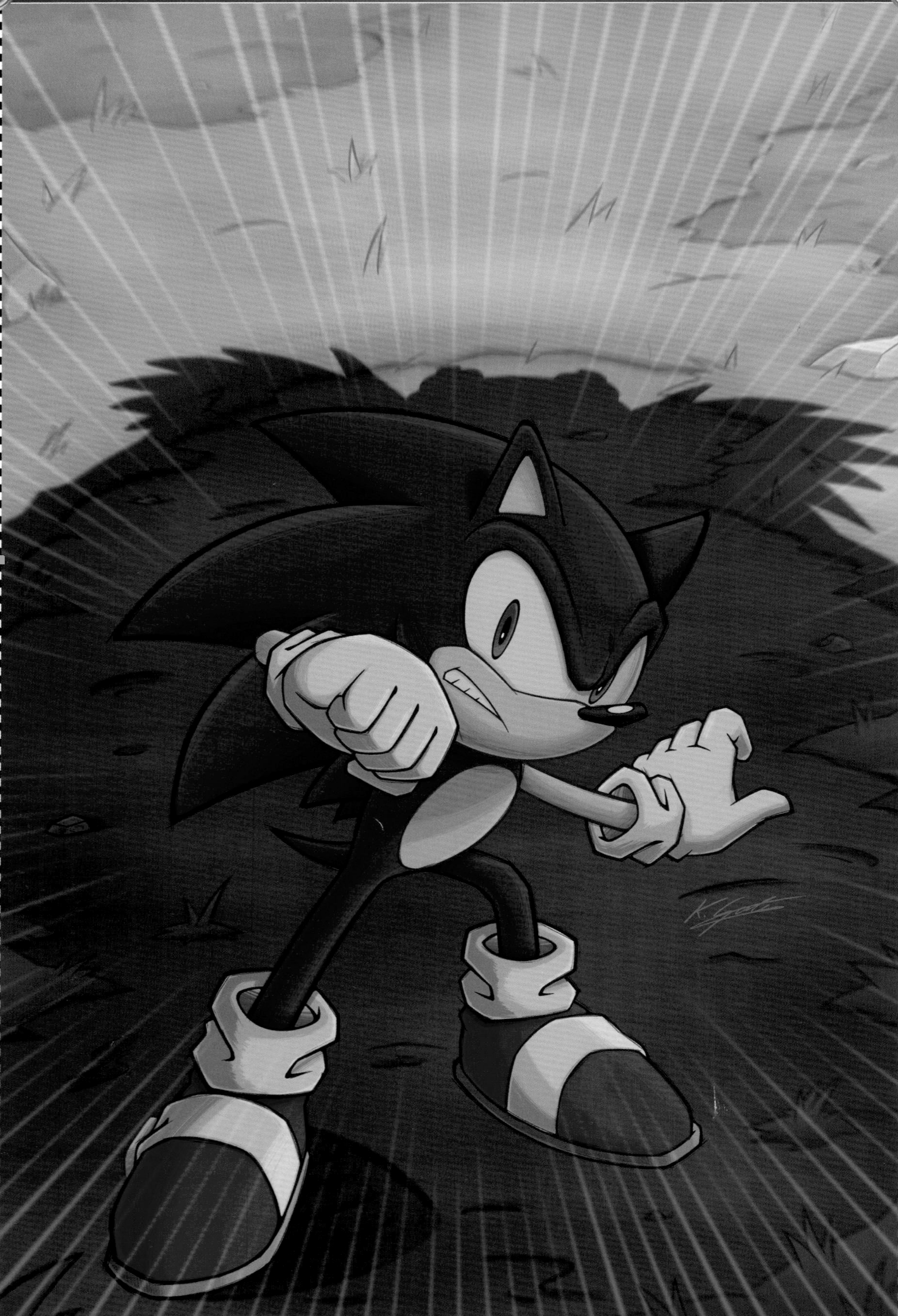

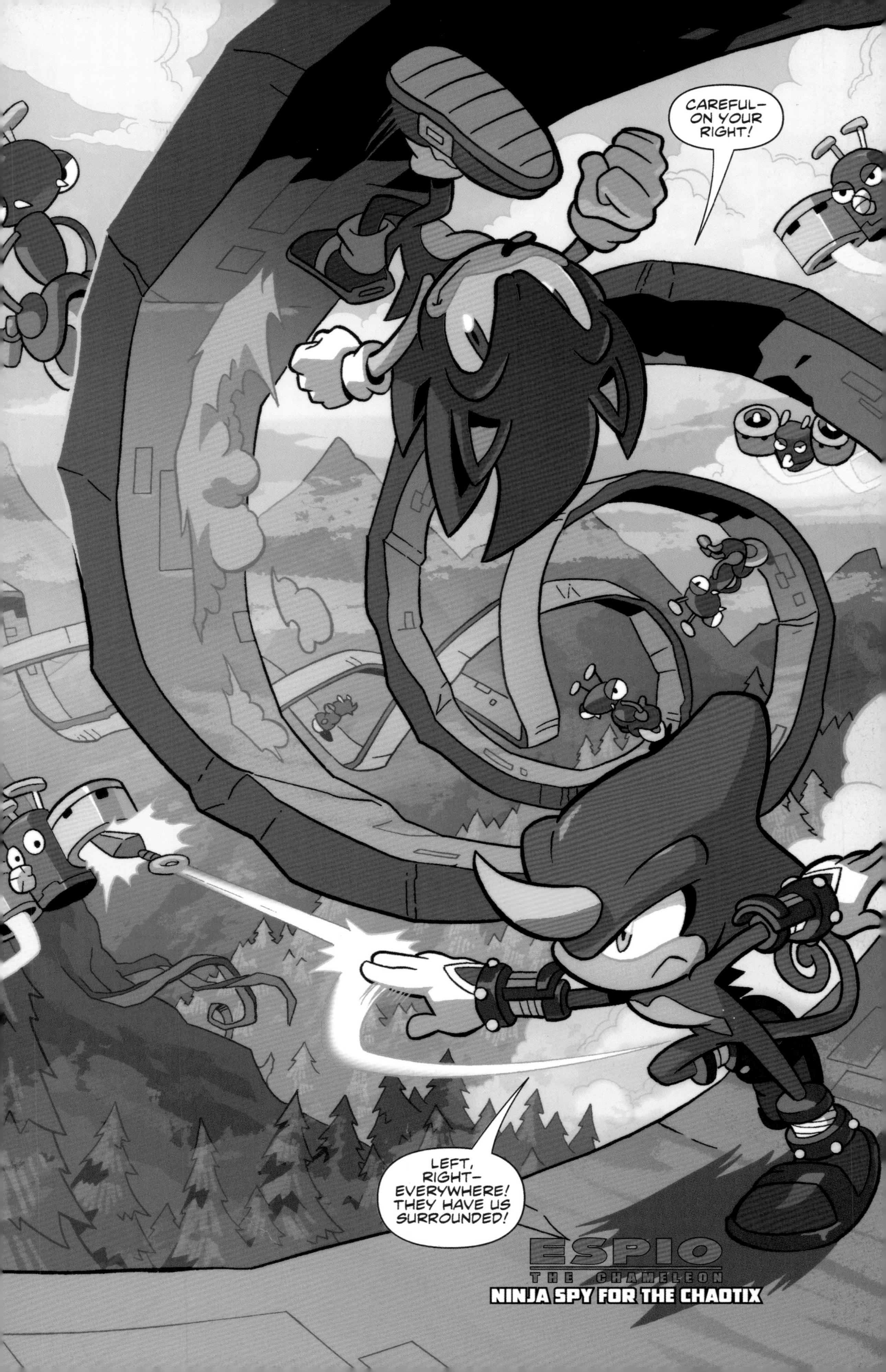
CAREFUL—
ON YOUR
RIGHT!
LEFT,
RIGHT—
EVERYWHERE!
THEY HAVE US
SURROUNDED!
ESPIO
THE CHAMELEON
NINJA SPY FOR THE CHAOTIX

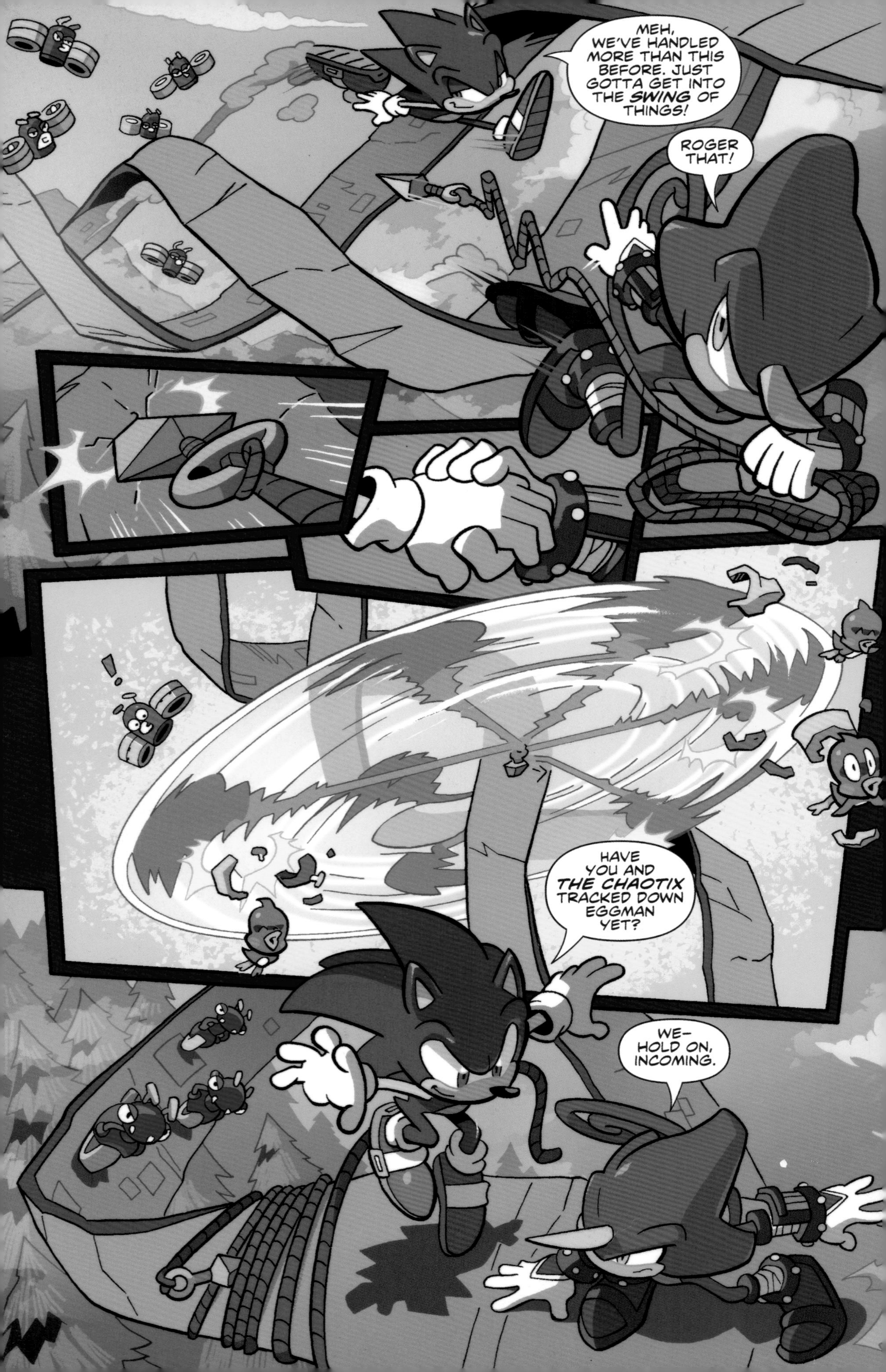
MEH, WE'VE HANDLED MORE THAN THIS BEFORE. JUST GOTTA GET INTO THE SWING OF THINGS!
ROGER THAT!
!
HAVE YOU AND THE CHAOTIX TRACKED DOWN EGGMAN YET?
WE— HOLD ON, INCOMING.

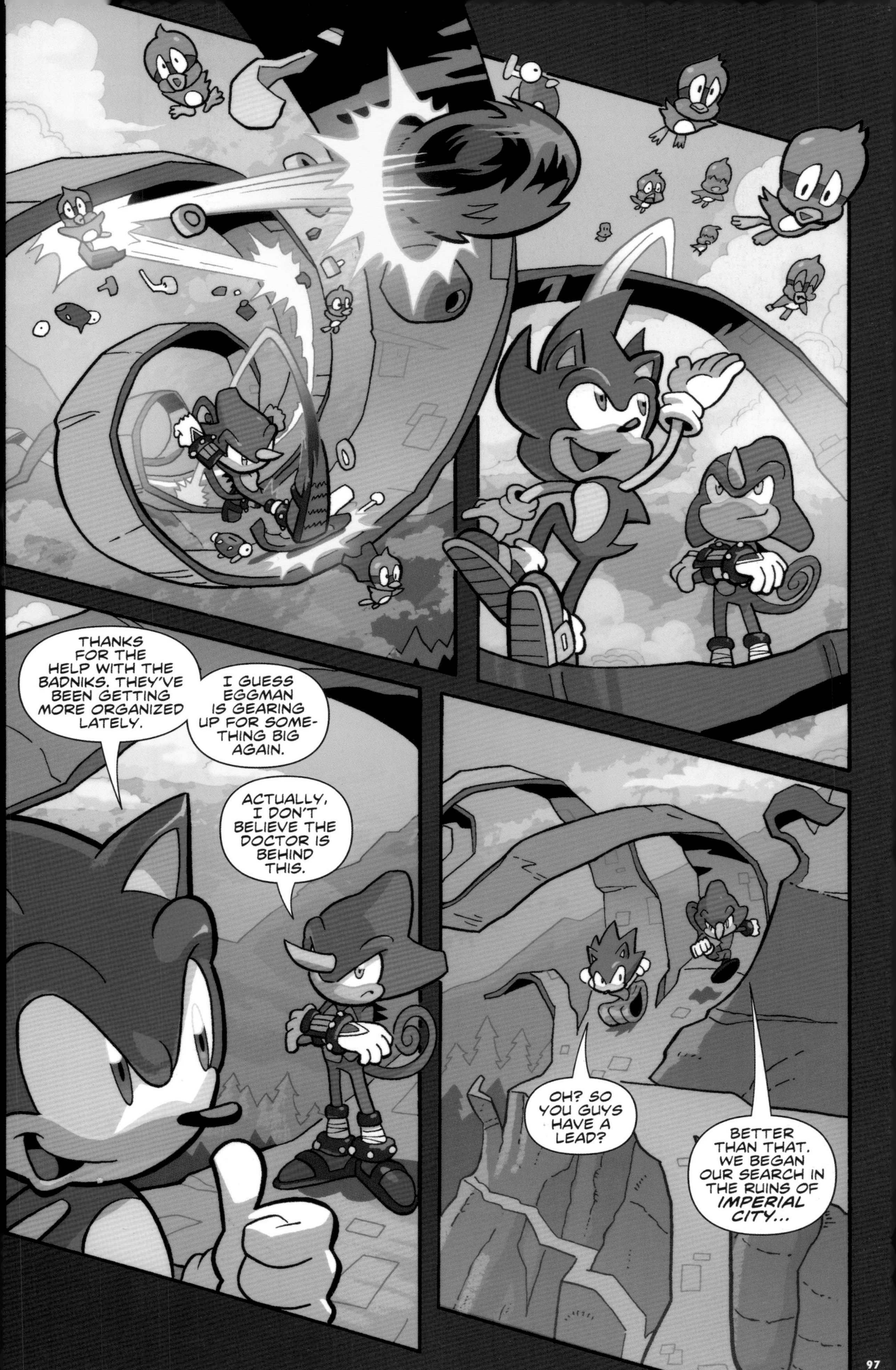

THANKS FOR THE HELP WITH THE BADNIKS. THEY'VE BEEN GETTING MORE ORGANIZED LATELY.
I GUESS EGGMAN IS GEARING UP FOR SOME-THING BIG AGAIN.
ACTUALLY, I DON'T BELIEVE THE DOCTOR IS BEHIND THIS.
OH? SO YOU GUYS HAVE A LEAD?
BETTER THAN THAT. WE BEGAN OUR SEARCH IN THE RUINS OF *IMPERIAL CITY*...

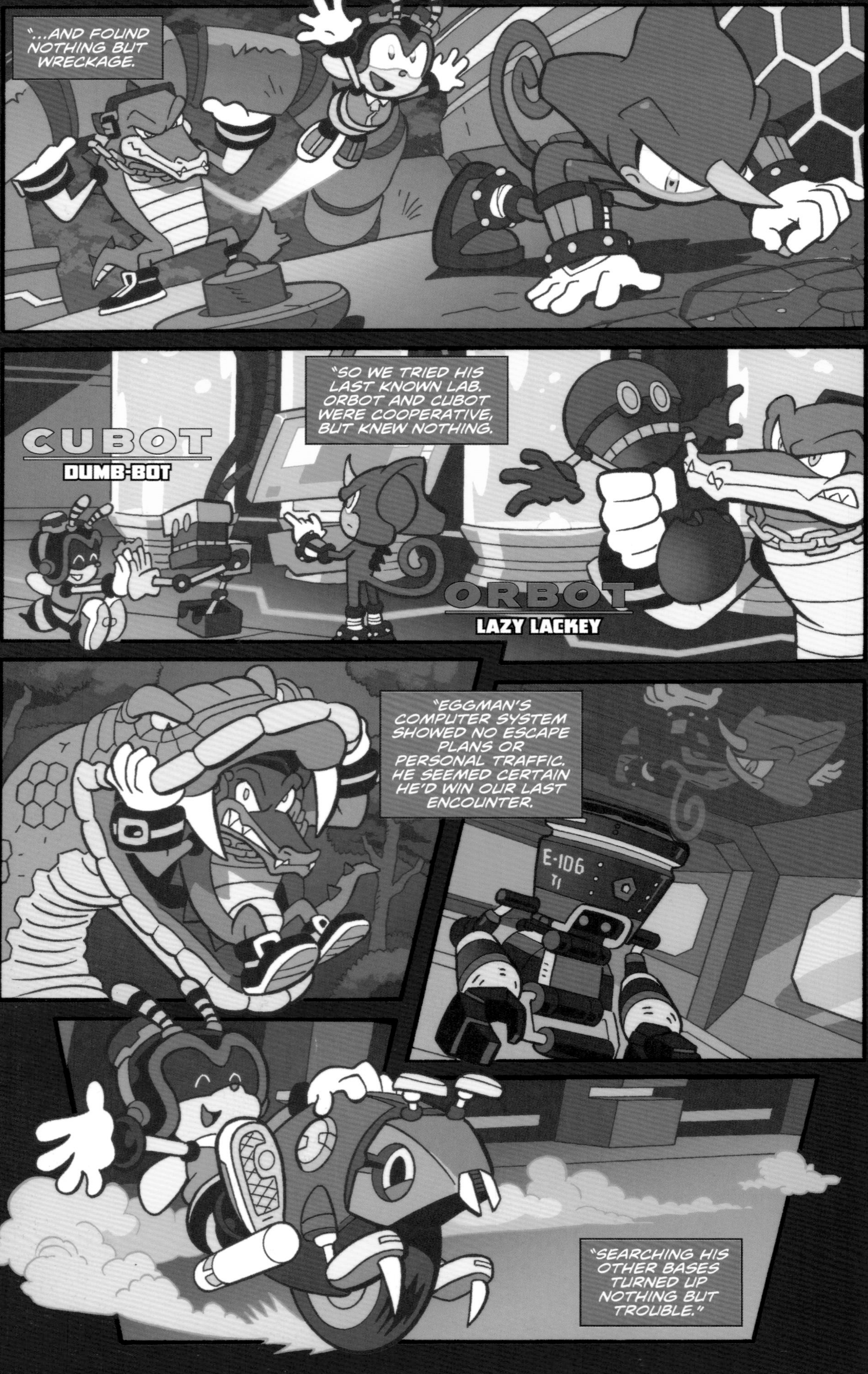
"...AND FOUND NOTHING BUT WRECKAGE.
"SO WE TRIED HIS LAST KNOWN LAB. ORBOT AND CUBOT WERE COOPERATIVE, BUT KNEW NOTHING.
CUBOT
DUMB-BOT
ORBOT
LAZY LACKEY
"EGGMAN'S COMPUTER SYSTEM SHOWED NO ESCAPE PLANS OR PERSONAL TRAFFIC. HE SEEMED CERTAIN HE'D WIN OUR LAST ENCOUNTER.
E-106
"SEARCHING HIS OTHER BASES TURNED UP NOTHING BUT TROUBLE."

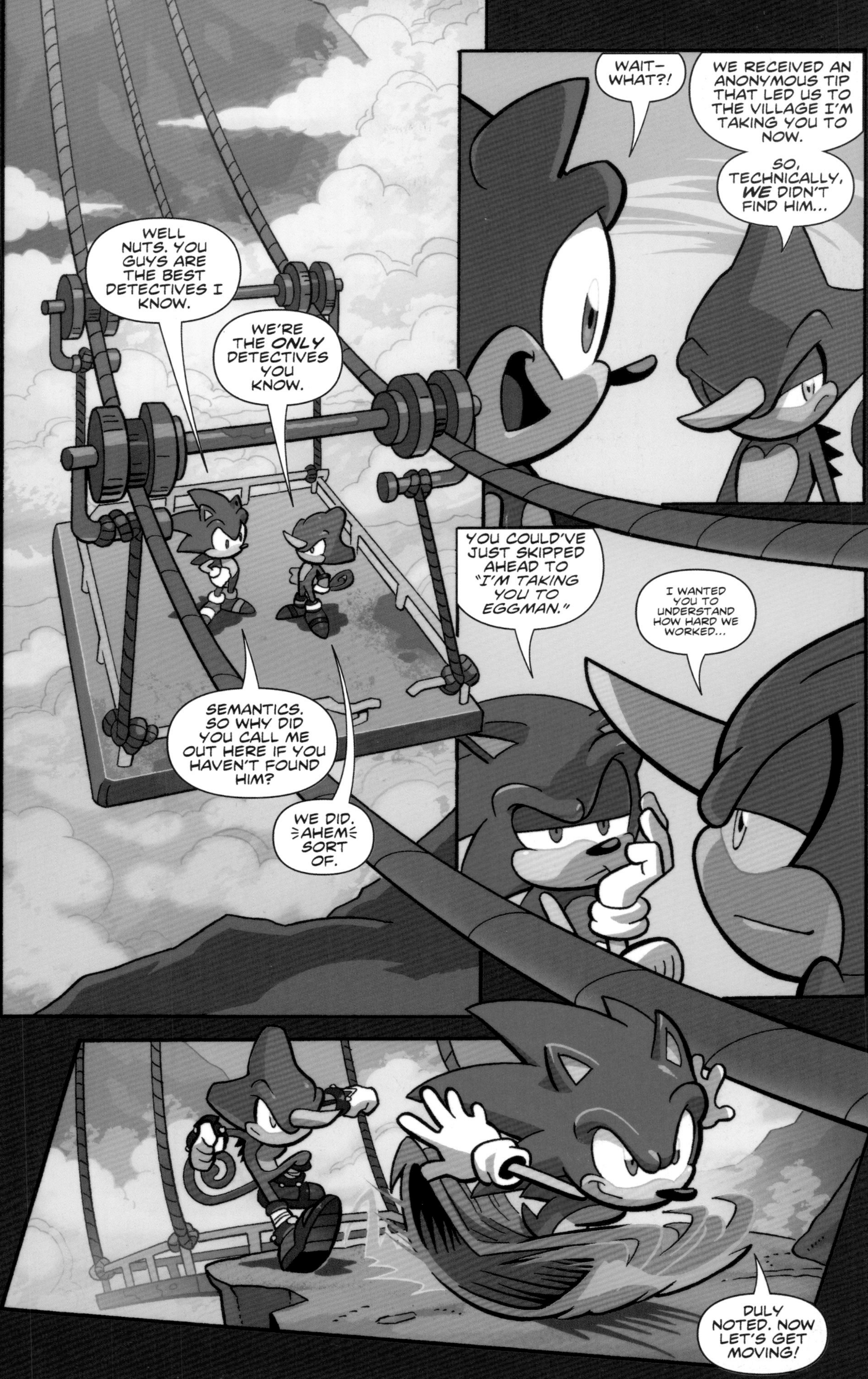
WELL NUTS. YOU GUYS ARE THE BEST DETECTIVES I KNOW.
WE'RE THE ONLY DETECTIVES YOU KNOW.
SEMANTICS. SO WHY DID YOU CALL ME OUT HERE IF YOU HAVEN'T FOUND HIM?
WE DID. AHEM SORT OF.
WAIT— WHAT?!
WE RECEIVED AN ANONYMOUS TIP THAT LED US TO THE VILLAGE I'M TAKING YOU TO NOW.
SO, TECHNICALLY, WE DIDN'T FIND HIM...
YOU COULD'VE JUST SKIPPED AHEAD TO "I'M TAKING YOU TO EGGMAN."
I WANTED YOU TO UNDERSTAND HOW HARD WE WORKED...
DULY NOTED. NOW LET'S GET MOVING!

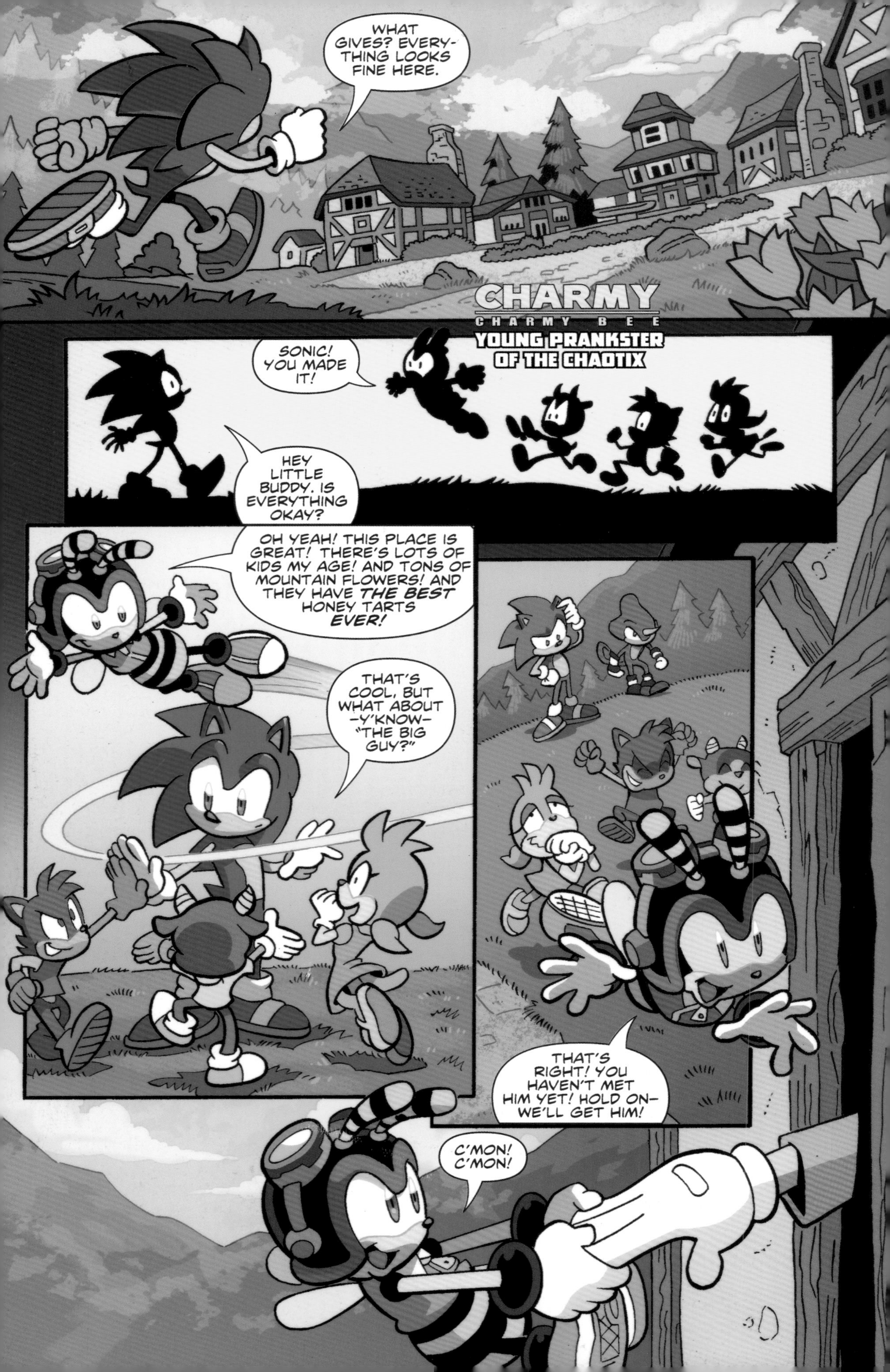
WHAT GIVES? EVERY-THING LOOKS FINE HERE.
CHARMY
CHARMY BEE
YOUNG PRANKSTER OF THE CHAOTIX
SONIC! YOU MADE IT!
HEY LITTLE BUDDY. IS EVERYTHING OKAY?
OH YEAH! THIS PLACE IS GREAT! THERE'S LOTS OF KIDS MY AGE! AND TONS OF MOUNTAIN FLOWERS! AND THEY HAVE THE BEST HONEY TARTS EVER!
THAT'S COOL, BUT WHAT ABOUT -Y'KNOW- "THE BIG GUY?"
THAT'S RIGHT! YOU HAVEN'T MET HIM YET! HOLD ON-WE'LL GET HIM!
C'MON! C'MON!

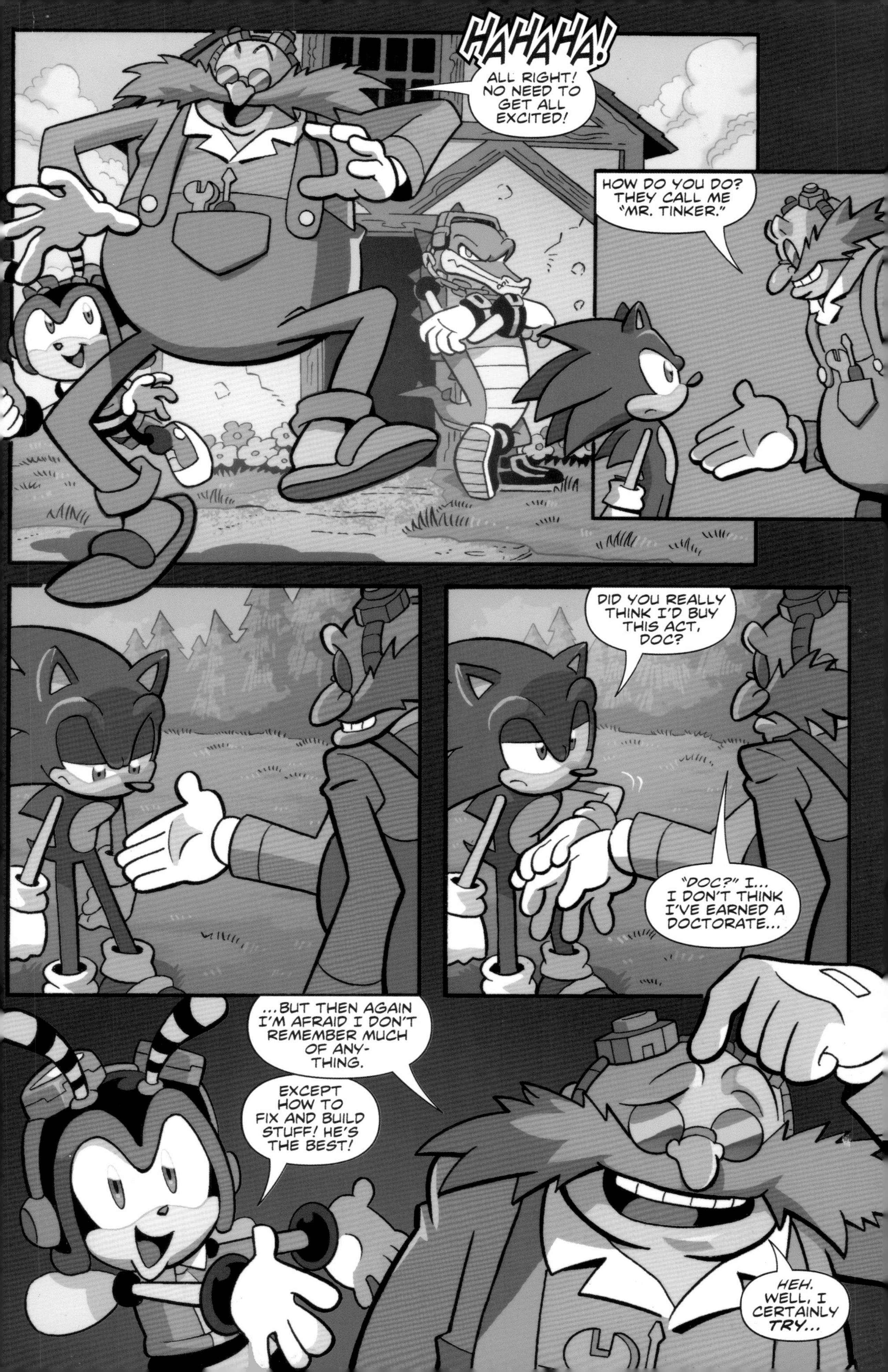
HAHAHA!
ALL RIGHT! NO NEED TO GET ALL EXCITED!
HOW DO YOU DO? THEY CALL ME "MR. TINKER."
DID YOU REALLY THINK I'D BUY THIS ACT, DOC?
"DOC?" I... I DON'T THINK I'VE EARNED A DOCTORATE...
...BUT THEN AGAIN I'M AFRAID I DON'T REMEMBER MUCH OF ANY-THING.
EXCEPT HOW TO FIX AND BUILD STUFF! HE'S THE BEST!
HEH. WELL, I CERTAINLY TRY...

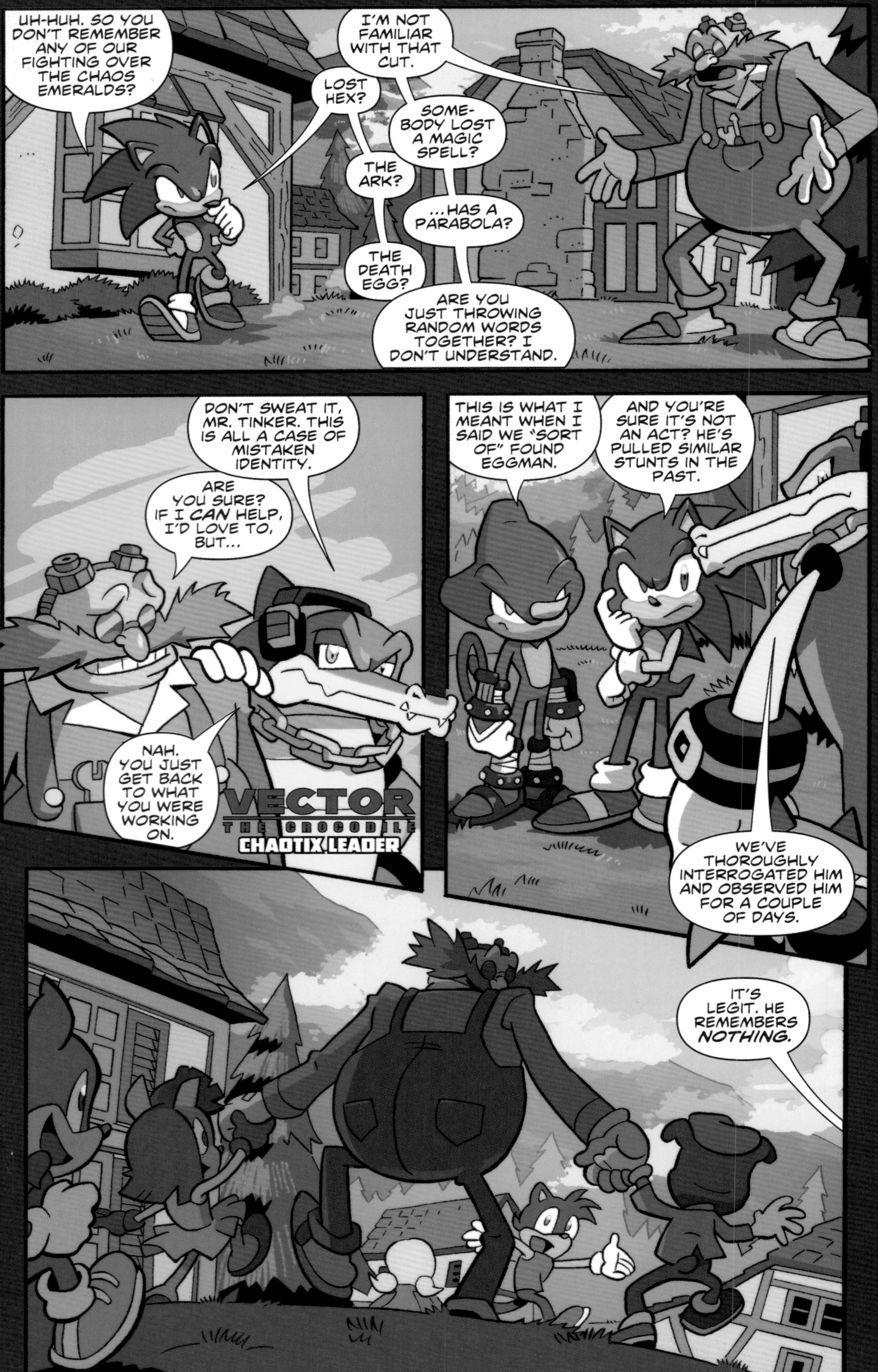
UH-HUH. SO YOU DON'T REMEMBER ANY OF OUR FIGHTING OVER THE CHAOS EMERALDS?
I'M NOT FAMILIAR WITH THAT CUT.
LOST HEX?
SOME-BODY LOST A MAGIC SPELL?
THE ARK?
...HAS A PARABOLA?
THE DEATH EGG?
ARE YOU JUST THROWING RANDOM WORDS TOGETHER? I DON'T UNDERSTAND.
DON'T SWEAT IT, MR. TINKER. THIS IS ALL A CASE OF MISTAKEN IDENTITY.
ARE YOU SURE? IF I CAN HELP, I'D LOVE TO, BUT...
NAH. YOU JUST GET BACK TO WHAT YOU WERE WORKING ON.
VECTOR
THE CROCODILE
CHAOTIX LEADER
THIS IS WHAT I MEANT WHEN I SAID WE "SORT OF" FOUND EGGMAN.
AND YOU'RE SURE IT'S NOT AN ACT? HE'S PULLED SIMILAR STUNTS IN THE PAST.
WE'VE THOROUGHLY INTERROGATED HIM AND OBSERVED HIM FOR A COUPLE OF DAYS.
IT'S LEGIT. HE REMEMBERS NOTHING.

YEAH, BUT...HE CAN BE *EXTREMELY* DANGEROUS.

NEVERMIND THE CLOSE CALLS I'VE HAD WHILE FIGHTING HIM. HE CAN THREATEN *WHOLE PLANETS* AT A TIME...

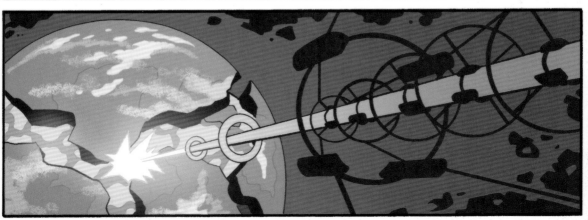

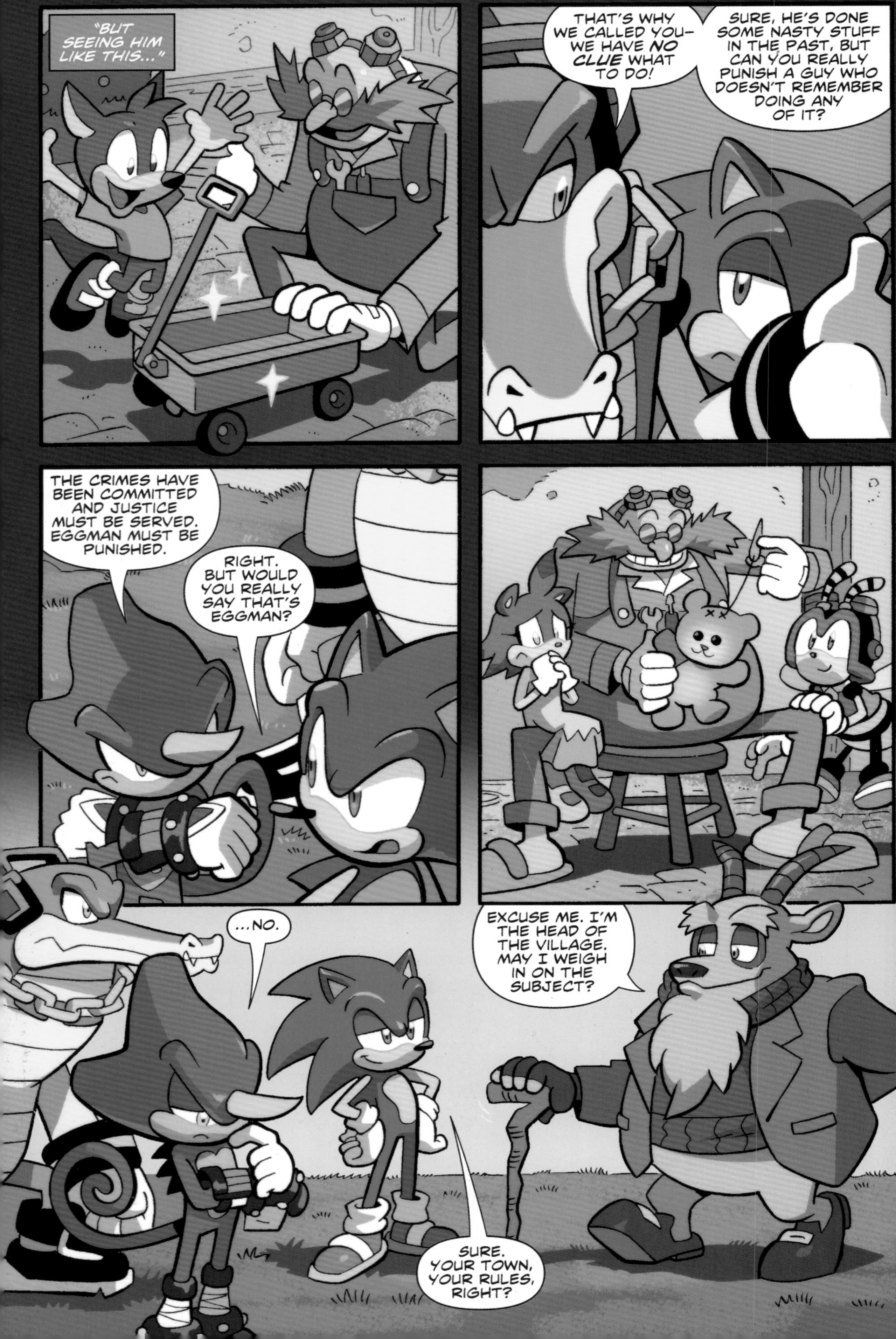
"BUT SEEING HIM LIKE THIS..."
THAT'S WHY WE CALLED YOU– WE HAVE NO CLUE WHAT TO DO!
SURE, HE'S DONE SOME NASTY STUFF IN THE PAST, BUT CAN YOU REALLY PUNISH A GUY WHO DOESN'T REMEMBER DOING ANY OF IT?
THE CRIMES HAVE BEEN COMMITTED AND JUSTICE MUST BE SERVED. EGGMAN MUST BE PUNISHED.
RIGHT. BUT WOULD YOU REALLY SAY THAT'S EGGMAN?
...NO.
EXCUSE ME. I'M THE HEAD OF THE VILLAGE. MAY I WEIGH IN ON THE SUBJECT?
SURE. YOUR TOWN, YOUR RULES, RIGHT?

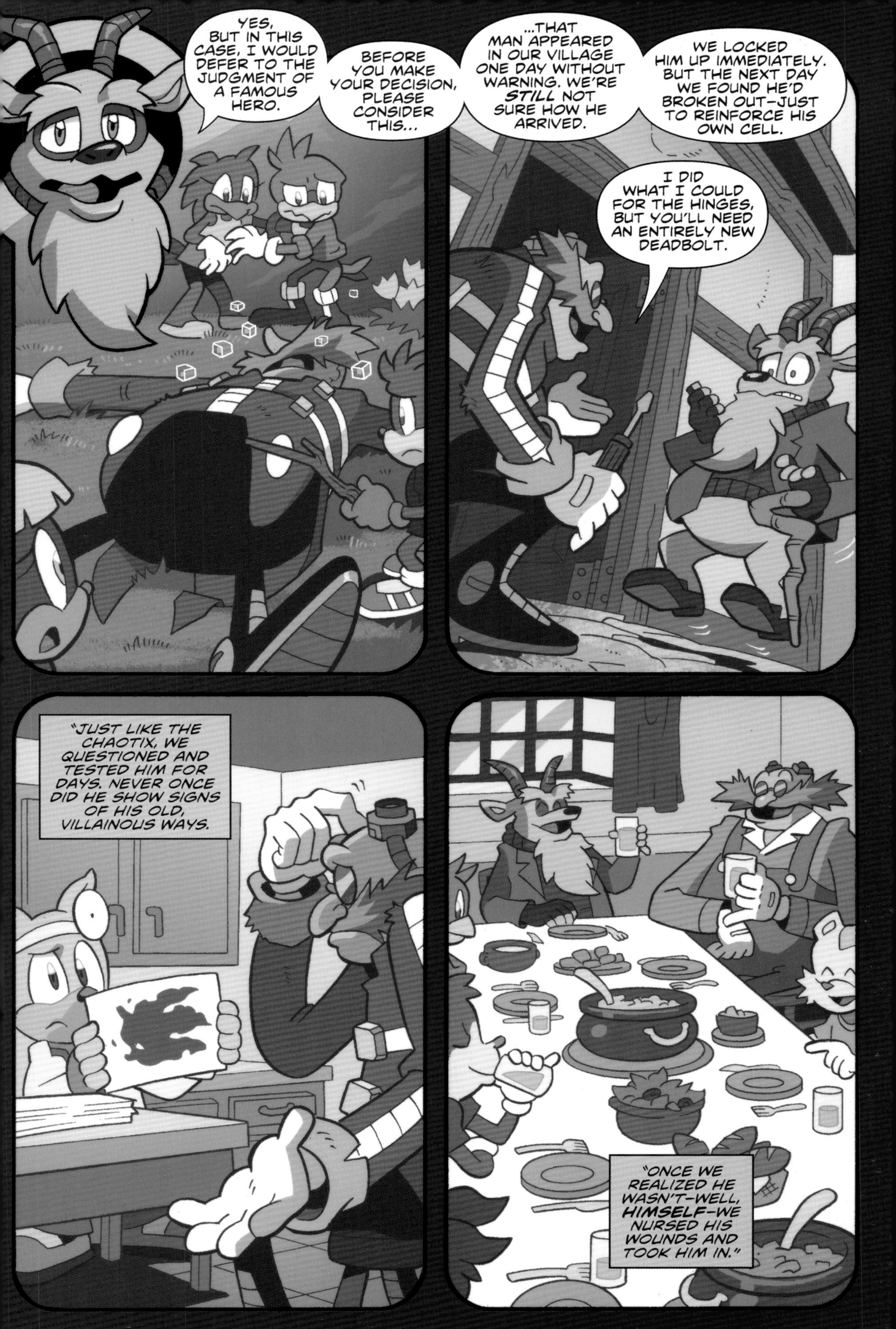

YES, BUT IN THIS CASE, I WOULD DEFER TO THE JUDGMENT OF A FAMOUS HERO.
BEFORE YOU MAKE YOUR DECISION, PLEASE CONSIDER THIS...
...THAT MAN APPEARED IN OUR VILLAGE ONE DAY WITHOUT WARNING. WE'RE *STILL* NOT SURE HOW HE ARRIVED.
WE LOCKED HIM UP IMMEDIATELY. BUT THE NEXT DAY WE FOUND HE'D BROKEN OUT—JUST TO REINFORCE HIS OWN CELL.
I DID WHAT I COULD FOR THE HINGES, BUT YOU'LL NEED AN ENTIRELY NEW DEADBOLT.
"JUST LIKE THE CHAOTIX, WE QUESTIONED AND TESTED HIM FOR DAYS. NEVER ONCE DID HE SHOW SIGNS OF HIS OLD, VILLAINOUS WAYS.
"ONCE WE REALIZED HE WASN'T—WELL, **HIMSELF**—WE NURSED HIS WOUNDS AND TOOK HIM IN."

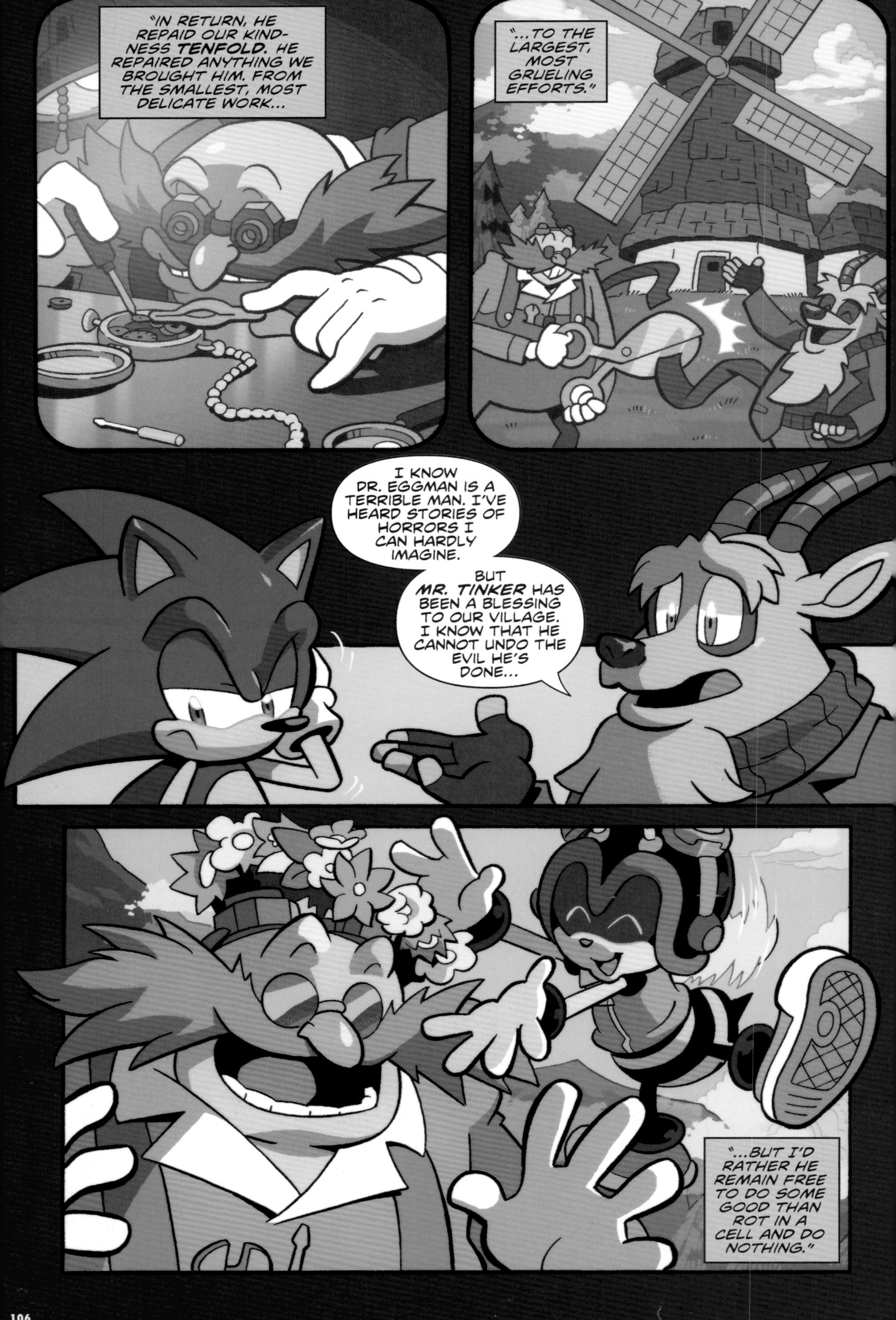
"IN RETURN, HE REPAID OUR KINDNESS **TENFOLD.** HE REPAIRED ANYTHING WE BROUGHT HIM. FROM THE SMALLEST, MOST DELICATE WORK...
"...TO THE LARGEST, MOST GRUELING EFFORTS."
I KNOW DR. EGGMAN IS A TERRIBLE MAN. I'VE HEARD STORIES OF HORRORS I CAN HARDLY IMAGINE.
BUT ***MR. TINKER*** HAS BEEN A BLESSING TO OUR VILLAGE. I KNOW THAT HE CANNOT UNDO THE EVIL HE'S DONE...
"...BUT I'D RATHER HE REMAIN FREE TO DO SOME GOOD THAN ROT IN A CELL AND DO NOTHING."

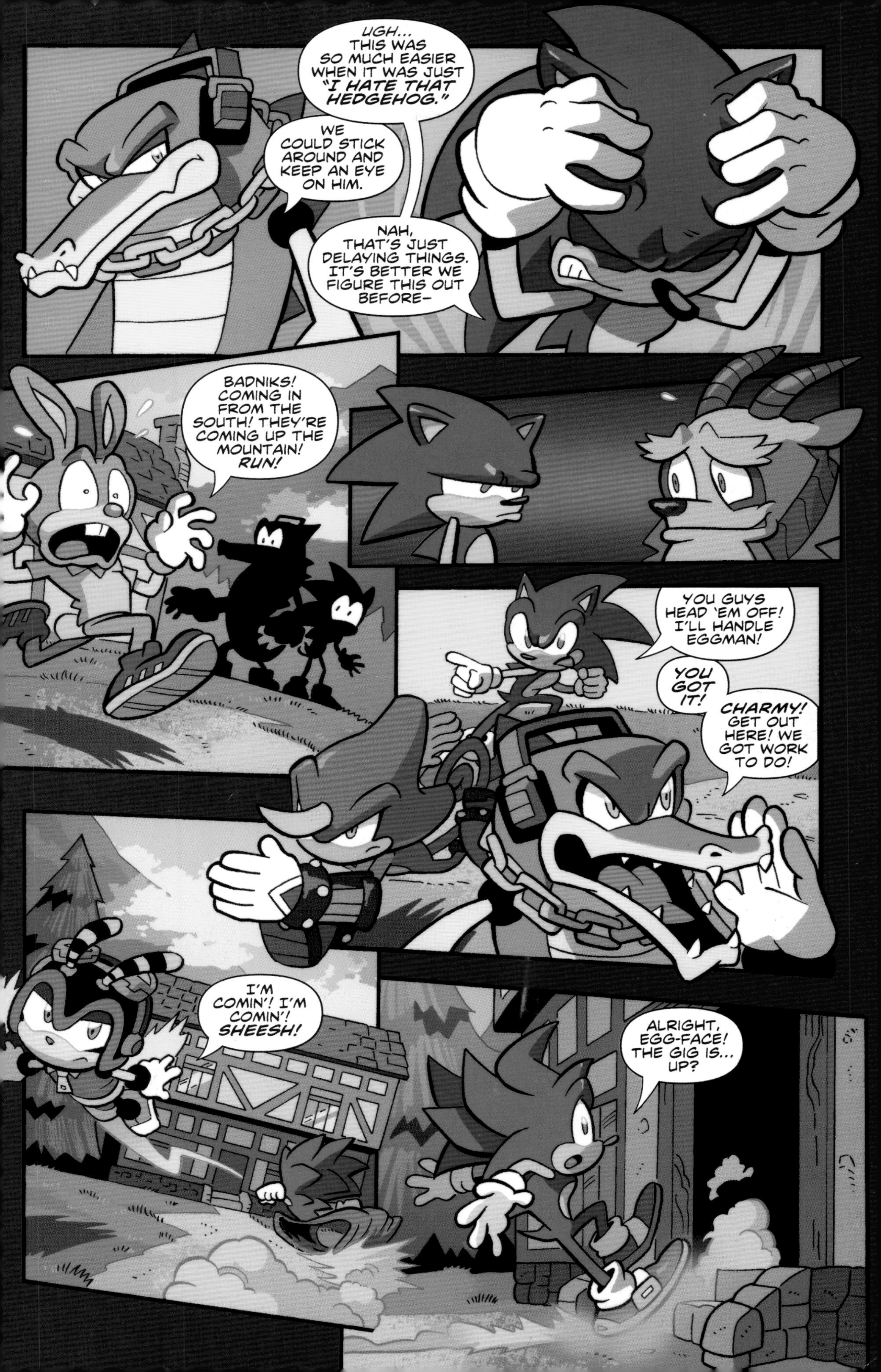
UGH... THIS WAS SO MUCH EASIER WHEN IT WAS JUST "I HATE THAT HEDGEHOG."
WE COULD STICK AROUND AND KEEP AN EYE ON HIM.
NAH, THAT'S JUST DELAYING THINGS. IT'S BETTER WE FIGURE THIS OUT BEFORE–
BADNIKS! COMING IN FROM THE SOUTH! THEY'RE COMING UP THE MOUNTAIN! RUN!
YOU GUYS HEAD 'EM OFF! I'LL HANDLE EGGMAN!
YOU GOT IT!
CHARMY! GET OUT HERE! WE GOT WORK TO DO!
I'M COMIN'! I'M COMIN'! SHEESH!
ALRIGHT, EGG-FACE! THE GIG IS... UP?

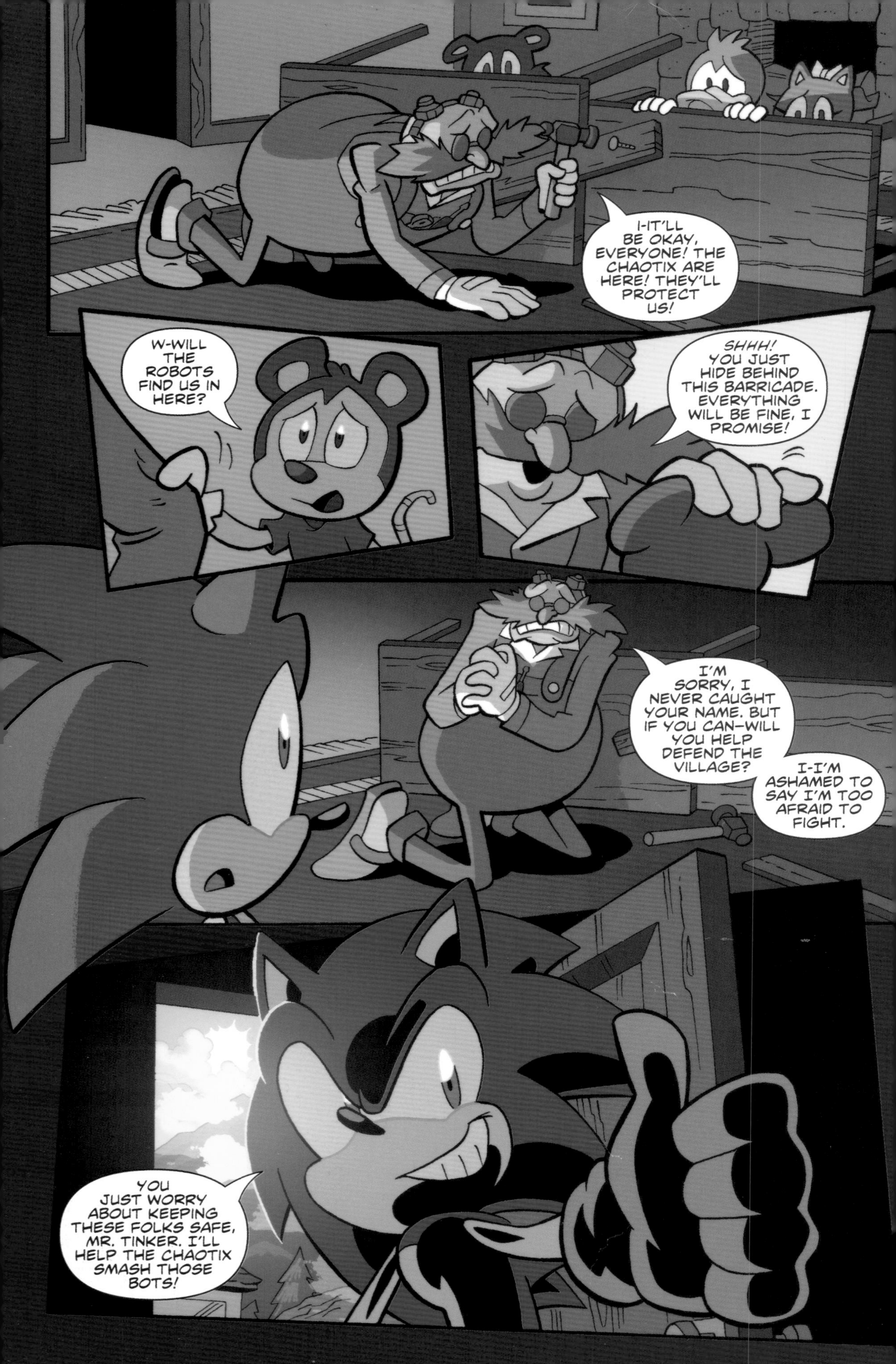
I-IT'LL BE OKAY, EVERYONE! THE CHAOTIX ARE HERE! THEY'LL PROTECT US!
W-WILL THE ROBOTS FIND US IN HERE?
SHHH! YOU JUST HIDE BEHIND THIS BARRICADE. EVERYTHING WILL BE FINE, I PROMISE!
I'M SORRY, I NEVER CAUGHT YOUR NAME. BUT IF YOU CAN–WILL YOU HELP DEFEND THE VILLAGE?
I-I'M ASHAMED TO SAY I'M TOO AFRAID TO FIGHT.
YOU JUST WORRY ABOUT KEEPING THESE FOLKS SAFE, MR. TINKER. I'LL HELP THE CHAOTIX SMASH THOSE BOTS!

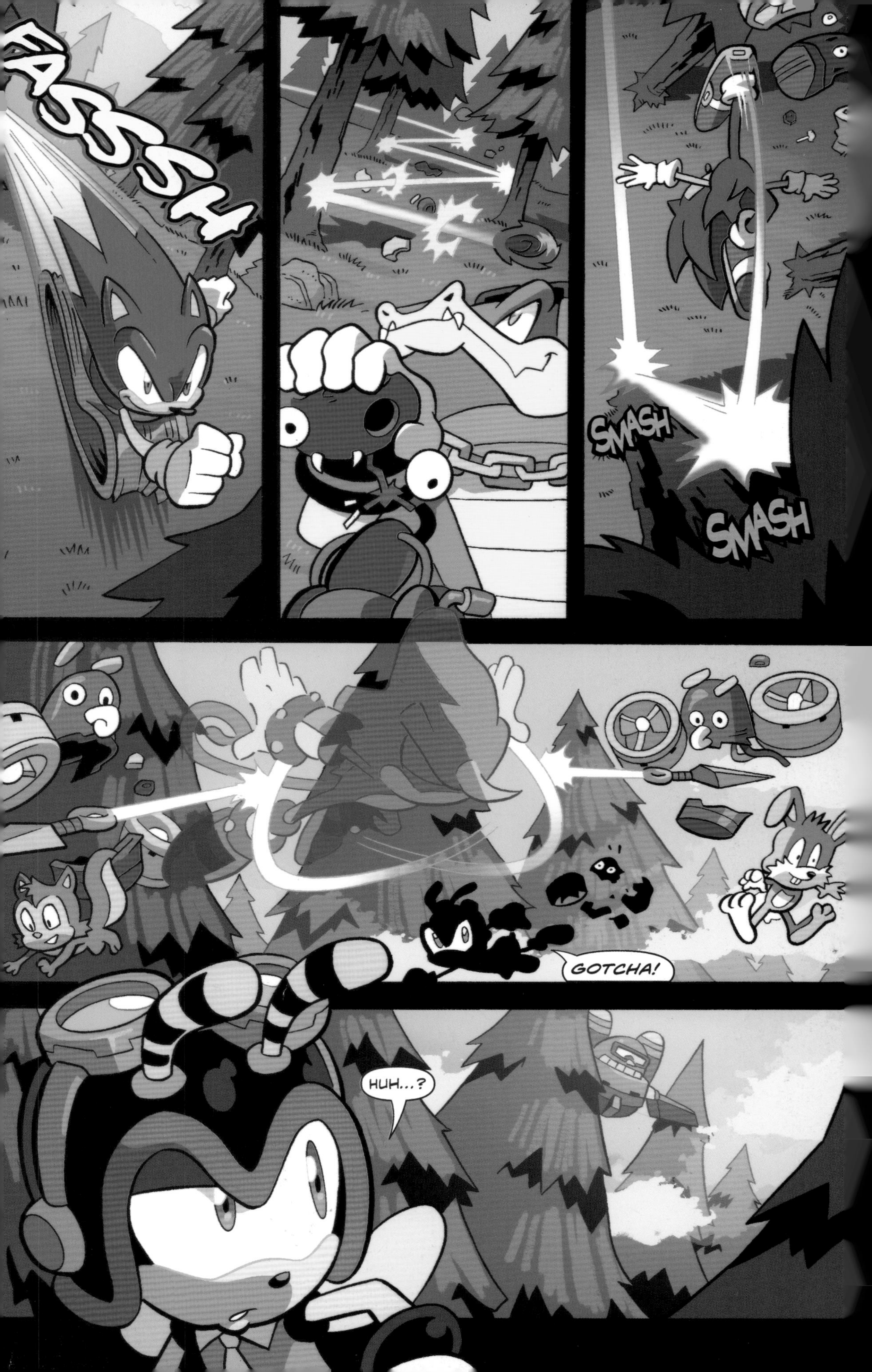
FASSSH
SMASH
SMASH
GOTCHA!
HUH...?

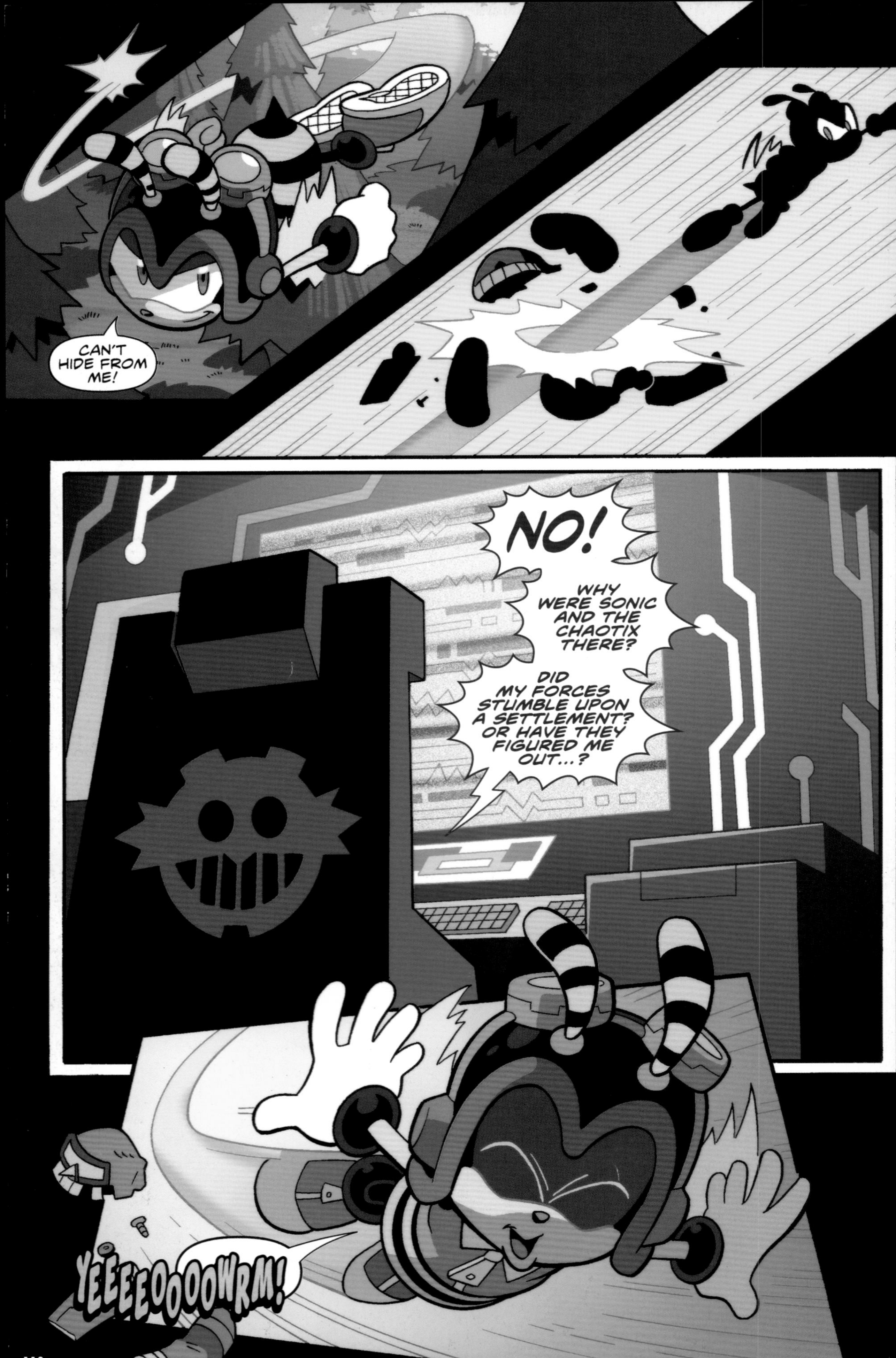
CAN'T HIDE FROM ME!
NO!
WHY WERE SONIC AND THE CHAOTIX THERE?
DID MY FORCES STUMBLE UPON A SETTLEMENT? OR HAVE THEY FIGURED ME OUT...?
YEEEEOOOOWRM!

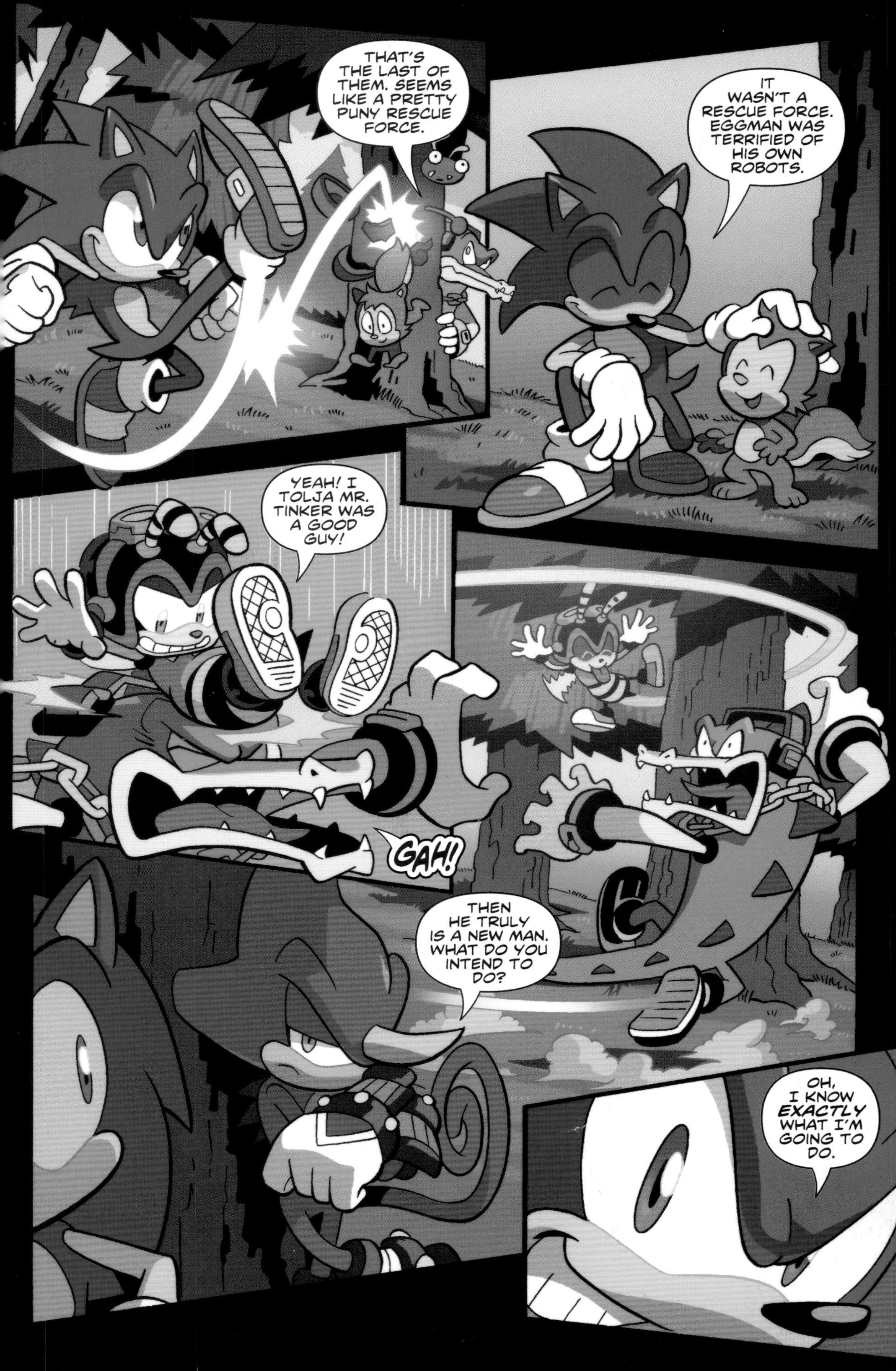

THAT'S THE LAST OF THEM. SEEMS LIKE A PRETTY PUNY RESCUE FORCE.
IT WASN'T A RESCUE FORCE. EGGMAN WAS TERRIFIED OF HIS OWN ROBOTS.
YEAH! I TOLJA MR. TINKER WAS A GOOD GUY!
GAH!
THEN HE TRULY IS A NEW MAN. WHAT DO YOU INTEND TO DO?
OH, I KNOW *EXACTLY* WHAT I'M GOING TO DO.

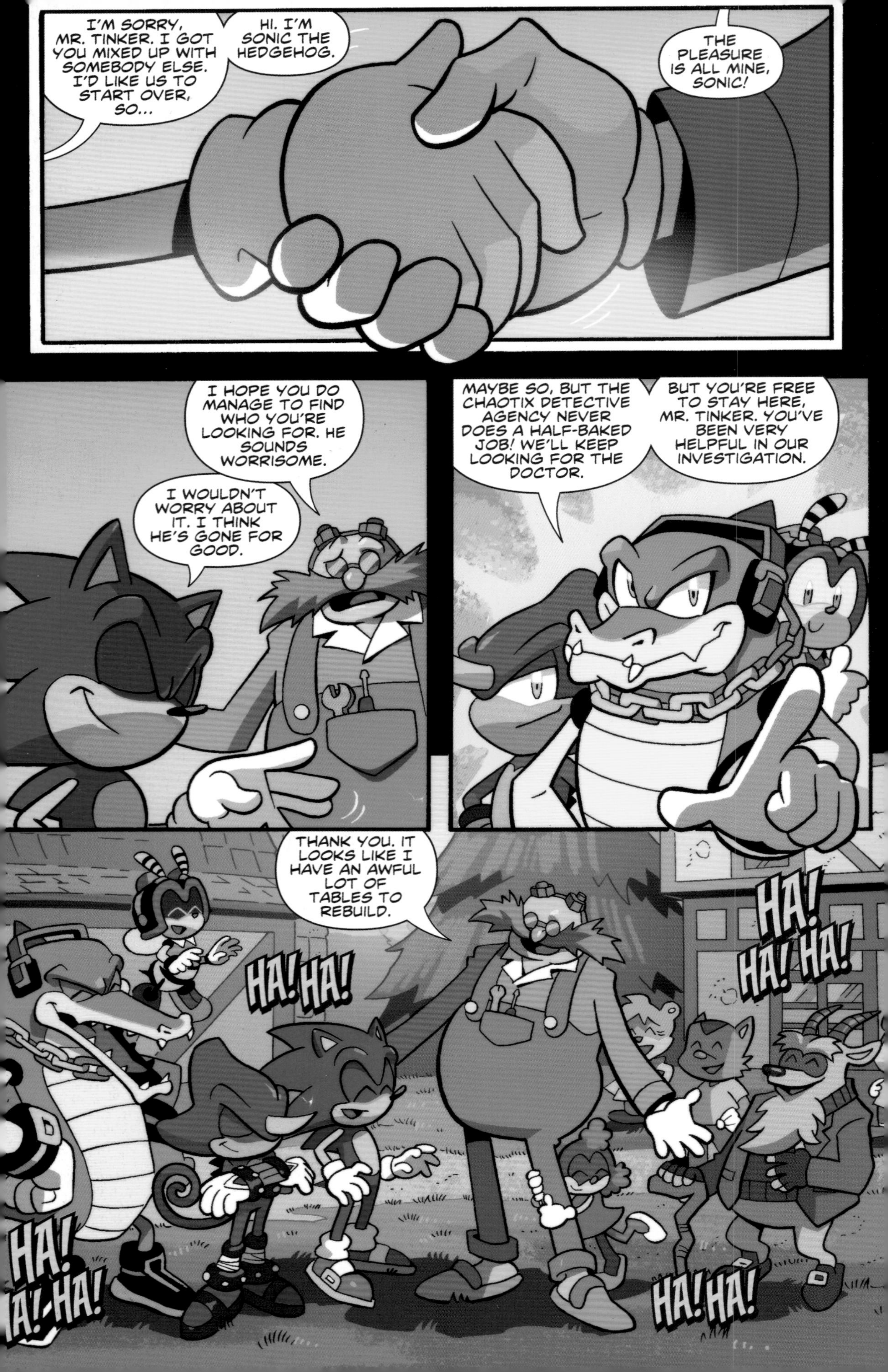
I'M SORRY, MR. TINKER. I GOT YOU MIXED UP WITH SOMEBODY ELSE. I'D LIKE US TO START OVER, SO...
HI. I'M SONIC THE HEDGEHOG.
THE PLEASURE IS ALL MINE, SONIC!
I HOPE YOU DO MANAGE TO FIND WHO YOU'RE LOOKING FOR. HE SOUNDS WORRISOME.
I WOULDN'T WORRY ABOUT IT. I THINK HE'S GONE FOR GOOD.
MAYBE SO, BUT THE CHAOTIX DETECTIVE AGENCY NEVER DOES A HALF-BAKED JOB! WE'LL KEEP LOOKING FOR THE DOCTOR.
BUT YOU'RE FREE TO STAY HERE, MR. TINKER. YOU'VE BEEN VERY HELPFUL IN OUR INVESTIGATION.
THANK YOU. IT LOOKS LIKE I HAVE AN AWFUL LOT OF TABLES TO REBUILD.
HA! HA!
HA! HA! HA!
HA! HA!
HA! HA!

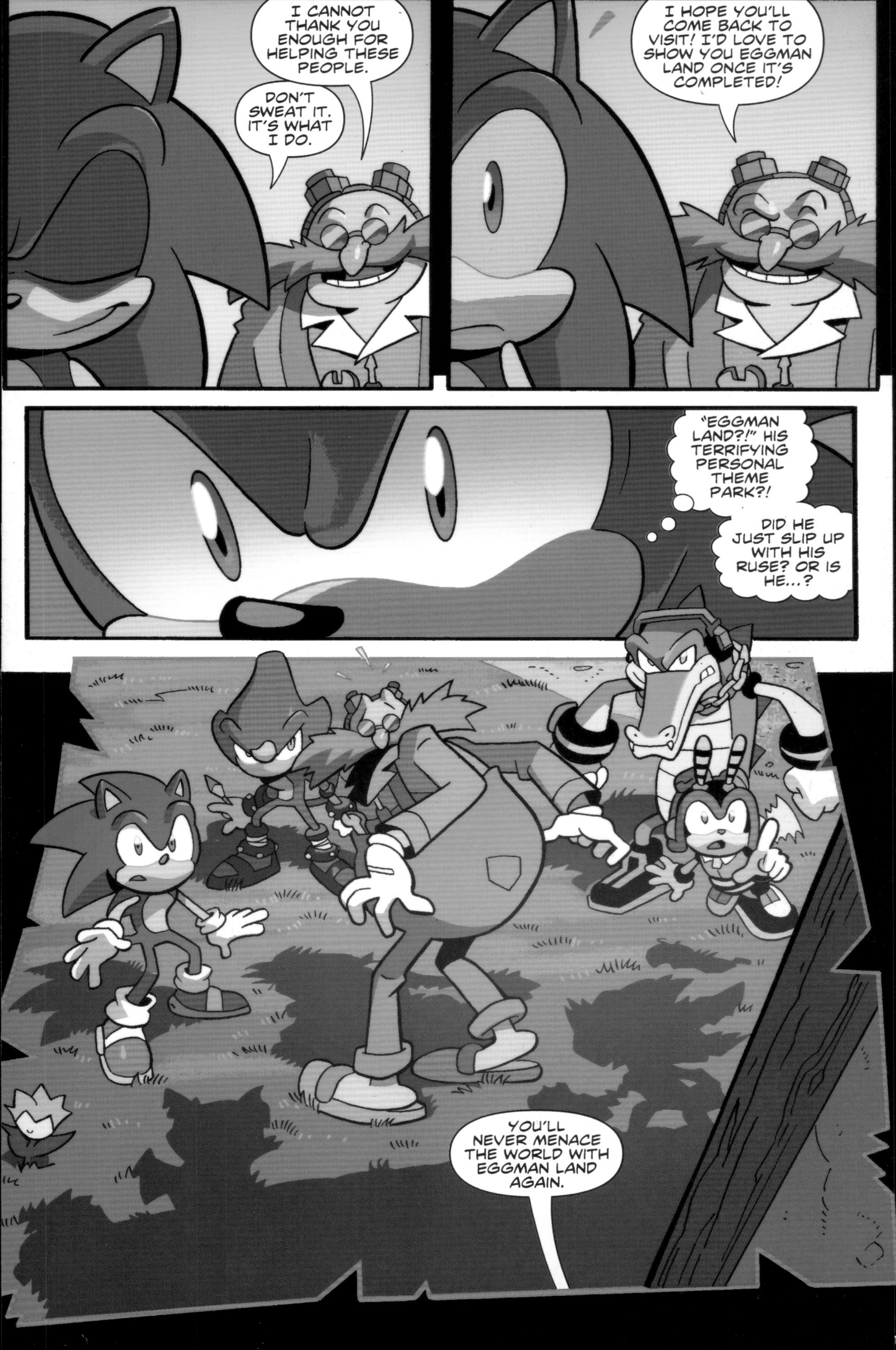

I CANNOT THANK YOU ENOUGH FOR HELPING THESE PEOPLE.
DON'T SWEAT IT. IT'S WHAT I DO.
I HOPE YOU'LL COME BACK TO VISIT! I'D LOVE TO SHOW YOU EGGMAN LAND ONCE IT'S COMPLETED!
"EGGMAN LAND?!" HIS TERRIFYING PERSONAL THEME PARK?!
DID HE JUST SLIP UP WITH HIS RUSE? OR IS HE...?
YOU'LL NEVER MENACE THE WORLD WITH EGGMAN LAND AGAIN.

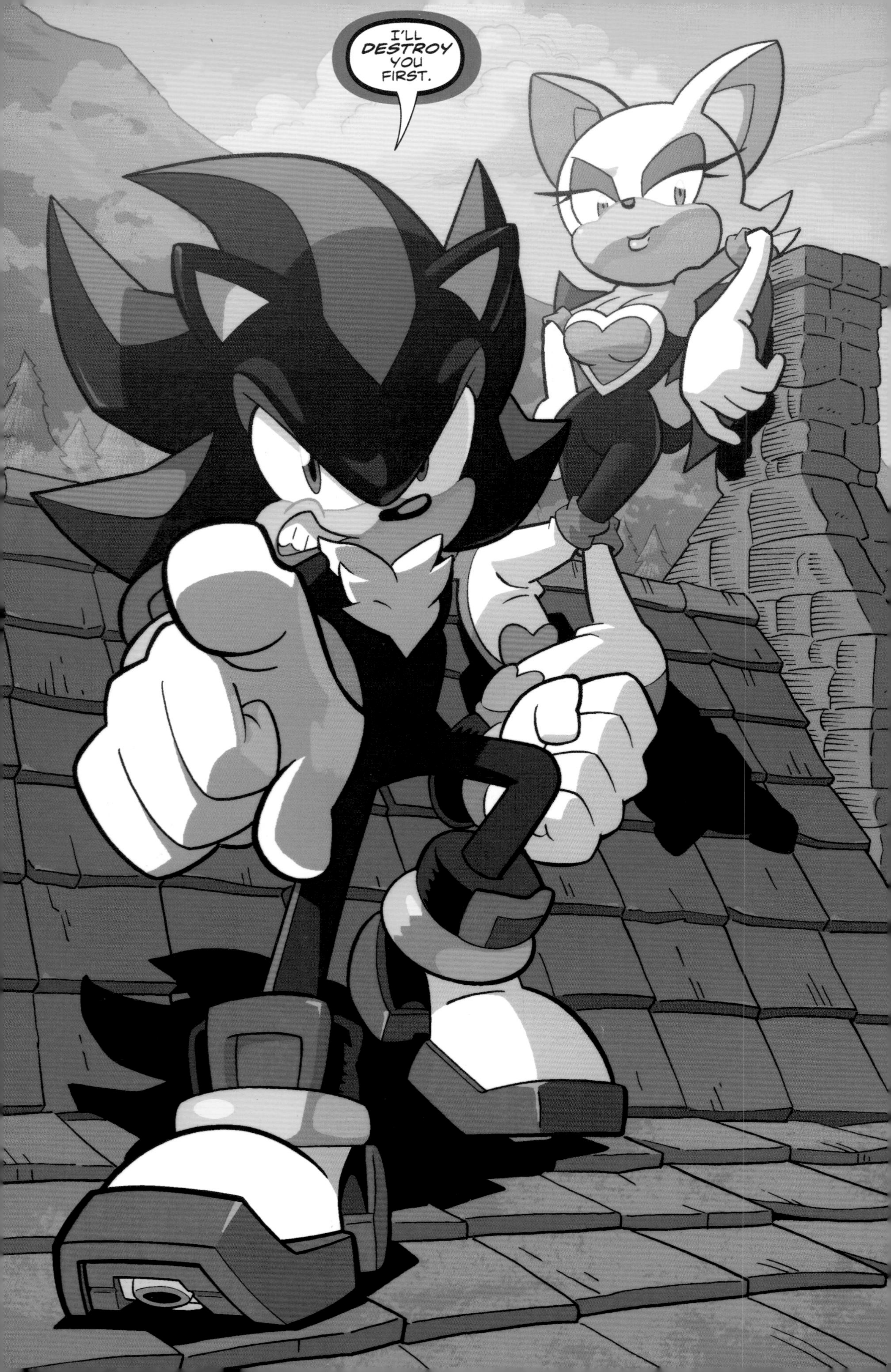
I'LL DESTROY YOU FIRST.

ART BY NATHALIE FOURDRAINE

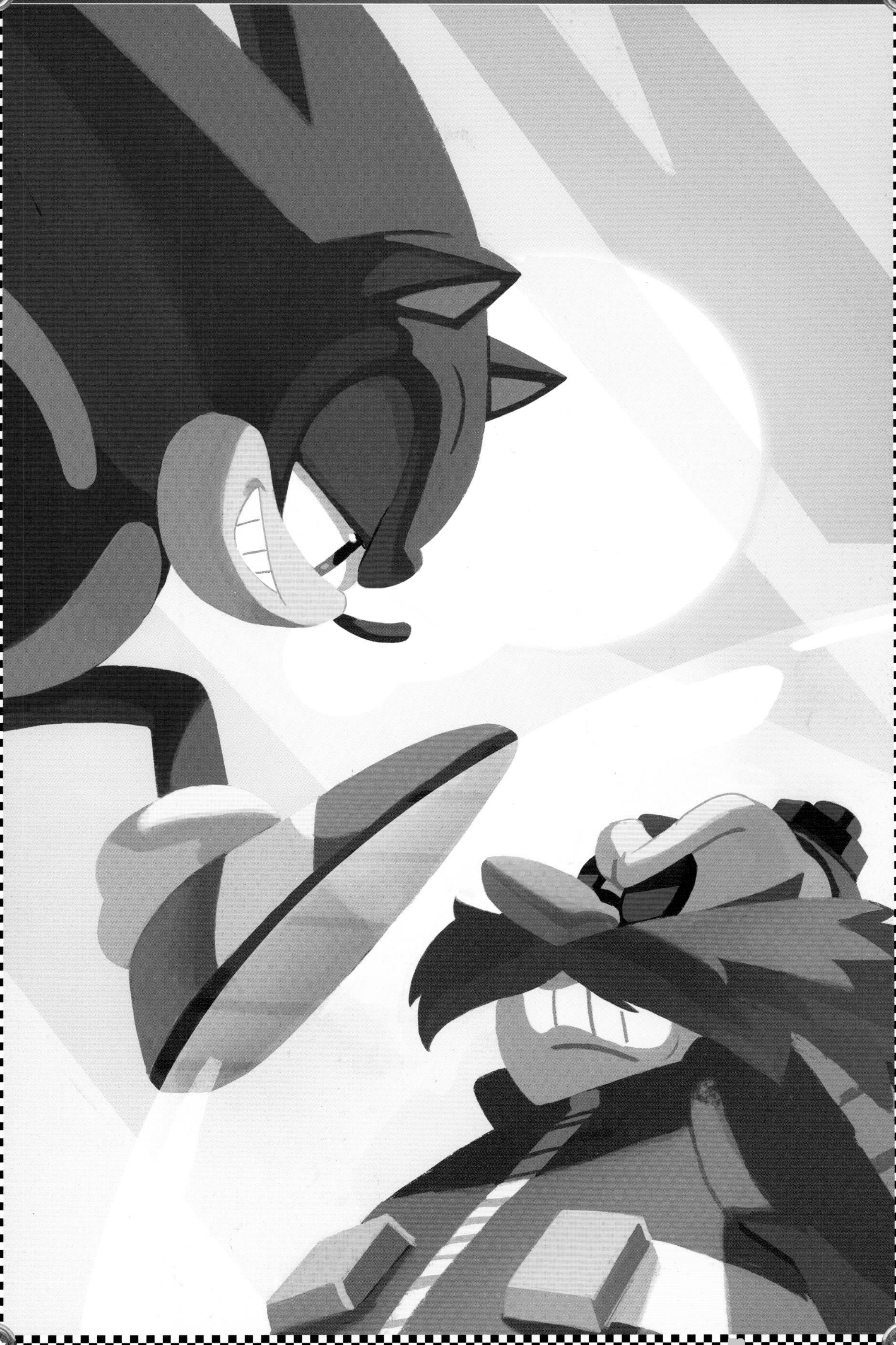

ART BY JONATHAN GRAY COLORS BY MATT HERMS

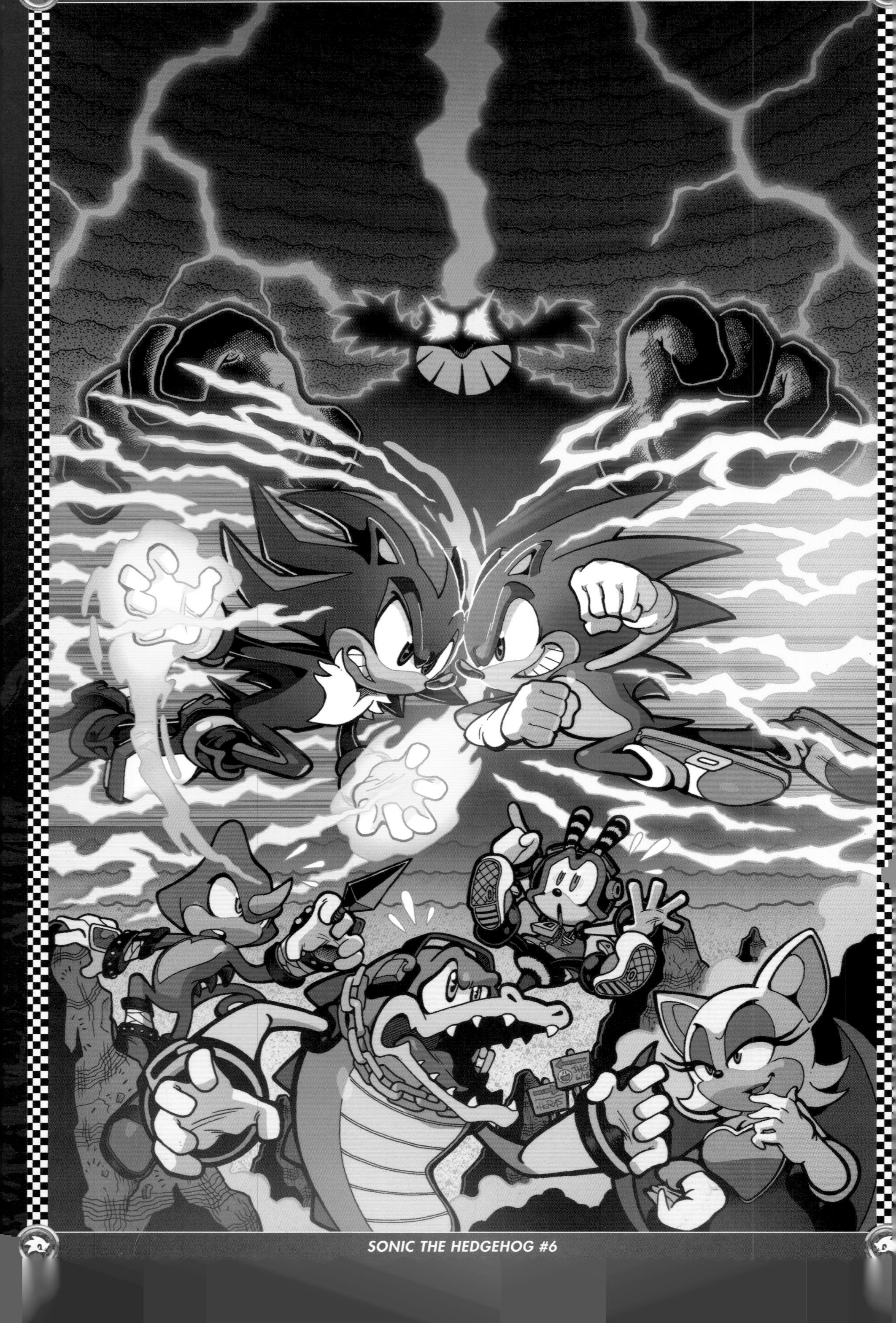

SONIC THE HEDGEHOG #6

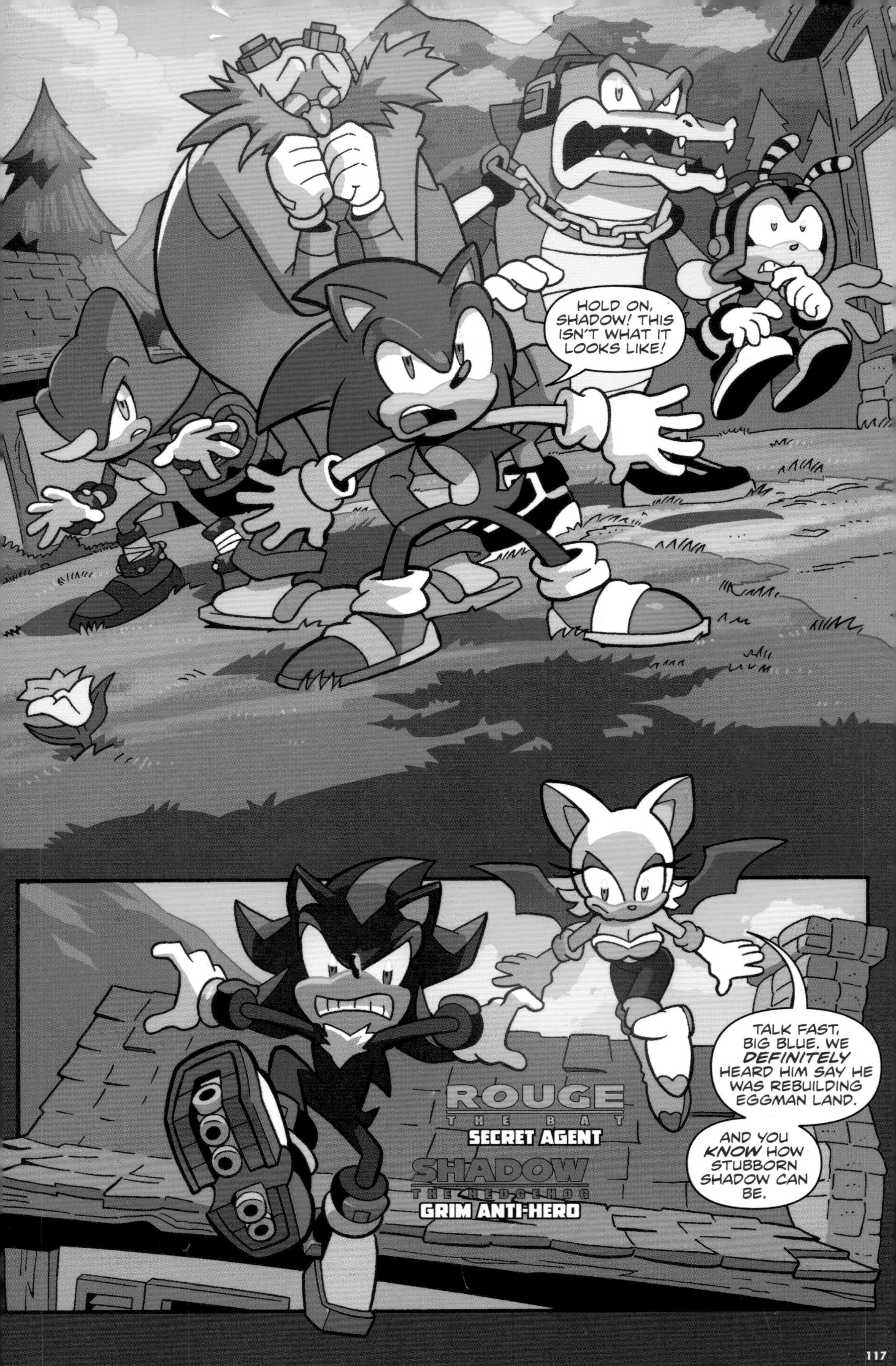
HOLD ON, SHADOW! THIS ISN'T WHAT IT LOOKS LIKE!
ROUGE THE BAT
SECRET AGENT
SHADOW THE HEDGEHOG
GRIM ANTI-HERO
TALK FAST, BIG BLUE. WE *DEFINITELY* HEARD HIM SAY HE WAS REBUILDING EGGMAN LAND.
AND YOU *KNOW* HOW STUBBORN SHADOW CAN BE.

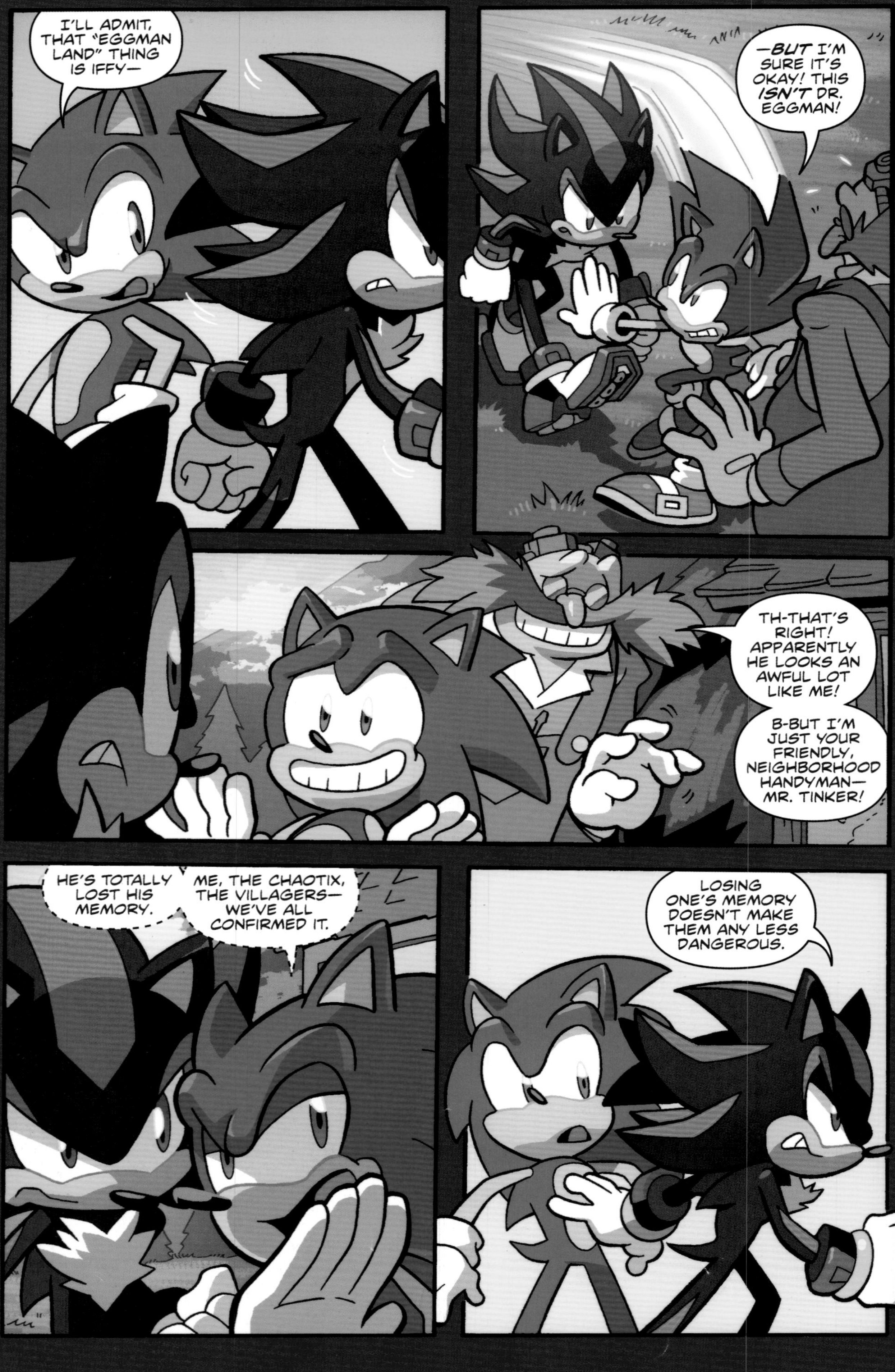
I'LL ADMIT, THAT "EGGMAN LAND" THING IS IFFY—
—BUT I'M SURE IT'S OKAY! THIS ISN'T DR. EGGMAN!
TH-THAT'S RIGHT! APPARENTLY HE LOOKS AN AWFUL LOT LIKE ME!
B-BUT I'M JUST YOUR FRIENDLY, NEIGHBORHOOD HANDYMAN— MR. TINKER!
HE'S TOTALLY LOST HIS MEMORY.
ME, THE CHAOTIX, THE VILLAGERS— WE'VE ALL CONFIRMED IT.
LOSING ONE'S MEMORY DOESN'T MAKE THEM ANY LESS DANGEROUS.

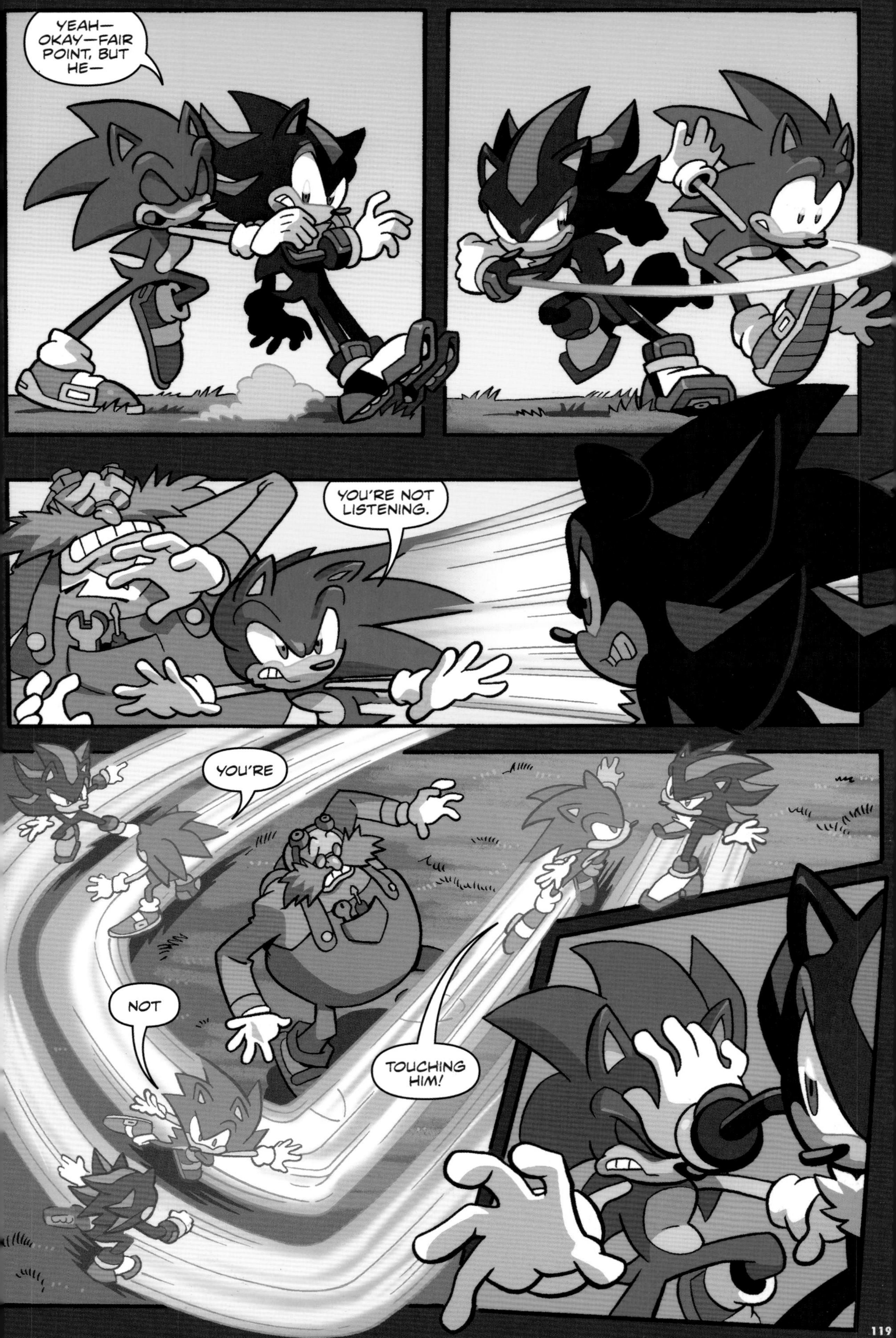
YEAH—
OKAY—FAIR
POINT, BUT
HE—
YOU'RE NOT
LISTENING.
YOU'RE
NOT
TOUCHING
HIM!

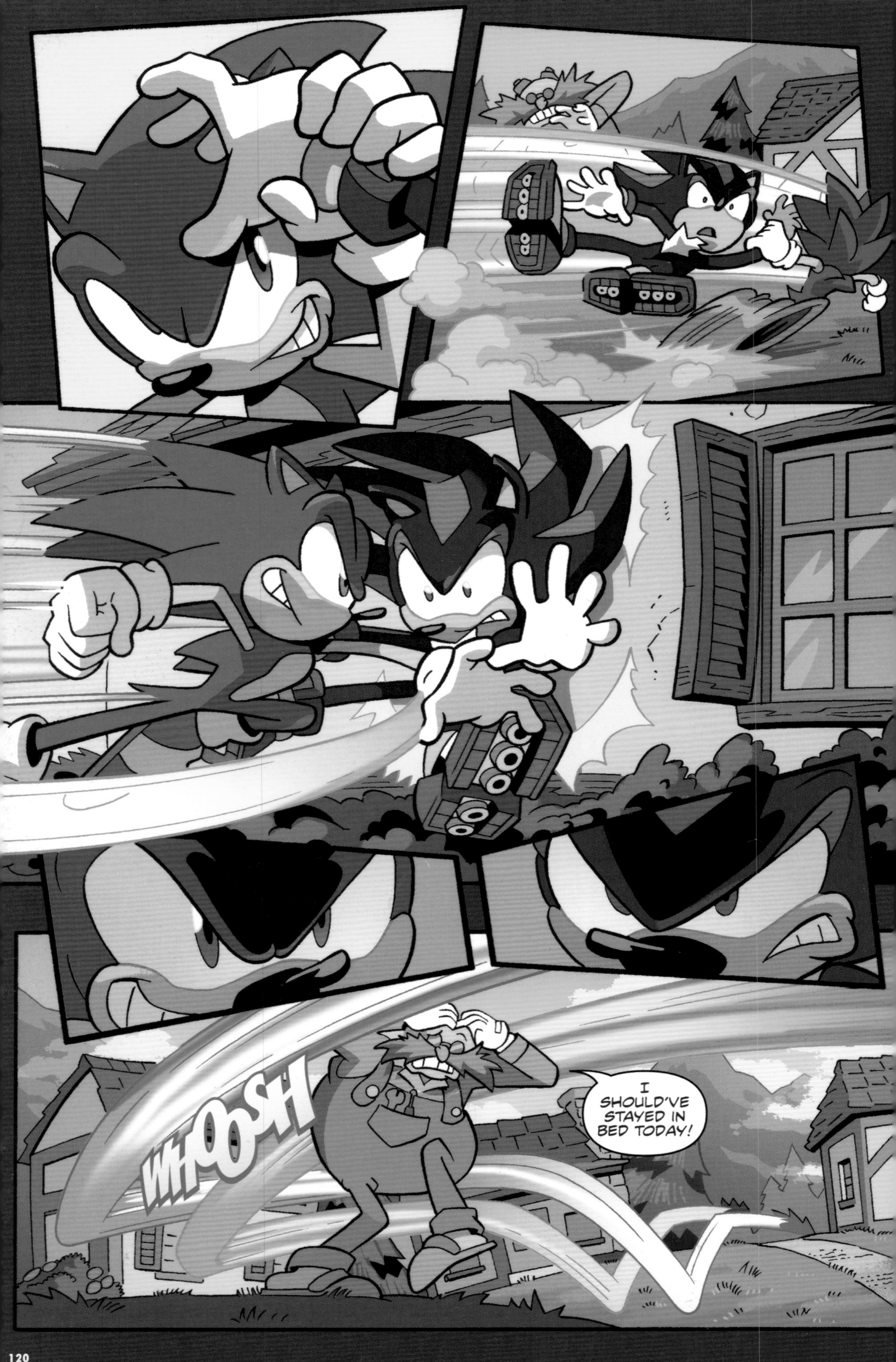
I SHOULD'VE STAYED IN BED TODAY!
WHOOSH

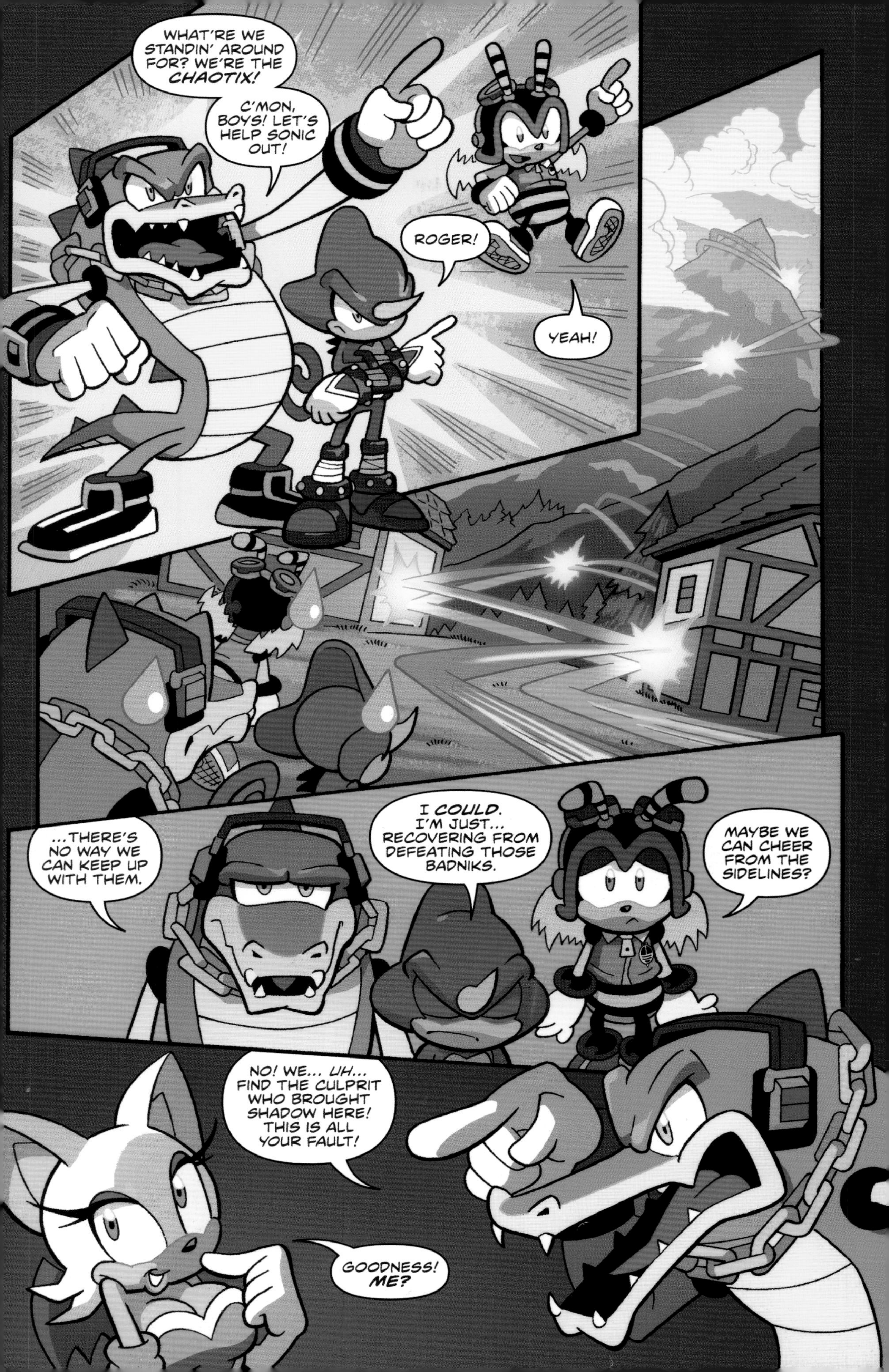
WHAT'RE WE STANDIN' AROUND FOR? WE'RE THE CHAOTIX!
C'MON, BOYS! LET'S HELP SONIC OUT!
ROGER!
YEAH!
...THERE'S NO WAY WE CAN KEEP UP WITH THEM.
I COULD. I'M JUST... RECOVERING FROM DEFEATING THOSE BADNIKS.
MAYBE WE CAN CHEER FROM THE SIDELINES?
NO! WE... UH... FIND THE CULPRIT WHO BROUGHT SHADOW HERE! THIS IS ALL YOUR FAULT!
GOODNESS! ME?

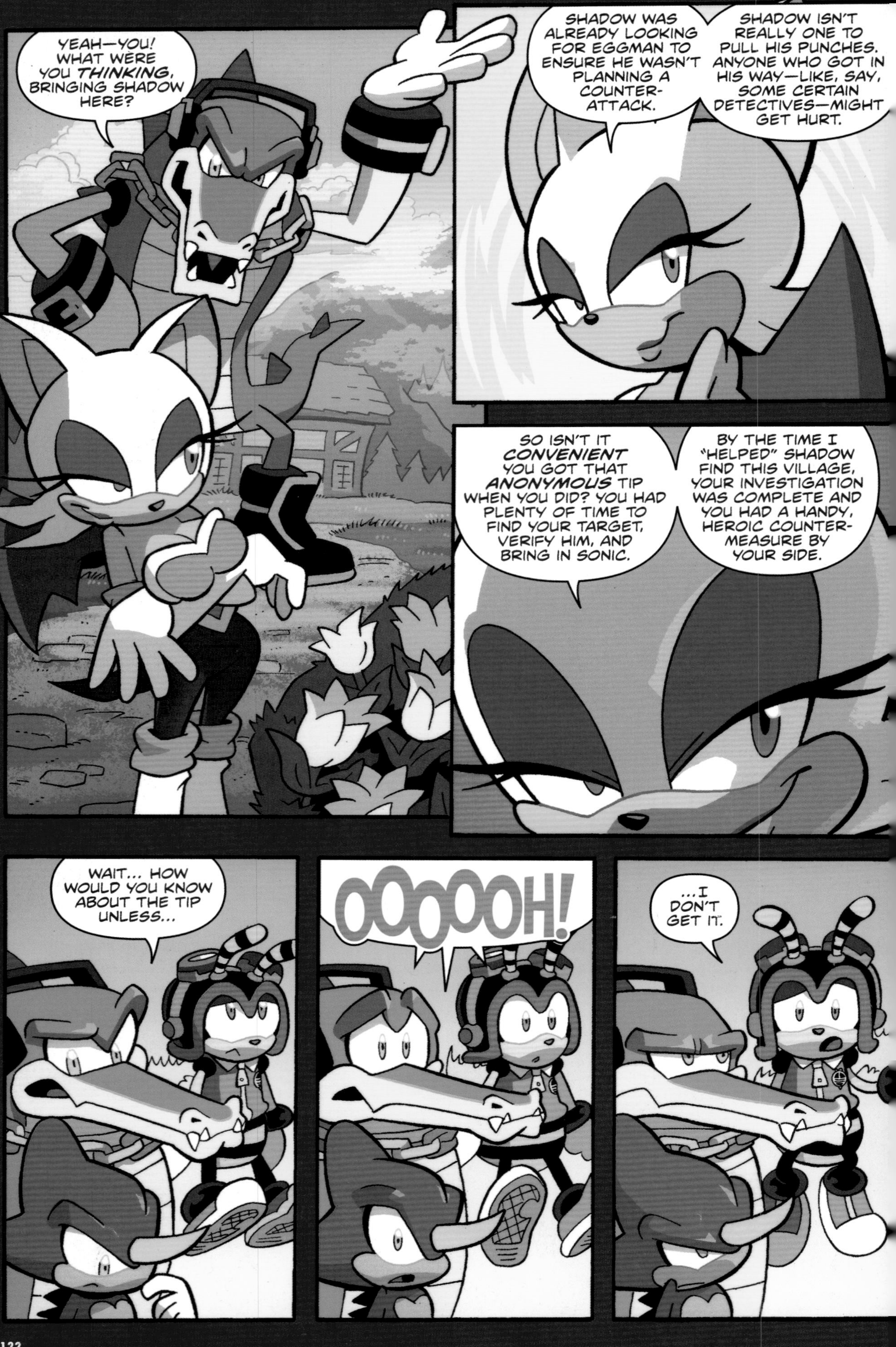

YEAH—YOU! WHAT WERE YOU THINKING, BRINGING SHADOW HERE?
SHADOW WAS ALREADY LOOKING FOR EGGMAN TO ENSURE HE WASN'T PLANNING A COUNTER-ATTACK.
SHADOW ISN'T REALLY ONE TO PULL HIS PUNCHES. ANYONE WHO GOT IN HIS WAY—LIKE, SAY, SOME CERTAIN DETECTIVES—MIGHT GET HURT.
SO ISN'T IT CONVENIENT YOU GOT THAT ANONYMOUS TIP WHEN YOU DID? YOU HAD PLENTY OF TIME TO FIND YOUR TARGET, VERIFY HIM, AND BRING IN SONIC.
BY THE TIME I "HELPED" SHADOW FIND THIS VILLAGE, YOUR INVESTIGATION WAS COMPLETE AND YOU HAD A HANDY, HEROIC COUNTER-MEASURE BY YOUR SIDE.
WAIT... HOW WOULD YOU KNOW ABOUT THE TIP UNLESS...
OOOOOH!
...I DON'T GET IT.

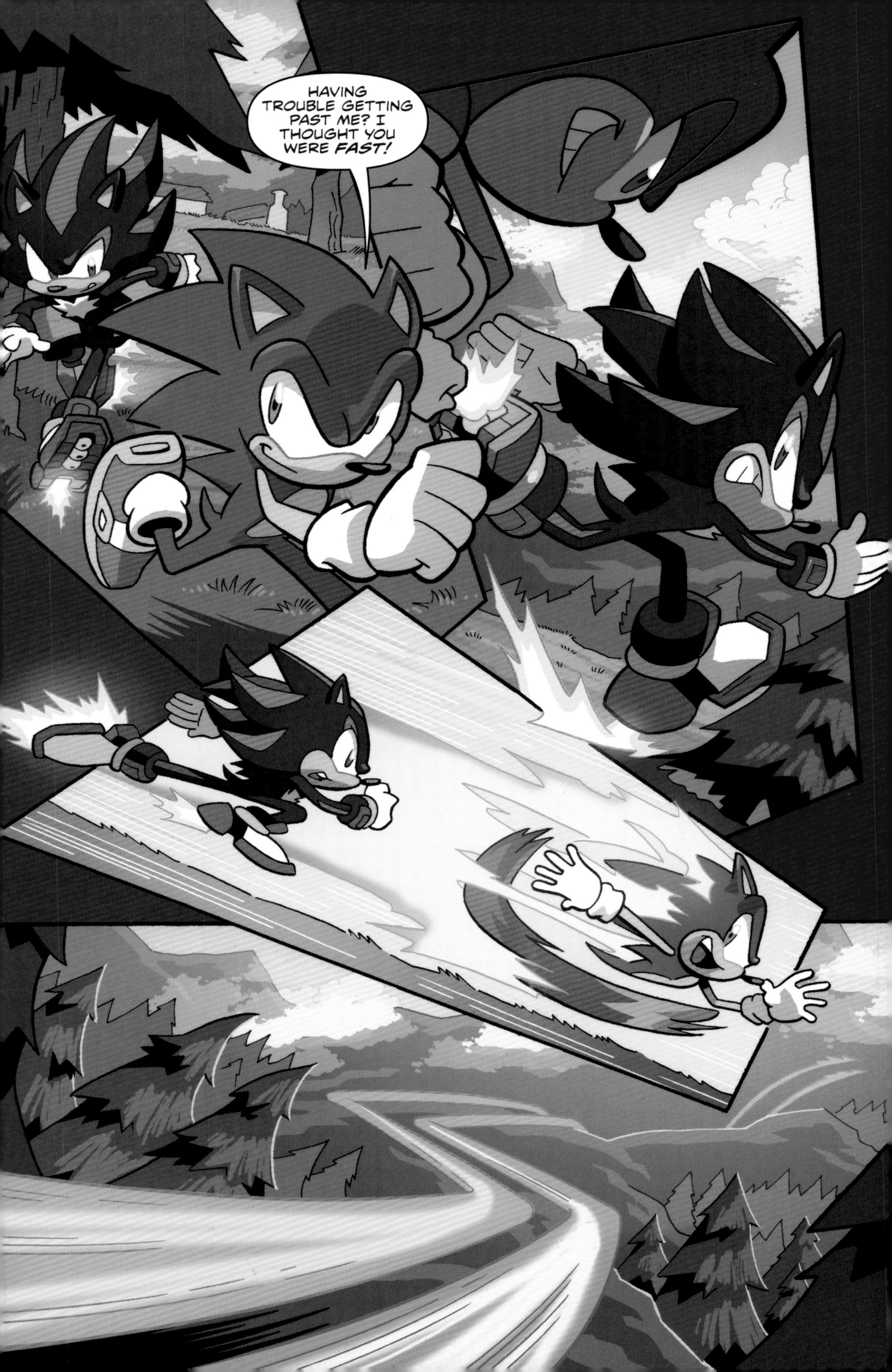
HAVING TROUBLE GETTING PAST ME? I THOUGHT YOU WERE *FAST!*

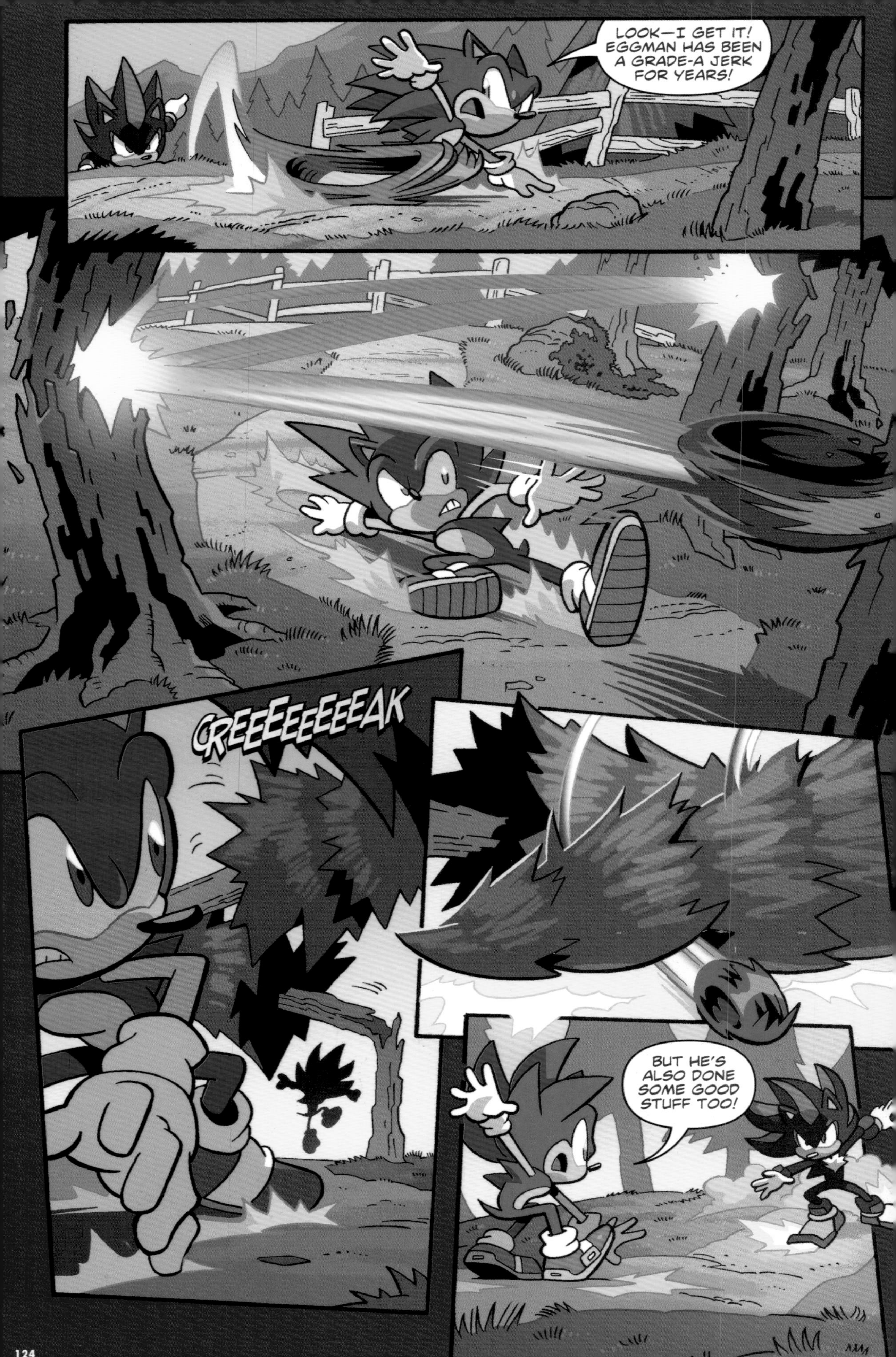
LOOK—I GET IT! EGGMAN HAS BEEN A GRADE-A JERK FOR YEARS!
CREEEEEEEEEAK
BUT HE'S ALSO DONE SOME GOOD STUFF TOO!

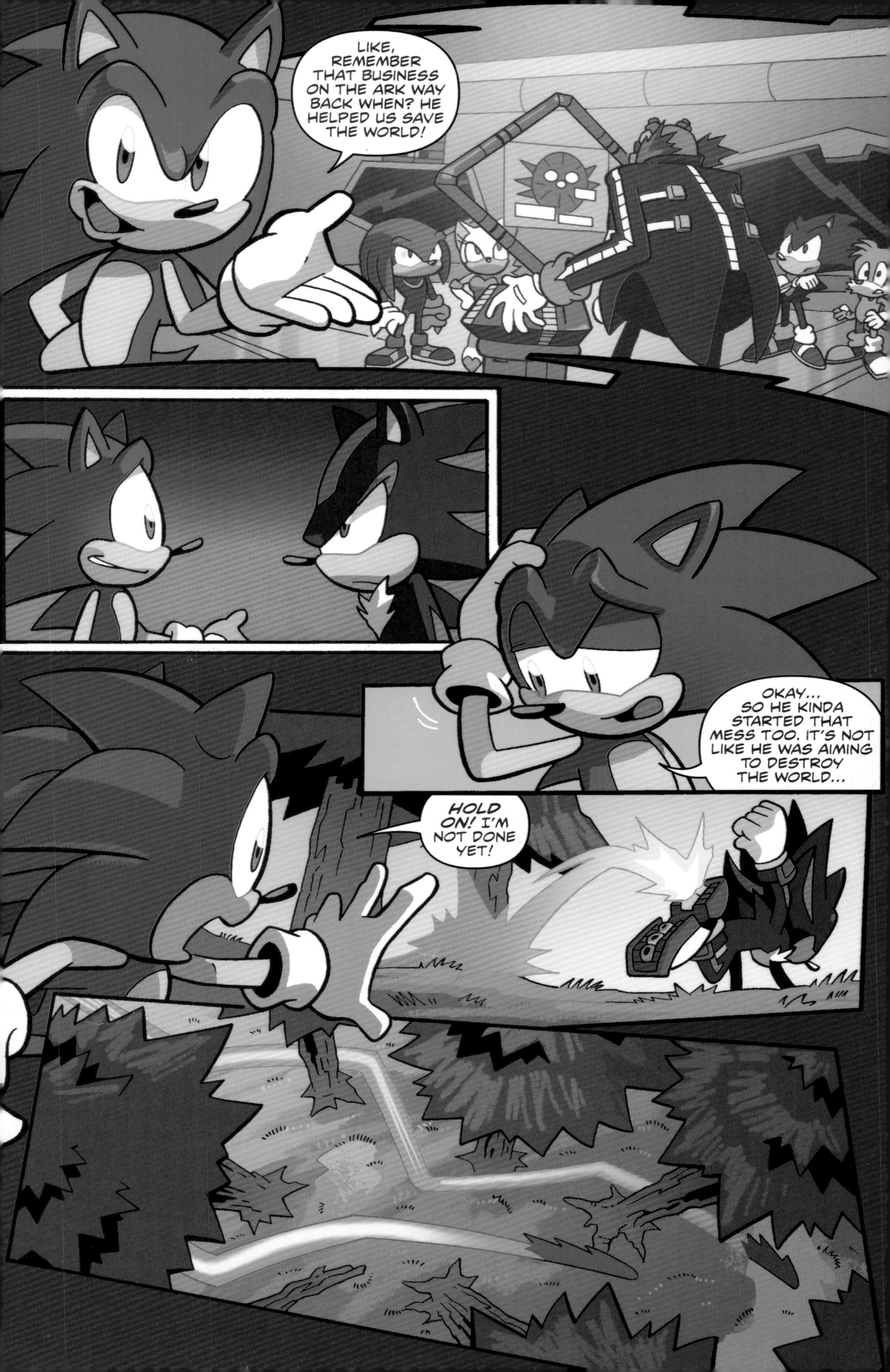
LIKE, REMEMBER THAT BUSINESS ON THE ARK WAY BACK WHEN? HE HELPED US SAVE THE WORLD!
OKAY... SO HE KINDA STARTED THAT MESS TOO. IT'S NOT LIKE HE WAS AIMING TO DESTROY THE WORLD...
HOLD ON! I'M NOT DONE YET!

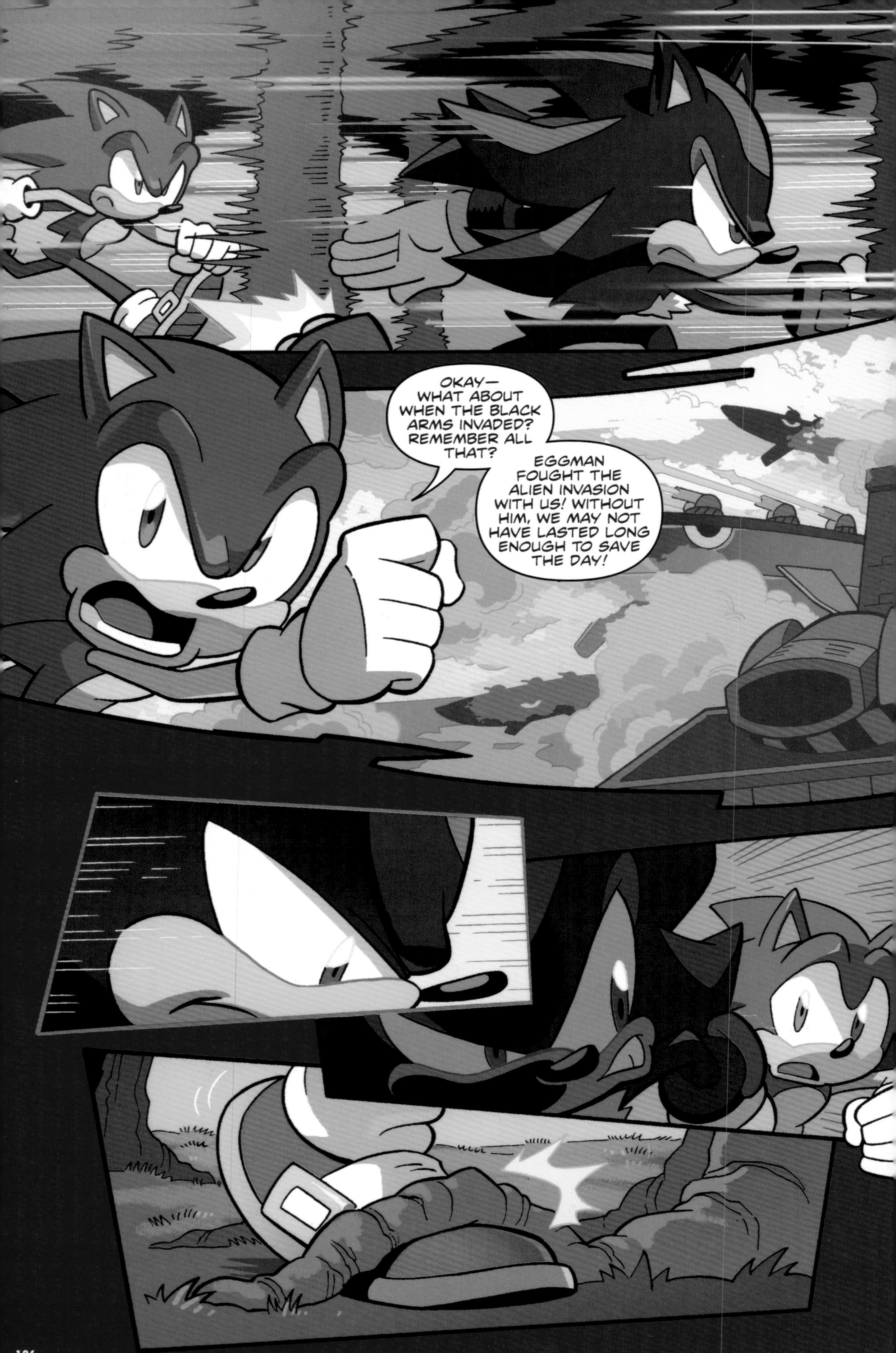
OKAY— WHAT ABOUT WHEN THE BLACK ARMS INVADED? REMEMBER ALL THAT?
EGGMAN FOUGHT THE ALIEN INVASION WITH US! WITHOUT HIM, WE MAY NOT HAVE LASTED LONG ENOUGH TO SAVE THE DAY!

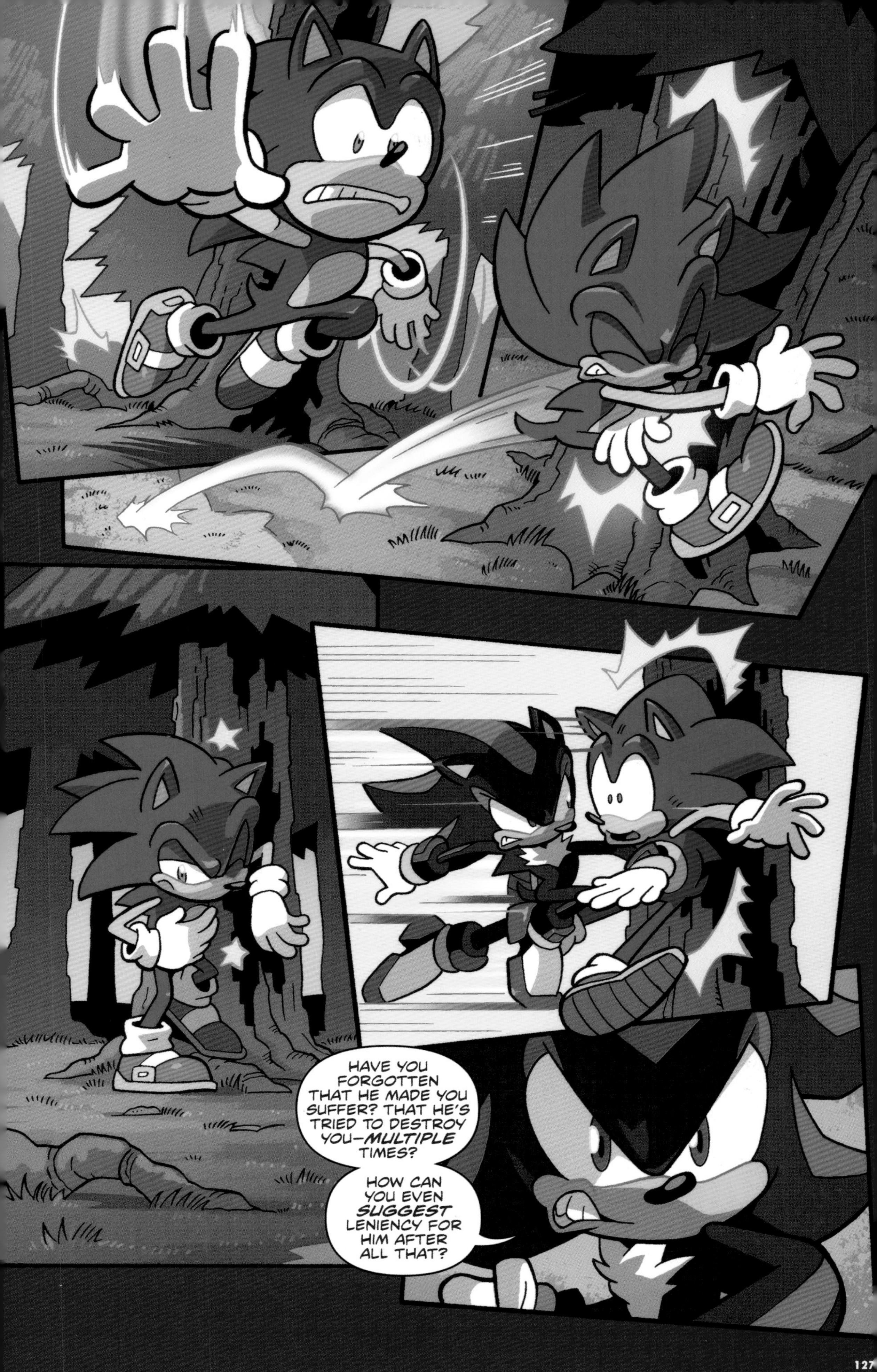
HAVE YOU FORGOTTEN THAT HE MADE YOU SUFFER? THAT HE'S TRIED TO DESTROY YOU—*MULTIPLE* TIMES?
HOW CAN YOU EVEN *SUGGEST* LENIENCY FOR HIM AFTER ALL THAT?

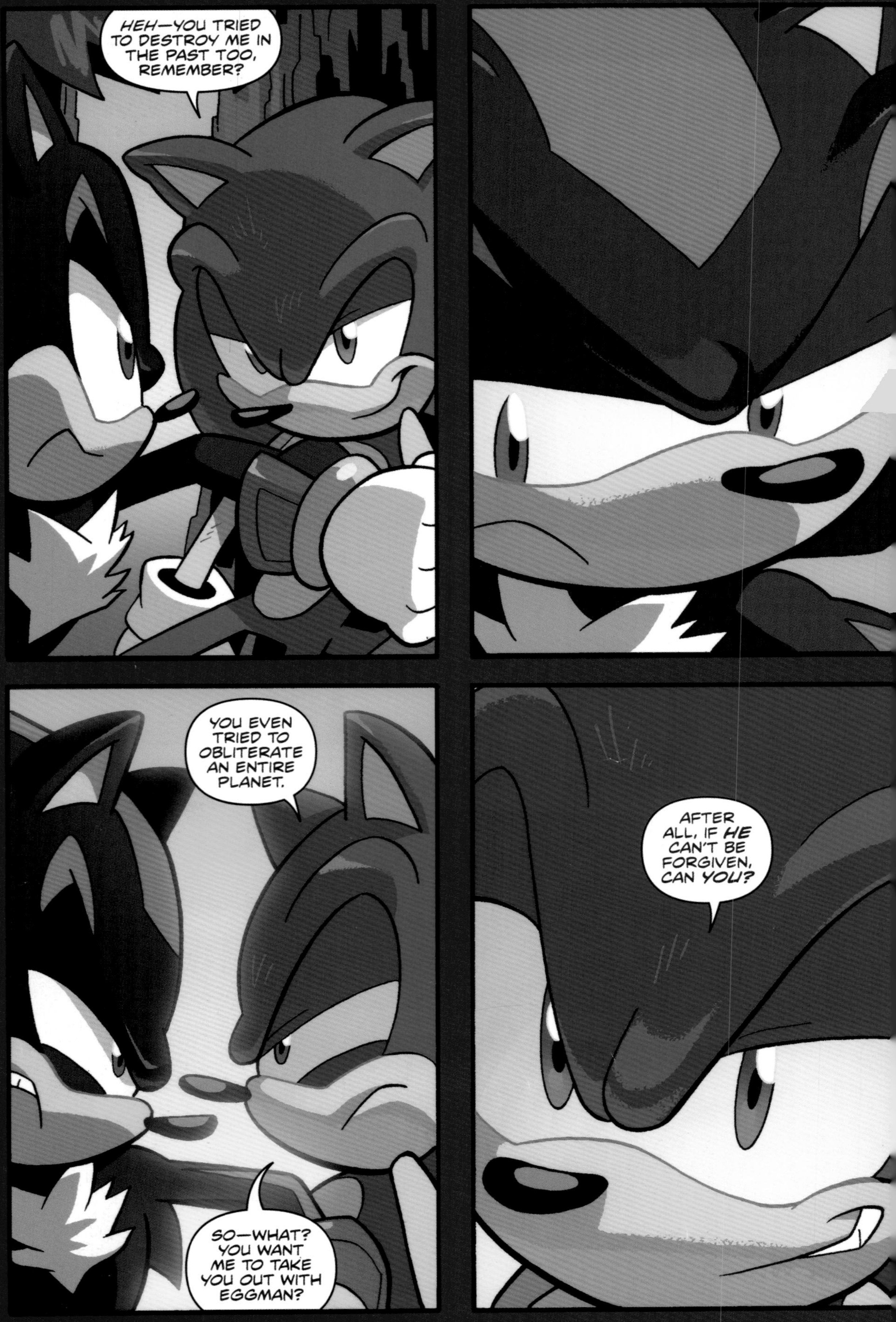
HEH—YOU TRIED TO DESTROY ME IN THE PAST TOO, REMEMBER?
YOU EVEN TRIED TO OBLITERATE AN ENTIRE PLANET.
SO—WHAT? YOU WANT ME TO TAKE YOU OUT WITH EGGMAN?
AFTER ALL, IF HE CAN'T BE FORGIVEN, CAN YOU?

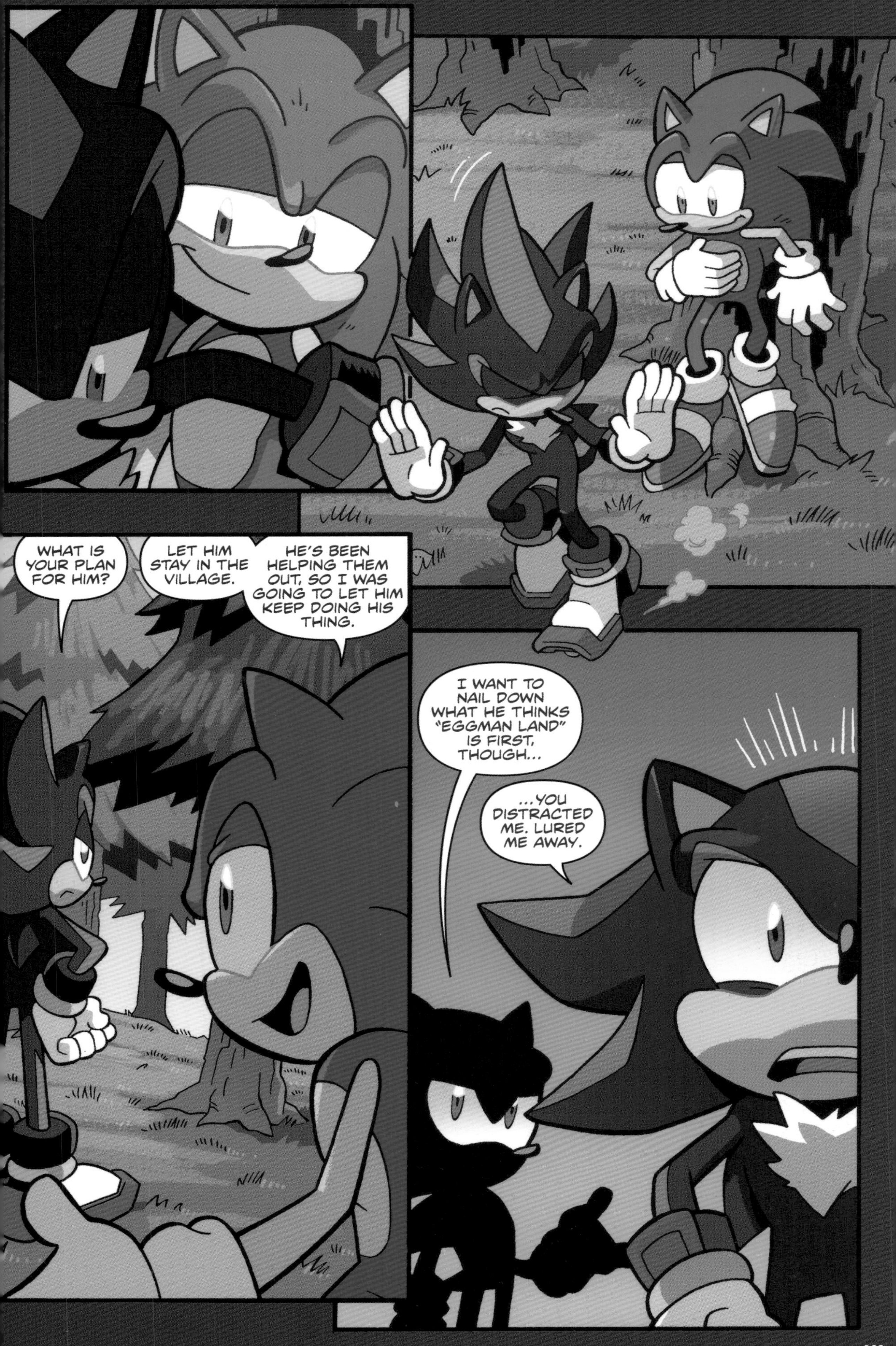
WHAT IS YOUR PLAN FOR HIM?
LET HIM STAY IN THE VILLAGE.
HE'S BEEN HELPING THEM OUT, SO I WAS GOING TO LET HIM KEEP DOING HIS THING.
I WANT TO NAIL DOWN WHAT HE THINKS "EGGMAN LAND" IS FIRST, THOUGH...
...YOU DISTRACTED ME. LURED ME AWAY.

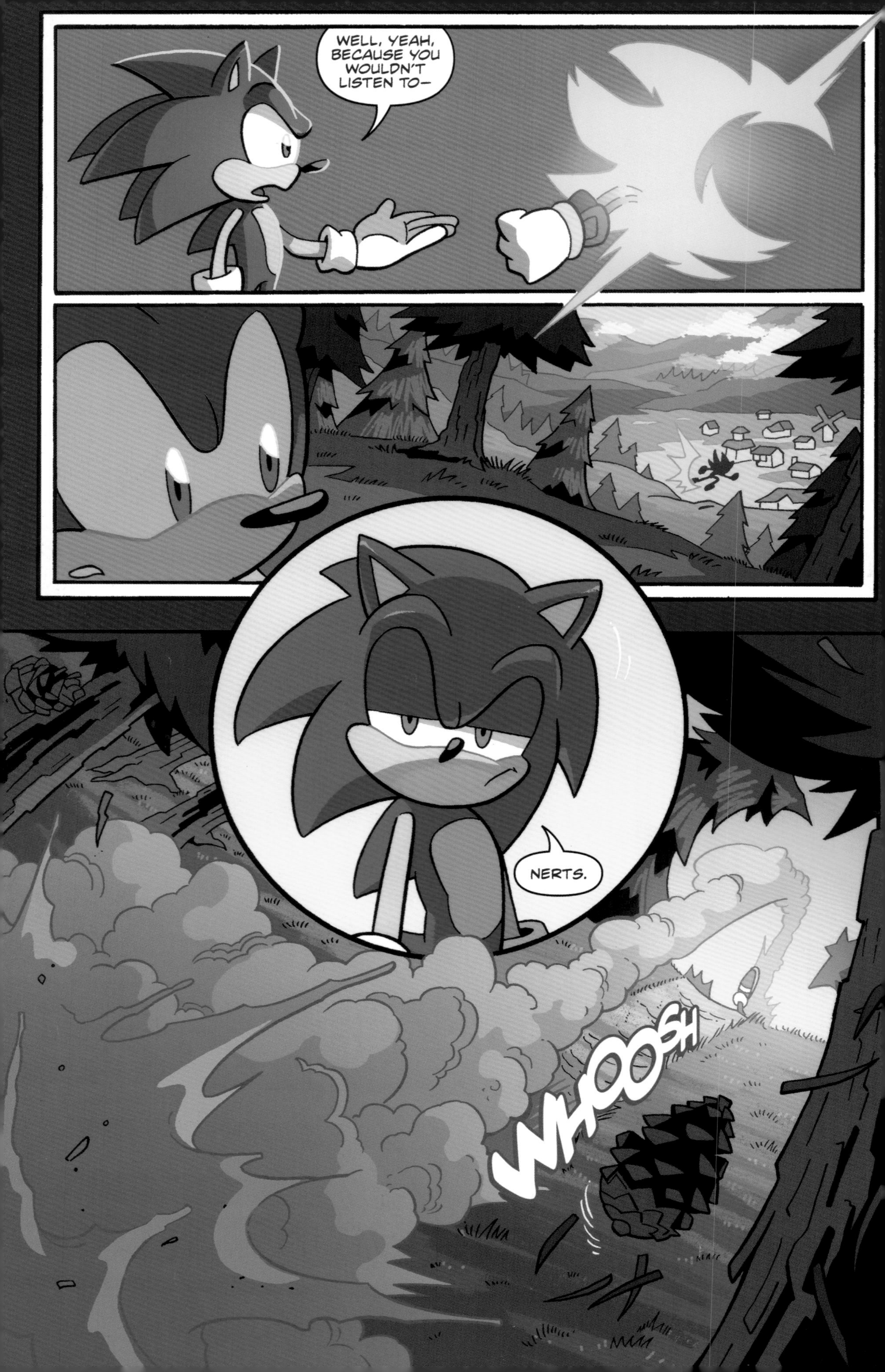
WELL, YEAH, BECAUSE YOU WOULDN'T LISTEN TO—
NERTS.
WHOOSH

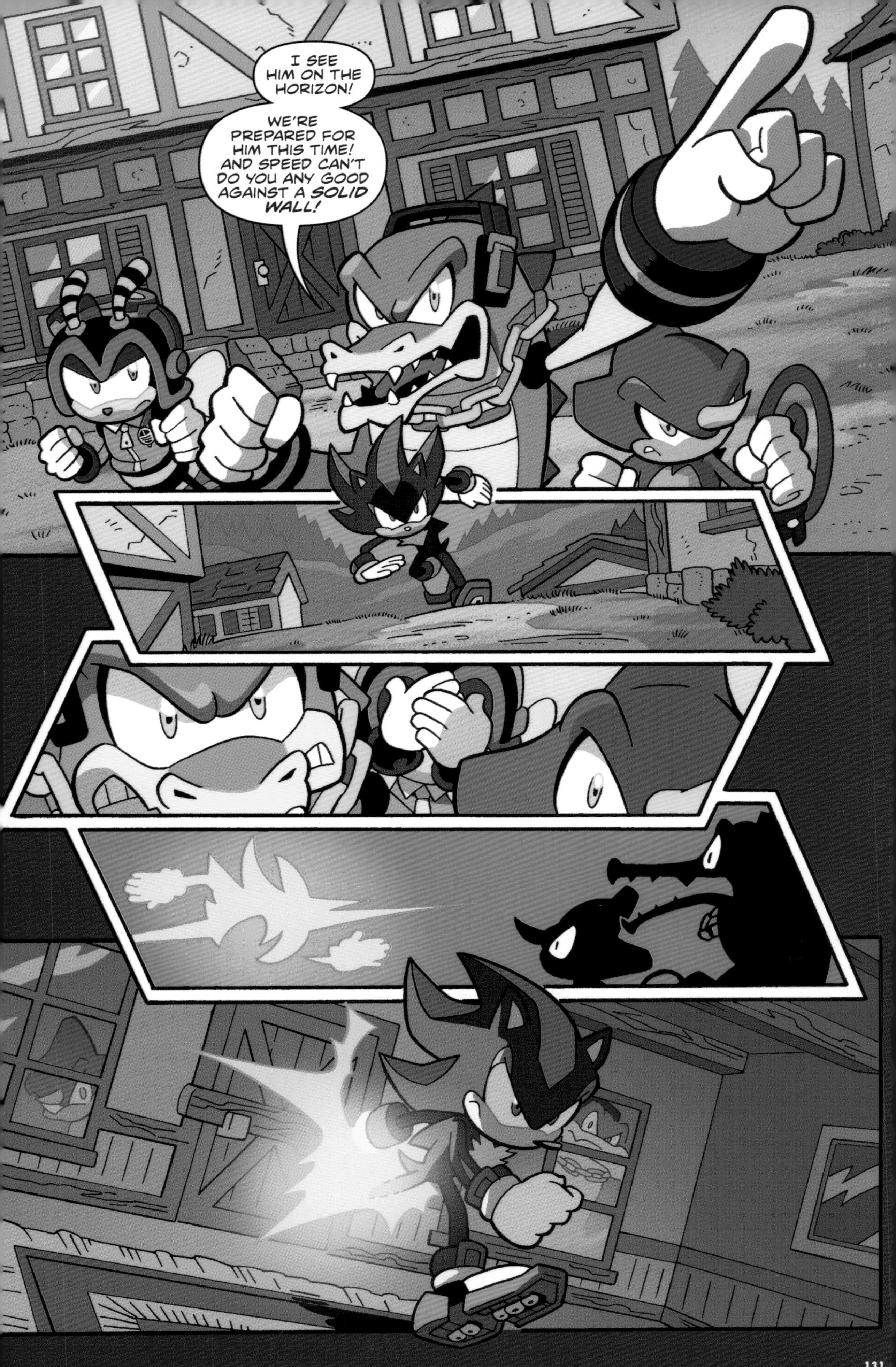
I SEE HIM ON THE HORIZON!
WE'RE PREPARED FOR HIM THIS TIME! AND SPEED CAN'T DO YOU ANY GOOD AGAINST A SOLID WALL!

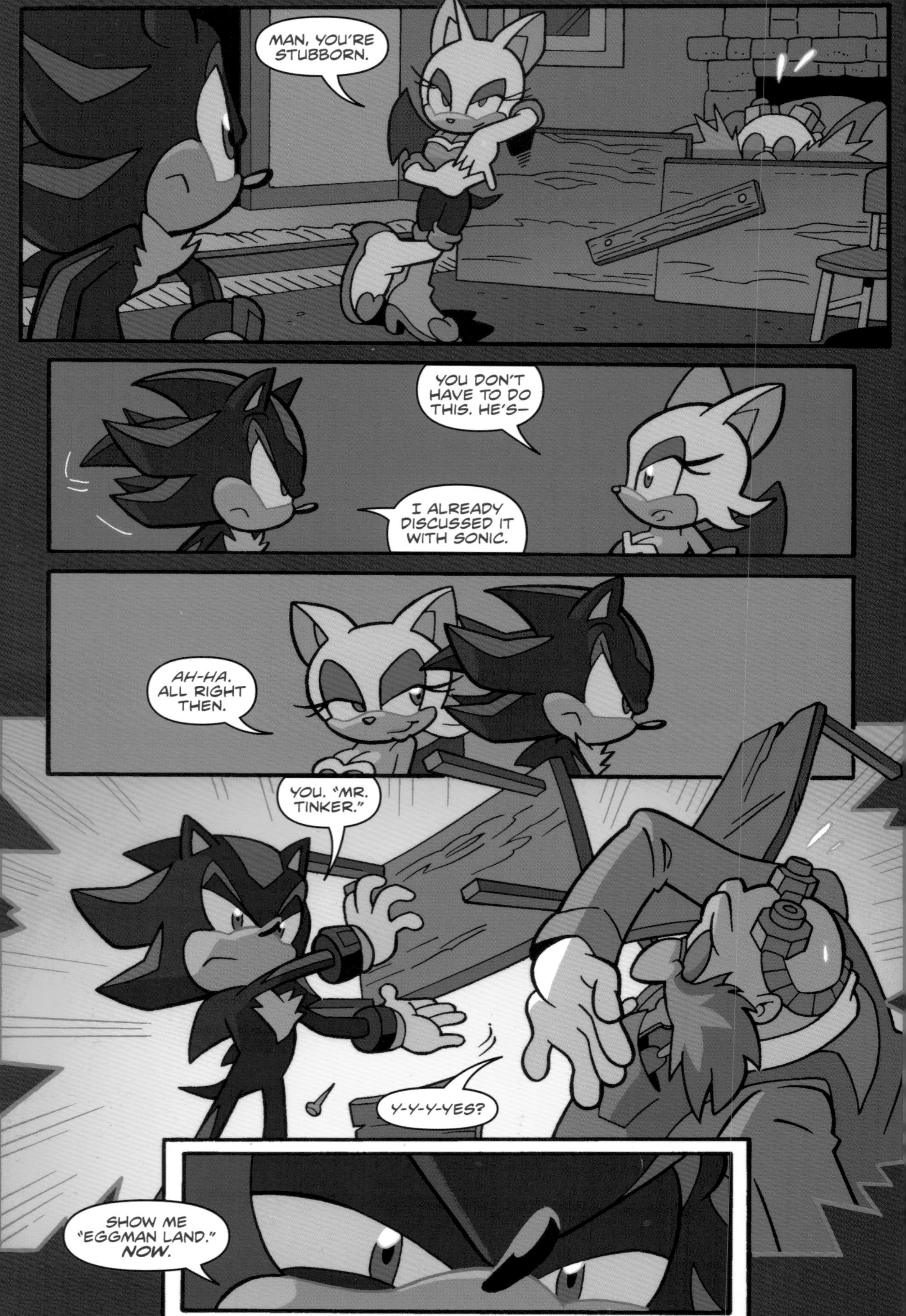
MAN, YOU'RE STUBBORN.
YOU DON'T HAVE TO DO THIS. HE'S—
I ALREADY DISCUSSED IT WITH SONIC.
AH-HA. ALL RIGHT THEN.
YOU. "MR. TINKER."
Y-Y-Y-YES?
SHOW ME "EGGMAN LAND." NOW.

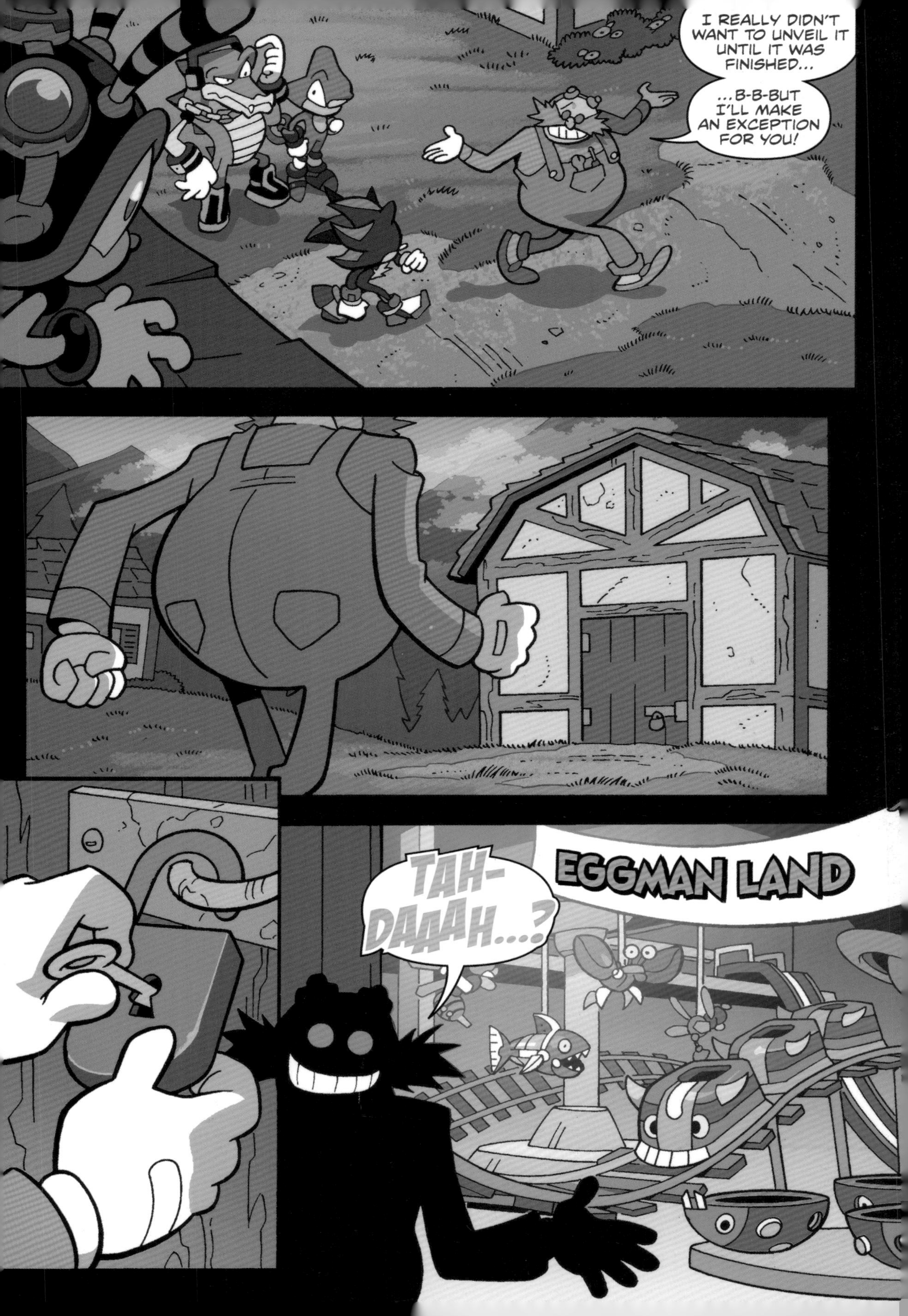
I REALLY DIDN'T WANT TO UNVEIL IT UNTIL IT WAS FINISHED...
...B-B-BUT I'LL MAKE AN EXCEPTION FOR YOU!
EGGMAN LAND
TAH-DAAAH...?

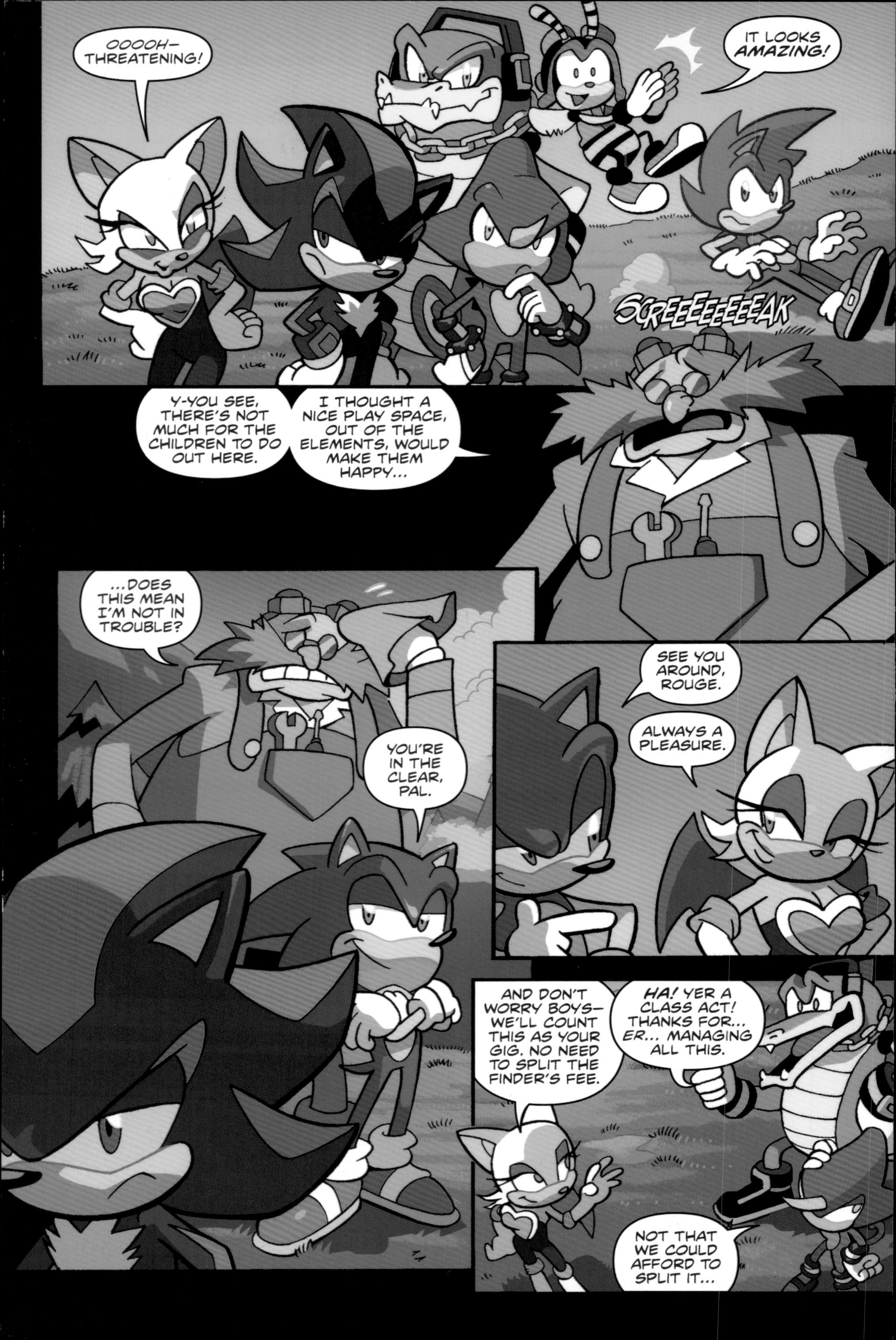
OOOOH—THREATENING!
IT LOOKS AMAZING!
SCREEEEEEEEEAK
Y-YOU SEE, THERE'S NOT MUCH FOR THE CHILDREN TO DO OUT HERE.
I THOUGHT A NICE PLAY SPACE, OUT OF THE ELEMENTS, WOULD MAKE THEM HAPPY...
...DOES THIS MEAN I'M NOT IN TROUBLE?
YOU'RE IN THE CLEAR, PAL.
SEE YOU AROUND, ROUGE.
ALWAYS A PLEASURE.
AND DON'T WORRY BOYS—WE'LL COUNT THIS AS YOUR GIG. NO NEED TO SPLIT THE FINDER'S FEE.
HA! YER A CLASS ACT! THANKS FOR... ER... MANAGING ALL THIS.
NOT THAT WE COULD AFFORD TO SPLIT IT...

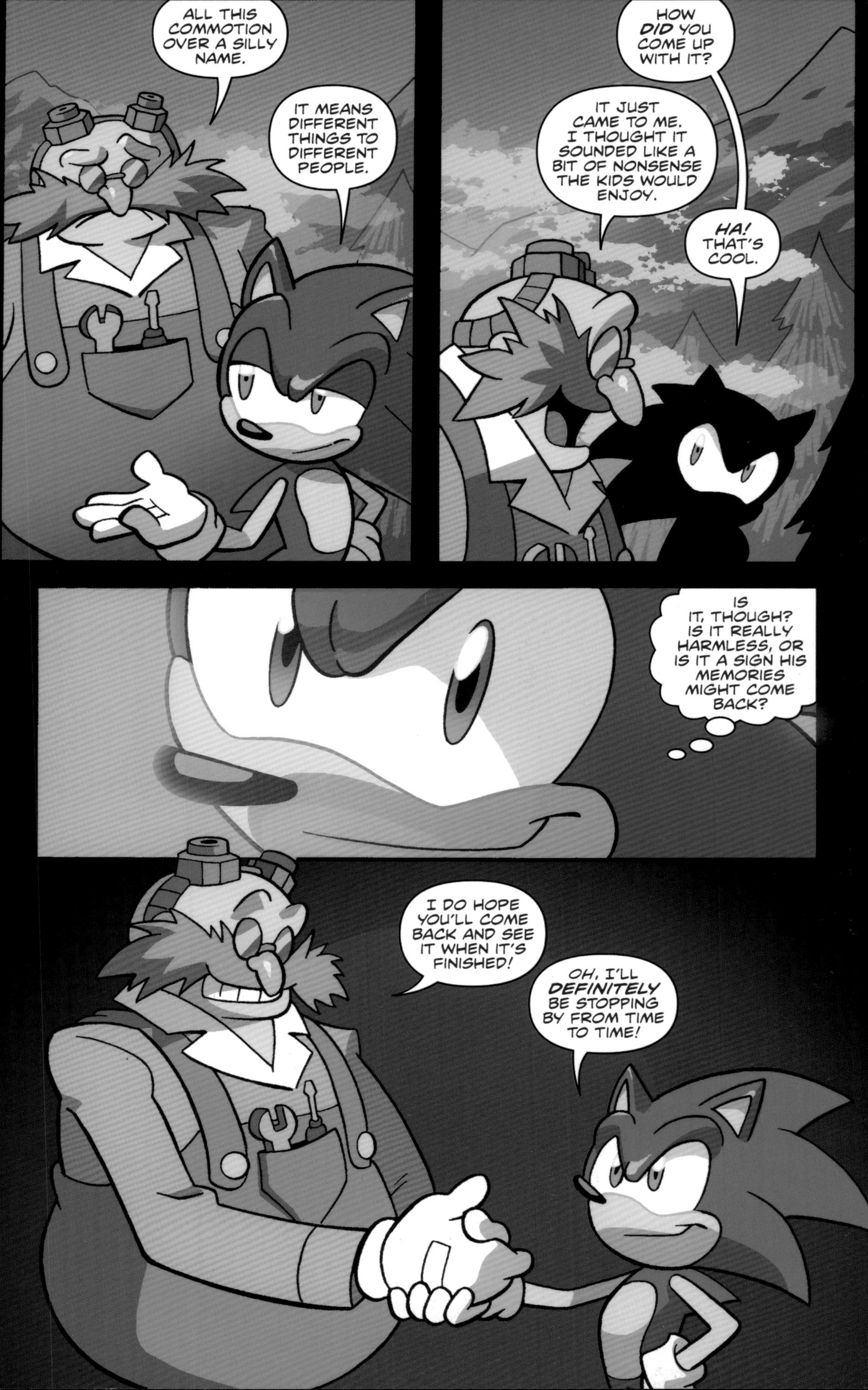
ALL THIS COMMOTION OVER A SILLY NAME.
IT MEANS DIFFERENT THINGS TO DIFFERENT PEOPLE.
HOW *DID* YOU COME UP WITH IT?
IT JUST CAME TO ME. I THOUGHT IT SOUNDED LIKE A BIT OF NONSENSE THE KIDS WOULD ENJOY.
HA! THAT'S COOL.
IS IT, THOUGH? IS IT REALLY HARMLESS, OR IS IT A SIGN HIS MEMORIES MIGHT COME BACK?
I DO HOPE YOU'LL COME BACK AND SEE IT WHEN IT'S FINISHED!
OH, I'LL *DEFINITELY* BE STOPPING BY FROM TIME TO TIME!

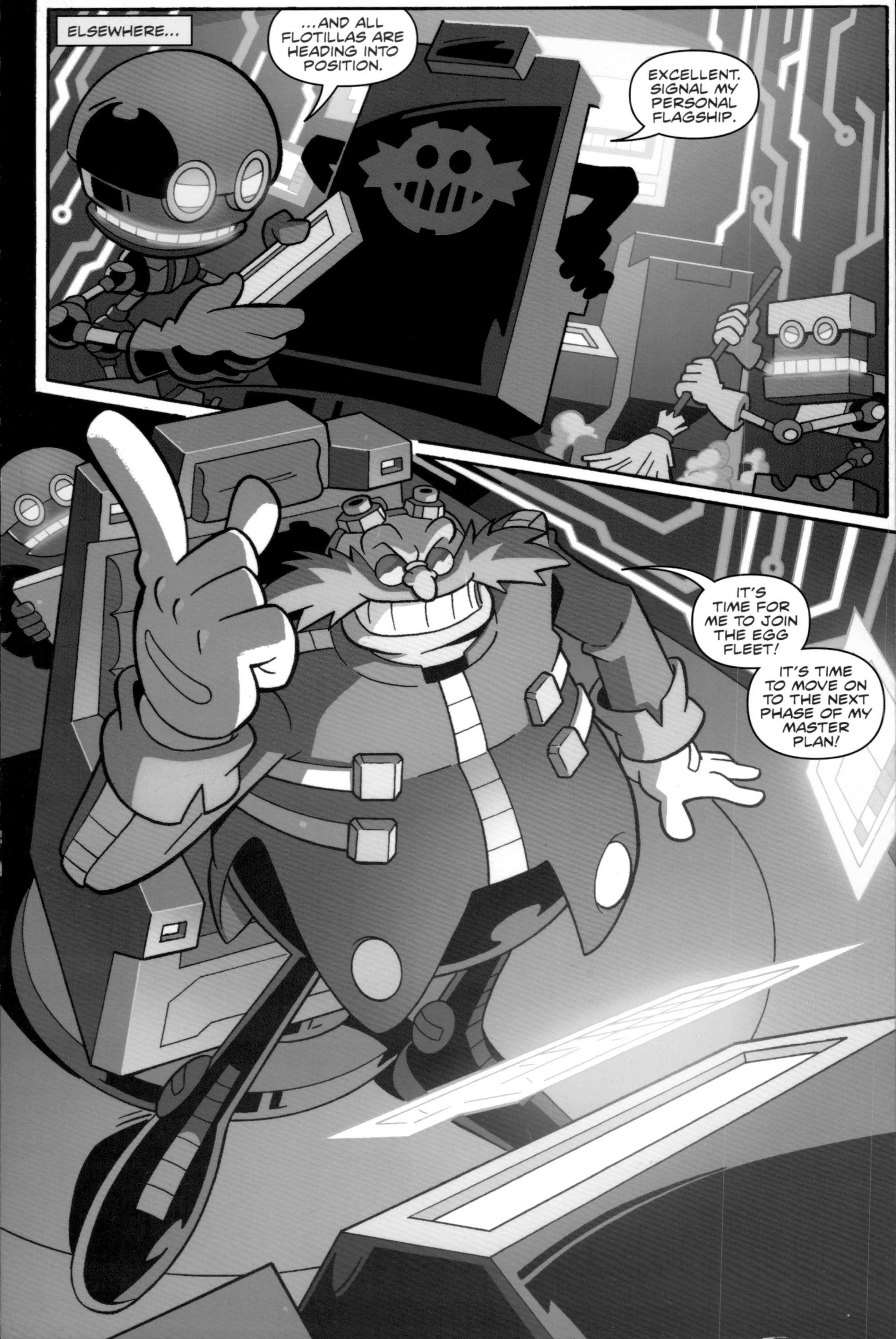
ELSEWHERE...
...AND ALL FLOTILLAS ARE HEADING INTO POSITION.
EXCELLENT. SIGNAL MY PERSONAL FLAGSHIP.
IT'S TIME FOR ME TO JOIN THE EGG FLEET!
IT'S TIME TO MOVE ON TO THE NEXT PHASE OF MY MASTER PLAN!

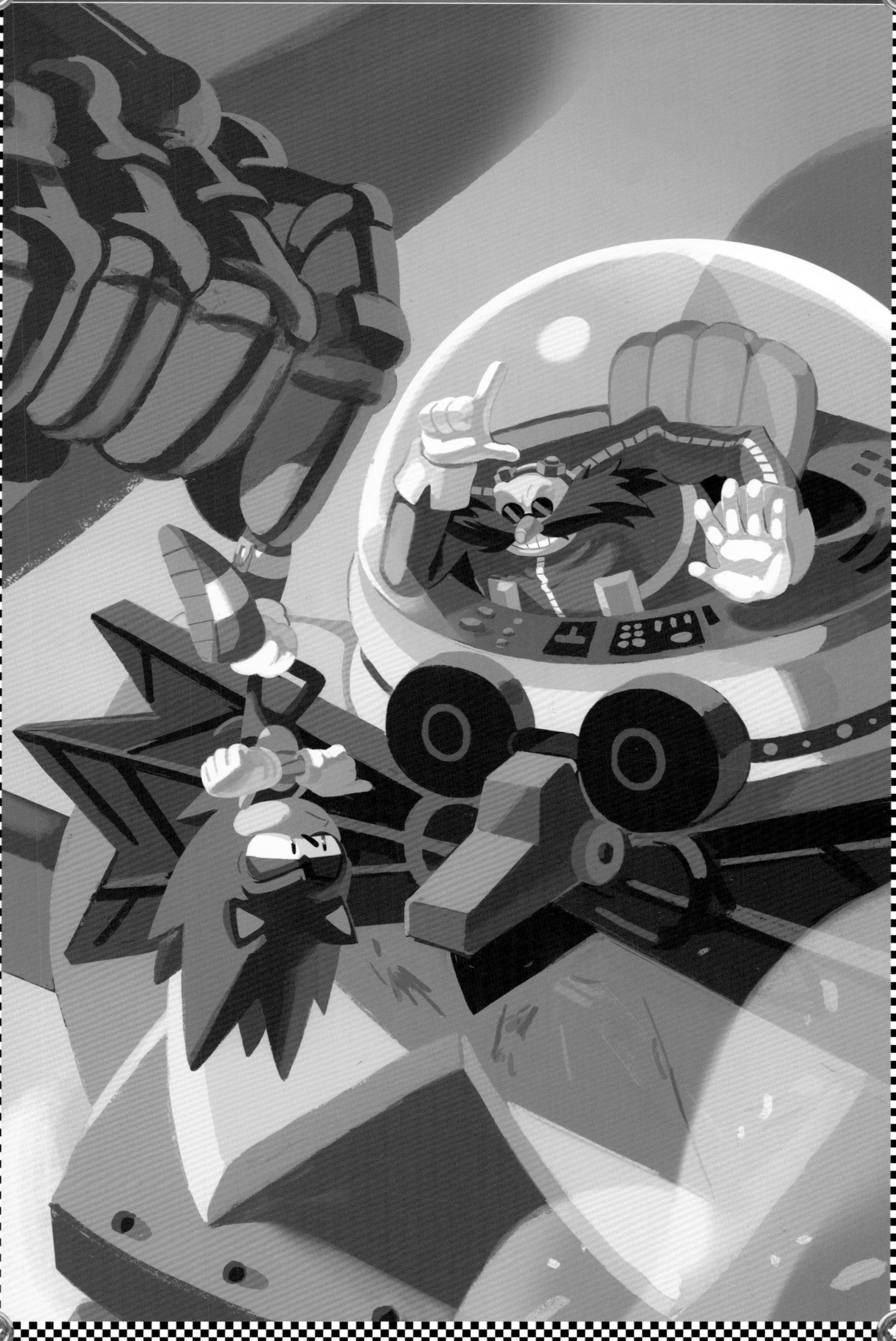

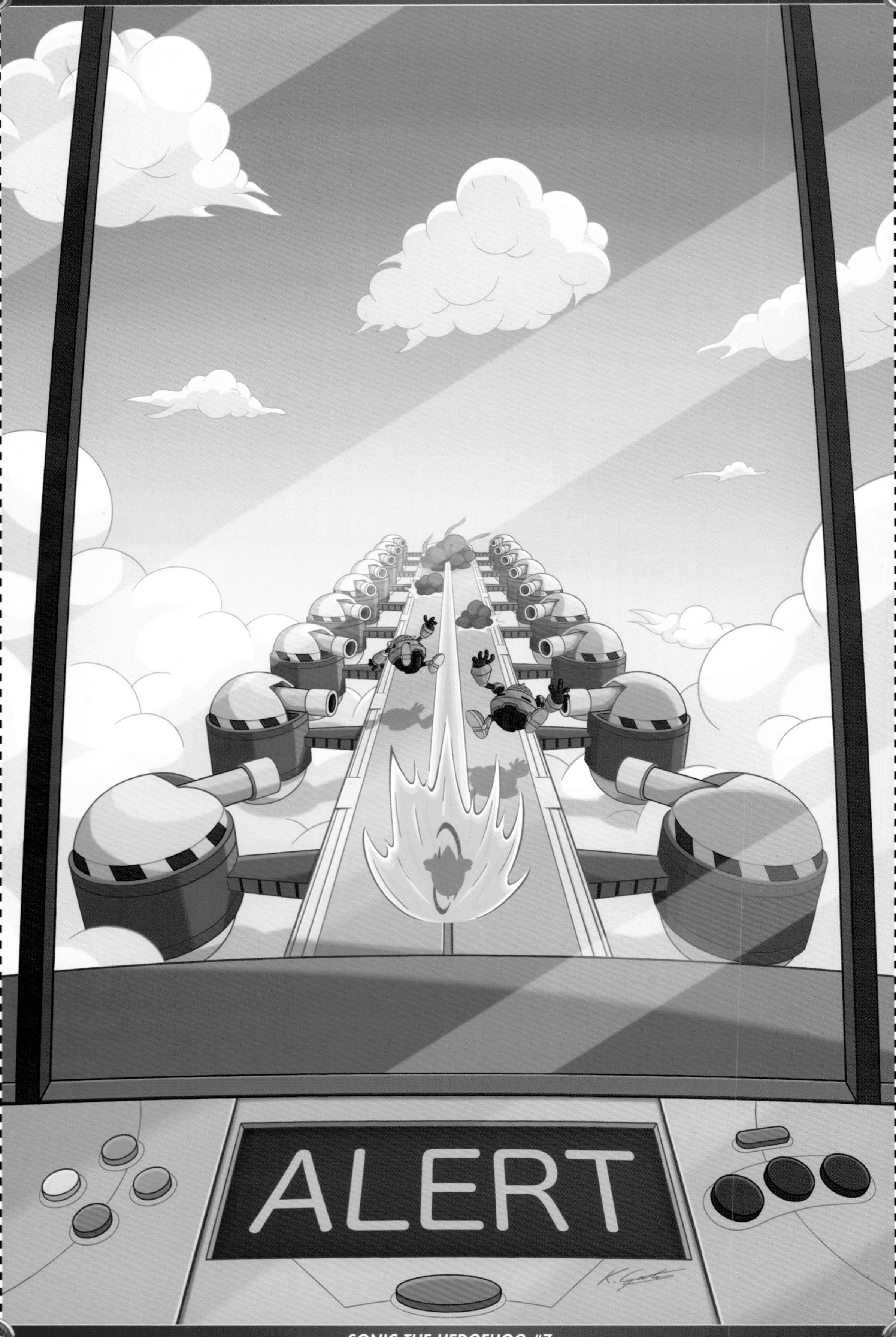
ALERT
K. Gates

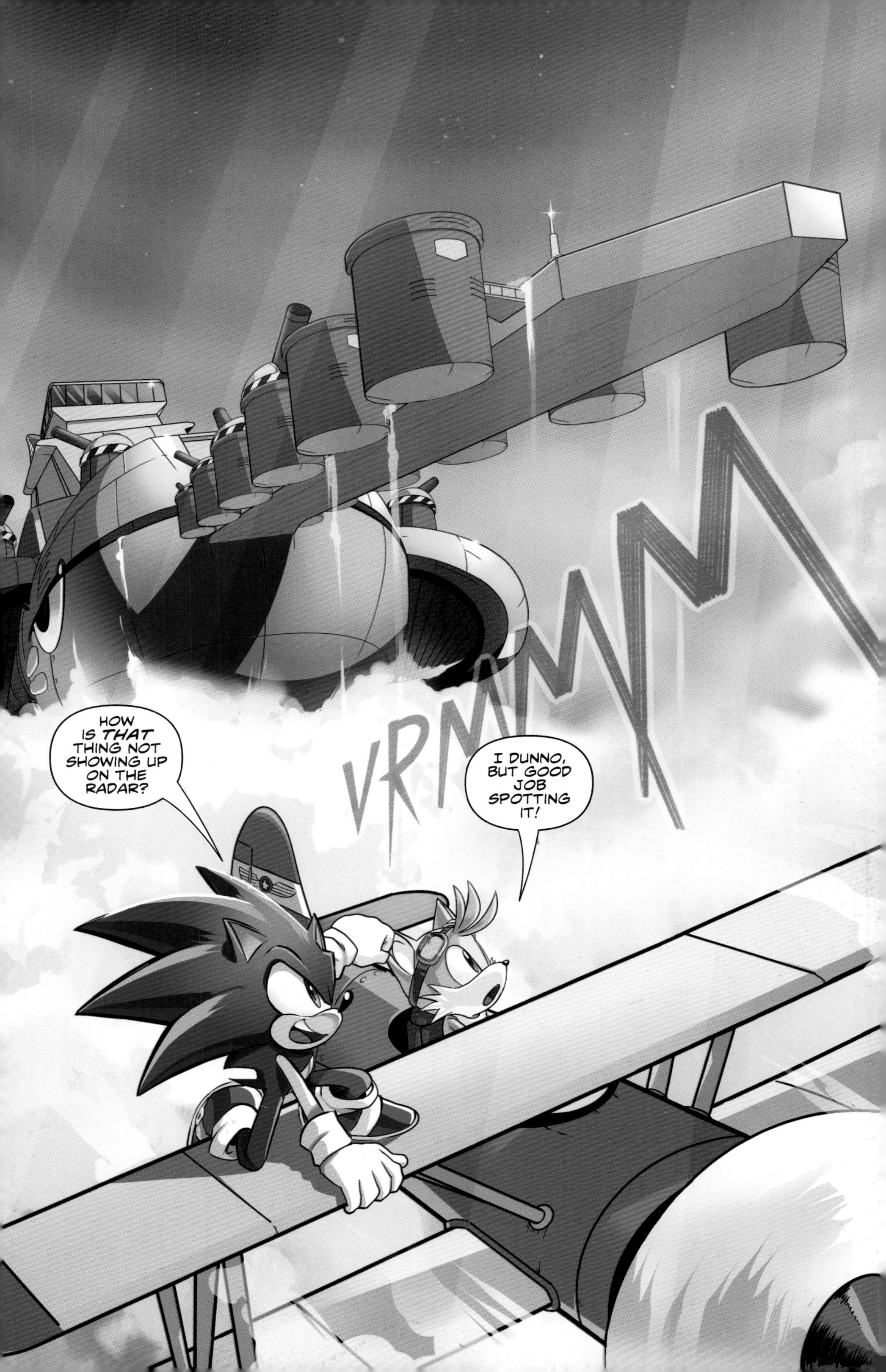
VRMMMMM
HOW IS THAT THING NOT SHOWING UP ON THE RADAR?
I DUNNO, BUT GOOD JOB SPOTTING IT!

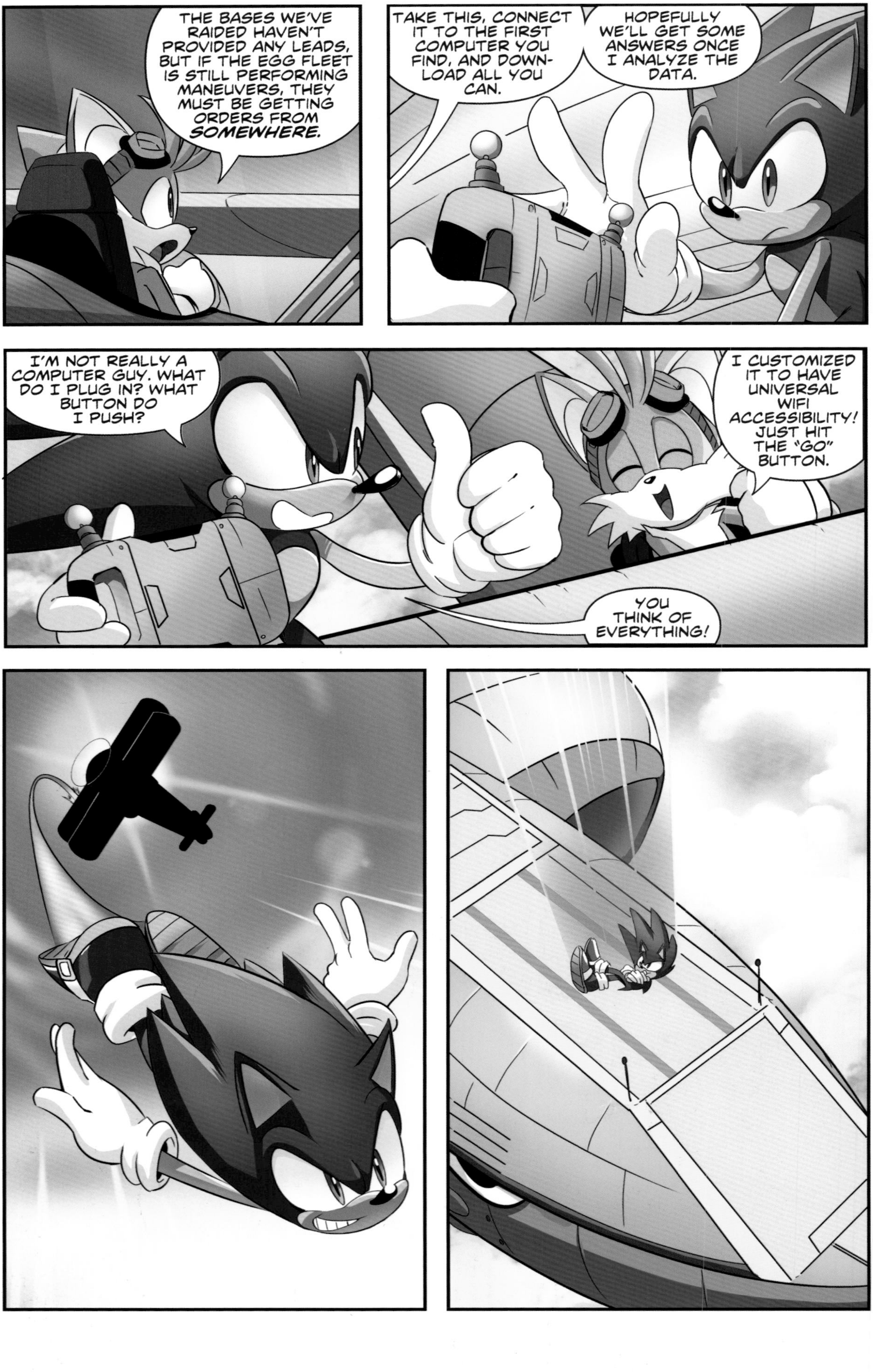
THE BASES WE'VE RAIDED HAVEN'T PROVIDED ANY LEADS, BUT IF THE EGG FLEET IS STILL PERFORMING MANEUVERS, THEY MUST BE GETTING ORDERS FROM *SOMEWHERE.*
TAKE THIS, CONNECT IT TO THE FIRST COMPUTER YOU FIND, AND DOWN-LOAD ALL YOU CAN.
HOPEFULLY WE'LL GET SOME ANSWERS ONCE I ANALYZE THE DATA.
I'M NOT REALLY A COMPUTER GUY. WHAT DO I PLUG IN? WHAT BUTTON DO I PUSH?
I CUSTOMIZED IT TO HAVE UNIVERSAL WIFI ACCESSIBILITY! JUST HIT THE "GO" BUTTON.
YOU THINK OF EVERYTHING!

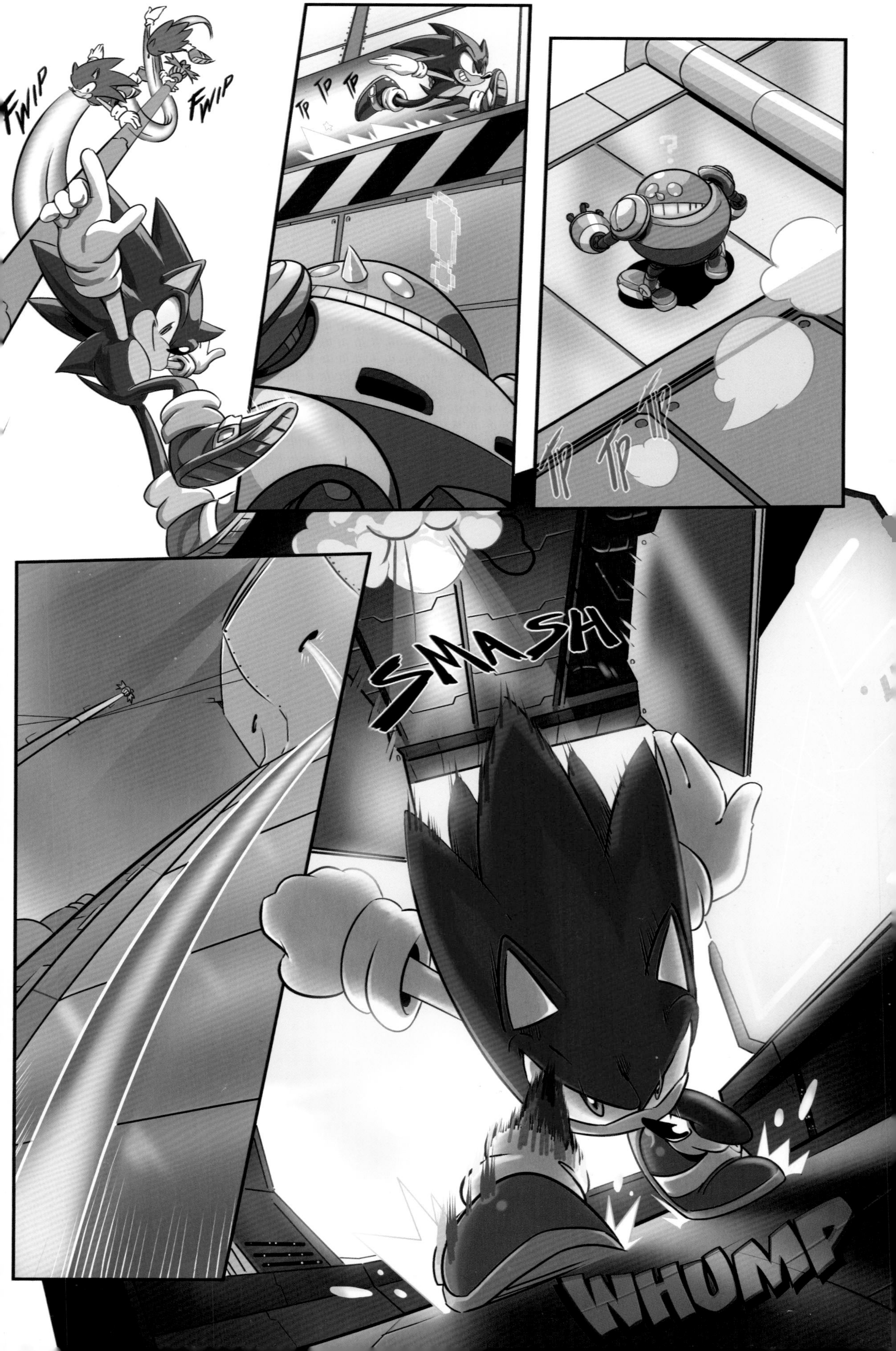
FWIP
FWIP
TP TP TP
TP TP TP
SMASH
WHUMP

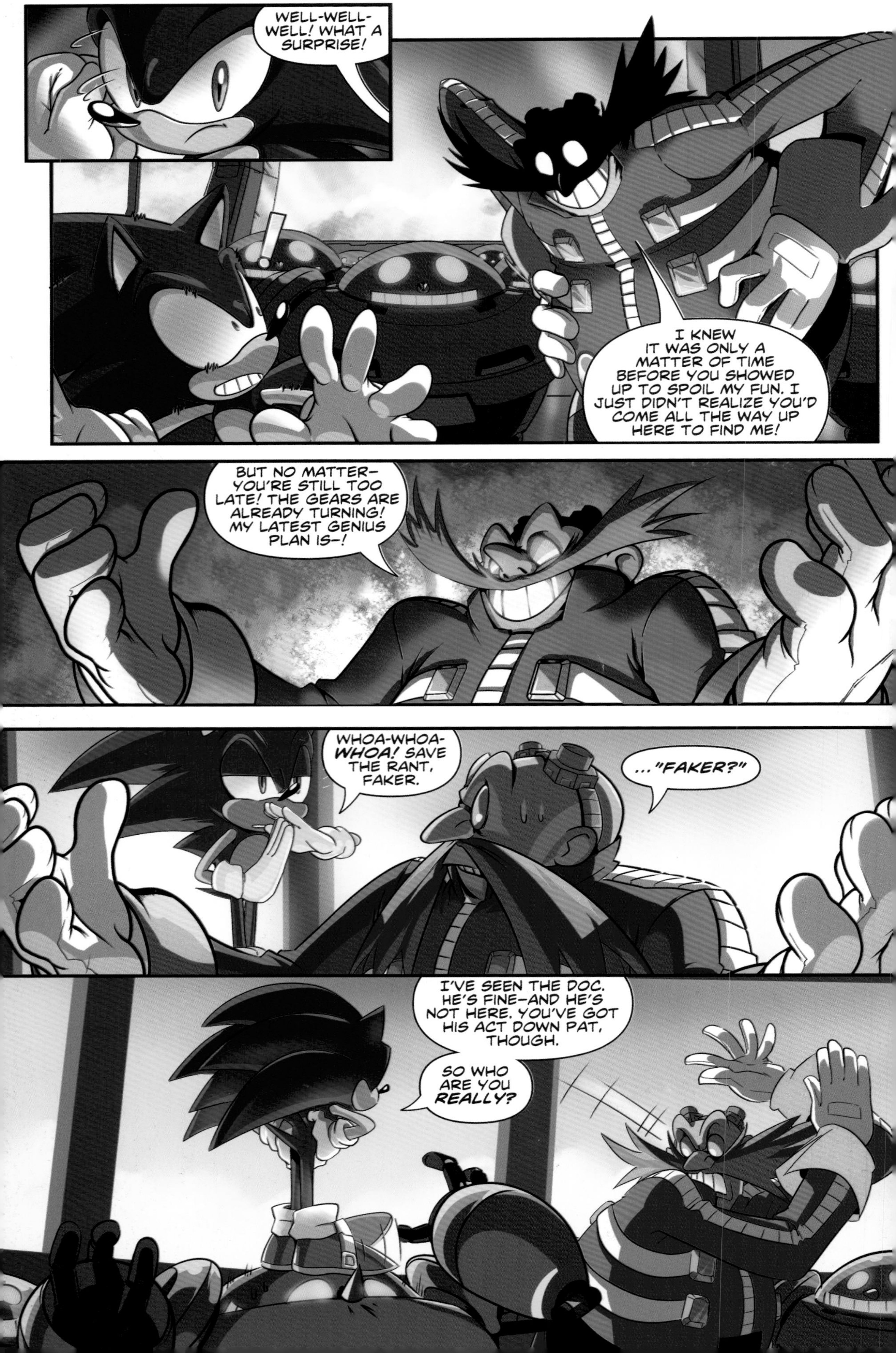
WELL-WELL-WELL! WHAT A SURPRISE!
I KNEW IT WAS ONLY A MATTER OF TIME BEFORE YOU SHOWED UP TO SPOIL MY FUN. I JUST DIDN'T REALIZE YOU'D COME ALL THE WAY UP HERE TO FIND ME!
BUT NO MATTER– YOU'RE STILL TOO LATE! THE GEARS ARE ALREADY TURNING! MY LATEST GENIUS PLAN IS–!
WHOA-WHOA-WHOA! SAVE THE RANT, FAKER.
..."FAKER?"
I'VE SEEN THE DOC. HE'S FINE–AND HE'S NOT HERE. YOU'VE GOT HIS ACT DOWN PAT, THOUGH.
SO WHO ARE YOU REALLY?

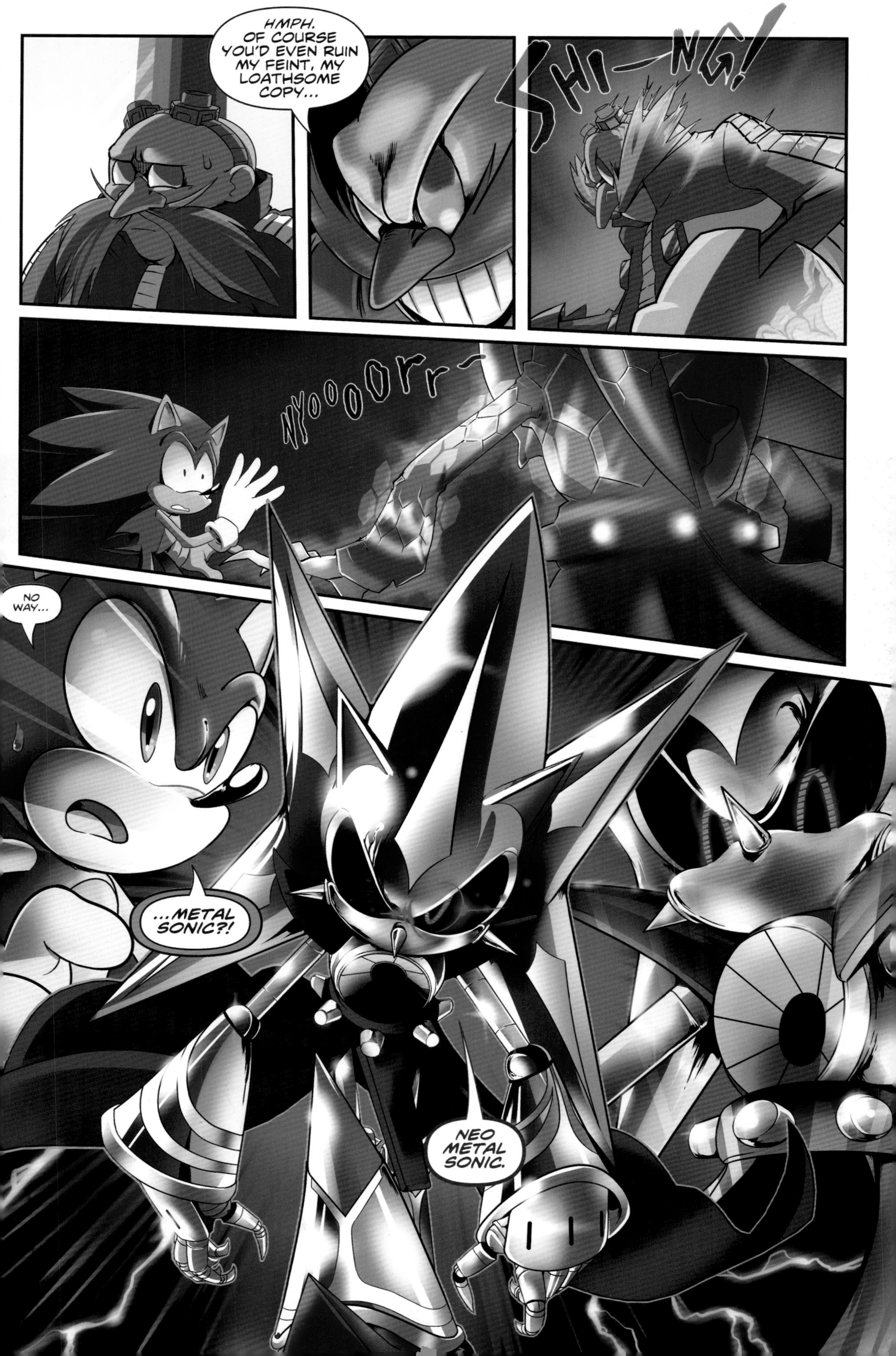
HMPH. OF COURSE YOU'D EVEN RUIN MY FEINT, MY LOATHSOME COPY...
SHI—NG!
NYOOOOOrr~
NO WAY...
...METAL SONIC?!
NEO METAL SONIC.

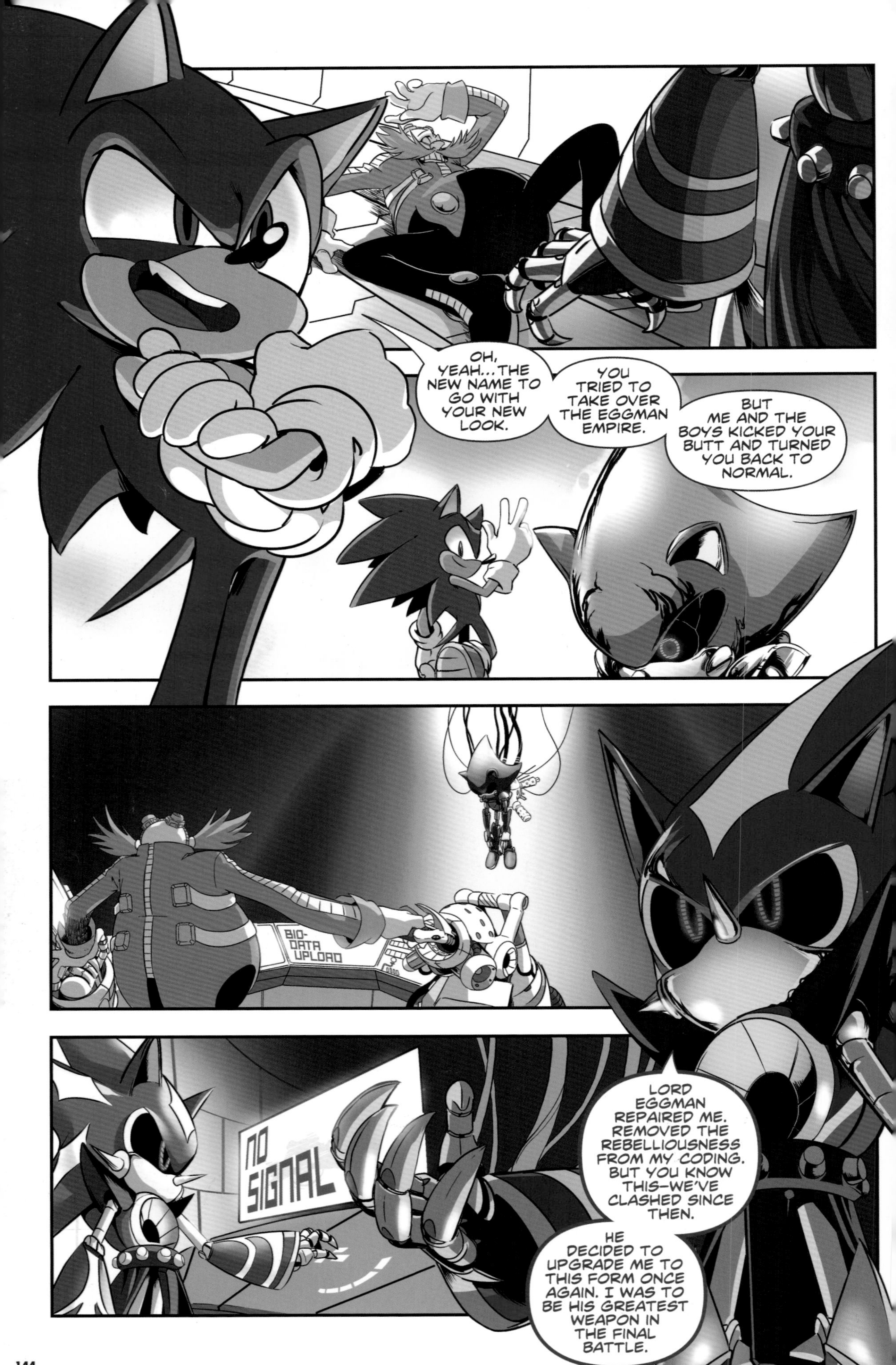
OH, YEAH... THE NEW NAME TO GO WITH YOUR NEW LOOK.
YOU TRIED TO TAKE OVER THE EGGMAN EMPIRE.
BUT ME AND THE BOYS KICKED YOUR BUTT AND TURNED YOU BACK TO NORMAL.
BIO-DATA UPLOAD
NO SIGNAL
LORD EGGMAN REPAIRED ME. REMOVED THE REBELLIOUSNESS FROM MY CODING. BUT YOU KNOW THIS—WE'VE CLASHED SINCE THEN.
HE DECIDED TO UPGRADE ME TO THIS FORM ONCE AGAIN. I WAS TO BE HIS GREATEST WEAPON IN THE FINAL BATTLE.

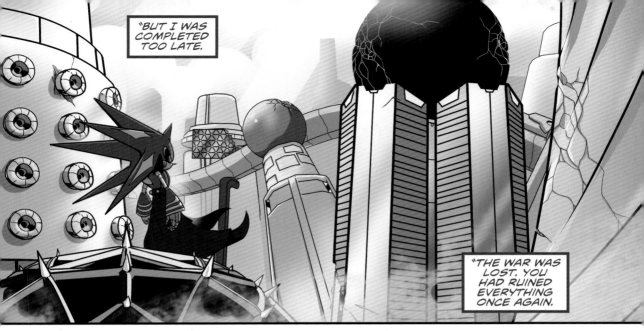

"BUT I WAS COMPLETED TOO LATE."

"THE WAR WAS LOST. YOU HAD RUINED EVERYTHING ONCE AGAIN."

"I WAS GIVEN THE DOCTOR'S BIO-DATA. HIS GENIUS. HIS DRIVE. HIS VISION."

"BUT I SERVE THE EGGMAN EMPIRE. THE ONLY ONE WHO CAN TRULY RULE IT IS DR. EGGMAN.

"I DECIDED I WOULD USE HIS PERSONA TO ENSURE HIS REIGN REMAINED UNBROKEN."

I WILL CONQUER THE WORLD FOR EGGMAN *AS* EGGMAN.

AND *YOU* WILL TELL ME WHERE HE IS SO I MAY HAND OVER CONTROL TO HIM.

145

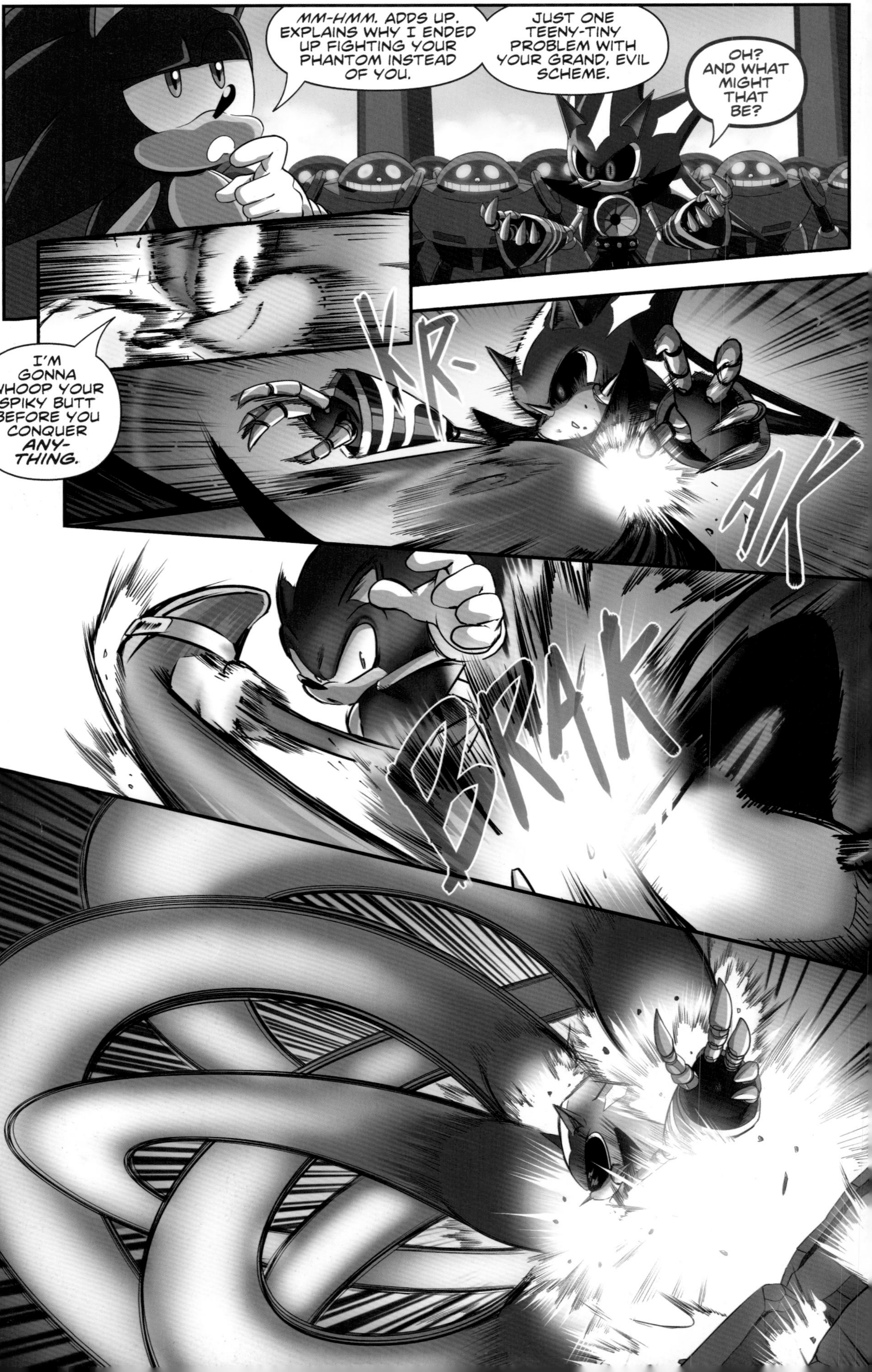
MM-HMM. ADDS UP. EXPLAINS WHY I ENDED UP FIGHTING YOUR PHANTOM INSTEAD OF YOU.
JUST ONE TEENY-TINY PROBLEM WITH YOUR GRAND, EVIL SCHEME.
OH? AND WHAT MIGHT THAT BE?
I'M GONNA WHOOP YOUR SPIKY BUTT BEFORE YOU CONQUER ANY-THING.
KR-
AK
BRAK

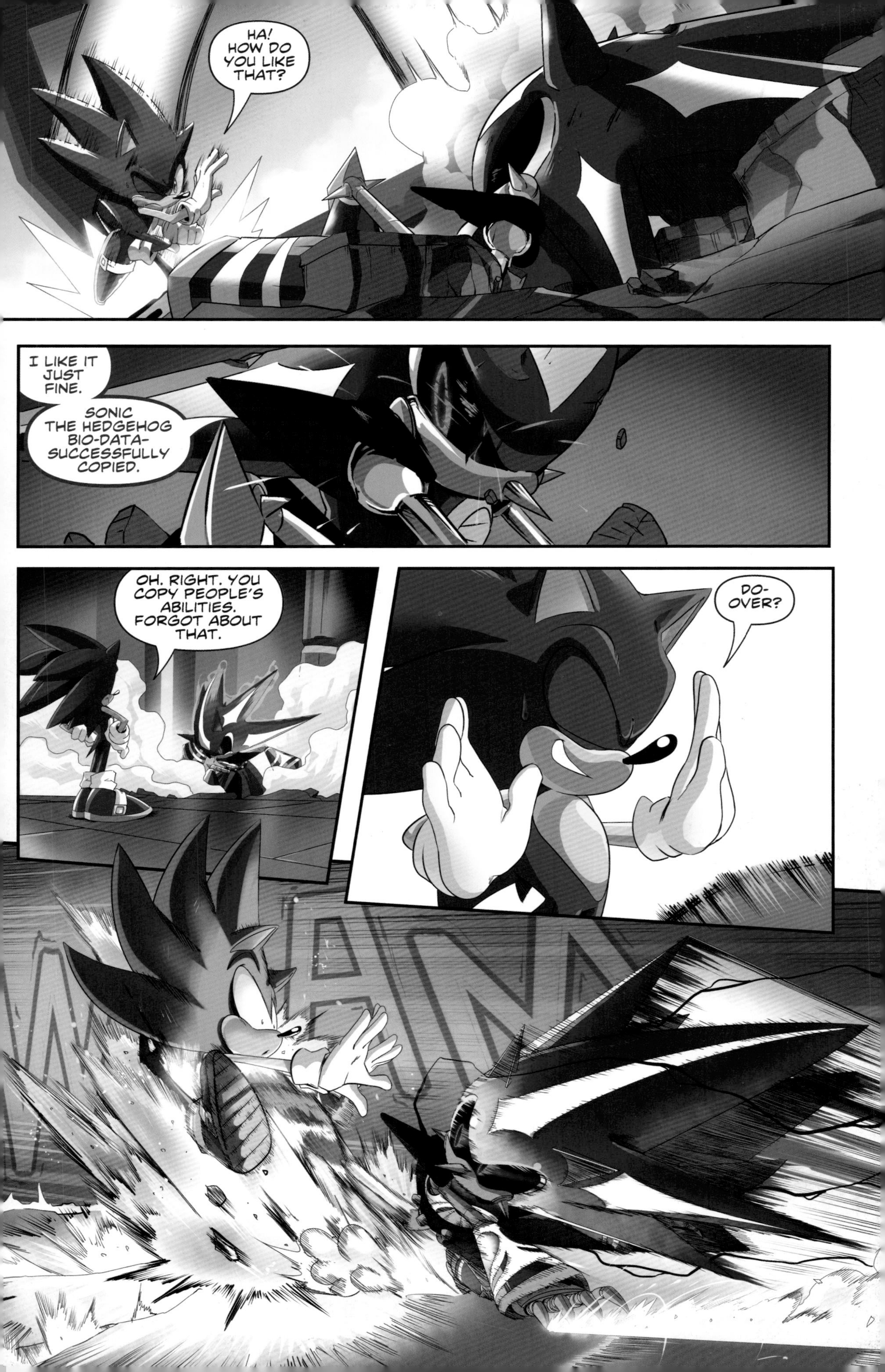
HA! HOW DO YOU LIKE THAT?
I LIKE IT JUST FINE.
SONIC THE HEDGEHOG BIO-DATA- SUCCESSFULLY COPIED.
OH. RIGHT. YOU COPY PEOPLE'S ABILITIES. FORGOT ABOUT THAT.
DO-OVER?

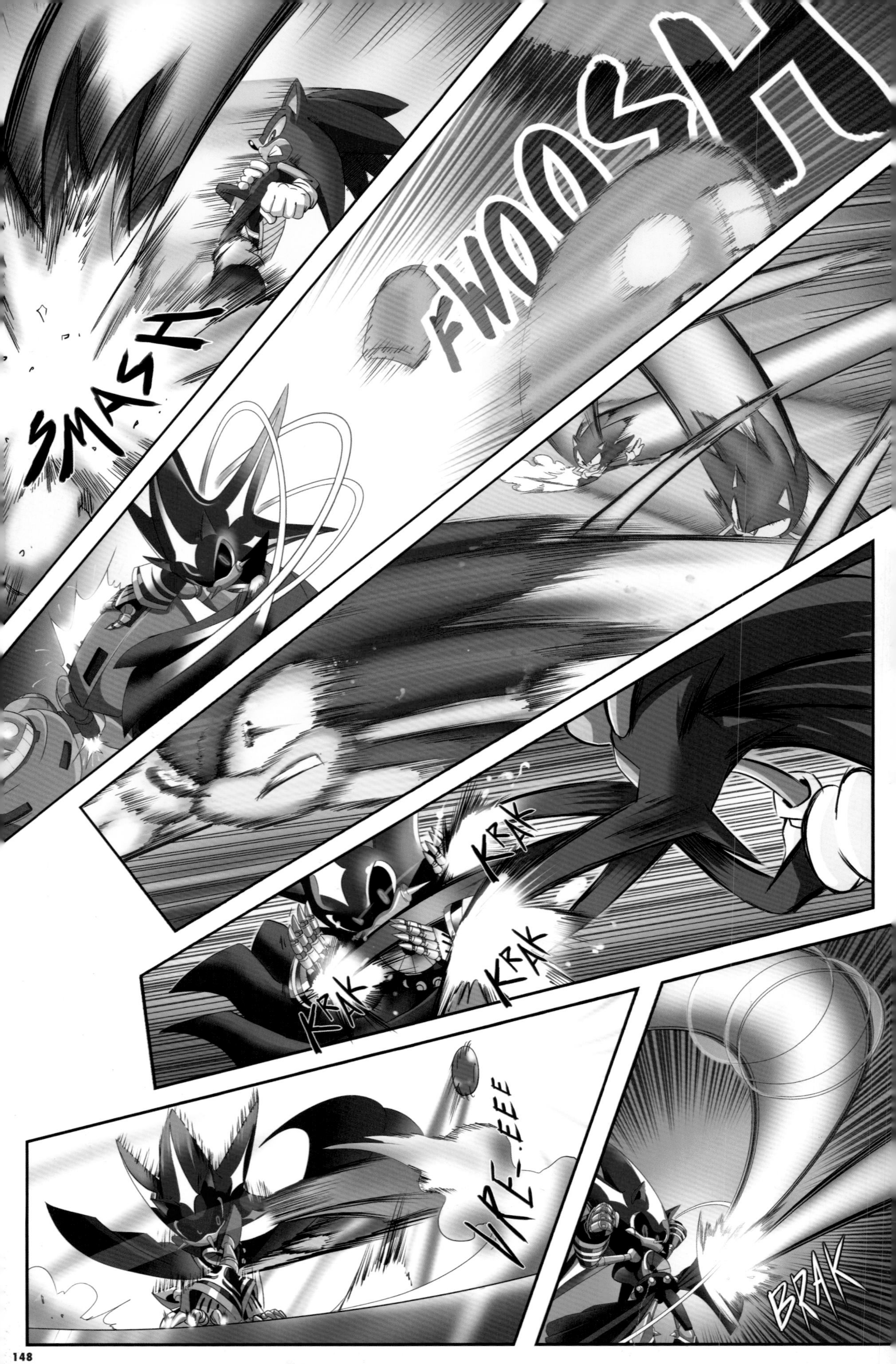
SMASH
FWOOSH
KRAK
KRAK
KRAK
VREE-EEE
BRAK

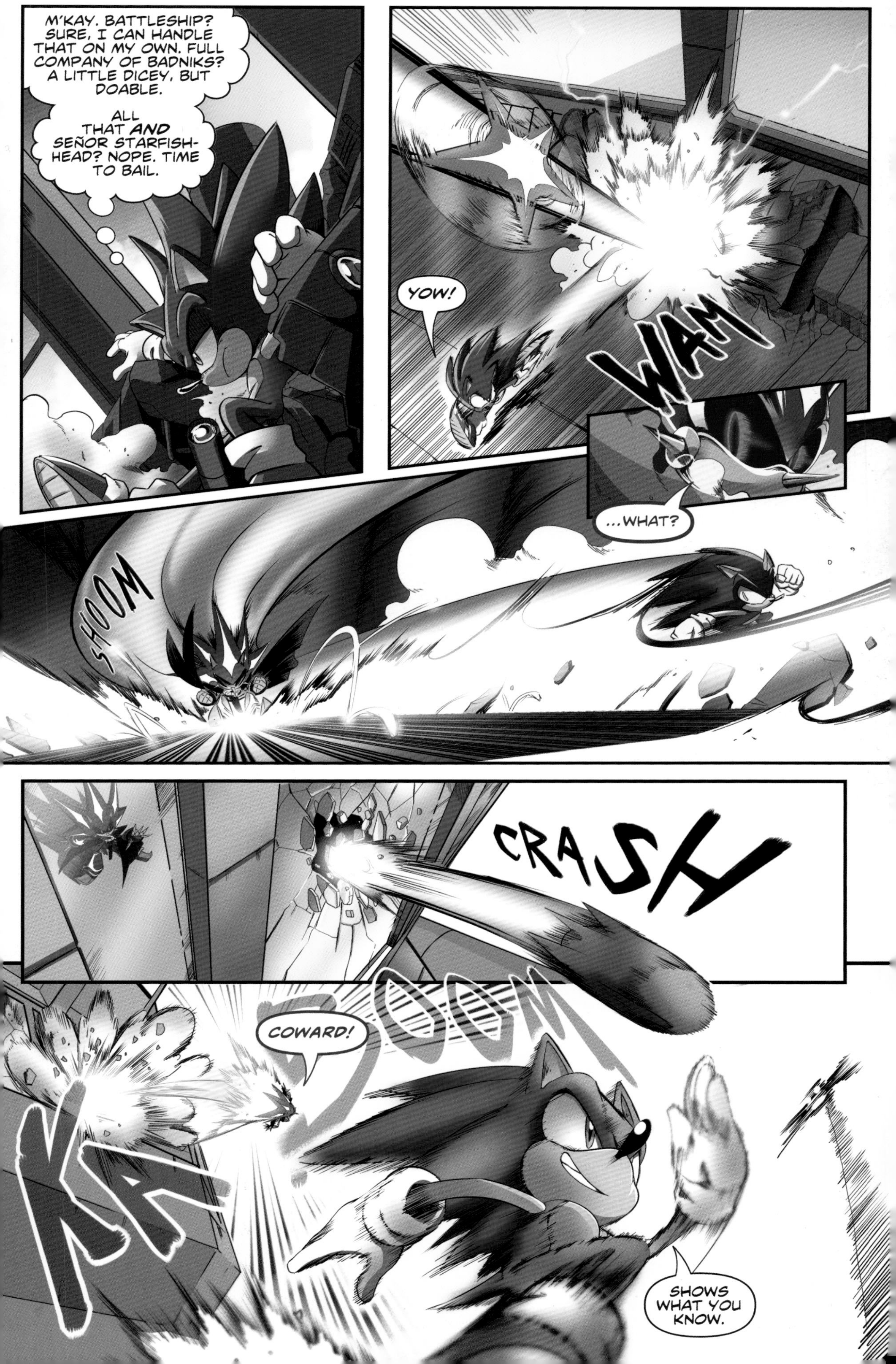
M'KAY. BATTLESHIP? SURE, I CAN HANDLE THAT ON MY OWN. FULL COMPANY OF BADNIKS? A LITTLE DICEY, BUT DOABLE.
ALL THAT AND SEÑOR STARFISH-HEAD? NOPE. TIME TO BAIL.
YOW!
WAM
...WHAT?
SHOOM
CRASH
COWARD!
BOOM
KA
SHOWS WHAT YOU KNOW.

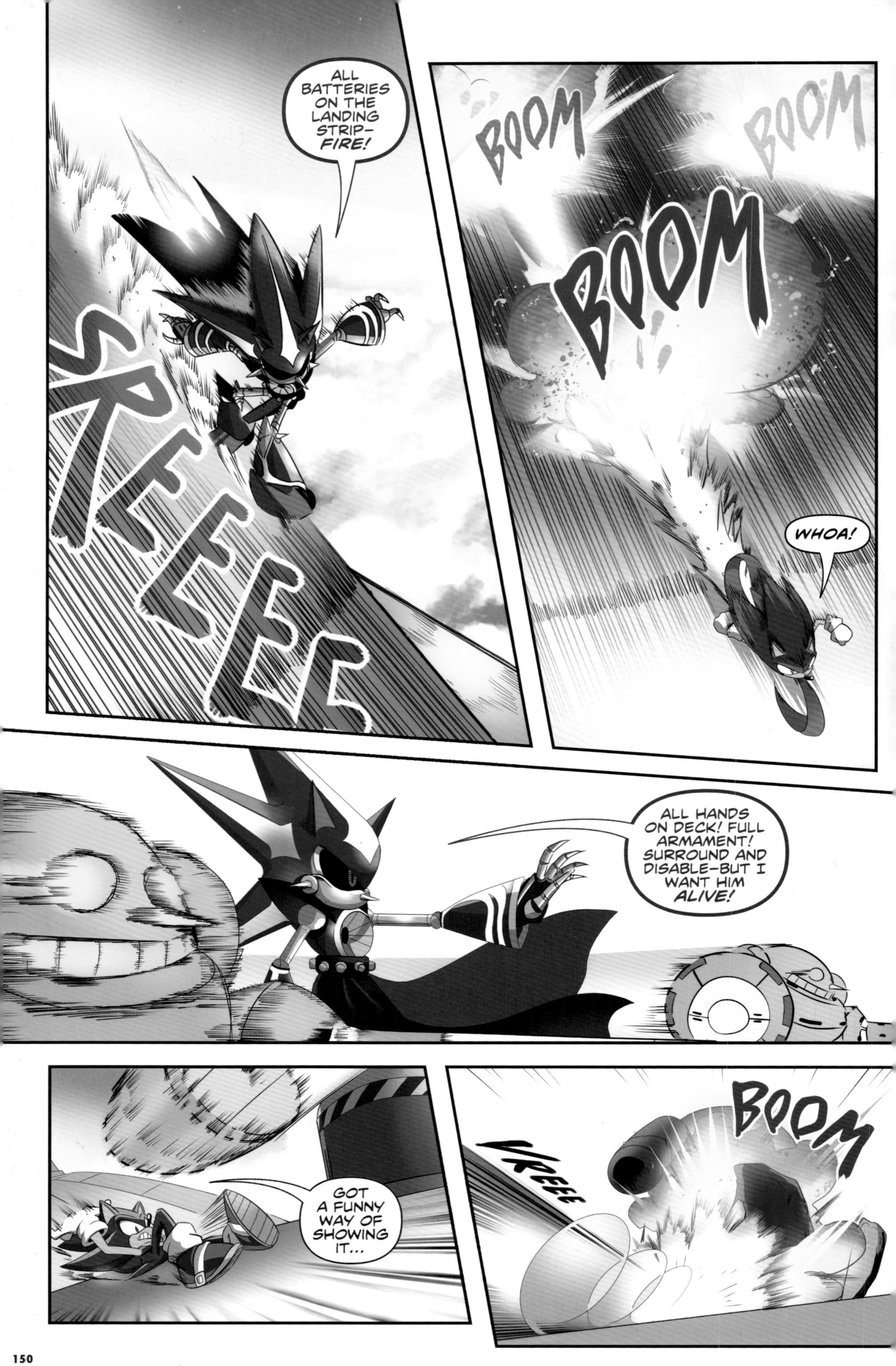

ALL BATTERIES ON THE LANDING STRIP– *FIRE!*
BOOM
BOOM
BOOM
WHOA!
ALL HANDS ON DECK! FULL ARMAMENT! SURROUND AND DISABLE–BUT I WANT HIM *ALIVE!*
GOT A FUNNY WAY OF SHOWING IT...
VREEE
BOOM

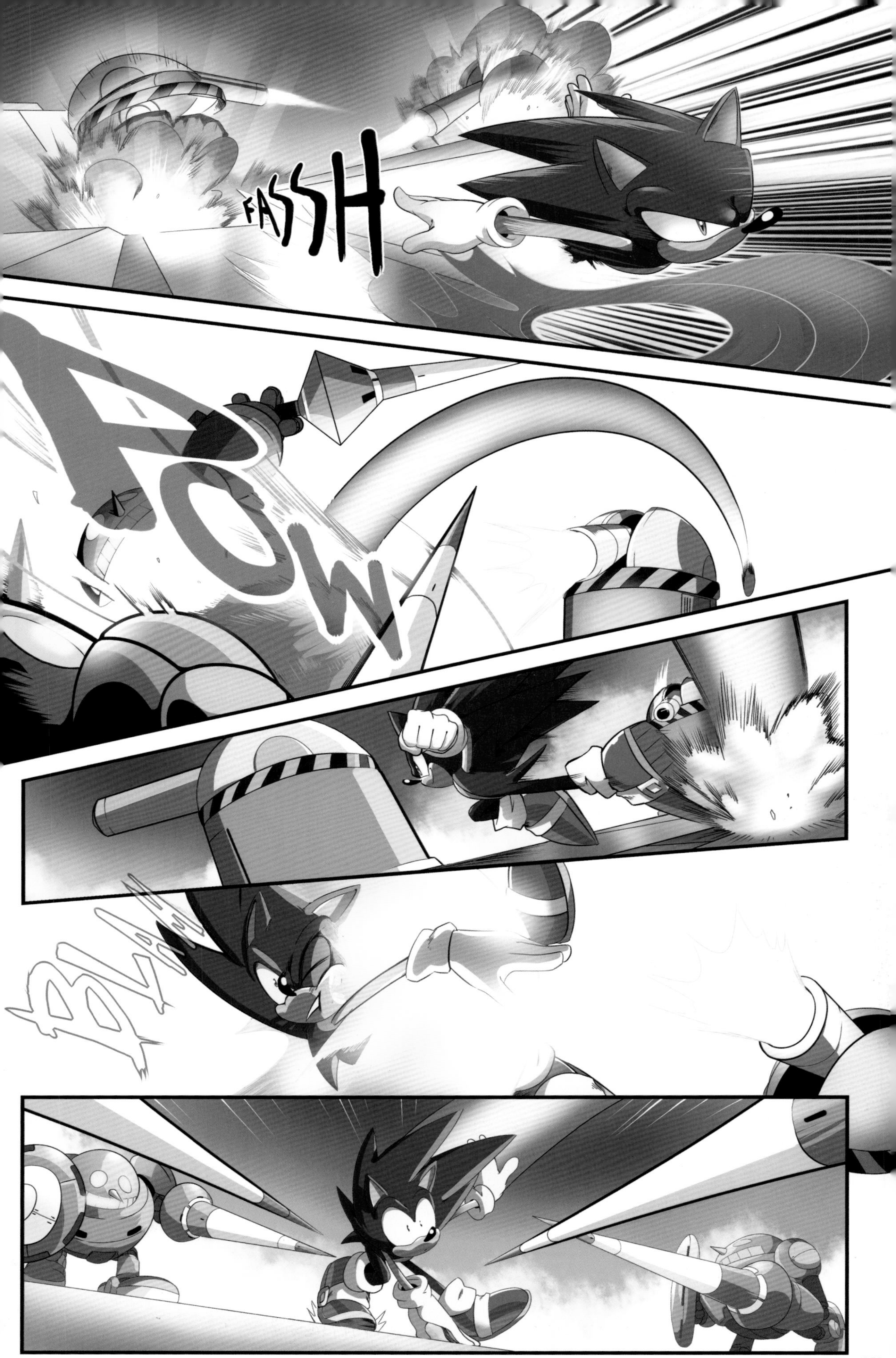
FASSH
POW
BLAM

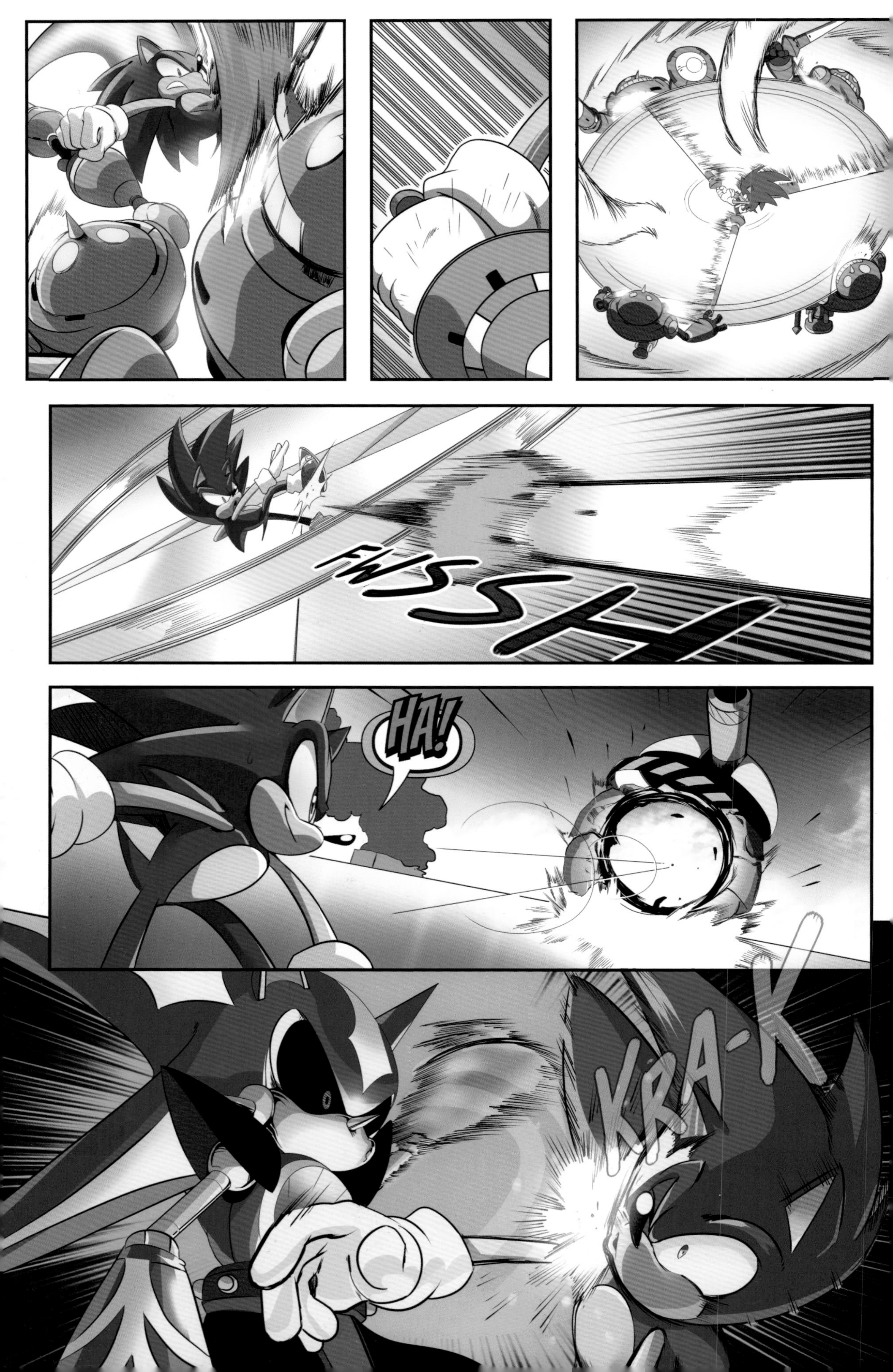
FWSSH
HA!
KRA-K

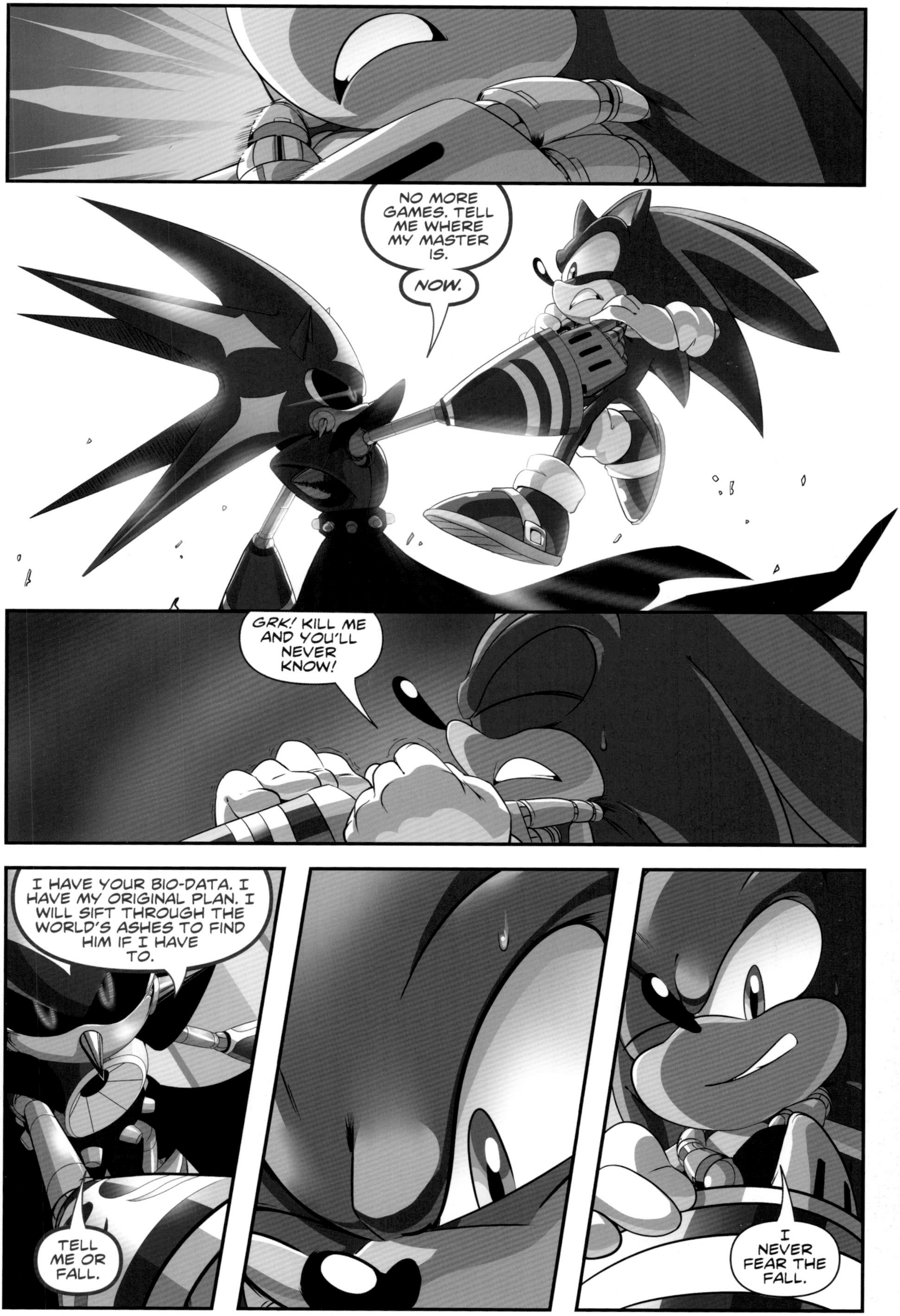
NO MORE GAMES. TELL ME WHERE MY MASTER IS.
NOW.
GRK! KILL ME AND YOU'LL NEVER KNOW!
I HAVE YOUR BIO-DATA. I HAVE MY ORIGINAL PLAN. I WILL SIFT THROUGH THE WORLD'S ASHES TO FIND HIM IF I HAVE TO.
TELL ME OR FALL.
I NEVER FEAR THE FALL.

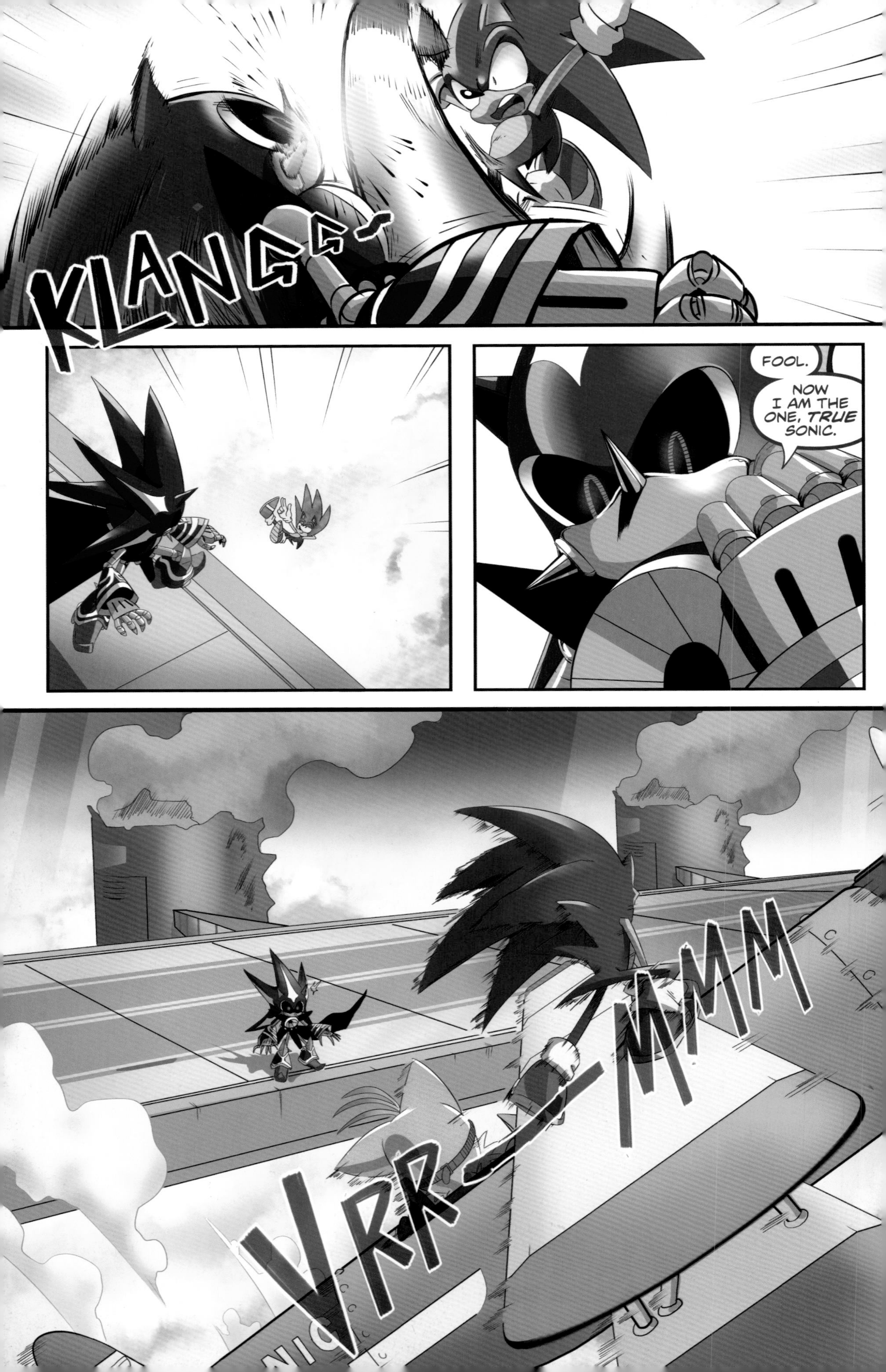
KLANGG-
FOOL.
NOW I AM THE ONE, TRUE SONIC.
VRR--MMMM

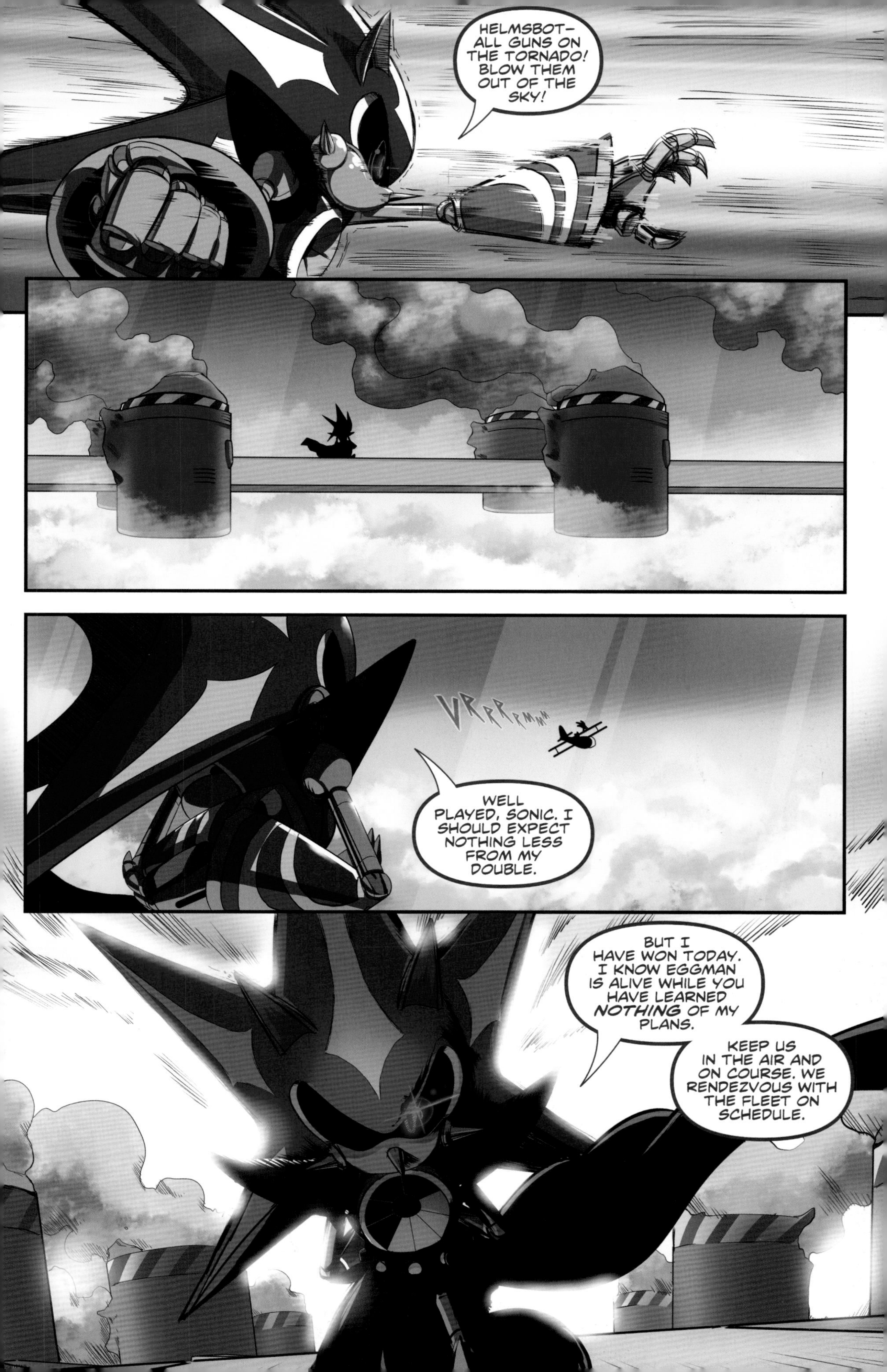
HELMSBOT— ALL GUNS ON THE TORNADO! BLOW THEM OUT OF THE SKY!
VRRRRMMM
WELL PLAYED, SONIC. I SHOULD EXPECT NOTHING LESS FROM MY DOUBLE.
BUT I HAVE WON TODAY. I KNOW EGGMAN IS ALIVE WHILE YOU HAVE LEARNED NOTHING OF MY PLANS.
KEEP US IN THE AIR AND ON COURSE. WE RENDEZVOUS WITH THE FLEET ON SCHEDULE.

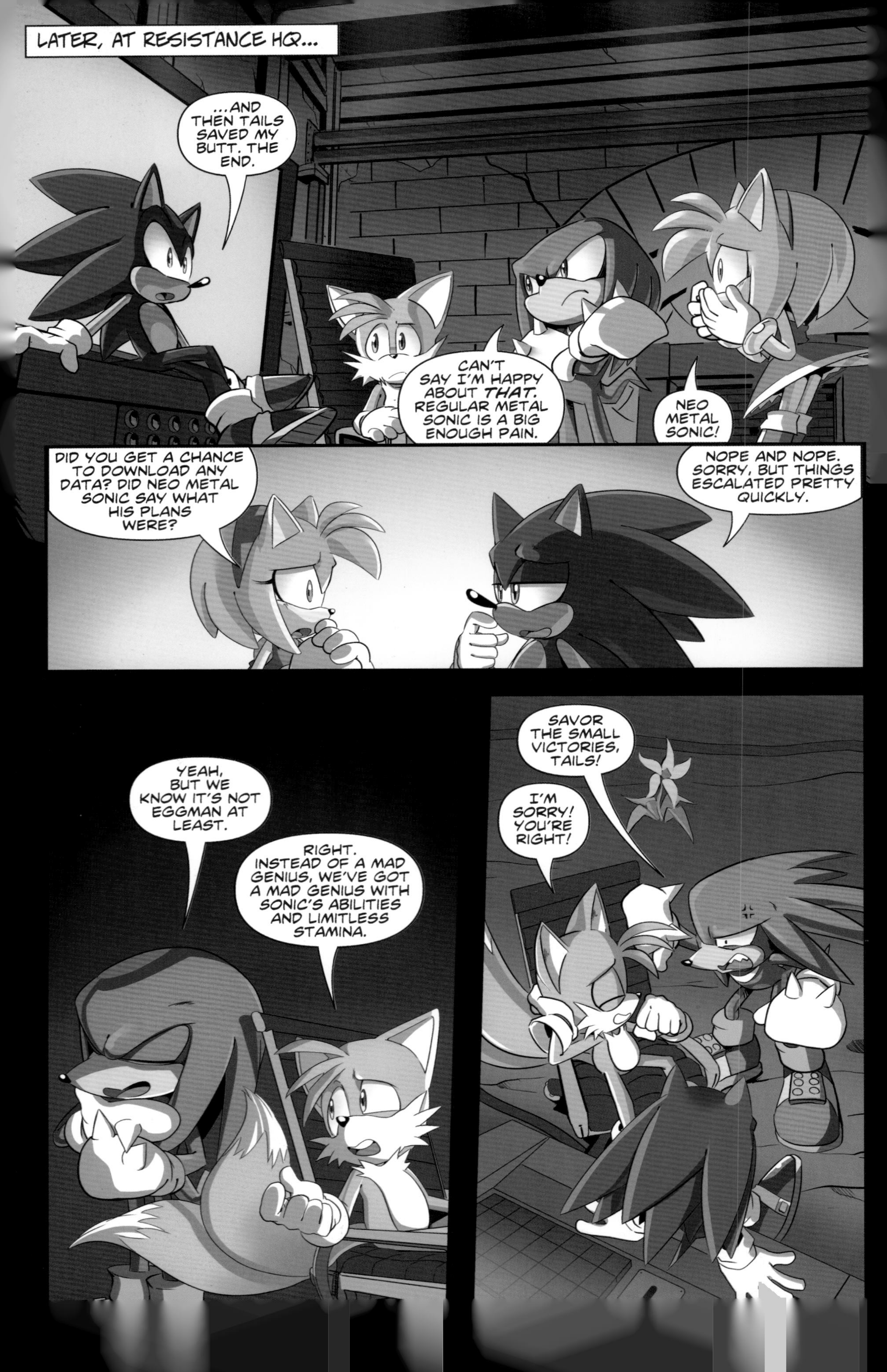
LATER, AT RESISTANCE HQ...
...AND THEN TAILS SAVED MY BUTT. THE END.
CAN'T SAY I'M HAPPY ABOUT THAT. REGULAR METAL SONIC IS A BIG ENOUGH PAIN.
NEO METAL SONIC!
DID YOU GET A CHANCE TO DOWNLOAD ANY DATA? DID NEO METAL SONIC SAY WHAT HIS PLANS WERE?
NOPE AND NOPE. SORRY, BUT THINGS ESCALATED PRETTY QUICKLY.
YEAH, BUT WE KNOW IT'S NOT EGGMAN AT LEAST.
RIGHT. INSTEAD OF A MAD GENIUS, WE'VE GOT A MAD GENIUS WITH SONIC'S ABILITIES AND LIMITLESS STAMINA.
SAVOR THE SMALL VICTORIES, TAILS!
I'M SORRY! YOU'RE RIGHT!

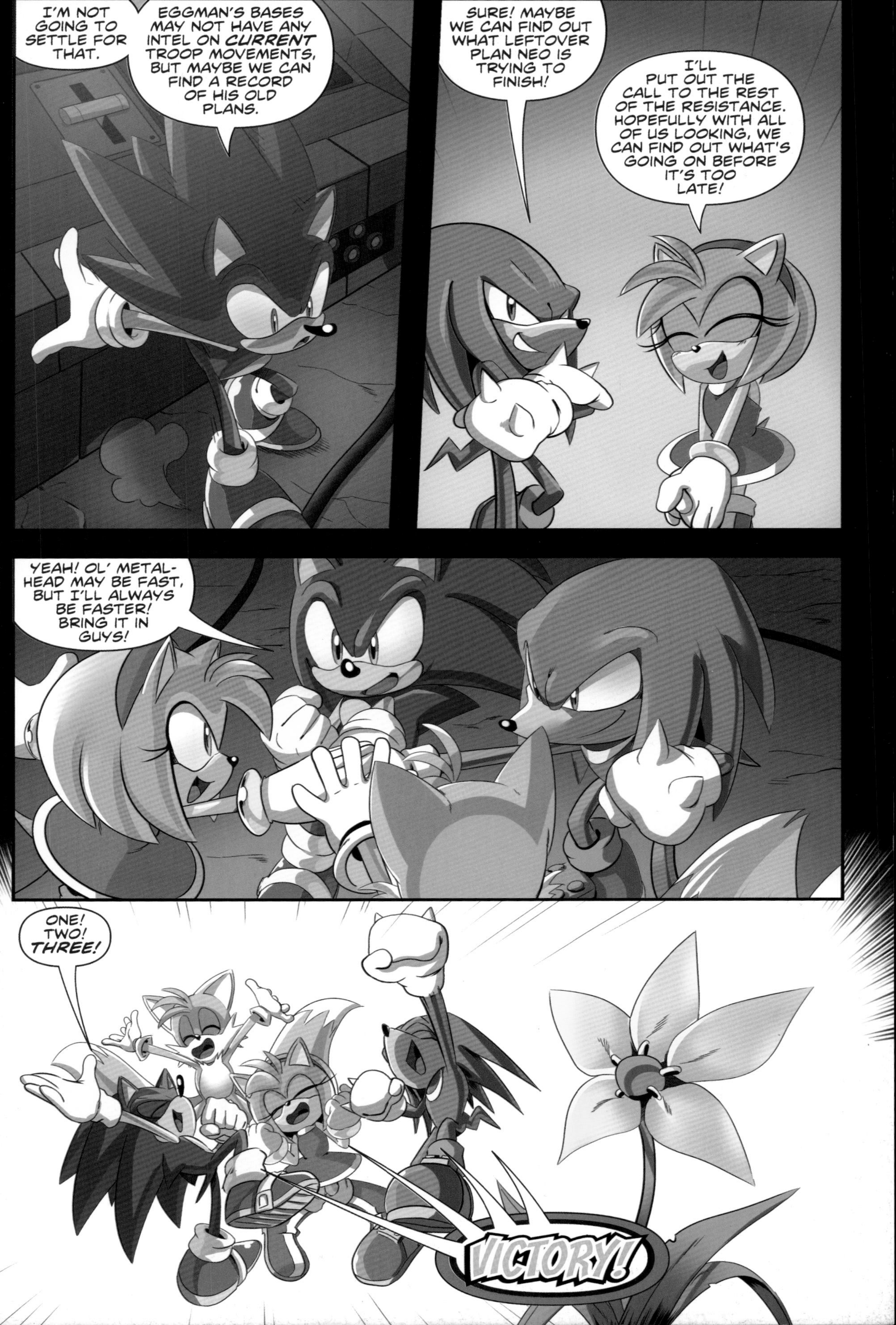
I'M NOT GOING TO SETTLE FOR THAT.
EGGMAN'S BASES MAY NOT HAVE ANY INTEL ON *CURRENT* TROOP MOVEMENTS, BUT MAYBE WE CAN FIND A RECORD OF HIS OLD PLANS.
SURE! MAYBE WE CAN FIND OUT WHAT LEFTOVER PLAN NEO IS TRYING TO FINISH!
I'LL PUT OUT THE CALL TO THE REST OF THE RESISTANCE. HOPEFULLY WITH ALL OF US LOOKING, WE CAN FIND OUT WHAT'S GOING ON BEFORE IT'S TOO LATE!
YEAH! OL' METAL-HEAD MAY BE FAST, BUT I'LL ALWAYS BE FASTER! BRING IT IN GUYS!
ONE! TWO! ***THREE!***
VICTORY!

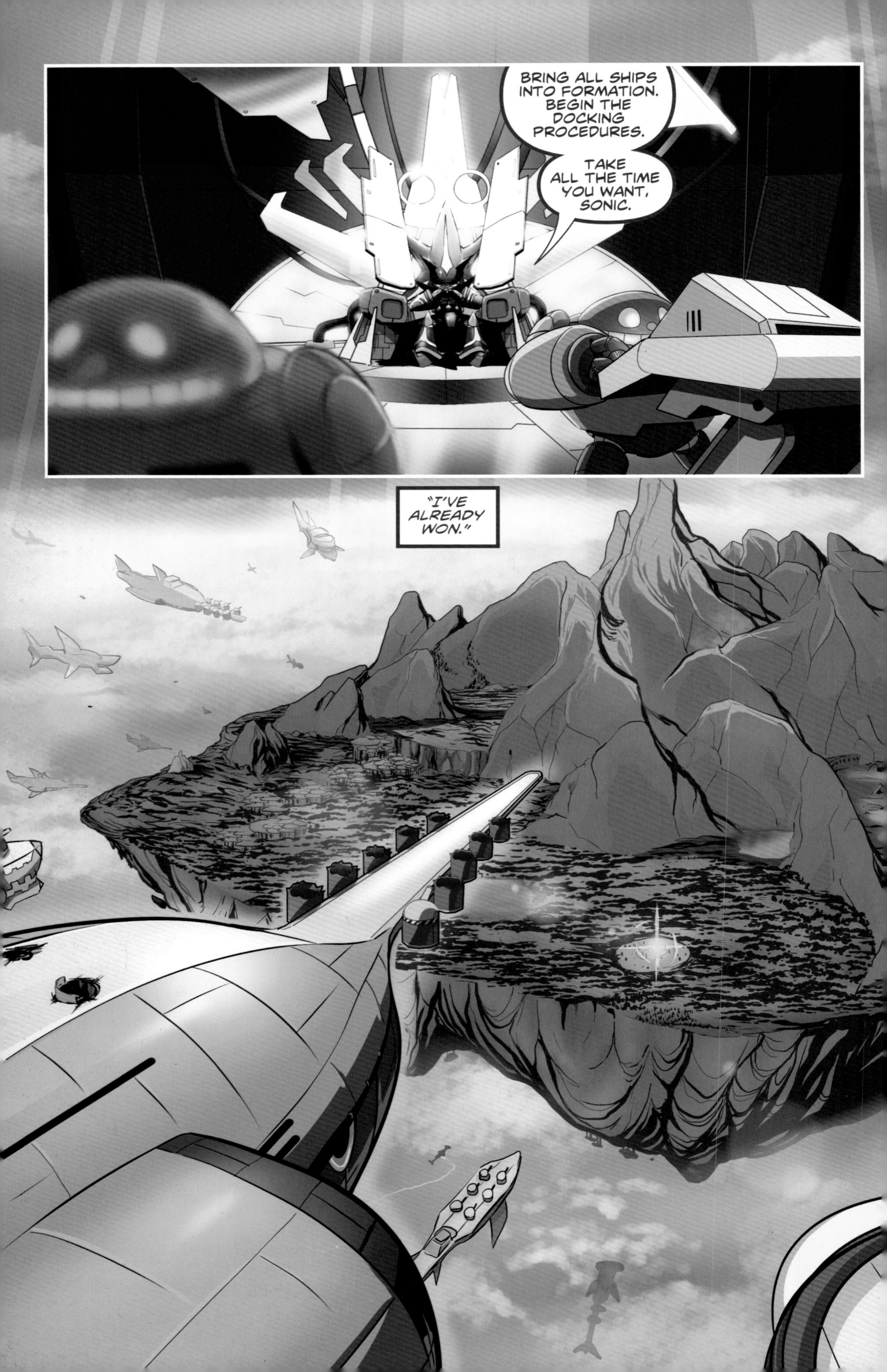
BRING ALL SHIPS INTO FORMATION. BEGIN THE DOCKING PROCEDURES.
TAKE ALL THE TIME YOU WANT, SONIC.
"I'VE ALREADY WON."

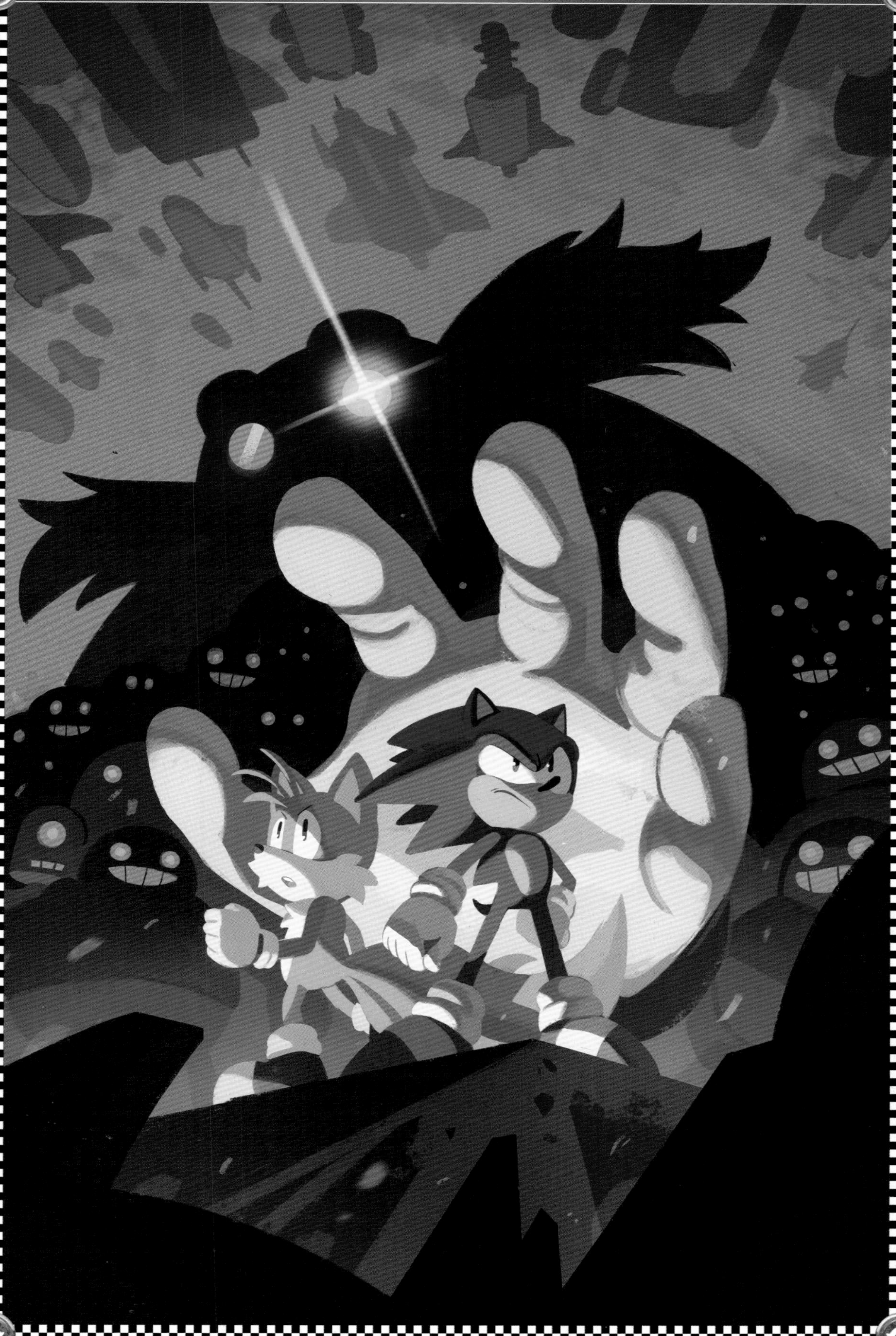

ART BY EVAN STANLEY COLORS BY MATT HERMS

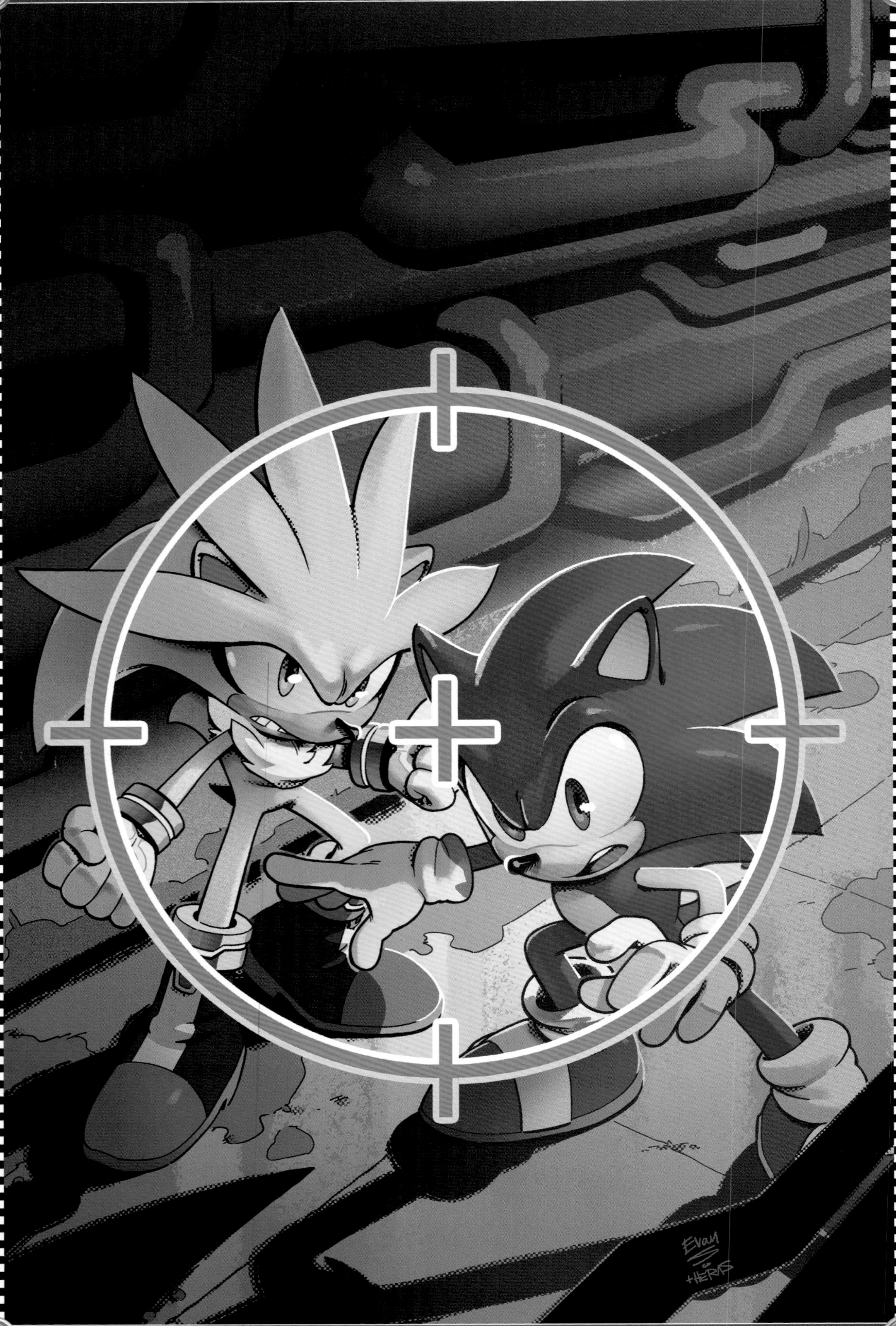

SONIC THE HEDGEHOG #8

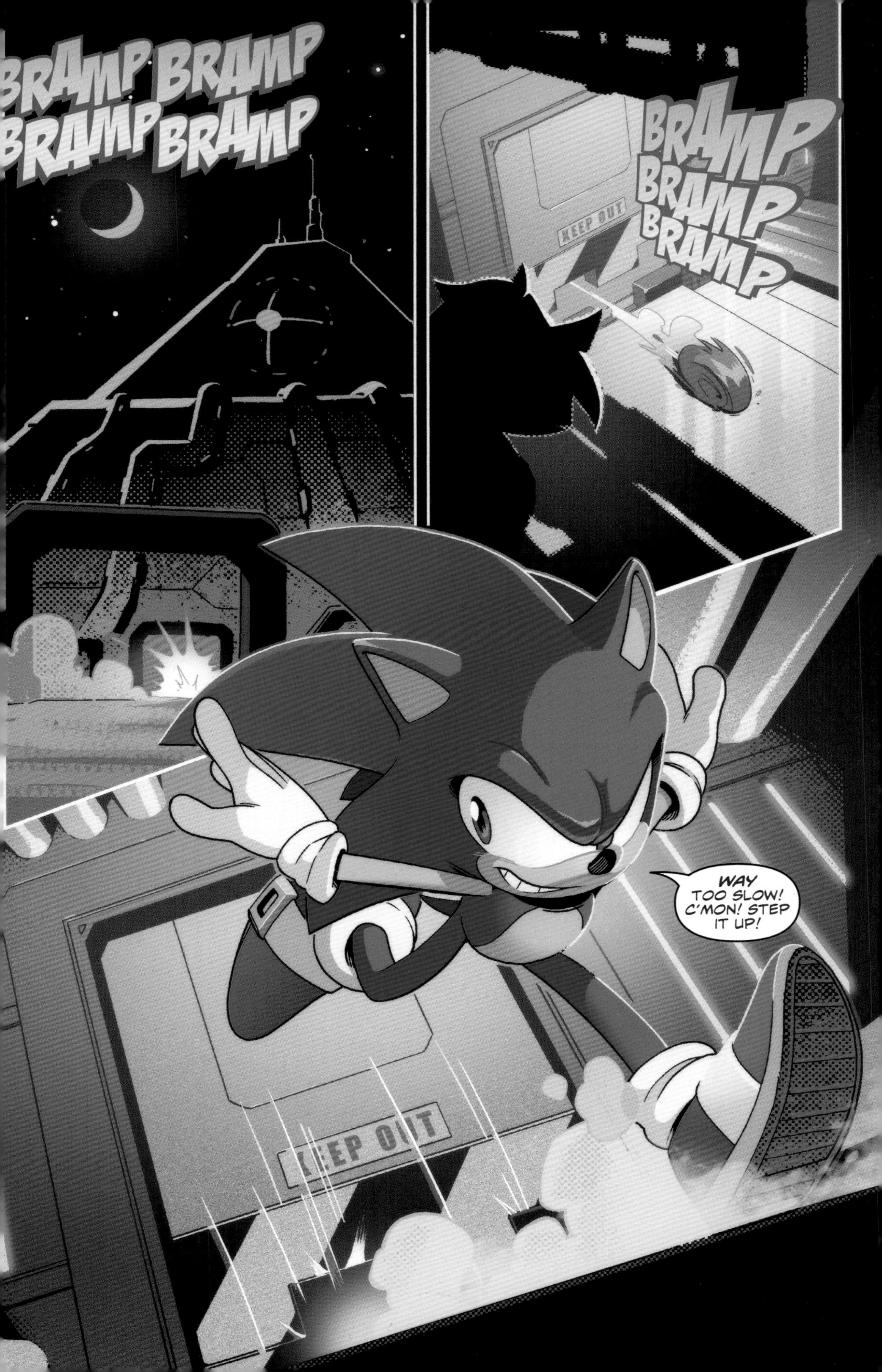
BRAMP BRAMP
BRAMP BRAMP
BRAMP
BRAMP
BRAMP
KEEP OUT
WAY TOO SLOW! C'MON! STEP IT UP!
KEEP OUT

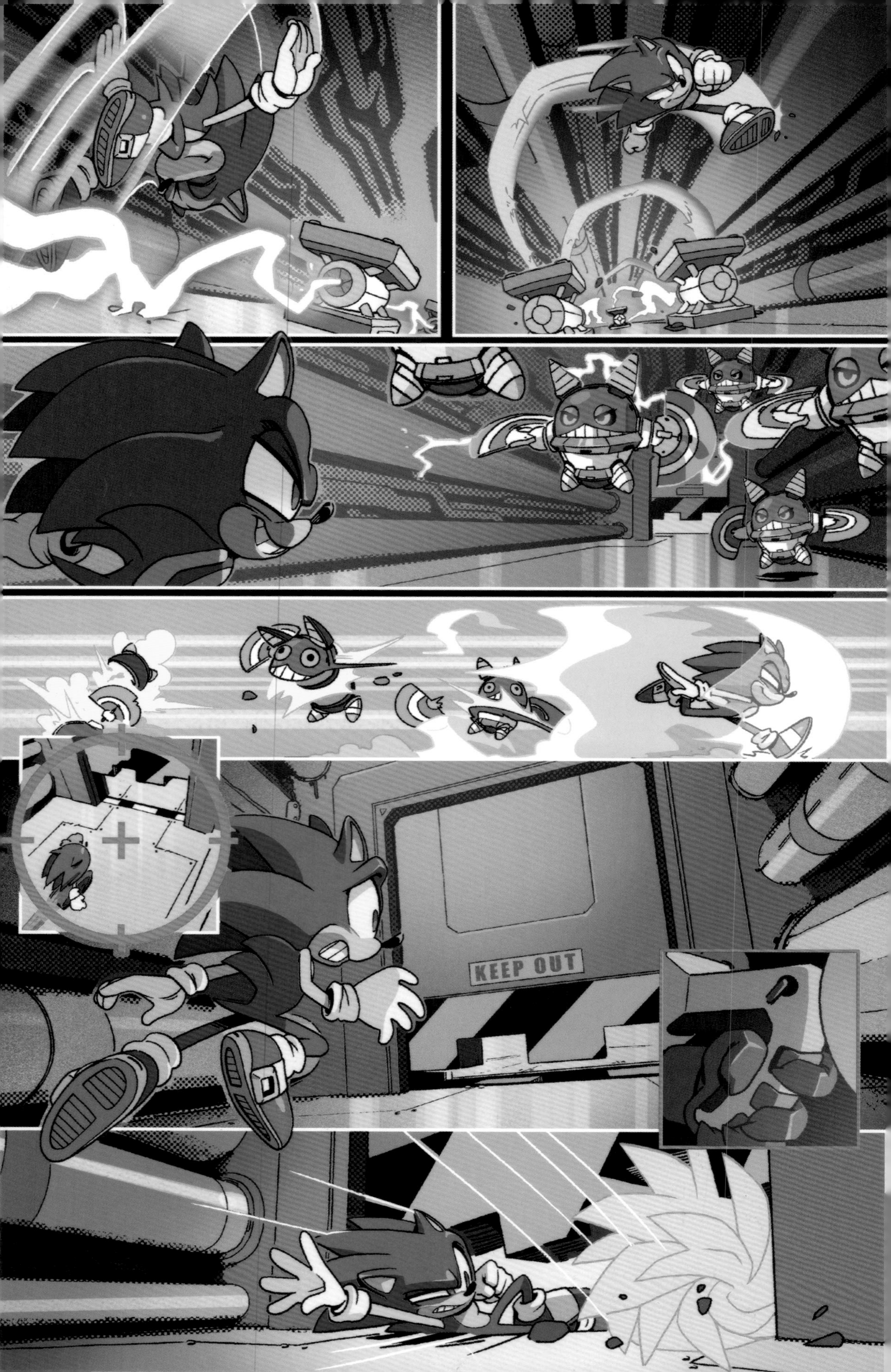
KEEP OUT

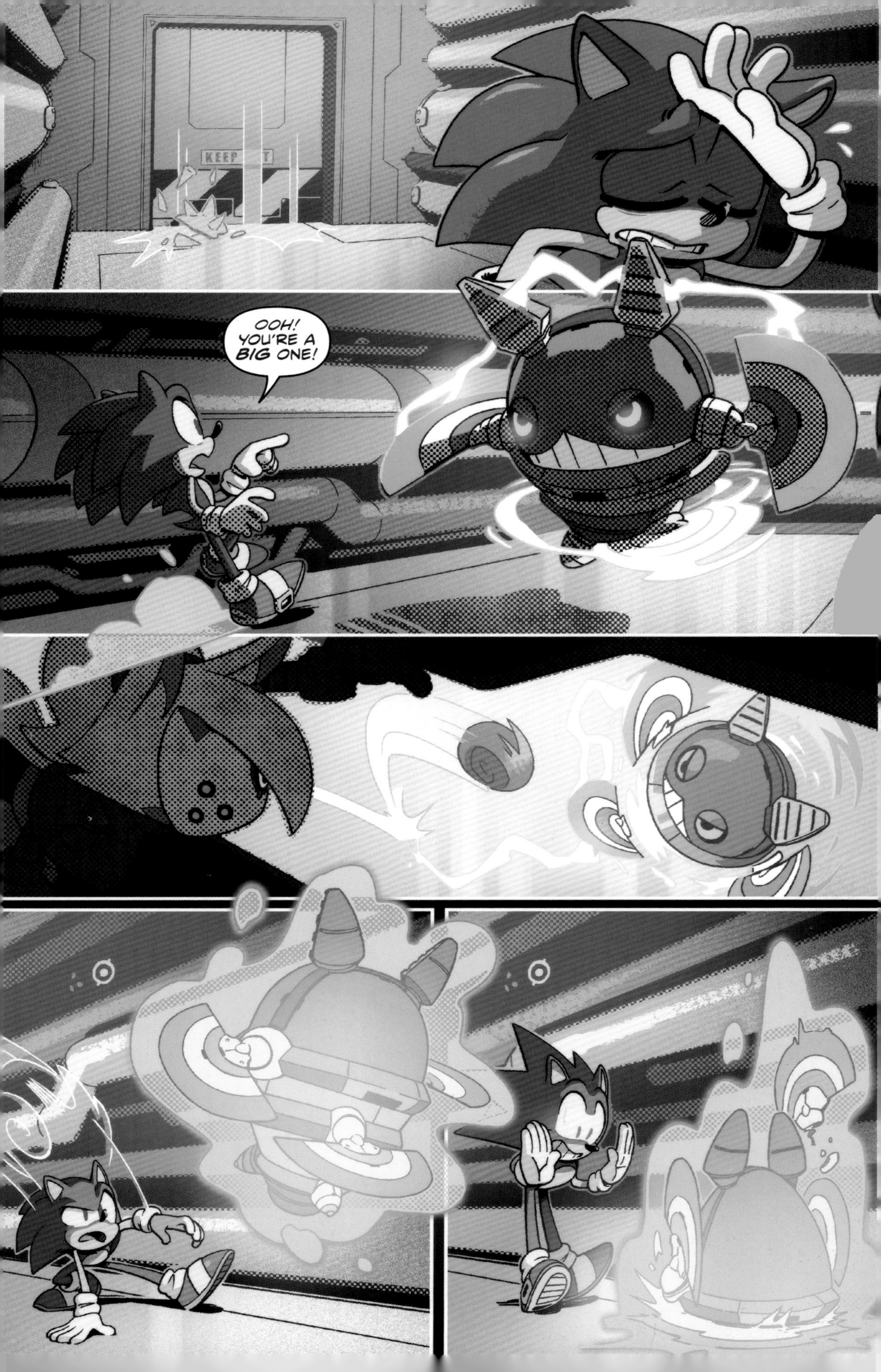
KEEP
OOH! YOU'RE A BIG ONE!

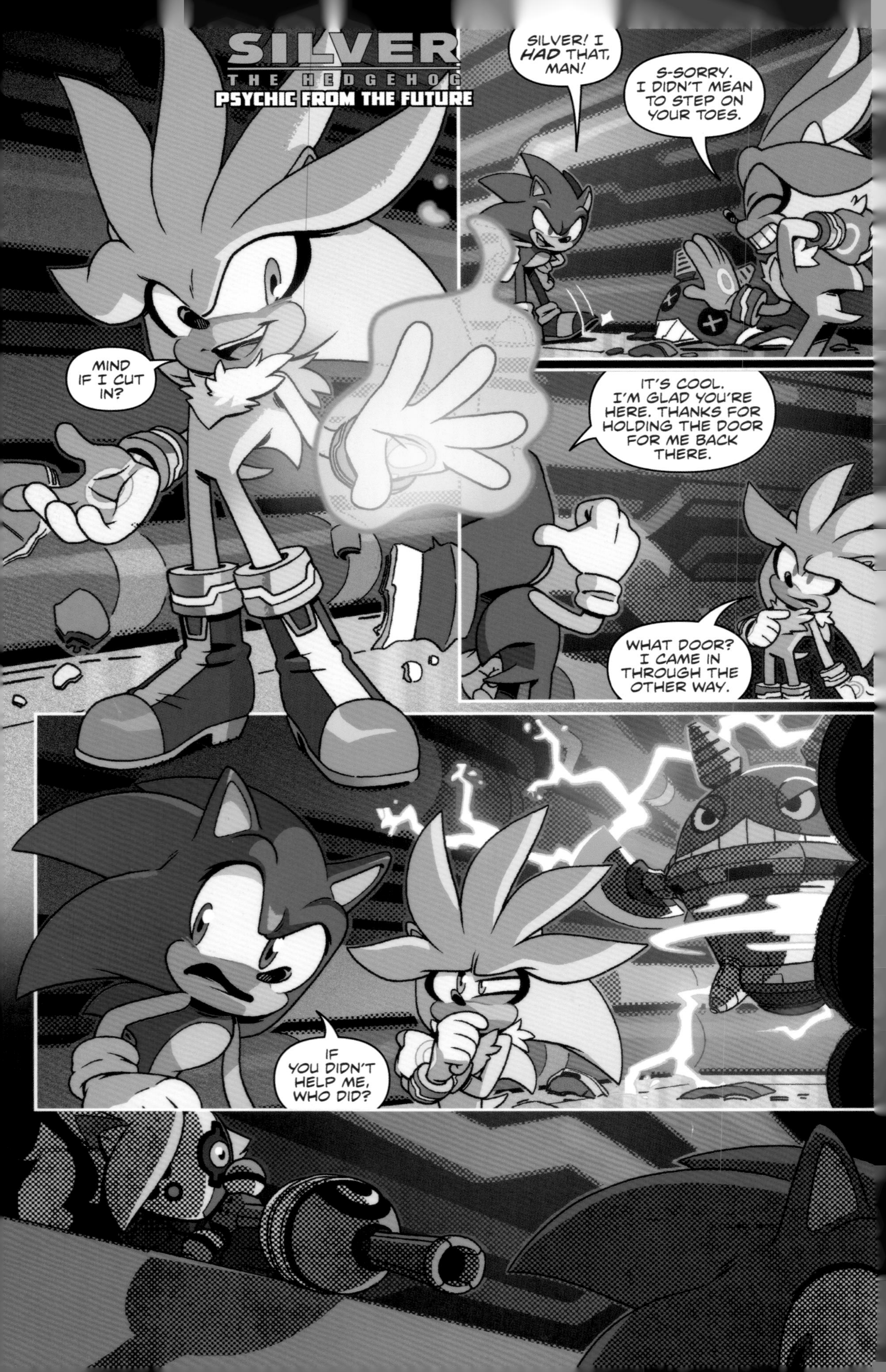
SILVER THE HEDGEHOG
PSYCHIC FROM THE FUTURE
MIND IF I CUT IN?
SILVER! I HAD THAT, MAN!
S-SORRY. I DIDN'T MEAN TO STEP ON YOUR TOES.
IT'S COOL. I'M GLAD YOU'RE HERE. THANKS FOR HOLDING THE DOOR FOR ME BACK THERE.
WHAT DOOR? I CAME IN THROUGH THE OTHER WAY.
IF YOU DIDN'T HELP ME, WHO DID?

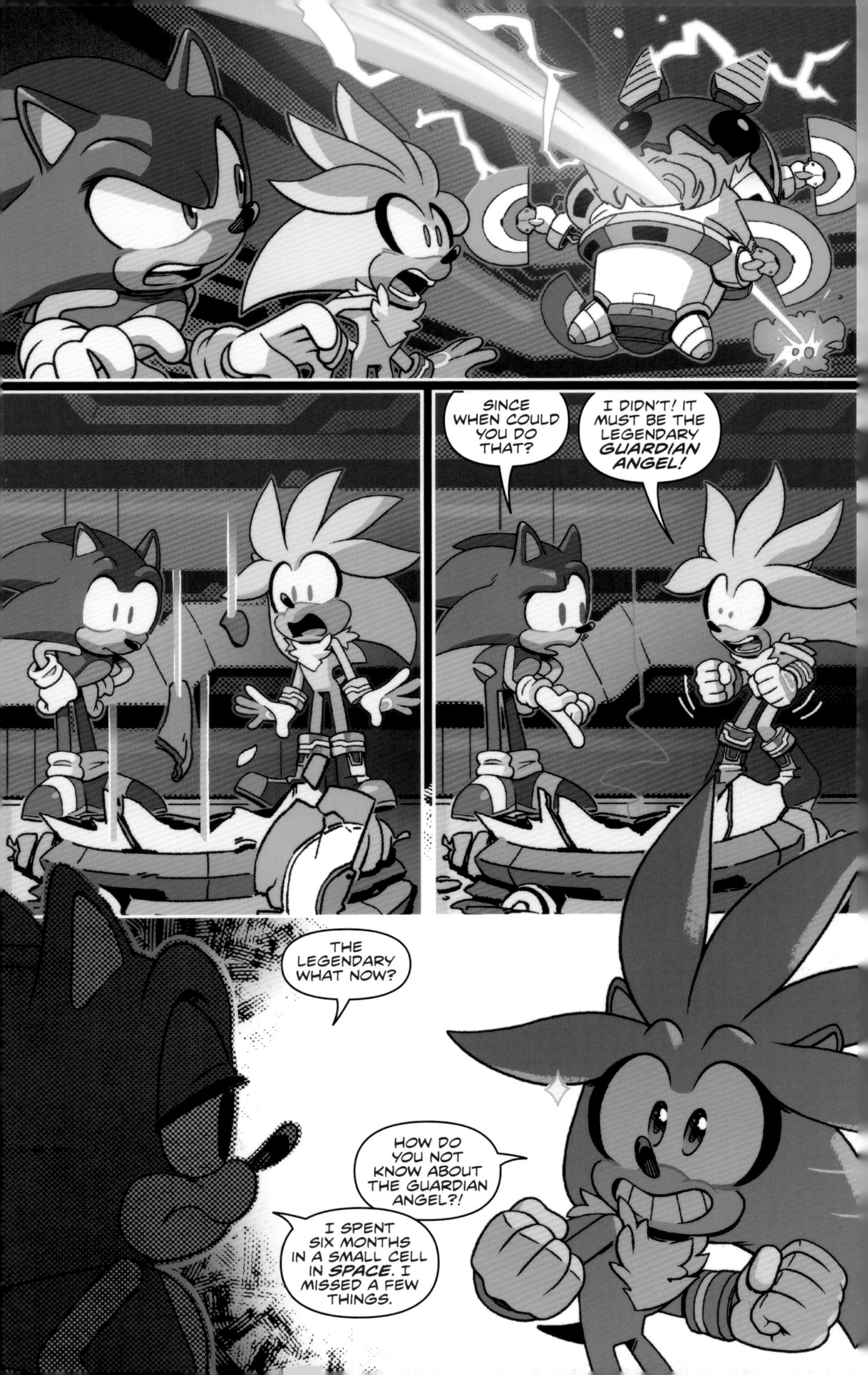
SINCE WHEN COULD YOU DO THAT?
I DIDN'T! IT MUST BE THE LEGENDARY GUARDIAN ANGEL!
THE LEGENDARY WHAT NOW?
HOW DO YOU NOT KNOW ABOUT THE GUARDIAN ANGEL?!
I SPENT SIX MONTHS IN A SMALL CELL IN SPACE. I MISSED A FEW THINGS.

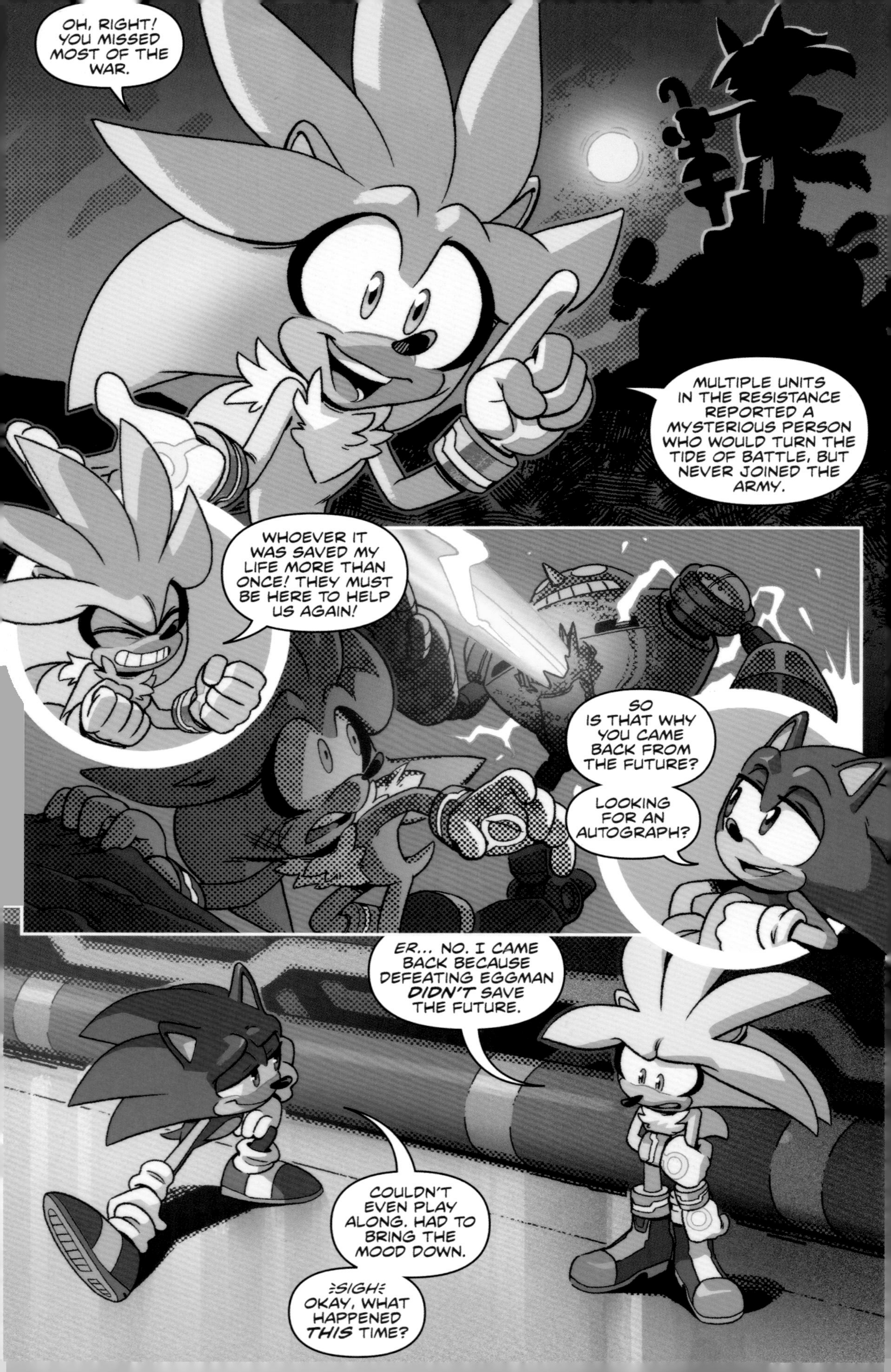
OH, RIGHT! YOU MISSED MOST OF THE WAR.
MULTIPLE UNITS IN THE RESISTANCE REPORTED A MYSTERIOUS PERSON WHO WOULD TURN THE TIDE OF BATTLE, BUT NEVER JOINED THE ARMY.
WHOEVER IT WAS SAVED MY LIFE MORE THAN ONCE! THEY MUST BE HERE TO HELP US AGAIN!
SO IS THAT WHY YOU CAME BACK FROM THE FUTURE?
LOOKING FOR AN AUTOGRAPH?
ER... NO. I CAME BACK BECAUSE DEFEATING EGGMAN DIDN'T SAVE THE FUTURE.
COULDN'T EVEN PLAY ALONG. HAD TO BRING THE MOOD DOWN.
SIGH OKAY, WHAT HAPPENED THIS TIME?

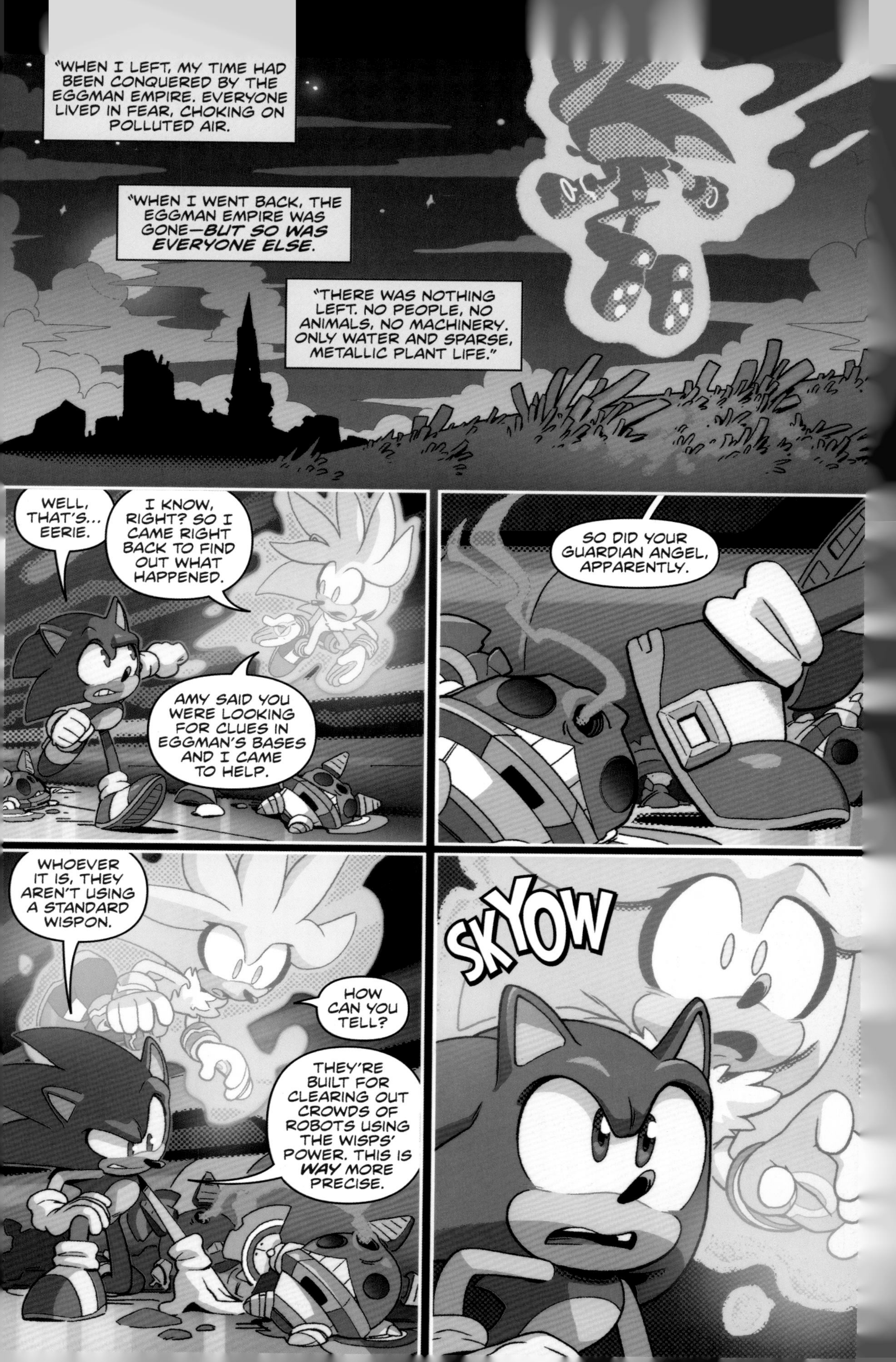

"WHEN I LEFT, MY TIME HAD BEEN CONQUERED BY THE EGGMAN EMPIRE. EVERYONE LIVED IN FEAR, CHOKING ON POLLUTED AIR.
"WHEN I WENT BACK, THE EGGMAN EMPIRE WAS GONE—*BUT SO WAS EVERYONE ELSE*.
"THERE WAS NOTHING LEFT. NO PEOPLE, NO ANIMALS, NO MACHINERY. ONLY WATER AND SPARSE, METALLIC PLANT LIFE."
WELL, THAT'S... EERIE.
I KNOW, RIGHT? SO I CAME RIGHT BACK TO FIND OUT WHAT HAPPENED.
AMY SAID YOU WERE LOOKING FOR CLUES IN EGGMAN'S BASES AND I CAME TO HELP.
SO DID YOUR GUARDIAN ANGEL, APPARENTLY.
WHOEVER IT IS, THEY AREN'T USING A STANDARD WISPON.
HOW CAN YOU TELL?
THEY'RE BUILT FOR CLEARING OUT CROWDS OF ROBOTS USING THE WISPS' POWER. THIS IS *WAY* MORE PRECISE.
SKYOW

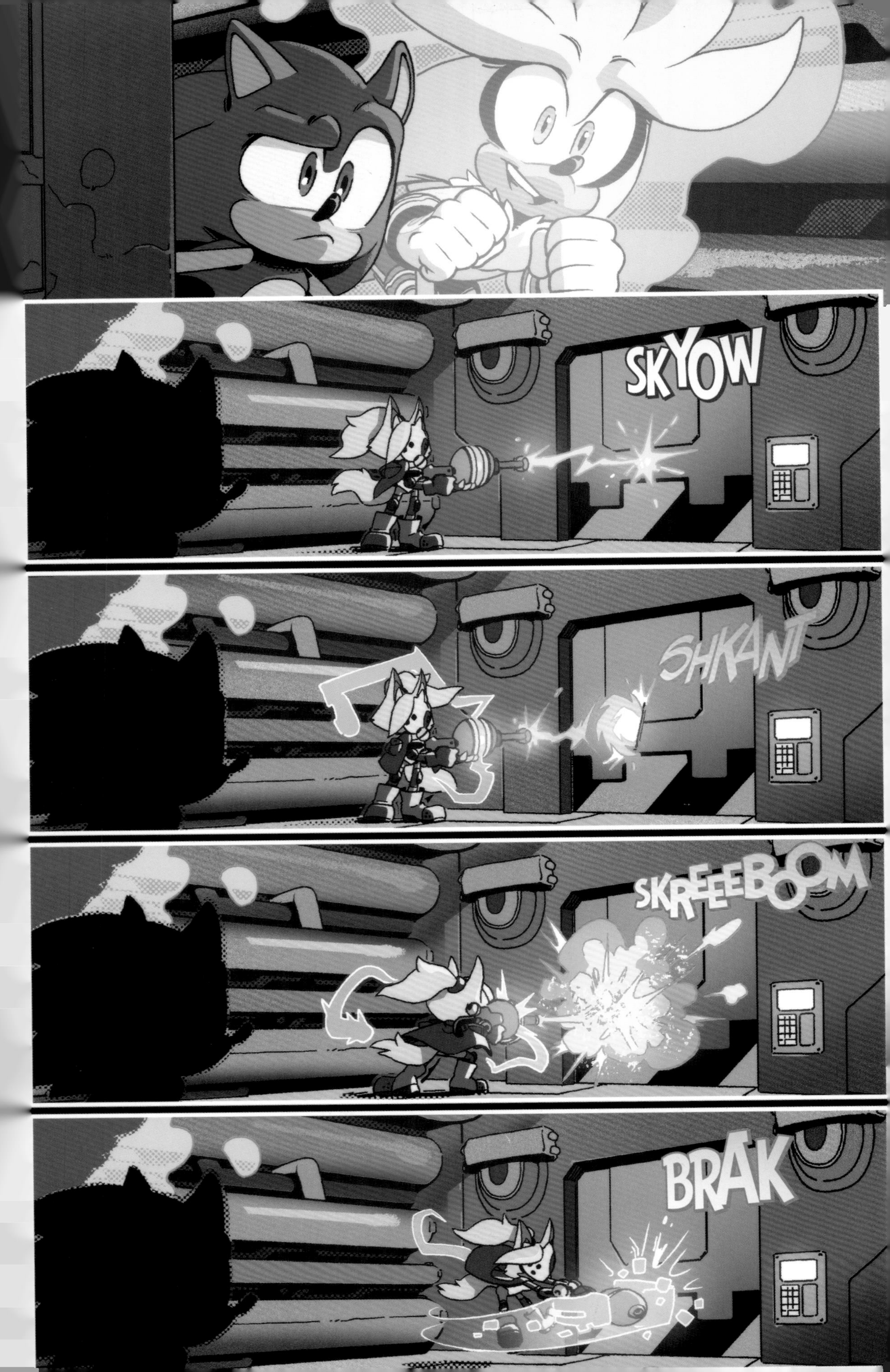
SKYOW
SHKANT
SKREEEBOOM
BRAK

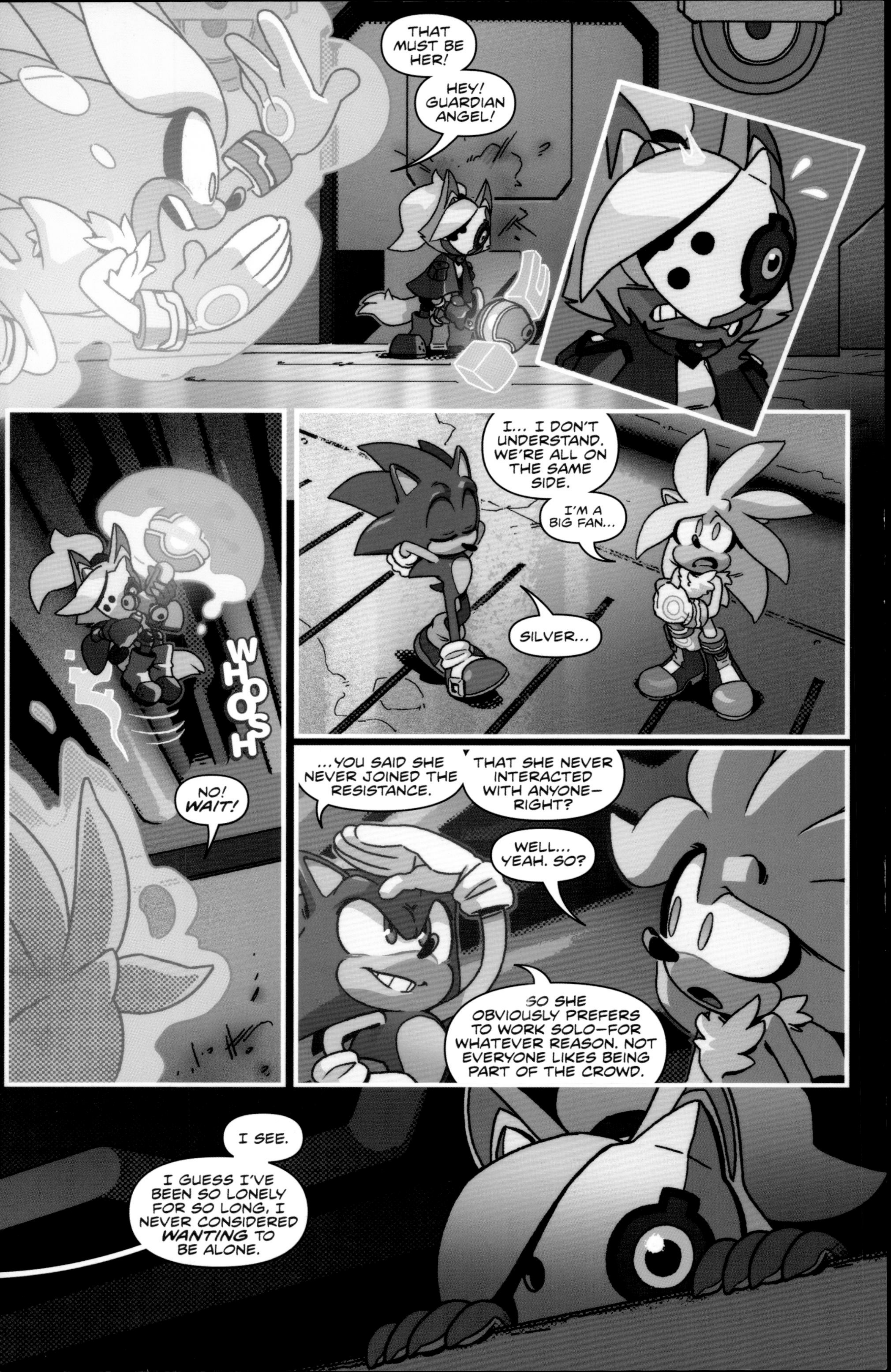

THAT MUST BE HER!
HEY! GUARDIAN ANGEL!
WHOOSH
NO! WAIT!
I... I DON'T UNDERSTAND. WE'RE ALL ON THE SAME SIDE.
I'M A BIG FAN...
SILVER...
...YOU SAID SHE NEVER JOINED THE RESISTANCE.
THAT SHE NEVER INTERACTED WITH ANYONE— RIGHT?
WELL... YEAH. SO?
SO SHE OBVIOUSLY PREFERS TO WORK SOLO—FOR WHATEVER REASON. NOT EVERYONE LIKES BEING PART OF THE CROWD.
I SEE.
I GUESS I'VE BEEN SO LONELY FOR SO LONG, I NEVER CONSIDERED *WANTING* TO BE ALONE.

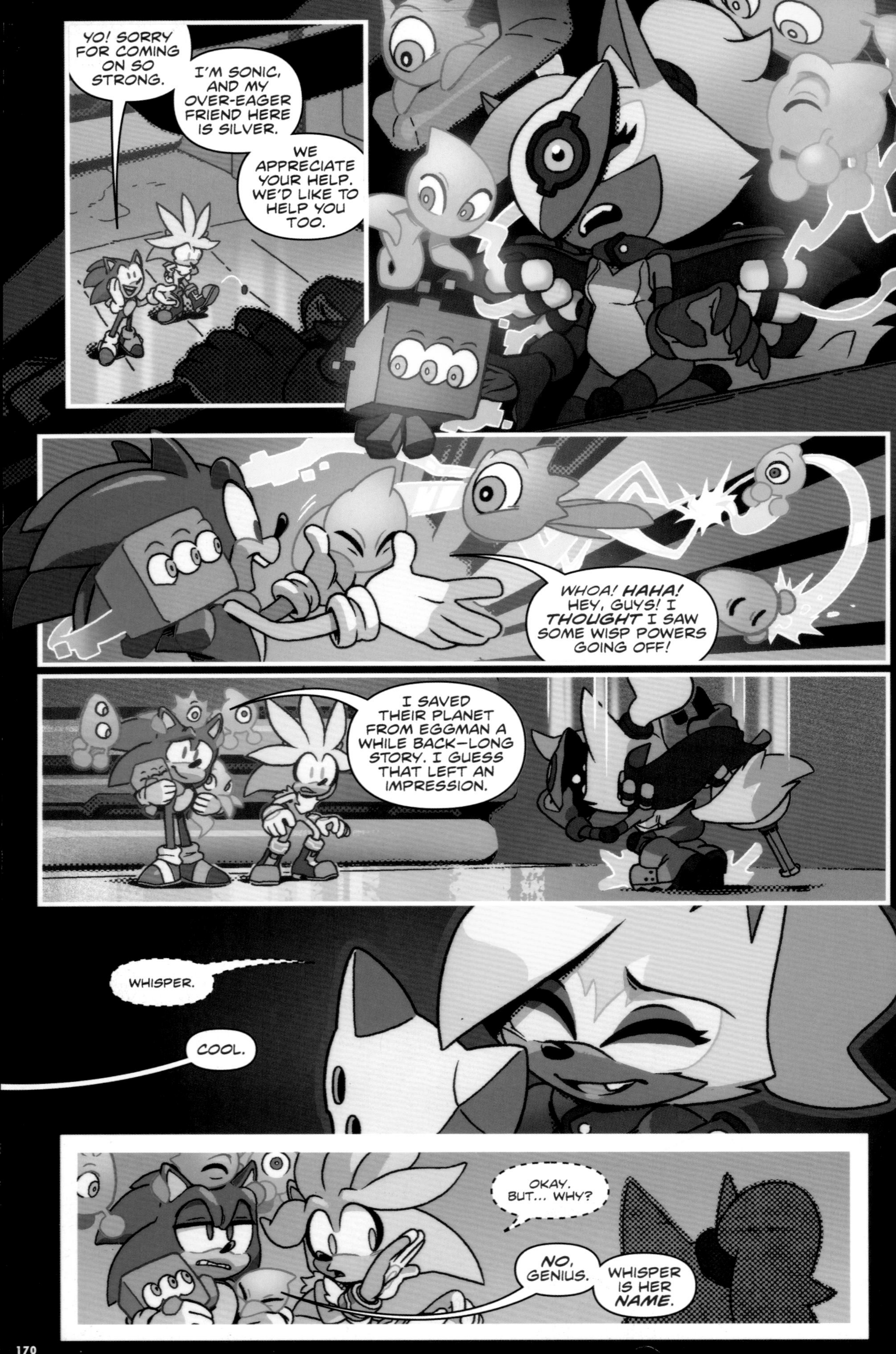

YO! SORRY FOR COMING ON SO STRONG.
I'M SONIC, AND MY OVER-EAGER FRIEND HERE IS SILVER.
WE APPRECIATE YOUR HELP. WE'D LIKE TO HELP YOU TOO.
WHOA! HAHA! HEY, GUYS! I THOUGHT I SAW SOME WISP POWERS GOING OFF!
I SAVED THEIR PLANET FROM EGGMAN A WHILE BACK—LONG STORY. I GUESS THAT LEFT AN IMPRESSION.
WHISPER.
COOL.
OKAY. BUT... WHY?
NO, GENIUS.
WHISPER IS HER NAME.

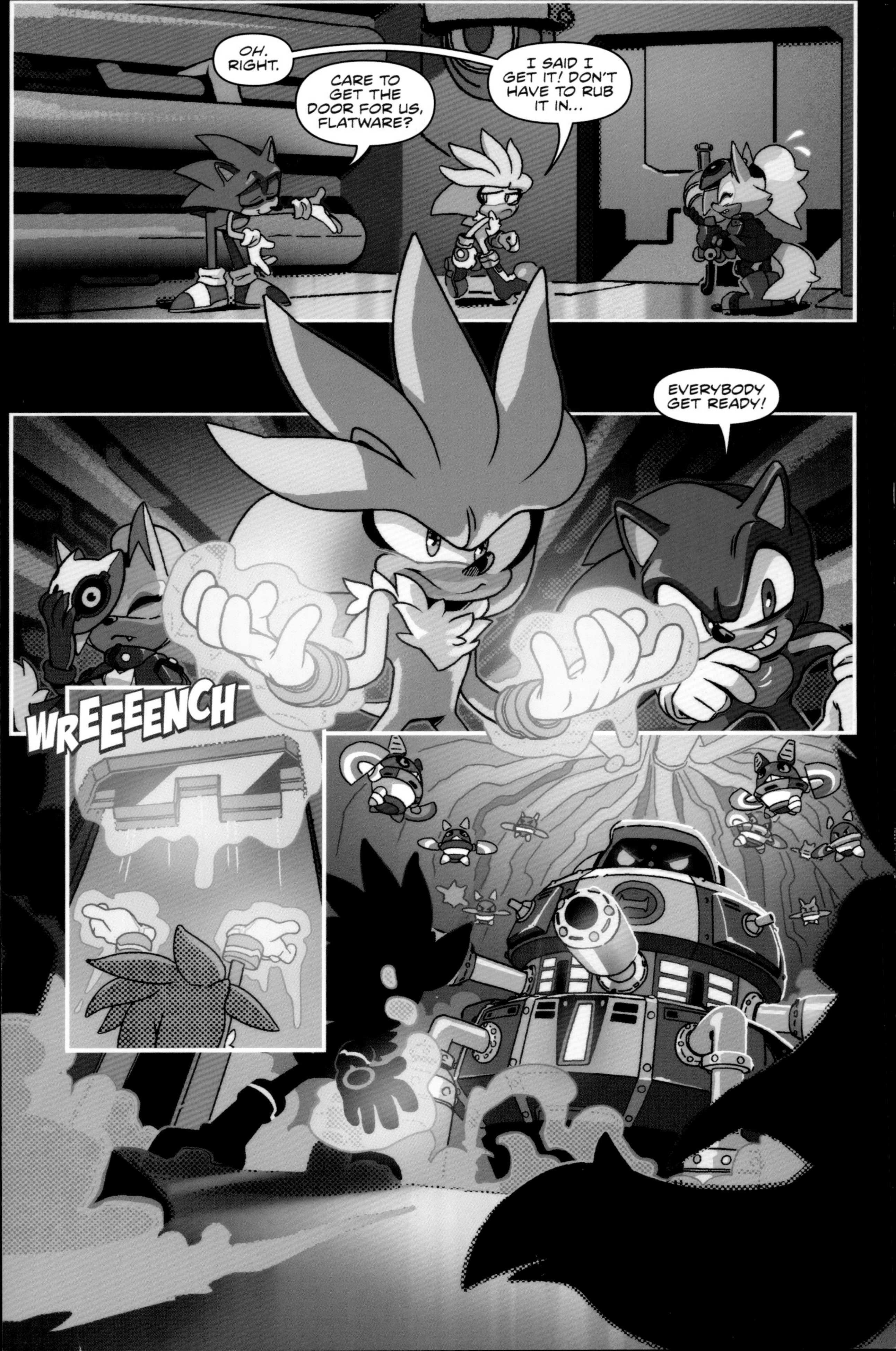
CARE TO GET THE DOOR FOR US, FLATWARE?
I SAID I GET IT! DON'T HAVE TO RUB IT IN...
OH. RIGHT.
EVERYBODY GET READY!
WREEEENCH

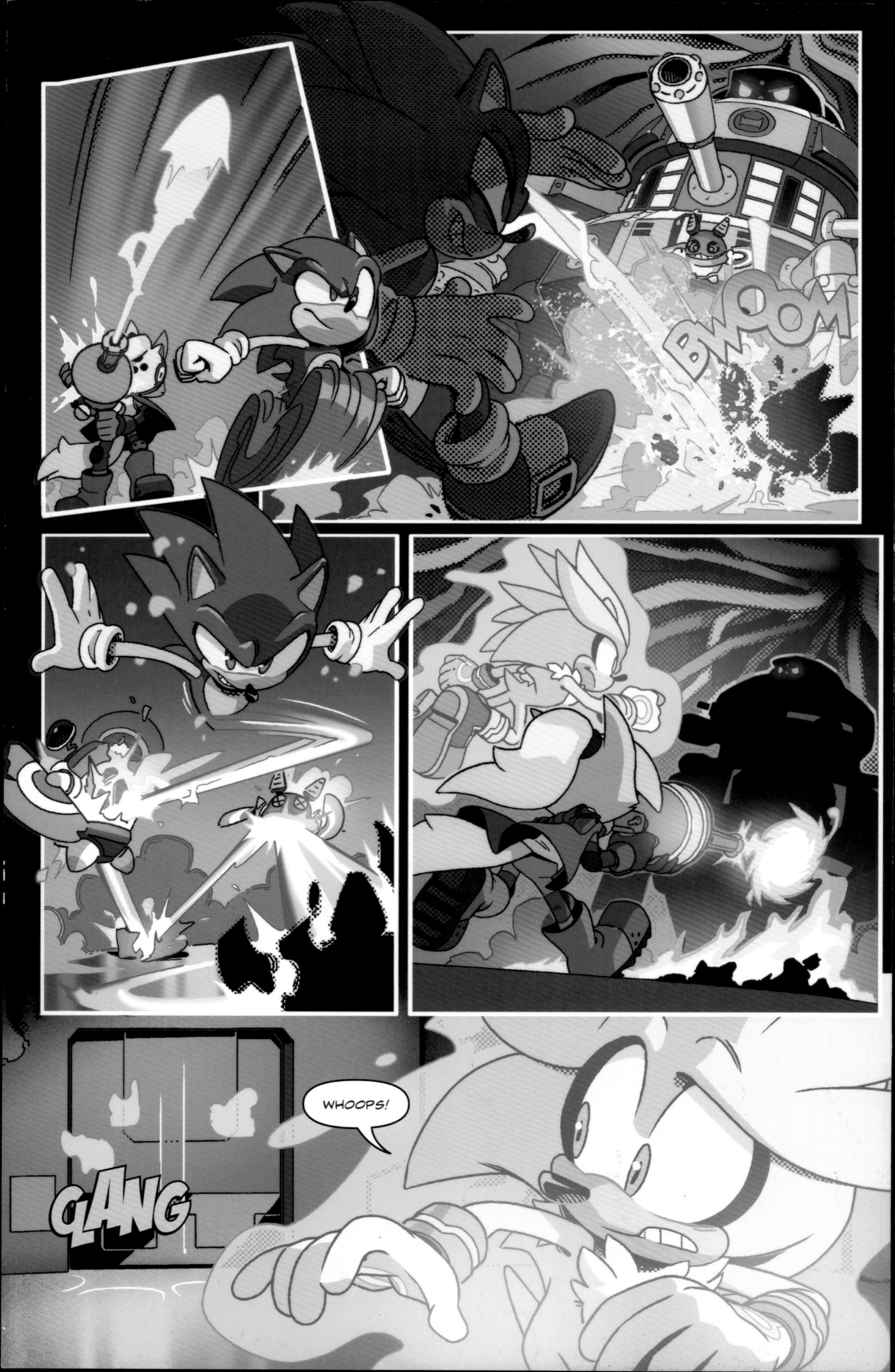
BWOOM
WHOOPS!
CLANG

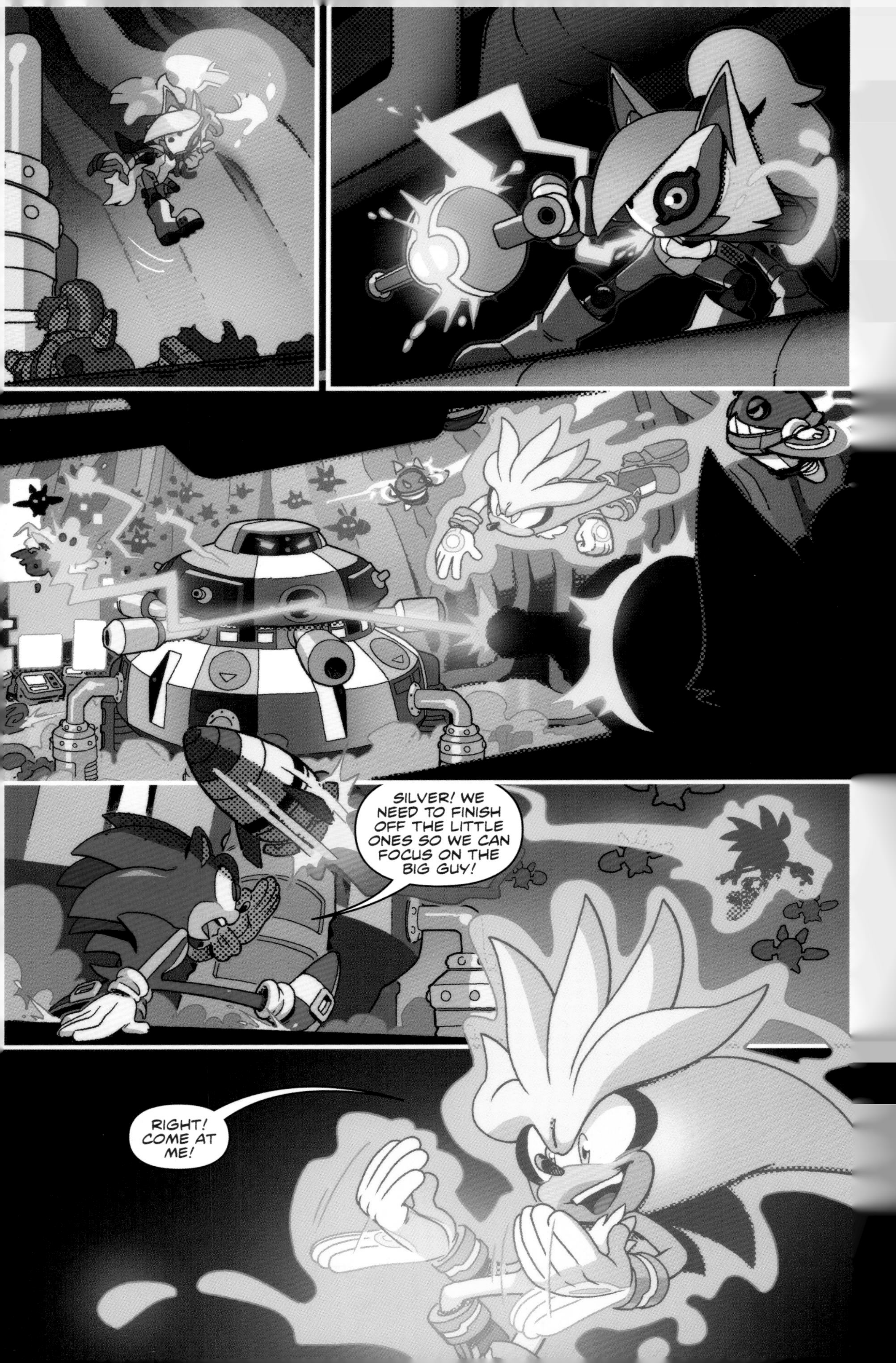
SILVER! WE NEED TO FINISH OFF THE LITTLE ONES SO WE CAN FOCUS ON THE BIG GUY!
RIGHT! COME AT ME!

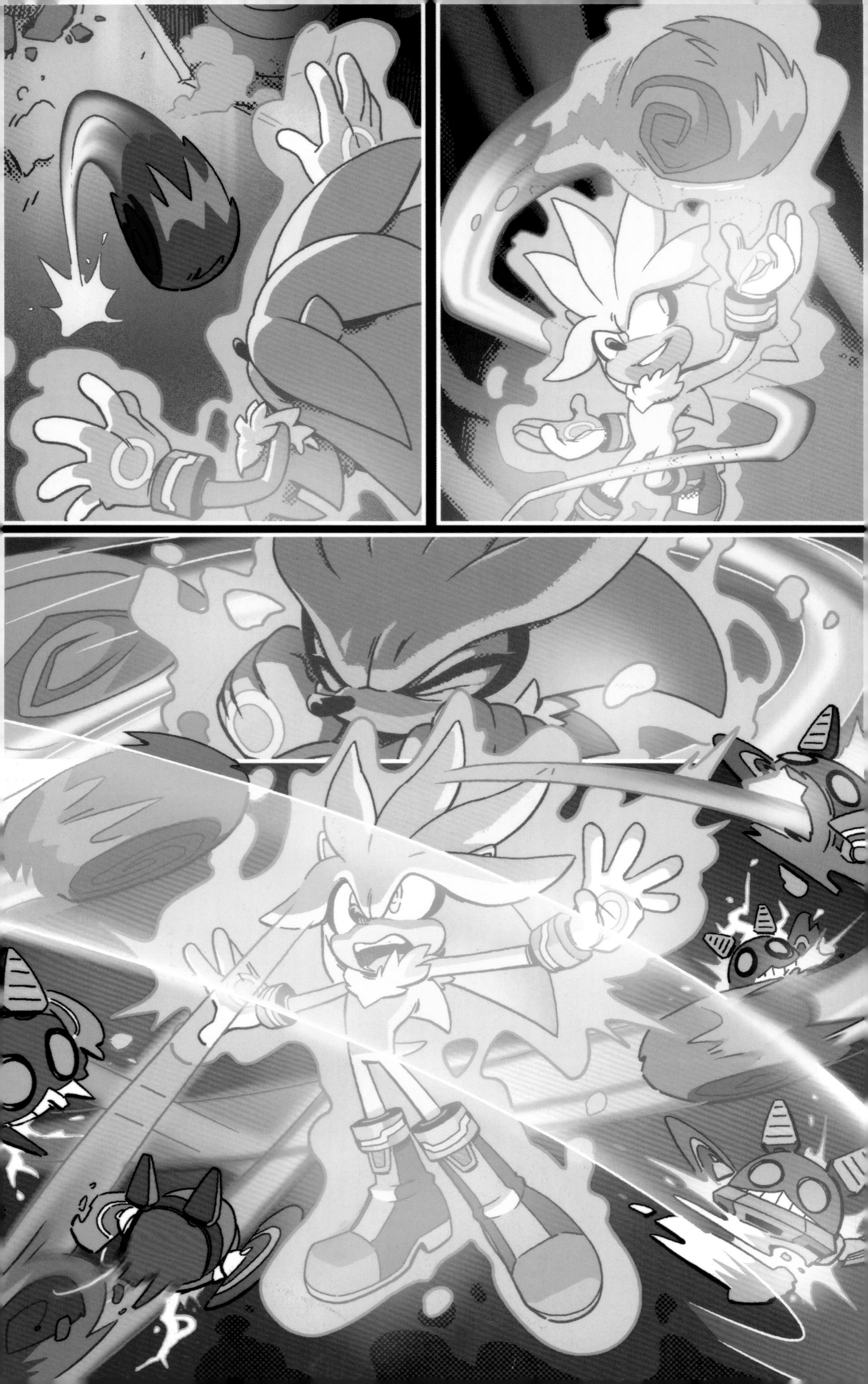

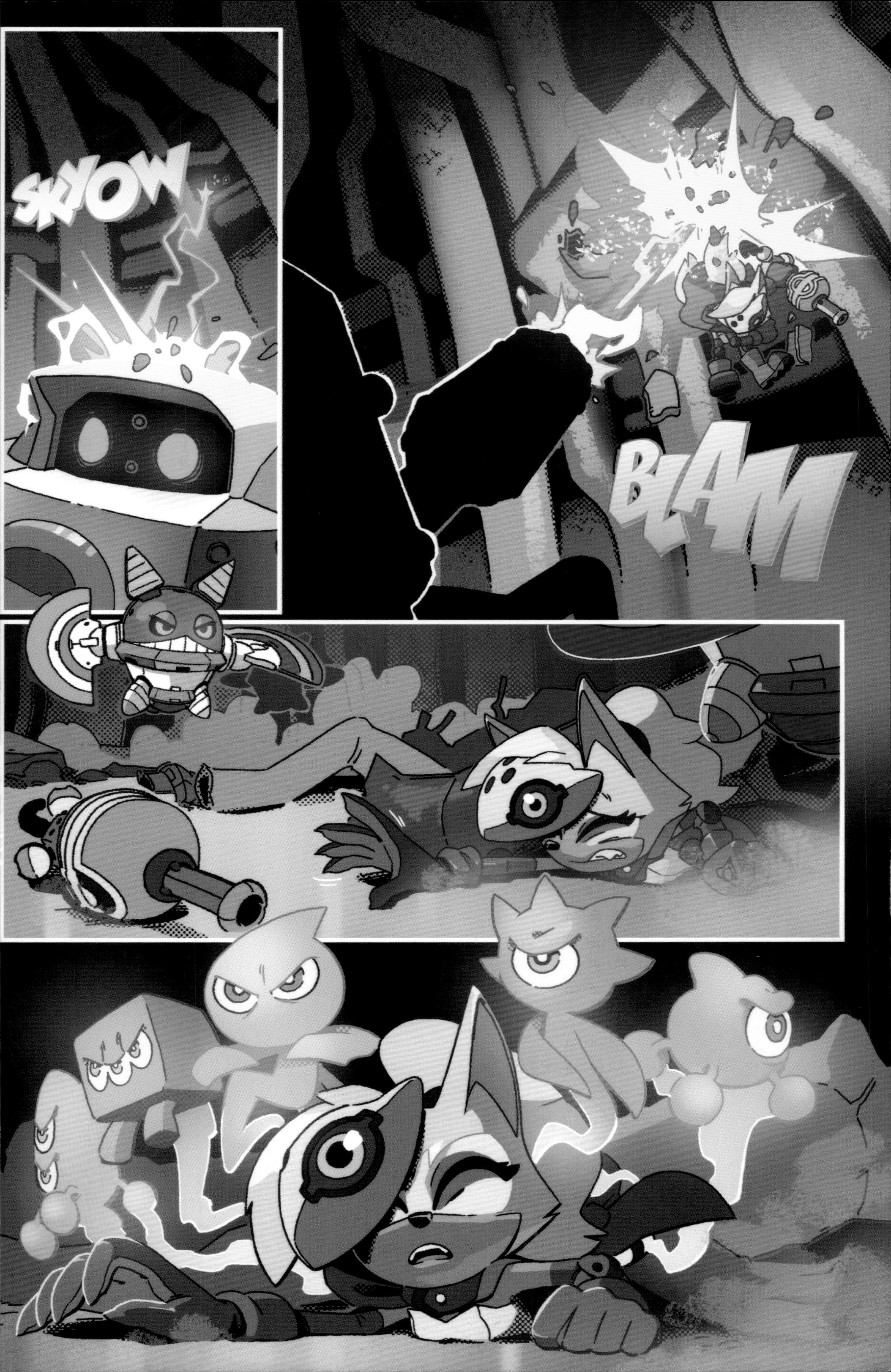
SKYOW
BLAM

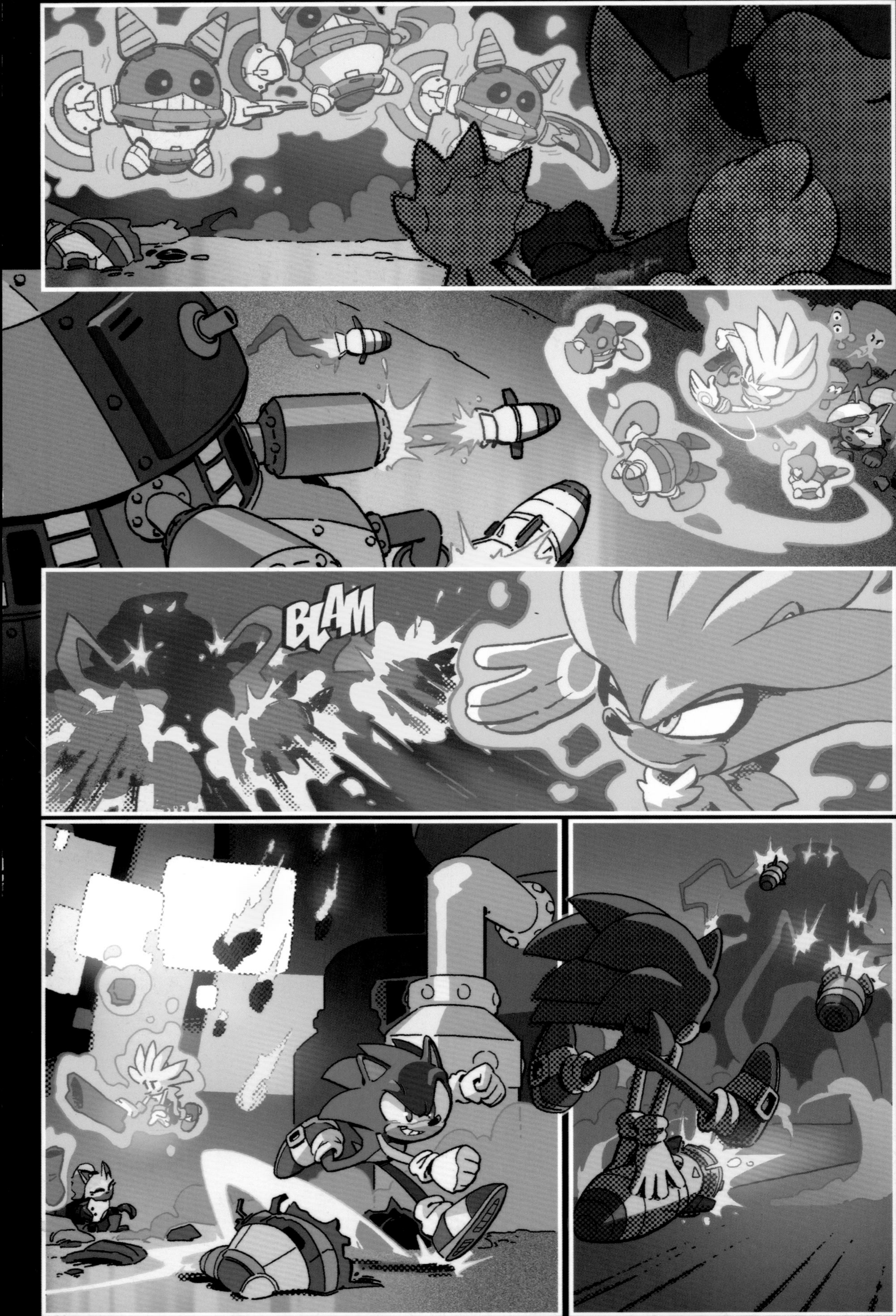
BLAM

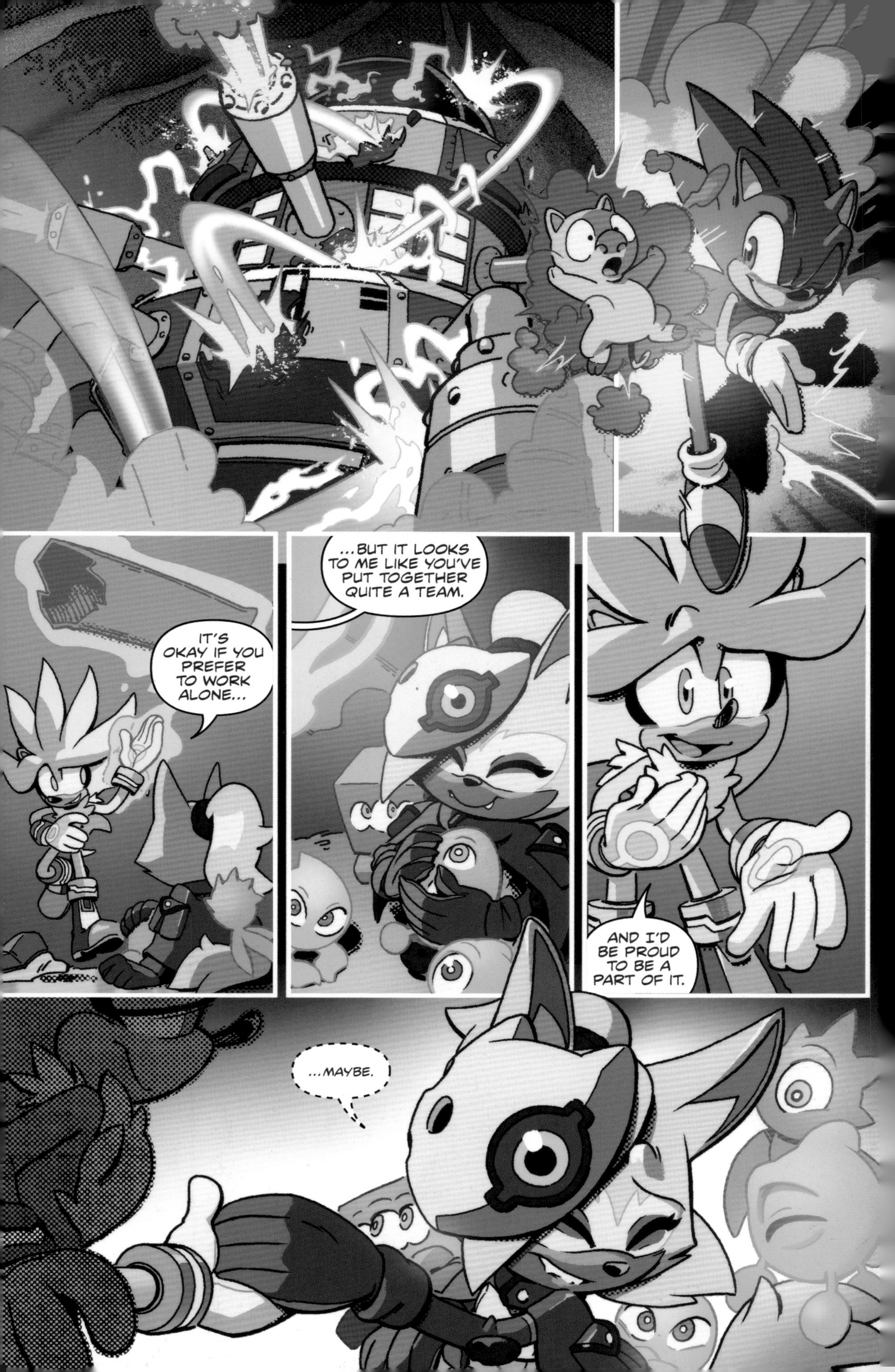
IT'S OKAY IF YOU PREFER TO WORK ALONE...
...BUT IT LOOKS TO ME LIKE YOU'VE PUT TOGETHER QUITE A TEAM.
AND I'D BE PROUD TO BE A PART OF IT.
...MAYBE.

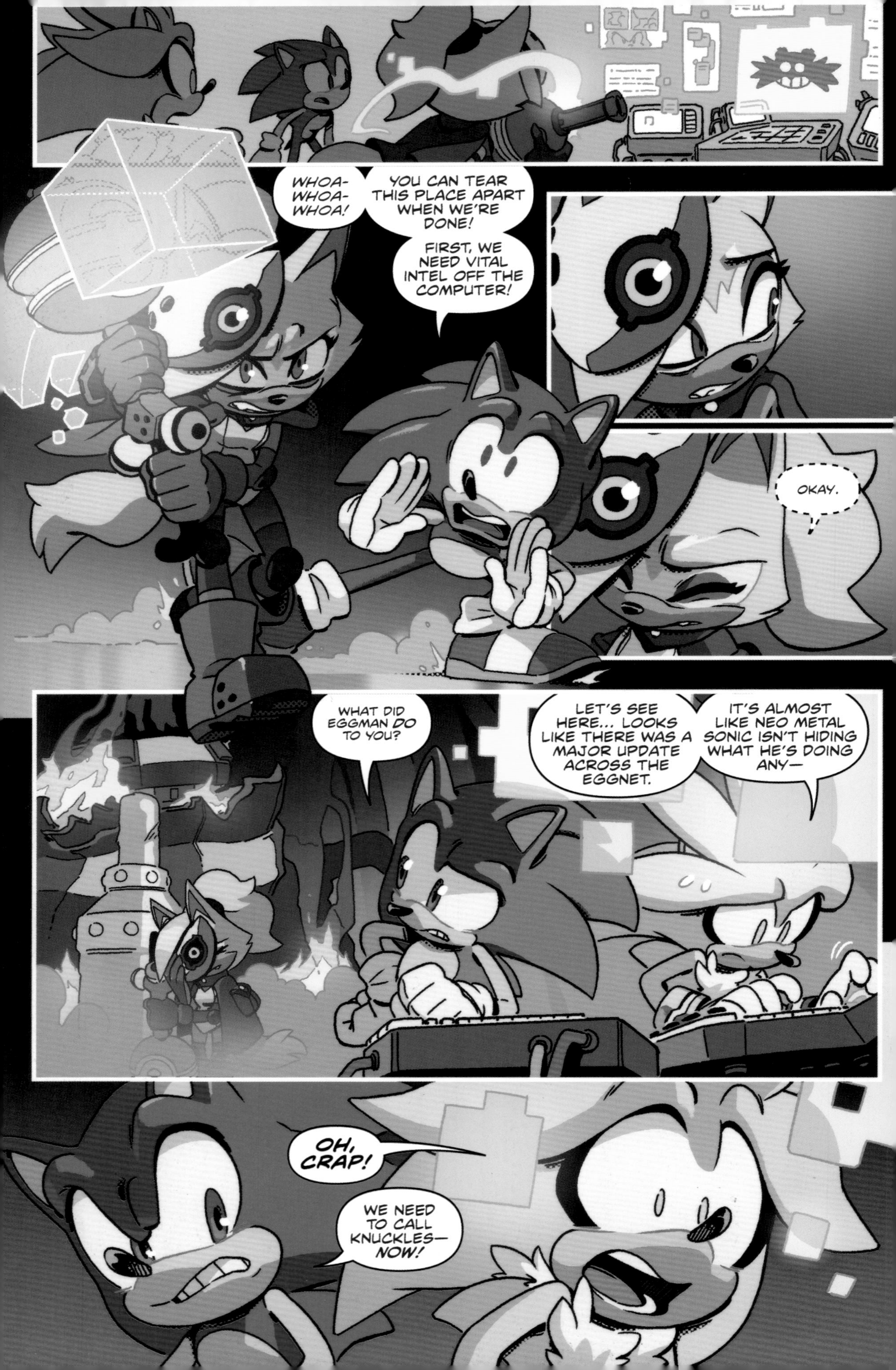
WHOA-WHOA-WHOA!
YOU CAN TEAR THIS PLACE APART WHEN WE'RE DONE!
FIRST, WE NEED VITAL INTEL OFF THE COMPUTER!
OKAY.
WHAT DID EGGMAN DO TO YOU?
LET'S SEE HERE... LOOKS LIKE THERE WAS A MAJOR UPDATE ACROSS THE EGGNET.
IT'S ALMOST LIKE NEO METAL SONIC ISN'T HIDING WHAT HE'S DOING ANY—
OH, CRAP!
WE NEED TO CALL KNUCKLES—NOW!

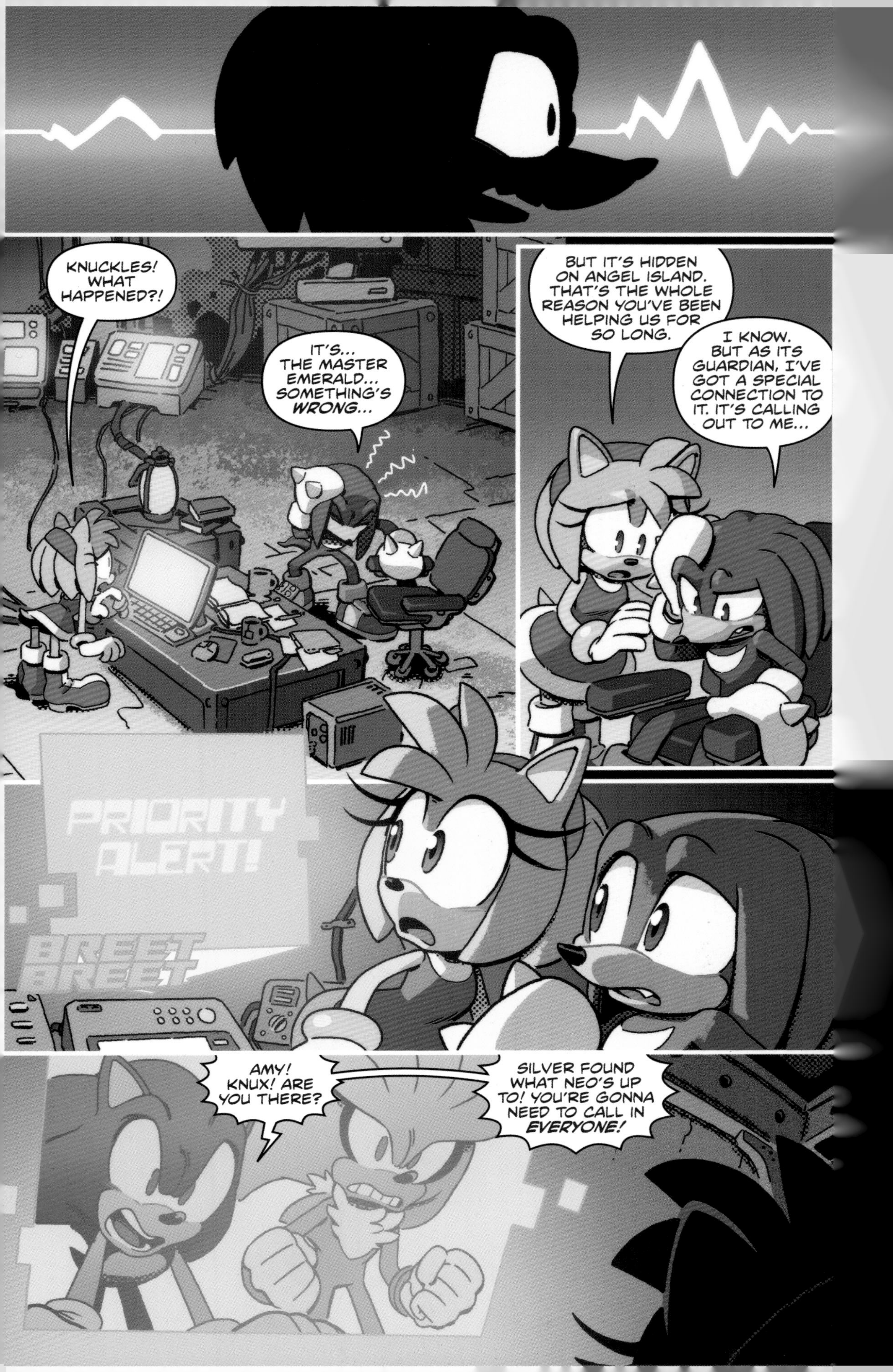
KNUCKLES! WHAT HAPPENED?!
IT'S... THE MASTER EMERALD... SOMETHING'S WRONG...
BUT IT'S HIDDEN ON ANGEL ISLAND. THAT'S THE WHOLE REASON YOU'VE BEEN HELPING US FOR SO LONG.
I KNOW. BUT AS ITS GUARDIAN, I'VE GOT A SPECIAL CONNECTION TO IT. IT'S CALLING OUT TO ME...
PRIORITY ALERT!
BREET BREET
AMY! KNUX! ARE YOU THERE?
SILVER FOUND WHAT NEO'S UP TO! YOU'RE GONNA NEED TO CALL IN EVERYONE!

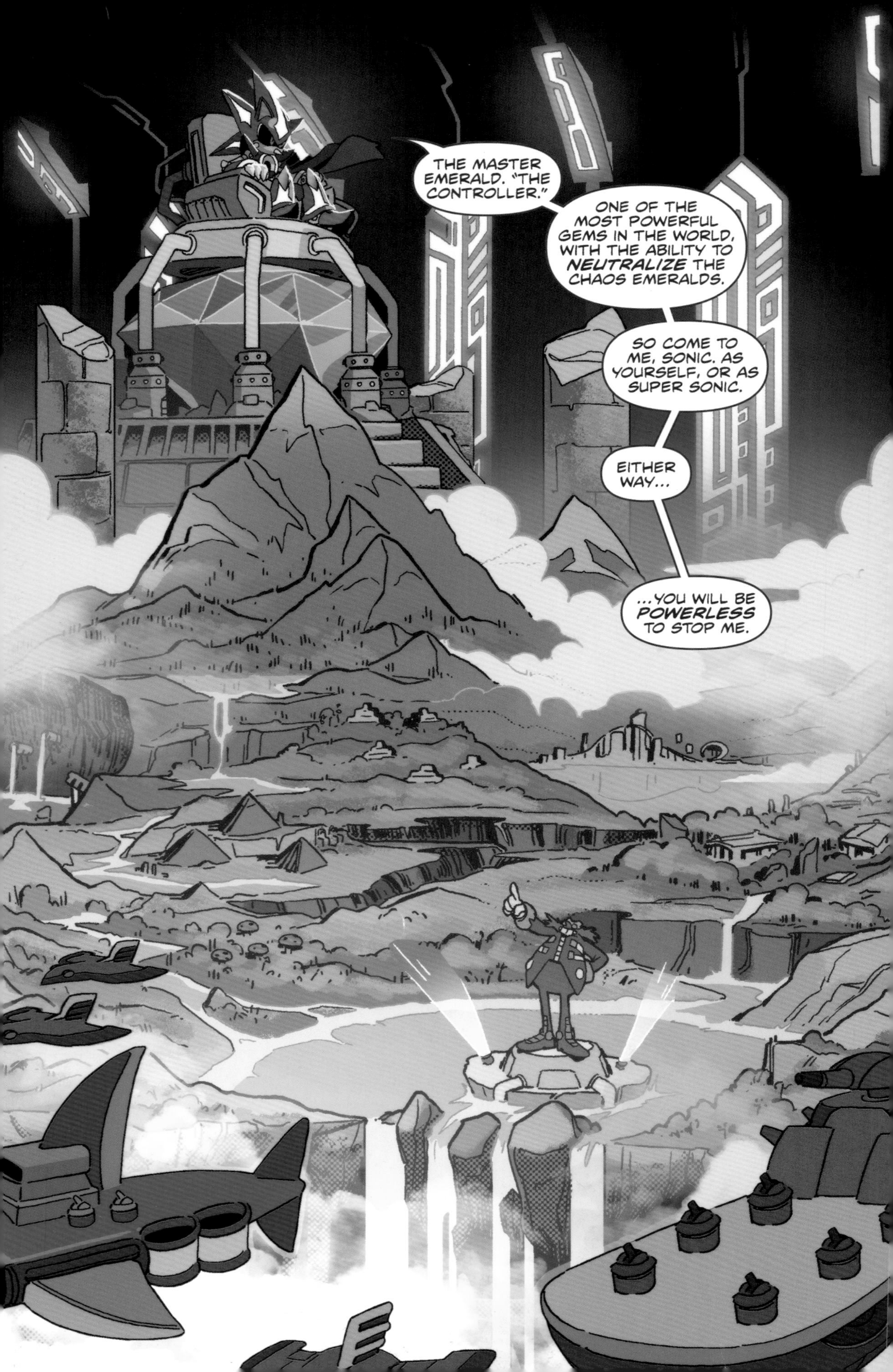
THE MASTER EMERALD. "THE CONTROLLER."
ONE OF THE MOST POWERFUL GEMS IN THE WORLD, WITH THE ABILITY TO **NEUTRALIZE** THE CHAOS EMERALDS.
SO COME TO ME, SONIC. AS YOURSELF, OR AS SUPER SONIC.
EITHER WAY...
...YOU WILL BE **POWERLESS** TO STOP ME.

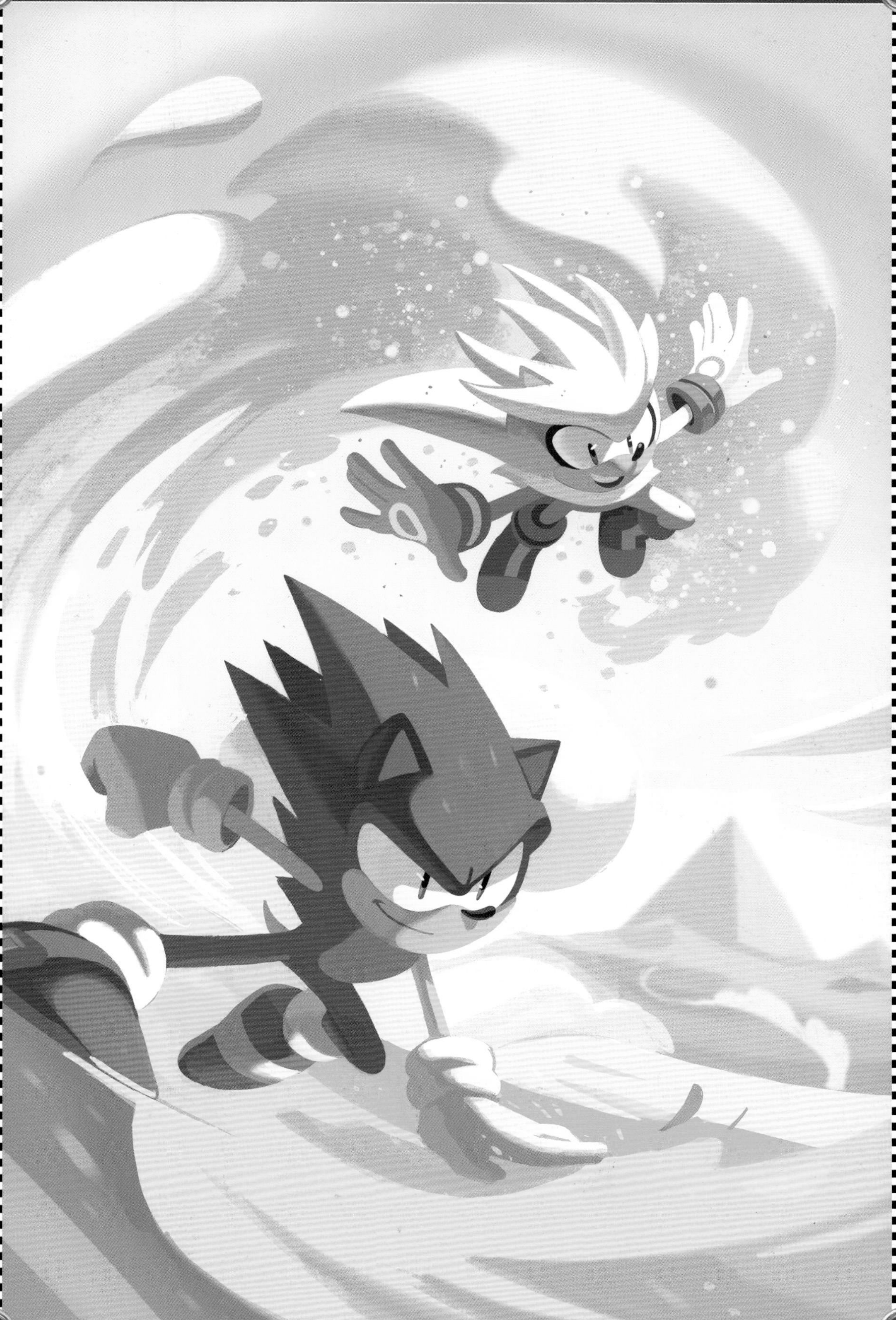

ART BY LAMAR WELLS & ADAM BRYCE THOMAS COLORS BY ADAM BRYCE THOMAS

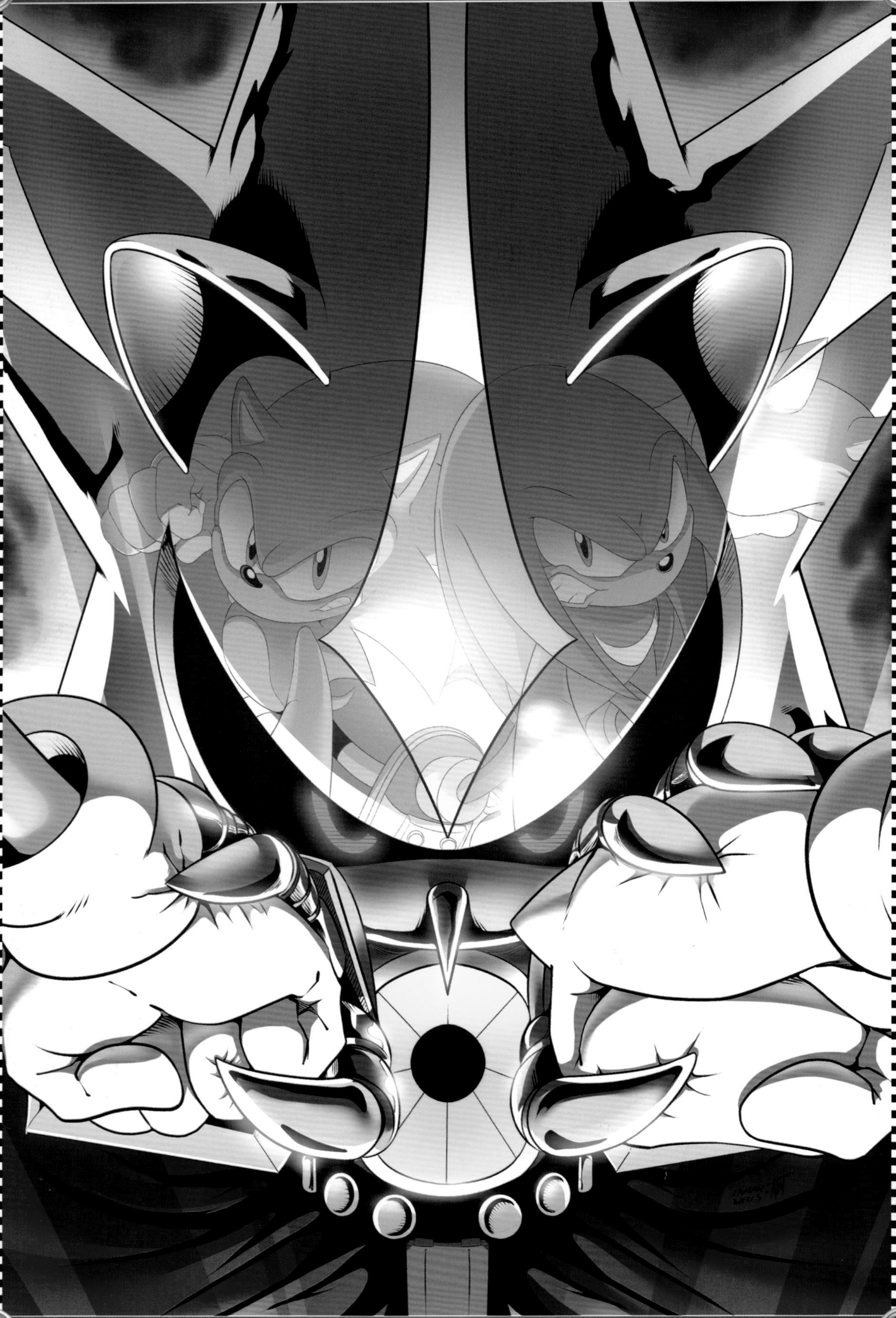

SONIC THE HEDGEHOG #9

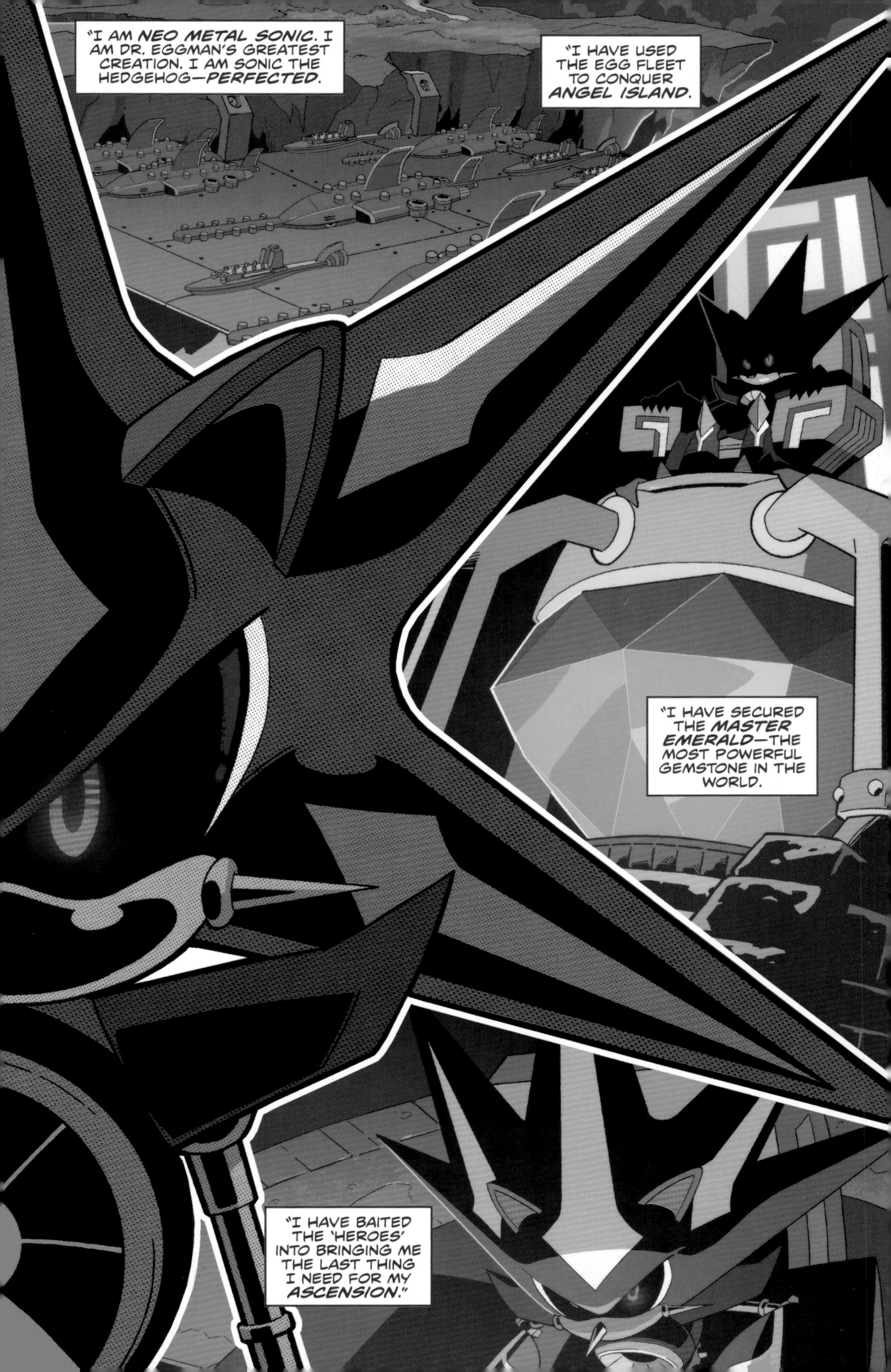
"I AM NEO METAL SONIC. I AM DR. EGGMAN'S GREATEST CREATION. I AM SONIC THE HEDGEHOG—PERFECTED.
"I HAVE USED THE EGG FLEET TO CONQUER ANGEL ISLAND.
"I HAVE SECURED THE MASTER EMERALD—THE MOST POWERFUL GEMSTONE IN THE WORLD.
"I HAVE BAITED THE 'HEROES' INTO BRINGING ME THE LAST THING I NEED FOR MY ASCENSION."

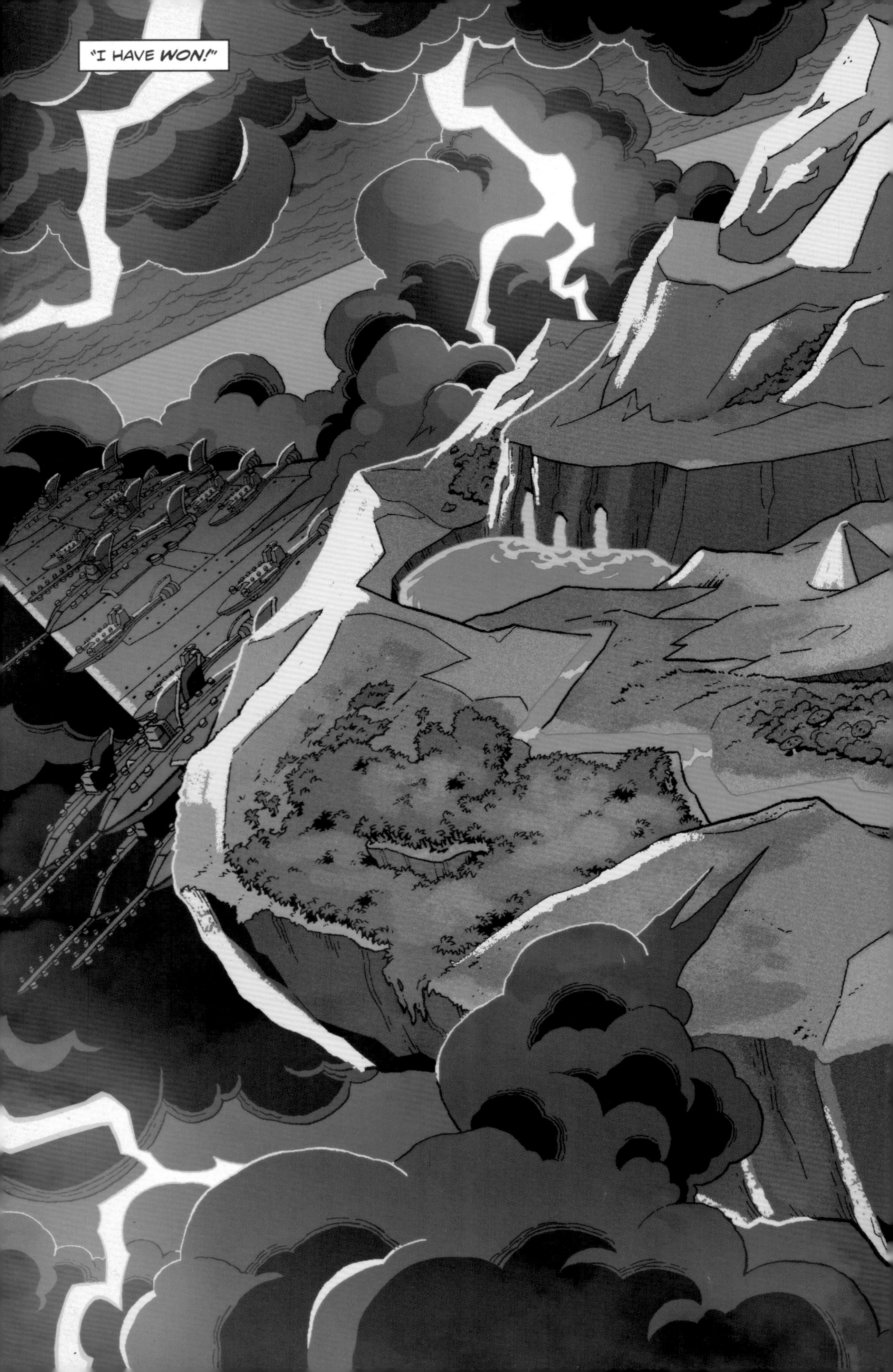
"I HAVE WON!"

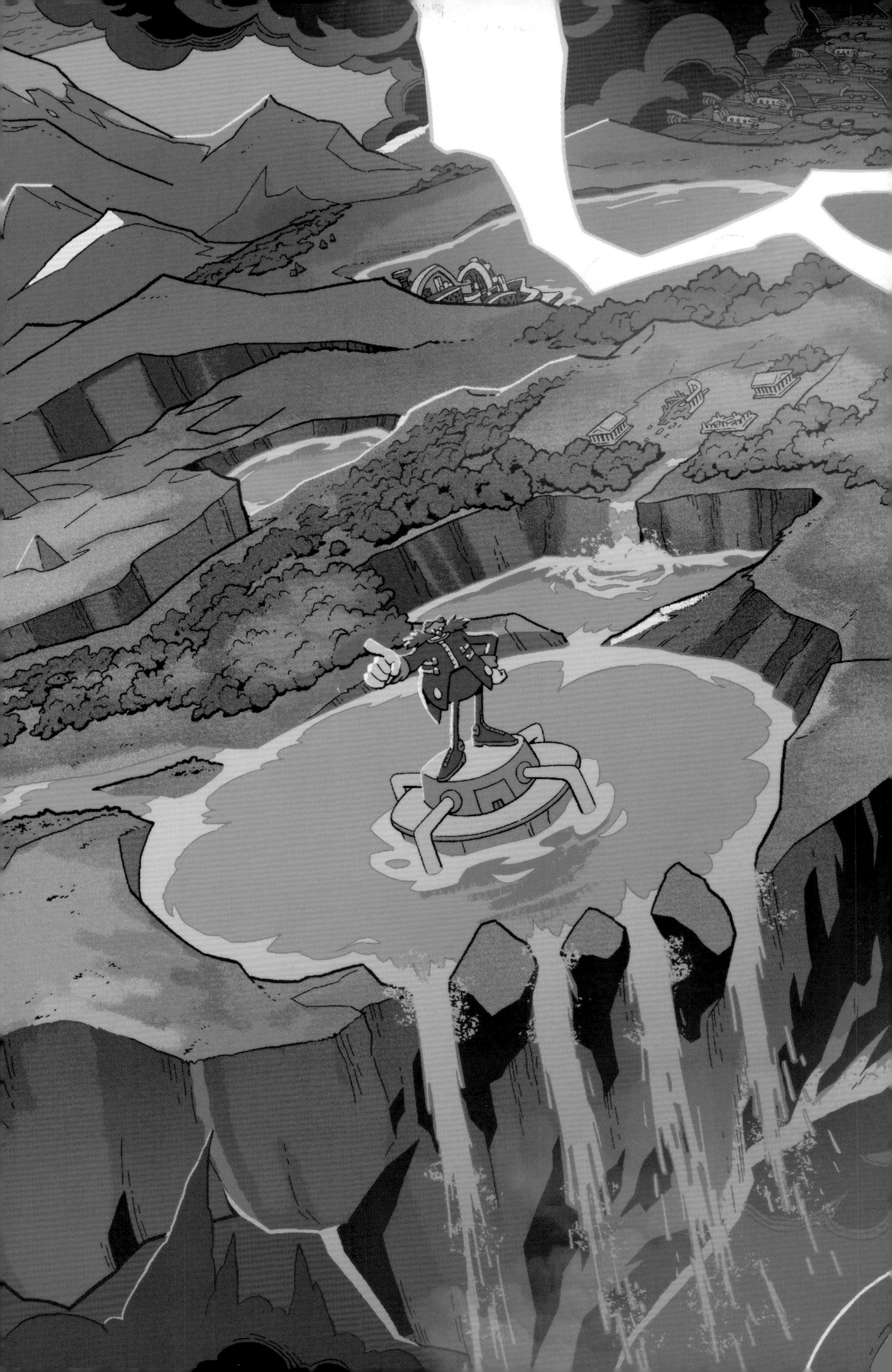

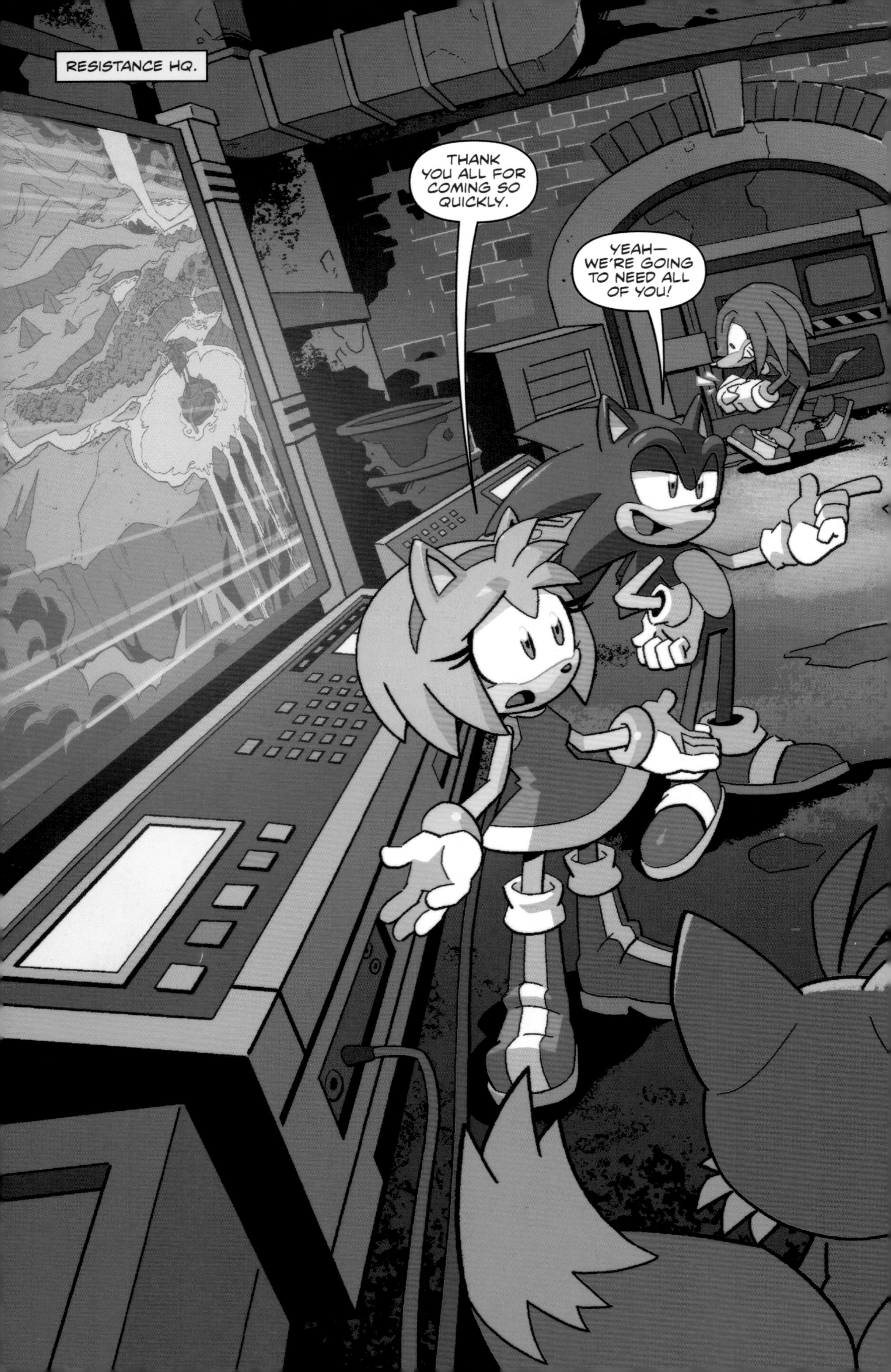
RESISTANCE HQ.
THANK YOU ALL FOR COMING SO QUICKLY.
YEAH— WE'RE GOING TO NEED ALL OF YOU!

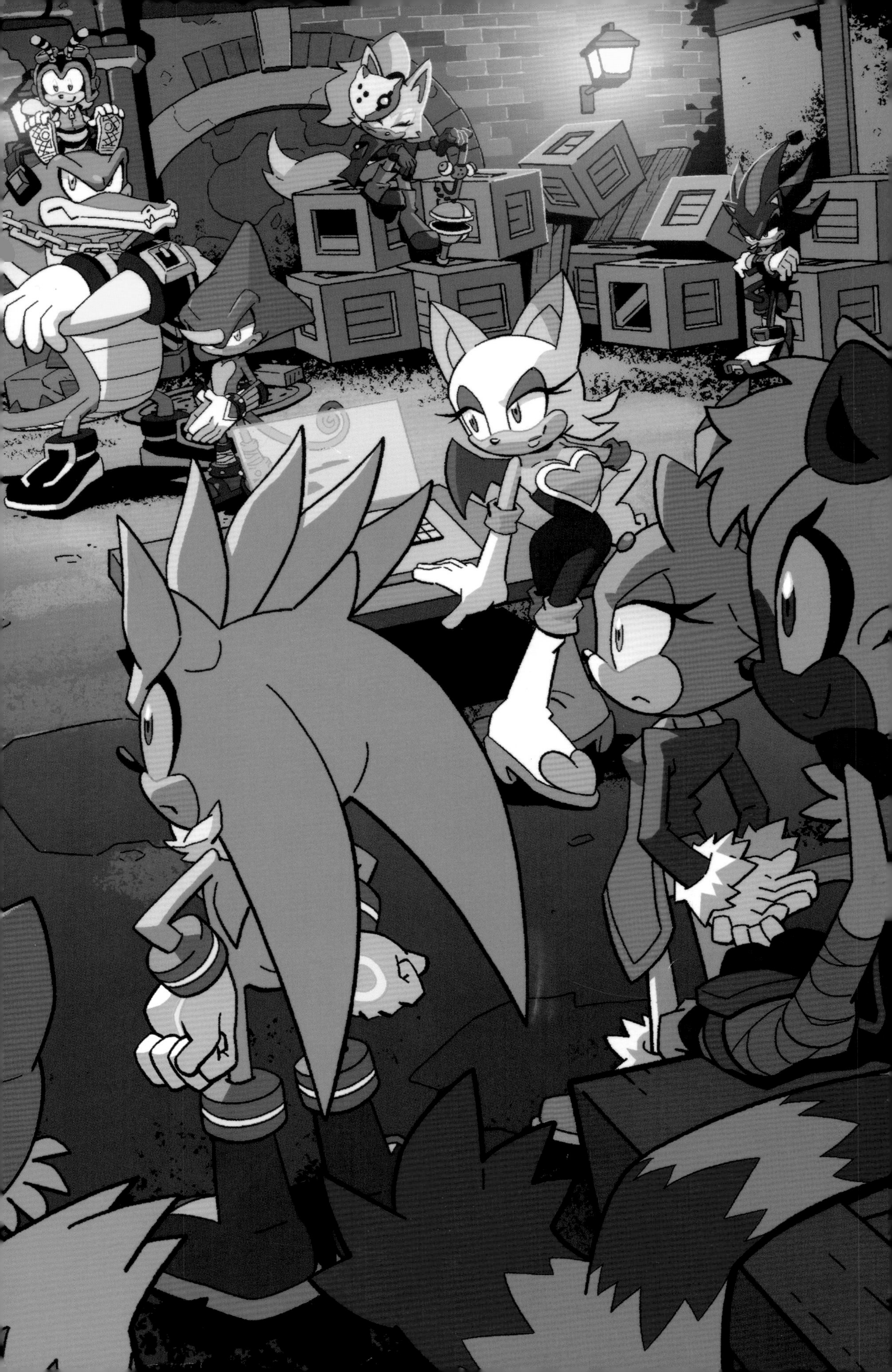

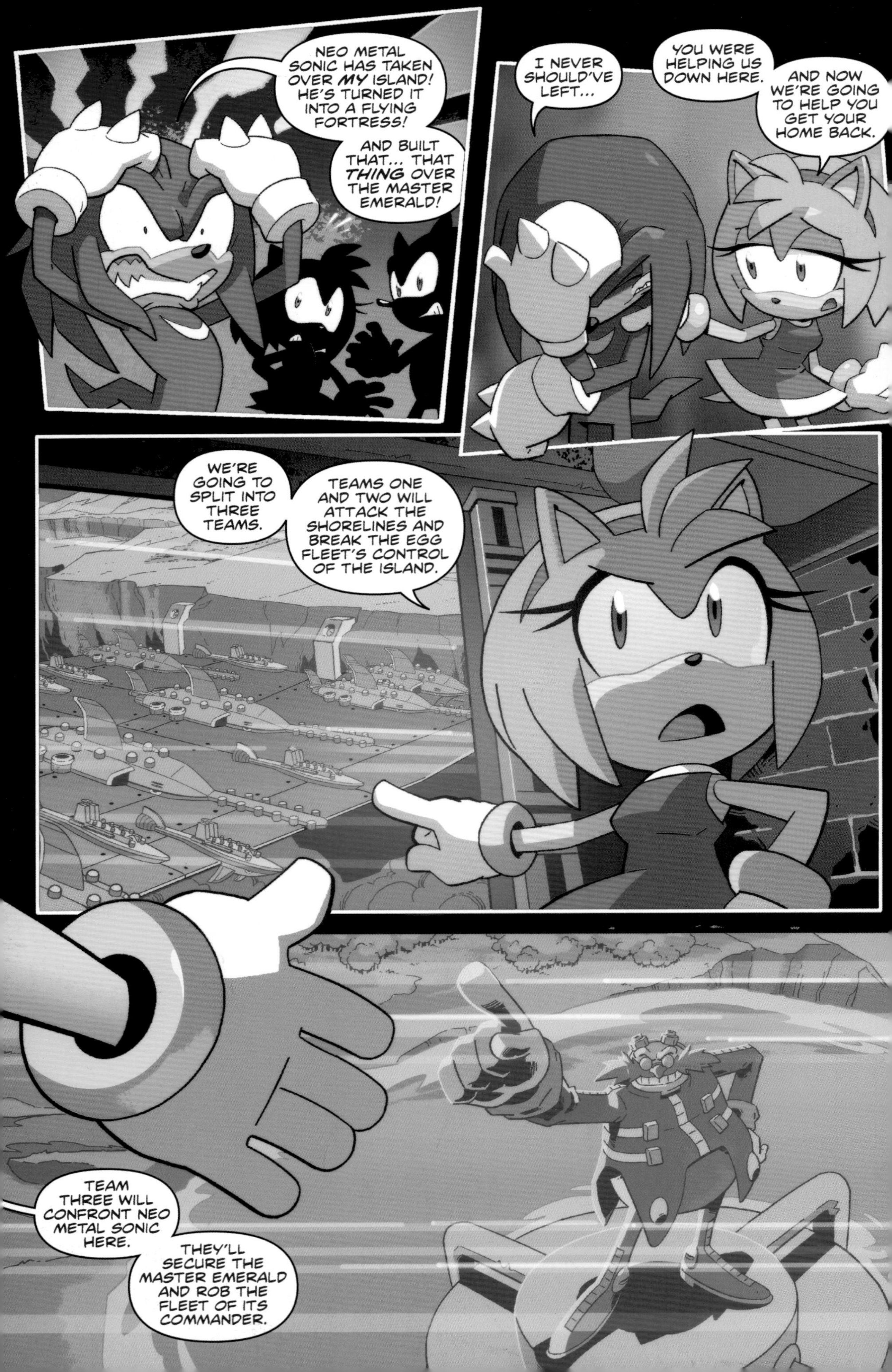
NEO METAL SONIC HAS TAKEN OVER *MY* ISLAND! HE'S TURNED IT INTO A FLYING FORTRESS!
AND BUILT THAT... THAT *THING* OVER THE MASTER EMERALD!
I NEVER SHOULD'VE LEFT...
YOU WERE HELPING US DOWN HERE.
AND NOW WE'RE GOING TO HELP YOU GET YOUR HOME BACK.
WE'RE GOING TO SPLIT INTO THREE TEAMS.
TEAMS ONE AND TWO WILL ATTACK THE SHORELINES AND BREAK THE EGG FLEET'S CONTROL OF THE ISLAND.
TEAM THREE WILL CONFRONT NEO METAL SONIC HERE.
THEY'LL SECURE THE MASTER EMERALD AND ROB THE FLEET OF ITS COMMANDER.

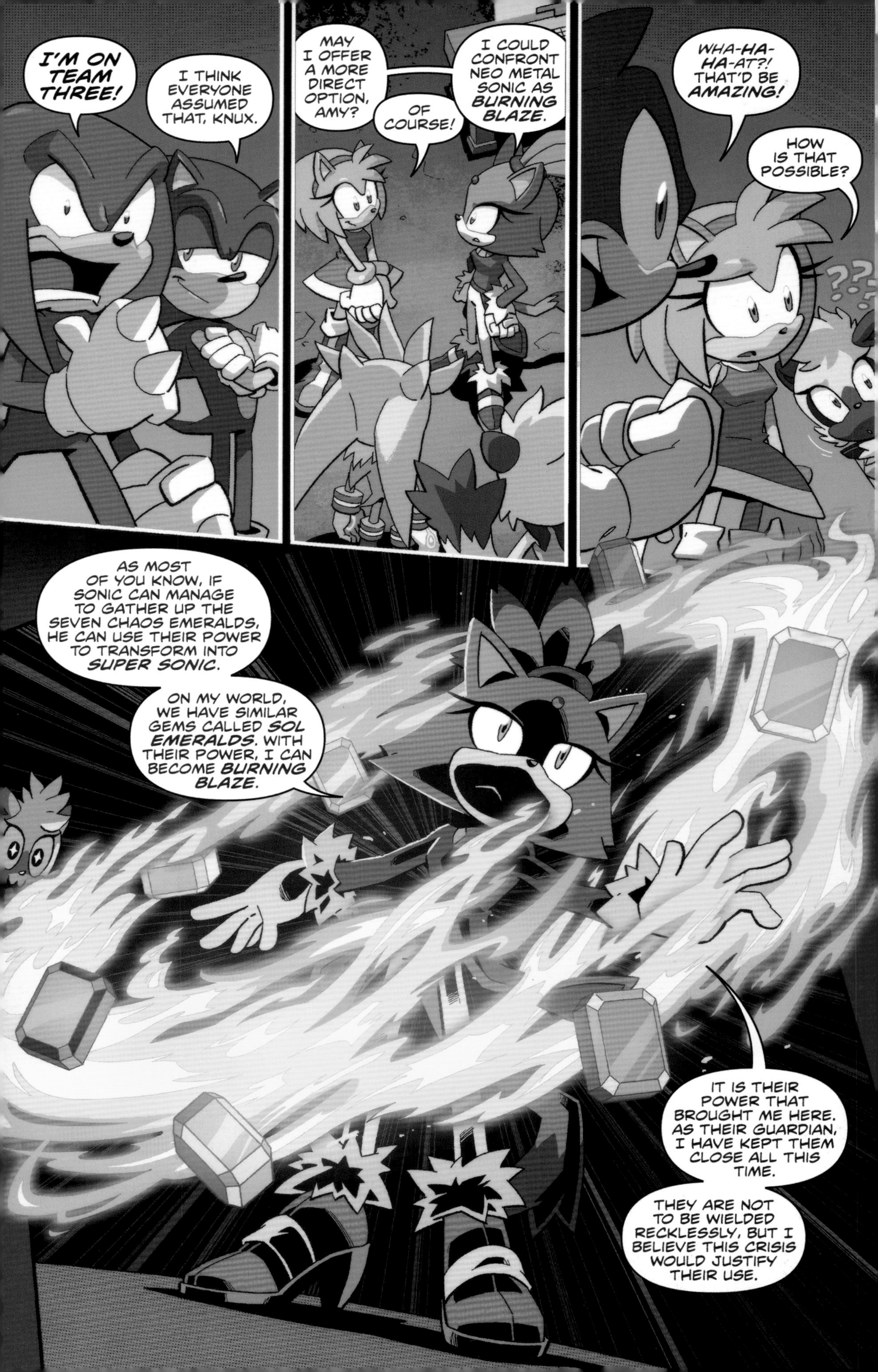
I'M ON TEAM THREE!
I THINK EVERYONE ASSUMED THAT, KNUX.
MAY I OFFER A MORE DIRECT OPTION, AMY?
OF COURSE!
I COULD CONFRONT NEO METAL SONIC AS BURNING BLAZE.
WHA-HA-HA-AT?! THAT'D BE AMAZING!
HOW IS THAT POSSIBLE?
???
AS MOST OF YOU KNOW, IF SONIC CAN MANAGE TO GATHER UP THE SEVEN CHAOS EMERALDS, HE CAN USE THEIR POWER TO TRANSFORM INTO SUPER SONIC.
ON MY WORLD, WE HAVE SIMILAR GEMS CALLED SOL EMERALDS. WITH THEIR POWER, I CAN BECOME BURNING BLAZE.
IT IS THEIR POWER THAT BROUGHT ME HERE. AS THEIR GUARDIAN, I HAVE KEPT THEM CLOSE ALL THIS TIME.
THEY ARE NOT TO BE WIELDED RECKLESSLY, BUT I BELIEVE THIS CRISIS WOULD JUSTIFY THEIR USE.

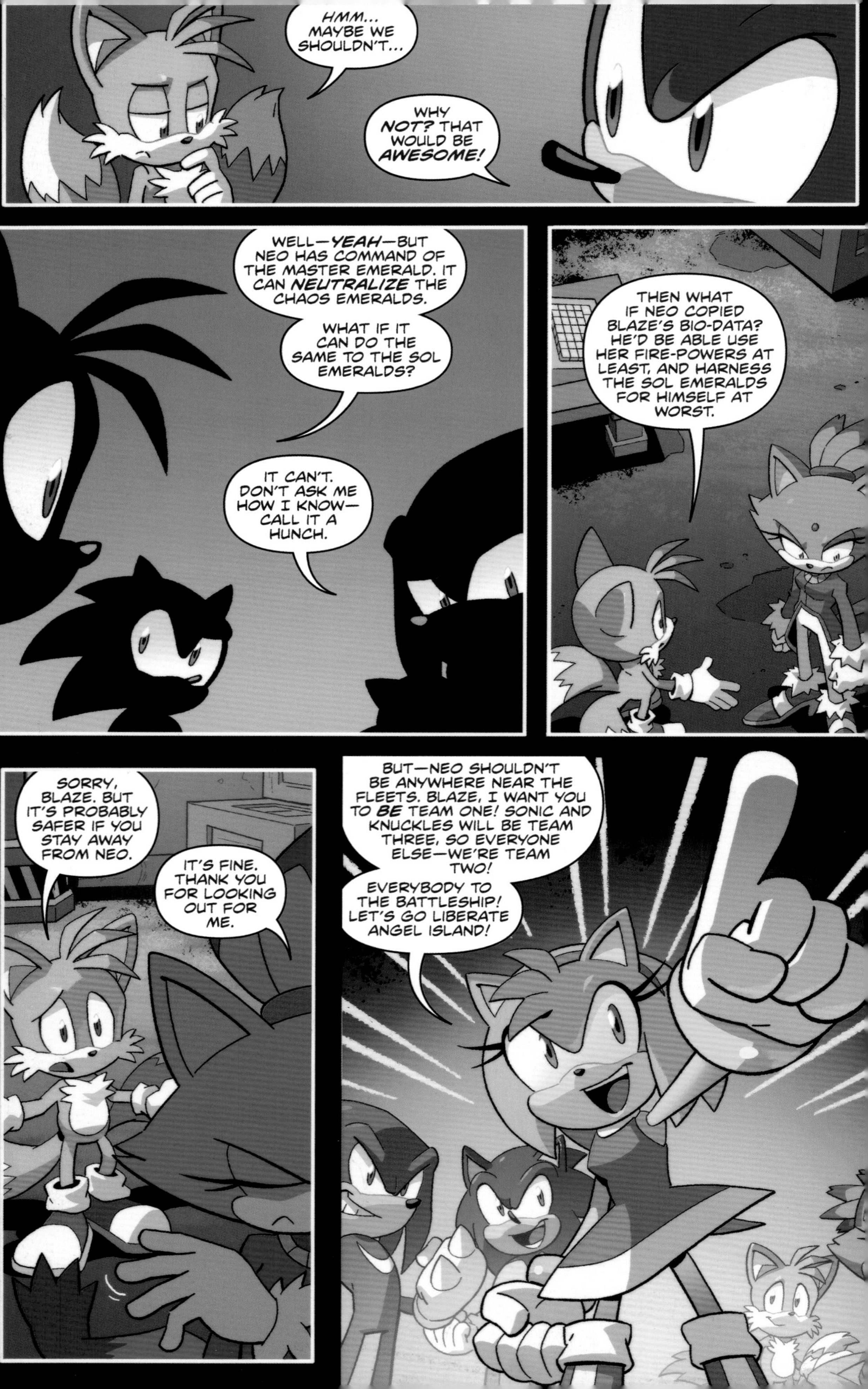
HMM... MAYBE WE SHOULDN'T...
WHY *NOT?* THAT WOULD BE *AWESOME!*
WELL—*YEAH*—BUT NEO HAS COMMAND OF THE MASTER EMERALD. IT CAN *NEUTRALIZE* THE CHAOS EMERALDS.
WHAT IF IT CAN DO THE SAME TO THE SOL EMERALDS?
IT CAN'T. DON'T ASK ME HOW I KNOW—CALL IT A HUNCH.
THEN WHAT IF NEO COPIED BLAZE'S BIO-DATA? HE'D BE ABLE USE HER FIRE-POWERS AT LEAST, AND HARNESS THE SOL EMERALDS FOR HIMSELF AT WORST.
SORRY, BLAZE. BUT IT'S PROBABLY SAFER IF YOU STAY AWAY FROM NEO.
IT'S FINE. THANK YOU FOR LOOKING OUT FOR ME.
BUT—NEO SHOULDN'T BE ANYWHERE NEAR THE FLEETS. BLAZE, I WANT YOU TO *BE* TEAM ONE! SONIC AND KNUCKLES WILL BE TEAM THREE, SO EVERYONE ELSE—WE'RE TEAM TWO!
EVERYBODY TO THE BATTLESHIP! LET'S GO LIBERATE ANGEL ISLAND!

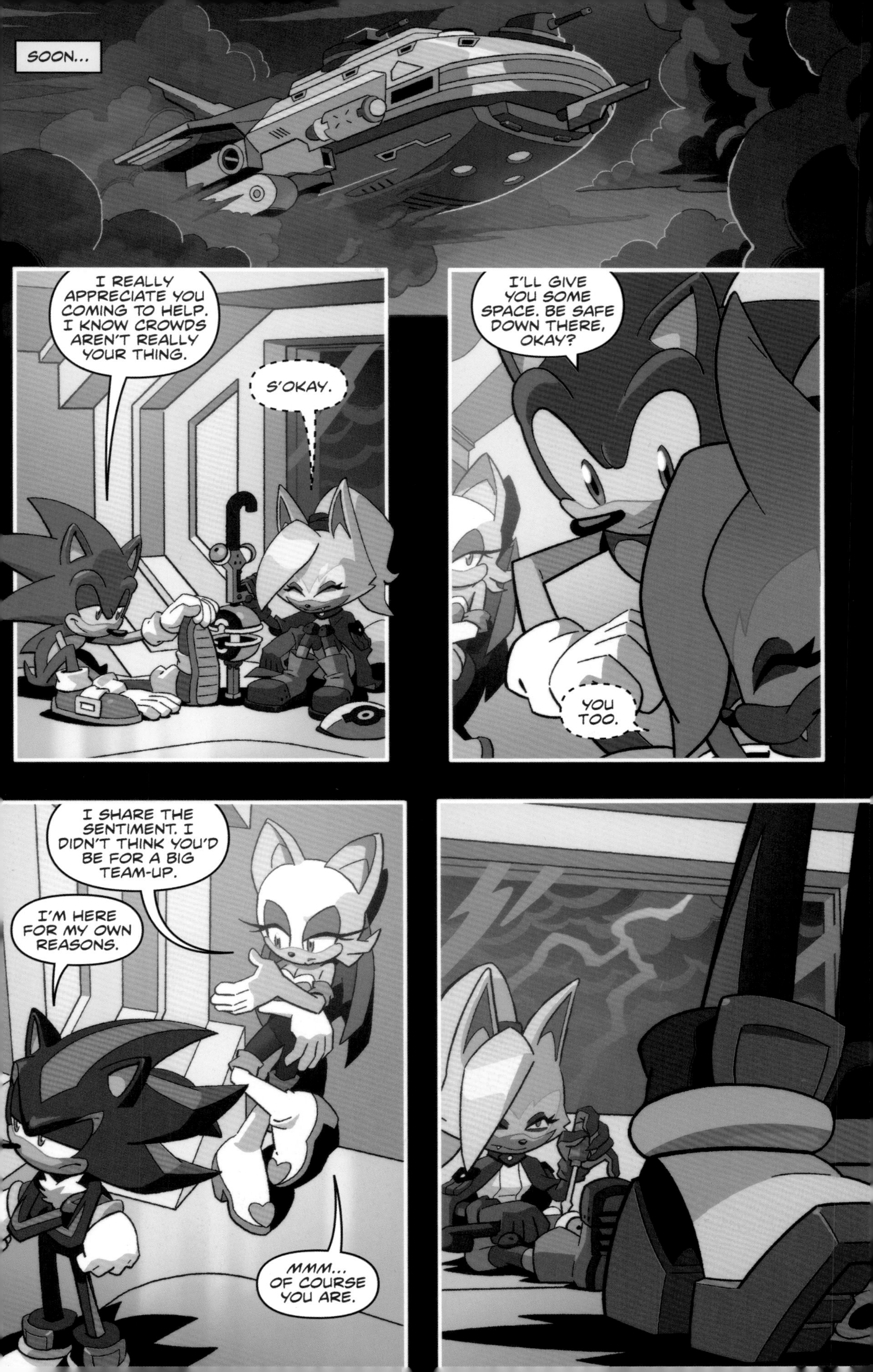

SOON...
I REALLY APPRECIATE YOU COMING TO HELP. I KNOW CROWDS AREN'T REALLY YOUR THING.
S'OKAY.
I'LL GIVE YOU SOME SPACE. BE SAFE DOWN THERE, OKAY?
YOU TOO.
I SHARE THE SENTIMENT. I DIDN'T THINK YOU'D BE FOR A BIG TEAM-UP.
I'M HERE FOR MY OWN REASONS.
MMM... OF COURSE YOU ARE.

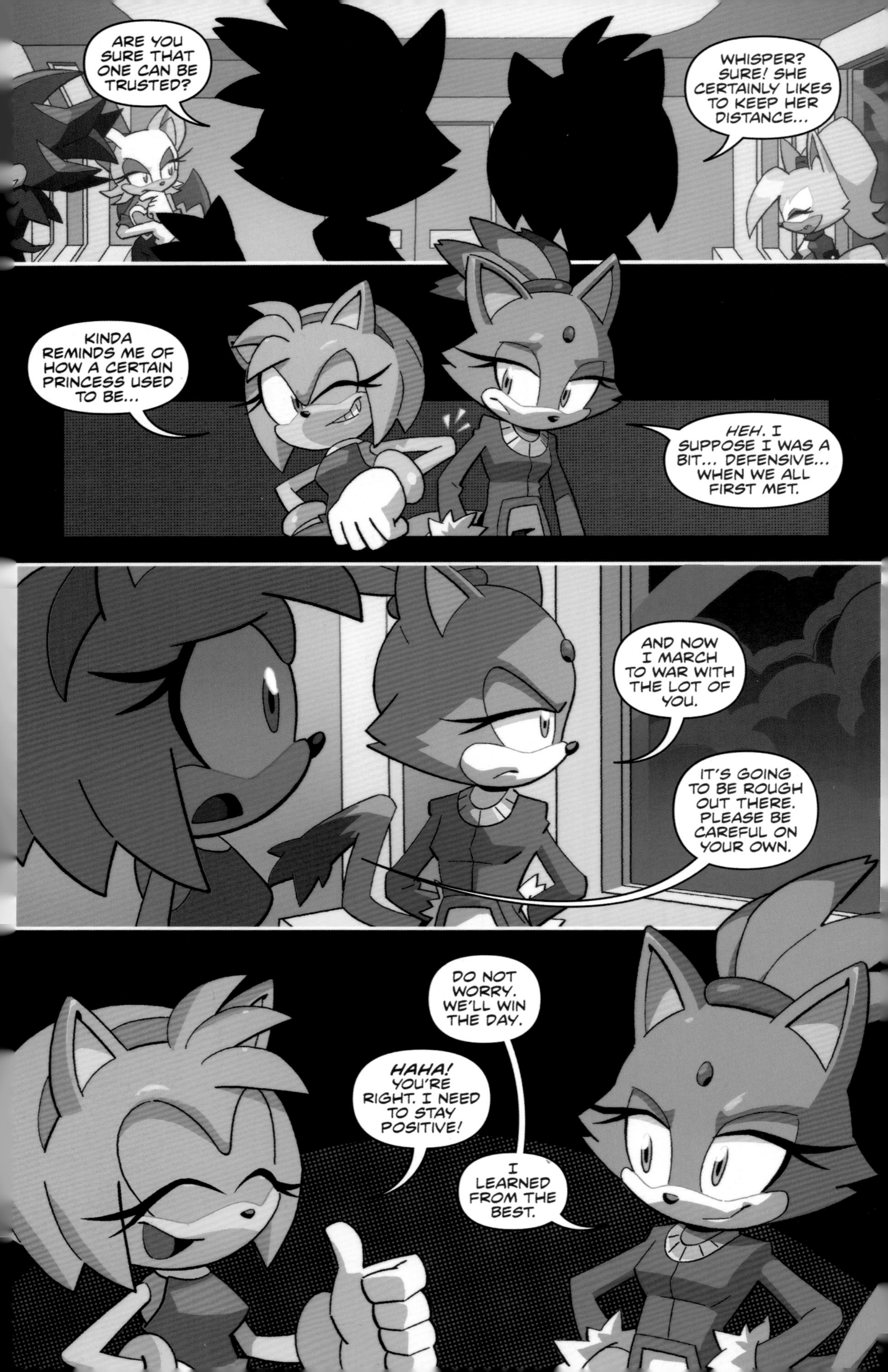

ARE YOU SURE THAT ONE CAN BE TRUSTED?
WHISPER? SURE! SHE CERTAINLY LIKES TO KEEP HER DISTANCE...
KINDA REMINDS ME OF HOW A CERTAIN PRINCESS USED TO BE...
HEH. I SUPPOSE I WAS A BIT... DEFENSIVE... WHEN WE ALL FIRST MET.
AND NOW I MARCH TO WAR WITH THE LOT OF YOU.
IT'S GOING TO BE ROUGH OUT THERE. PLEASE BE CAREFUL ON YOUR OWN.
DO NOT WORRY. WE'LL WIN THE DAY.
I LEARNED FROM THE BEST.
HAHA! YOU'RE RIGHT. I NEED TO STAY POSITIVE!

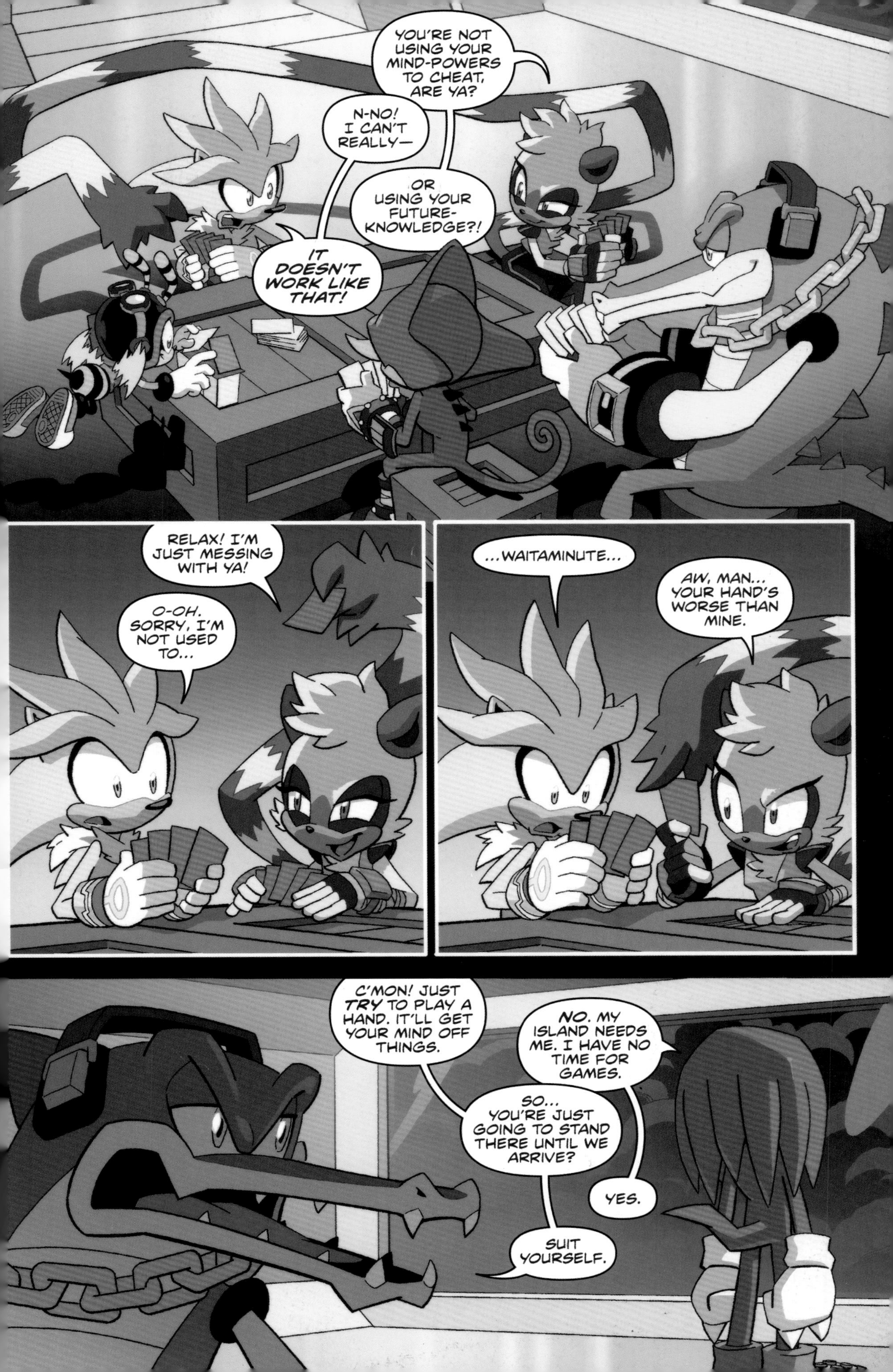

YOU'RE NOT USING YOUR MIND-POWERS TO CHEAT, ARE YA?
N-NO! I CAN'T REALLY—
OR USING YOUR FUTURE-KNOWLEDGE?!
IT DOESN'T WORK LIKE THAT!
RELAX! I'M JUST MESSING WITH YA!
O-OH. SORRY, I'M NOT USED TO...
...WAITAMINUTE...
AW, MAN... YOUR HAND'S WORSE THAN MINE.
C'MON! JUST TRY TO PLAY A HAND. IT'LL GET YOUR MIND OFF THINGS.
NO. MY ISLAND NEEDS ME. I HAVE NO TIME FOR GAMES.
SO... YOU'RE JUST GOING TO STAND THERE UNTIL WE ARRIVE?
YES.
SUIT YOURSELF.

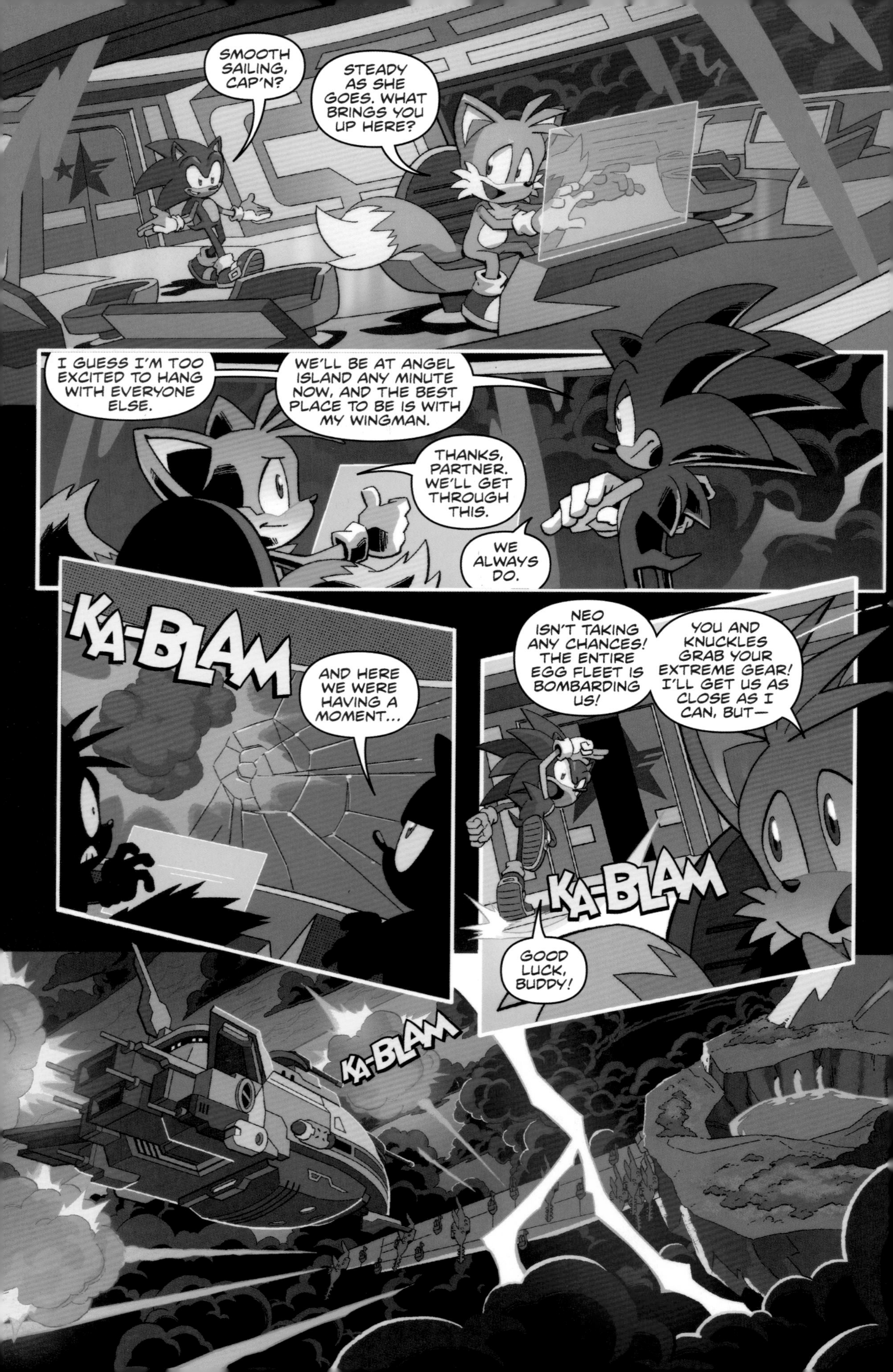
SMOOTH SAILING, CAP'N?
STEADY AS SHE GOES. WHAT BRINGS YOU UP HERE?
I GUESS I'M TOO EXCITED TO HANG WITH EVERYONE ELSE.
WE'LL BE AT ANGEL ISLAND ANY MINUTE NOW, AND THE BEST PLACE TO BE IS WITH MY WINGMAN.
THANKS, PARTNER. WE'LL GET THROUGH THIS.
WE ALWAYS DO.
KA-BLAM
AND HERE WE WERE HAVING A MOMENT...
NEO ISN'T TAKING ANY CHANCES! THE ENTIRE EGG FLEET IS BOMBARDING US!
YOU AND KNUCKLES GRAB YOUR EXTREME GEAR! I'LL GET US AS CLOSE AS I CAN, BUT—
KA-BLAM
GOOD LUCK, BUDDY!
KA-BLAM

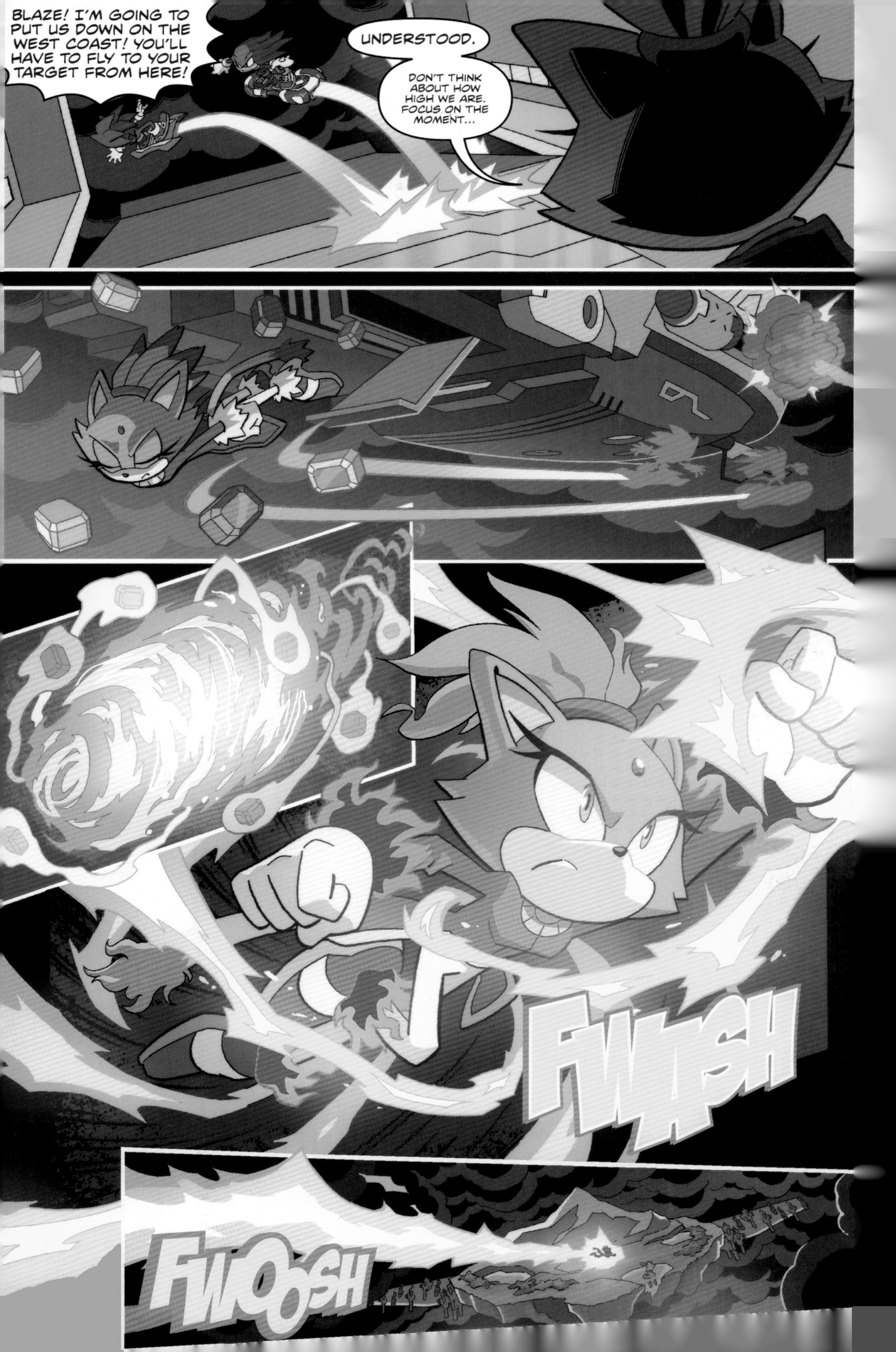
BLAZE! I'M GOING TO PUT US DOWN ON THE WEST COAST! YOU'LL HAVE TO FLY TO YOUR TARGET FROM HERE!
UNDERSTOOD.
DON'T THINK ABOUT HOW HIGH WE ARE. FOCUS ON THE MOMENT...
FWASH
FWOOSH

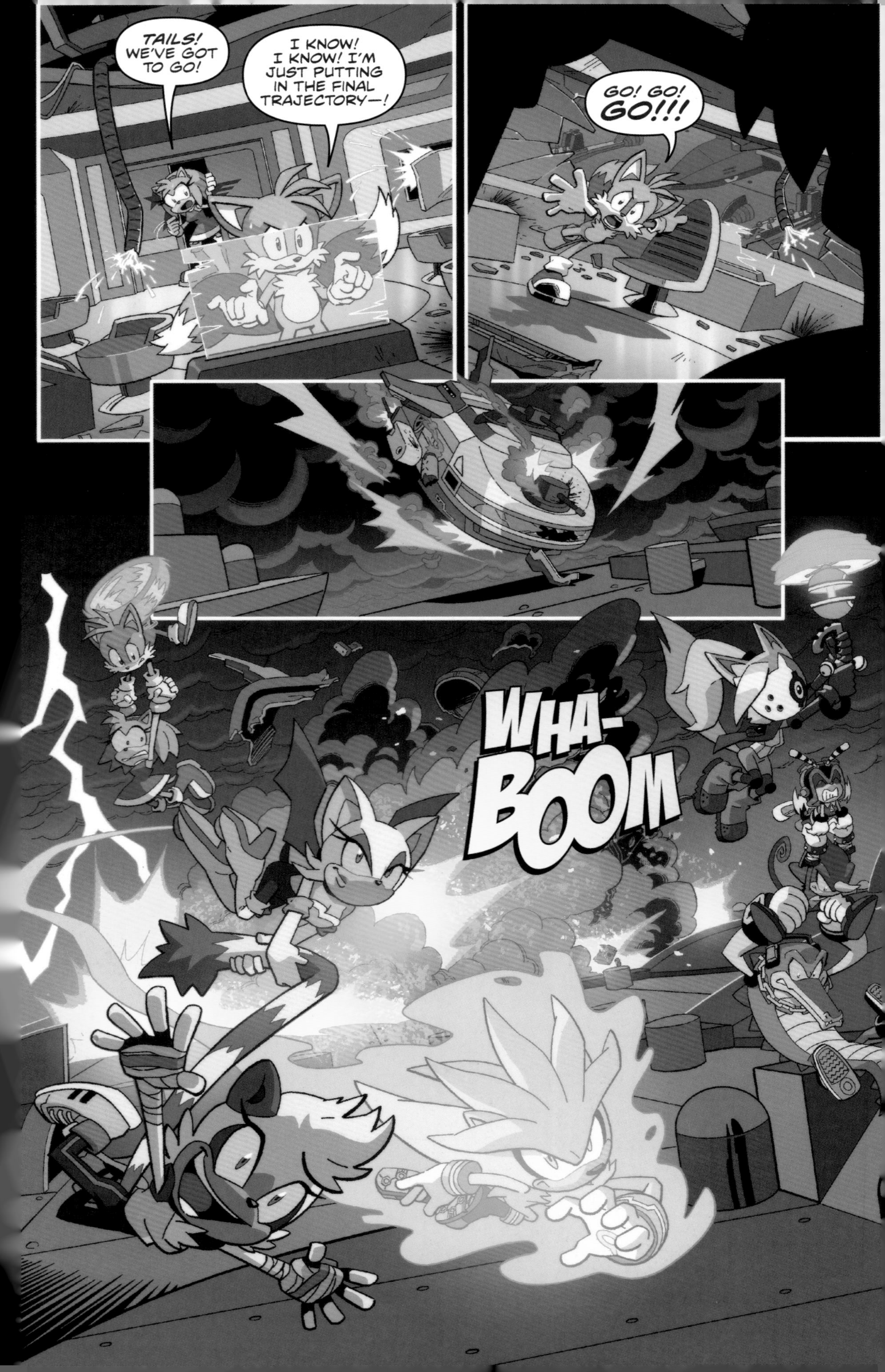

TAILS! WE'VE GOT TO GO!
I KNOW! I KNOW! I'M JUST PUTTING IN THE FINAL TRAJECTORY—!
GO! GO! GO!!!
WHA-BOOM

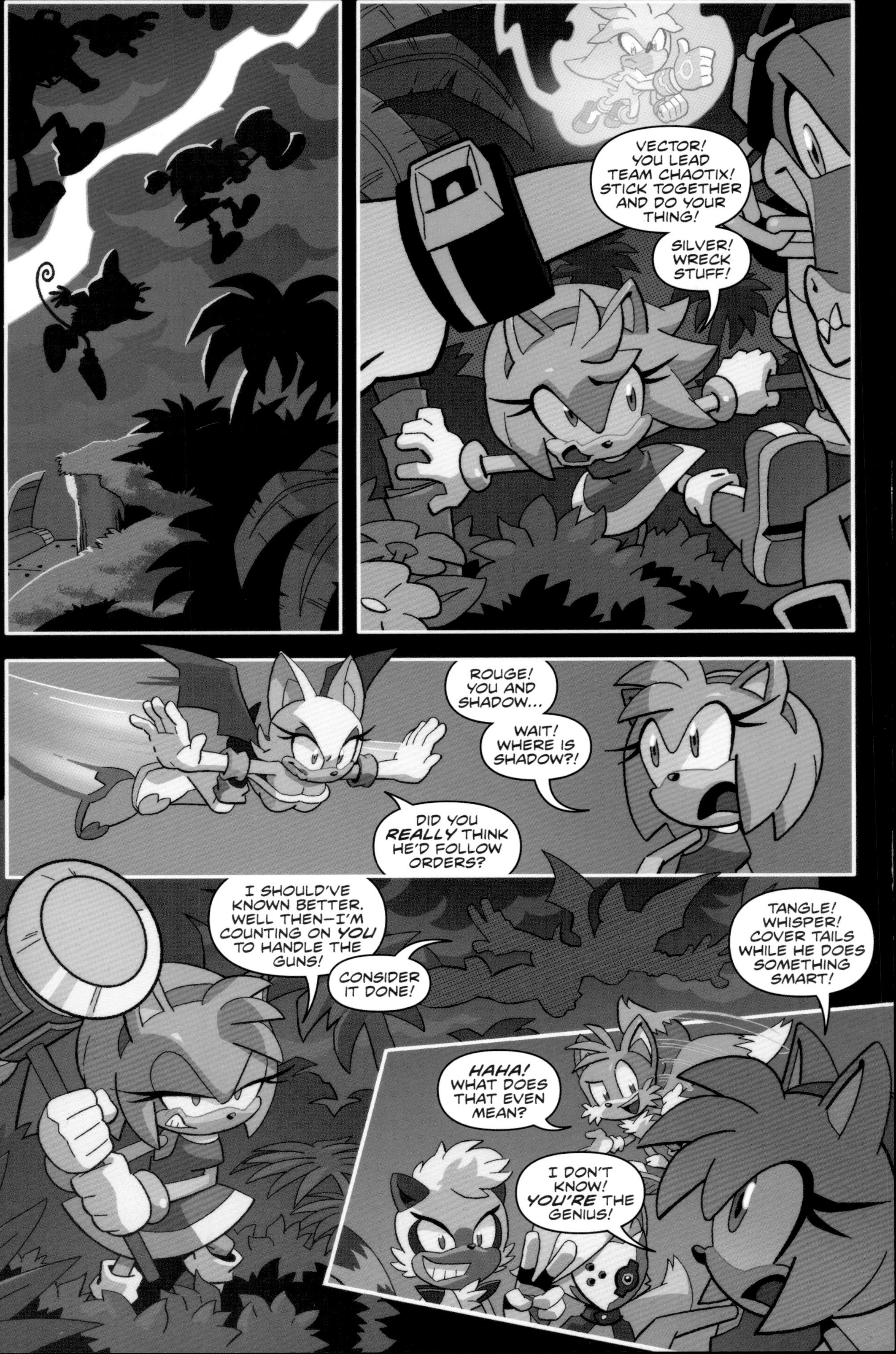
VECTOR! YOU LEAD TEAM CHAOTIX! STICK TOGETHER AND DO YOUR THING!
SILVER! WRECK STUFF!
ROUGE! YOU AND SHADOW...
WAIT! WHERE IS SHADOW?!
DID YOU **REALLY** THINK HE'D FOLLOW ORDERS?
I SHOULD'VE KNOWN BETTER. WELL THEN—I'M COUNTING ON **YOU** TO HANDLE THE GUNS!
CONSIDER IT DONE!
TANGLE! WHISPER! COVER TAILS WHILE HE DOES SOMETHING SMART!
HAHA! WHAT DOES THAT EVEN MEAN?
I DON'T KNOW! **YOU'RE** THE GENIUS!

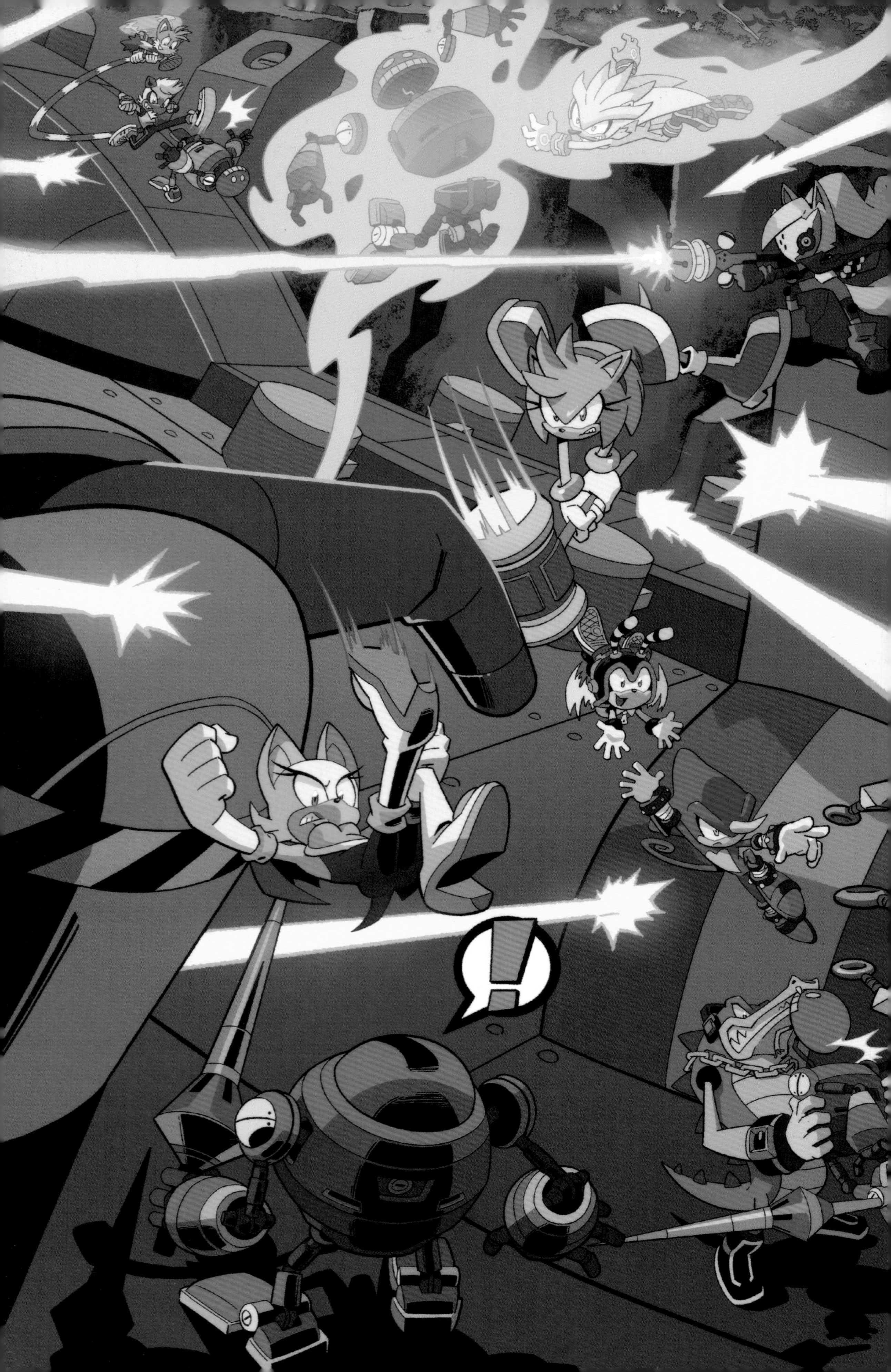
!

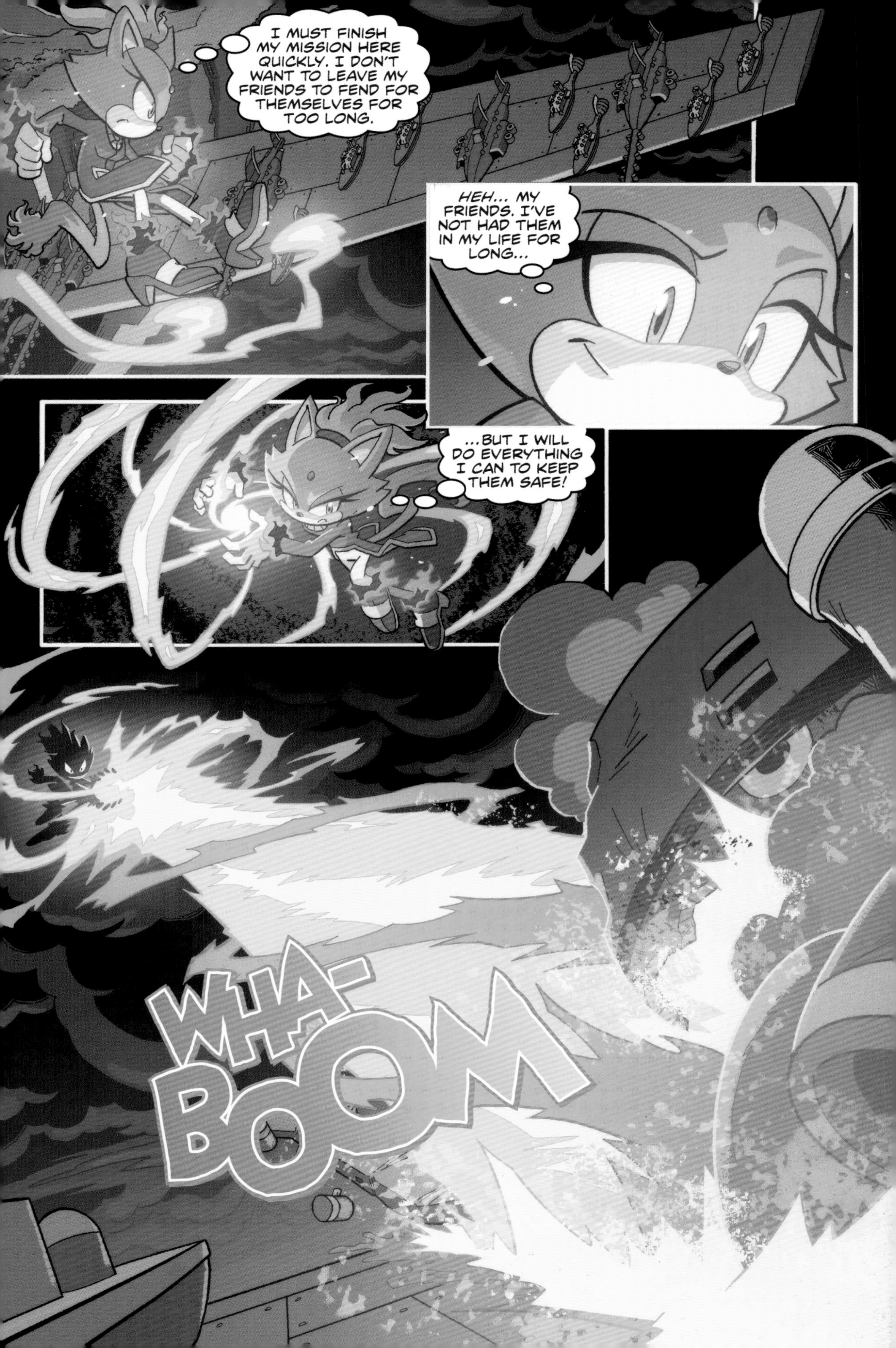
I MUST FINISH MY MISSION HERE QUICKLY. I DON'T WANT TO LEAVE MY FRIENDS TO FEND FOR THEMSELVES FOR TOO LONG.
HEH... MY FRIENDS. I'VE NOT HAD THEM IN MY LIFE FOR LONG...
...BUT I WILL DO EVERYTHING I CAN TO KEEP THEM SAFE!
WHA-BOOM

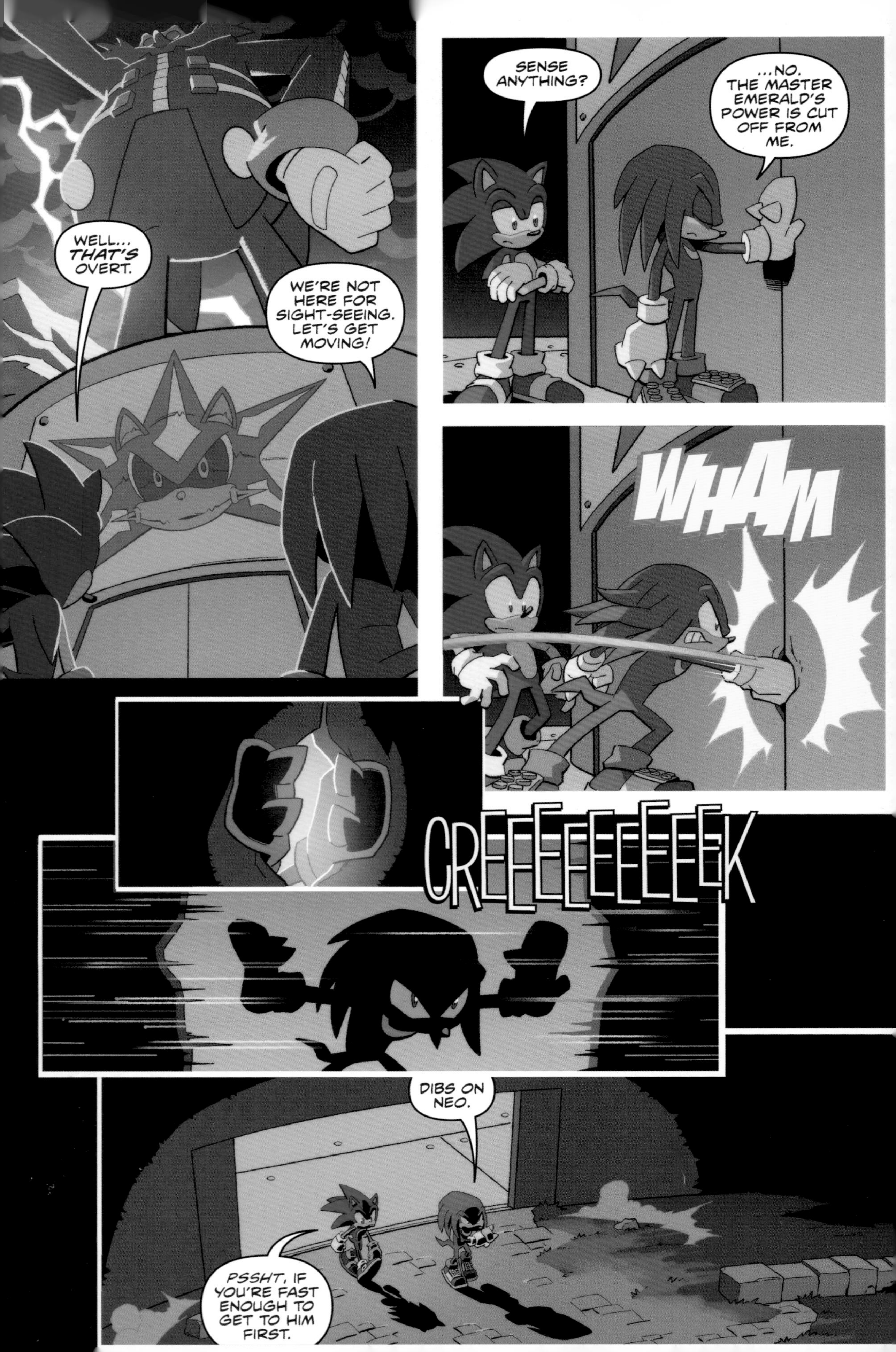
WELL... THAT'S OVERT.
WE'RE NOT HERE FOR SIGHT-SEEING. LET'S GET MOVING!
SENSE ANYTHING?
...NO. THE MASTER EMERALD'S POWER IS CUT OFF FROM ME.
WHAM
CREEEEEEEEEEK
DIBS ON NEO.
PSSHT, IF YOU'RE FAST ENOUGH TO GET TO HIM FIRST.

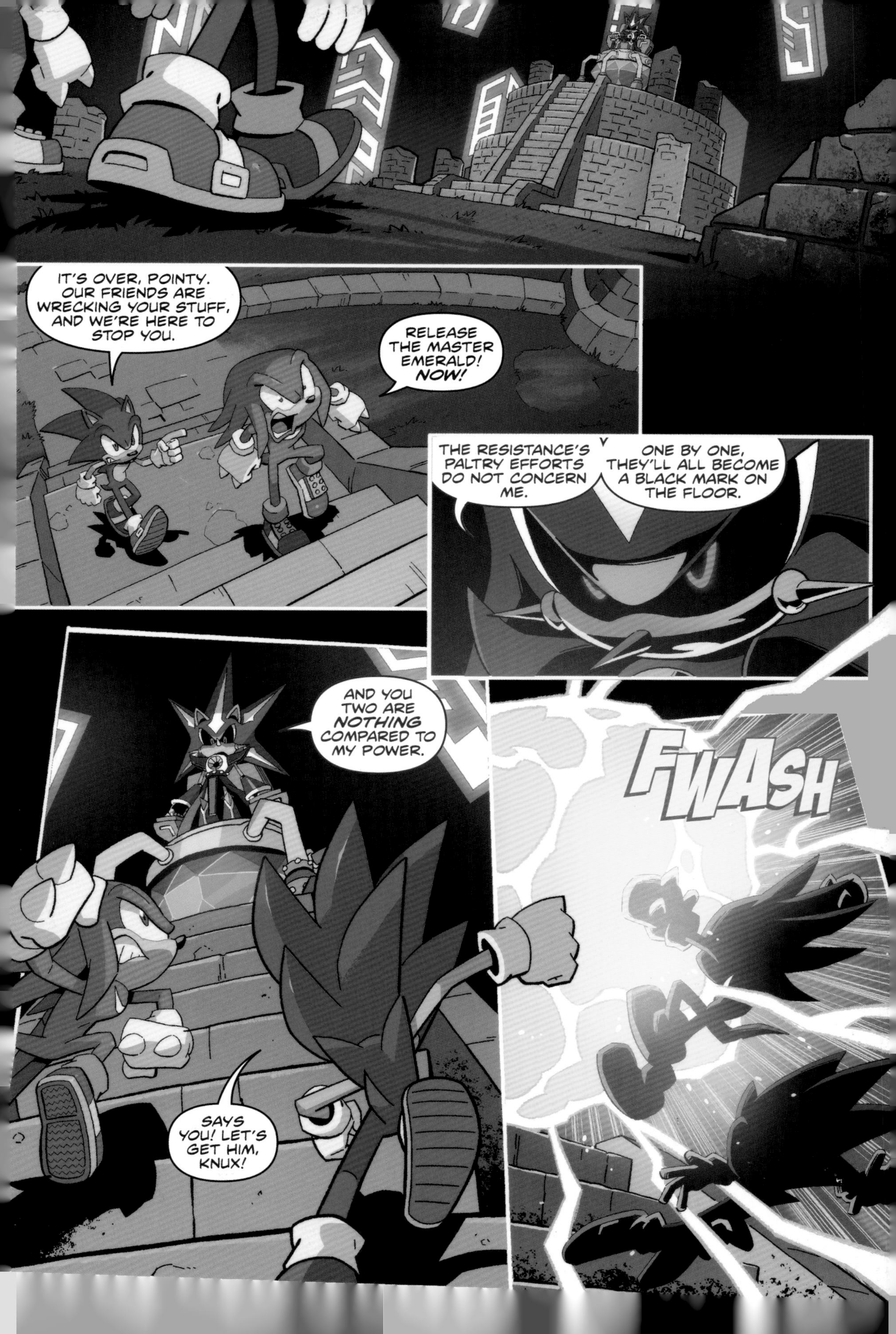

IT'S OVER, POINTY. OUR FRIENDS ARE WRECKING YOUR STUFF, AND WE'RE HERE TO STOP YOU.
RELEASE THE MASTER EMERALD! *NOW!*
THE RESISTANCE'S PALTRY EFFORTS DO NOT CONCERN ME.
ONE BY ONE, THEY'LL ALL BECOME A BLACK MARK ON THE FLOOR.
AND YOU TWO ARE *NOTHING* COMPARED TO MY POWER.
SAYS YOU! LET'S GET HIM, KNUX!
FWASH

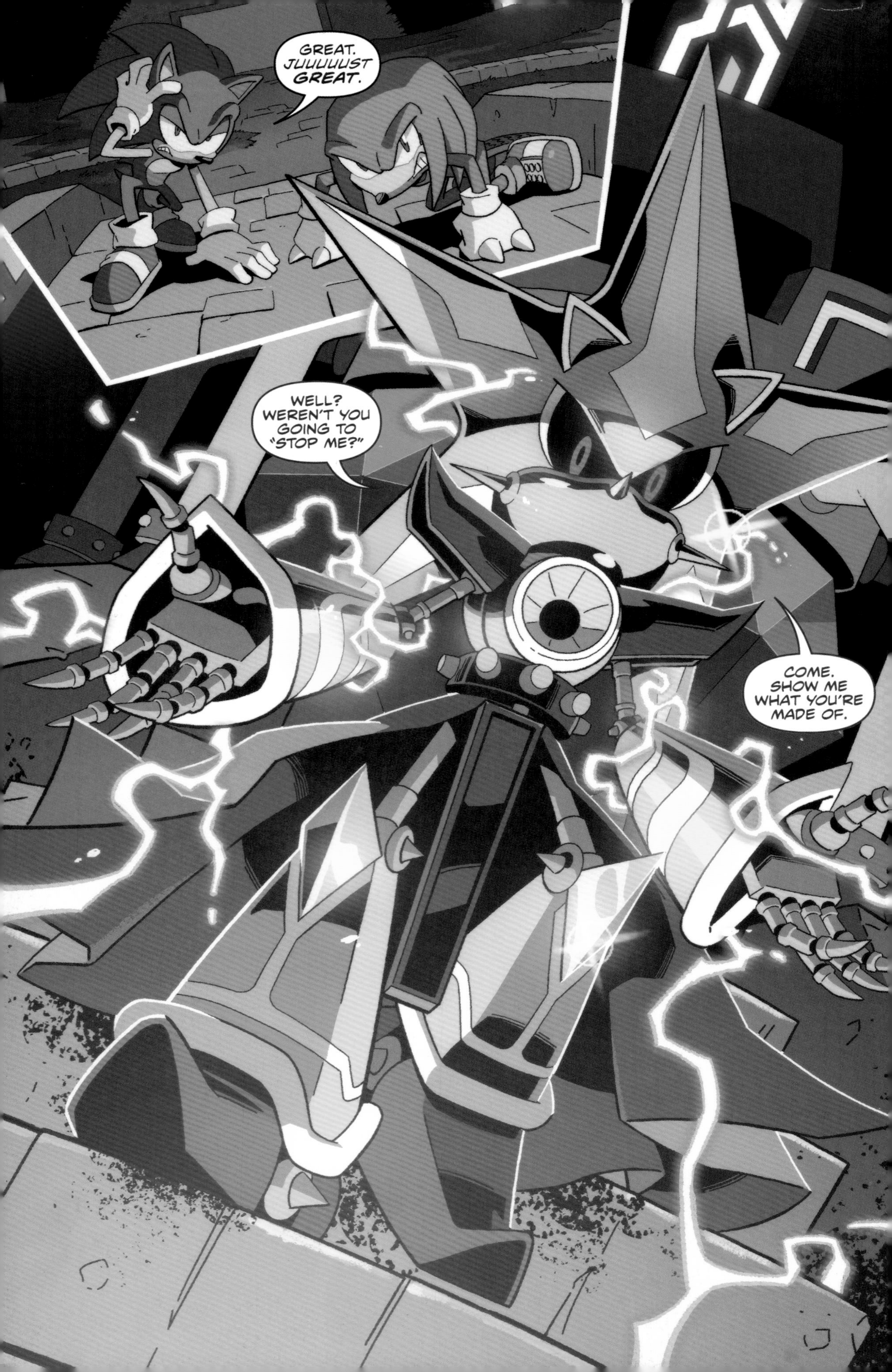
GREAT. JUUUUUST GREAT.
WELL? WEREN'T YOU GOING TO "STOP ME?"
COME. SHOW ME WHAT YOU'RE MADE OF.

ART BY NATHALIE FOURDRAINE

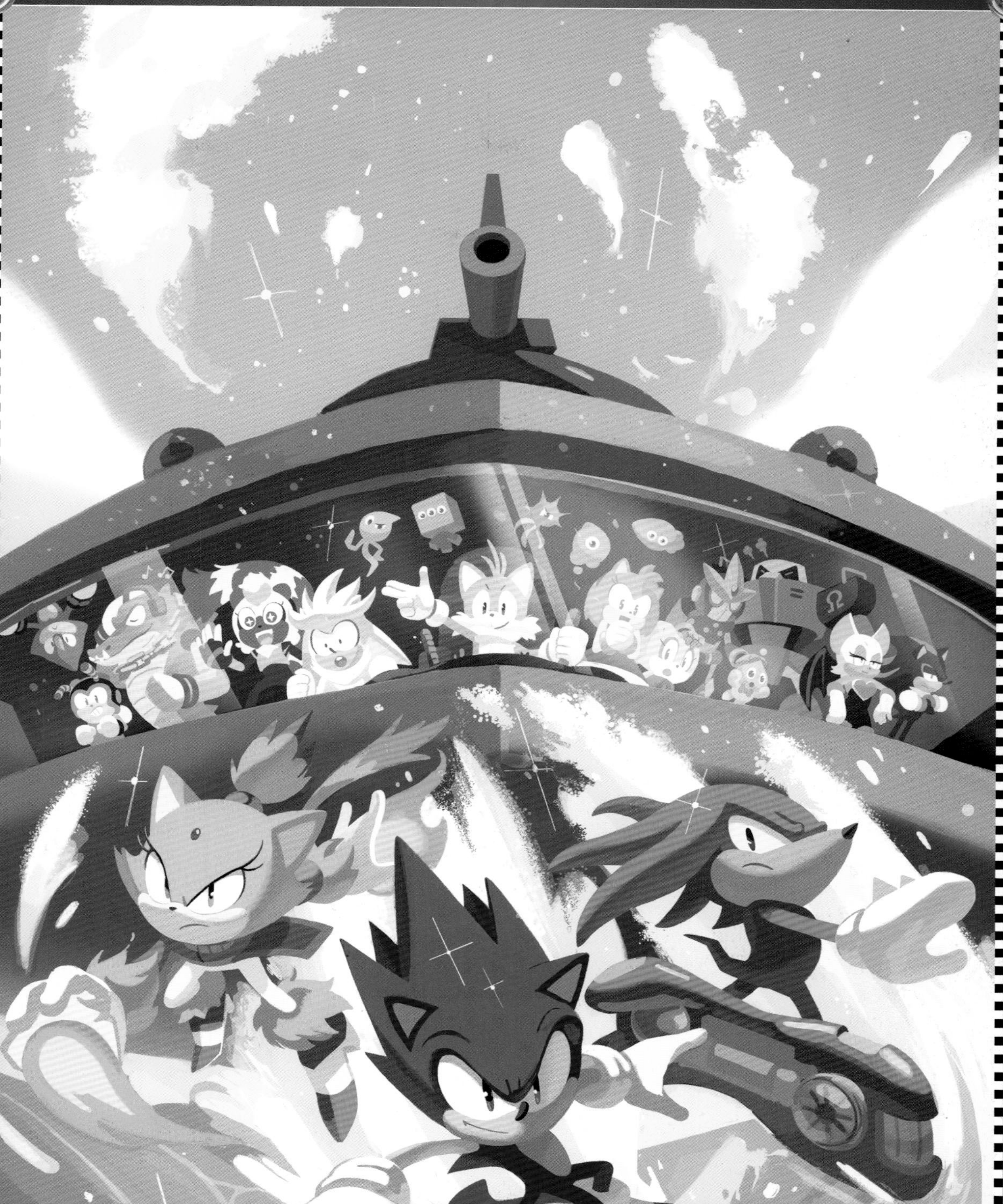

ART BY ADAM BRYCE THOMAS

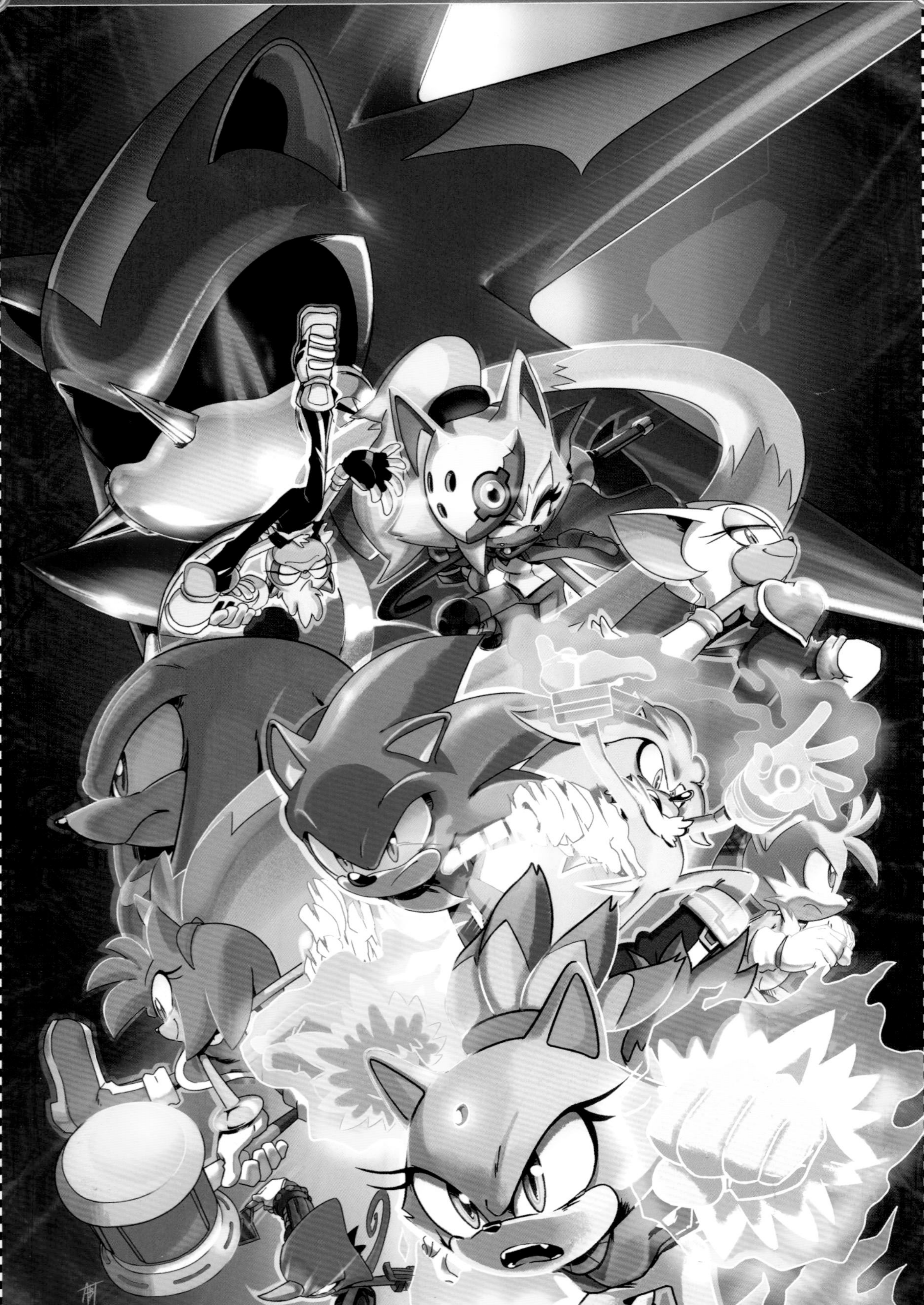
ABT

SONIC THE HEDGEHOG #10

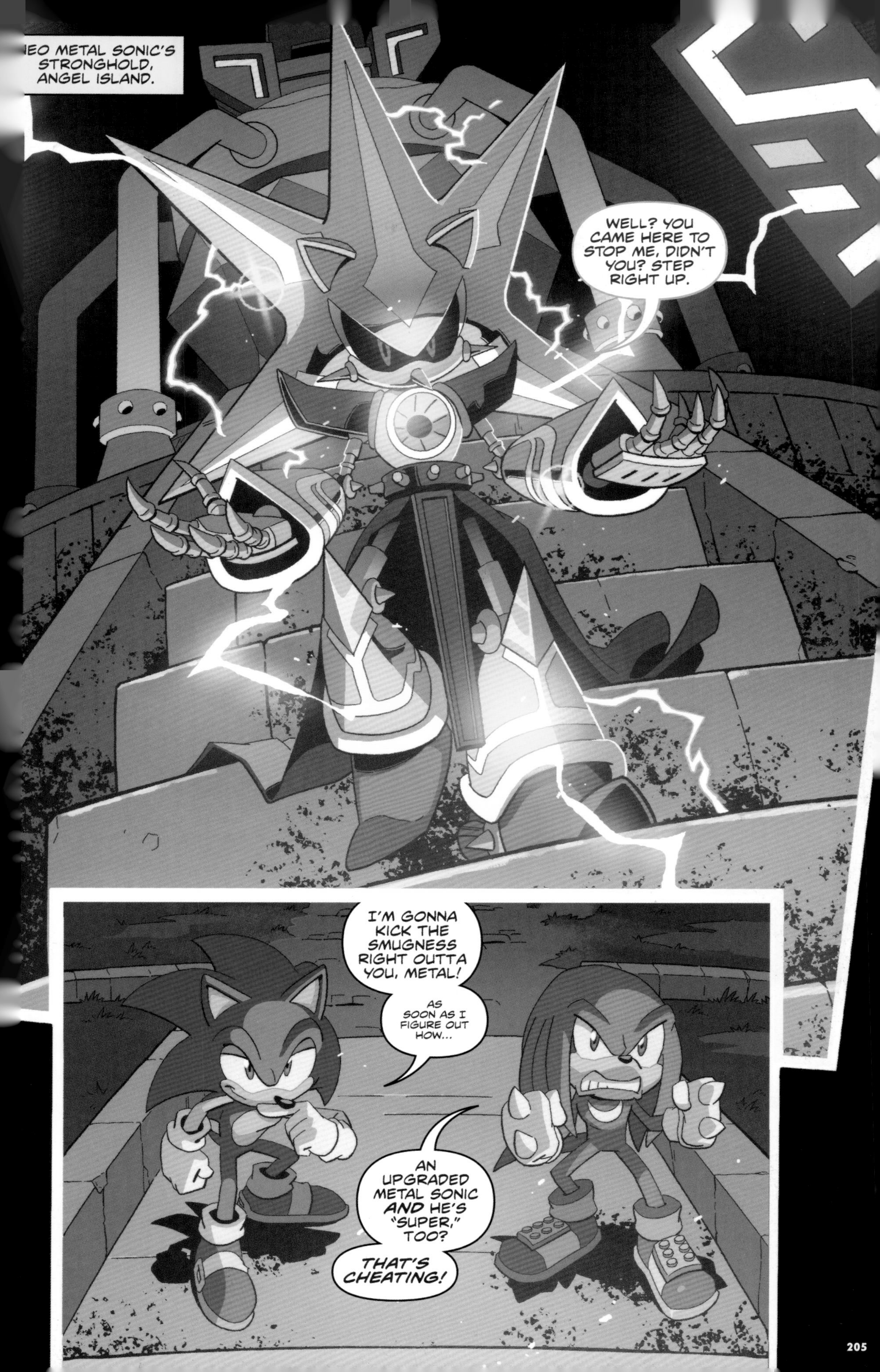
NEO METAL SONIC'S STRONGHOLD, ANGEL ISLAND.
WELL? YOU CAME HERE TO STOP ME, DIDN'T YOU? STEP RIGHT UP.
I'M GONNA KICK THE SMUGNESS RIGHT OUTTA YOU, METAL!
AS SOON AS I FIGURE OUT HOW...
AN UPGRADED METAL SONIC AND HE'S "SUPER," TOO?
THAT'S CHEATING!

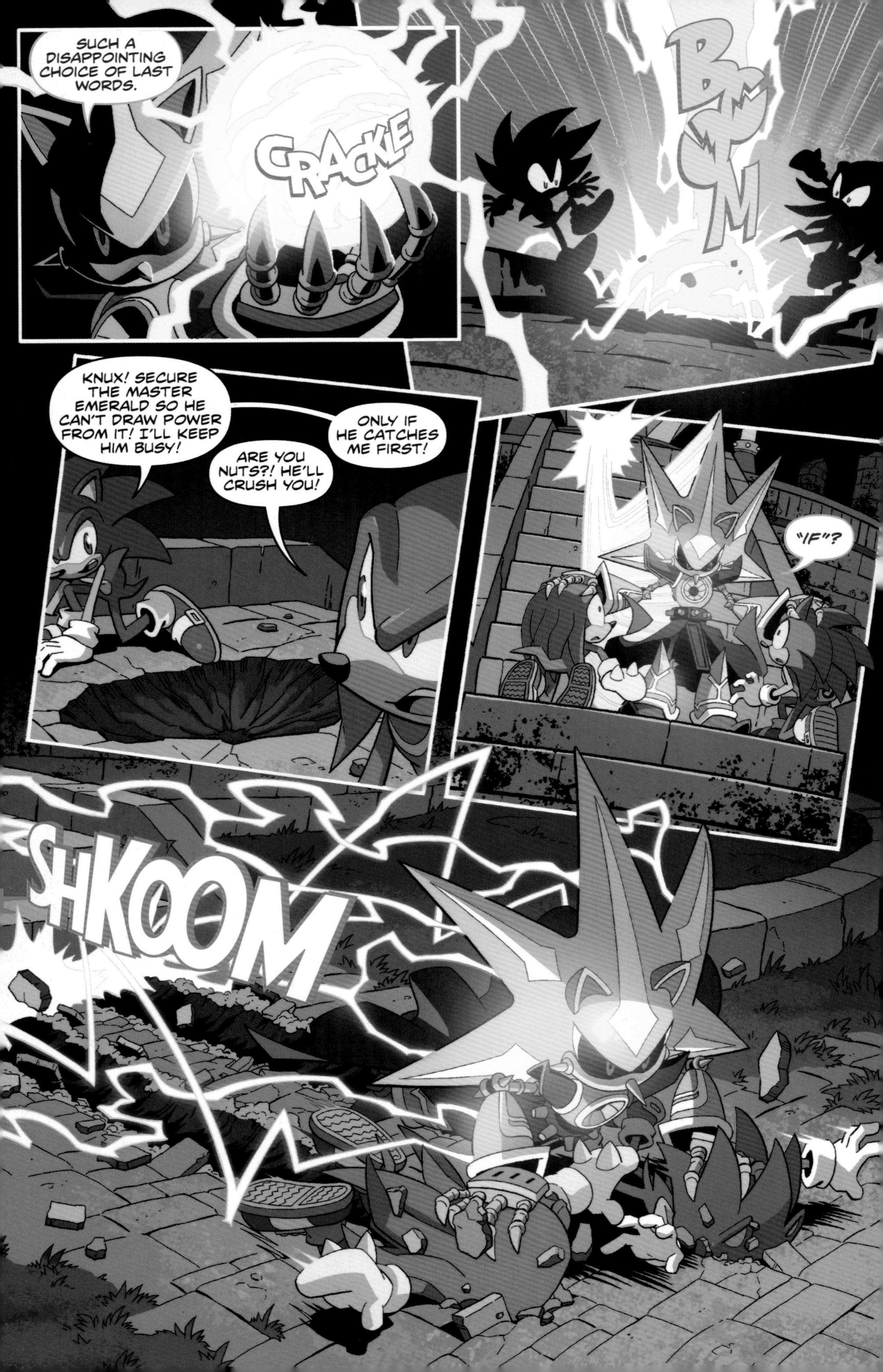
SUCH A DISAPPOINTING CHOICE OF LAST WORDS.
CRACKLE
BOOM
KNUX! SECURE THE MASTER EMERALD SO HE CAN'T DRAW POWER FROM IT! I'LL KEEP HIM BUSY!
ARE YOU NUTS?! HE'LL CRUSH YOU!
ONLY IF HE CATCHES ME FIRST!
"IF"?
SHKOOM

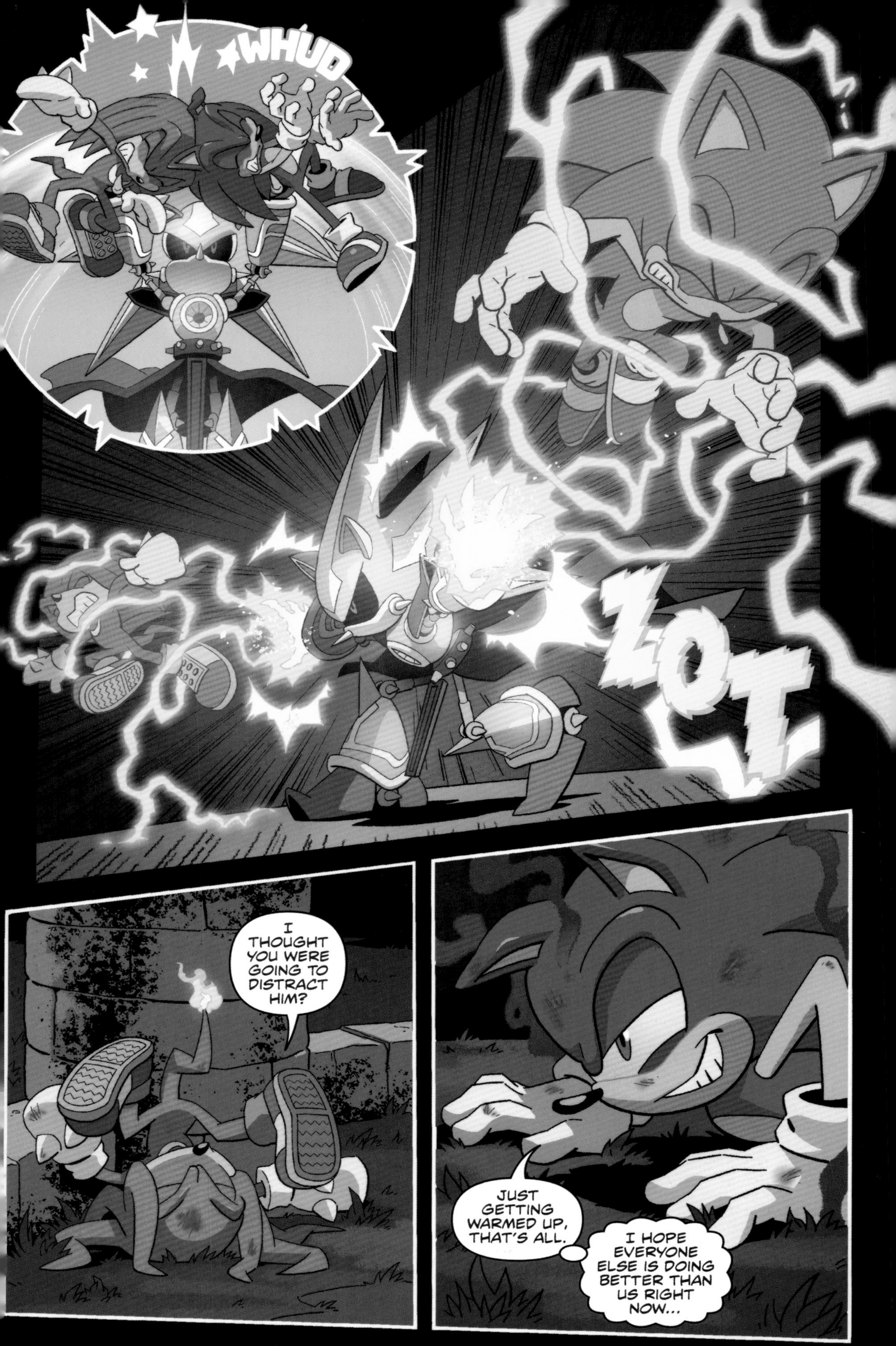
WHUD
ZOT
I THOUGHT YOU WERE GOING TO DISTRACT HIM?
JUST GETTING WARMED UP, THAT'S ALL.
I HOPE EVERYONE ELSE IS DOING BETTER THAN US RIGHT NOW...

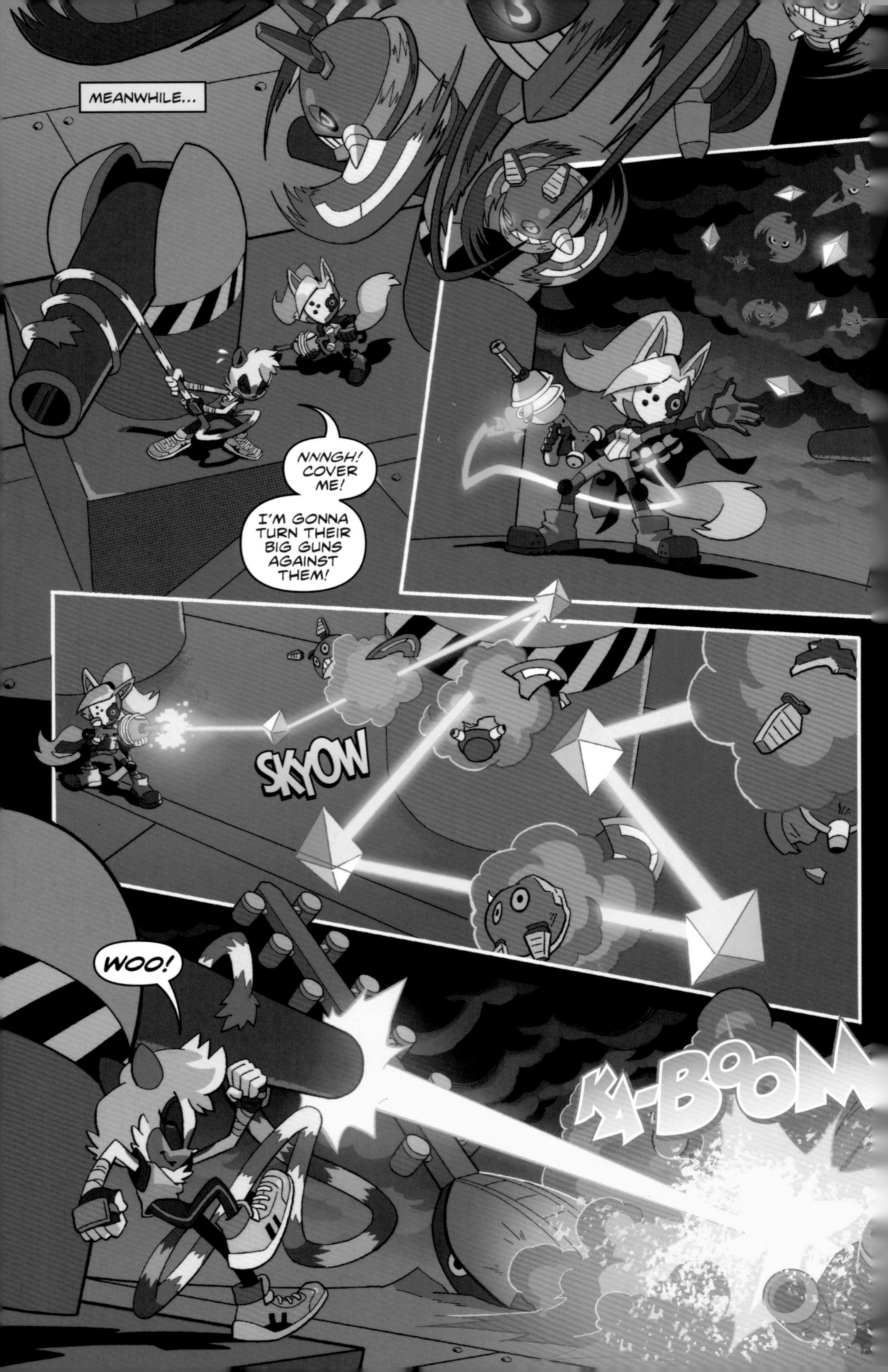
MEANWHILE...
NNNGH! COVER ME!
I'M GONNA TURN THEIR BIG GUNS AGAINST THEM!
SKYOW
WOO!
KA-BOOM

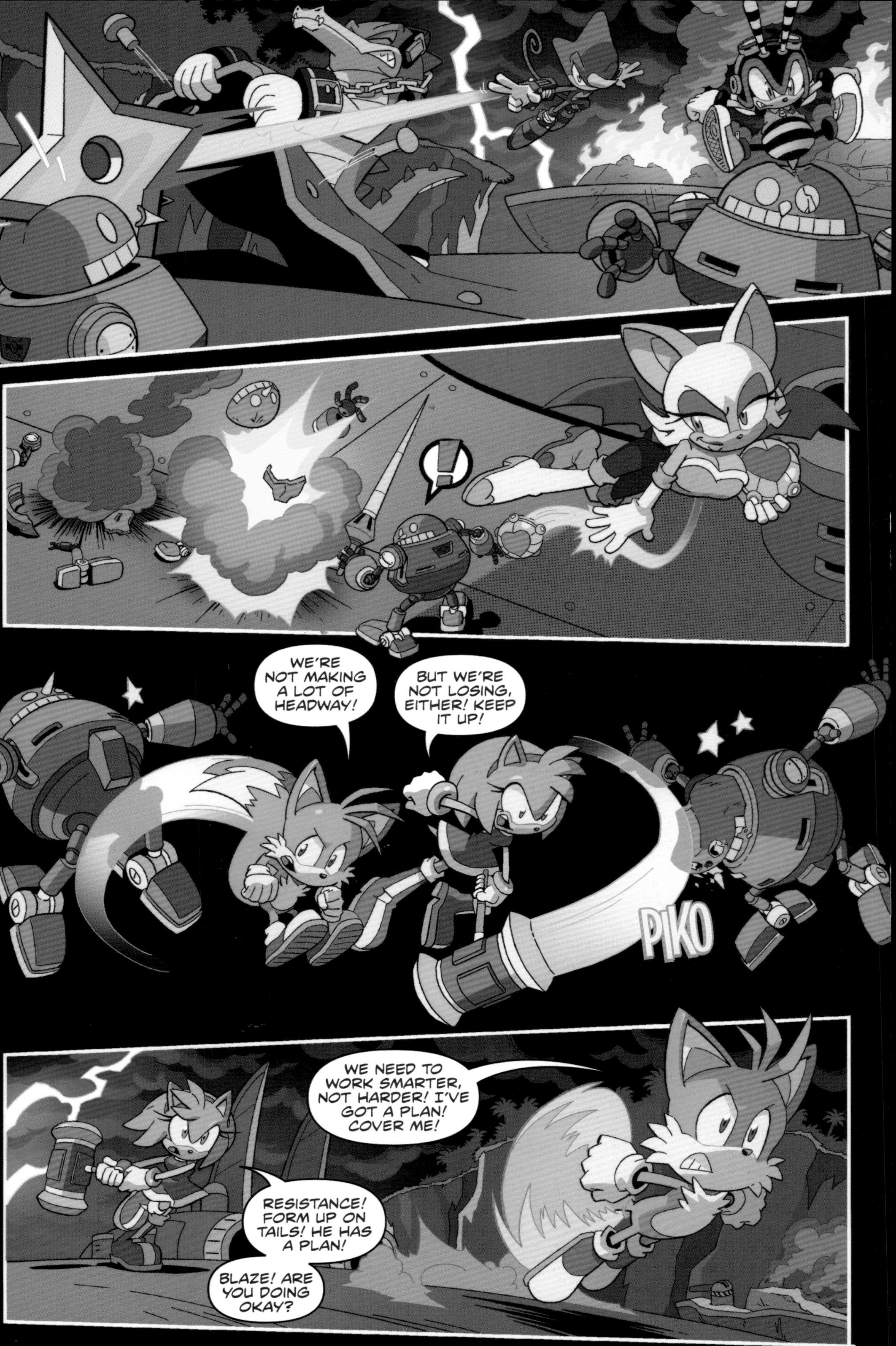
!
WE'RE NOT MAKING A LOT OF HEADWAY!
BUT WE'RE NOT LOSING, EITHER! KEEP IT UP!
PIKO
WE NEED TO WORK SMARTER, NOT HARDER! I'VE GOT A PLAN! COVER ME!
RESISTANCE! FORM UP ON TAILS! HE HAS A PLAN!
BLAZE! ARE YOU DOING OKAY?

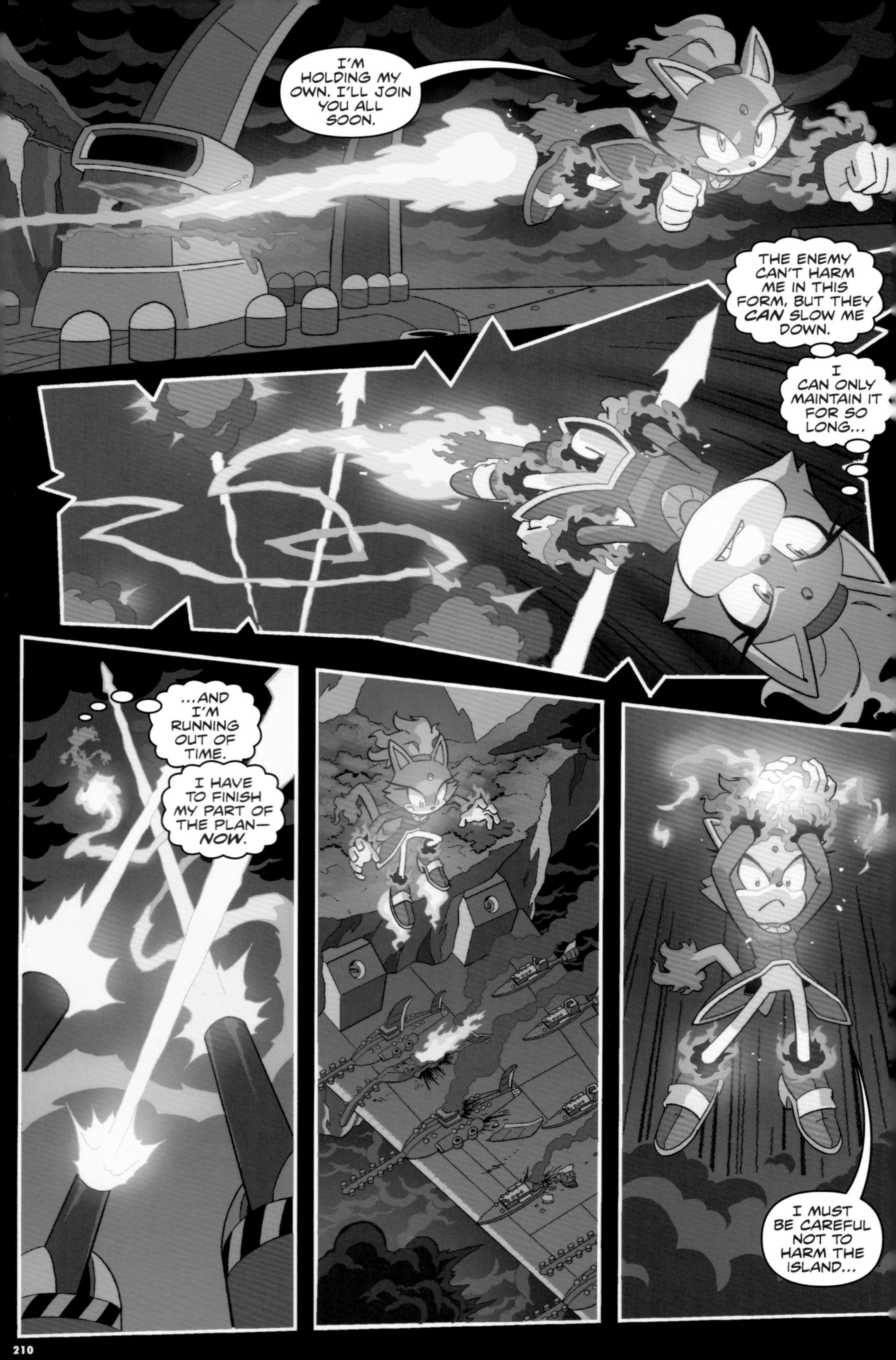
I'M HOLDING MY OWN. I'LL JOIN YOU ALL SOON.
THE ENEMY CAN'T HARM ME IN THIS FORM, BUT THEY CAN SLOW ME DOWN.
I CAN ONLY MAINTAIN IT FOR SO LONG...
...AND I'M RUNNING OUT OF TIME.
I HAVE TO FINISH MY PART OF THE PLAN—NOW.
I MUST BE CAREFUL NOT TO HARM THE ISLAND...

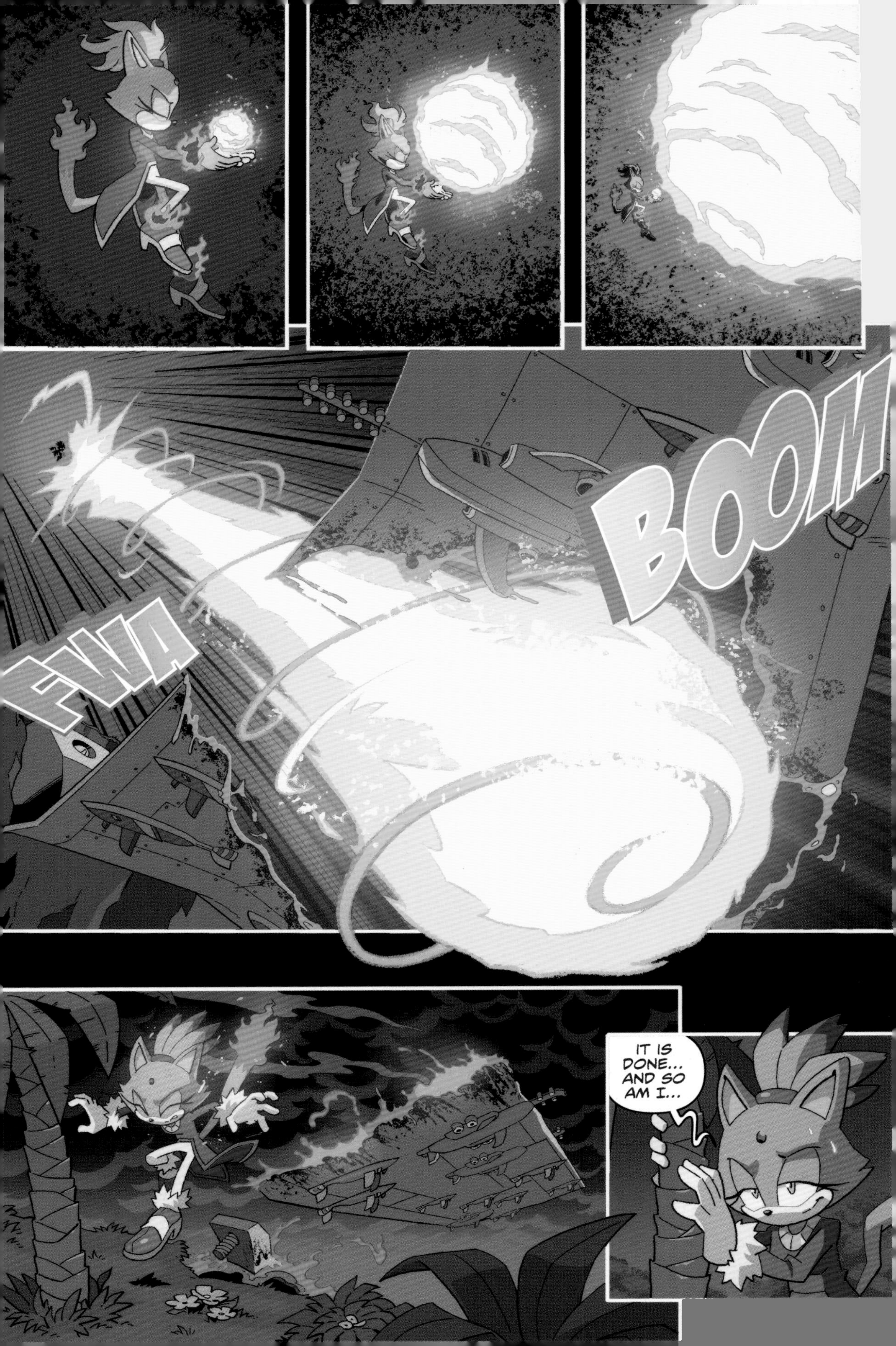
BOOM
FWA
IT IS DONE... AND SO AM I...

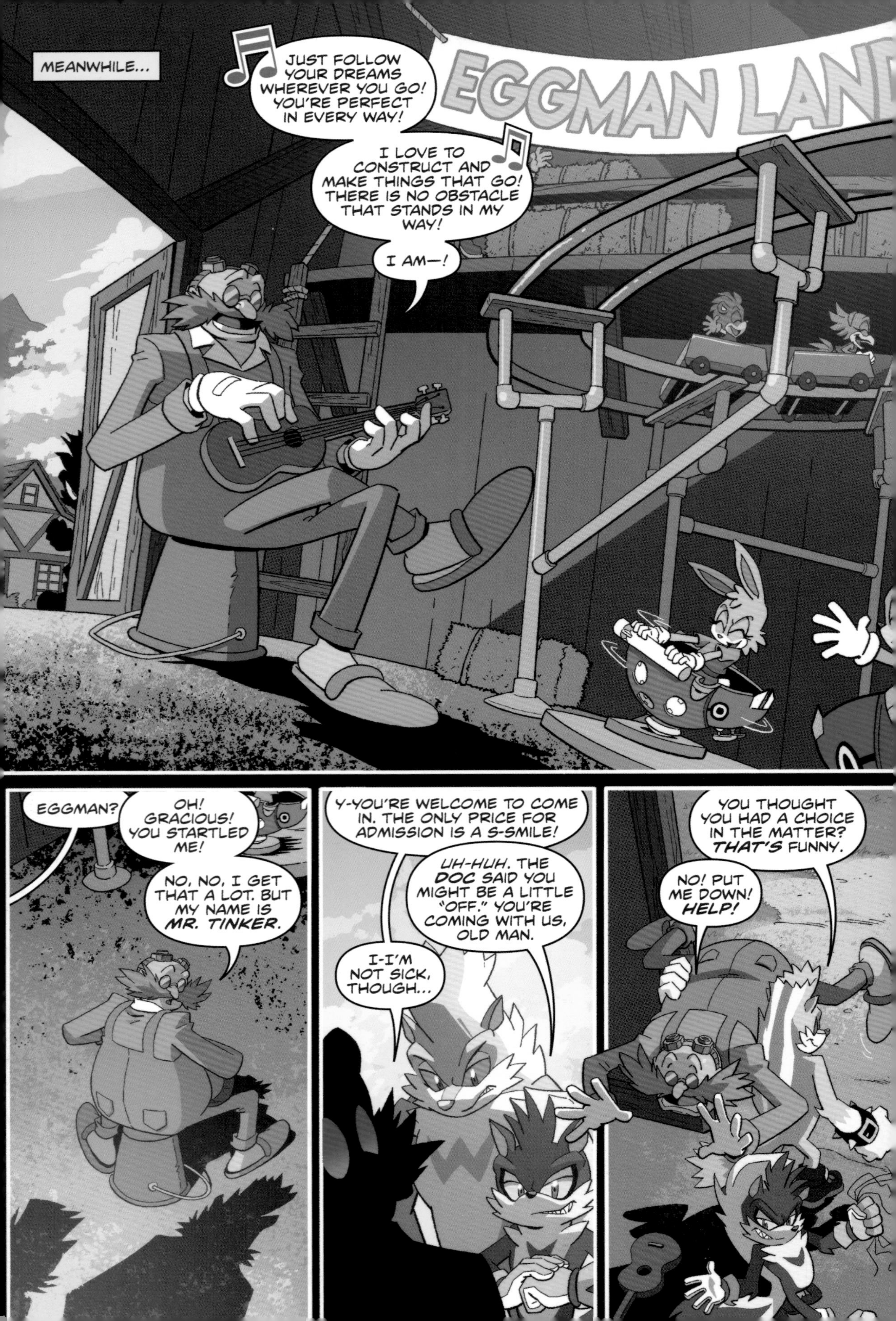
MEANWHILE...
JUST FOLLOW YOUR DREAMS WHEREVER YOU GO! YOU'RE PERFECT IN EVERY WAY!
EGGMAN LAND
I LOVE TO CONSTRUCT AND MAKE THINGS THAT GO! THERE IS NO OBSTACLE THAT STANDS IN MY WAY!
I AM—!
EGGMAN?
OH! GRACIOUS! YOU STARTLED ME!
NO, NO, I GET THAT A LOT. BUT MY NAME IS MR. TINKER.
Y-YOU'RE WELCOME TO COME IN. THE ONLY PRICE FOR ADMISSION IS A S-SMILE!
UH-HUH. THE DOC SAID YOU MIGHT BE A LITTLE "OFF." YOU'RE COMING WITH US, OLD MAN.
I-I'M NOT SICK, THOUGH...
YOU THOUGHT YOU HAD A CHOICE IN THE MATTER? THAT'S FUNNY.
NO! PUT ME DOWN! HELP!

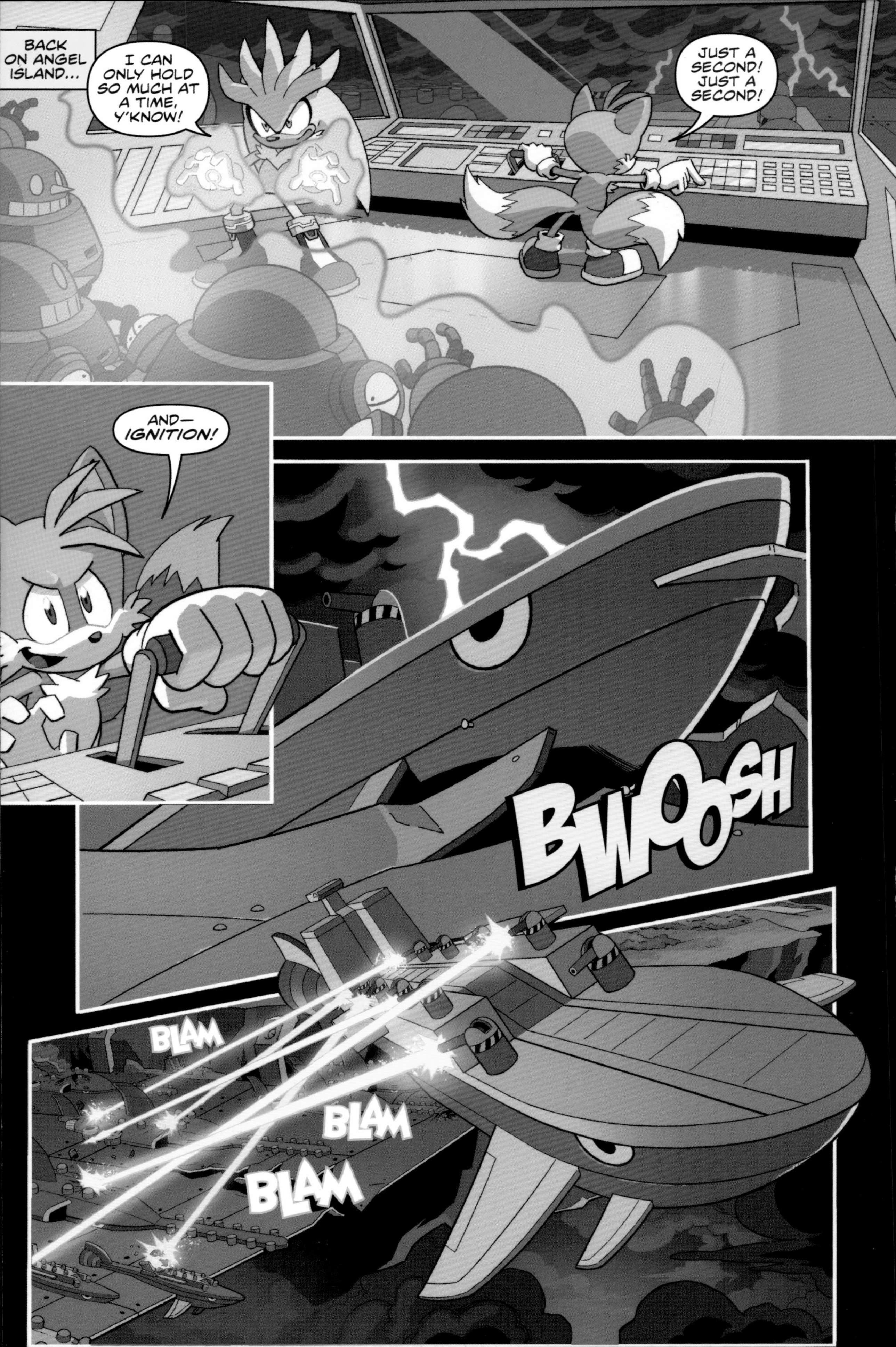

BACK ON ANGEL ISLAND...
I CAN ONLY HOLD SO MUCH AT A TIME, Y'KNOW!
JUST A SECOND! JUST A SECOND!
AND— IGNITION!
BWOOSH
BLAM
BLAM
BLAM

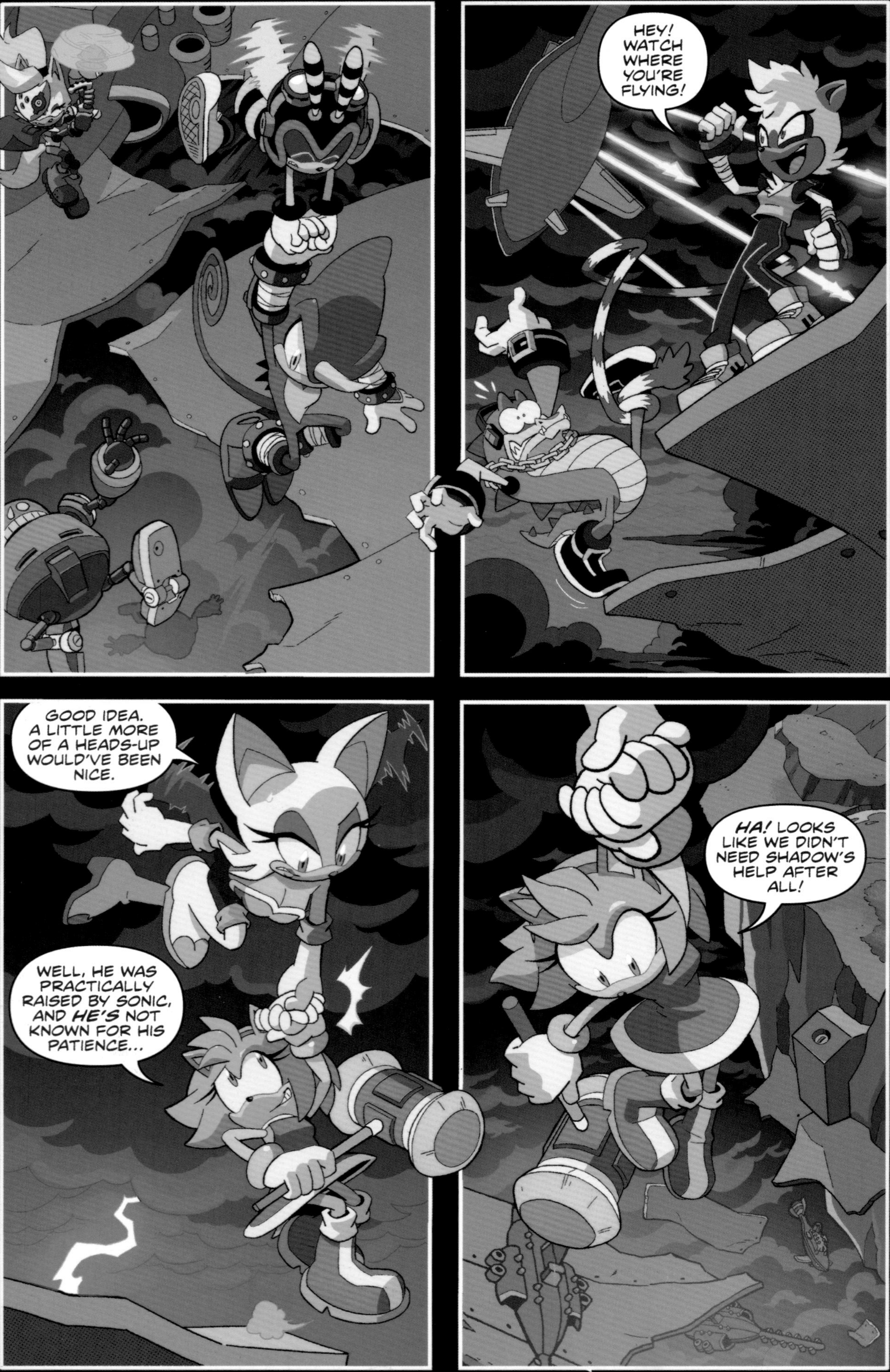
HEY! WATCH WHERE YOU'RE FLYING!
GOOD IDEA. A LITTLE MORE OF A HEADS-UP WOULD'VE BEEN NICE.
WELL, HE WAS PRACTICALLY RAISED BY SONIC, AND *HE'S* NOT KNOWN FOR HIS PATIENCE...
HA! LOOKS LIKE WE DIDN'T NEED SHADOW'S HELP AFTER ALL!

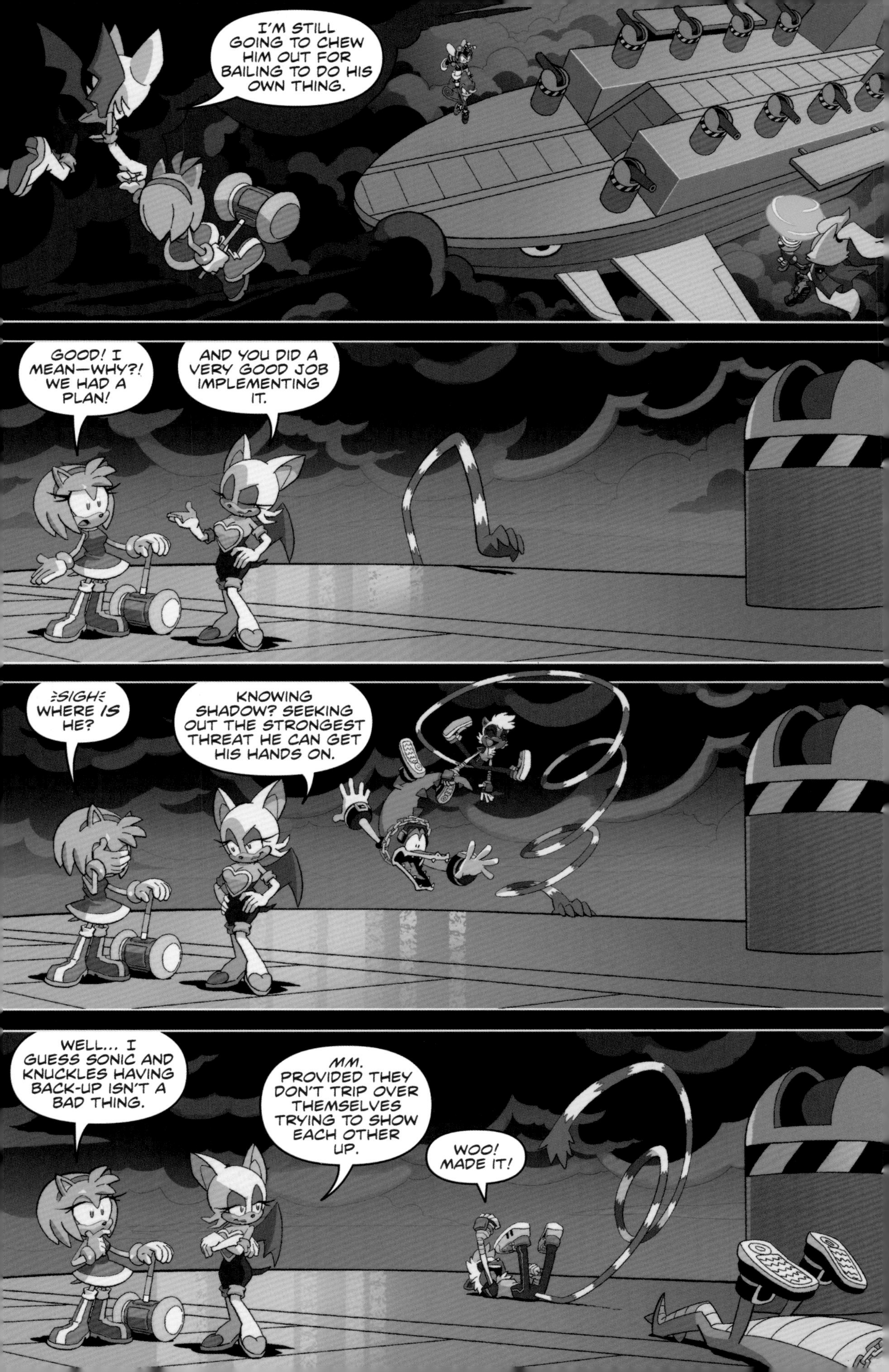
I'M STILL GOING TO CHEW HIM OUT FOR BAILING TO DO HIS OWN THING.
GOOD! I MEAN—WHY?! WE HAD A PLAN!
AND YOU DID A VERY GOOD JOB IMPLEMENTING IT.
=SIGH= WHERE *IS* HE?
KNOWING SHADOW? SEEKING OUT THE STRONGEST THREAT HE CAN GET HIS HANDS ON.
WELL... I GUESS SONIC AND KNUCKLES HAVING BACK-UP ISN'T A BAD THING.
MM. PROVIDED THEY DON'T TRIP OVER THEMSELVES TRYING TO SHOW EACH OTHER UP.
WOO! MADE IT!

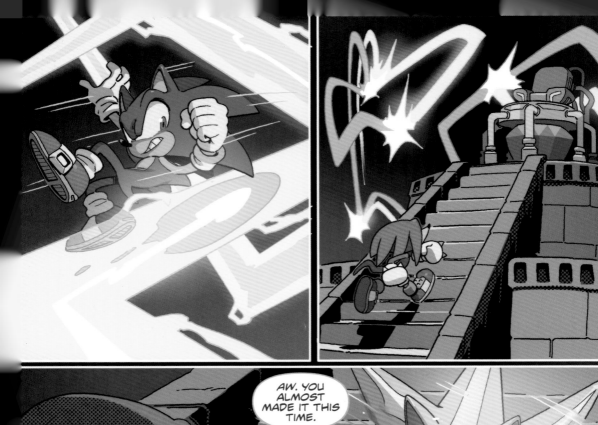

AW. YOU ALMOST MADE IT THIS TIME.

I AM DISAPPOINTED. TRULY. YOU'RE DEFEATED, AND I DIDN'T EVEN NEED TO UNLEASH MY FINAL FORM.

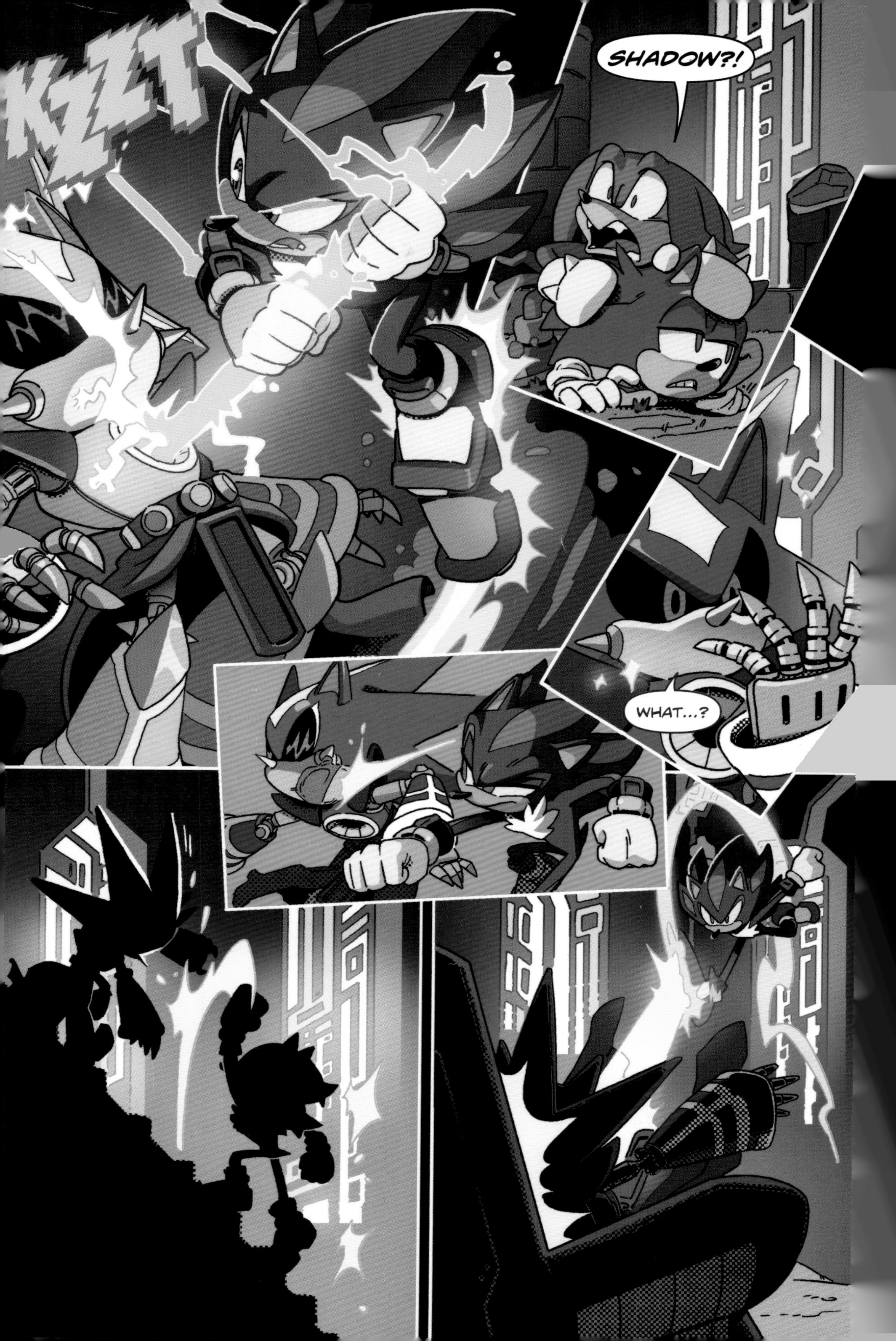
KZZT
SHADOW?!
WHAT...?

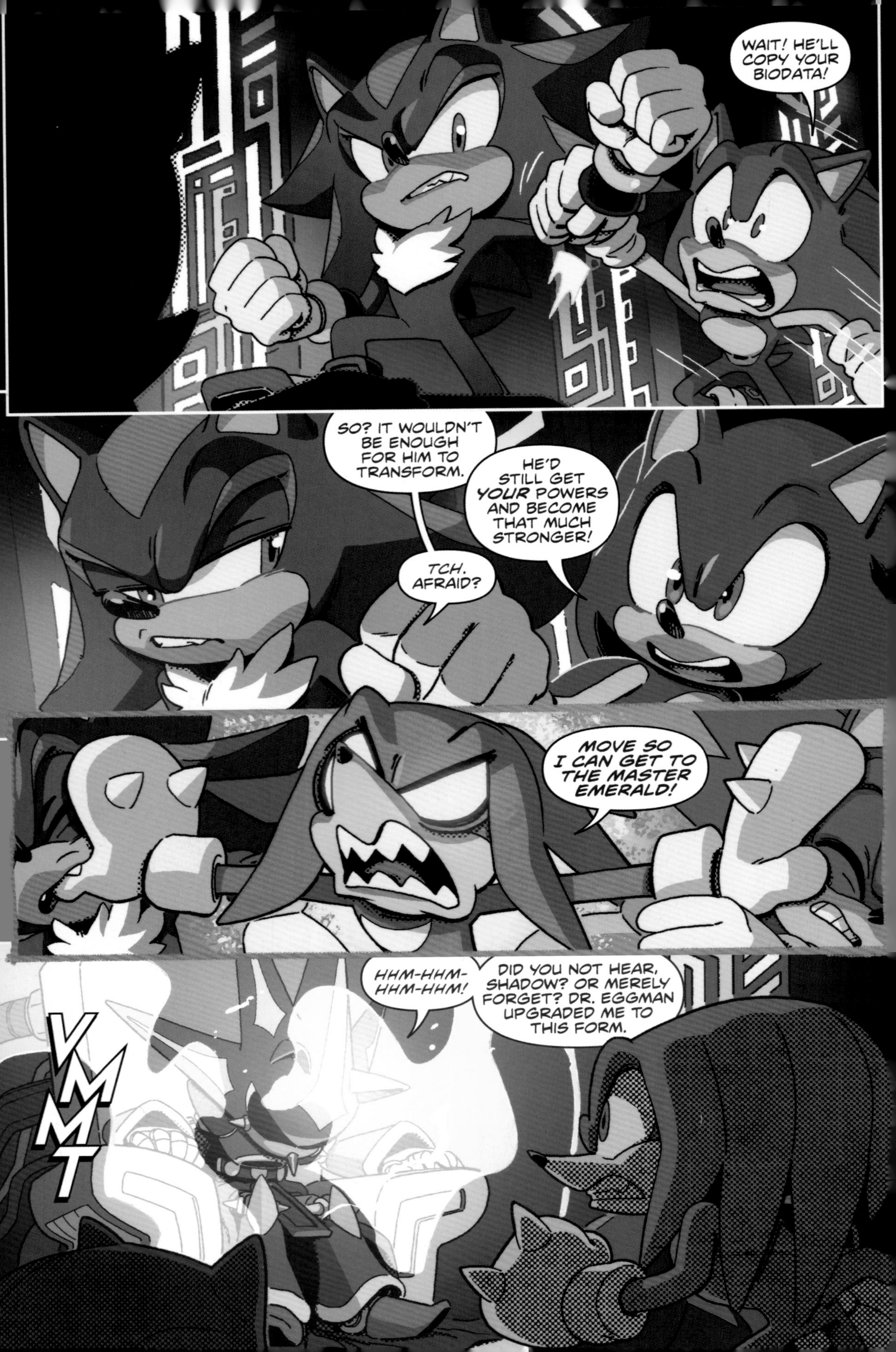
WAIT! HE'LL COPY YOUR BIODATA!
SO? IT WOULDN'T BE ENOUGH FOR HIM TO TRANSFORM.
HE'D STILL GET YOUR POWERS AND BECOME THAT MUCH STRONGER!
TCH. AFRAID?
MOVE SO I CAN GET TO THE MASTER EMERALD!
VMMT
HHM-HHM-HHM-HHM!
DID YOU NOT HEAR, SHADOW? OR MERELY FORGET? DR. EGGMAN UPGRADED ME TO THIS FORM.

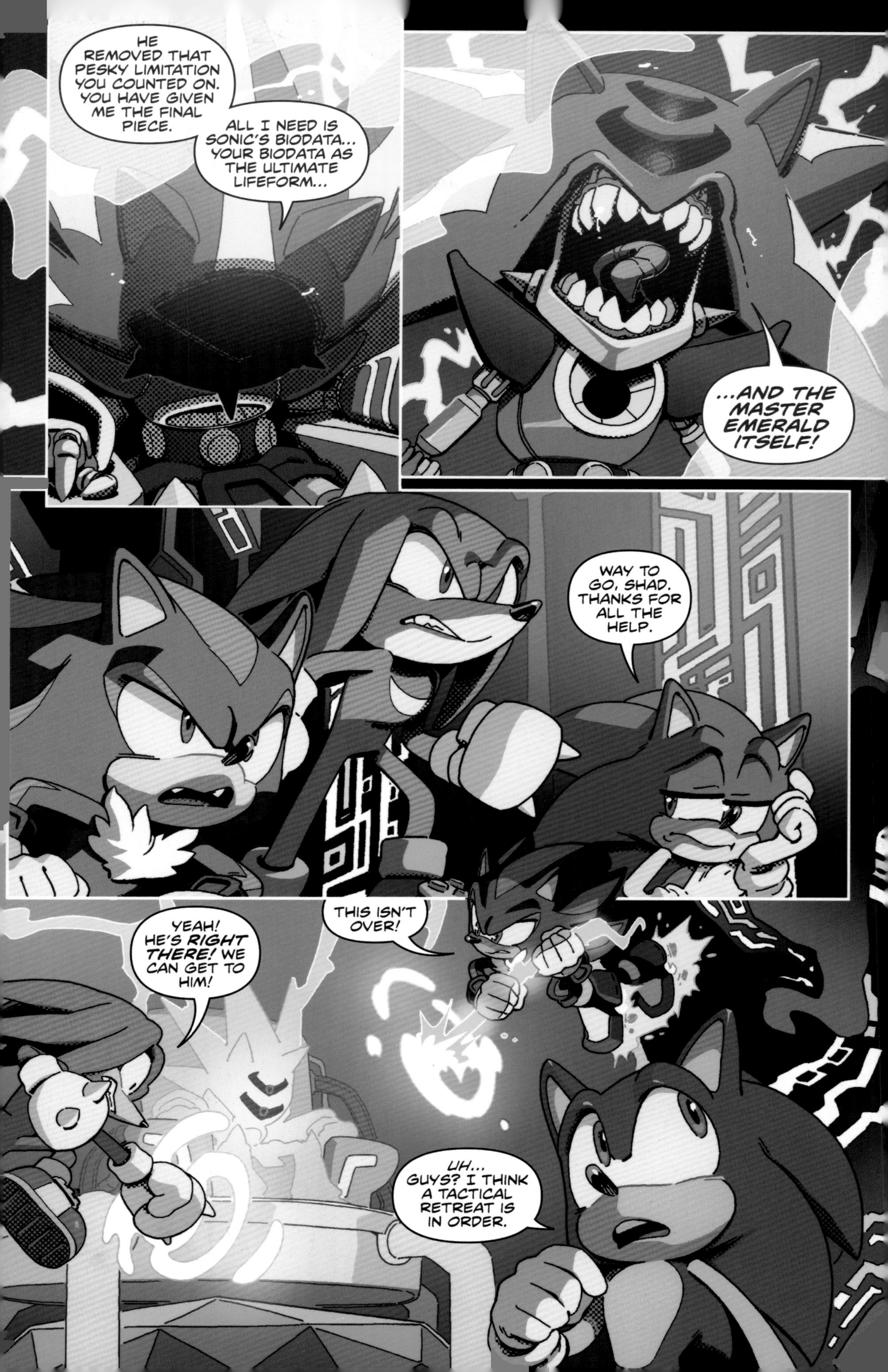
HE REMOVED THAT PESKY LIMITATION YOU COUNTED ON. YOU HAVE GIVEN ME THE FINAL PIECE.
ALL I NEED IS SONIC'S BIODATA... YOUR BIODATA AS THE ULTIMATE LIFEFORM...
...AND THE MASTER EMERALD ITSELF!
WAY TO GO, SHAD. THANKS FOR ALL THE HELP.
YEAH! HE'S *RIGHT THERE!* WE CAN GET TO HIM!
THIS ISN'T OVER!
UH... GUYS? I THINK A TACTICAL RETREAT IS IN ORDER.

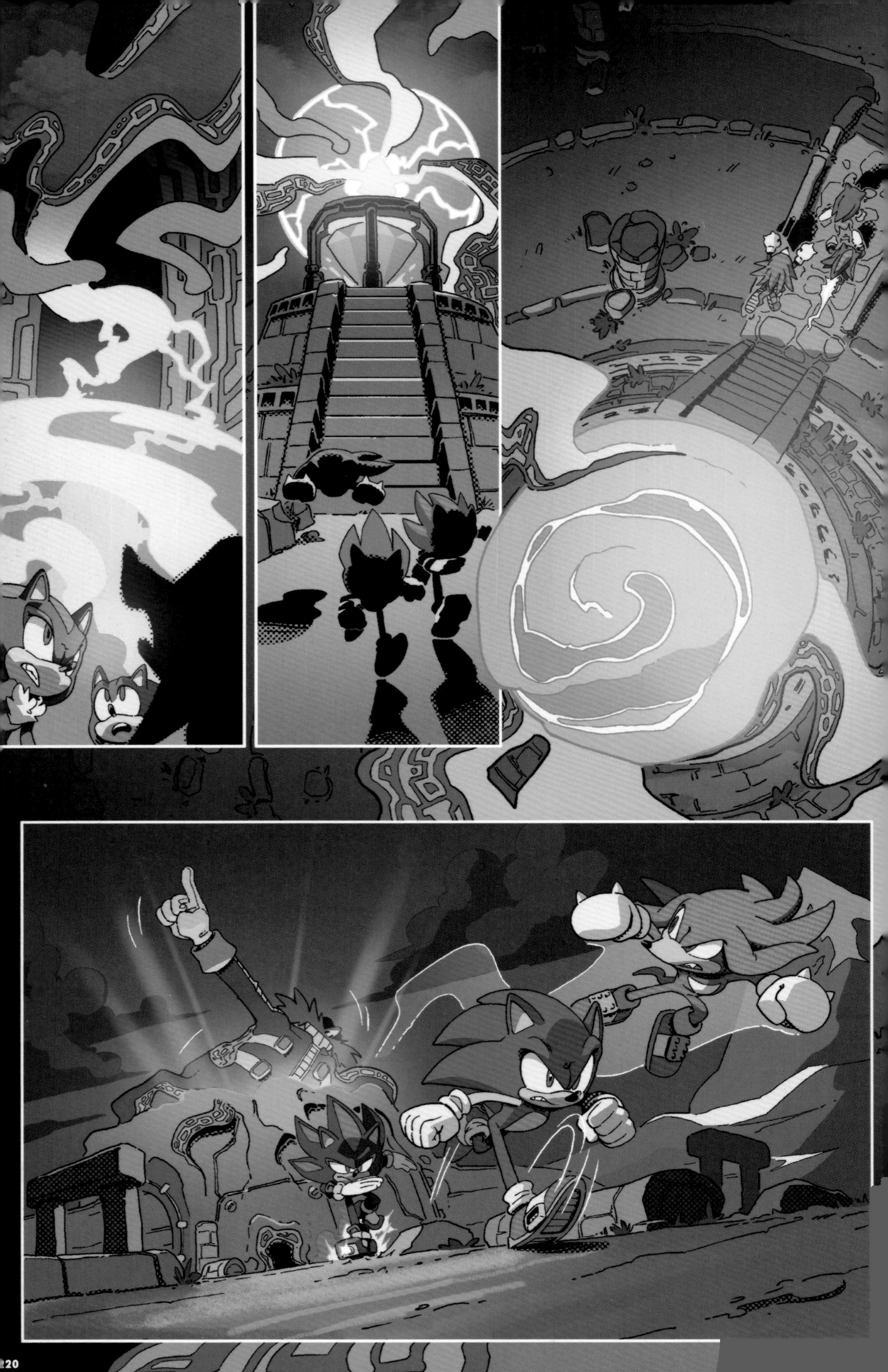

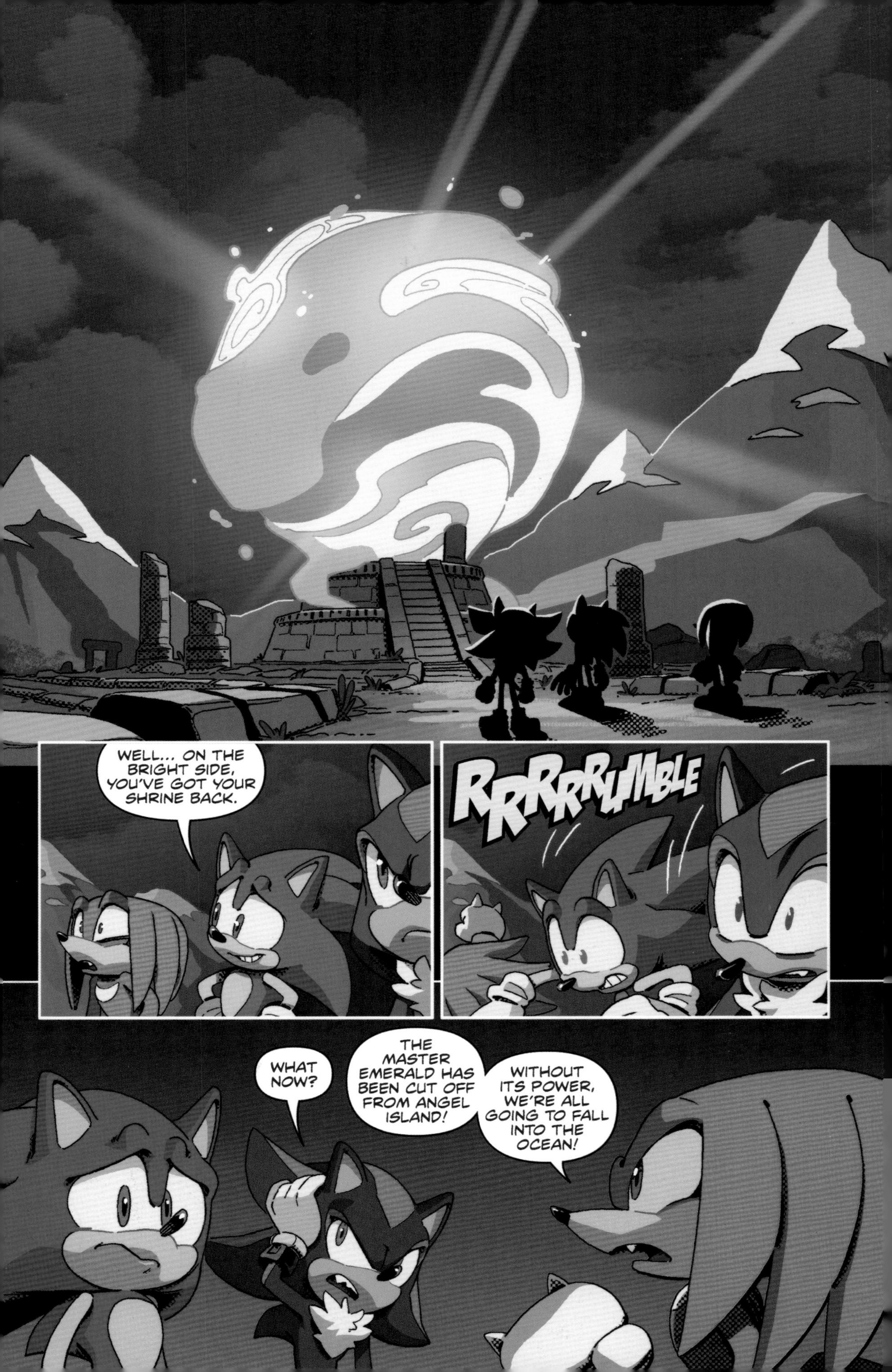
WELL... ON THE BRIGHT SIDE, YOU'VE GOT YOUR SHRINE BACK.
RRRRRUMBLE
WHAT NOW?
THE MASTER EMERALD HAS BEEN CUT OFF FROM ANGEL ISLAND!
WITHOUT ITS POWER, WE'RE ALL GOING TO FALL INTO THE OCEAN!

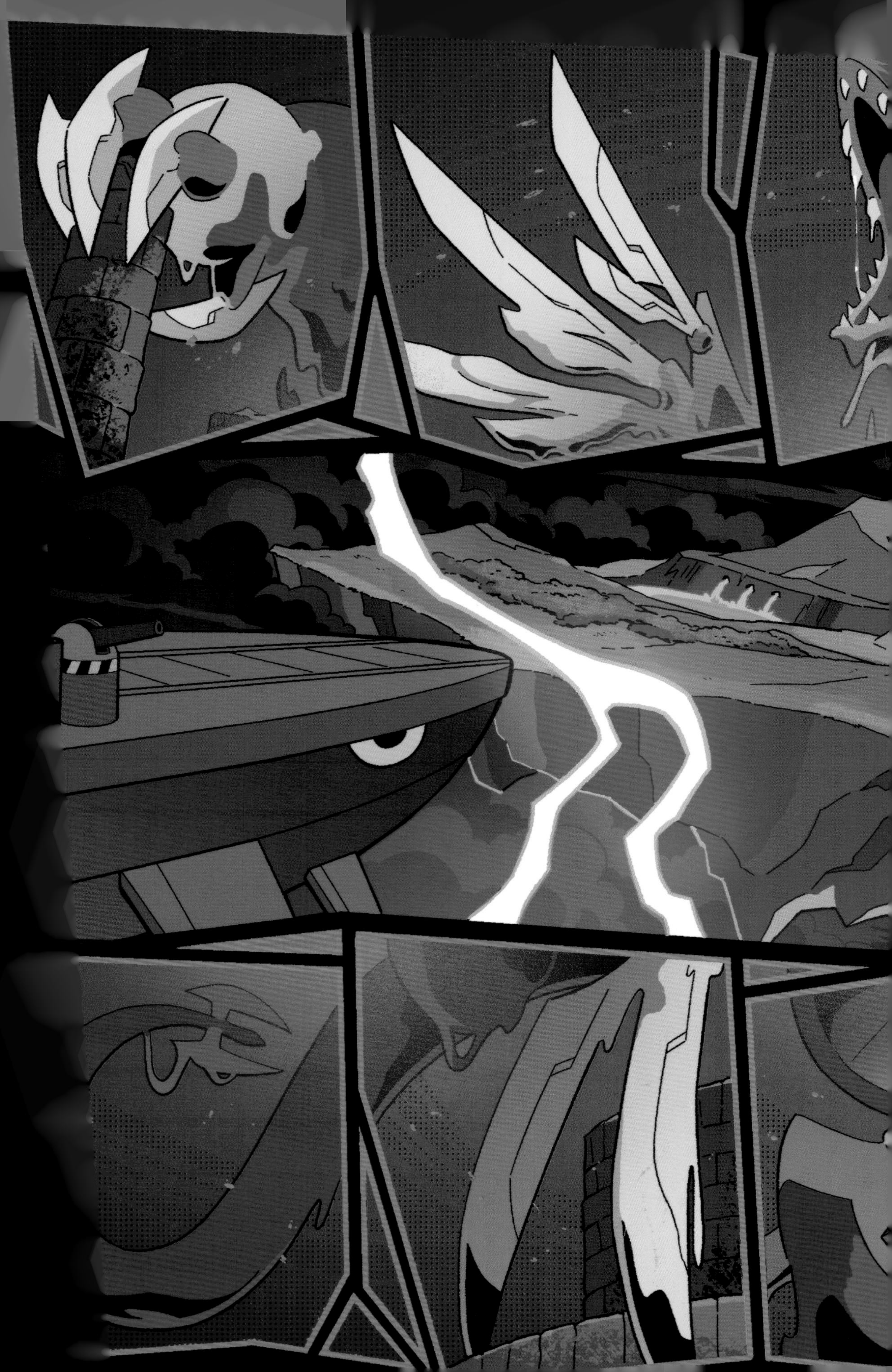

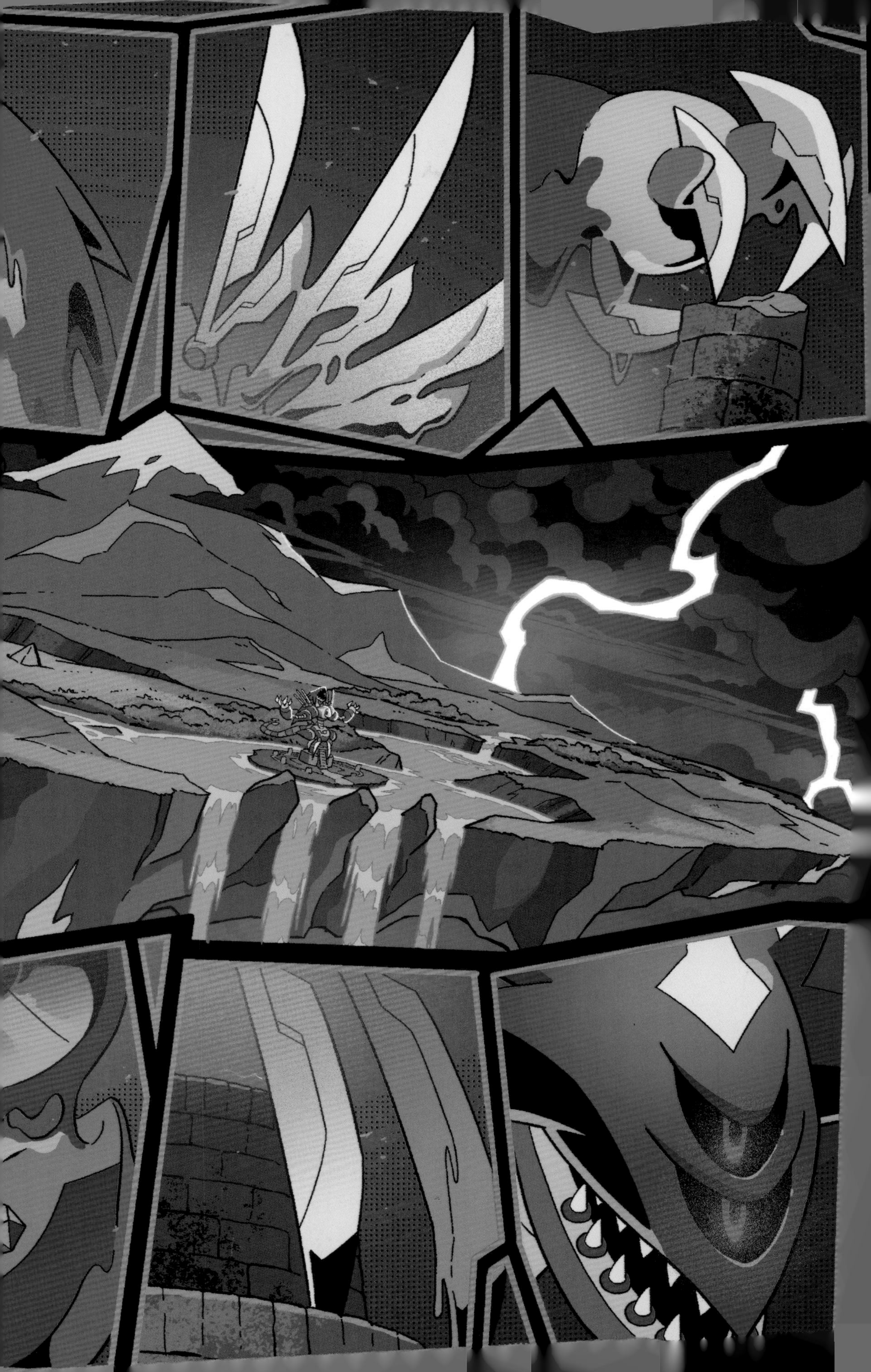

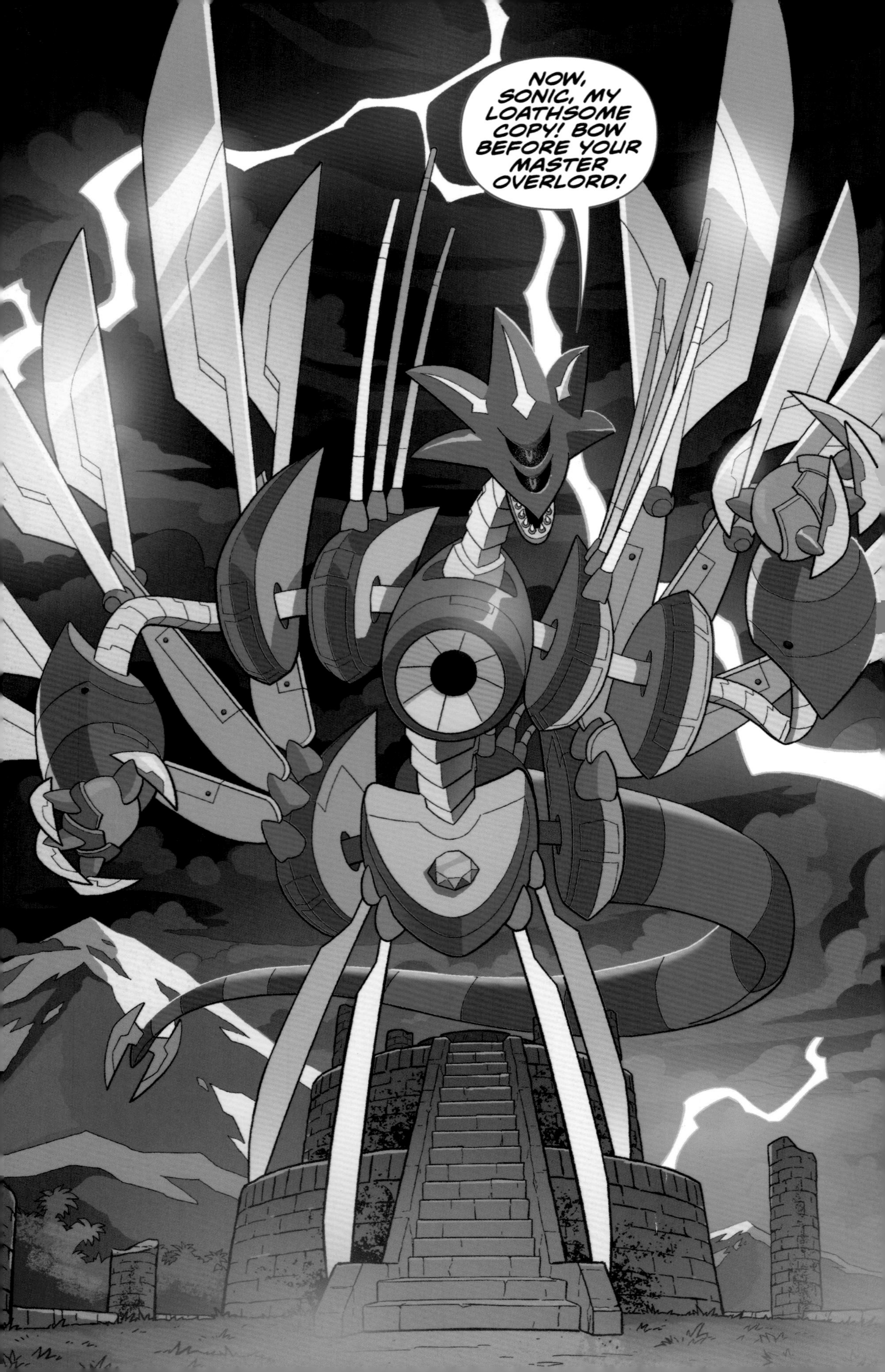
NOW, SONIC, MY LOATHSOME COPY! BOW BEFORE YOUR MASTER OVERLORD!

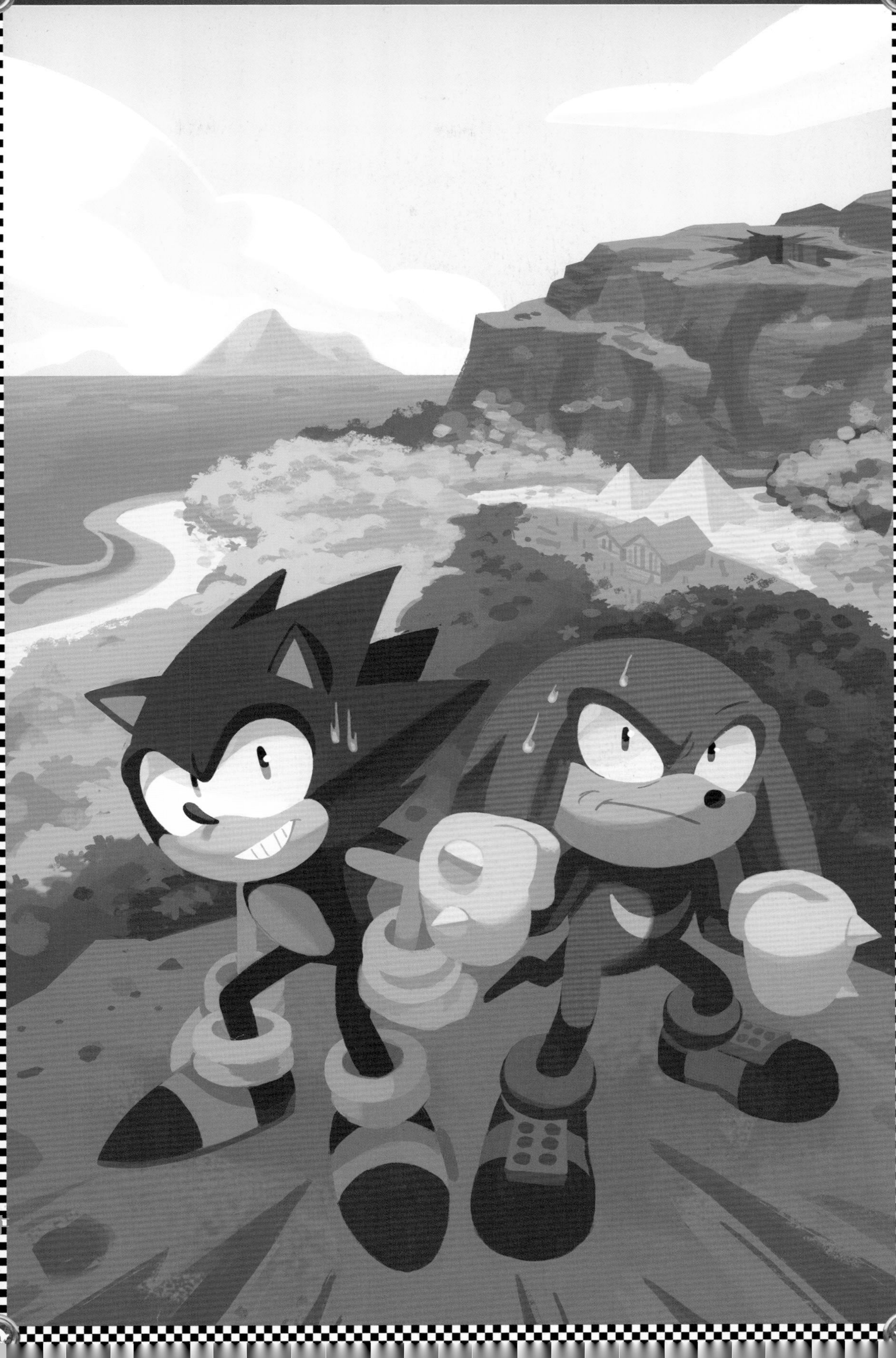

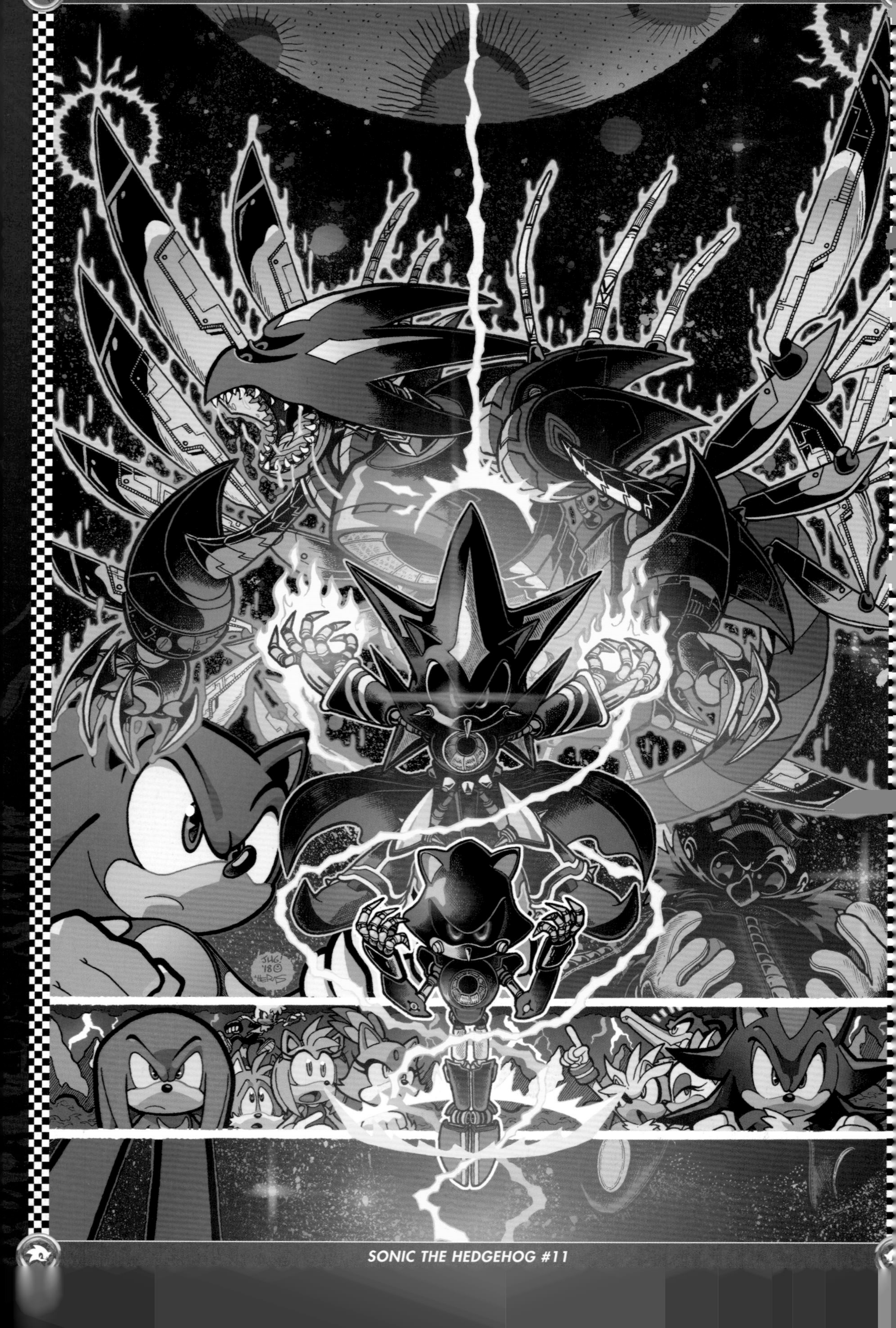
JHG! '18 © HERMS

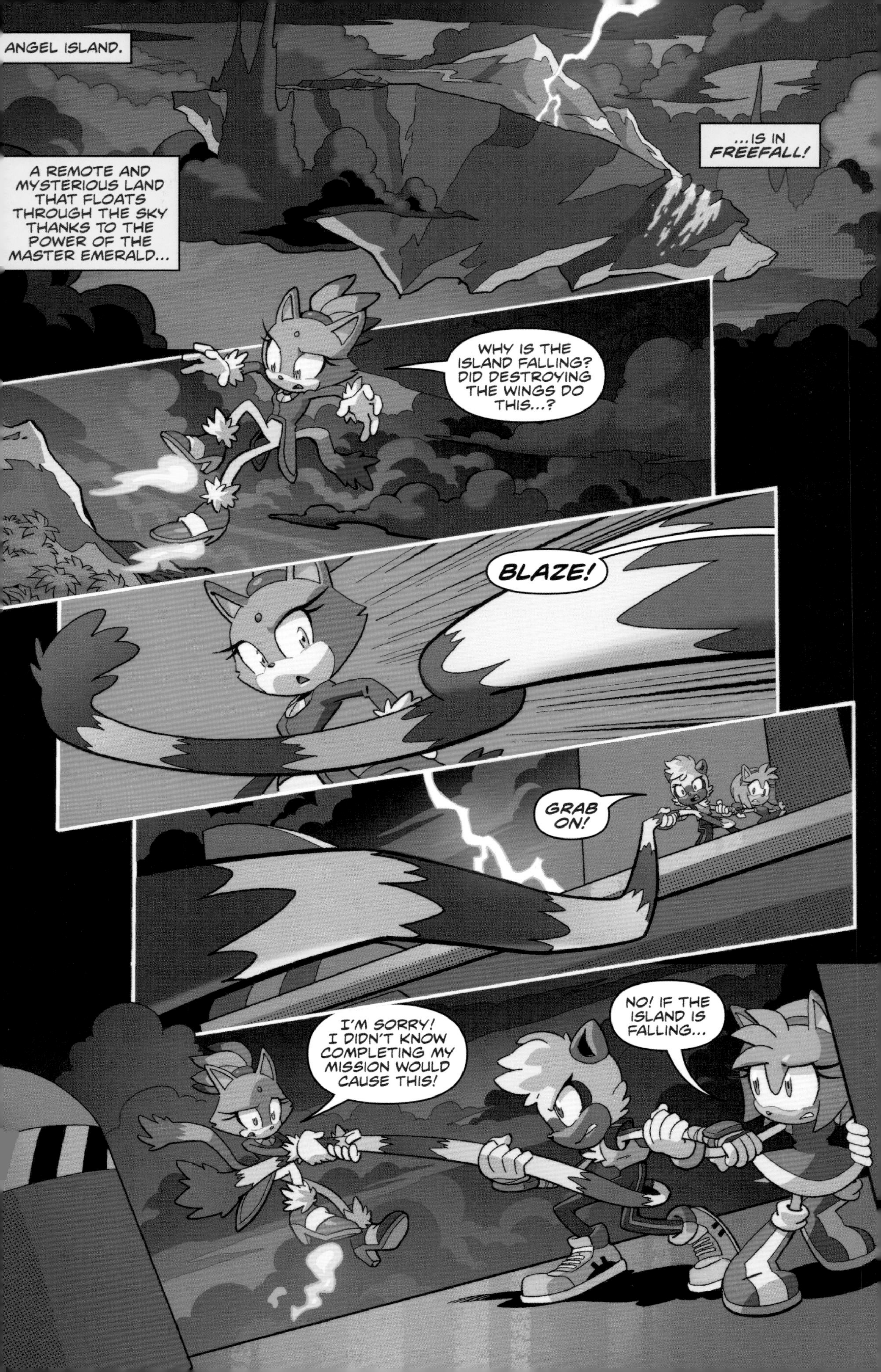
ANGEL ISLAND.
A REMOTE AND MYSTERIOUS LAND THAT FLOATS THROUGH THE SKY THANKS TO THE POWER OF THE MASTER EMERALD...
...IS IN FREEFALL!
WHY IS THE ISLAND FALLING? DID DESTROYING THE WINGS DO THIS...?
BLAZE!
GRAB ON!
I'M SORRY! I DIDN'T KNOW COMPLETING MY MISSION WOULD CAUSE THIS!
NO! IF THE ISLAND IS FALLING...

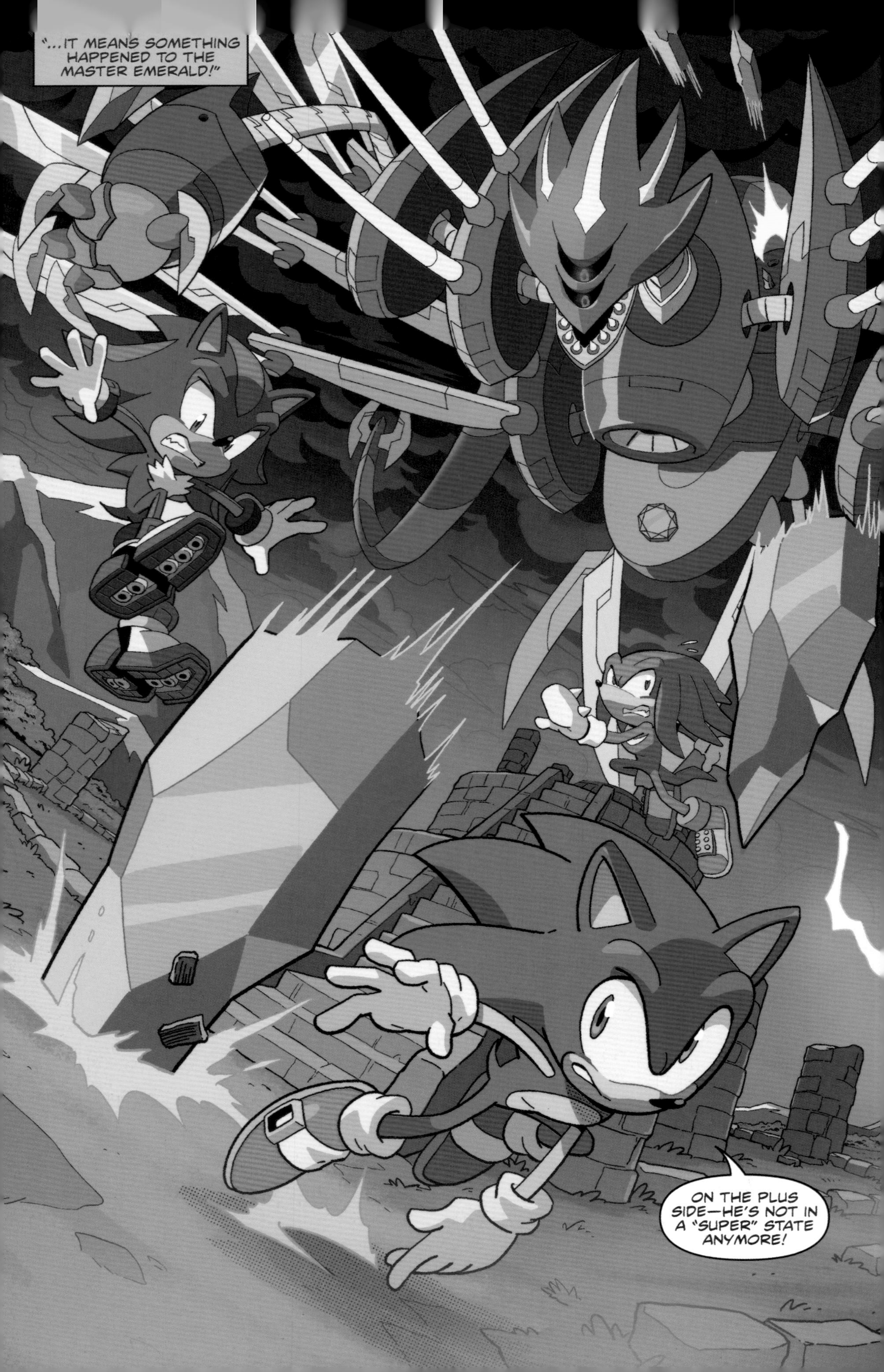
"...IT MEANS SOMETHING HAPPENED TO THE MASTER EMERALD!"
ON THE PLUS SIDE—HE'S NOT IN A "SUPER" STATE ANYMORE!

AMY! DO YOU READ ME? NEO TOOK THE MASTER EMERALD AND TRANSFORMED!

PLEASE TELL ME BURNING BLAZE IS STILL AROUND FOR HEAVY SUPPORT!

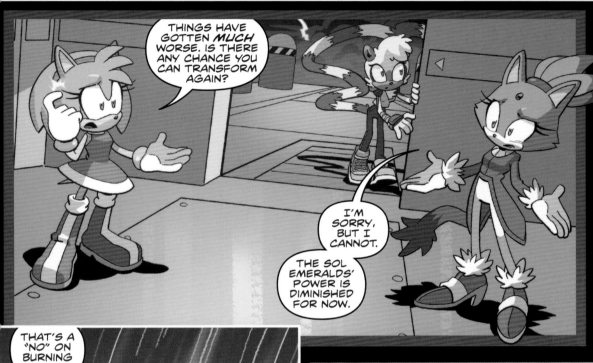

THINGS HAVE GOTTEN *MUCH* WORSE. IS THERE ANY CHANCE YOU CAN TRANSFORM AGAIN?

I'M SORRY, BUT I CANNOT.

THE SOL EMERALDS' POWER IS DIMINISHED FOR NOW.

THAT'S A "NO" ON BURNING BLAZE!

AND WE DON'T HAVE THE CHAOS EMERALDS, SO NO "SUPER SONIC" FOR ME, EITHER...

I WILL *NOT* LOSE TO THAT THING!

OKAY, OKAY... GOT IT! I HAVE A PLAN!

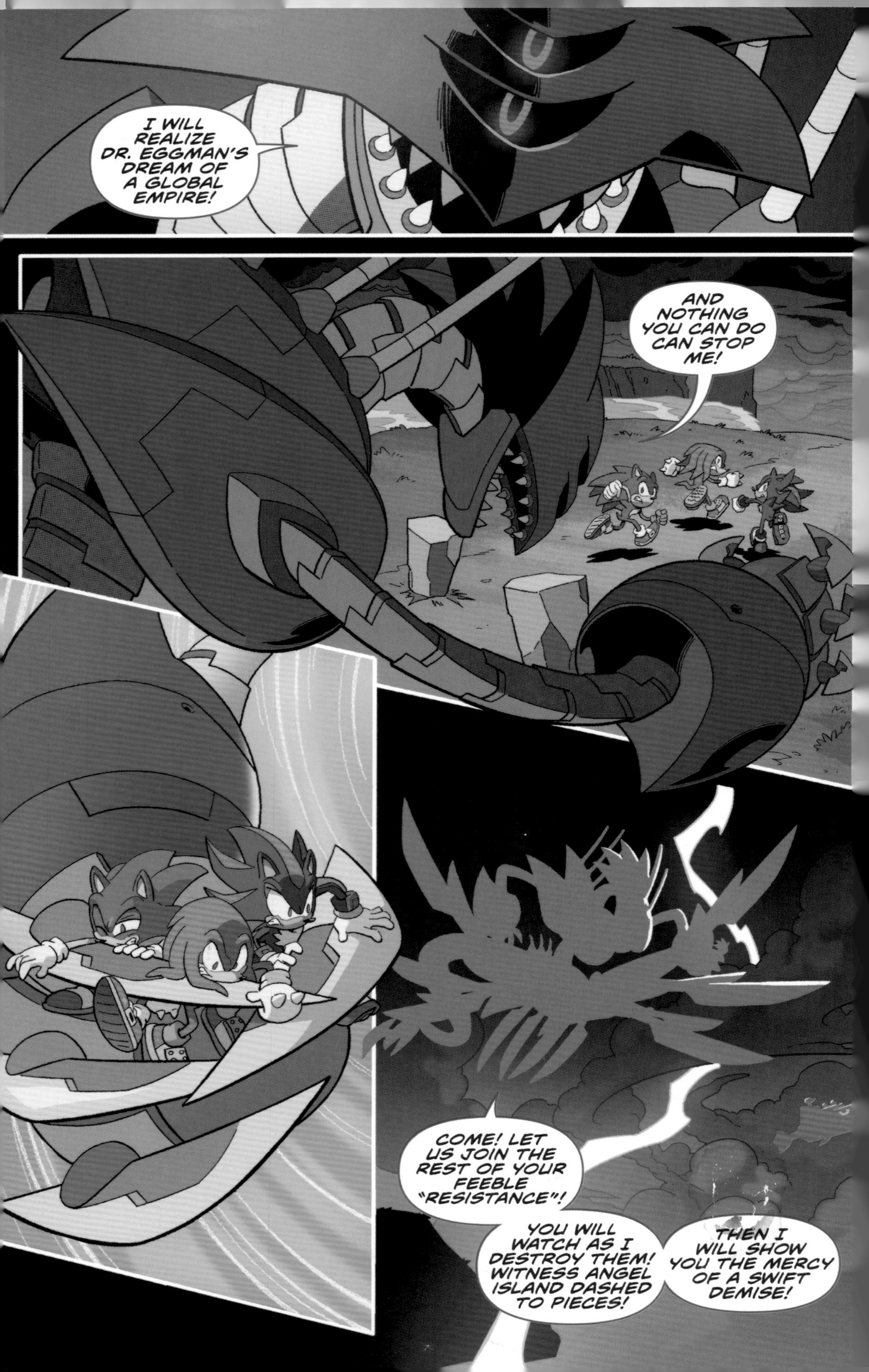
I WILL REALIZE DR. EGGMAN'S DREAM OF A GLOBAL EMPIRE!
AND NOTHING YOU CAN DO CAN STOP ME!
COME! LET US JOIN THE REST OF YOUR FEEBLE "RESISTANCE"!
YOU WILL WATCH AS I DESTROY THEM! WITNESS ANGEL ISLAND DASHED TO PIECES!
THEN I WILL SHOW YOU THE MERCY OF A SWIFT DEMISE!

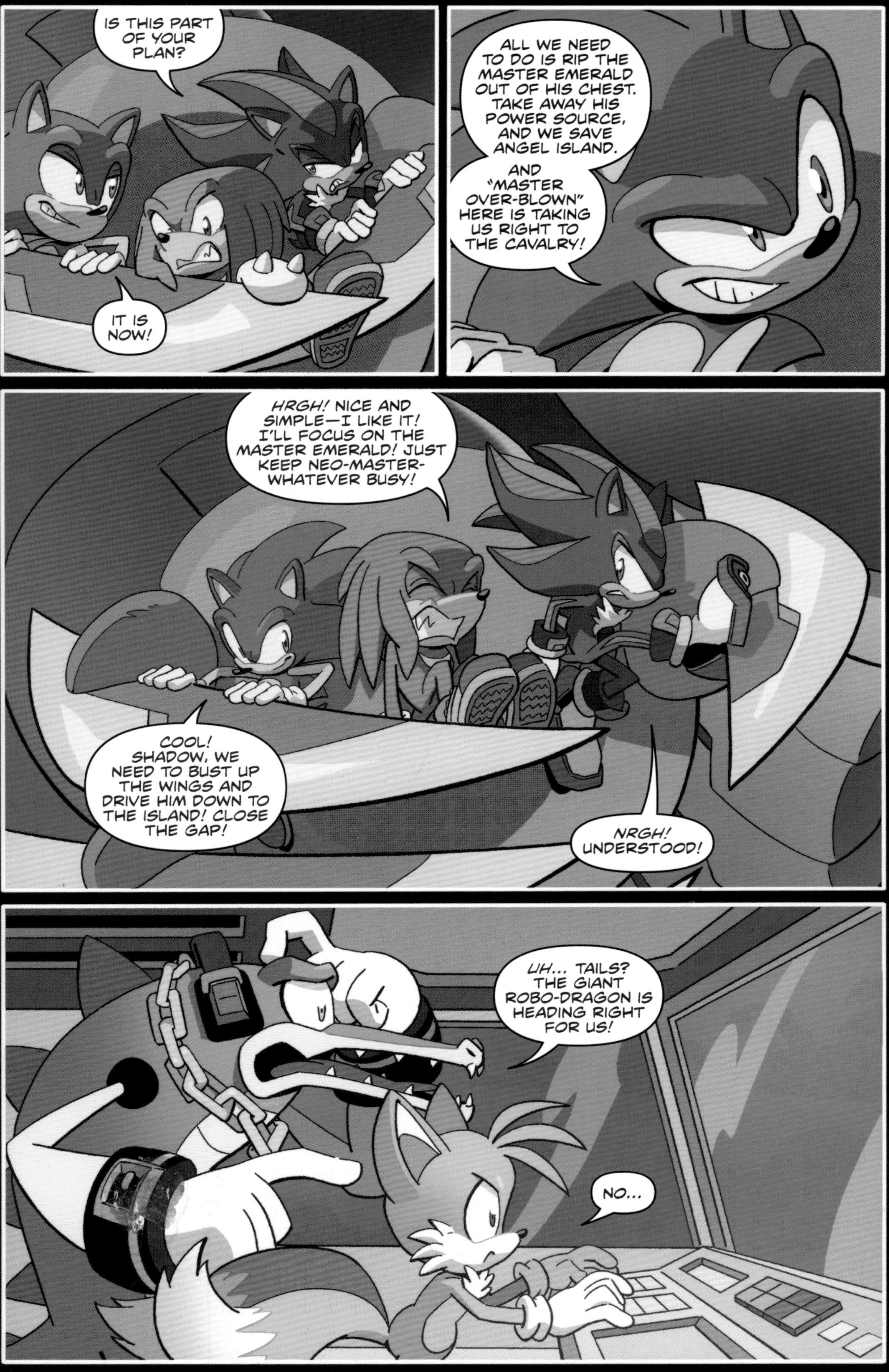
IS THIS PART OF YOUR PLAN?
IT IS NOW!
ALL WE NEED TO DO IS RIP THE MASTER EMERALD OUT OF HIS CHEST. TAKE AWAY HIS POWER SOURCE, AND WE SAVE ANGEL ISLAND.
AND "MASTER OVER-BLOWN" HERE IS TAKING US RIGHT TO THE CAVALRY!
HRGH! NICE AND SIMPLE—I LIKE IT! I'LL FOCUS ON THE MASTER EMERALD! JUST KEEP NEO-MASTER-WHATEVER BUSY!
COOL! SHADOW, WE NEED TO BUST UP THE WINGS AND DRIVE HIM DOWN TO THE ISLAND! CLOSE THE GAP!
NRGH! UNDERSTOOD!
UH... TAILS? THE GIANT ROBO-DRAGON IS HEADING RIGHT FOR US!
NO...

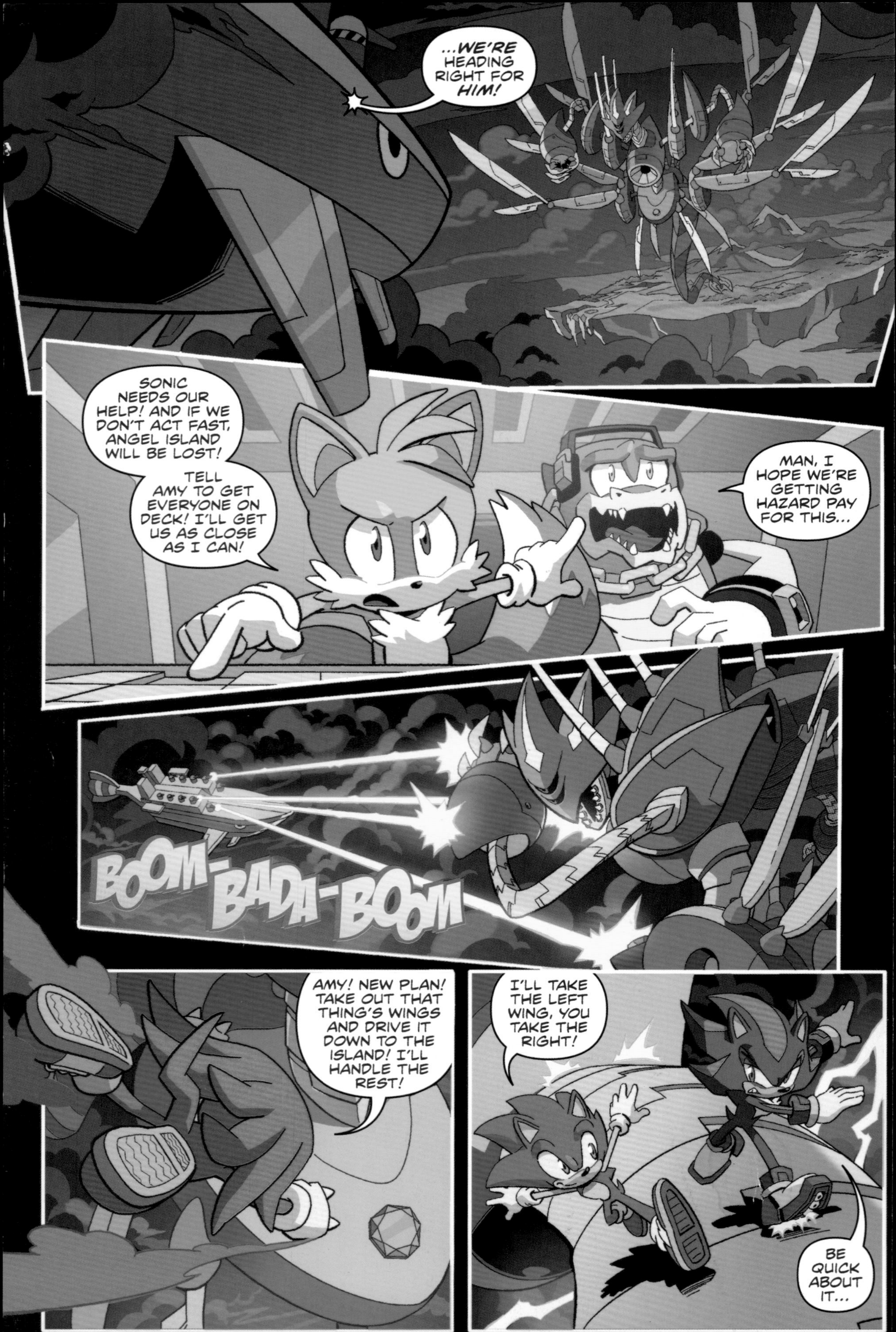

...WE'RE HEADING RIGHT FOR HIM!
SONIC NEEDS OUR HELP! AND IF WE DON'T ACT FAST, ANGEL ISLAND WILL BE LOST!
TELL AMY TO GET EVERYONE ON DECK! I'LL GET US AS CLOSE AS I CAN!
MAN, I HOPE WE'RE GETTING HAZARD PAY FOR THIS...
BOOM-BADA-BOOM
AMY! NEW PLAN! TAKE OUT THAT THING'S WINGS AND DRIVE IT DOWN TO THE ISLAND! I'LL HANDLE THE REST!
I'LL TAKE THE LEFT WING, YOU TAKE THE RIGHT!
BE QUICK ABOUT IT...

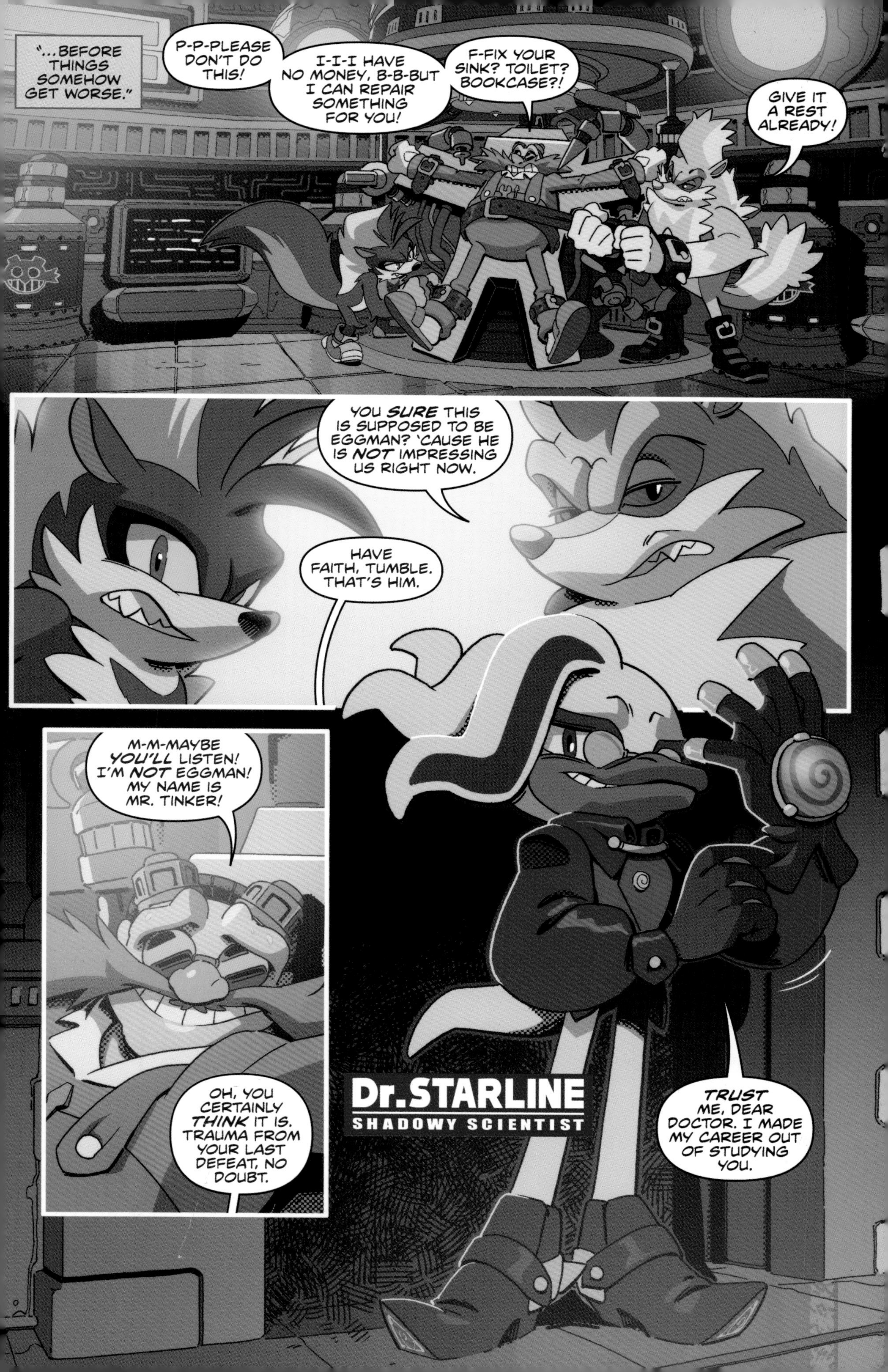
"...BEFORE THINGS SOMEHOW GET WORSE."
P-P-PLEASE DON'T DO THIS!
I-I-I HAVE NO MONEY, B-B-BUT I CAN REPAIR SOMETHING FOR YOU!
F-FIX YOUR SINK? TOILET? BOOKCASE?!
GIVE IT A REST ALREADY!
YOU SURE THIS IS SUPPOSED TO BE EGGMAN? 'CAUSE HE IS NOT IMPRESSING US RIGHT NOW.
HAVE FAITH, TUMBLE. THAT'S HIM.
M-M-MAYBE YOU'LL LISTEN! I'M NOT EGGMAN! MY NAME IS MR. TINKER!
OH, YOU CERTAINLY THINK IT IS. TRAUMA FROM YOUR LAST DEFEAT, NO DOUBT.
Dr. STARLINE
SHADOWY SCIENTIST
TRUST ME, DEAR DOCTOR. I MADE MY CAREER OUT OF STUDYING YOU.

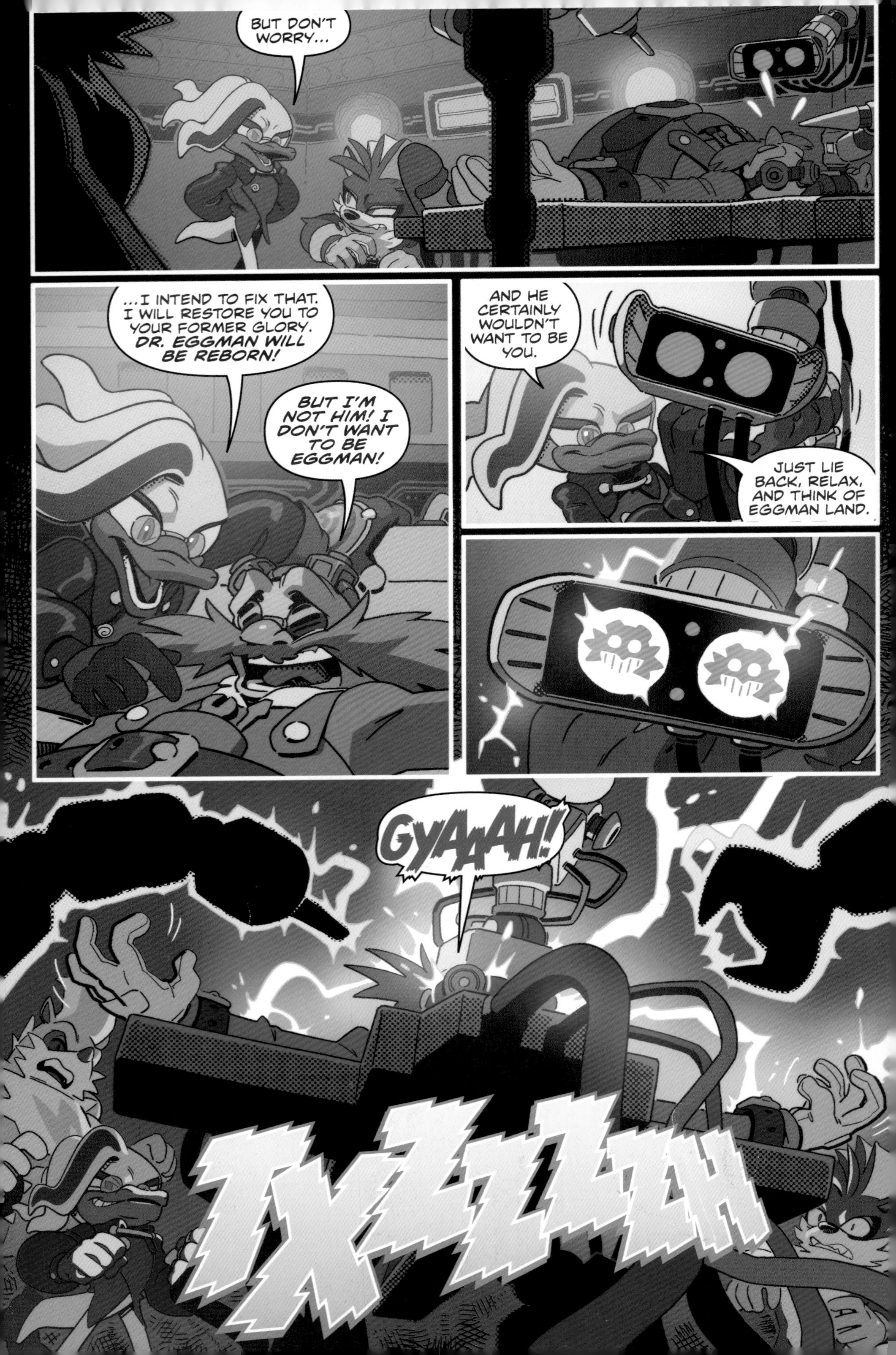
BUT DON'T WORRY...
...I INTEND TO FIX THAT. I WILL RESTORE YOU TO YOUR FORMER GLORY. *DR. EGGMAN WILL BE REBORN!*
BUT I'M NOT HIM! I DON'T WANT TO BE EGGMAN!
AND HE CERTAINLY WOULDN'T WANT TO BE YOU.
JUST LIE BACK, RELAX, AND THINK OF EGGMAN LAND.
GYAAAH!
TXZZZZH

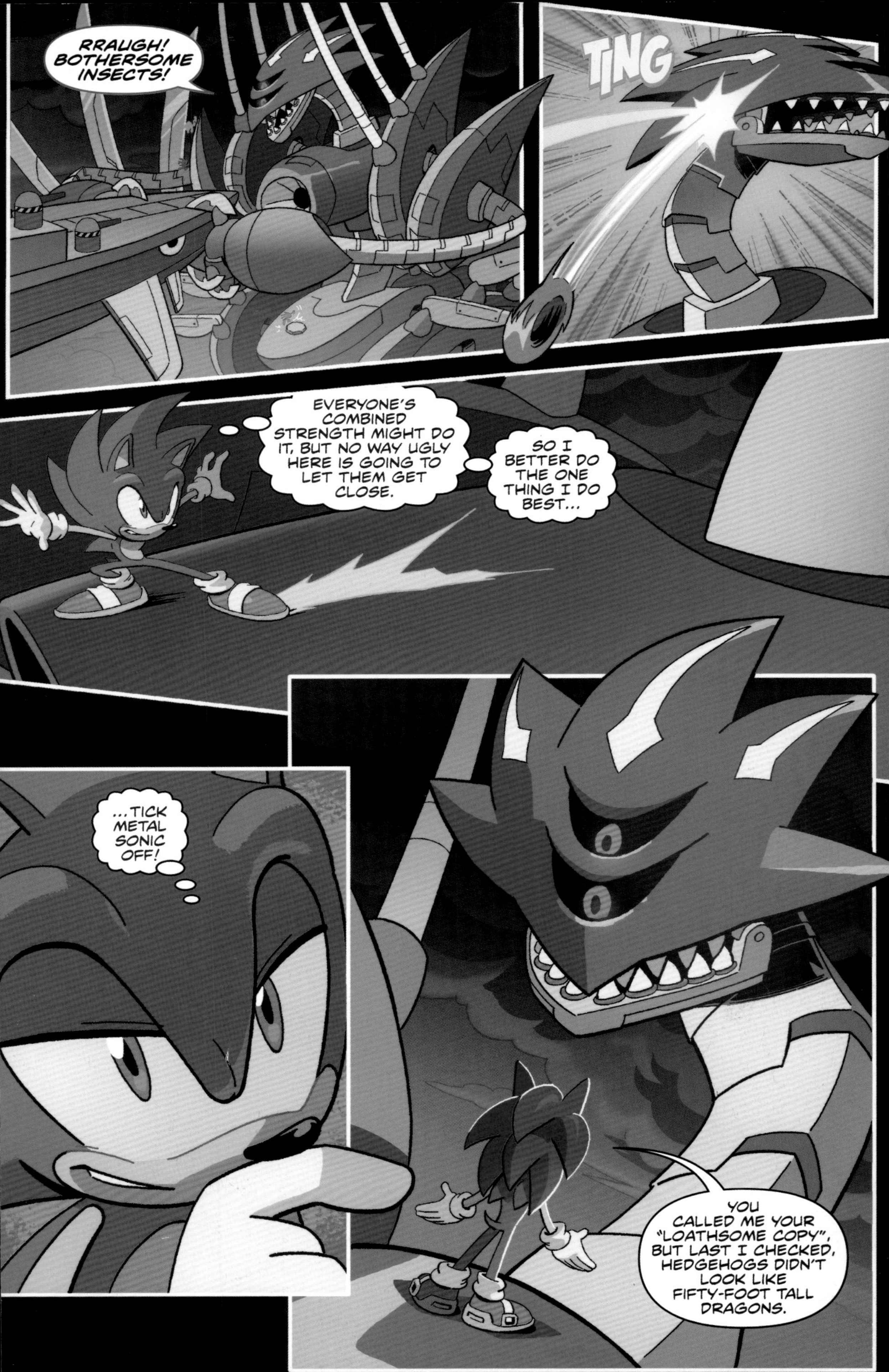
RRAUGH! BOTHERSOME INSECTS!
TING
EVERYONE'S COMBINED STRENGTH MIGHT DO IT, BUT NO WAY UGLY HERE IS GOING TO LET THEM GET CLOSE.
SO I BETTER DO THE ONE THING I DO BEST...
...TICK METAL SONIC OFF!
YOU CALLED ME YOUR "LOATHSOME COPY", BUT LAST I CHECKED, HEDGEHOGS DIDN'T LOOK LIKE FIFTY-FOOT TALL DRAGONS.

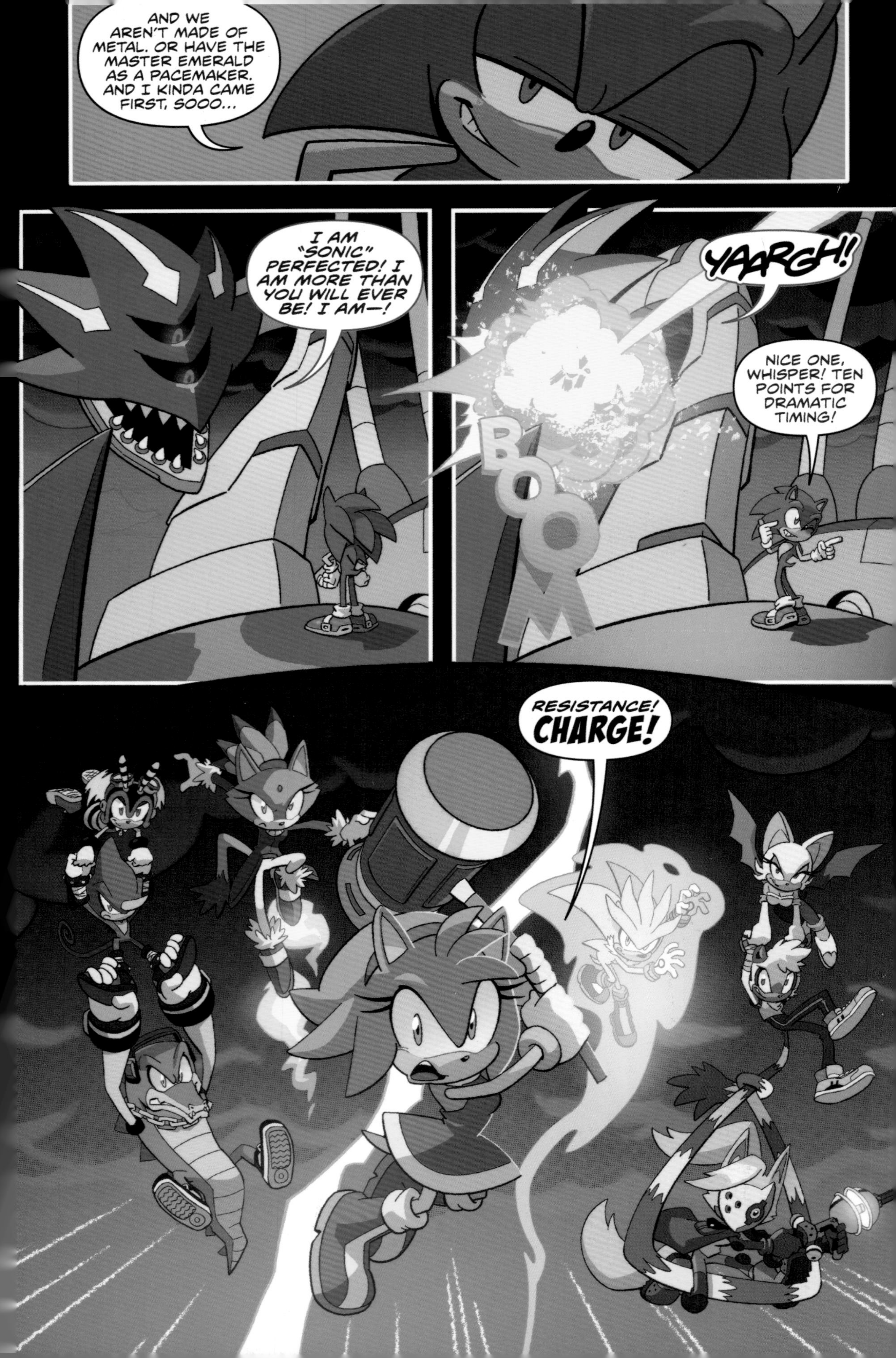
AND WE AREN'T MADE OF METAL. OR HAVE THE MASTER EMERALD AS A PACEMAKER. AND I KINDA CAME FIRST, SOOO...
I AM "SONIC" PERFECTED! I AM MORE THAN YOU WILL EVER BE! I AM—!
YAARGH!
BOOM
NICE ONE, WHISPER! TEN POINTS FOR DRAMATIC TIMING!
RESISTANCE! CHARGE!

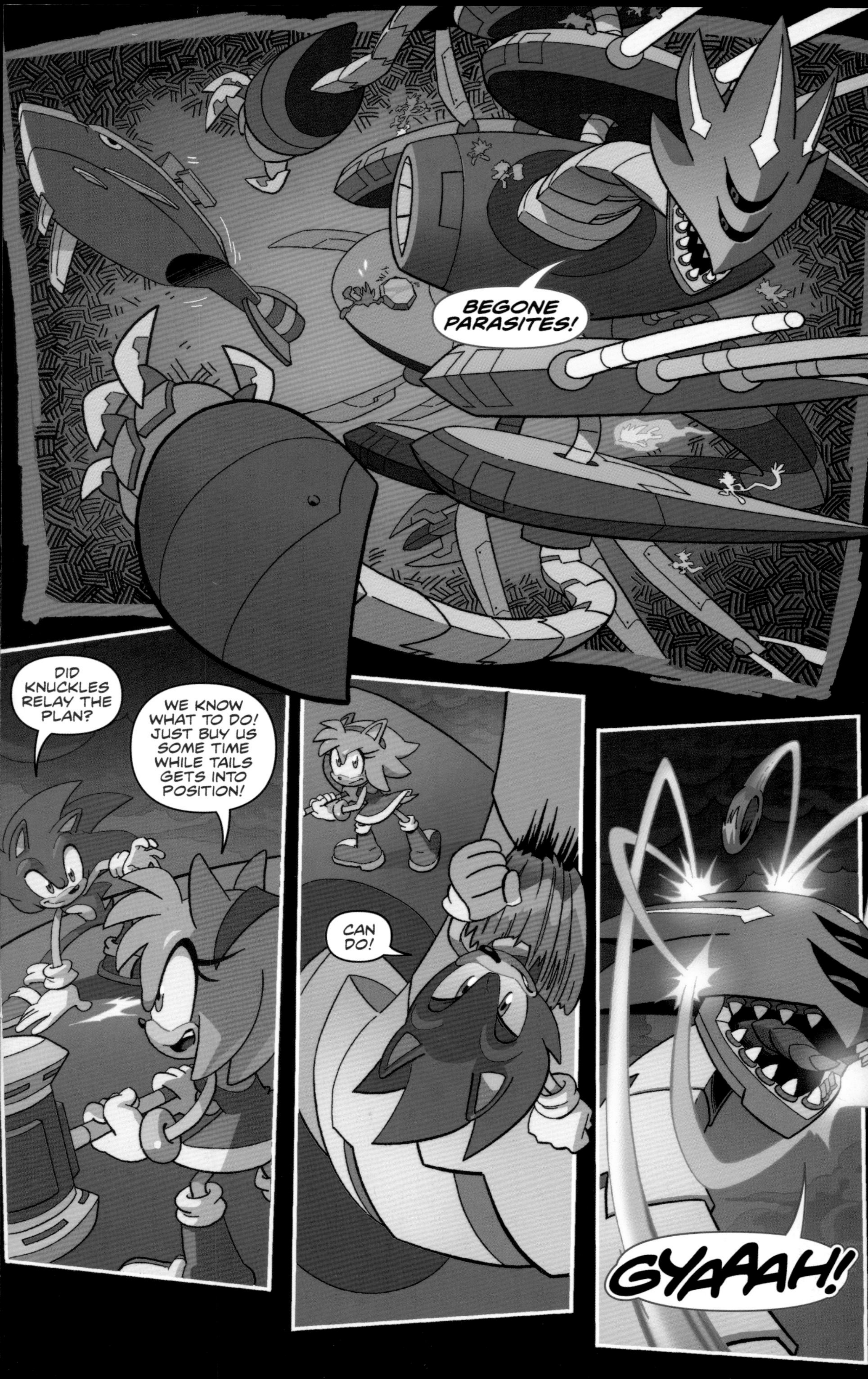
BEGONE PARASITES!
DID KNUCKLES RELAY THE PLAN?
WE KNOW WHAT TO DO! JUST BUY US SOME TIME WHILE TAILS GETS INTO POSITION!
CAN DO!
GYAAAH!

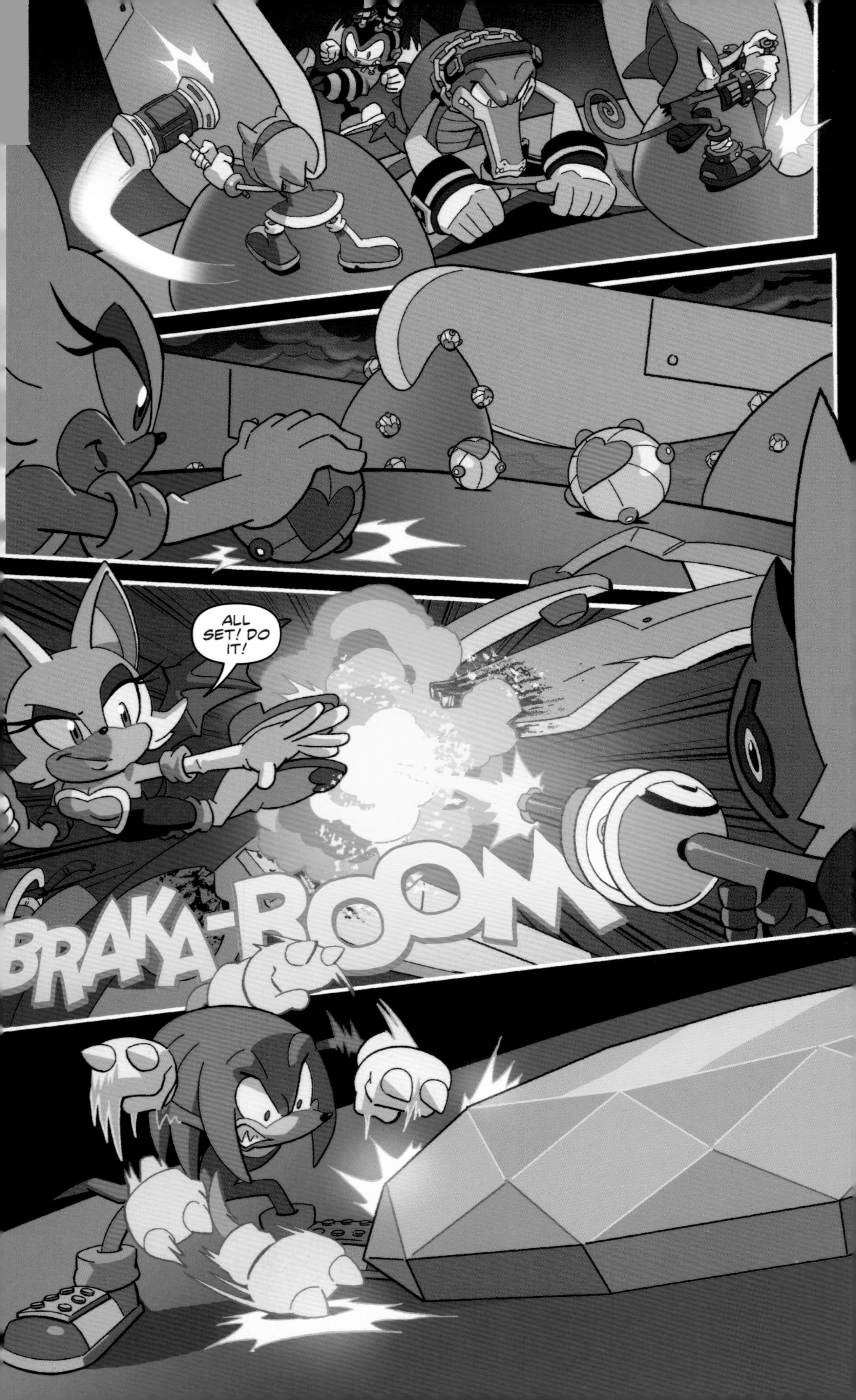
ALL SET! DO IT!
BRAKA-BOOM

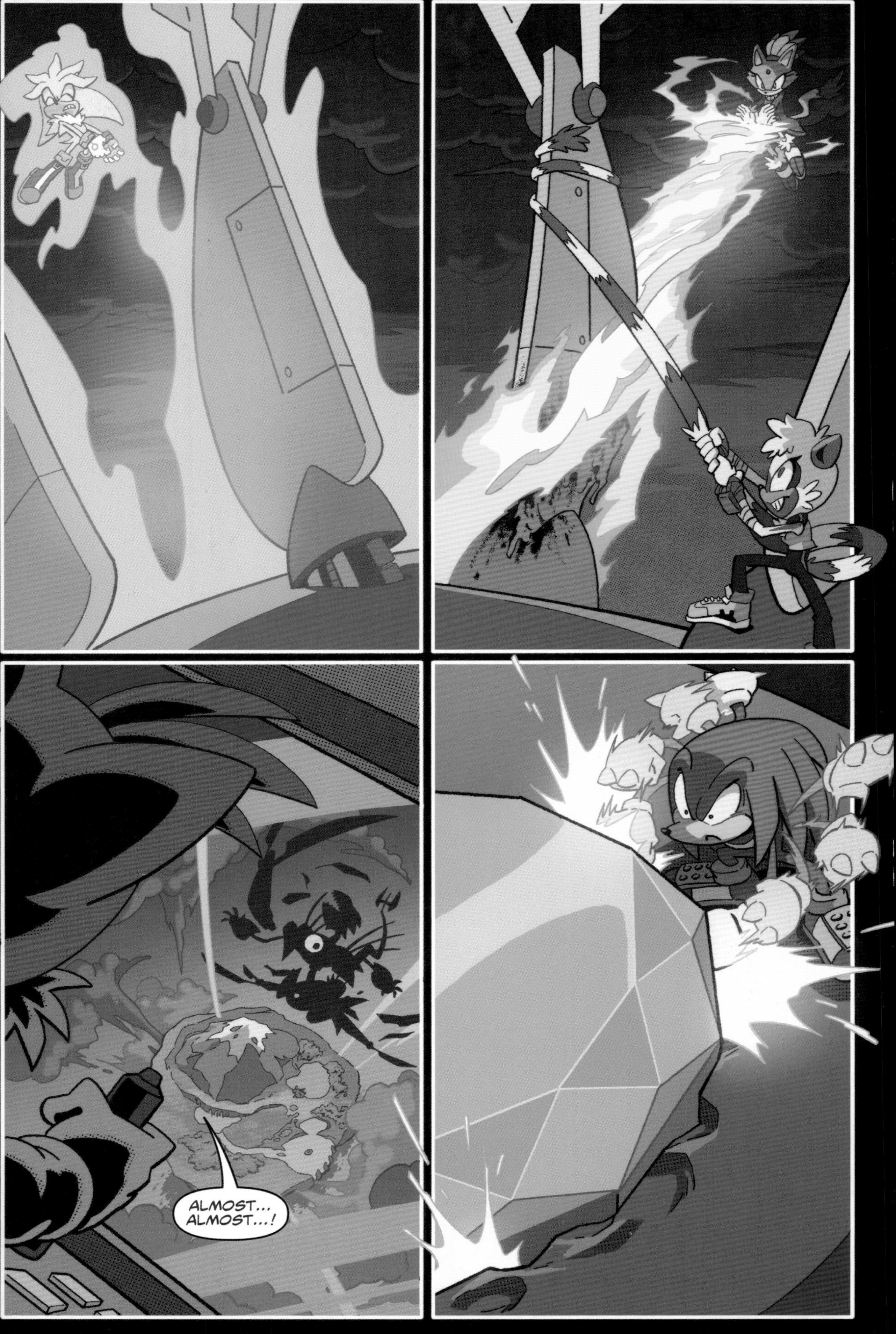
ALMOST...
ALMOST...!

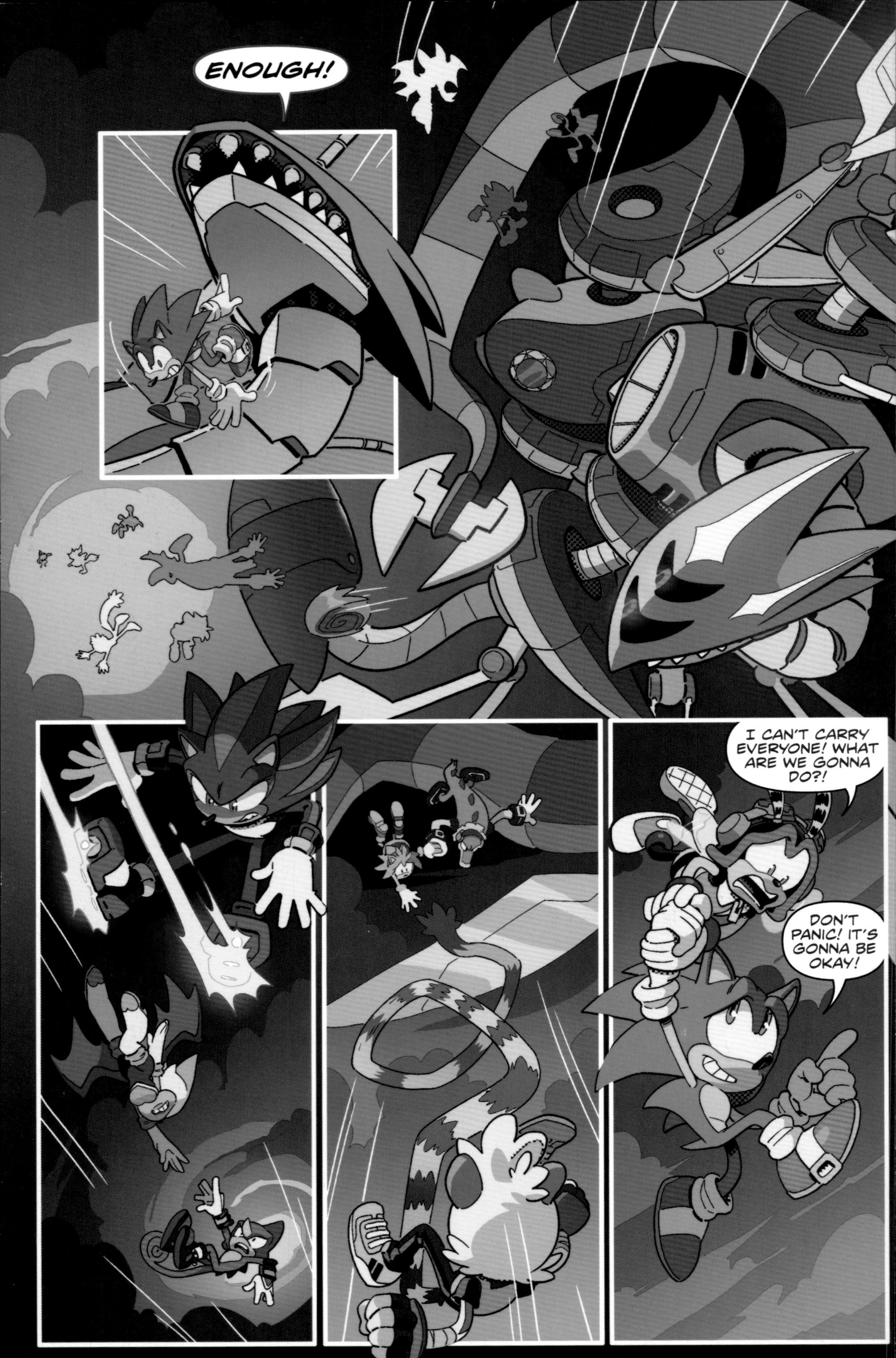
ENOUGH!
I CAN'T CARRY EVERYONE! WHAT ARE WE GONNA DO?!
DON'T PANIC! IT'S GONNA BE OKAY!

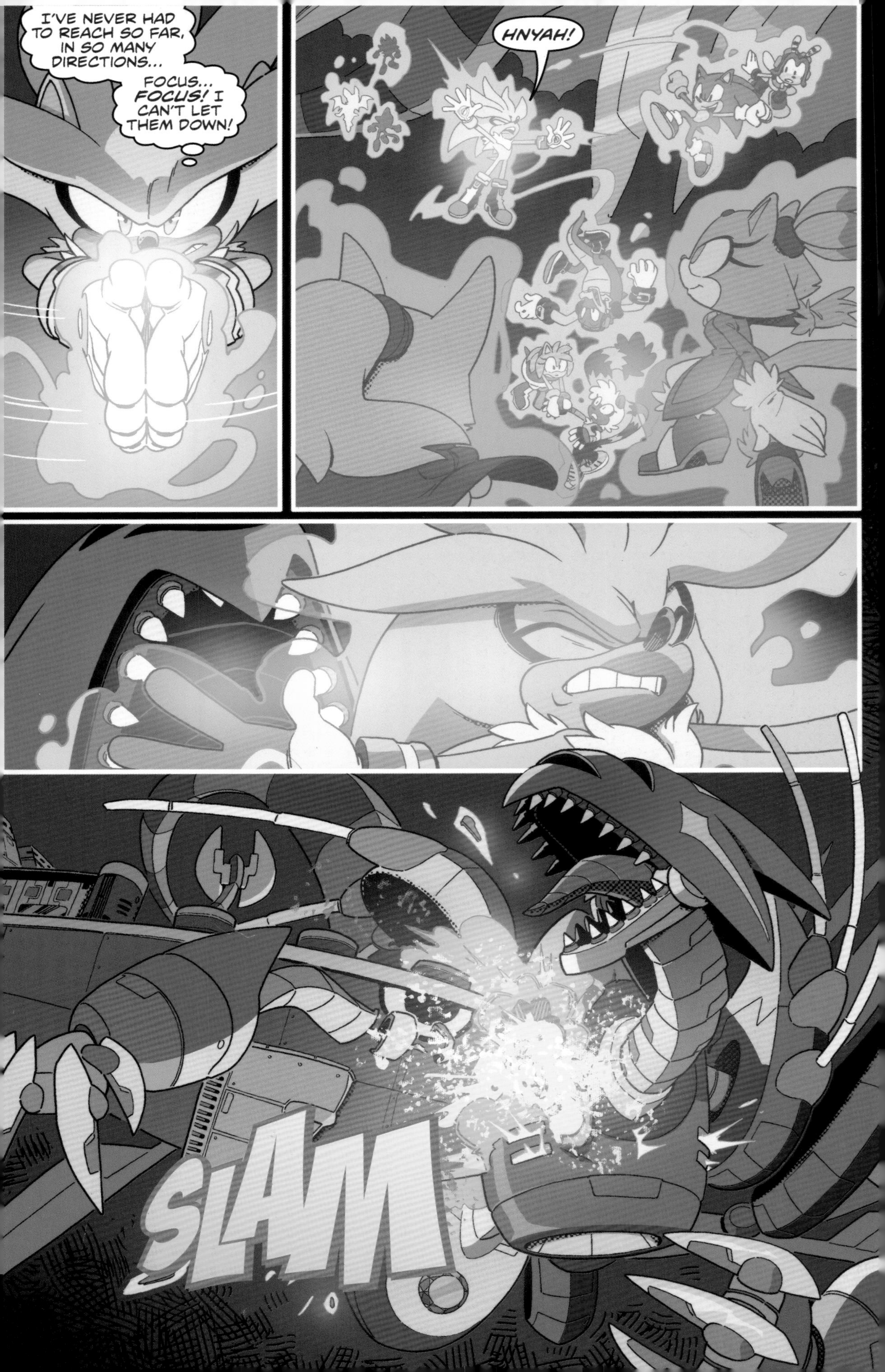
I'VE NEVER HAD TO REACH SO FAR, IN SO MANY DIRECTIONS...
FOCUS... FOCUS! I CAN'T LET THEM DOWN!
HNYAH!
SLAM

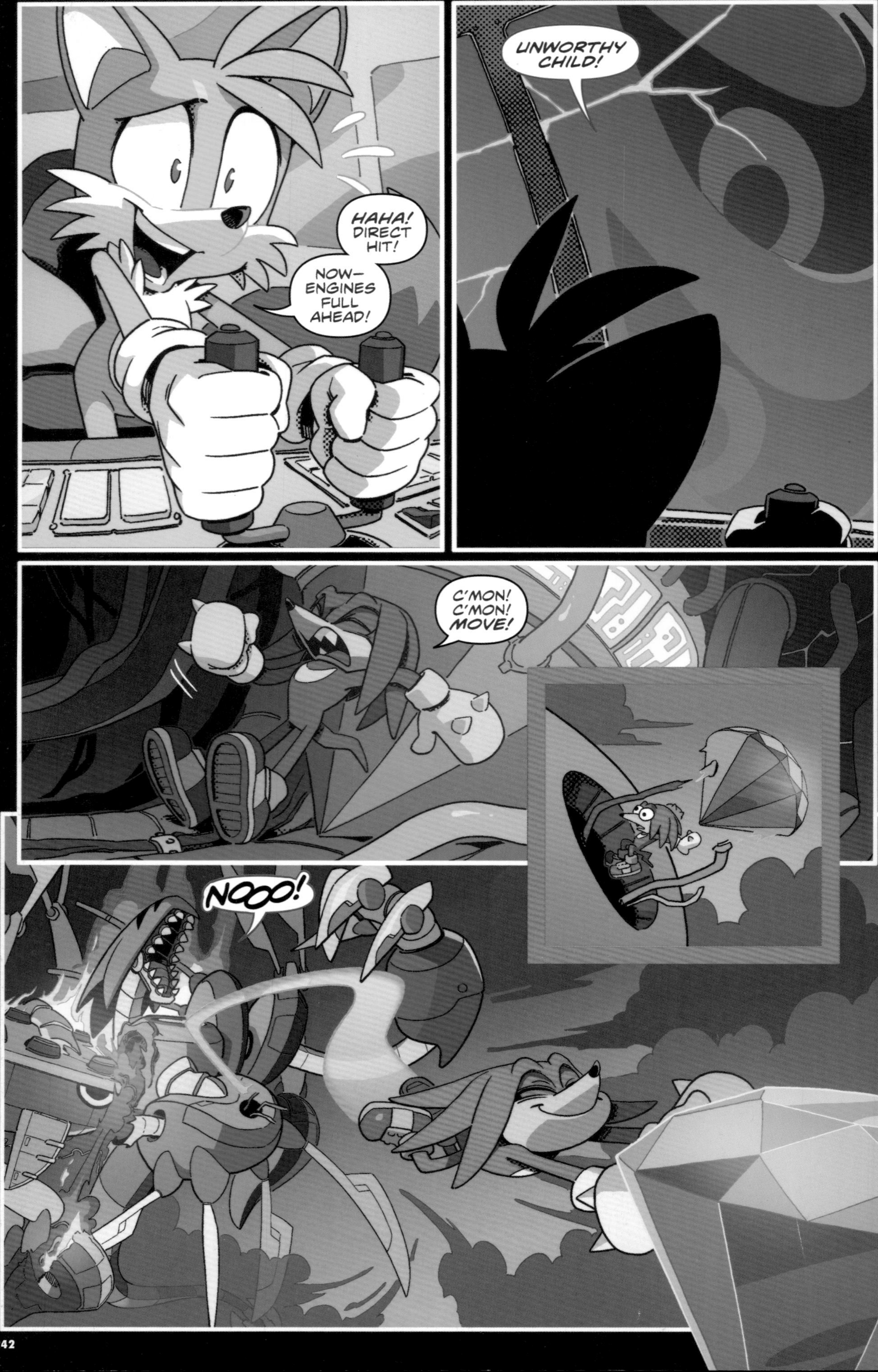
HAHA! DIRECT HIT!
NOW— ENGINES FULL AHEAD!
UNWORTHY CHILD!
C'MON! C'MON! MOVE!
NOOO!

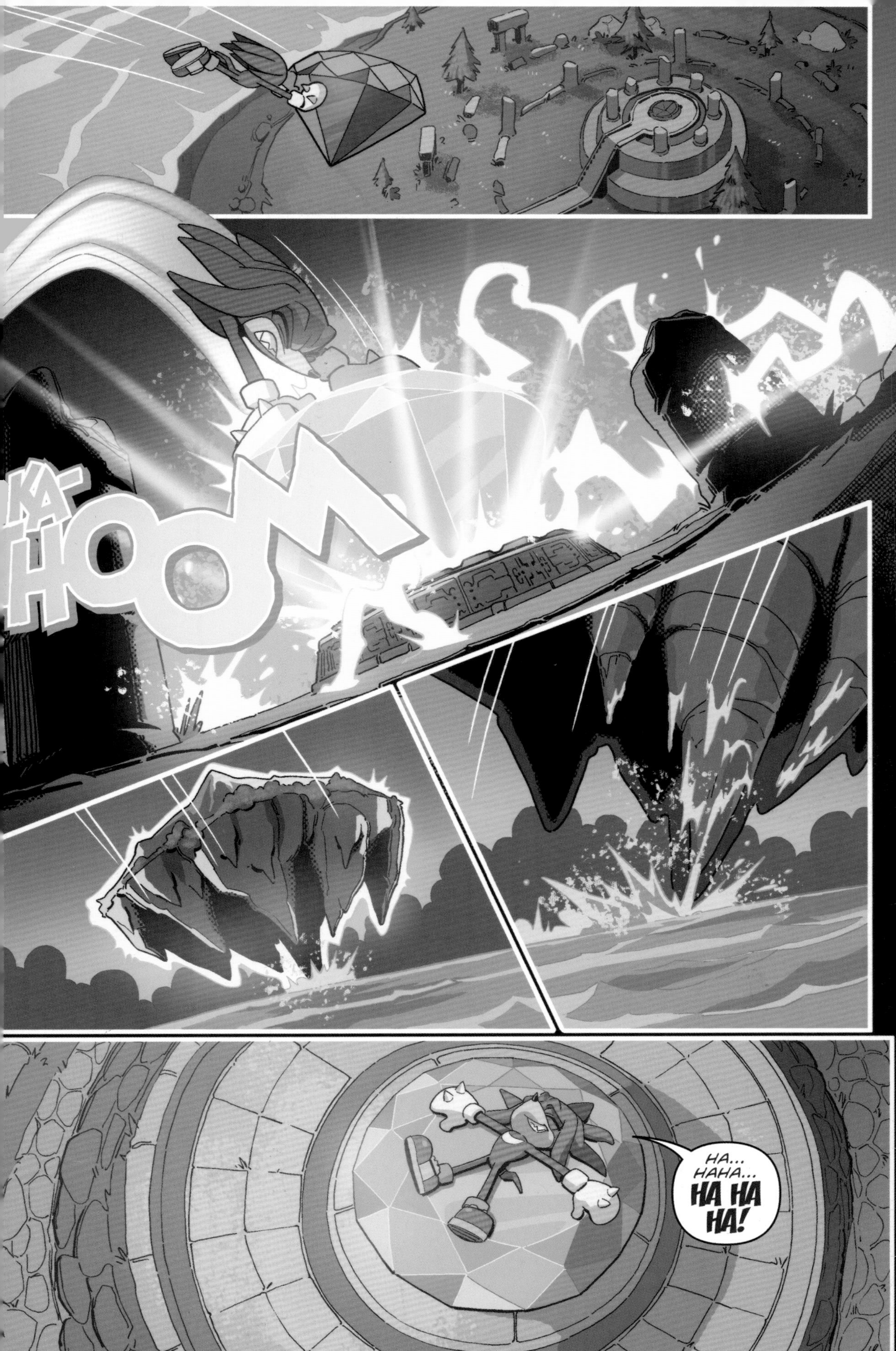
KA-
HOOM
HA...
HAHA...
HA HA
HA!

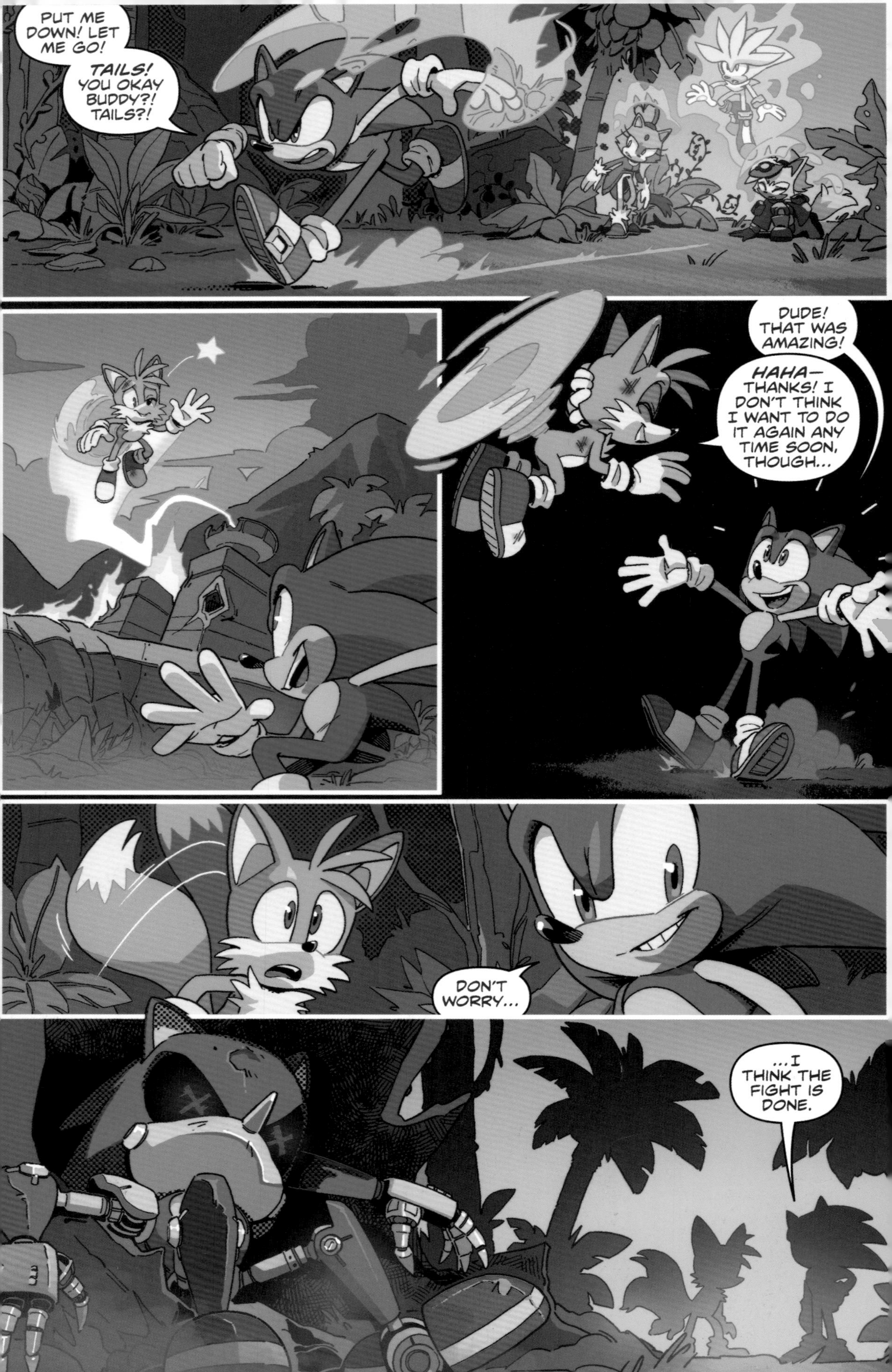
PUT ME DOWN! LET ME GO!
TAILS! YOU OKAY BUDDY?! TAILS?!
DUDE! THAT WAS AMAZING!
HAHA— THANKS! I DON'T THINK I WANT TO DO IT AGAIN ANY TIME SOON, THOUGH...
DON'T WORRY...
...I THINK THE FIGHT IS DONE.

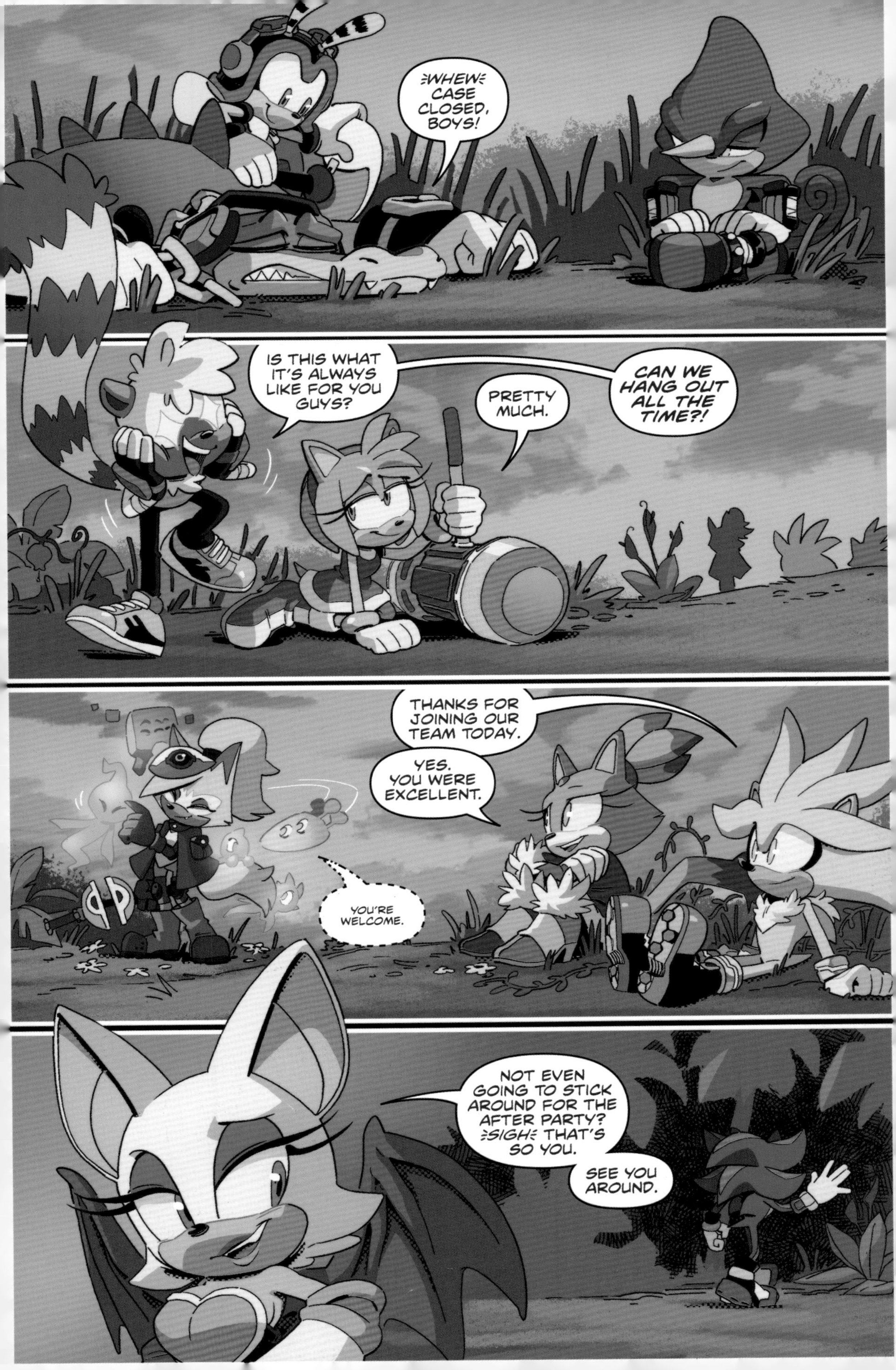

≈WHEW≈ CASE CLOSED, BOYS!
IS THIS WHAT IT'S ALWAYS LIKE FOR YOU GUYS?
PRETTY MUCH.
CAN WE HANG OUT ALL THE TIME?!
THANKS FOR JOINING OUR TEAM TODAY.
YES. YOU WERE EXCELLENT.
YOU'RE WELCOME.
NOT EVEN GOING TO STICK AROUND FOR THE AFTER PARTY? ≈SIGH≈ THAT'S SO YOU.
SEE YOU AROUND.

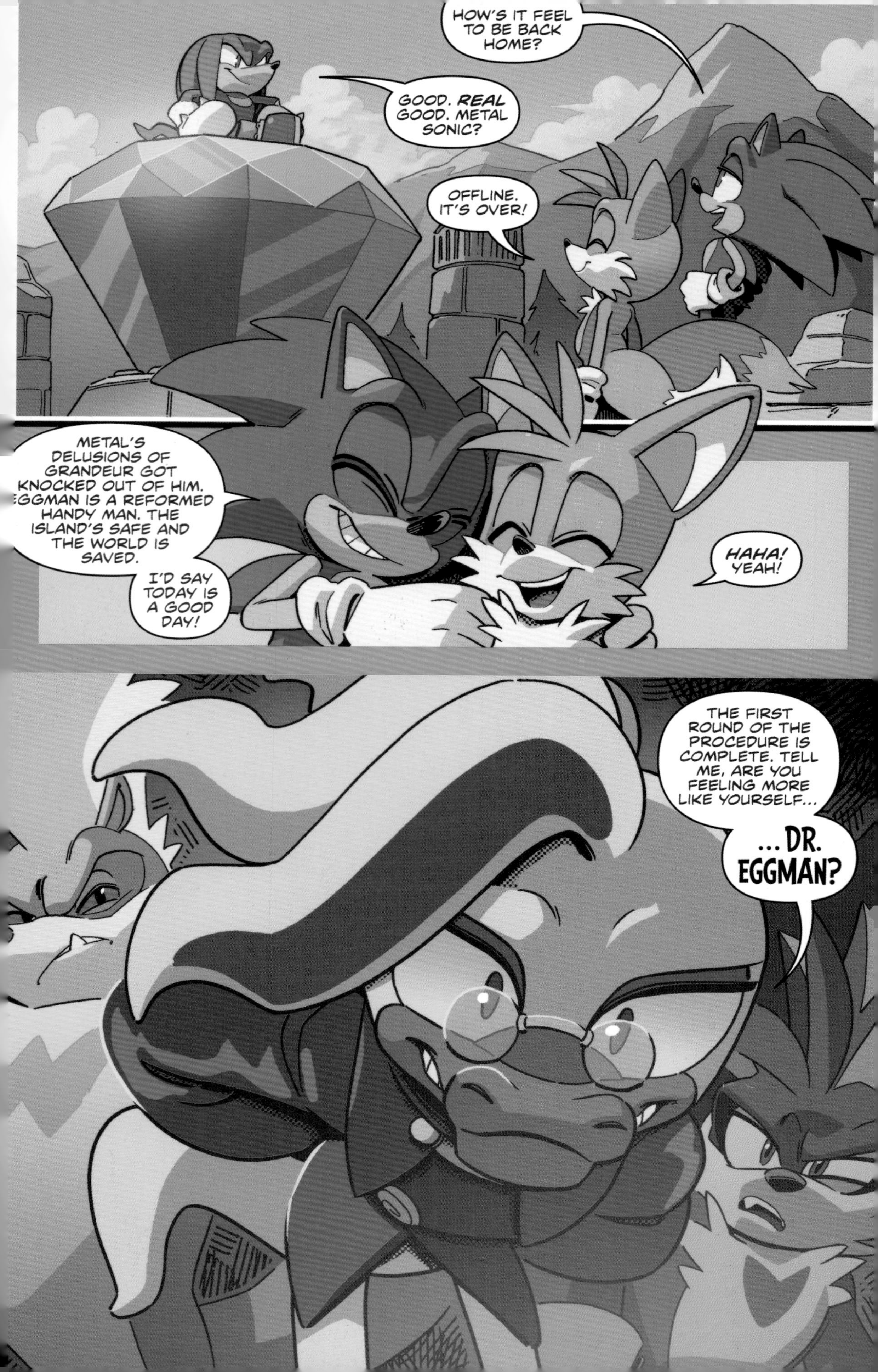
HOW'S IT FEEL TO BE BACK HOME?
GOOD. REAL GOOD. METAL SONIC?
OFFLINE. IT'S OVER!
METAL'S DELUSIONS OF GRANDEUR GOT KNOCKED OUT OF HIM. EGGMAN IS A REFORMED HANDY MAN. THE ISLAND'S SAFE AND THE WORLD IS SAVED.
I'D SAY TODAY IS A GOOD DAY!
HAHA! YEAH!
THE FIRST ROUND OF THE PROCEDURE IS COMPLETE. TELL ME, ARE YOU FEELING MORE LIKE YOURSELF...
... DR. EGGMAN?

ART BY NATHALIE FOURDRAINE

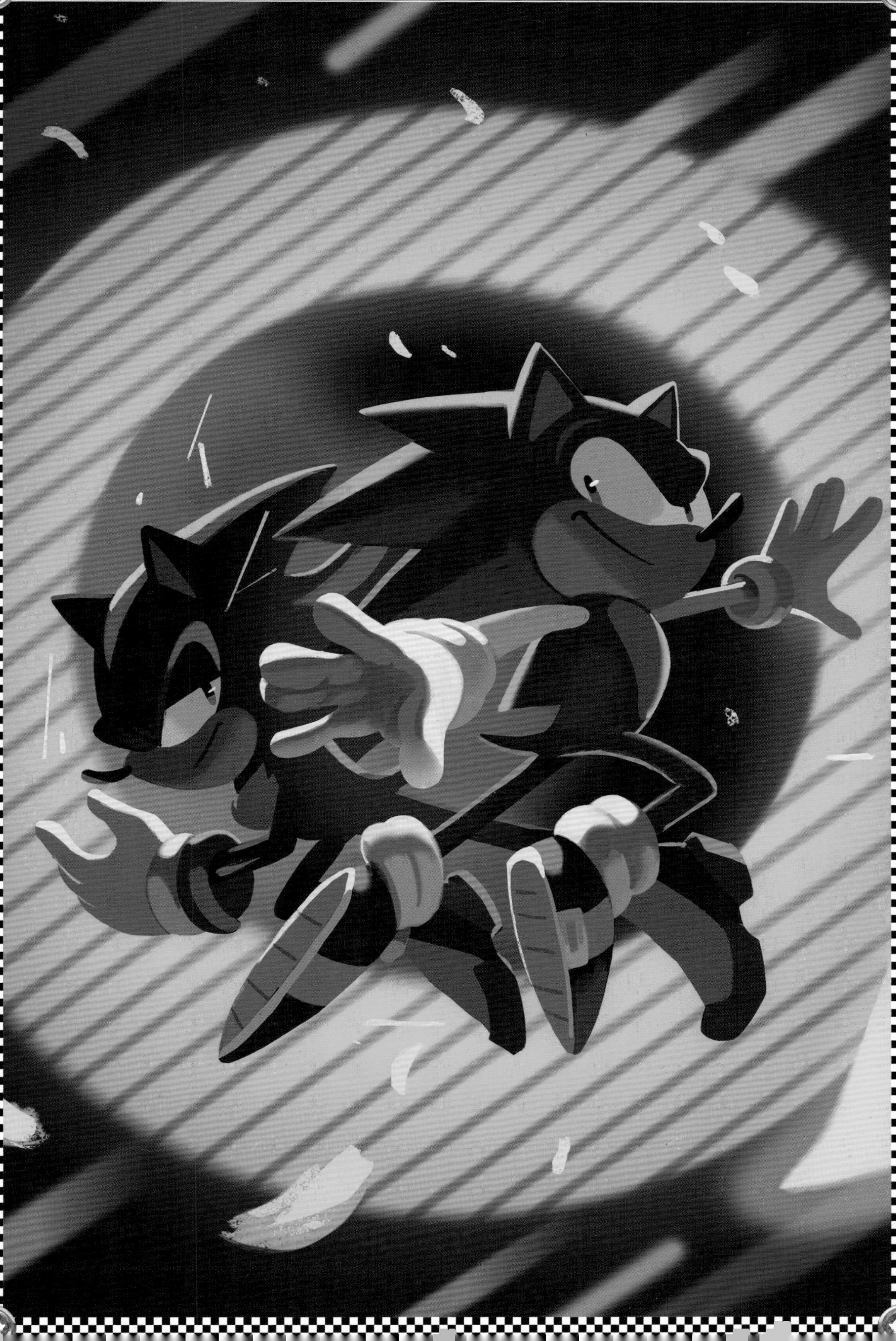

ART BY EVAN STANLEY COLORS BY MATT HERMS

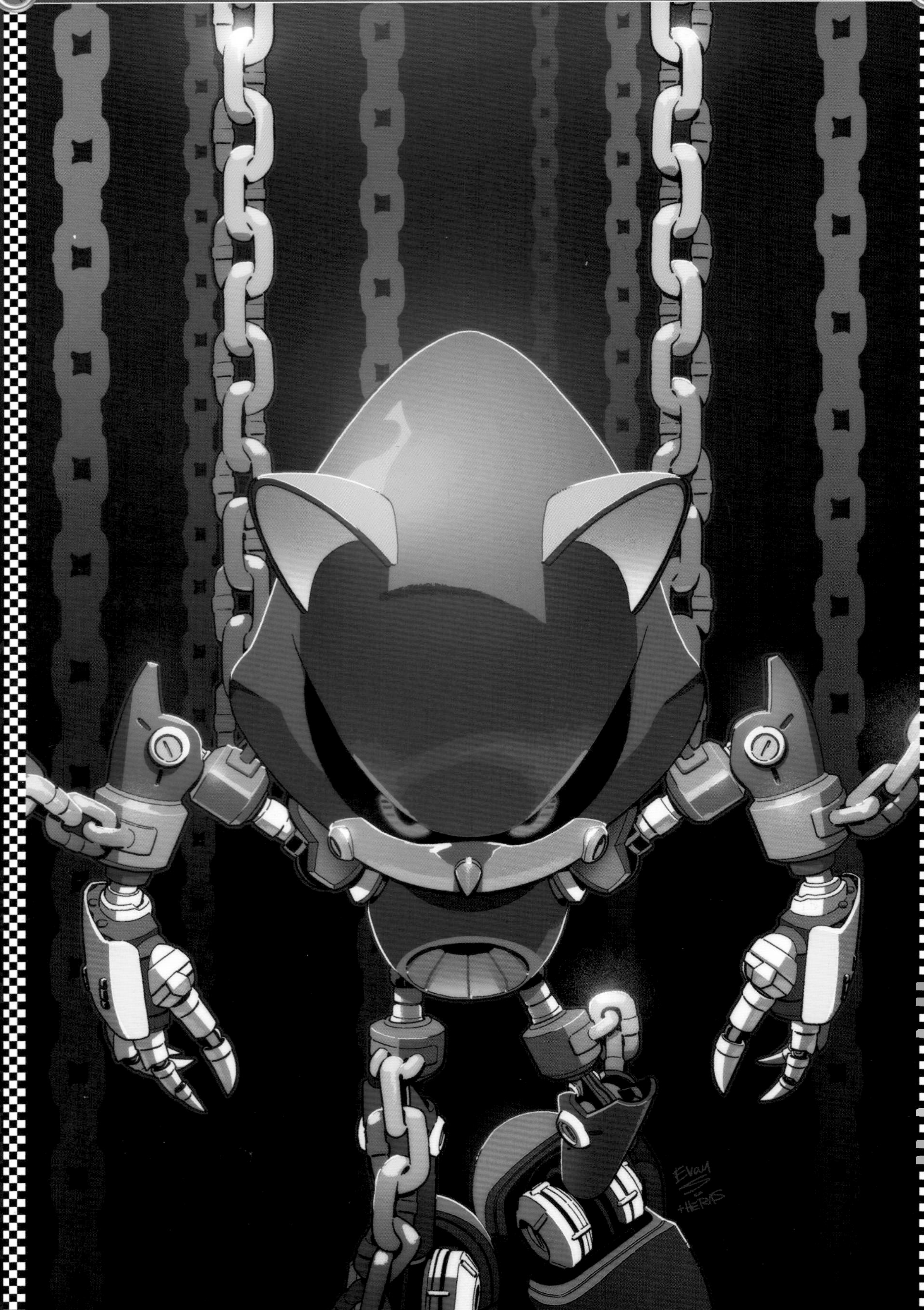

SONIC THE HEDGEHOG #12

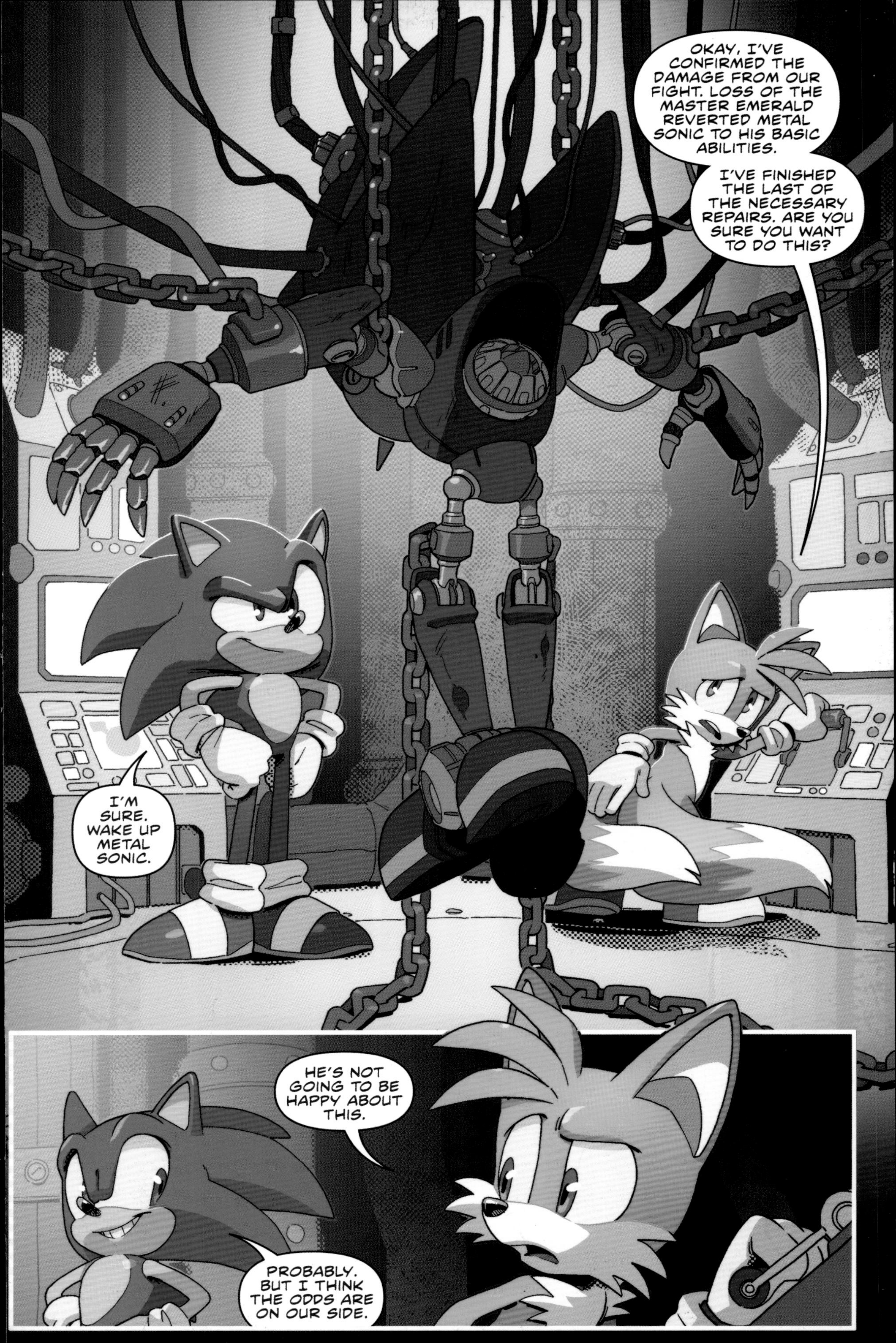
OKAY, I'VE CONFIRMED THE DAMAGE FROM OUR FIGHT. LOSS OF THE MASTER EMERALD REVERTED METAL SONIC TO HIS BASIC ABILITIES.
I'VE FINISHED THE LAST OF THE NECESSARY REPAIRS. ARE YOU SURE YOU WANT TO DO THIS?
I'M SURE. WAKE UP METAL SONIC.
HE'S NOT GOING TO BE HAPPY ABOUT THIS.
PROBABLY. BUT I THINK THE ODDS ARE ON OUR SIDE.

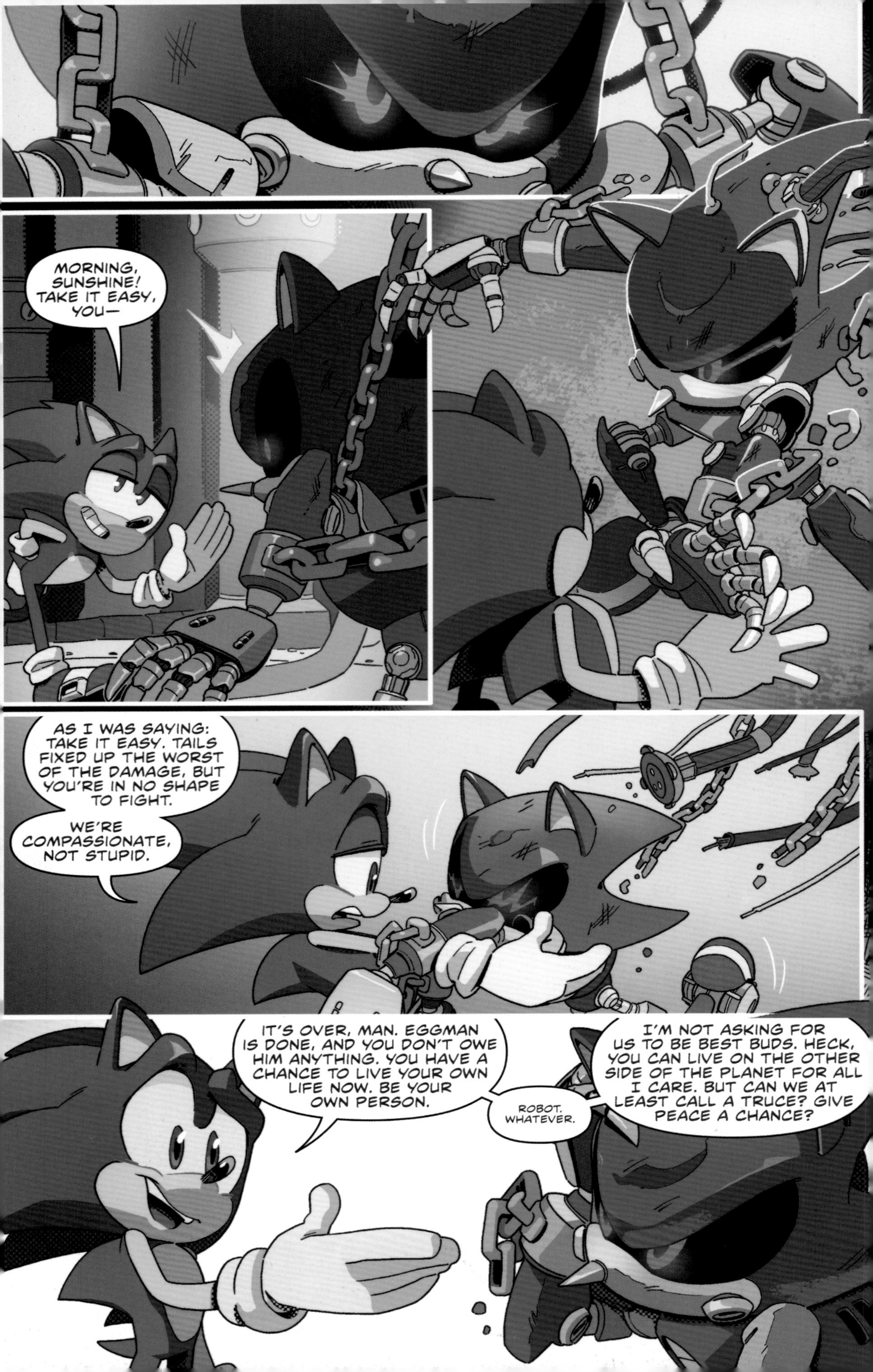
MORNING, SUNSHINE! TAKE IT EASY, YOU—
AS I WAS SAYING: TAKE IT EASY. TAILS FIXED UP THE WORST OF THE DAMAGE, BUT YOU'RE IN NO SHAPE TO FIGHT.
WE'RE COMPASSIONATE, NOT STUPID.
IT'S OVER, MAN. EGGMAN IS DONE, AND YOU DON'T OWE HIM ANYTHING. YOU HAVE A CHANCE TO LIVE YOUR OWN LIFE NOW. BE YOUR OWN PERSON.
ROBOT. WHATEVER.
I'M NOT ASKING FOR US TO BE BEST BUDS. HECK, YOU CAN LIVE ON THE OTHER SIDE OF THE PLANET FOR ALL I CARE. BUT CAN WE AT LEAST CALL A TRUCE? GIVE PEACE A CHANCE?

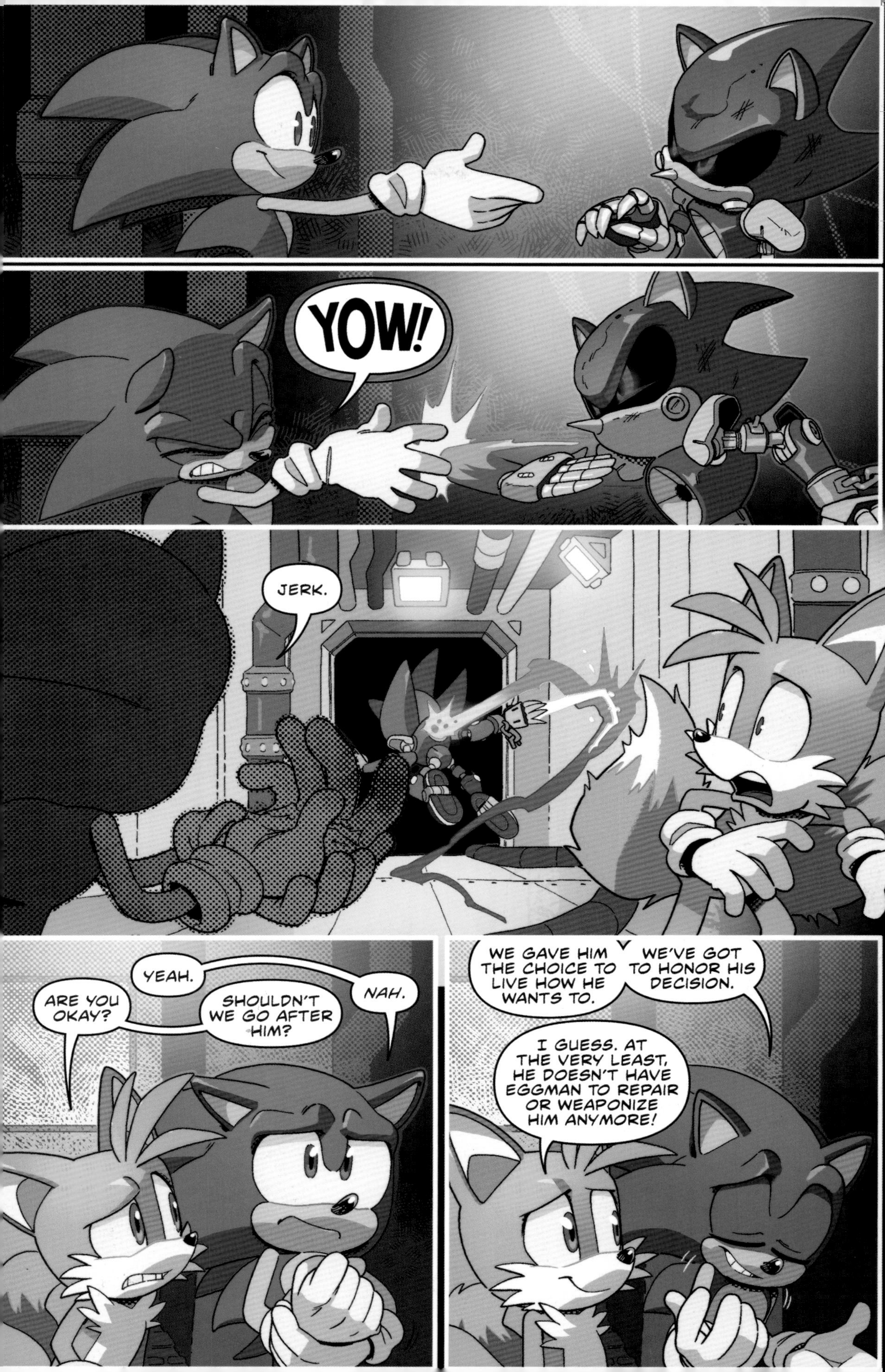
YOW!
JERK.
ARE YOU OKAY?
YEAH.
SHOULDN'T WE GO AFTER HIM?
NAH.
WE GAVE HIM THE CHOICE TO LIVE HOW HE WANTS TO.
WE'VE GOT TO HONOR HIS DECISION.
I GUESS. AT THE VERY LEAST, HE DOESN'T HAVE EGGMAN TO REPAIR OR WEAPONIZE HIM ANYMORE!

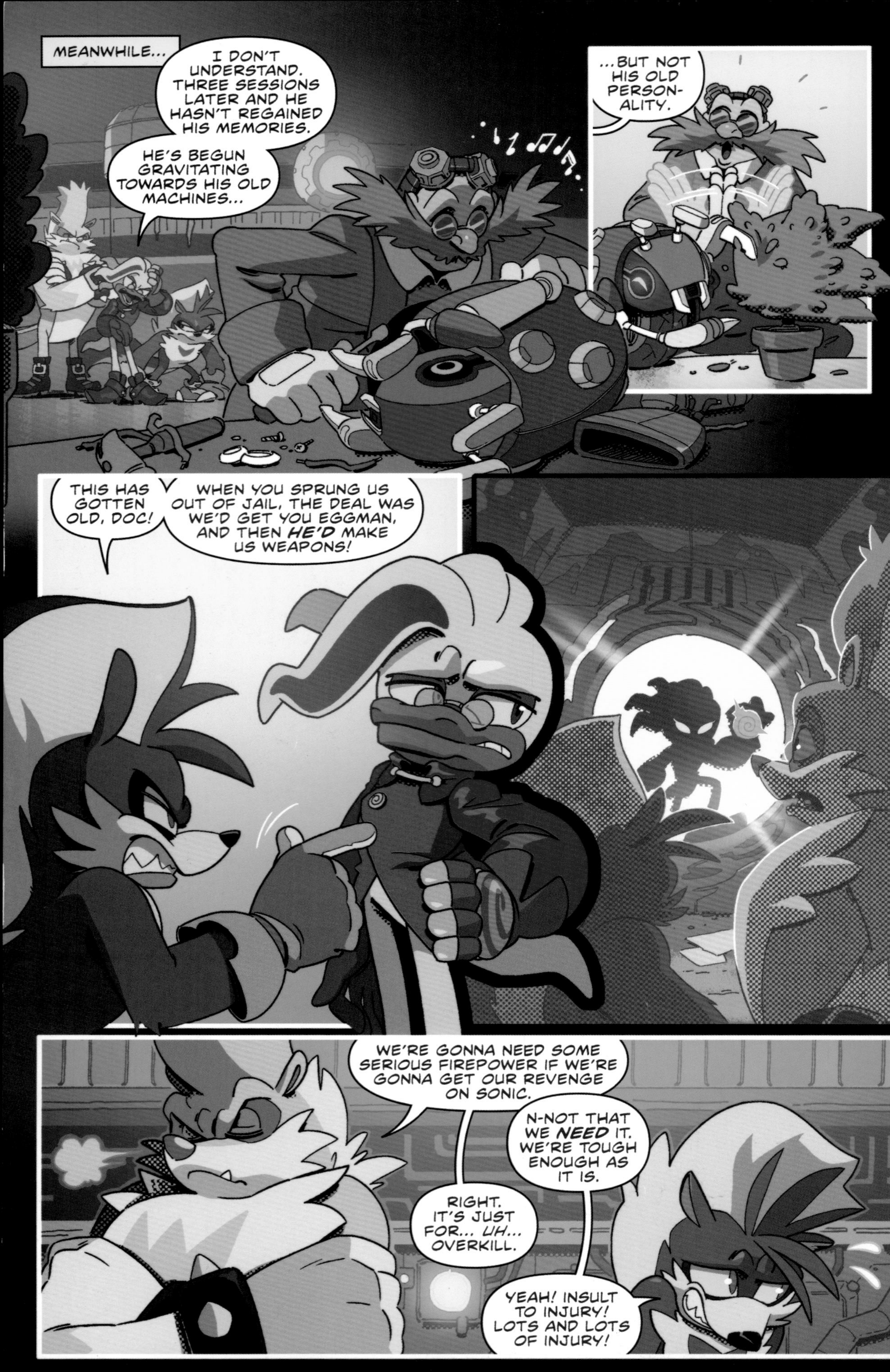
MEANWHILE...
I DON'T UNDERSTAND. THREE SESSIONS LATER AND HE HASN'T REGAINED HIS MEMORIES.
HE'S BEGUN GRAVITATING TOWARDS HIS OLD MACHINES...
...BUT NOT HIS OLD PERSON-ALITY.
THIS HAS GOTTEN OLD, DOC!
WHEN YOU SPRUNG US OUT OF JAIL, THE DEAL WAS WE'D GET YOU EGGMAN, AND THEN HE'D MAKE US WEAPONS!
WE'RE GONNA NEED SOME SERIOUS FIREPOWER IF WE'RE GONNA GET OUR REVENGE ON SONIC.
N-NOT THAT WE NEED IT. WE'RE TOUGH ENOUGH AS IT IS.
RIGHT. IT'S JUST FOR... UH... OVERKILL.
YEAH! INSULT TO INJURY! LOTS AND LOTS OF INJURY!

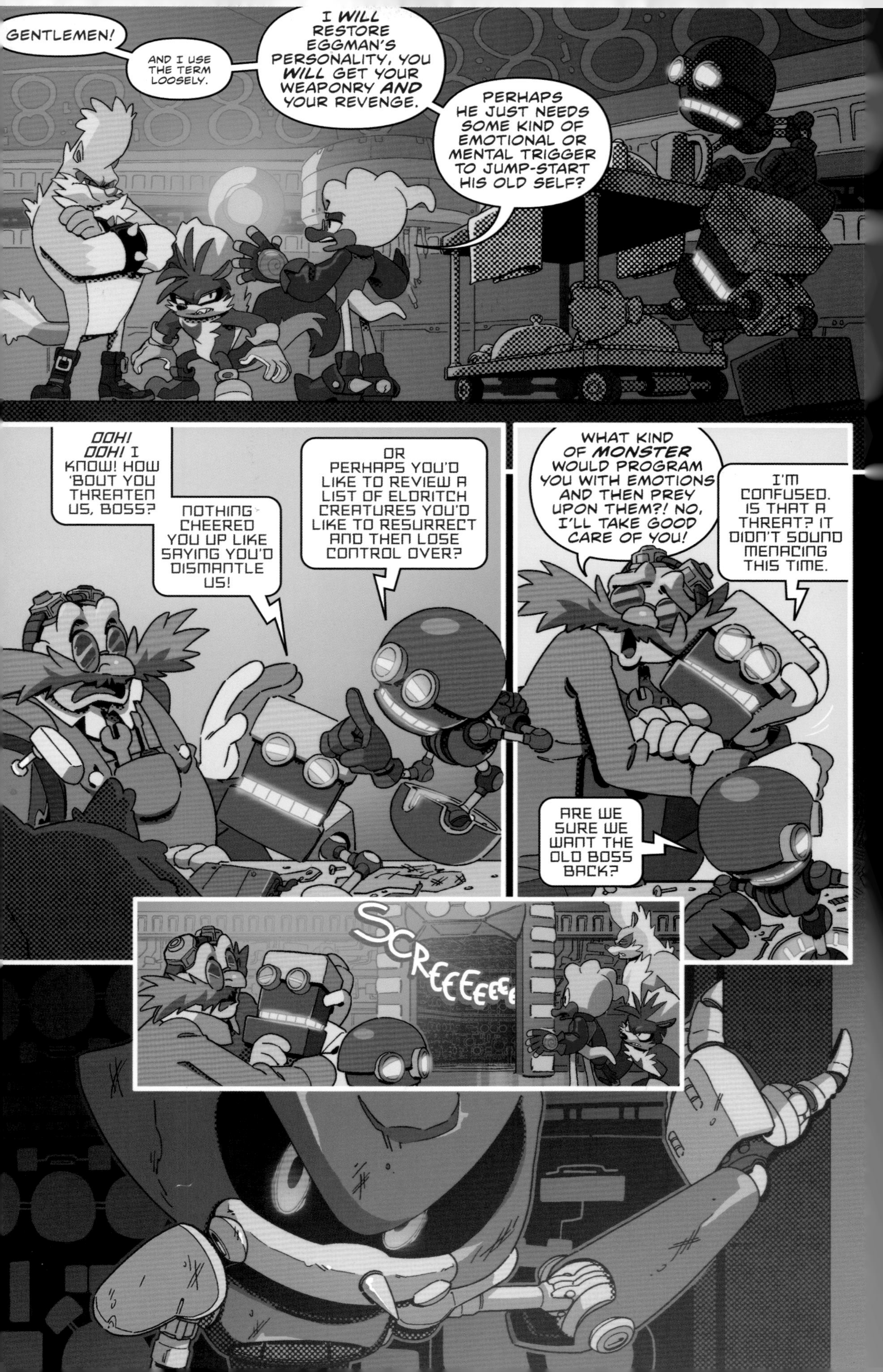
GENTLEMEN!
AND I USE THE TERM LOOSELY.
I WILL RESTORE EGGMAN'S PERSONALITY. YOU WILL GET YOUR WEAPONRY AND YOUR REVENGE.
PERHAPS HE JUST NEEDS SOME KIND OF EMOTIONAL OR MENTAL TRIGGER TO JUMP-START HIS OLD SELF?
OOH! OOH! I KNOW! HOW 'BOUT YOU THREATEN US, BOSS?
NOTHING CHEERED YOU UP LIKE SAYING YOU'D DISMANTLE US!
OR PERHAPS YOU'D LIKE TO REVIEW A LIST OF ELDRITCH CREATURES YOU'D LIKE TO RESURRECT AND THEN LOSE CONTROL OVER?
WHAT KIND OF MONSTER WOULD PROGRAM YOU WITH EMOTIONS AND THEN PREY UPON THEM?! NO, I'LL TAKE GOOD CARE OF YOU!
I'M CONFUSED. IS THAT A THREAT? IT DIDN'T SOUND MENACING THIS TIME.
ARE WE SURE WE WANT THE OLD BOSS BACK?
SCREEEEEEE

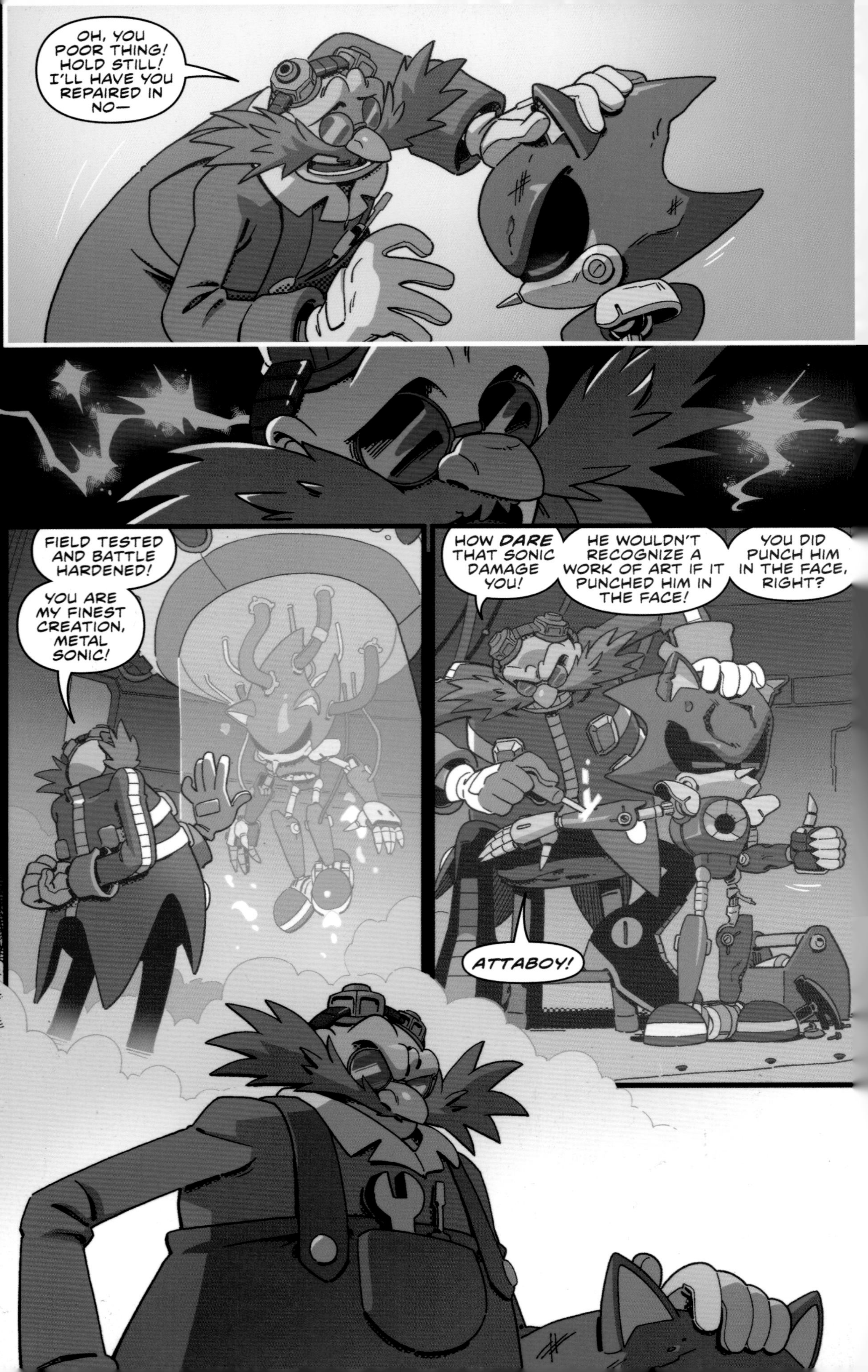
OH, YOU POOR THING! HOLD STILL! I'LL HAVE YOU REPAIRED IN NO—
FIELD TESTED AND BATTLE HARDENED!
YOU ARE MY FINEST CREATION, METAL SONIC!
HOW *DARE* THAT SONIC DAMAGE YOU!
HE WOULDN'T RECOGNIZE A WORK OF ART IF IT PUNCHED HIM IN THE FACE!
YOU DID PUNCH HIM IN THE FACE, RIGHT?
ATTABOY!

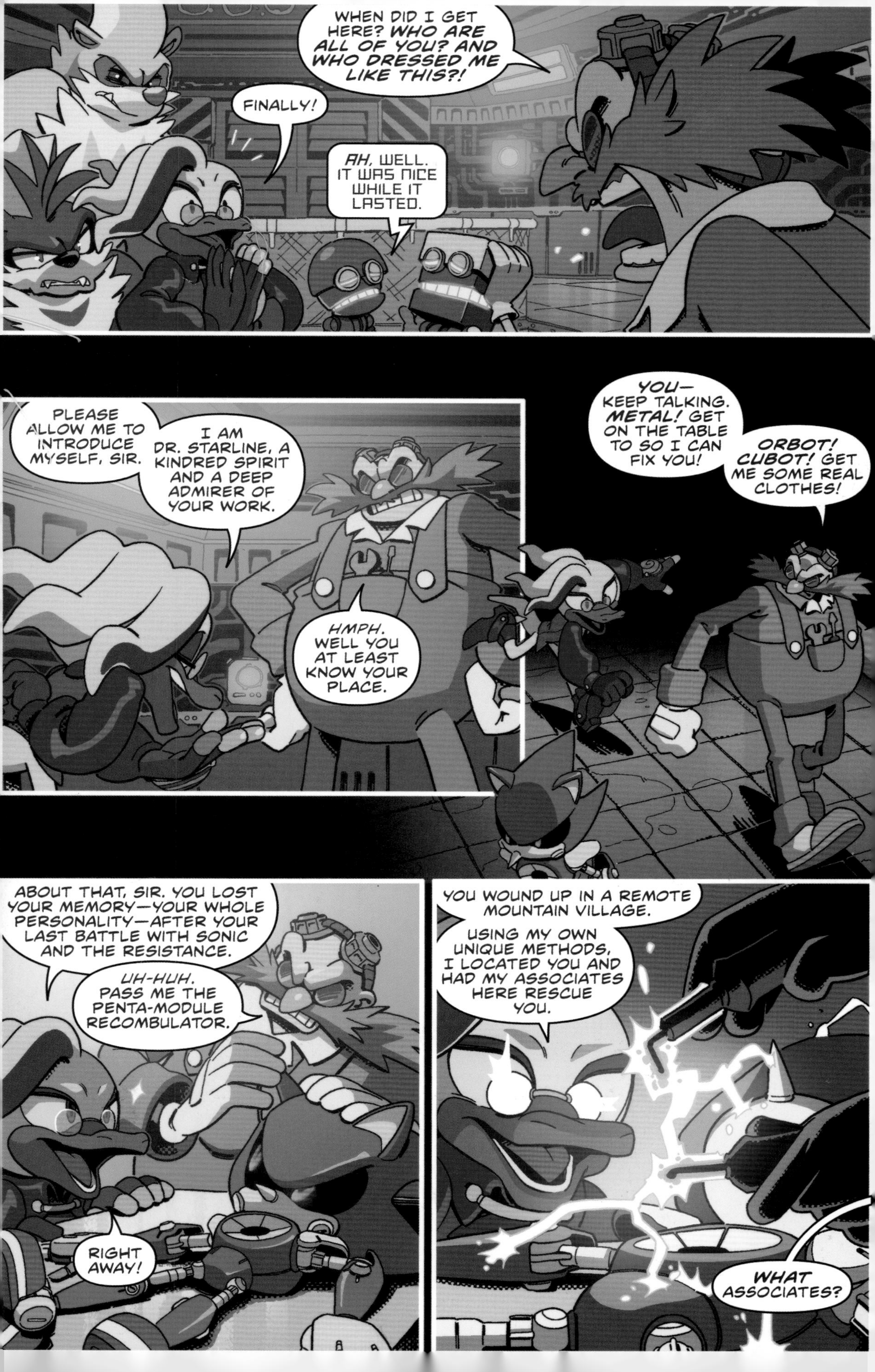

WHEN DID I GET HERE? WHO ARE ALL OF YOU? AND WHO DRESSED ME LIKE THIS?!
FINALLY!
AH, WELL. IT WAS NICE WHILE IT LASTED.
PLEASE ALLOW ME TO INTRODUCE MYSELF, SIR.
I AM DR. STARLINE, A KINDRED SPIRIT AND A DEEP ADMIRER OF YOUR WORK.
HMPH. WELL YOU AT LEAST KNOW YOUR PLACE.
YOU— KEEP TALKING. METAL! GET ON THE TABLE TO SO I CAN FIX YOU!
ORBOT! CUBOT! GET ME SOME REAL CLOTHES!
ABOUT THAT, SIR. YOU LOST YOUR MEMORY—YOUR WHOLE PERSONALITY—AFTER YOUR LAST BATTLE WITH SONIC AND THE RESISTANCE.
UH-HUH. PASS ME THE PENTA-MODULE RECOMBULATOR.
RIGHT AWAY!
YOU WOUND UP IN A REMOTE MOUNTAIN VILLAGE.
USING MY OWN UNIQUE METHODS, I LOCATED YOU AND HAD MY ASSOCIATES HERE RESCUE YOU.
WHAT ASSOCIATES?

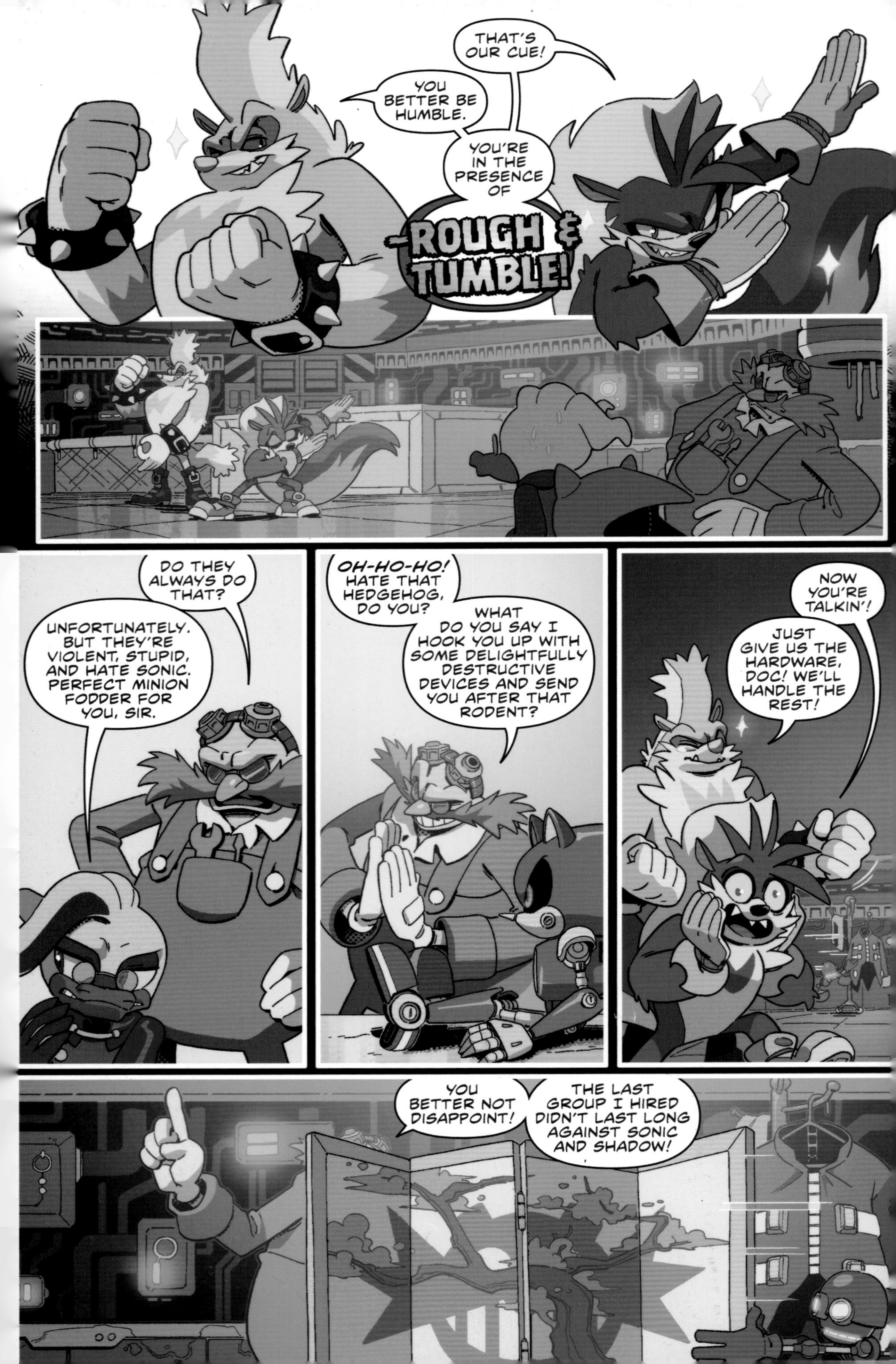
YOU BETTER BE HUMBLE.
THAT'S OUR CUE!
YOU'RE IN THE PRESENCE OF
ROUGH & TUMBLE!
DO THEY ALWAYS DO THAT?
UNFORTUNATELY. BUT THEY'RE VIOLENT, STUPID, AND HATE SONIC. PERFECT MINION FODDER FOR YOU, SIR.
OH-HO-HO! HATE THAT HEDGEHOG, DO YOU?
WHAT DO YOU SAY I HOOK YOU UP WITH SOME DELIGHTFULLY DESTRUCTIVE DEVICES AND SEND YOU AFTER THAT RODENT?
NOW YOU'RE TALKIN'!
JUST GIVE US THE HARDWARE, DOC! WE'LL HANDLE THE REST!
YOU BETTER NOT DISAPPOINT!
THE LAST GROUP I HIRED DIDN'T LAST LONG AGAINST SONIC AND SHADOW!

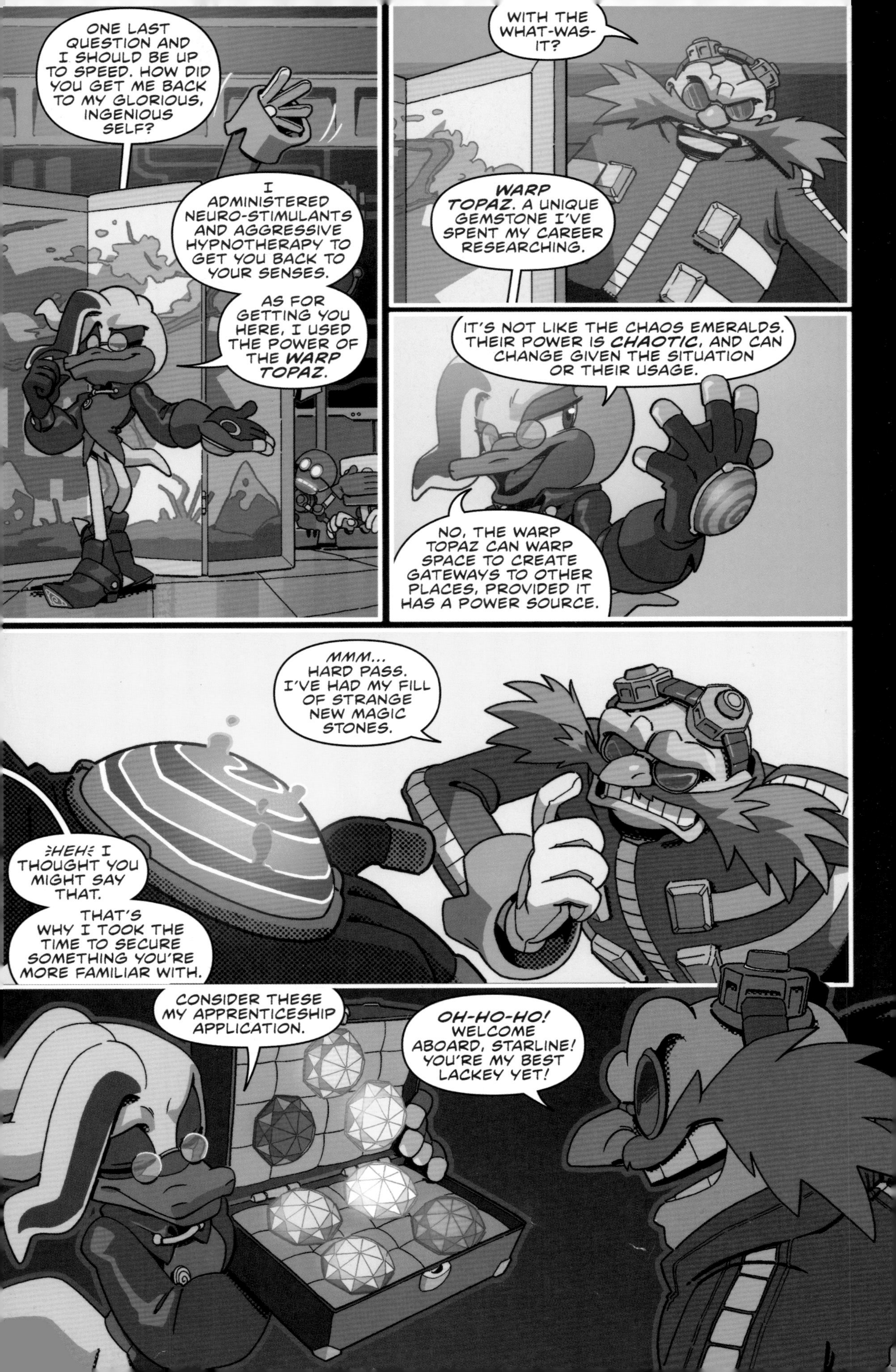
ONE LAST QUESTION AND I SHOULD BE UP TO SPEED. HOW DID YOU GET ME BACK TO MY GLORIOUS, INGENIOUS SELF?
I ADMINISTERED NEURO-STIMULANTS AND AGGRESSIVE HYPNOTHERAPY TO GET YOU BACK TO YOUR SENSES.
AS FOR GETTING YOU HERE, I USED THE POWER OF THE *WARP TOPAZ*.
WITH THE WHAT-WAS-IT?
WARP TOPAZ. A UNIQUE GEMSTONE I'VE SPENT MY CAREER RESEARCHING.
IT'S NOT LIKE THE CHAOS EMERALDS. THEIR POWER IS *CHAOTIC*, AND CAN CHANGE GIVEN THE SITUATION OR THEIR USAGE.
NO, THE WARP TOPAZ CAN WARP SPACE TO CREATE GATEWAYS TO OTHER PLACES, PROVIDED IT HAS A POWER SOURCE.
MMM... HARD PASS. I'VE HAD MY FILL OF STRANGE NEW MAGIC STONES.
HEH I THOUGHT YOU MIGHT SAY THAT.
THAT'S WHY I TOOK THE TIME TO SECURE SOMETHING YOU'RE MORE FAMILIAR WITH.
CONSIDER THESE MY APPRENTICESHIP APPLICATION.
OH-HO-HO! WELCOME ABOARD, STARLINE! YOU'RE MY BEST LACKEY YET!

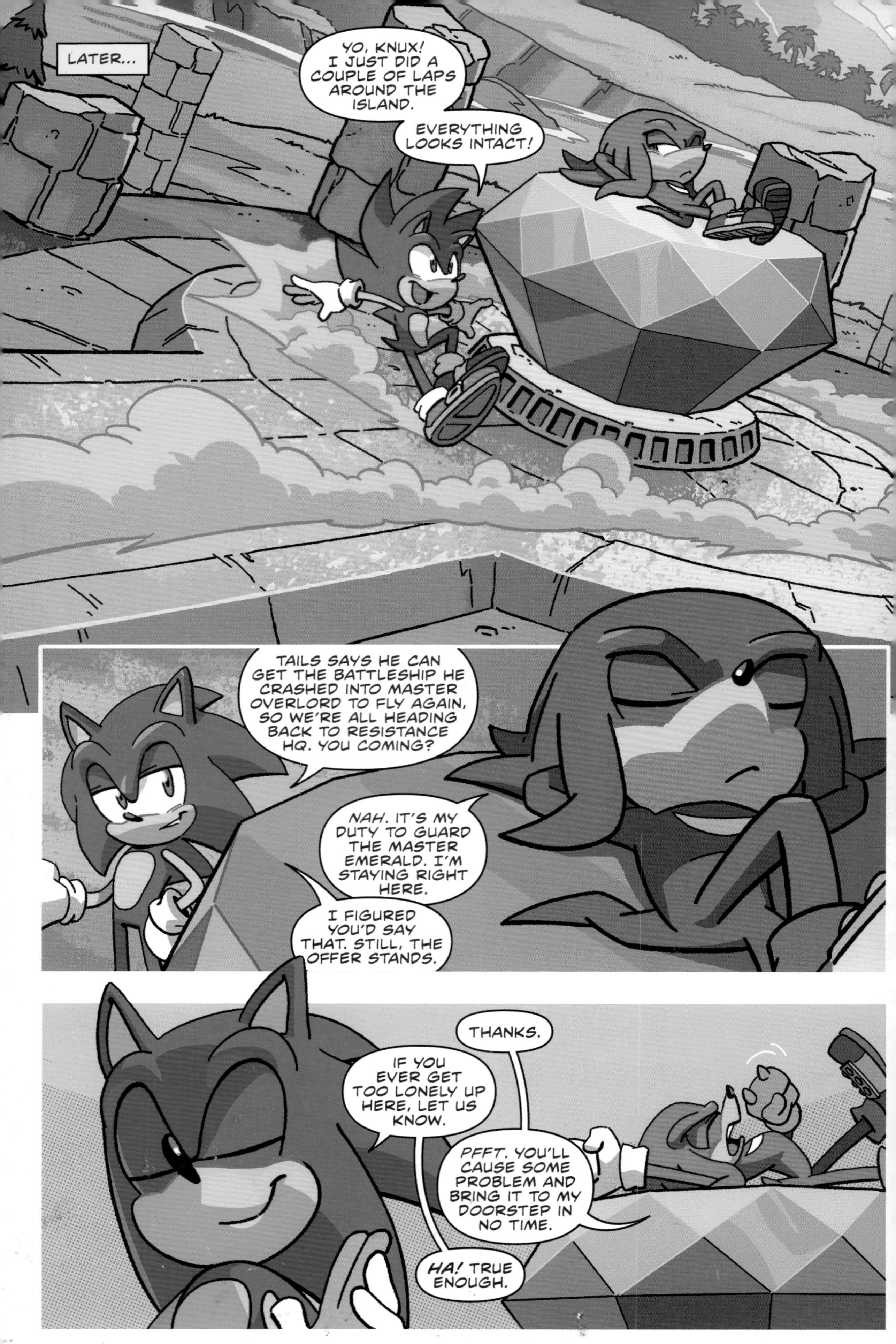
LATER...
YO, KNUX! I JUST DID A COUPLE OF LAPS AROUND THE ISLAND.
EVERYTHING LOOKS INTACT!
TAILS SAYS HE CAN GET THE BATTLESHIP HE CRASHED INTO MASTER OVERLORD TO FLY AGAIN, SO WE'RE ALL HEADING BACK TO RESISTANCE HQ. YOU COMING?
NAH. IT'S MY DUTY TO GUARD THE MASTER EMERALD. I'M STAYING RIGHT HERE.
I FIGURED YOU'D SAY THAT. STILL, THE OFFER STANDS.
THANKS.
IF YOU EVER GET TOO LONELY UP HERE, LET US KNOW.
PFFT. YOU'LL CAUSE SOME PROBLEM AND BRING IT TO MY DOORSTEP IN NO TIME.
HA! TRUE ENOUGH.

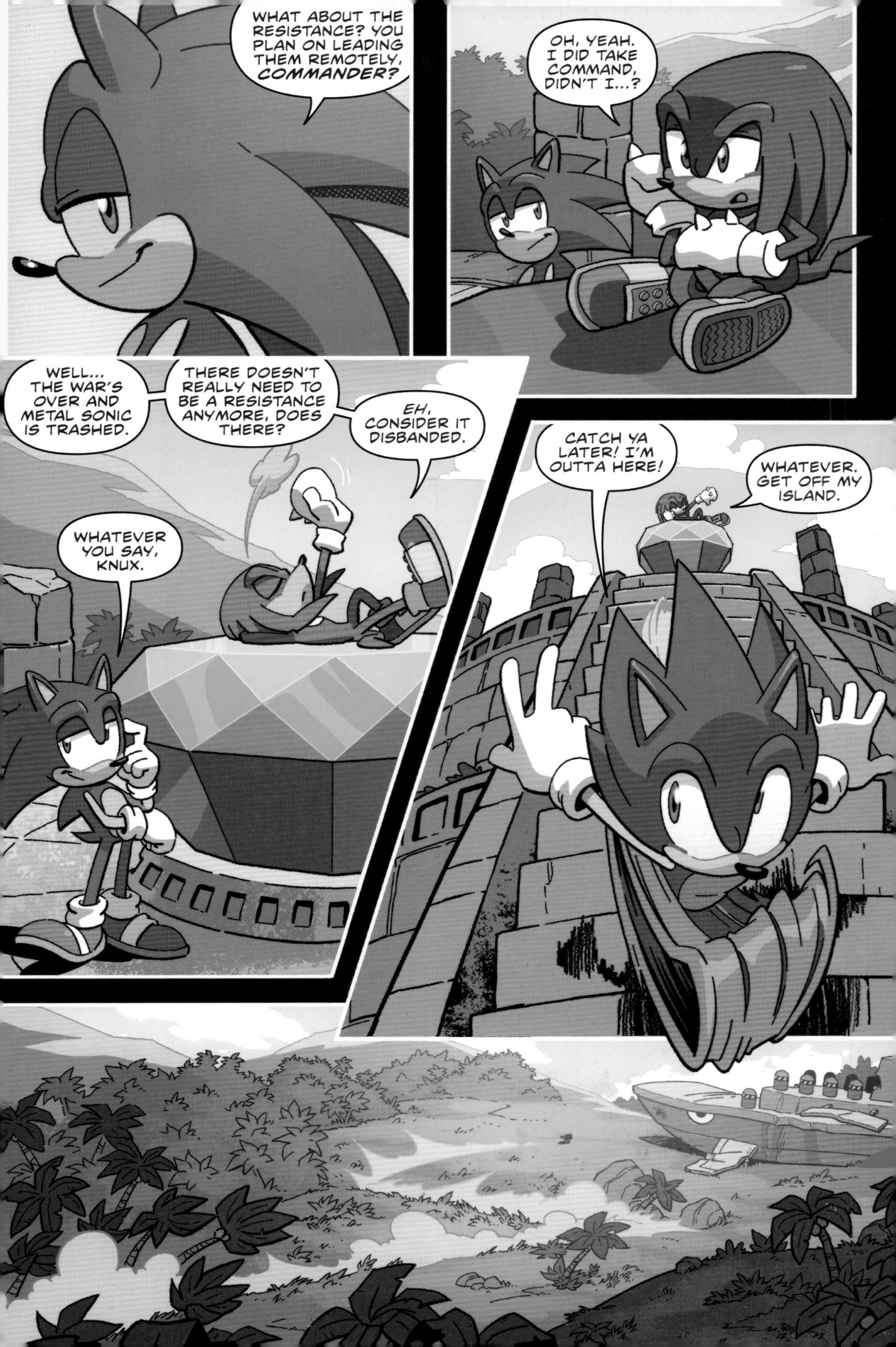

WHAT ABOUT THE RESISTANCE? YOU PLAN ON LEADING THEM REMOTELY, *COMMANDER?*
OH, YEAH. I DID TAKE COMMAND, DIDN'T I...?
WELL... THE WAR'S OVER AND METAL SONIC IS TRASHED.
THERE DOESN'T REALLY NEED TO BE A RESISTANCE ANYMORE, DOES THERE?
EH, CONSIDER IT DISBANDED.
WHATEVER YOU SAY, KNUX.
CATCH YA LATER! I'M OUTTA HERE!
WHATEVER. GET OFF MY ISLAND.

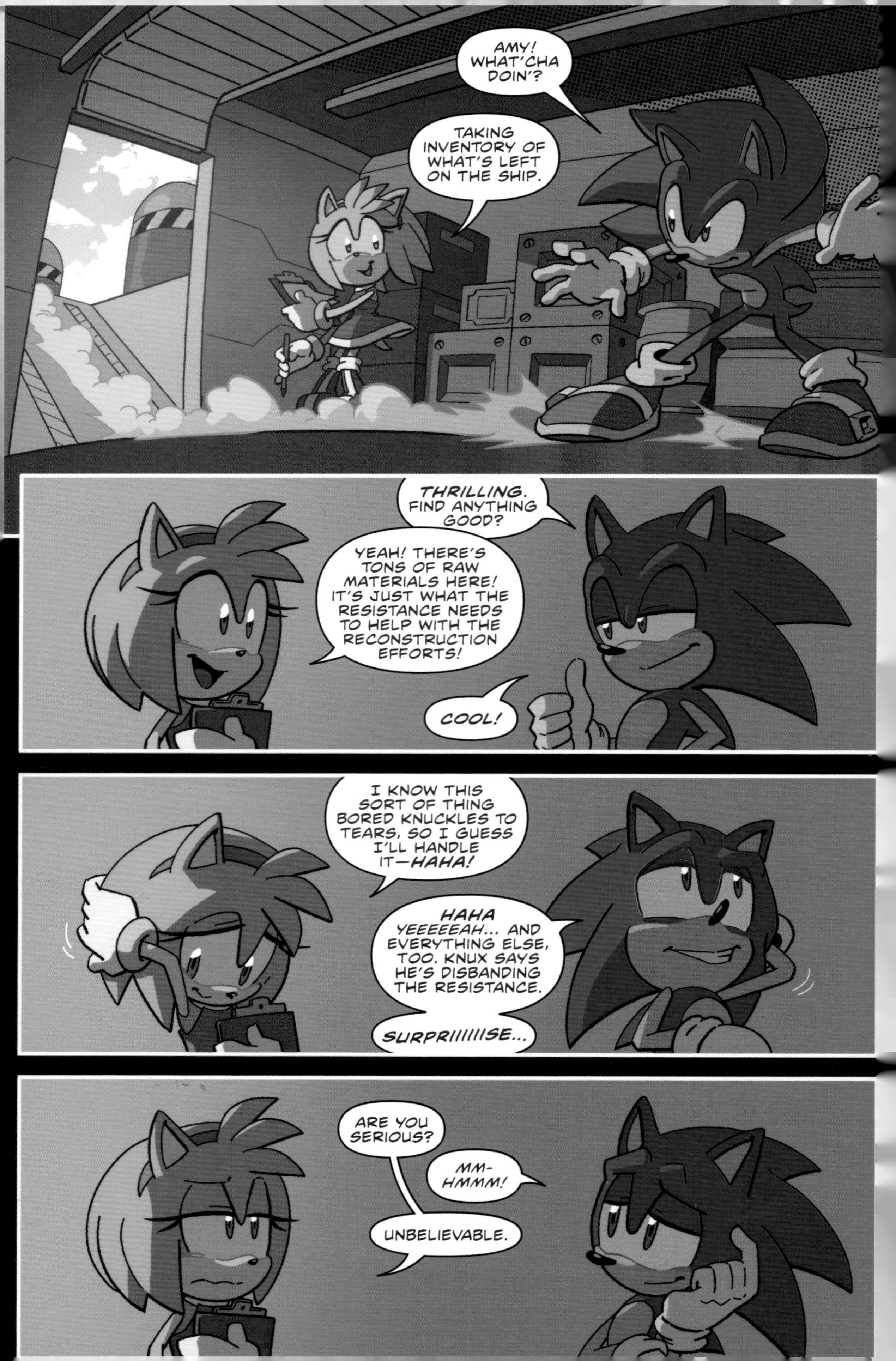
AMY! WHAT'CHA DOIN'?
TAKING INVENTORY OF WHAT'S LEFT ON THE SHIP.
THRILLING. FIND ANYTHING GOOD?
YEAH! THERE'S TONS OF RAW MATERIALS HERE! IT'S JUST WHAT THE RESISTANCE NEEDS TO HELP WITH THE RECONSTRUCTION EFFORTS!
COOL!
I KNOW THIS SORT OF THING BORED KNUCKLES TO TEARS, SO I GUESS I'LL HANDLE IT—HAHA!
HAHA YEEEEEAH... AND EVERYTHING ELSE, TOO. KNUX SAYS HE'S DISBANDING THE RESISTANCE.
SURPRIIIIIISE...
ARE YOU SERIOUS?
MM-HMMM!
UNBELIEVABLE.

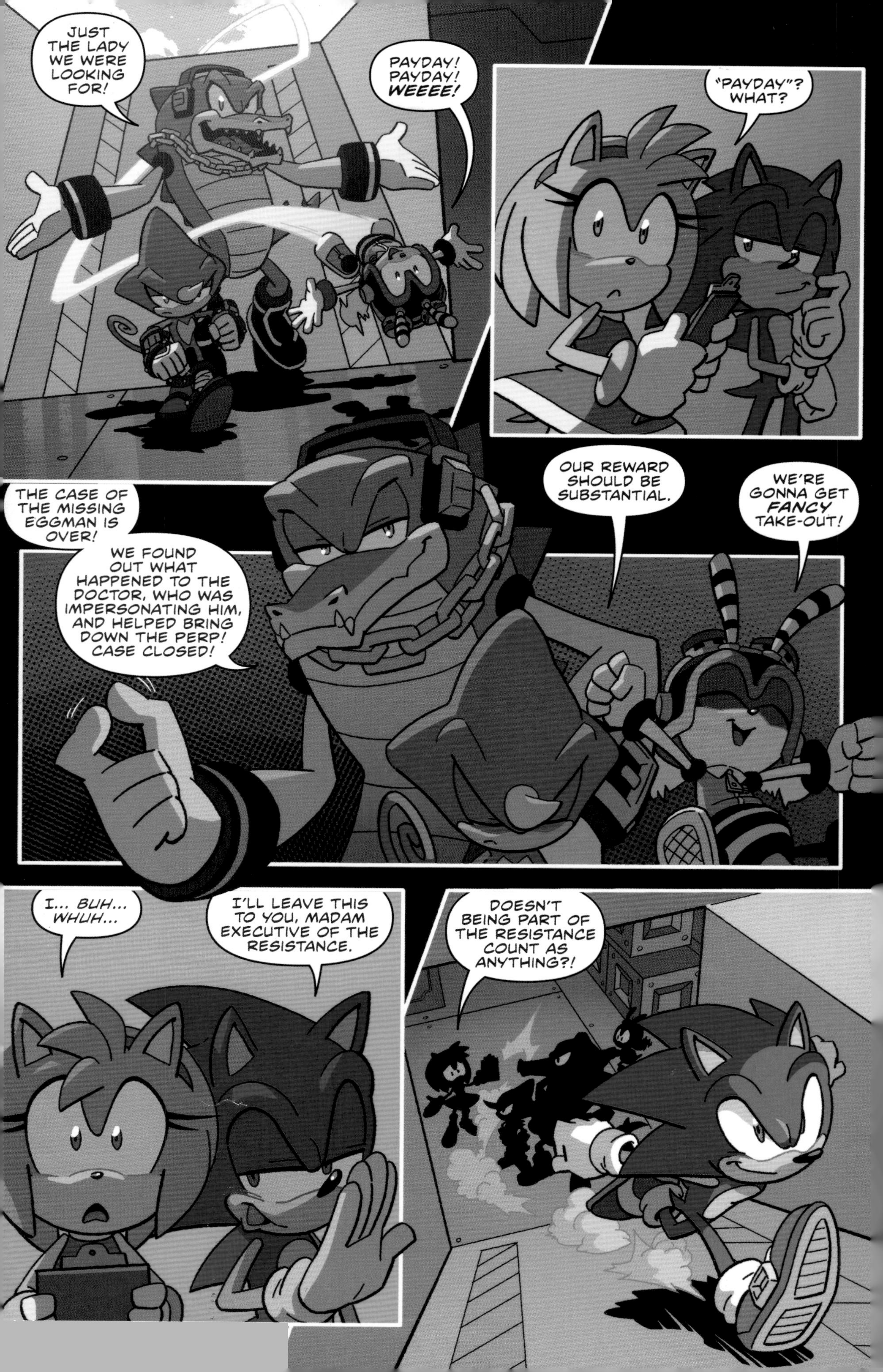
JUST THE LADY WE WERE LOOKING FOR!
PAYDAY! PAYDAY! WEEEE!
"PAYDAY"? WHAT?
THE CASE OF THE MISSING EGGMAN IS OVER!
WE FOUND OUT WHAT HAPPENED TO THE DOCTOR, WHO WAS IMPERSONATING HIM, AND HELPED BRING DOWN THE PERP! CASE CLOSED!
OUR REWARD SHOULD BE SUBSTANTIAL.
WE'RE GONNA GET FANCY TAKE-OUT!
I... BUH... WHUH...
I'LL LEAVE THIS TO YOU, MADAM EXECUTIVE OF THE RESISTANCE.
DOESN'T BEING PART OF THE RESISTANCE COUNT AS ANYTHING?!

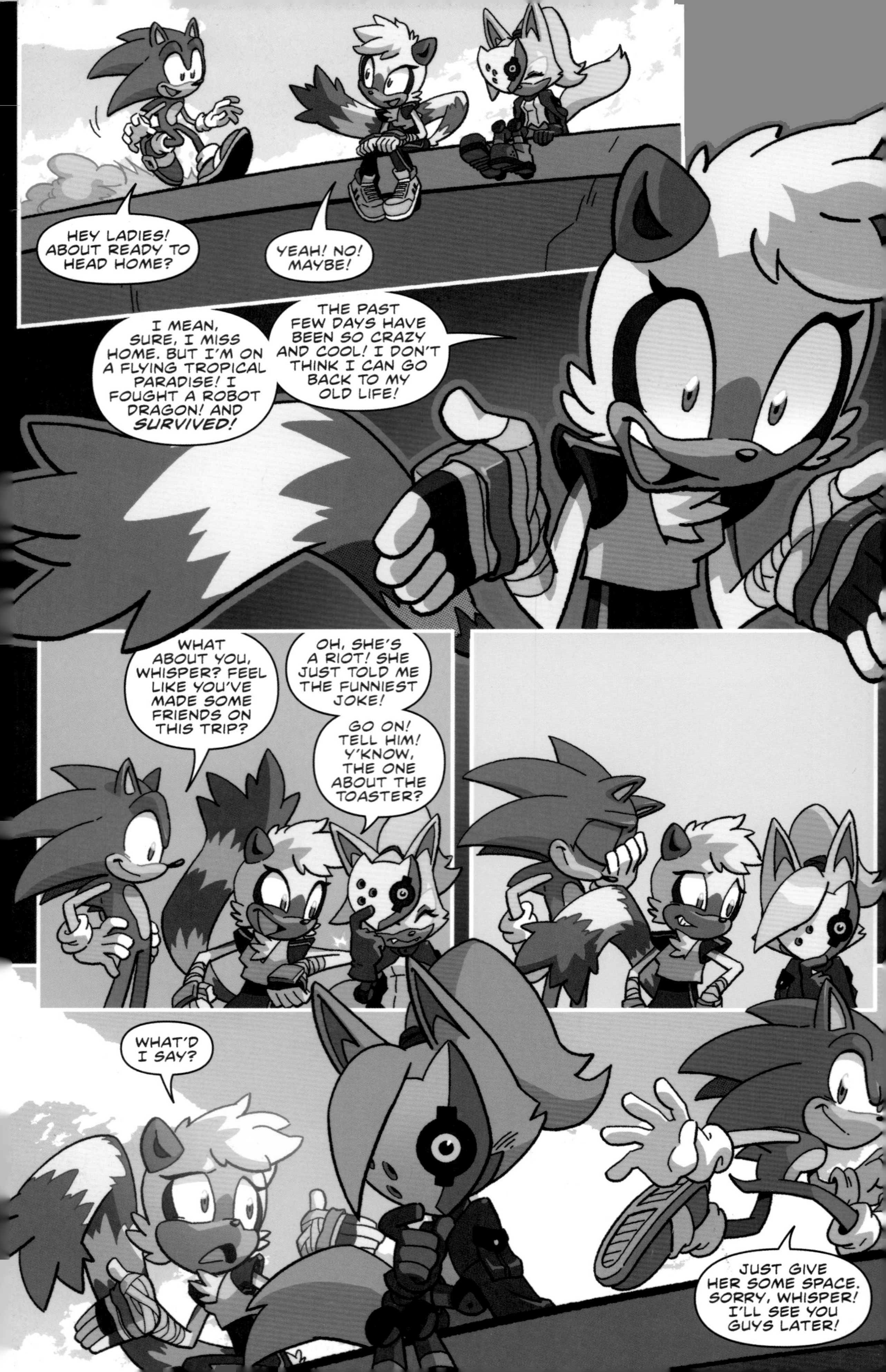

HEY LADIES! ABOUT READY TO HEAD HOME?
YEAH! NO! MAYBE!
I MEAN, SURE, I MISS HOME. BUT I'M ON A FLYING TROPICAL PARADISE! I FOUGHT A ROBOT DRAGON! AND SURVIVED!
THE PAST FEW DAYS HAVE BEEN SO CRAZY AND COOL! I DON'T THINK I CAN GO BACK TO MY OLD LIFE!
WHAT ABOUT YOU, WHISPER? FEEL LIKE YOU'VE MADE SOME FRIENDS ON THIS TRIP?
OH, SHE'S A RIOT! SHE JUST TOLD ME THE FUNNIEST JOKE!
GO ON! TELL HIM! Y'KNOW, THE ONE ABOUT THE TOASTER?
WHAT'D I SAY?
JUST GIVE HER SOME SPACE. SORRY, WHISPER! I'LL SEE YOU GUYS LATER!

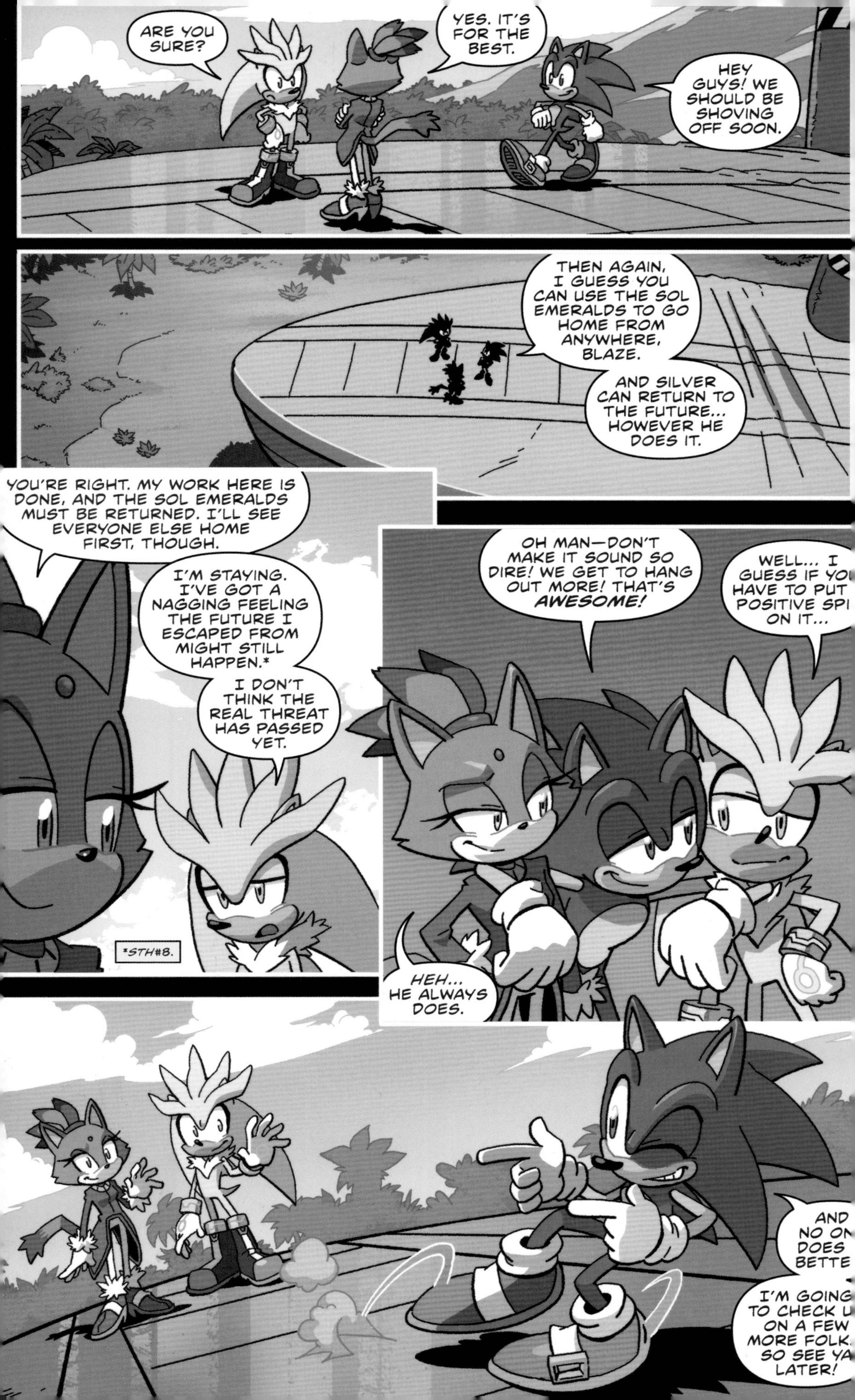
ARE YOU SURE?
YES. IT'S FOR THE BEST.
HEY GUYS! WE SHOULD BE SHOVING OFF SOON.
THEN AGAIN, I GUESS YOU CAN USE THE SOL EMERALDS TO GO HOME FROM ANYWHERE, BLAZE.
AND SILVER CAN RETURN TO THE FUTURE... HOWEVER HE DOES IT.
YOU'RE RIGHT. MY WORK HERE IS DONE, AND THE SOL EMERALDS MUST BE RETURNED. I'LL SEE EVERYONE ELSE HOME FIRST, THOUGH.
I'M STAYING. I'VE GOT A NAGGING FEELING THE FUTURE I ESCAPED FROM MIGHT STILL HAPPEN.*
I DON'T THINK THE REAL THREAT HAS PASSED YET.
*STH#8.
OH MAN—DON'T MAKE IT SOUND SO DIRE! WE GET TO HANG OUT MORE! THAT'S **AWESOME!**
WELL... I GUESS IF YO HAVE TO PUT POSITIVE SPI ON IT...
HEH... HE ALWAYS DOES.
AND NO ON DOES BETTE
I'M GOING TO CHECK U ON A FEW MORE FOLK SO SEE YA LATER!

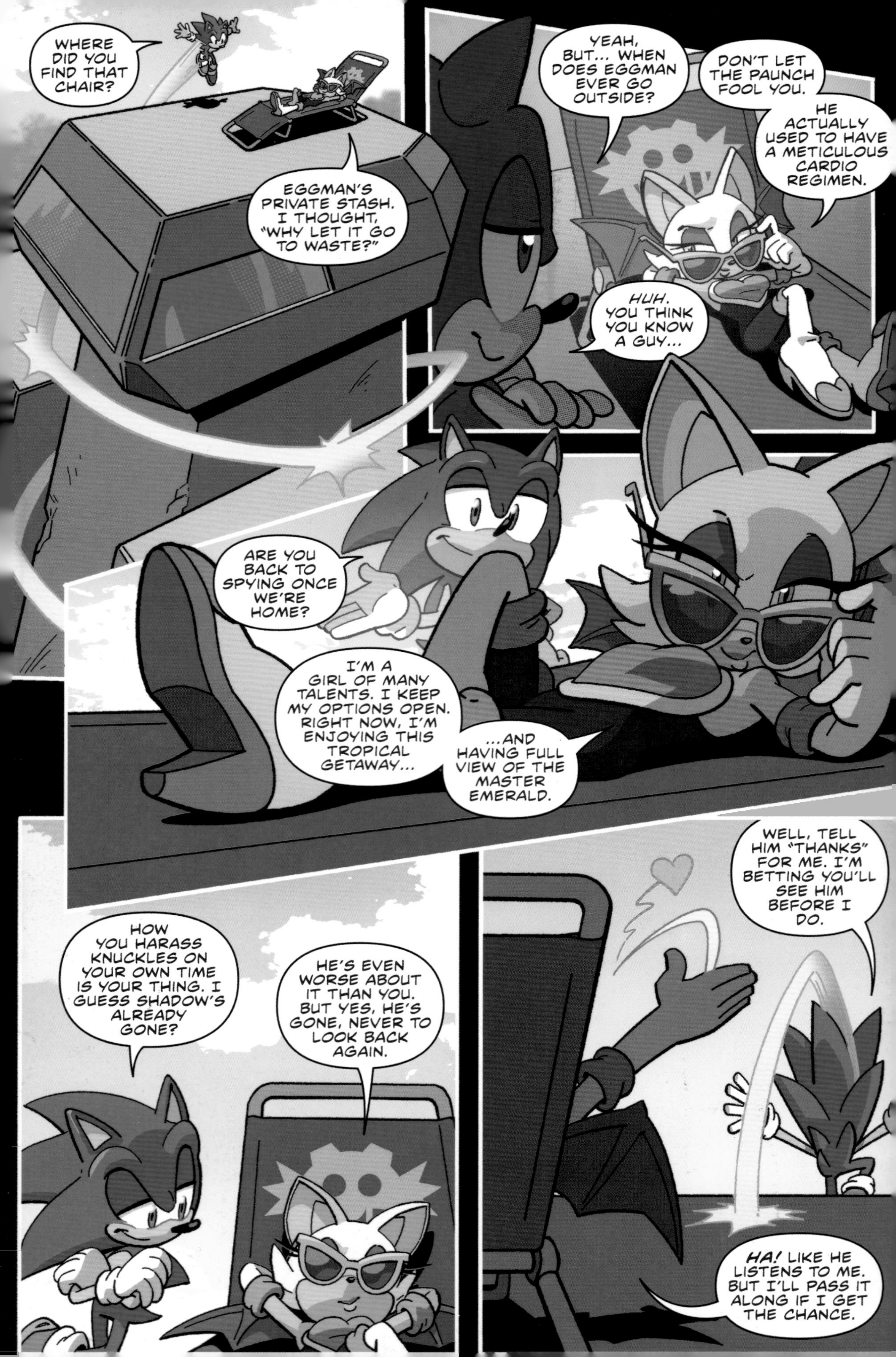

WHERE DID YOU FIND THAT CHAIR?
EGGMAN'S PRIVATE STASH. I THOUGHT, "WHY LET IT GO TO WASTE?"
YEAH, BUT... WHEN DOES EGGMAN EVER GO OUTSIDE?
DON'T LET THE PAUNCH FOOL YOU.
HE ACTUALLY USED TO HAVE A METICULOUS CARDIO REGIMEN.
HUH. YOU THINK YOU KNOW A GUY...
ARE YOU BACK TO SPYING ONCE WE'RE HOME?
I'M A GIRL OF MANY TALENTS. I KEEP MY OPTIONS OPEN. RIGHT NOW, I'M ENJOYING THIS TROPICAL GETAWAY...
...AND HAVING FULL VIEW OF THE MASTER EMERALD.
HOW YOU HARASS KNUCKLES ON YOUR OWN TIME IS YOUR THING. I GUESS SHADOW'S ALREADY GONE?
HE'S EVEN WORSE ABOUT IT THAN YOU. BUT YES, HE'S GONE, NEVER TO LOOK BACK AGAIN.
WELL, TELL HIM "THANKS" FOR ME. I'M BETTING YOU'LL SEE HIM BEFORE I DO.
HA! LIKE HE LISTENS TO ME. BUT I'LL PASS IT ALONG IF I GET THE CHANCE.

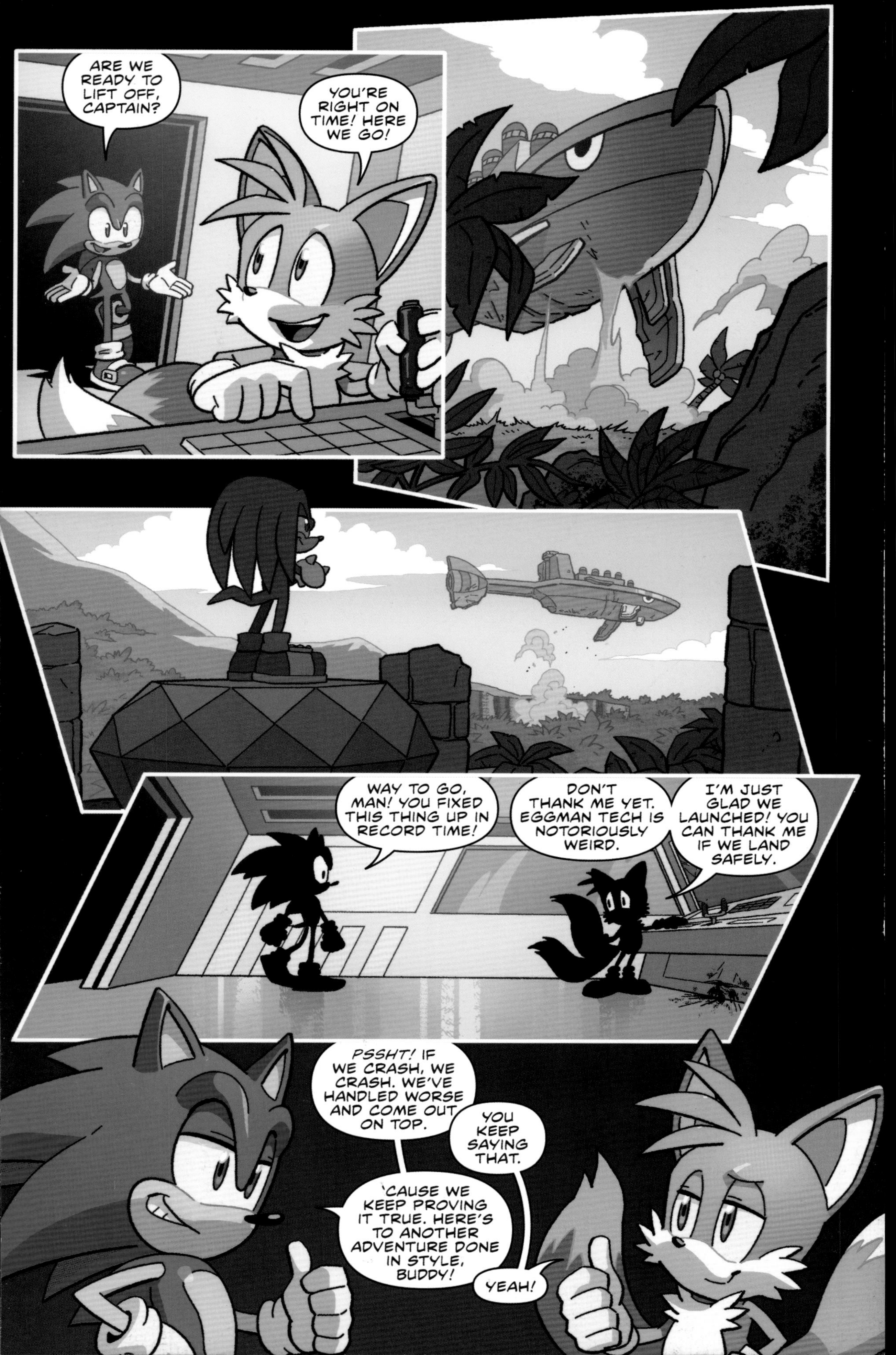
ARE WE READY TO LIFT OFF, CAPTAIN?
YOU'RE RIGHT ON TIME! HERE WE GO!
WAY TO GO, MAN! YOU FIXED THIS THING UP IN RECORD TIME!
DON'T THANK ME YET. EGGMAN TECH IS NOTORIOUSLY WEIRD.
I'M JUST GLAD WE LAUNCHED! YOU CAN THANK ME IF WE LAND SAFELY.
PSSHT! IF WE CRASH, WE CRASH. WE'VE HANDLED WORSE AND COME OUT ON TOP.
YOU KEEP SAYING THAT.
'CAUSE WE KEEP PROVING IT TRUE. HERE'S TO ANOTHER ADVENTURE DONE IN STYLE, BUDDY!
YEAH!

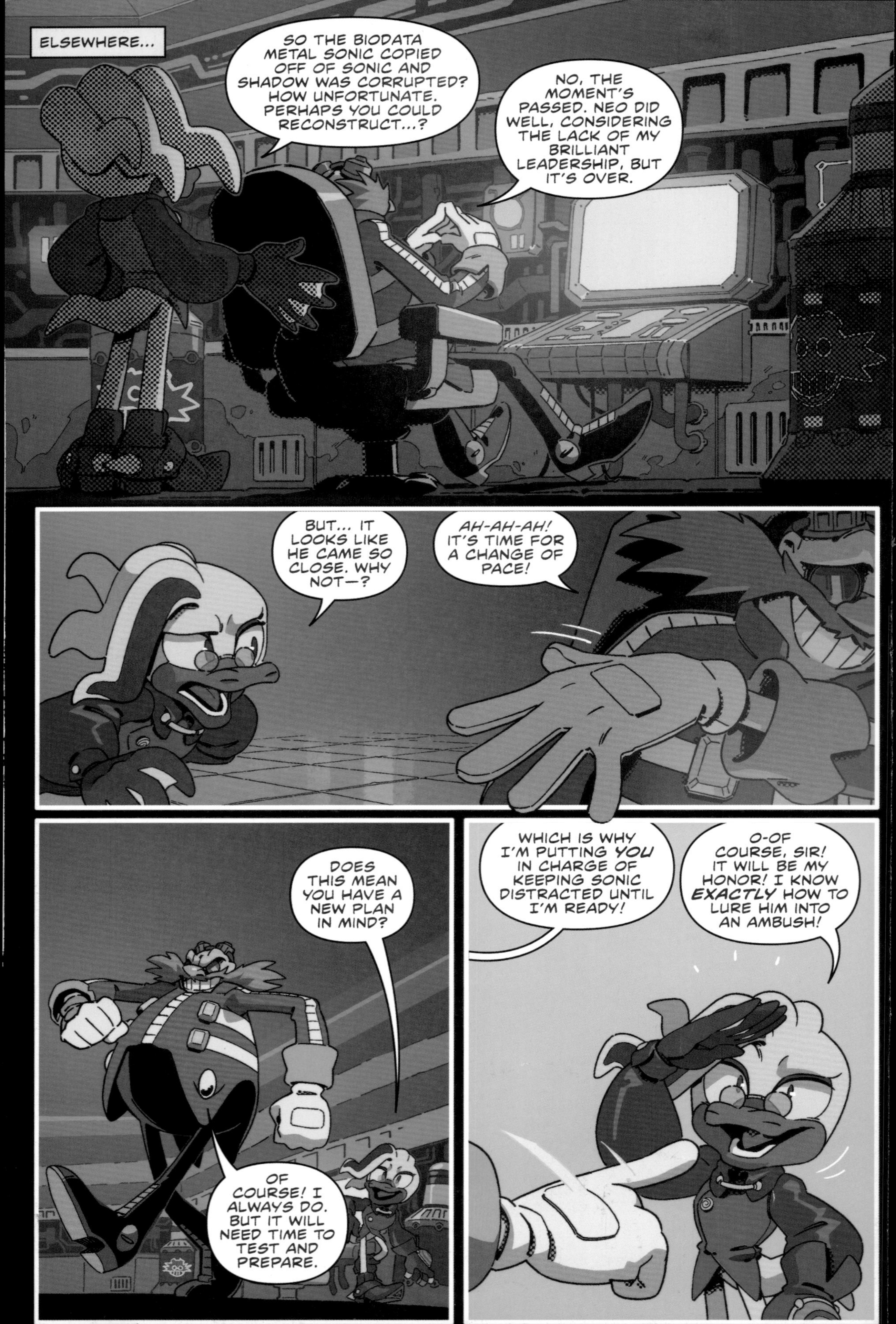
ELSEWHERE...
SO THE BIODATA METAL SONIC COPIED OFF OF SONIC AND SHADOW WAS CORRUPTED? HOW UNFORTUNATE. PERHAPS YOU COULD RECONSTRUCT...?
NO, THE MOMENT'S PASSED. NEO DID WELL, CONSIDERING THE LACK OF MY BRILLIANT LEADERSHIP, BUT IT'S OVER.
BUT... IT LOOKS LIKE HE CAME SO CLOSE. WHY NOT—?
AH-AH-AH! IT'S TIME FOR A CHANGE OF PACE!
DOES THIS MEAN YOU HAVE A NEW PLAN IN MIND?
OF COURSE! I ALWAYS DO. BUT IT WILL NEED TIME TO TEST AND PREPARE.
WHICH IS WHY I'M PUTTING YOU IN CHARGE OF KEEPING SONIC DISTRACTED UNTIL I'M READY!
O-OF COURSE, SIR! IT WILL BE MY HONOR! I KNOW EXACTLY HOW TO LURE HIM INTO AN AMBUSH!

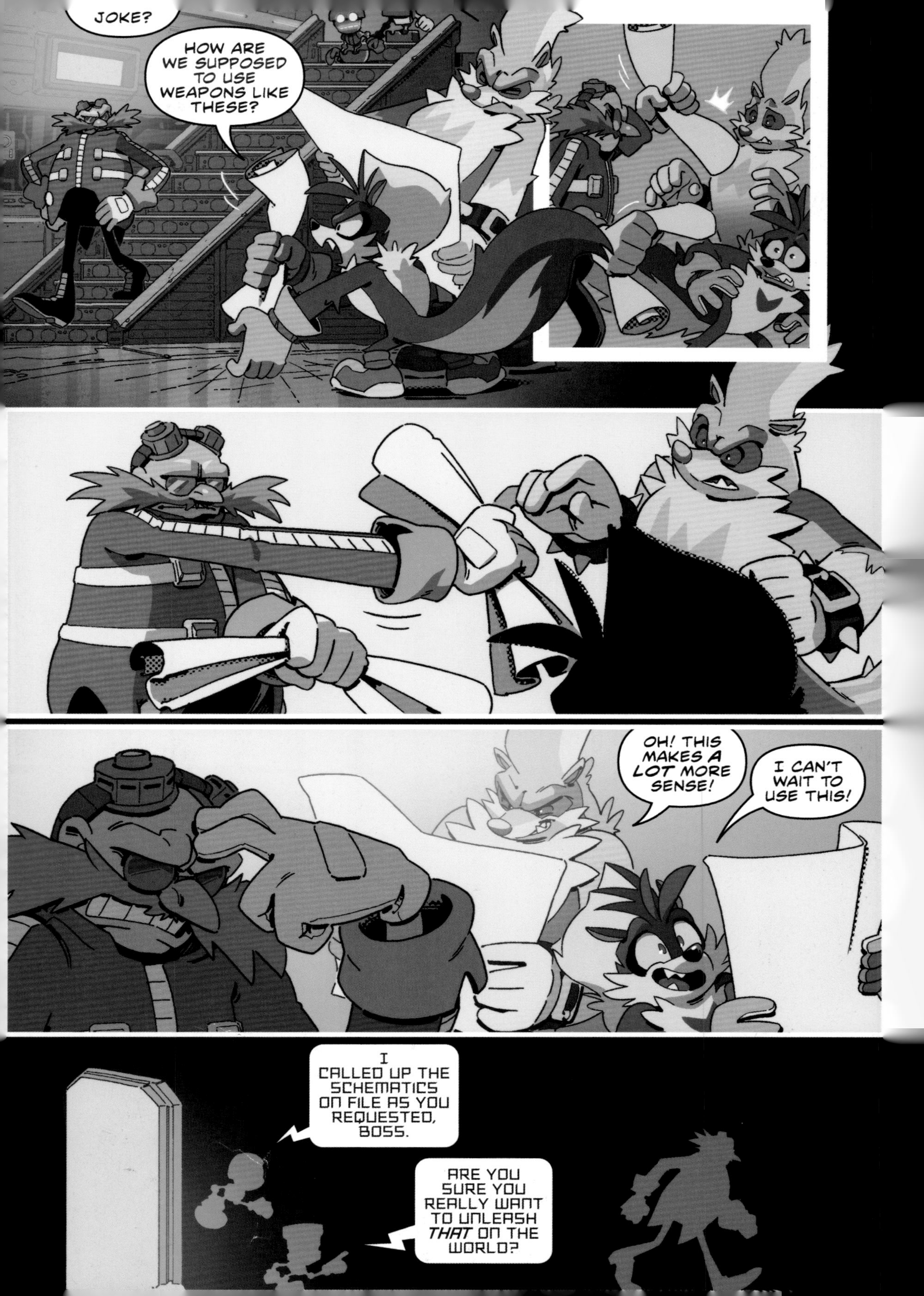
JOKE?
HOW ARE WE SUPPOSED TO USE WEAPONS LIKE THESE?
OH! THIS MAKES *A LOT* MORE SENSE!
I CAN'T WAIT TO USE THIS!
I CALLED UP THE SCHEMATICS ON FILE AS YOU REQUESTED, BOSS.
ARE YOU SURE YOU REALLY WANT TO UNLEASH *THAT* ON THE WORLD?

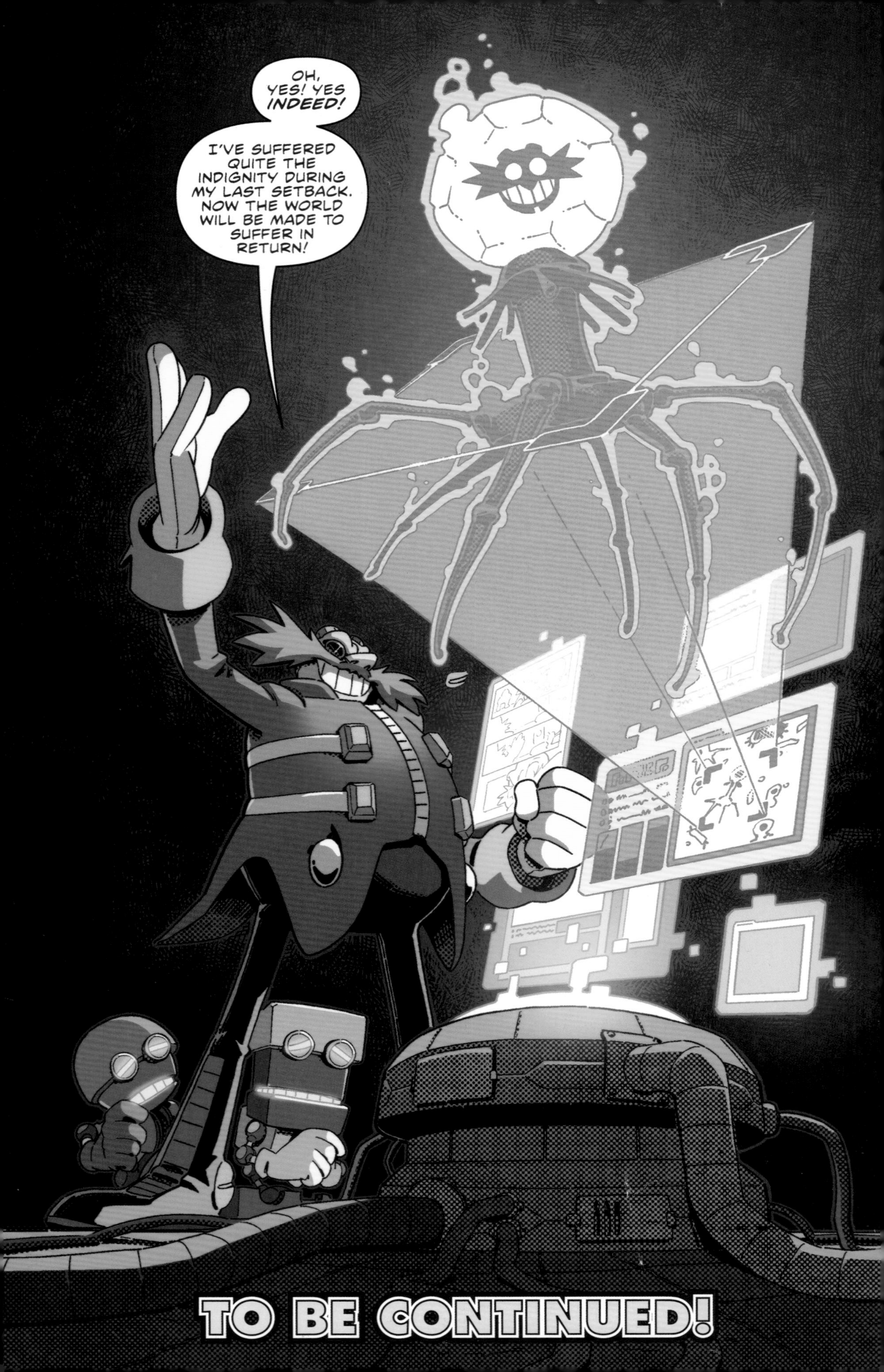
OH, YES! YES INDEED!
I'VE SUFFERED QUITE THE INDIGNITY DURING MY LAST SETBACK. NOW THE WORLD WILL BE MADE TO SUFFER IN RETURN!
TO BE CONTINUED!

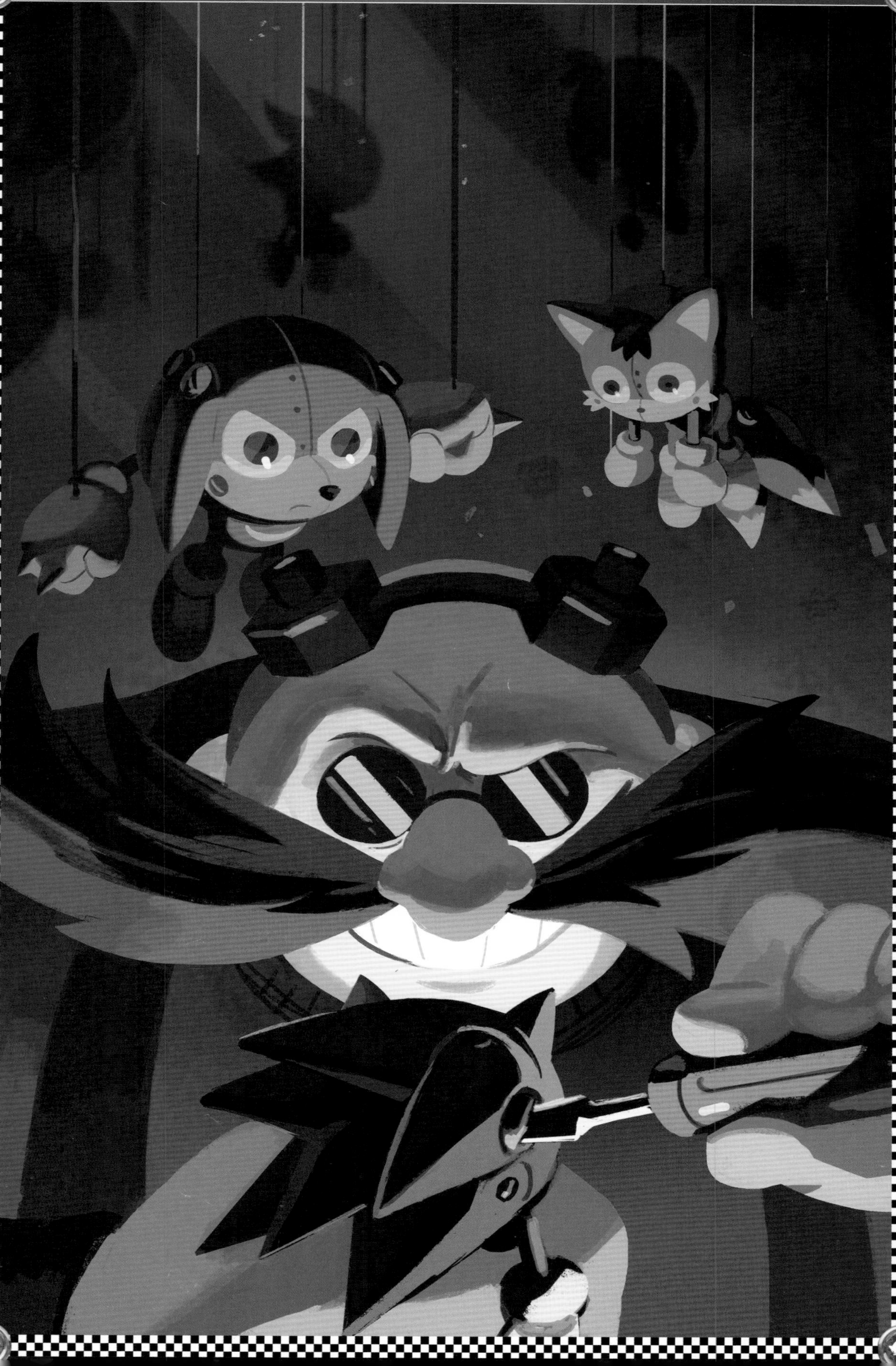

ART BY TRACY YARDLEY

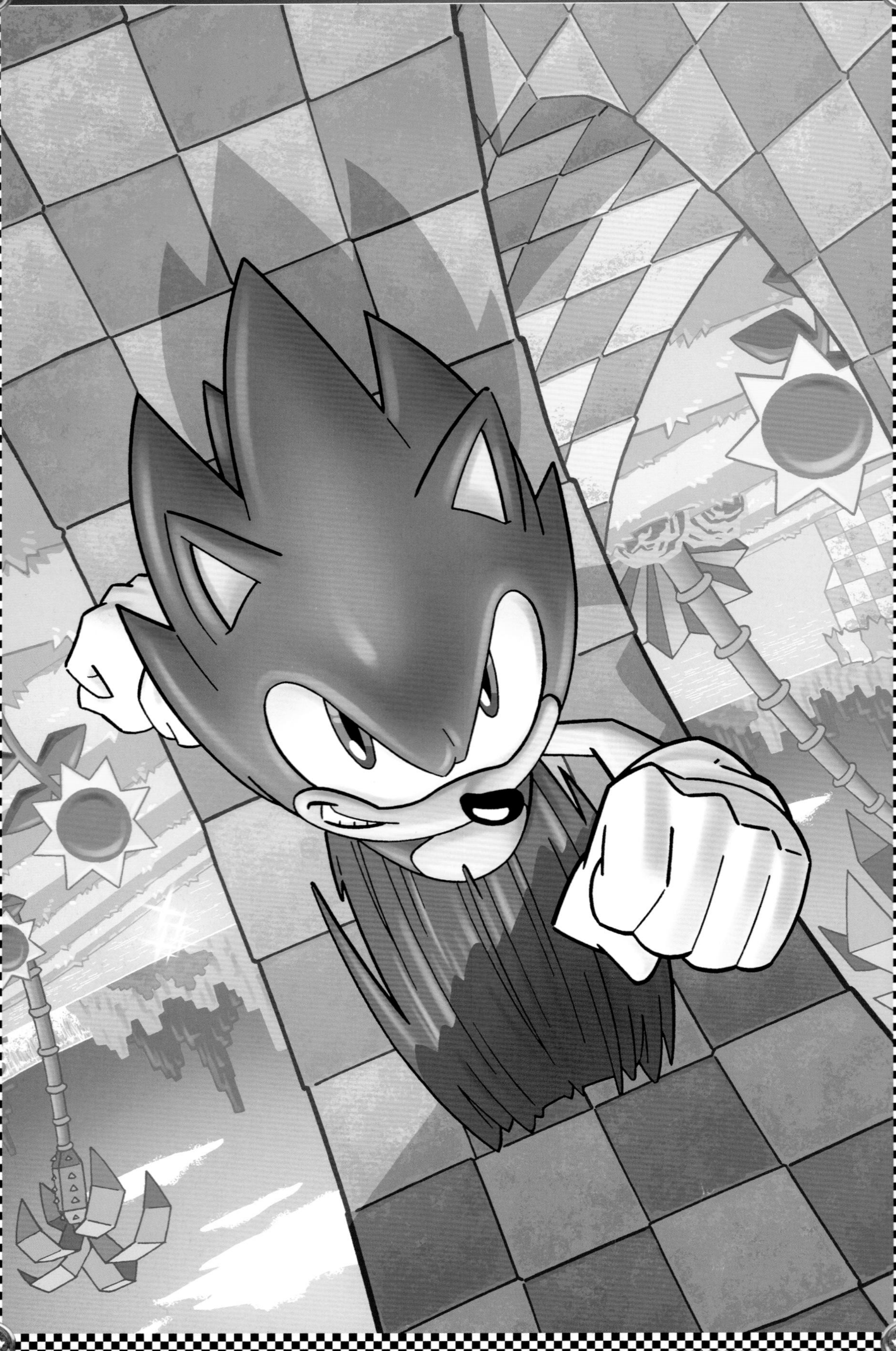

ART BY JONATHAN GRAY COLORS BY MATT HERMS

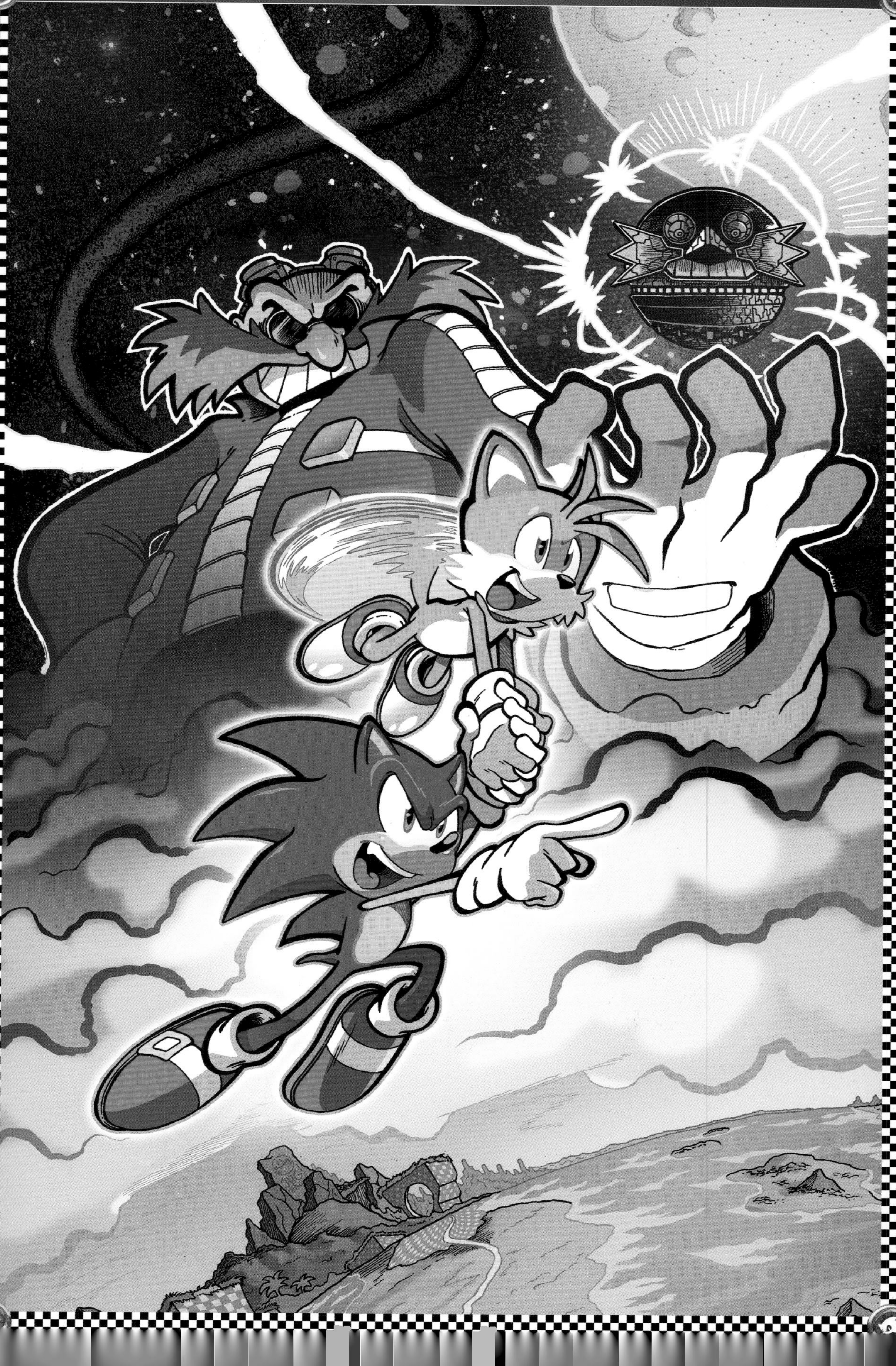

ART BY EDWIN HUANG

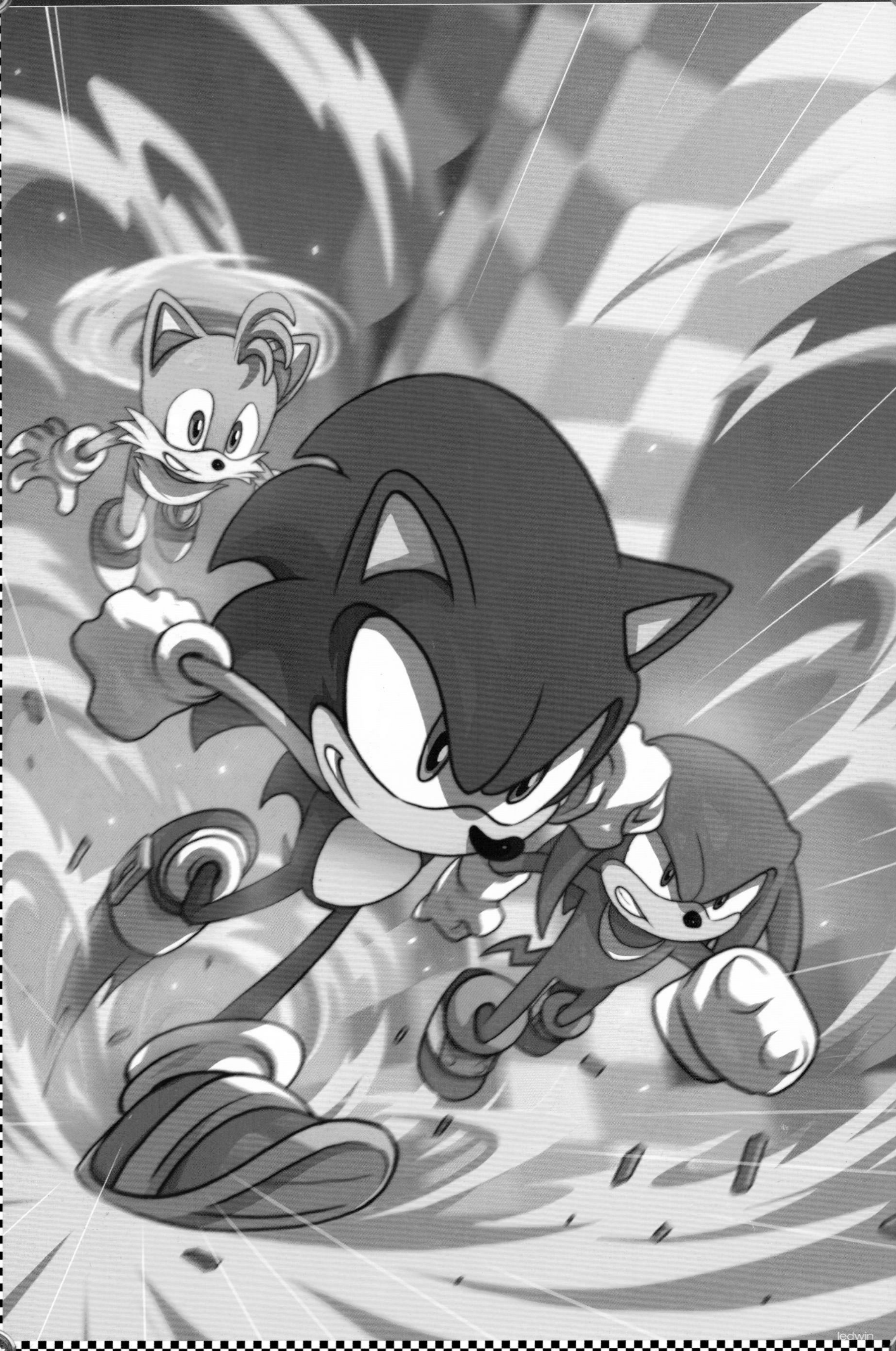

ART BY RAFA KNIGHT

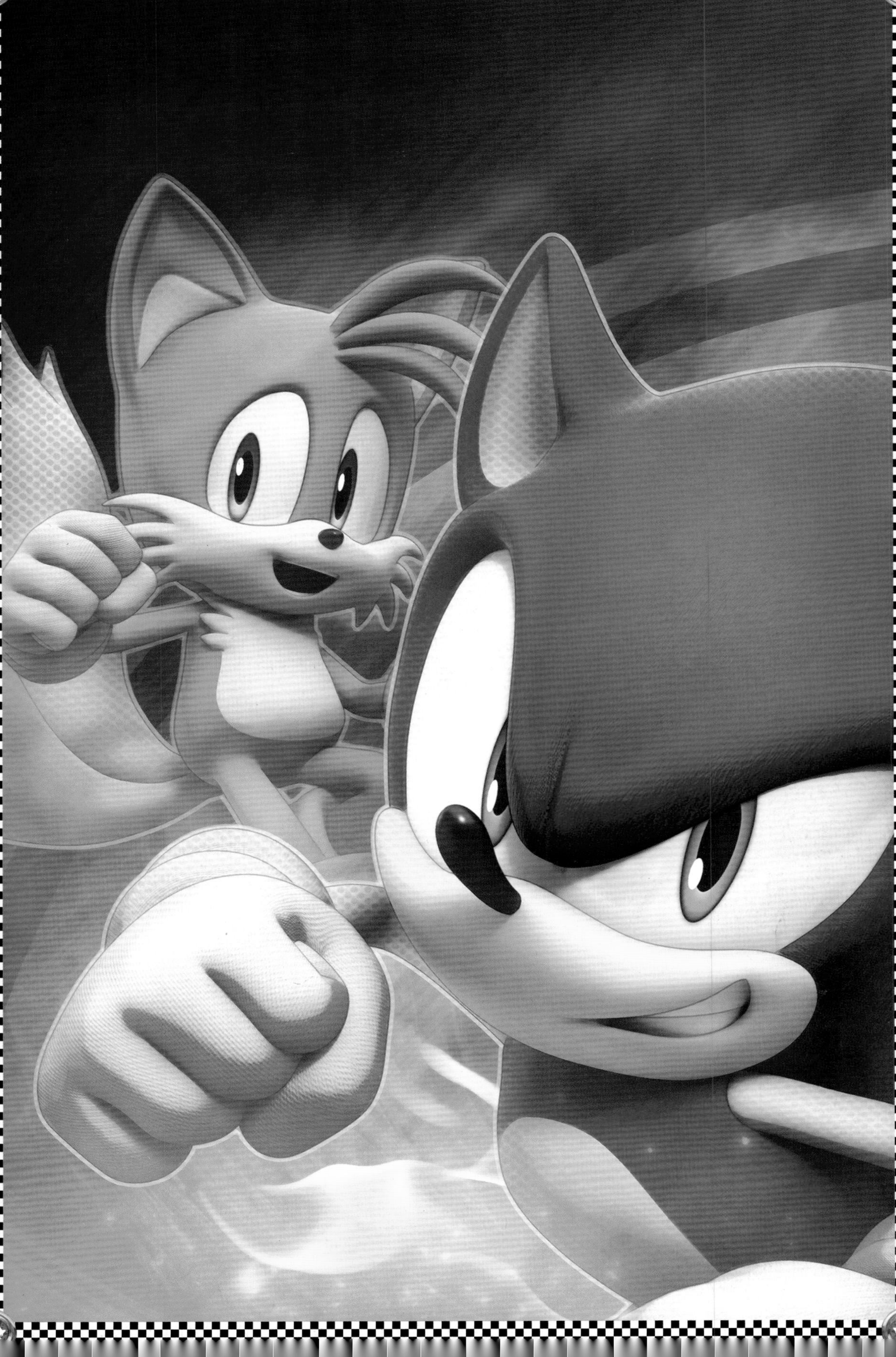

ART BY KIERAN GATES

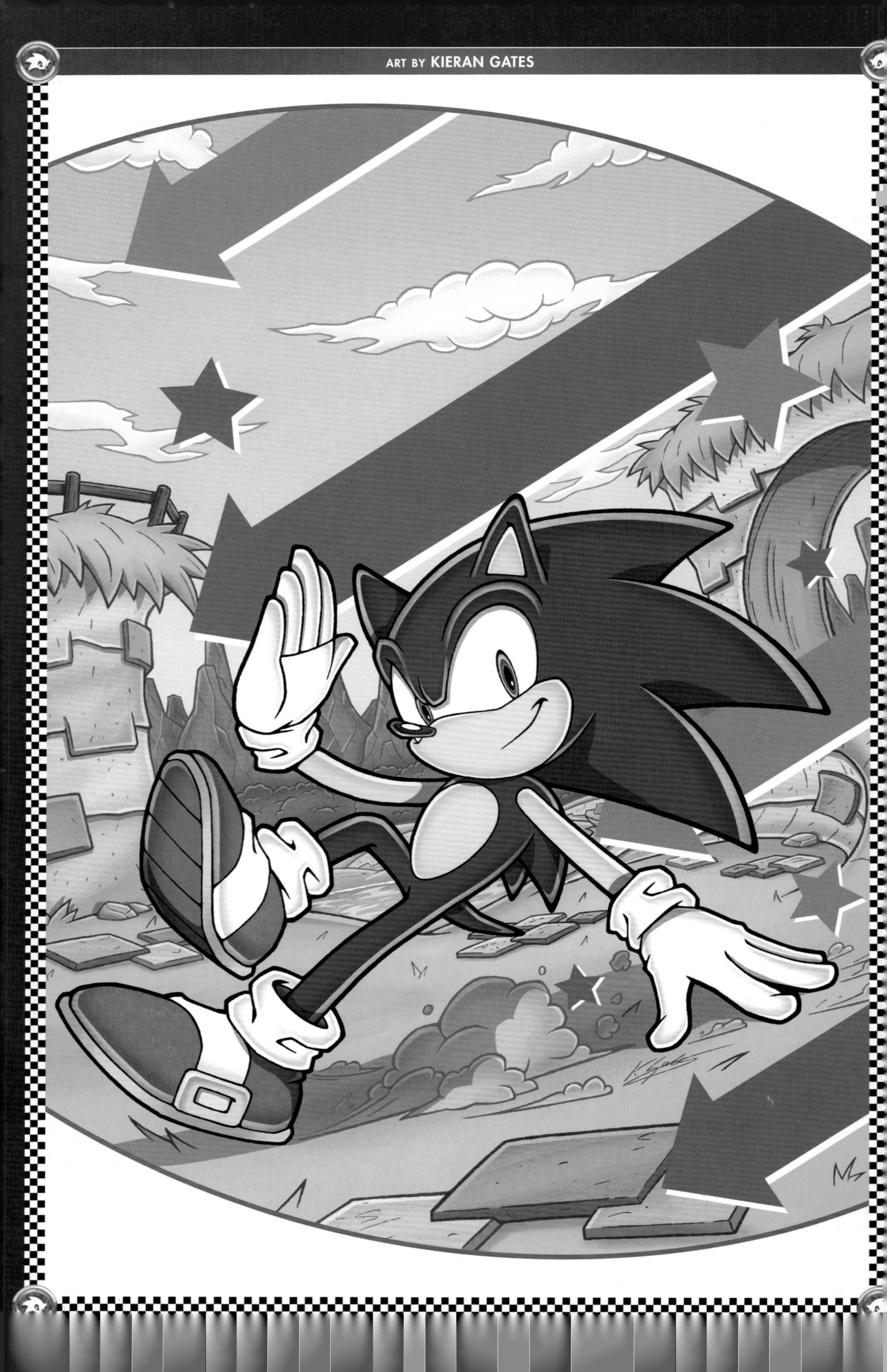

ART BY ADAM BRYCE THOMAS

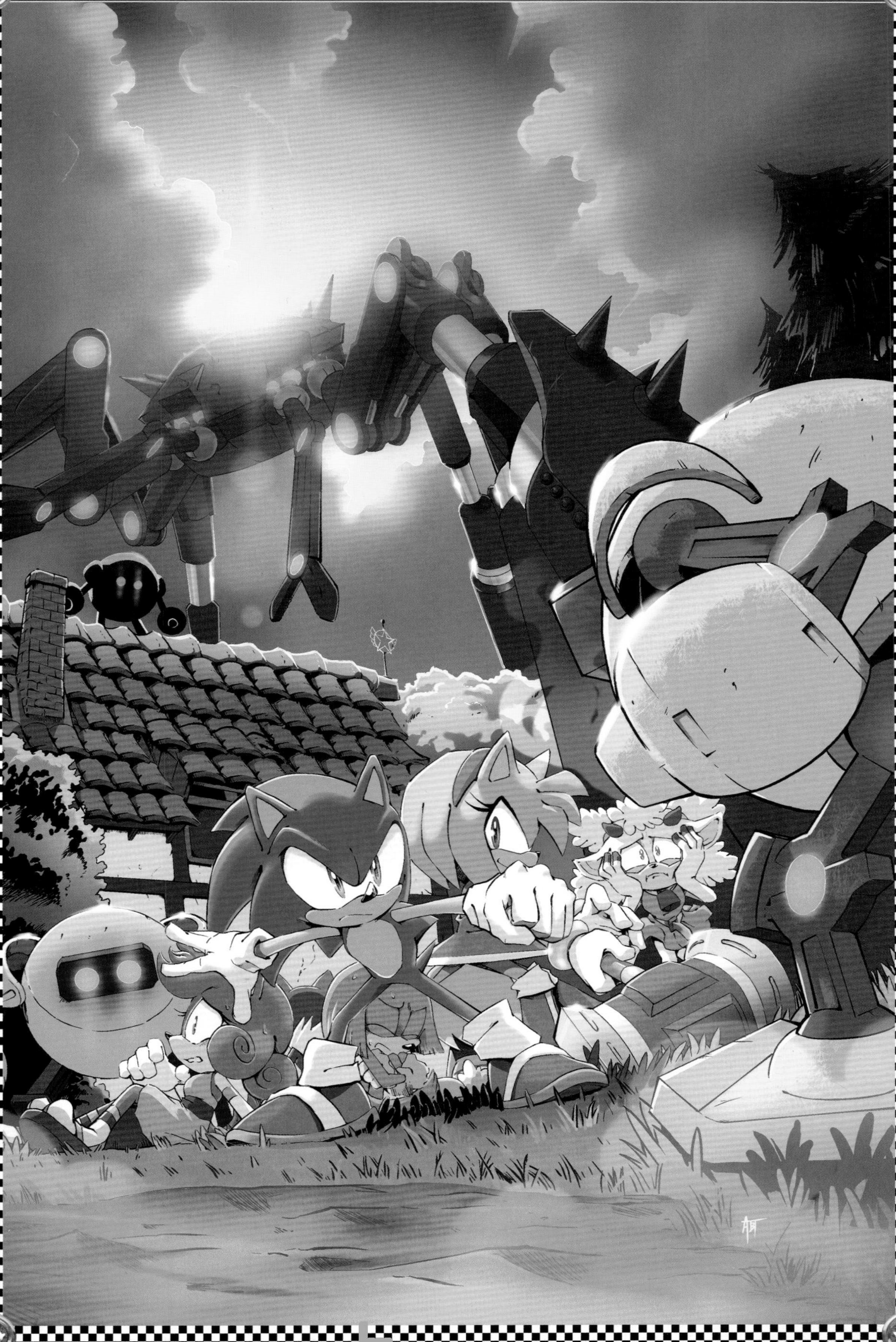

ART BY JONATHAN GRAY COLORS BY MATT HERMS

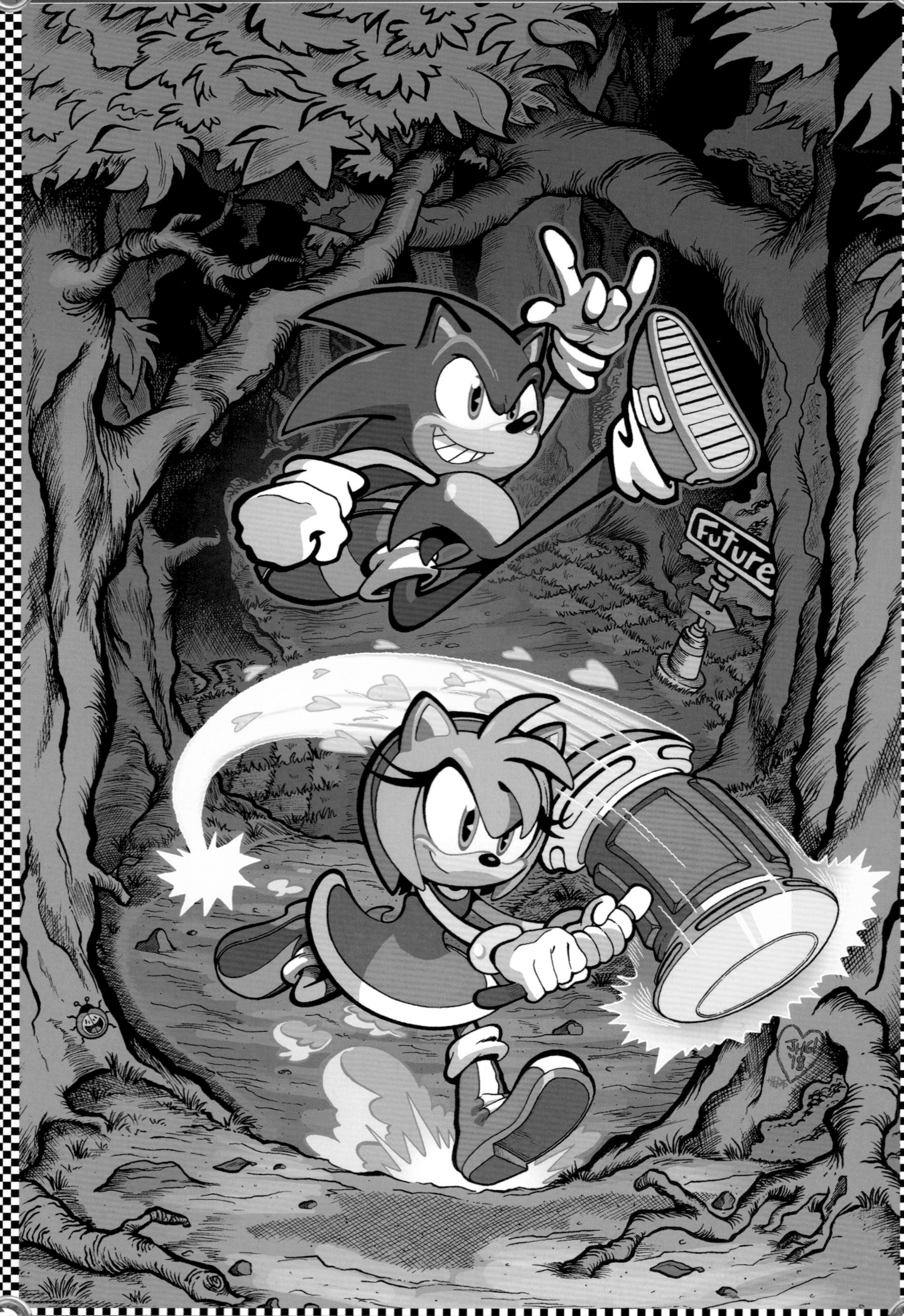
FUTURE

ART BY JENNIFER HERNANDEZ

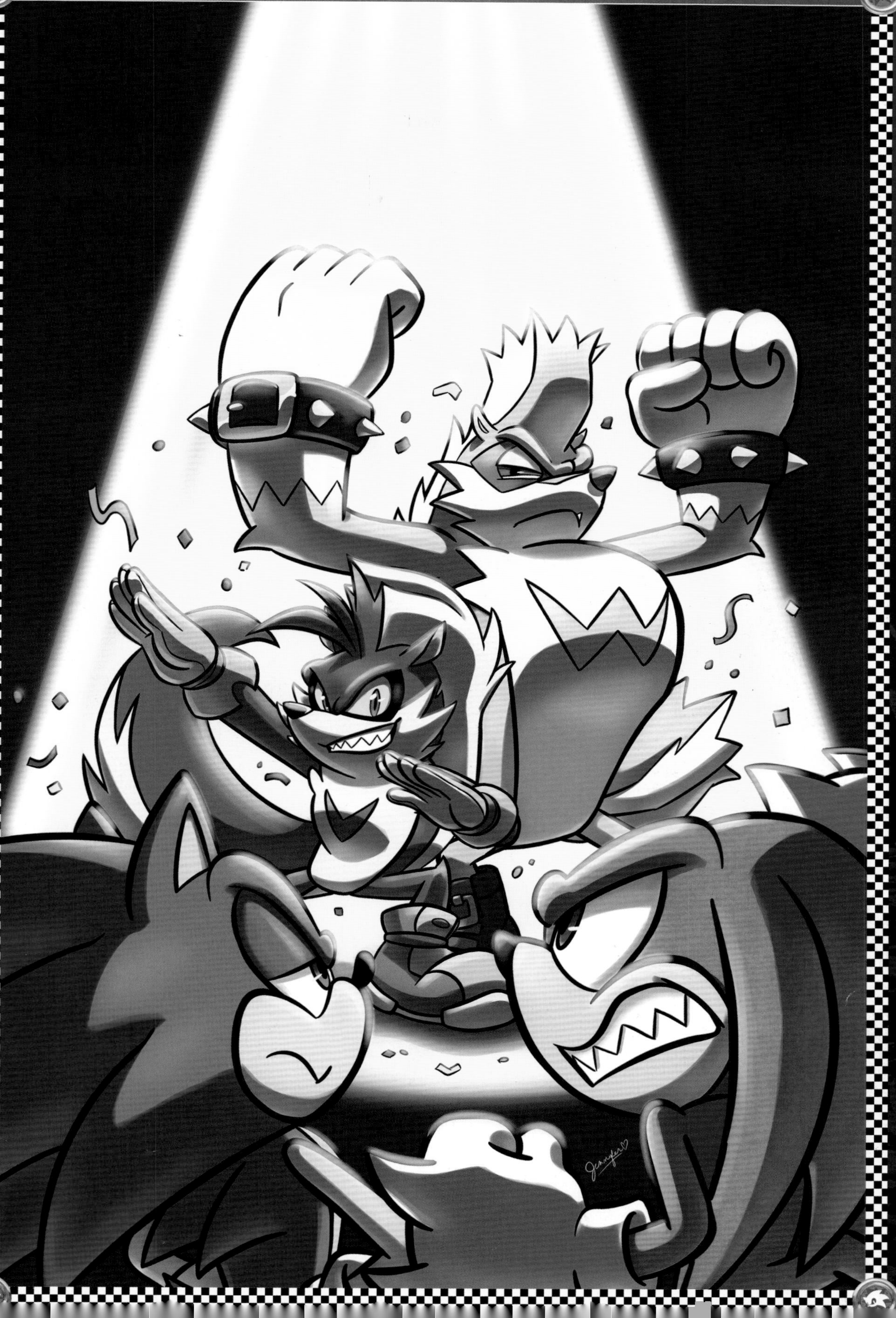
Jennifer

ART BY JAMAL PEPPERS COLORS BY HEATHER BRECKEL

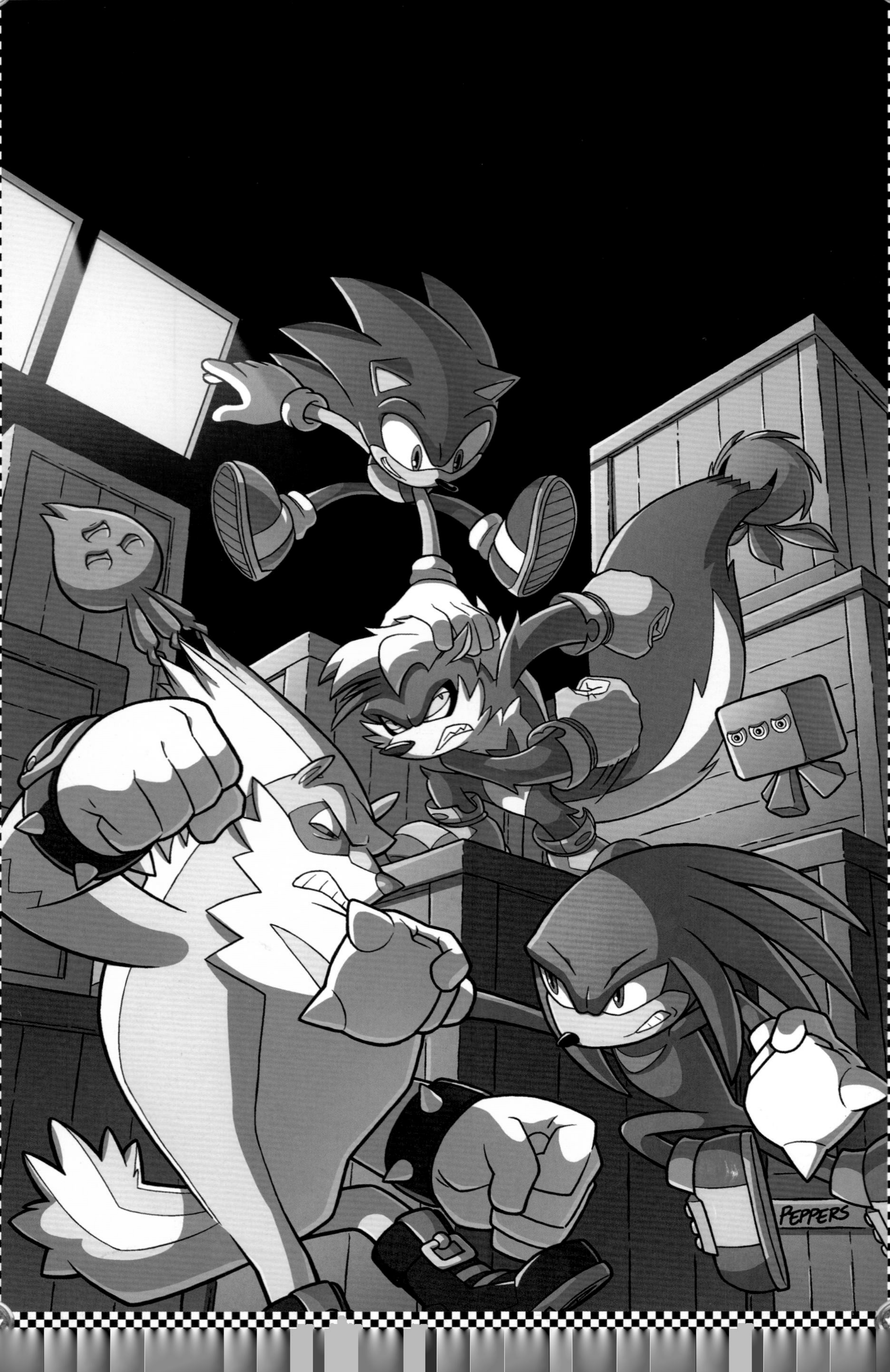
PEPPERS

ART BY EVAN STANLEY COLORS BY MATT HERMS

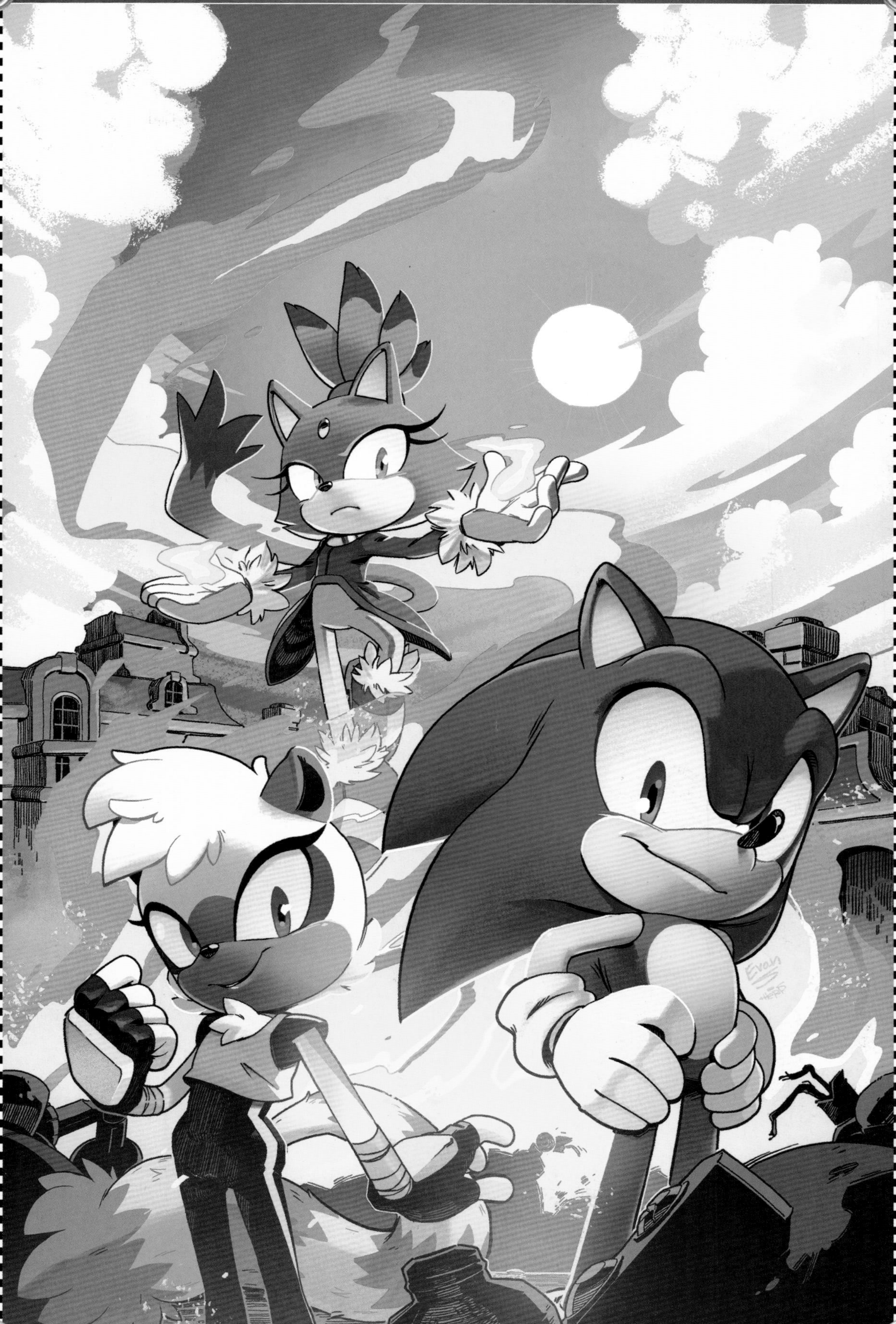

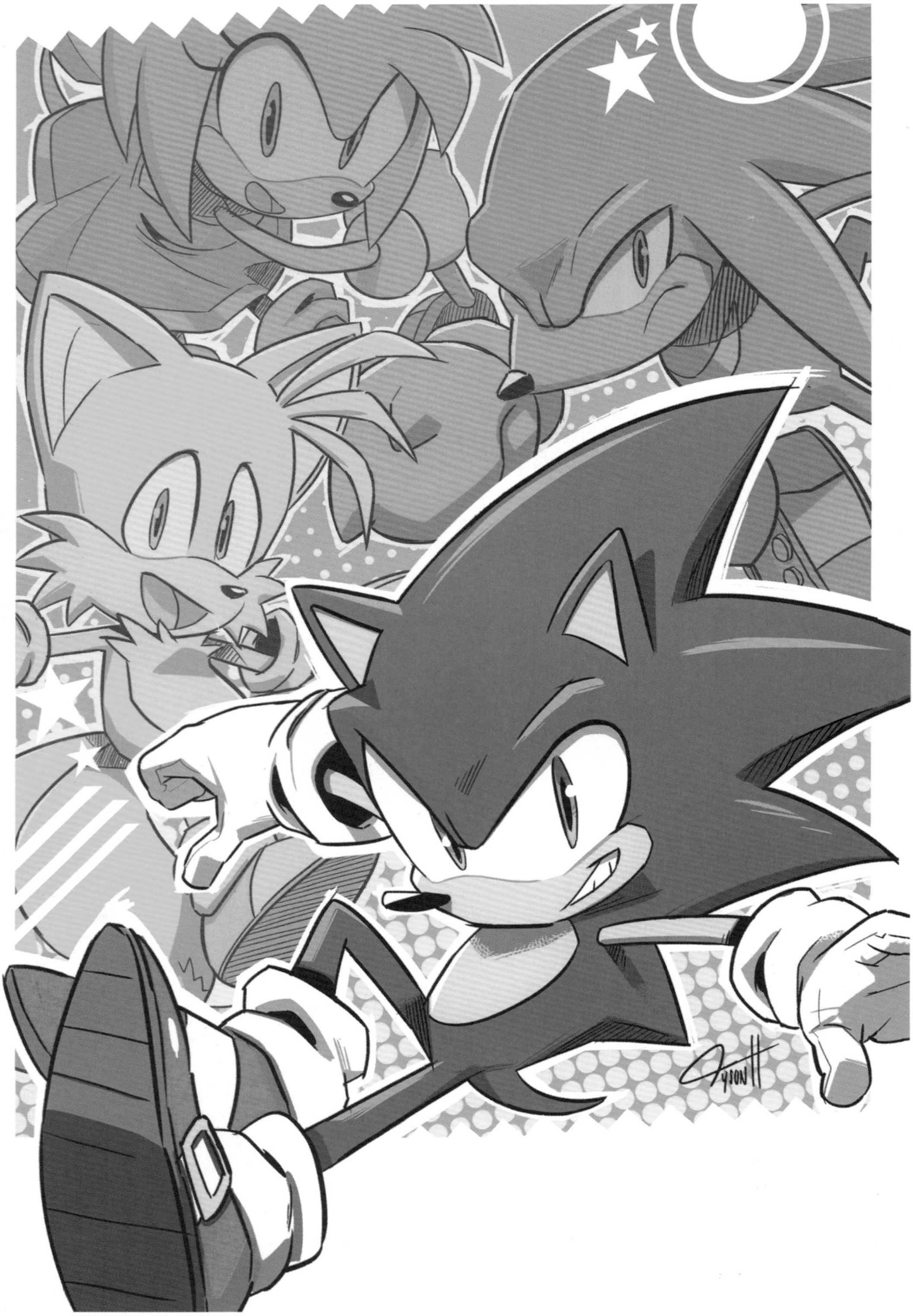

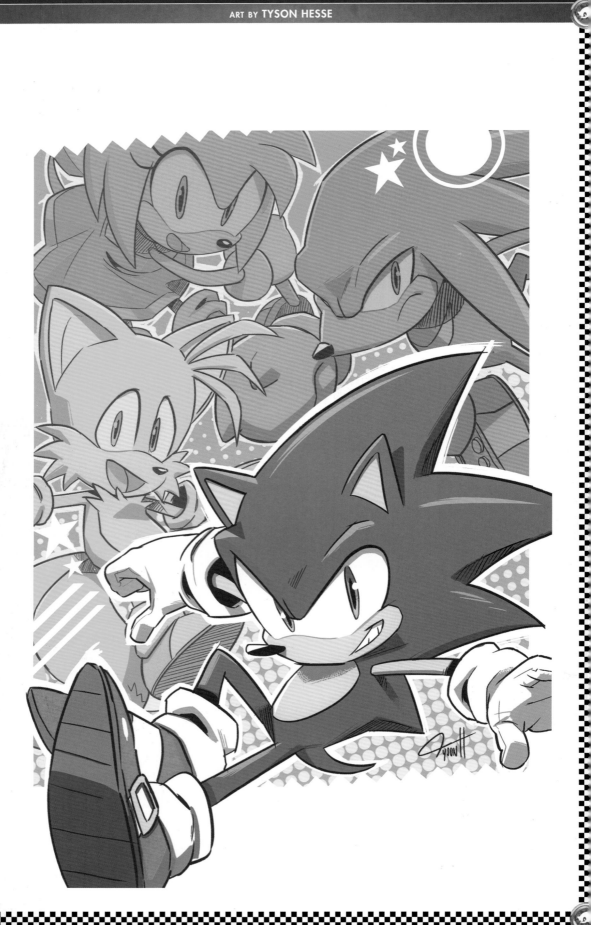

ART BY JAMAL PEPPERS

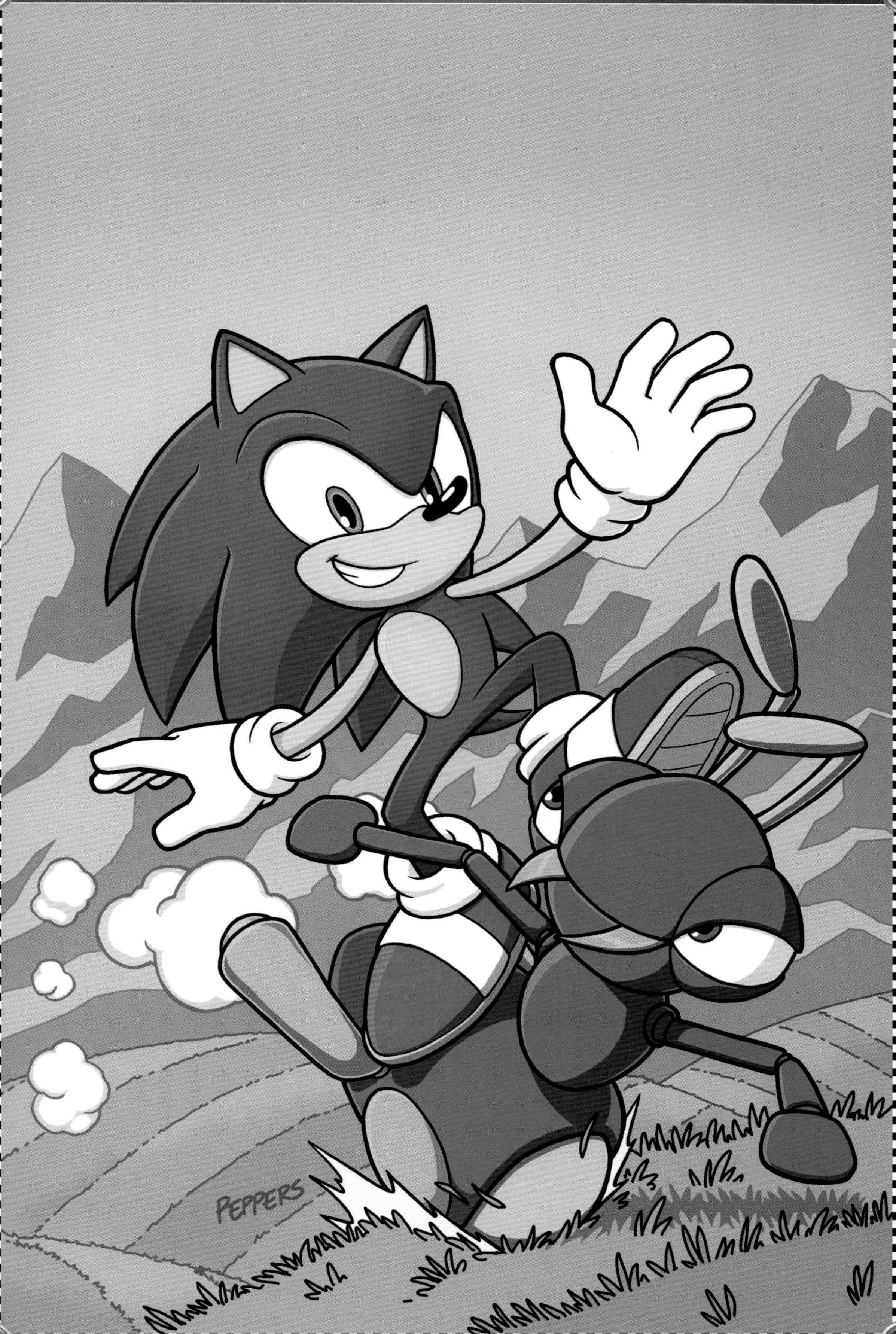
PEPPERS

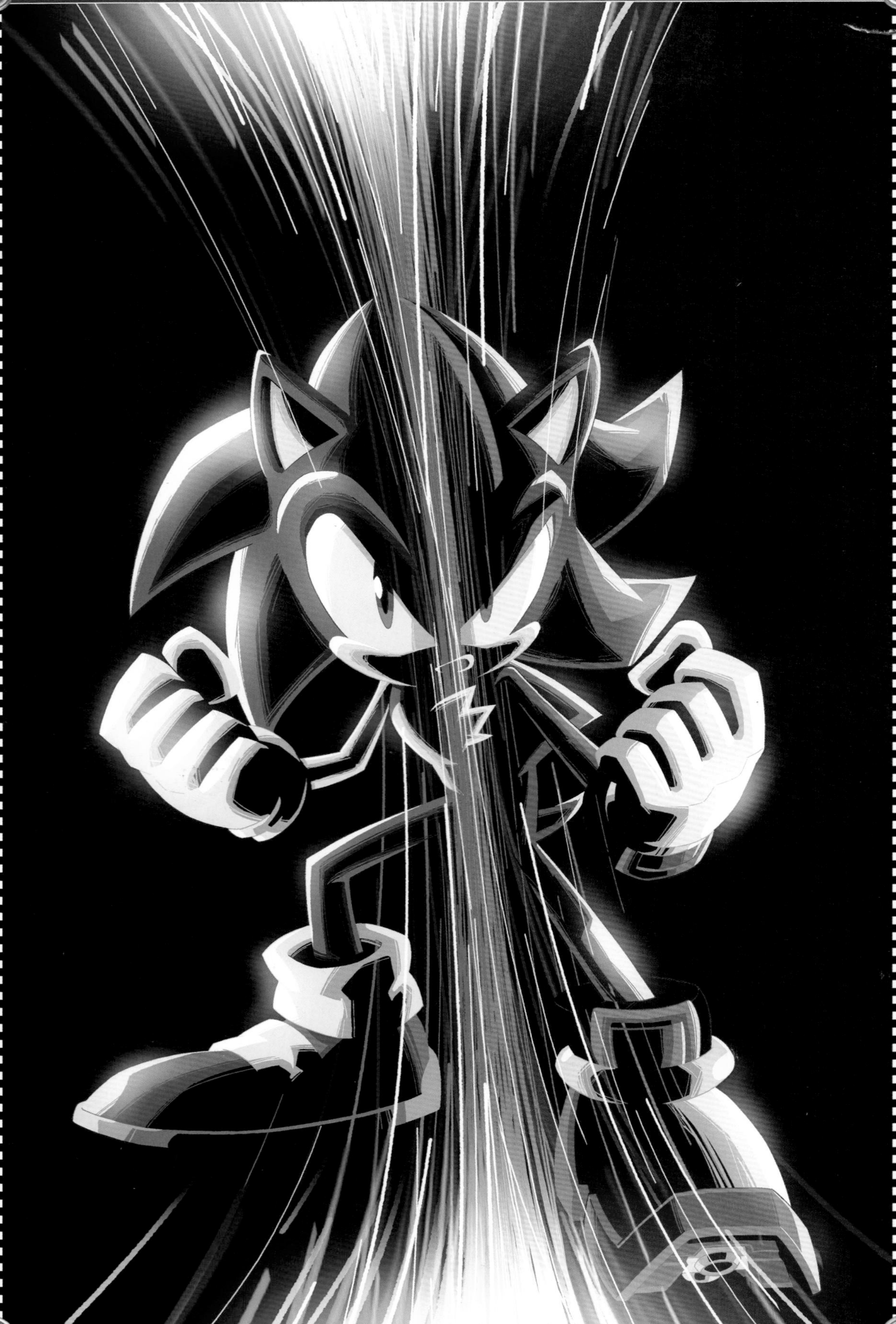

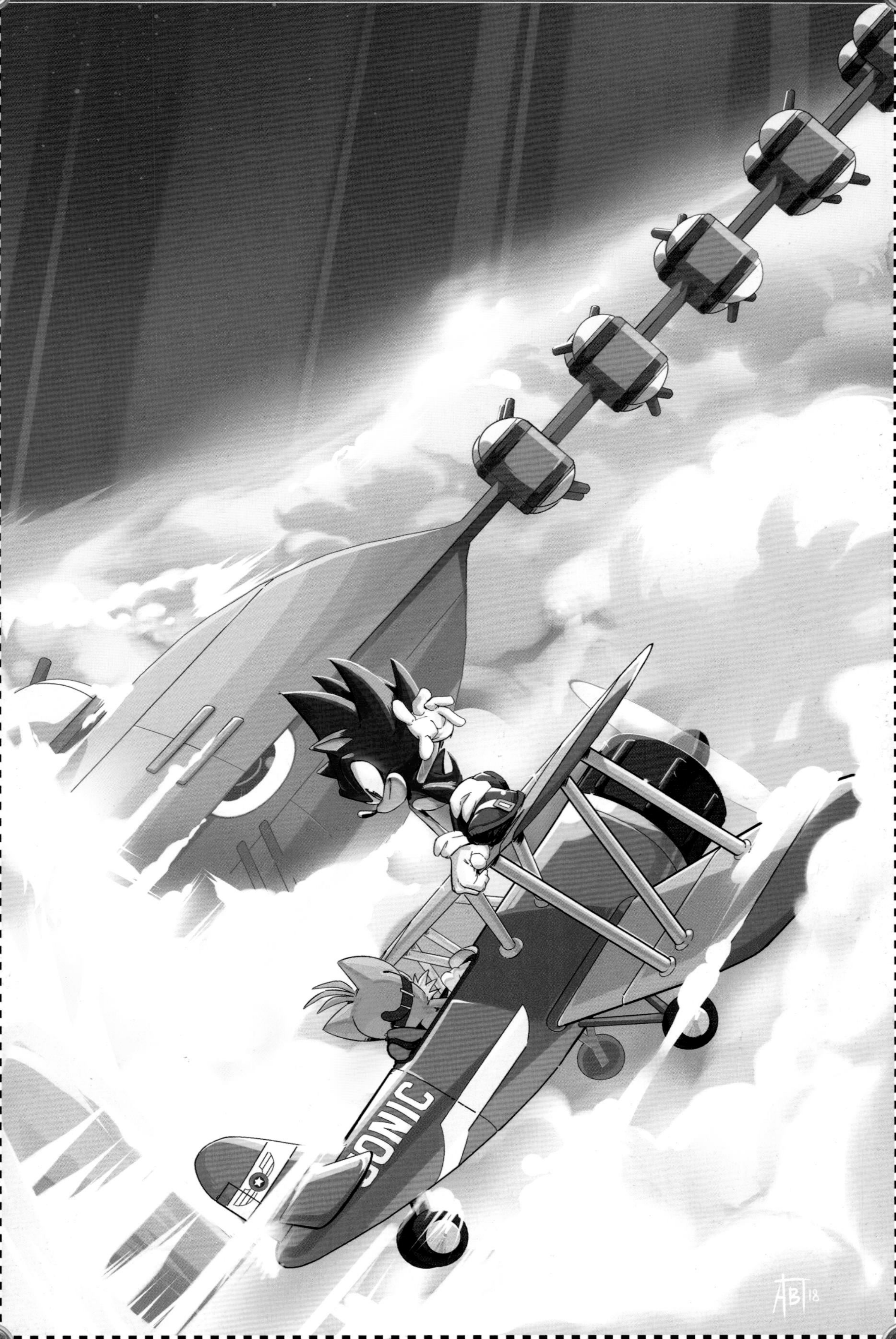
SONIC
ABT 18

ART BY EVAN STANLEY COLORS BY MATT HERMS

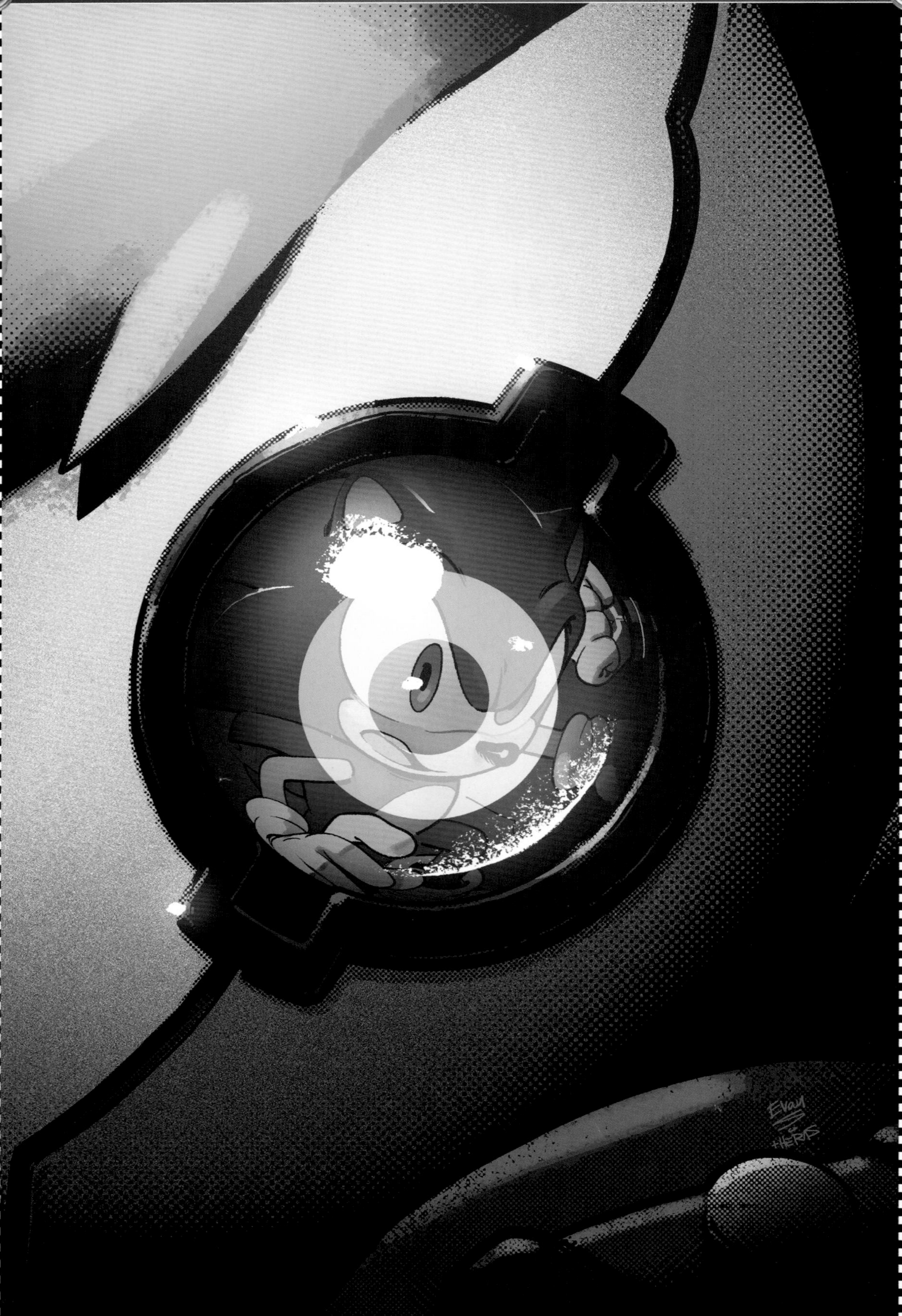

EVAN
HERMS

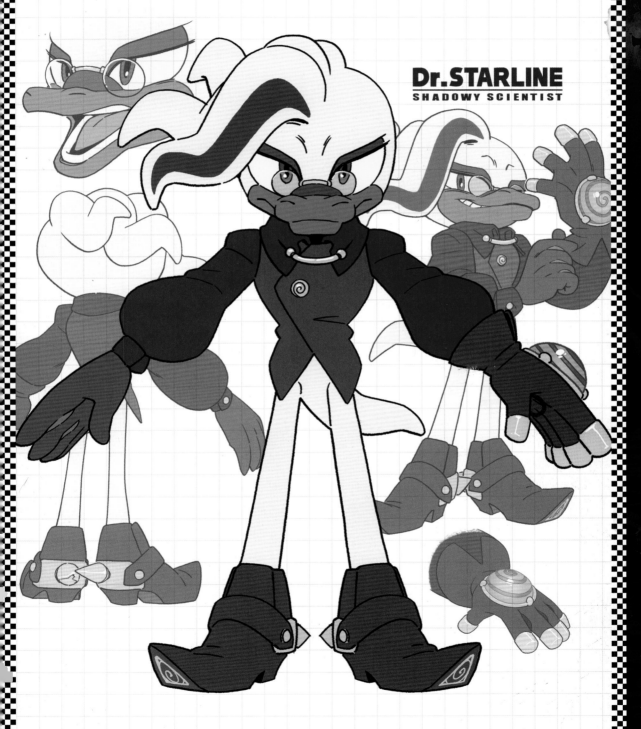

Dr.STARLINE
SHADOWY SCIENTIST

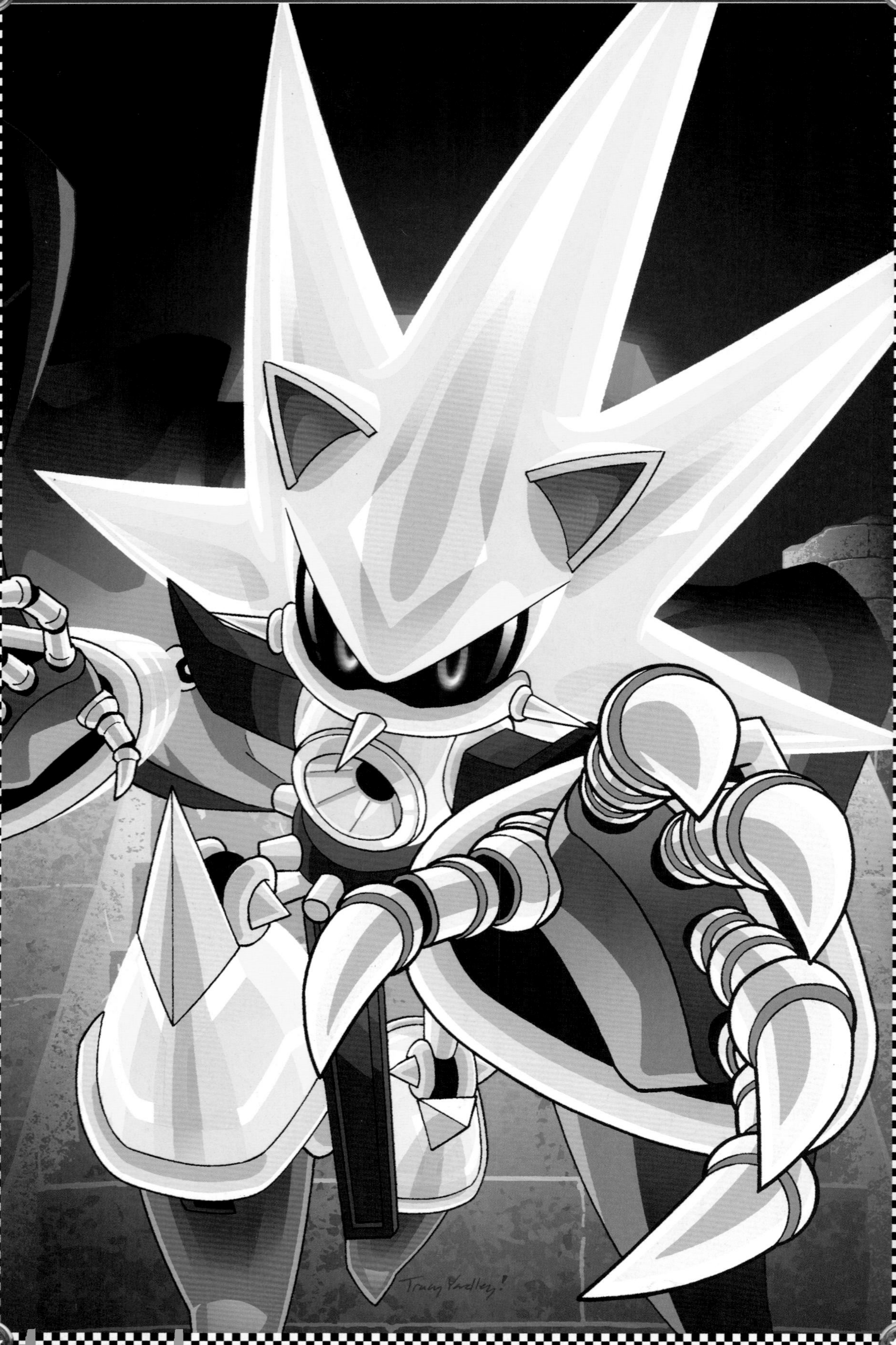
Tracy Yardley!

ART BY LAMAR WELLS & ADAM BRYCE THOMAS COLORS BY ADAM BRYCE THOMAS

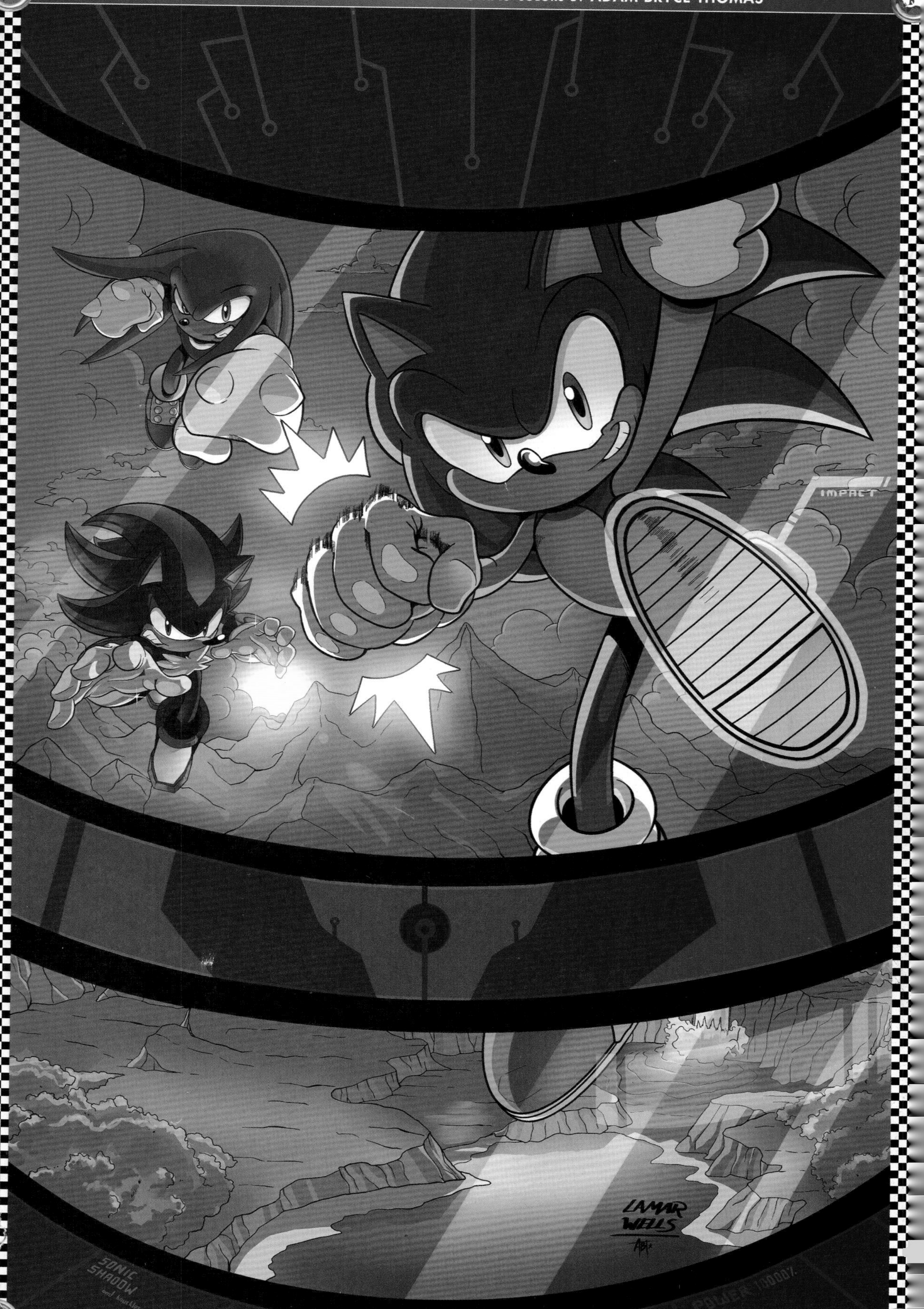
IMPACT
LAMAR WELLS
SONIC
SHADOW
and knuckles
POWER 1000%

ART BY TRACY YARDLEY

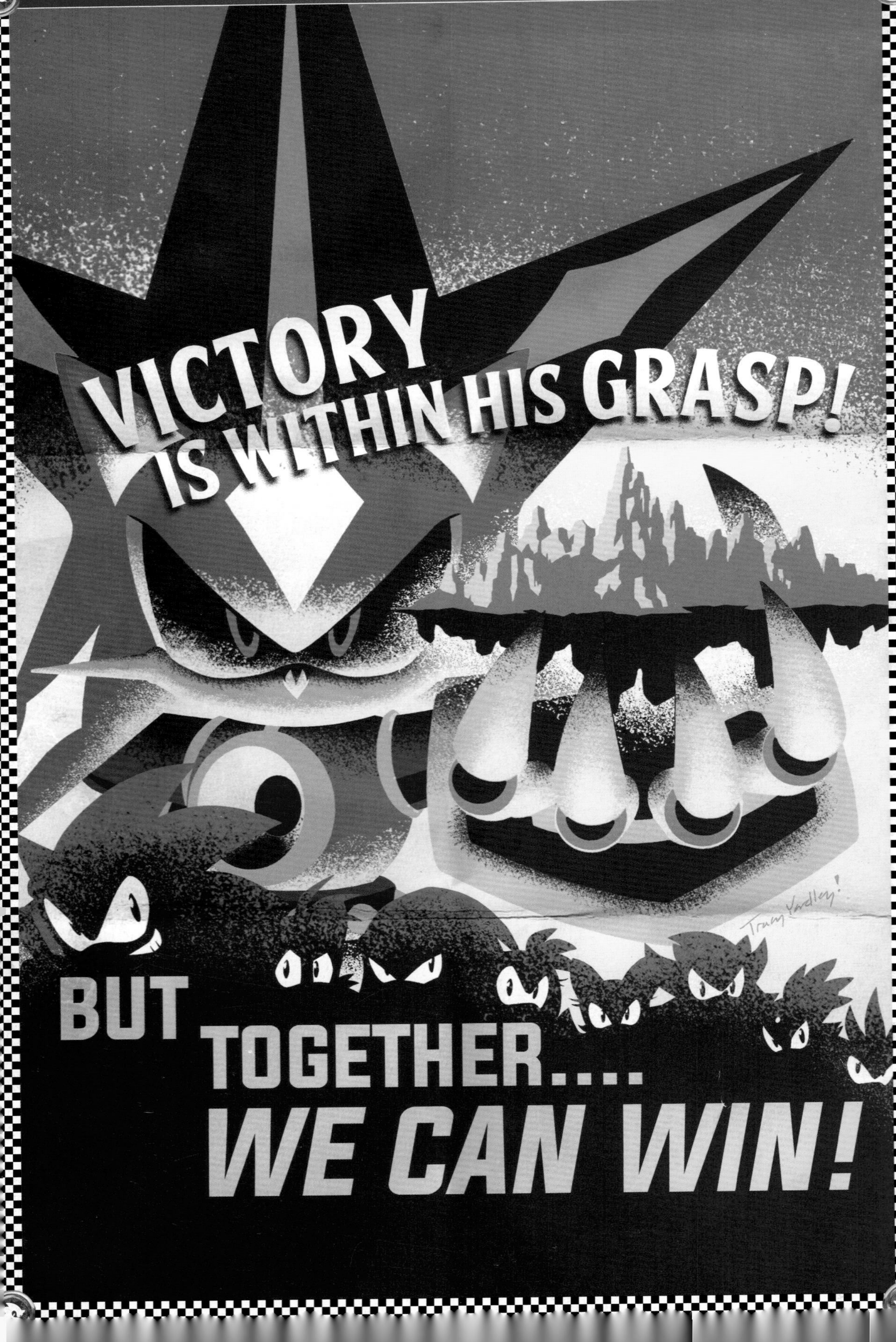
VICTORY
IS WITHIN HIS GRASP!
Tracy Yardley!
BUT
TOGETHER....
WE CAN WIN!